Praise for *The Adventures of Lucky Pierre:*

"Robert Coover remains our foremost verbal wizard, our laugher in the dark, Samuel Beckett reborn: *Lucky Pierre* is a hilarious, radical, and essential book. Long live excess!"
—T. Coraghessan Boyle

"The leading citizen of a fabulistic metropolis called Cinecity, [Lucky Pierre] is famed for his 'regal mechanism,' the only thing more tumescent than which is Coover's jauntily purple prose. . . . Maybe America's most famous experimental writer, certainly its dirtiest."
—*Entertainment Weekly*

"Coover writes for the mind's eye. . . . Other authors have played with a flow of verbiage, like the babble of insane shamans, but no other has stopped a reader dead every third word with images. In *The Adventures of Lucky Pierre,* it's sexual images, images that can't help but be created as you read. . . . Coover . . . works on a new textual frontier."
—*Los Angeles Times Book Review*

"Disturbingly funny . . . Tenderness . . . pervades when L.P.'s tale ends . . . an ardent acknowledgment of the transient surfaces upon which our lives, our selves, flicker and play before they dim, and fall forever into silence."
—*The Village Voice*

"Robert Coover is a colossal subversive. His fiction is among the most looted of the old guard, by writers who crave his raucous imagination and adulterous relationship to storytelling. At seventy Coover is still a brilliant myth-maker, a potty-mouthed Svengali, and an evil technician of metaphors. He is among our language's most important inventors, and it is more crucial than ever to read him."
—Ben Marcus

"One of our boldest literary experimenters."
—*Seattle Times/Post Intelligencer*

"[A] remarkable, perverse take on the history of narrative cinema, seen through the lubricated lens of pornography. The comic pratfalls of Buster Keaton, the surreal displacements and anxieties of Luis Buñuel, and the political and formal radicalism of Jean-Luc Godard are all in evidence."
—*The Times Literary Supplement* (UK)

"The world has yet to meet the artist capable of topping Robert Coover's superb, wonderfully wicked, exuberant staying power . . . until, perhaps, Lucky Pierre."
—Robert Antoni

"Coover's novels are . . . lively, entertaining, challenging, sexy, funny, and beautifully written. . . . *The Adventures of Lucky Pierre* is a wild ride, reading like a collaboration between Terry Southern and Philip K. Dick for a film for David Cronenberg."
—*The Commercial Appeal* (Memphis)

"A wild, pornographic, funny, postmodern rant . . . In the tradition of *Tristram Shandy* or *Finnegans Wake*, this is a story that can be opened at any point and read at length with great pleasure." —*Kirkus Reviews* (starred review)

"Coover . . . lures readers—in large part by giving them a good time—to confront their assumptions about reality. . . . He writes about sex as it's never been written about before, with a sly, detached precision that captures the unillusioned and undeterred Freudian id. Mr. Coover can be seen as the inverse of another writer about sex, the Marquis de Sade." —*The New York Times*

"Wildly imaginative and vividly rendered." —*Booklist*

Praise for Robert Coover:

"Mr. Coover's work has long occupied a place of honor. . . . He goes at his task with an almost alarming linguistic energy, a Burgessy splatter of vocabulary, and a ferocious love of everything comic and grotesque." —Salman Rushdie

"Mr. Coover is among the best we now have writing. . . . Nothing in Mr. Coover's writing is quite what it seems to be. In the pattern of the leaves there is always the smile of the Cheshire Cat." —*The New York Times*

"As his dazzling career continues to demonstrate, Mr. Coover is a big one-man Big Bang of exploding creative force." —*The New York Times Book Review*

The Adventures of Lucky Pierre

Also by Robert Coover

Short Fiction

Pricksongs & Descants
In Bed One Night & Other Brief Encounters
A Night at the Movies
The Grand Hotels (of Joseph Cornell)

Plays

A Theological Position

Novels

The Origin of the Brunists
The Universal Baseball Association, Inc., J. Henry Waugh, Prop.
The Public Burning
A Political Fable
Spanking the Maid
Gerald's Party
Whatever Happened to Gloomy Gus of the Chicago Bears?
Pinocchio in Venice
John's Wife
Briar Rose
Ghost Town

The Adventures of Lucky Pierre

Directors' Cut

Robert Coover

Grove Press
New York

Portions of this book have appeared in different form in the following publications: the literary magazines *New American Review*, *Antaeus*, *Penthouse*, *Granta*, *Witness*, *Playboy*, *A Hard Day's Night* (Japan), *Coe Review*, *Fiction International*, *3rd Bed*, *Nexos* (Mexico), *Balcones*, *Trema* (France), and *Golden Handcuffs*, and the anthology *After Yesterday's Crash*.

Published simultaneously in Canada
Printed in the United States of America

FIRST GROVE PRESS EDITION

Library of Congress Cataloging-in-Publication Data
Coover, Robert.
The adventures of Lucky Pierre : directors' cut / Robert Coover.
p. cm.
ISBN 0-8021-4041-6 (pbk.)
1. Motion picture actors and actresses—Fiction. 2. Women motion picture producers and directors—Fiction. 3. Motion picture industry—Fiction. 4. Erotic films—Fiction. 5. Actors—Fiction. I. Title.
PS3553.O633 A66 2002
813'.54—dc21 2002033856

Grove Press
841 Broadway
New York, NY 10003

04 05 06 07 08 10 9 8 7 6 5 4 3 2 1

For Saint Buster, Saint Luis, and Saint Jean-Luc,
who kept the light burning in the dark century.

The best in this kind are but shadows; and the worst are no worse, if imagination amend them.—Saint Will

Contents

Titles & Reel 1: Cecilia

(**Cantus.**) In the darkness, softly. A whisper becoming a tone, the echo of a tone. Doleful, a soft incipient lament blowing in the night like a wind, like the echo of a wind, a plainsong wafting distantly through the windy chambers of the night, wafting unisonously through the spaced chambers of the bitter night, alas, the solitary city, she that was full of people, thus a distant and hollow epiodion laced with sibilants bewailing the solitary city.

And now, the flickering of a light, a pallor emerging from the darkness as though lit by a candle, a candle guttering in the cold wind, a forgotten candle, hid and found again, casting its doubtful luster on this faint white plane, now visible, now lost again in the tenebrous absences behind the eye.

And still the hushing plaint, undeterred by light, plying its fricatives like a persistent woeful wind, the echo of woe, affanato, piangevole, a piangevole wind rising in the fluttering night through its perfect primes, lamenting the beautiful princess become an unclean widow, an emergence from C, a titular C, tentative and parenthetical, the widow then, weeping sore in the night, the candle searching the pale expanse for form, for the suggestion of form, a balm for the anxious eye, weeping she weepeth.

The glimmering light, the light of the world, now firmer at the center, flickers unsteadily at the outer edges, implications of tangible paraboloids amid the soft anguish, the plainsong exploring its mode, third position athwart, for among all her lovers there are none to comfort her, and the eye finding a horizon, discovering at last a distant geography of synclinal nodes, barren, windblown, now blurring, now defined.

Now defined: a strange valley, brighter at its median and upon the crests than down the slopes, the hint there perhaps of vegetation, like a grove of pines buried in the snow, and still the chant, epicedial, sospirante, she is driven like a hunted animal, C to C and F again, she findeth no rest. How many have died here?

The plainchant, blowing through the gloomy valley like an afflicted widow, continues to mourn the solitary city. Overtaken amid the narrow defiles. Continues to grieve, ignoring the gradual illuminations, a grief caught in secret acrostics, gone into captivity. All her gates are desolate. The eye courses the valley to its yawning embouchure, past a scattering of obscure excrescences with bright tips, courses the dark defile to its radical, this pinched and woebegone pit, mourning its uprooted yew, her priests sigh, her virgins are afflicted. Gravis. Innig. In bitterness, yes, con amarezza, she is with bitterness.

Beyond this gnurled foramen, crumpled crater too afflicted to expose its core to chant or candle, lies a quieter brighter field, yet one ringed about with indices of a multitude of transgressions, tight with uncertainty and attenuation, and, as it were, mere propylaeum to the ruptured conventicle of extravagance and savagery just beyond, just below. . . .

Ah! What a sight, this wild terrain cleft violently end to end and exposed like an open grave! The light flares and wanes, flutters, as though caught in a sudden gale, as though eclipsed by a flight of harts. Oh woe, her princes are denied a pasture, nature is convulsed, and a terrible commotion, sundered by plosives, sounds all about. Angoscioso and disperato, rising and falling intervals in the tremulous matinal gloom.

Black bars radiate from this turbulent arena, laid on the surrounding hills like the stripes of a rod in the day of wrath, and at the end of the black bars, like whipstocks for the maimed, letters. Flickering neumes: VAGINAL ORIFICE, LABIA MAJORA. And not a propylaeum: a PERINEUM. ANUS: the afflicted pit. Alas, despised because they have seen her nakedness. C to C and F again. Like the echo of letters, the shadow of codes, the breath of labia, yea, she sigheth, and turneth backward, a simple canticle, notations writ on the posteriors of a kneeling woman, this kneeling woman, these posteriors: URETHRA, CLITORIS, black indications quavering in this ghostly crepuscular light, the light of the world, the light of a solitary city at the end of night, the coldest hour.

Between the spreading intrados of the massive thighs, below the bitter valley, through a filigree of letters suspended mysteriously in the archway—MONS VENERIS, now sharp, now diffuse—beyond and through all this can be seen the distant teats, hanging in the wind, blowing in the dawn wind, oh, therefore she came down wonderfully, her last end forgotten, heavy teats ready for milking, their fat nipples swollen with promise. They sway in the wind, and something is indeed falling from them, yes, like frozen milk: Snow! Snow is falling, falling from the big teats, snow is swirling in the bitter wind, under the pale corrugated belly of the wintry dawn, blowing out of the ANUS and the VAGINAL CANAL, it is snowing on the city.

O Lord, behold my affliction! A vast desolation, the city, the afflicted city, far as the eye can see, stones heaped up to the end of the earth, lying dead in the winter, dead in the storm; whose hands could have raised up so much emptiness? the enemy hath magnified himself. Yet decrescendo, this, the intervals blurred now by the grinding whine of low-geared motors, for in spite of everything dim towers, ruby-tipped, rise obstinately through the blowing snow, a multitude of lamps blink red and green in fugal progressions down below, chimneys puff out black inversions and raise a defiant clamor of colliding steel, and the snow itself is swallowed up by a million dark alleys, just as their fearful obscurities are obliterated by the blinding snow.

Through the city, through the snow, under the gray belly of metropolitan morning, walks a man, walks the shadow of a solitary man, like the figure in pedestrian-crossing signs, a photogram of a walking man, caught in an empty white triangle, a three-sided barrenness, walking alone in a lifelike parable of empty triads, between a pair of dotted lines, defined as it were by his own purpose: forever to walk between these lines, snow or no snow, taking his risks—or rather, perhaps that *is* a pedestrian-crossing sign, blurred by the blowing snow, and, yes, the man is just this moment passing under it, trammeling the imaginary channel, the dotted straight and narrow, at right angles. There he is, huddled miserably against the snow and wind and the early hour, shrinking miserably into his own wraps, meeting the pedestrians, those shadows of men making their dotted crossings, at right angles, meeting some head-on as well, brushing through the cold and restless crowds, as horns sound and airbrakes wheeze, sirens wail, all her people sigh—they seek bread—the last whimpering echo of a plainsong guttering like a candle in the morning traffic.

His hat jammed down upon his ears and scowling brows, his overcoat lapels turned up to the hat brim, scarf around his chin, he is all but buried in his winter habit. Only his eyes stare forth, aglitter with vexation and the resolution to press on, and below them his nose, pinched and flared with indignation, his pink cheeks puffed out, blowing frosty clouds of breath through chattering teeth. His mouth, under his mustache, is drawn into a rigid pucker around his two front teeth; my god, it is cold, what the fuck am I doing out here? His hands are stuffed deep in his overcoat pockets, and—poking forth from his thick herringbone wraps like a testy one-eyed malcontent—his penis, ramrod stiff in the morning wind, glistening with ice crystals, livid at the tip, batting aggressively against the sullen crowds, this swirling mass of dark bodies too cold for identities, struggling through the snow, their senses harrowed, intent solely on keeping their brains from freezing.

Oh, my poor doomed ass, I'm in real trouble, he whimpers to himself as he trundles along, tears trickling down his cheeks, teeth clattering, frozen snot in his mustache, up against it, expletives the only thing that can keep him warm, that he can pretend will keep him warm, shouldering his way through a thickening stupefaction, sidestepping the suicides, aching with cold and feeling sorry for himself, sick of keeping it up but scared not to, picking them up, putting them down, there he goes, a living legend, who knows, maybe the last of his kind, seen through a whirl of blowing snow, through a scrim of messages, an unfocused word-filter, lamenting the world's glacial entropy and the snow down his neck, bobbing along in this cold sea of pathetic mourners, this isocephalic compaction of misery and affliction, the dying city and he in it, sending it all to hell yet refusing to quit, refusing to tip over and get trampled into the slush, and so celebrating consciousness after all, in his own wretched way, the man of the moment, the lord of the leg-over, the star, the one and only: Lucky Pierre.

The swish and blast of the passing traffic modulate into a kind of measureless rhythm, not a pulsation so much as an aimless rising and falling, sometimes blunted, sometimes drawn brassily forth. Subways rumble underfoot, airdrills rattle in alleys, and there's the thunder of jets overhead like occasional celestial farts. Tipped wastebaskets spill bottles, newspapers, pamphlets, dead fetuses, throwaway cameras and mobiles, coils of black cable, burnt spoons, old shoes. Cars, spinning gracefully in the icy streets, smash decorously into one another, effecting dampened cymbals, sending heads and carcasses flying through their shattering windshields and crumpling percussively into snowbanks. Above the crowds, a billboard asks: WHAT IS MY PRICK DOING IN YOUR CUNT, LIZZIE? Six blocks away and around the corner, a theater marquee replies: FUCKING ME! FUCKING ME! OH SO NICELY!

A little old lady, leaning on a cane, hesitates at a curb, peers up at the light, now changing from green to red. Her spectacles are frosted over; icicles hang from her nose; her free hand trembles at her breast, clutching an old frayed shawl. The man, our hero, trying to beat the light, comes charging up, but not in time, skids to a stop, glissandos right into the old lady's humped-over backside, bowling her heels over head into the street with a jab of his stiff penis. There is a brief plaint like the squawk of a turkey as a refuse truck runs her down. Old as she was, it's still all a bit visceral, but soon enough the traffic rolling by has flattened her out, her vitals blending into the dirty slush, her old rags soaking up the rest.

—Pity, someone mutters.

—Life's tough.

—Goddamn street cleaners, never around when you need them.

The light changes, the old lady is trampled away. There's the blur of hurrying feet, kicking, pounding, slogging through the blood, slush, and snow. Thousands of feet. Going all directions. *Whush, crump, crump, stomp.* Crushing butts, condoms, chewed bones, dead batteries, gum wrappers. Someone's pocket watch. Film tins and beer cans. *Crump, crump, crump,* a kind of rasper continuo. Wind-up toys and belt buckles. Lost dentures. Projector sprocket. Used needles. Ticket stubs. All those frozen feet, shuffling along, *whush, whush,* almost whispering: That's right, Maggie, lift your arse and—*whush, crump, crump*—tickle my balls! Oh shit, it's cold! *It's too fucking cold!*

No. Stop thinking about it. Change locations. Think warm, think green. Come on, lift your arse and, whush, crump, give it a try. Think nymphet. That's better. Behind a tree maybe, peeking out at one side, at the other showing her sweet little buns, blazing in the sunlight. Sunlight! Imagine! At the edge of a meadow, say, there she is, go for it. Hup two three. Through the wildflowers, into the sun-dappled forest—she takes off, her bright tail flashing like a doe's scut, what a sight!—over fallen trunks, crackling branches, and dry leaves, pick 'em up, put 'em down, you're moving now, splashing through a tinkling brook, up warm mossy rocks, keep it going! Some kind of music. . . .

(*Front end of a heavy bus, barreling through the city street, spitting up snow, whipping it into black froth: blaaaat! Printed on its destination sign in the grimy front window:* THE ADVENTURES OF LUCKY PIERRE.)

Cantilena maybe, piped on a syrinx, good. Cissy'd like that, all' antico, right. The nymphet's scintillating butt luring him, there and then not there, winking like a flickering zoetrope image through the trees and the dappled light, drawing him closer and closer, his breath heaving, his heart pumping, he's got her, they are thrashing about now, their limbs entwined, no snow, no wind, this is great!—no, she's scampered off!—no, he has her, she has him, that's it, keep going, they tumble, keep going, damn it, they tumble in slow motion out of the forest into the soft grass of the meadow, crushing daisies and buttercups, flutes fading, silence drenching now the sunny green space, his heart thumping in his ears, street sounds diminishing to nothing more than a playful whisper in the fading forest—

(*Sudden roar of the bus, splattering through snow, blackened with soot, its foglights glowing dully, horn blaring. Sprayed crudely along one muddy side, under the greasy windows:* DIRECTORS' CUT. *City streets, buildings, people, traffic, go whipping by.*)

Sshh! Getting there! Not just one but nine of them now, a pretty anthology in the sunny meadow, that's right, nine nymphets upside down in a tight circle, poised upon their little shoulders, back to back, cheeks to cheeks, peachily radiant in the sunlight, legs spread like the petals of a flower. He hovers busily, his limbs churning, stinger in view, high off the ground, admiring the corolla, many-stemmed, each with its own style and stigma, the variegated pappi blowing in the soft summer breeze; then he drops down—here we go!—to nibble playfully at the keels, suck at the stamina, slip in and out of septa. Distantly: the returning sound of muted trumpets—

BlaaaAAAAAAATT! He jumps back to the curb, but too late, a bus bearing down on him—*THWOCK!*—whacks his boner as it goes roaring by: He screams with pain, spins with the impact, and is bowled into the crowd, now crossing with the light, spilling a dozen of them. He catches a glimpse of the bus gunning it on down the street, trailing black fumes like projected shadows, an advertisement spread across its rear—I CAN SEE HER CUNT, GUSSY!—and what looks like the eye of a gaping pig in the back window, staring out at him. The crowds, rushing and tumbling over him, curse and weep:

—What is it like, Nelly?

He hobbles to the edge of the flow, nursing his bruised cock, looking for a reason to go on, looking for something to wrap it in. He finds a bum sleeping under a newspaper and appropriates page one with its banner head: A LARGE HAIRY MOUTH SUCKING HIS PURPLE DICK.

Aw, hey, listen: fuck it. That's it. No more. Quit.

He sits on the curb, snuffling, huddled miserably over his battered rod, wrapped now in crumpled newsprint, trying to coax green dreams out of his iced-up lobes, trying in vain to recall all the pleasant things he had from days of old, all the delightful things of the pecker and the eye, feeling the cold creep up his ass all the while, no sorrow like my sorrow: bitter snatch of the diatonic aubade. Something seems to leave him, some spring released, a slipping away. . . .

No! he cries in sudden panic, leaping up. Forget that shit, waste those frames! *Move* it, damn you: hup two three *four!* He's running flat out now, prick waggling frantically, stiff-arming the opposition, recocking the spring, leaping the lifeless, goal in view, central heating, hot tub, all that, gonna make it—*oof!* sorry, ma'am!

—Good *morning,* L.P.! Oooh! How *nice!*

—Good morning, love! (*whoof!*) After you!

—Why, *thank* you, Mr. P!

—Morning, sir! Thank you, sir!

Ah, damn it, is it nothing to you, all ye that pass by?

Parallelograms of bright light rotate and intersect kaleidoscopically, in rhythm with a fluttering thump like feet pumping an organ or a propeller blowing in the winter wind, at times almost syllabic: by-aye-aye-aye-aye. . . . Within the shifting planes of flashing light can be seen stabler shapes, real and reflected, the backside of a person in uniform, a recurrent allusion to an infinite series of lighted passageways, the mutating images of drifting automobiles. And beneath the whump and flutter, the steady damp hum of a cave or a vast chamber. Through this whirl, as though projected through it, comes a man, intense, unhurried yet purposeful, his quick stride reflected in the gleaming marble floors. As he mounts the half-dozen stairs of this outer vestibule, a young woman in a natural lamb's-wool sweater and tweed button-through skirt with beige suede waistcoat, carrying a mobile phone and clipboard, passes him on his right, descending. Another woman crosses left to right in the foreground like a screen wipe, momentarily eclipsing the man from view.

When she has passed, he is seen with his foot poised decisively on the top step. Everything has stopped. Cold. The woman in the suede waistcoat has arrived at the shiny space before the revolving doors, the abrupt stilling of their motion suggested by a luminous blur, and she has turned to glance appreciatively up at the man. The man is removing his dark felt hat, or perhaps is tipping it, glancing off to his left as though recognizing someone, or noticing something important. Backlight radiates in the blond hair of the woman behind him; she has brought a purple felt-tip pen suggestively to her lips.

—Good morning, L.P.!

—Morning, Mr. P! Some storm, eh?

—Fuck me, you can say that again!

—What? Some storm, you mean? Is this a retake?

There is snow still in the rolled brim of the man's lifted hat and on the shoulders of his stylish herringbone overcoat. His jaw is firmly set, his brows slightly arched above his frozen leftward glance. He seems poised there on the top step as if on the threshold of some grand but unspecific adventure. Unseen high heels click on the marble floors. The fluttering sound of the revolving doors diminishes but can still be heard behind the continuing conversations, though nothing moves.

—*Love* the coat, L.P.!

—Help you off—?

—Careful! *Ow!*

—Oops! 'Scuse me, Mr. P!

—It's still numb, but it's starting to hurt.

—Well, chin up! Or . . . whatever. . . .

The man anchored on the top step, glancing left, has a thin mustache, curled slightly at the tips. His eyes are alert, his face impassive. His right hand lifts the hat with snow in its brim, his left carries an attaché case; both are gloved in kidskin. The wide lapels of his belted overcoat are turned down around a white ribbed cashmere scarf. The head of his penis, poking rigidly out between the rugged leather buttons of his coat, is pale blue—something between robin's-egg and wisteria—and is brightly ornamented with glittering ice crystals. Past his right elbow, in front of the doors locked in blurry midwhirl, the waistcoated woman with the clipboard continues to smile fixedly up at him, around the purple pen in her teeth, with sly admiration.

—Going up!

—All right, let it run!

There is a sudden unfocused rush toward the elevators in which the man in the herringbone overcoat is momentarily lost to view, but he is soon rediscovered, pushing through the crowd, wet felt hat tipped low over his brow, teeth bared.

—Cold enough for you, L.P.?

—Are you kidding? Hold it!

—If you insist.

—No, I meant—

—But—*brrr!*—feels like you could have used a mitten!

—Are we shooting *The Cunt Auction* today, Mr. P?

—Next week, I think. Ask Cissy.

—Ready for the second freeze, L.P.?

—Yeah, hit me.

—Good morning, sir!

The uniformed elevator operator smiles, stepping aside for him to enter. He brushes by, grazing the tips of her proffered breasts, his coat now over his arm. Two young girls board the elevator with him, and the operator closes the doors and begins the ascent, announcing the floors as they climb. The two girls, gazing up at the man as though suddenly smitten, draw together behind him and take deep breaths, their breasts lifting, as he removes his hat and stretches forth his left arm and, without impatience yet with a sense of the importance of the moment, as with all moments in his life, glances at his watch. And, once again, everything stops.

—Fourth floor. Five. Six.

—It's *him,* I tell you!

—Yes, step in, move to the back, please!

—H'lo, L.P. You're looking a bit blue.

—Wow! I've never met a real, you know, *artist* before!

The gesture of extending and bending his arm has hiked the man's jacket sleeve a perineum's length above his shirt cuff, exposing a ruby cufflink, vivid as a nipple. His coat is folded ceremonially over his right arm; he carries his attaché case in his right hand, his felt hat in his raised left, the one with the gold watch on the wrist at which he gazes inquiringly, face-to-face, suggesting a kind of dialogue between seen and seer. The suit jacket is a chalk-striped worsted with natural shoulders and narrow lapels, the cotton dress shirt powder-blue with satin stripes. The cavernous drone of the vestibule has vanished instantly with the closing of the elevator doors; there is now a dense weighted hush, almost tangible, and, distantly, a soft rushing whisper, like a muffled whistle, painting the still image with the movement of sound.

—Twenty-one. Twenty-two.

—Gosh, look! It sparkles!

—Excuse me! Out, please! See you later, L.P.!

—It's like a popsicle!

—Ciao!

—With an iced plum on the end!

The concealed fluorescent lighting, playing off the teak paneling, suffuses the elevator with a rich ruddy glow. There are sensuous glints of crimson in the gold watch on the man's raised wrist and in the soft auburn hair of the operator. He wears a burgundy silk tie, which contrasts with the operator's lime-green one, and the stem of a pipe pokes from one jacket pocket, adding the casual touch. His fixed expression is firm, even cold, bespeaking, like his impeccable taste, a man of power and influence, yet there is a warm glint in his brown eyes, teasing humor in his thin mustache, one brow arched thoughtfully as he stares intently at the round watch as at a navel or a crystal ball. The operator smiles cheerfully with the left side of her face, and presumably with the unseen right as well. Behind her, the two girls with lifted breasts and parted lips peek up over the man's right shoulder, their heads drawn together, their infatuate gaze fastened upon him as if upon an ineffable mystery.

—What flavor is it?

—*Bllmmf!*

—Thirty-nine. Forty. . . .

—My turn!

—Don' wush mwe! I fink he's—*awlck!*

—Ahh—*grunt!*—that helps!

—Step back, please! Let them out!

—*Whoof!* Thank you, my dear, I can almost feel it now. . . .

—Thank *you,* sir! That was delish!

—Fifty-one.

The two girls with parted lips seem enamored of his right ear; his own gaze is locked still upon his watch, as if this steadfast gaze were the mechanism by which its hands, if it has hands, have ceased to turn, his tense inquiry stilling thus the notorious unmoved mover. An illusion of course (such is the very substance of his vocation), for if all else has seemingly stopped, the operator's inexorable voice-over count continues.

—Fifty-ninth floor. Watch your step, please.

—Morning, L.P.!

—You going up or down?

—Don't ask. . . .

—That was yummy, but it was so cold it made my teeth ache!

—Sixty-five. Sixty-six.

—You think there's more?

—There always is. . . .

—Your floor, sir.

—Pull up your pants, L.P. Third freeze coming up!

—No, wait—!

—Too late, sir. They're rolling.

The receptionist, just cradling the crimson desk phone, looks up from her desktop monitor as the man, taking a deep breath and dropping his coat behind, his fly gaping and pants unbuckled, exits the elevator, smoothing down his mustache, moistening his lips. He strides purposefully, shaking off his jacket, kicking his shoes aside, toward the receptionist's desk, watched by the smiling operator in the obscure empty chamber of the elevator behind him. A dark-eyed woman in a tangerine skirt, carrying a file folder, crosses right to left behind him, moving toward the elevator. She pauses, her long brown hair swirling loosely about her shoulders as she turns her head to glance up at the man, perhaps in surprise, or perhaps pretending surprise, as, stepping out of his trousers, he bears down upon the receptionist.

—Good morning, sir!

—Cissy was just looking for you, Mr. P!

—Hold it!

The receptionist, in profile, smiles up with dazzling white teeth at the man. Her back is arched, her breasts jutting forward in the classic manner, her golden skirt taut with secretarial attentiveness. The man has stopped dead in midstride.

—Call for you on two.

—Morning, sir!

—I think it's the Mayor.

—I'll take it in my office.

He is gazing down on the receptionist, a faint ironic smile playing on his frozen lips, lifting slightly the curled ends of his mustache. His right foot is planted firmly on the tiled floor, his left leg bent at the knee. He carries his attaché case slightly forward in his right hand, like a weapon or an offering. He wears a soft cream-colored undershirt beneath the open blue shirt, snug continental briefs to match, the thumb of his left hand hooked in the waistband. His left toe seems just to have left the floor about a foot behind his planted right heel, and behind the poised toe, all the way back into the paneled elevator which has discharged him: a hasty scatter of rumpled clothing.

—Coffee, L.P.?

—Market reports, sir.

—Who's that brunette over there doing the filing?

—A new girl, sir. Would you like to break her in?

—In a moment. . . .

The powder-blue shirt, unbuttoned and tails free, is loose and flowing with the man's forward motion. His hairy belly, partly concealed by the blur of attaché case, is tanned and hard, the briefs below stretched like a flying jib against the rising mast within. Just behind him, a worsted jacket raises one chalk-striped sleeve starchily from the floor as though in greeting, or farewell, or reaching perhaps for the ruby cufflink nailed into the air above it, and a silk tie hovers over his shoulder in midflight like a dark red bat.

—Mr. P!

This scream is launched at a high soprano squeal but suddenly plummets to a grinding basso profundo. At the same time certain things begin, very slowly, to happen:

The man's right knee flexes.

His calf muscle ripples.

His left toe rises, his knee doubling.

The silk tie curls like a licking tongue, then sags.

The fingers on his right hand release their grip on the attaché case.

The thumb of his left hand descends with glacial force, pushing down on the waistband of the masted briefs.

The jacket sleeve begins its graceful collapse.

The cufflink arcs away from the sleeve's yawning reach.

The tangerine-skirted fileclerk behind him brings the file slowly toward her face as though donning a ritual mask, hair lifting, strands stretching.

The operator, still smiling, commences a step backward into the elevator.

The burgundy tie slides downward through the air like a kite on a loose string.

The receptionist's thighs lift away from the office chair.

The fingers on her right hand stiffen, and the crimson designer phone begins to separate itself from her hand.

The fileclerk's mouth slowly opens and a low rumbling sound emerges, like that of an old bear deep in a damp cave.

The cufflink falls at her feet with a hollow pop and rises again off the tiled floor. The jacket sleeve ripples softly at the conclusion of its fall.

The operator completes her step back into the elevator. Shadows pass across her face. Her left arm rises slowly.

The rumble gradually augments in volume and pitch as the silk tie crumples to the floor.

The attaché case flies straight ahead. The phone receiver seems to float.

The man's right knee starts to straighten, as the left leg continues to double.

The receptionist twists gracefully to her right. Her knee comes into contact with her chair as her feet leave the floor, and the chair too begins to lift and sail toward the wall behind the desk.

Papers rise from the desktop; a letter basket begins to tilt, the elevator doors to close. Behind the fileclerk's roar, there are sounds like the collision of soft metals, the grating of rusted hinges, apples tumbling in a deep barrel.

The man's rosy erection, springing free at last, rises like a clenched fist.

The cufflink completes its fall and glides into the elevator shaft.

The man's right hand arrives at the desktop as his right foot leaves the floor. His hips swivel and lift, and his buttocks, bared by the lowered briefs, rise like a floating buoy above the sea of flying paper, canopied by the high fluttering banners of his powder-blue shirttails. The dark-eyed fileclerk in the tangerine skirt, watching from behind, is now screaming in a baritone.

The elevator doors close. There is a deep resonant boom and a thunderous rattle as the crimson phone strikes the desktop, the steel chair caroms off the wall. The attaché case soars out of view. A bronze cast of his famous organ, regally tumescent, lifts away from the desktop like a launched rocket, propelled by the fileclerk's tenor scream.

The man doubles at the waist, his feet rising rapidly above the desktop, the underpants now nearly at his knees. The receptionist's face disappears behind the desk; her golden hips arch upward and her thighs spread awkwardly. A garter snaps with a fulminous pop like a jeroboam of champagne blowing its cork. The scream peaks into alto and is cut off as the fileclerk's teeth clamp down on the file folder, but simultaneously a new cry is heard from behind the desk, a halftone lower than that of the fileclerk but rising rapidly: *O-o-o-o-o-o-o-ow!*

The man's left knee has, in midair, doubled up clear of the briefs, but they catch now around his left ankle and right thigh, and he fails to clear the desk—his hand releases the waistband and reaches out. His right buttock makes crushing contact with the desktop and flattens. Papers take off, pens and pencils fly like thrown darts, and a stapler leaps from the desk like a frightened animal breaking from cover. There is, beneath the receptionist's fading cry, a sound much like that of a rug being beaten, and then a deep bass plaint soaring toward a clear G-sharp:

—*G-A-A-A*-A-A-W-W-W-D-A-A-*A-A-M-M-M!*

His buttocks bounce off the desktop like a beach ball, rising above his head. His legs spread, stretching the cream-colored underpants into a narrow taut band between ankle and thigh. He ducks his head to somersault into the wall and fallen chair, grabbing at the desktop monitor as he goes and taking it with him, his shirttails now around his ears, just as the receptionist completes her own flip, her golden skirt now hiked waist high, the popped strands of her black garterbelt fluttering as her otherwise bare bottom slaps the tiled floor. Phone, bronze cock, coffee cup, ashtrays, stapler, monitor, keyboard, and baskets crash and rattle explosively.

The receptionist raises herself on her elbows to watch the man as he bounces off the wall, his legs still tangled in the shorts. He lies there awhile, stretched out, eyes closed, his penis, the real one, dipping and swaying uncertainly.

—Ah, shit, he says in that dull sensuous monotone so beloved by millions throughout the world.

There was a time once. It wasn't like this. He could soar over trees, if he wanted to. In that time. Groves of trees, whole fucking forests. Buildings too, probably, but maybe there weren't any. It must have been a long time ago. The skies were blue. There were green meadows. Far as the eye could see. Flowers. Real ones. Two or three running steps, and then: lift! Your body just dropped its weight off like an old coat and up you went! And when you touched down again, it was soft and springy underfoot; this is true, it's how it really was. Springtimes then. There were dense endless springtimes. Not here, no. Yet . . . it must have been here. Only, it must have been . . . different then. Is that possible? How is it not possible, if he remembers it? Days were all of a piece in that time, and there were fantastic adventures in every direction. Then suddenly it was over, everything started closing in, running down, freezing up. Cleo. Yes. She spoiled it. Not malice, no, she was just a child, it was just her way; it was *his* fault, as it always was. Last of the superdays. . . . The cool clear water washes over him once again, fills his eyes, swirls round his chest, chills his groin. Her body rippling beneath the emerald-green waters, pale, shimmery, like patterns on an oscilloscope. She wriggles to the surface, flashing her hard young pussy at him, its tight red ringlets, pink shadows—an epiphanic burst of shattered light, then down she plunges again, deeper and deeper, trailing bubbles, her long limbs glowing, down where the water's a bright blue, deep aqua. Where it's dangerous. The feel then of her slender waist, the way she thrashes about, the blows striking thickly, pleasurably, against his chest, against his thighs, the springy dance of her wild red curls, the bubbles bursting against his eyes—god, what did all that glory have to do with a coldwater flat? With the goddamn pain in his ass?

He stumbles into his office, alla zoppa, loathing the world. Cecilia follows with the clothes. As he passes, her assistants slap him affectionately on the butt.

—Nice try, sir!

—Whew! Nasty bruise there on your fanny, Mr. P.

—Don't worry, sir, we'll edit it out.

—Should we call the doctor, L.P.? She might have something to put on that.

—Not today, Cissy, I'm not up for it.

In his office, he pushes a button and a floor panel slides back, revealing a heated recessed whirlpool bath. The office is paneled in dark cherry and is equipped with built-in audio and film gear, computer workstations, pinball machines and video games, projection screens, an editing bench, bicycle and weight machines, a dropdown kingsize version of the legendary Marvelous Bed (he has the original in his flat), and a real mahogany desk from the old days. Deep jungle-green carpeting has been laid wall to wall around the bath; on the walls, shag shots of himself fucking beautiful women, framed in light boxes, making the glossy bodies seem to glow like fleshy lightbulbs. Mechanized gyro-mirrors are spaced about, giving the room several extra dimensions, and in a couple of them, while his assistant adjusts the dimmer and color switches of the concealed lighting to a softer rosier tone, he examines his bruises.

—Last damned time I'm gonna try that with briefs on, Cissy. I'm getting too old for cockeyed stunts like that!

—Speaking of cockeyed and stunted, L.P., you don't look your old self up front either.

—It's been a helluva morning.

Members of his staff enter with correspondence for him to sign, sex manual photos to autograph, project treatments, scripts, and storyboards for his approval: *Home Movies, Lucky Pierre's Fucking Academy, The Bachelor Party, The Maidenhead Xpic,* a true-life cliffhanger called *The Falling Star.*

—Put them over there.

His bed-sized desktop is cluttered with tapes and film clips, black-letter ballads, aphrodisiac samples, publicity stills, ex voti, tobacco tins, desperate epigrams, and a flocculent scattering of diverse pubic hairs. Beside a tailor's dummy for a cocksock there is a framed photograph of a woman being banged by three hundred masked men at a lynching, which is signed *Dearest Lucky, my hero! I miss you terribly! Luv, Cleo.* He pushes aside a stack of project folders and video cassettes to clear a space, chooses his quill from the loins of a brass Robin Goodfellow, dips it into the stretched hairless cunny of an ancient Shelah-na-Gig, a gift from Cinecity's Mayor, signs his magic name a few dozen times, then dick-stamps the rest. In green. Color of the day. Production assistants help him peel off the cream-colored undershirt and minister gently to his backside bruises, while Cissy tosses the old clothes down a chute and adds bath salts to the water. He attempts a few warm-up presses, but he is still frozen up inside, each movement a painful crunching of ice crystals deep in the tendons and near the bone. Something else is moving, though, so not all's in vain.

—Do you want to work in your PJs today, L.P.?

—No—*grunt!*—let's do the shirtsleeves thing, the dress shirt with the cuffs turned up. And the pants with the woolly codpiece.

He rises, wheezing, then crawls on his hands and knees over to another button: From a little mahogany stool near the bath there emerges a hand-painted disposable fur-lined chamberpot, a touch of old-fashioned elegance and a reminder of a simpler, happier time. He staggers to his feet, helped by Cecilia, and sits to shit.

—Let's put some synthetic pasture down out there too, Cissy. My elbow got an awful crack on that tile floor!

—How's that sequence supposed to end, L.P.? she asks with an expectant smile, taking a note about the carpeting.

—I wanted to melt a freeze frame, that's all. I thought it'd make me feel better.

—I got that part. But then—?

—Well, then the whole thing is supposed to keep speeding up until the grunts and groans are just weird little spiccato pips of sounds, see, and we're fucking each other so fast that we don't seem to be moving, or even seem to be fucking backwards, you know, stroboscopic, like the wheels of a train as it gets up speed.

—Aha, backwards. Nice idea, L.P., but it won't work.

—You telling me?

On one of the television screens, there are news reports about a *thawnow* computer virus unleashed by anarchist hackers that is causing a citywide systems meltdown on the circuit, about the increase in film piracy and street theater crimes, and about the use of old film archives to ease the fuel shortage, the Mayor explaining the city's new genre classification ratings (Burn-1 to X-Burn) and its icon-based energy priorities.

—I see, says the reporter, who is glimpsed briefly in a cutaway shot flashing her challenging white smile directly at him—or at any viewer, for that matter—her green eyes sparkling with her need to know, hard but hot, her head aflame with her wild red hair. He has, if memory serves him (it does, but not as continuity, more like a popping clapperboard that startles him from time to time), a date with her tonight. At their coldwater flat, where it all began, if *began* is the word in a life like his. To get there, he has to go back out into those blizzardy streets. He must be crazy. Then it's true, the reporter continues, saliva glistening at the corners of her parted lips. Hierarchies, favoritism, the eradication of lesser genres, the narrowing of dialogue—City Hall is indeed in the grip of a new fundamentalism, as some have argued?

—These are hard times, my dear, replies the Mayor, standing beside her desk under her display case of canes and whips, monumentally regal in her brass-buttoned black velvet jacket and matching wraparound skirt, split to the top of her bold bare hipbone. A sign on her desktop reads PRO BONO PUBICO. Such times call for absolute purity of production values and directorial intransigence in their pursuit, she says. The hard core of our society must be protected for all our sakes; heat must be invested in heat. That said, we would like to know—at your convenience, of course, your *earliest* convenience—the names and agents of your argumentative sources.

The reporter flashes her trust-me grin, which in fact can mean anything, as he knows all too well, and the Mayor responds from on high—towering over Cleo, and indeed over everyone, as she does—with an icy smile, a flash of statuesque thigh, and a cool wink of her own. Seems to be aimed at him, sitting there on his fur-lined pot. This show is probably what the Mayor was calling about. Cora never wants him to miss her when she is on television.

Cissy clicks the set off just as the camera cuts back to the reporter, remarking, not for the first time, that redheaded women are an aesthetic disaster on daytime digitized color transmissions; it was like someone scratching glass with their fingernails every time that woman showed up there. There's an edgy irresistible excitement about her, true, though he's learned not to say so around Cissy. Cissy calls up baroque chamber music from the central server, goes over to prepare coffee at the bar, heat up his muffins. And that skin, she adds. Like death warmed over. The least they could do is pancake away the shine.

Though he feels vaguely irritated by her presumption—bossed around in his own domain, as it were—he shrugs it off. She was just following his orders, after all: freedom from the trivia of the daily round, no art possible without it. So, sure, switch it off. What the hell does he care about the bureaucratic mess in City Hall? The Mayor has always been supportive, never questions his budgets, he owes Cora a lot—all of this, for example—but her confusing political problems he can do without. They'd just constipate him. And as for dear Cleo. . . . He bends over, and one of the production assistants wipes his ass with a sponge the size of a stenographer's notebook.

—I publish this manifesto to man, the historico-political animal! he declaims grandly from his stoop, and Cecilia laughs gaily. She is absolutely the happiest person he knows.

The young woman who has wiped him drops the sponge into the pot like a ballot, and then, instead of flushing it, pushes a button, and the whole apparatus folds odorlessly in on itself and disappears. He steps down into the swirling hot bath.

Oh! Oh my god! Terrific! Oh ho ho! Unbelievable! Yes! Toes, feet, calves, legs, his frosted balls jump for joy when the hot water churns up around them. Where's the heat coming from? Don't ask, just sink away, up to the shoulders; this is it, it's all happening right here, here in this great warm frothing pool, here and now, forget everything else, oh man, soak it up!

—It's good to be here, Cissy. It's so *good* to be here! Let's stay in this evening and look at old movies!

His eyes brim over with tears of pleasure and thankfulness. Cissy brings him his muffins and coffee, filling him in on the day's scheduled filming while she feeds him. Now and then she smiles happily at him, and just the joy, the simple grace of that smile, its generosity, sends a shiver up his spine. Her long golden hair is pulled into a knot behind her head, making her seem more bright-eyed and apple-cheeked than ever. She's wearing rust-colored jersey culottes today, with a black-, silver-, and tan-striped cashmere sweater, short nubbly knit mauve jacket, and matching scarf—a little wild maybe, what with the orange boots, painted buckles, and green streak in her hair (that's for him), but then that's his Cissy, his Girl Frig-a-daeg. Certainly the culottes are right for her; must have been invented for just her kind of little soft round fanny, *mmm*, that classic mass of ass, plump rump, cool cul, his sweet Cecilia. He stretches out in the hot water, watching her move that super crupper. Lotta bottom. Soft croft. Well, a little too soft maybe, a little too soft all over, kind of tummy you can't help but notice, and breasts a bit over the top for such a little thing, but so what? If she's maybe not the most beautiful woman in the city, she's buns down the most beautiful fuck. An artist. She is. And she knows how to take care of a man. When he's blue. When he's cold.

—It's too goddamn cold out there, Cissy. Out there on the streets. It's just too goddamn cold.

She laughs.

—What are you laughing at? I'm serious!

—You know what's wonderful about you, L.P.? It's how you can say exactly the same thing twice and yet get something so different out of it each time.

—No, listen, Cissy, I'm not kidding now, this morning—

—Just a minute, L.P. . . .

He sighs, closes his eyes, sinks deeper, feeling the hot water curl up into the grottos behind his ears. It's as though, now that the immediate sensations of that bitter walk are past, the real terror of it is finally getting to him. I-I was going to—

—Okay, L.P. Go ahead.

—Quit! My god, Cissy, I was going to quit! It was awful! There were, I don't know, like voices, telling me to fuck it, like they were projected onto the blowing snow or something, saying there wasn't any point in going on, I wasn't going to make it and what's more it didn't matter! Oh shit, I don't even know how to tell you, Cissy, it's never happened to me before—not just like that, I mean—I've had my bad moments, I've been down before, but this was terrible. I was walking on this thin crust, like it was my own skin or something, and underneath it was all empty—that sounds dumb, but that's exactly how it was, this hollow skin, and so fucking cold, the wind, snow blowing down my neck, feet frozen, even my eyeballs locked up. I had to stare straight ahead, and everything I looked at just froze up solid—people, traffic, even the rats—instant statuary! I felt like some kind of goddamn ice-age Midas, a fucking cock-carrying Medusa! Oh my god! What's happening to me, Cissy? I'm scared! I'm scared to go back *out* there! What am I gonna do?

—That's great, L.P.!

—*Great?* What do you mean, great? I'm bawling my *eyes* out! It's *awful!*

—No, I mean, I just taped it, she says with a warm smile. It's got a nice ring, L.P. Genuine. I'm sure we can use it. I loved the way you said "that sounds *dumb,* but that's *exactly* how it *was!*"

—Aw hell, Cissy, he grumps, and rolls over on his belly. Soap my back, will you?

Unnhh. That's better. Cissy doesn't simply soap a back, she plays it like a keyboard instrument. The rest of the crew help her lather his ass and thighs, while Cissy runs nimble arpeggios up and down his spine, presses tonics, inversions, and augmented sevenths out of his tensed muscles. Carezzando, martellato, amorevole. She squeezes out the ice crystals, thumps away the bad news, strokes the discords down the drain with the ever-changing bathwater. Uff! . . . mmm . . . yeah! . . . getting clean. . . . What could have put him into such a mood in the first place?

—Well, who did you fuck last night?

—Cally.

—Cally?

—Mmm. Onstage at the Foxy.

—Really? Gosh, I missed it, L.P. I didn't know—

—Neither did I. I thought she was a young danseuse named Cherie.

Should have known better, name like that had to be a put-on, and besides, she was too beautiful, only one woman in the world beautiful as that. Fooled again: the story of his life.

—I thought we were in the throne room of a deserted palace.

—A palace! Why, L.P., I didn't know there *were* any palaces anymore!

—That's right, there aren't.

—But then, how—?

—Well, uh, she . . . she showed me this weird ring. She said she was really a princess under a spell, and I—

Cissy leans back into rich mirthful laughter, flipping suds off the ends of her fingers.

—Oh, L.P.! That's marvelous! You're so innocent!

—You're right, Cissy, right again. How is it no one else has ever noticed?

He'd met the girl, the pseudo-Cherie, earlier in the day, interviewing her for the monkey's role in *The Organ Grinder,* a successful old caper they were reshooting; it was a great piece of sodomy and bestiality in its day—classic, really—and now Cissy had a lot of ideas for improving on it. Cally had played his co-lead in the silent version; maybe she was upset that he was looking for a new monkey for the remake. More likely, she did it for no reason at all. Cally's like that, lady of a thousand faces, turns up everywhere—he's pretty sure she was one of girls in the elevator in this morning's *Fashion Freezes,* for example. Whatever, there he was, humping madly away, thinking he was in the throne room with mirrored walls and fat-assed nymphs in the cupolas, fucking the frantic virgin granddaughter of the last king in the world's memory, when all of a sudden the lights came up and everybody gave him a standing ovation. Probably what did it, all right. That damned Cally.

—The Mayor came onstage after and gave me a dozen roses.

—Oh, L.P., I *love* it!

Cissy is laughing too hard to continue the backrub, so he rolls over on his back once more and sinks away, under the surface, letting the hot water push up against his ears and nose, spread his hair, soothe his eyes, help him forget the stuttery freeze-and-dissolve start to his day. While the production assistants work away at his pectorals, practicing their scales, learning proportion and the subtle art of dynamics, Cissy projects a series of shifting abstract patterns down from the ceiling and orchestrates the lights, tinting his visions with cerise, azure, emerald, and topaz. Soft hands lift his butt for the traditional cock-washing ceremony, speaking ritual fuckwords over him as they soap him up, manipulate his adductors, stroke him erect. Numbers flicker before his eyes; then Cissy plunges him into a deep cyaneous whirl, far below the surface—and yes, there she is, she or her virtual image, lying at the bottom, her golden hair floating free now from its simple knot, nearly green in the bathyal blues, her bared rippling flesh aglow, her sweet smile drawing him, drawing him, deeper, deeper: his true love and soulsister Cecilia, plump and complaisant, responding to his profoundest yearnings, making the world beautiful for him. What more could he ask? Slowly, majestically, he floats by, bloated with pent-up desire and gratitude, and explosively yet effortlessly looses his seed upon her: it feels for a moment like his whole body from crown to loins is joyously rent apart as though an egg were being cracked, then made whole again, healed, sealed up, renewed. As the first of the seed trickles down upon her like the trailing sparks of a fireworks display, her mouth opens, her eyes close, her limbs begin to writhe and twist. Her body seems to be trying to catch the falling seed, or to escape it, but there is no escape; the denser spray reaches her now, settling over her like the fall of snow, like those imitation snowfalls in the little glass balls: she throws her head back and thrashes about, ever more wildly as the seed cloud covers her, overwhelming her with terrifyingly relentless serial orgasms, her whole body pitching and lurching now as though plugged into an electrical circuit or thrown on a frypan, the water turning murky and turbulent, heaving him about, upending him; he's lost his bearings, he can't see, the water's in his eyes and nose and mouth and there's nothing to grab hold of—*HELP!*

He beats his way to the surface, squawking, gasping for breath, but the storm waves crash over him, submerging him again; he no longer knows which way is up or where shore might be, knows only as he is swept under, swallowing seawater, that suddenly, unexpectedly, it is all over. How can this have happened? What went wrong? Where the hell's the stuntman? He waits, foundering inside the raging sea, for his whole life to flash before his eyes, thinking: I might at least know at last, if too late, who I am! But with water filling his nose and throat, he cannot even remember two minutes ago, much less a lifetime; how did he get here and where's here? He seems to recall a cruise ship at sea, the captain's tower, he had one hand on the wheel, if he remembers rightly, the other up the skirts of a doe-eyed melon-breasted lady passenger, an heiress of some sort, or a princess, wildly beautiful, and with the other he was ripping his fly open and pulling his rampantly tumescent cock out—ah, that's right, so which hand was on the wheel? Probably how he got in trouble, not for the first time, if, alas, the last. His memory of the lady passenger, her breasts popping from her gown as though spring-loaded as his hand navigated her thighs (and what happened to her when the ship went down? has he just seen her, her luminous body barnacled with royal jewels, wriggling wraithlike below him in the tatters of her million-dollar gown, blowing bubbly kisses at him?), revives him momentarily and he battles his way to the surface once more, buoyed by his faith in happy endings and confident of his scripted prowess and resilience—or perhaps he is only dreaming that he is battling his way to the surface, just as his memory of the lady passenger may be only a dream, the dream of a drowning man, a man washed forever from the frame, lost at sea, one now, out of focus, among the unseen millions of dead and dying, sinking like a stone into watery oblivion.

A barren landscape, sparsely grassed. Near the sea, for waves can be heard softly lapping an unseen shore. Slow dolly over the crest of a pale hill to view the narrow bay below, clogged with tangled dark algae and what might be a limbless waterlogged body, rising and falling with the tidal ebb and flow, its head buried in the thick mass of floating seaweed. Giant hands appear, gliding tentatively over the hills and valleys but shying from the shore. One of the hands moves inland from the bay past a shallow sinkhole or animal burrow and over an arid ridge toward a tiny muddy mound imbedded in dark wet weeds. One finger touches the top of the mound delicately, moves it from side to side.

—She's beautiful! So furry!

—Especially under her nose!

—But, look, Euterpe! Her breasts are crushed!

—The poor thing! Is she still alive?

—I think so. Help me pull her out of the water. We'll take her to Calliope.

The pale terrain, now seen as the torso of a lifeless castaway, is dragged out of an algae-clotted bay not unlike that between the unfortunate creature's hairy thighs by eight comely nymphs, naked except for bits of wispy translucent material that flutter about their glowing bodies like swirling mist.

—Be careful, Polyhymnia! She's been stabbed by something between her legs.

—Is it something living?

—It might have been, but I think it must have drowned. Watch out, though. It may still have its claws in her.

The nymphs spread the castaway out to dry, arms outflung. They slap and stroke the body, hoping to bring it back to life again, pumping the knees back and forth against the chest, kissing the gaping mouth, blowing in the ears and nostrils.

—Look! There, under that thing that's stabbing her!

—It's her breasts! They must have fallen!

The nymphs touch their own breasts, trying to imagine this calamity, then, doubling the castaway's knees back, joggle the fallen breasts.

—Careful, Thalia! They might fall off!

—Do you think they just slid down or were they there all the time?

—Maybe her mother was a cow.

—We could try to push them back up again. . . .

—First let's see if we can pull that wormy thing out. Maybe it'll help revive her.

—Ick! It's disgusting! Like a dead sea slug!

—Easy, Erato! Don't break it off! We'll never get it out!

A few of the nymphs tug on it gently, trying to work it free, while the others worry with the displaced breasts.

—Look out! The thing's still alive!

—It's growing bones inside!

The nymphs squeal and fall back, watching the strange apparition rising before their eyes.

—It's magic!

—It must be some demon!

—Is it eating her?
—See how big it's grown!
—Maybe it's feeding on her fallen breasts!
—That's why they're so tiny!
—What do you think it is?
—I don't know, Melpomene, but it sort of *looks* like a woowallah!

The nymphs titter nervously and edge closer, reaching out with their fingertips to poke at it.

—Do you think she was playing with her woowallah and it got stuck inside her?
—It's not so cold now!
—If you tip it over, it just stands up again!

A redheaded nymph, more brazen than the rest, squats over it and slowly takes it inside her. It *feels* like a woowallah, she exclaims, only nicer! She rises off it, then lowers herself again.

—Clio! You shouldn't do that! It might bite!
—It may get stuck into you like it's stuck in her!
—You may get stuck *together!*

The rash nymph rises and falls upon the woowallah-like thing, slowly at first, then with increasing abandon, gripping it at the root with one hand, pinching her own nipples with the other, gasping and whimpering as though in sudden terror.

—It's already got hold of her!
—It'll kill her!
—Someone go get a knife!
—Throw yourself off, Clio! Save yourself!
—Here! Help me! Let's pull her away before it's too late!

The nymphs tear their screaming companion off the strange tuberous beast between the castaway's thighs just as a thick sap spurts from the tip of it.

—Look out!
—We saved her!
—In the nick of time!
—It's spitting venom!
—Excreting it, you mean!
—Yuck! I got some of it on me!
—Wash it off! Quick!

—Are you all right, Clio?
—Of course I'm all right. It was great!
—Great . . . ! the castaway echoes faintly, eyes still closed.
—She's alive!
—Clio did it!
—She pumped the bad stuff out!
—Killed that parasitic thing, too! Look how squishy it's gone!
—But what's wrong with her voice?
—It must be her fallen breasts!
—Or maybe she got too much water in her throat!
—Hello? Hello? Oh no! She's gone again!
—Maybe we ought to pump her out again like Clio did!
—Right!
—My turn!
—Don't fight! We can all have a go!

A handsome silver-haired nymph, beating out the others, plants herself astride the castaway and attempts to stuff the limp noodly creature up between her legs. It doesn't feel like a woowallah at all, she complains, and she takes it out again to look at it, doubling it back and forth between her fingers. I think it's broken.

—Maybe you have to pull on it again, Urania.
—Rub it in your hair!
—Squeeze the breasts underneath!

The other nymphs crowd around to help.

—Watch out for the sticky stuff!
—It's no use. Its bones are gone. Clio ruined it.
—And the poor dear's asleep again.
—She's suffered so much!
—But at least she's breathing!
—You can say that! She snores worse than you, Terpsichore!
—Perhaps she's under an evil spell.
—That would explain the hair on her face.
—Let's take her to Calliope. She'll know what to do.

As the nymphs lift the unconscious castaway and wend their way up toward the nymphaeum at the center of the lush tropical island, making celestial music as they go, there is a commercial break, so he takes the occasion to order up another drink, sitting by himself there on a stool at the neighborhood bar where he often goes to escape the ceaseless hassles of office and studio, or so it says in the script. On the old-fashioned nine-screen television over the bar, a trio of pubescent beauties are demonstrating the hymen-cracking virtues of three different "new improved" Lucky Pierre dildos: tumescent, semitumescent, and knotted. He can see the logic of running a dildo ad in the middle of all this girlish chatter about woowallahs, but, as the condition of his own woowallah when last seen was none of the above, there is an implicit suggestion amounting to a joke at his own expense that annoys him, and he makes a mental note to speak to Cissy about it. How many of the millions watching right now have the least notion of how difficult it is to perform that sort of cued limpness? And *hold* it? How many even noticed that, as Cleo was pulled off him, it dipped, according to the script, "as though to nuzzle in the fallen breasts once more"?

—I've got one of the old ones, says a woman at the other end of the bar. What's improved about the new ones?

—It's the action, says the bartender. Unbelievable. It's like the real thing.

—Oh yeah? What real thing?

The bartender winks at him, pours him another. He should be getting back, but outside the snowstorm has worsened, and anyway his hair is still wet. That film reminds me of my childhood, the woman at the other end of the bar says, and she comes over with her drink and hikes herself up onto the stool beside him, crossing her legs with a flesh-on-flesh *shush*. When I was six years old, my grandfather was dying. He said he was suffering from a terrible triangulated pain whose points or angles were on each side of his groin near the hipbones and in the hole between his old gray withered cheeks below.

—Uh, yes, well, if you don't mind, miss—

She unzips his pants, reaches inside, and pulls out his cock, effectively taking it hostage. Shouldn't have been inside there anyway, but he was trying to keep it warm.

—He asked me to stop up the bottom hole with my finger and then to suck the pain out of the tube in the middle of the triangle, she continues, clutching his organ tightly in her fist and thumbing its head rhythmically to focus his attention. He said it had to be done to a certain steady beat, which he marked out by slapping my bottom. Sometimes, even feeble as he was, he hit it so hard

I cried, and then he'd kiss it, for he truly loved me and meant me no harm. What terrified me at the time was that I couldn't imagine, if I should suffer some day as my poor grandfather did, how I'd ever get the pain out without one of those tubes, and when I sobbed out my fears to him one day, he said to dry my eyes, sweet child, he'd give me his. But he died trying, so it didn't stay. Ever since then, I've been looking for one that would, she says, squeezing, and, free hand between her legs, crosses them the other way.

He winces, nods at the bartender, who snaps his fingers, and two bouncers come over, haul her skirt over her head and knot it, and throw the woman out the door. For a moment: a bone-chilling draft. Hard to tell what time it is out there. Daylight, but dark with the clouds of snow whipped up by the whistling wind.

—Sad stories, says the bartender, as the doors close and the wind's howl fades. I guess you hear them every day.

—She was storyboarding, he replies, hunched over his drink. Palming off a treatment. One of the hazards of the trade.

—I get it, says the bartender. You mean she probably never even had a grandfather.

—Or if she did or does, he's most likely her agent.

On the multiple video screens overhead, the interrupted desert island flick has returned. The nymphs' wise leader has explicated the esoteric mysteries behind their treasured woowallahs, and he, or at least his appendage, is now being received as a god by these creatures who have never seen a man before. He is evidently not displeased by this. Palms sway in the breeze. The music of flutes and lyres and the sound of waves softly lapping a shore ride in over the dampered stormwinds at his back, the clink of bottles and glasses behind the bar. Would that he might find such simple peace and happiness again!

—Oh man, what a life, sighs the bartender, following his gaze up to the screens, which look like an oversized tic-tac-toe board, crossed with O's and X's of flesh. Beautiful! But what I don't understand is where in this day and age they found that island.

—About six blocks from here. We built it in the studio.

—No kidding! But all that water—?

—A windowed pool and a few optical effects. What you do is—

—Okay, please! laughs the bartender, I don't wanna know! It'd just spoil the magic! But when are they gonna start digitizing this new stuff of yours and putting it out on the circuit? There's some old pirated classics out there we can download and jerk off on, but—

—Never. No continuity out there. No discipline. Television is sloppy enough. It's the movies I love. And the movies love me.

When asked, he tells the nymphs his name, whereupon the one to whom he's been carried, Calliope, announces: Then he is our Father Pierrus, and the nymph Euterpe adds solemnly: And we are his little Pierrodies! Well, more or less solemnly. Cissy can never play a scene like this one completely straight; she always looks a bit like something's about to crack her up. But if her acting is sometimes undone by her natural gaiety, as a filmmaker she is always deadly serious, no matter how frivolous or self-parodic the script.

As the nymphs, guided by their new deity's instructions, proceed to use him in a variety of amorous ways, Cecilia mirrors her opening sequence by exploring the topography of the desert island as though stroking a living body, and indeed it does seem to breathe and undulate as though feeling itself stroked. His own body, possessed by nympholeptic bliss, is similarly caressed by her cameras as it was when it first washed up on shore, and when the nine nymphs bow down in front of the temple to worship his erection it appears almost to calcify, to become a kind of lingam of stone or marble, rising mightily above their quivering buttocks, aglow in the golden tropical twilight. Each movement is intricately choreographed, each shot angled and furnitured immaculately and studiously framed. At one point, Cissy/Euterpe cups her hand around his penis and blows across the top of it as though it were a flute or a bottle, making a strange whispery music, and the creamily lit pucker of her perfect lips at the edge of his pouting corona has a balanced asymmetry of shape and color so stunningly beautiful it brings tears to his eyes.

—She really knows how to toot a skin-flute, says the bartender. I'd love to get played like that! Are they releasing a single?

—Sure. In a virtual-reality version with gender-specific tactile effects, if you want them.

—Hey, you bet I do! I'll pick one up on the way home!

On the screen Father Pierrus, also known as the Great Woowallah, is now nestled between the sleek sinewy thighs of hairless Polyhymnia, played silently by Cassie, bestowing his godly blessings upon her, while Clara, as Urania, wearing her woowallah strapped on with a thonged hip harness, penetrates him from behind.

—Wow! laughs the bartender. With nine of these nymphos, the possibilities are almost endless!

—That's true. In fact, the director's original idea was to include every conceivable combination and order, but the variations were so numerous it actually would not be possible to witness them all in one lifetime, even if watched twenty-four hours a day on fast forward, much less to film them all or to do that much fucking.

—Hey, I believe it. All but the last. The bartender winks again, pours another.

It's the way Cissy approaches filmmaking. So soft and pliable in so many ways, she is uncompromising when pursuing the aesthetic implications of her films. There are no details too small to escape her artist's eye. Even her title sequences are intricately designed works of art. He loves her for it: for her professional rigor, her integrity, her craft, her boundless energy and imagination. He loves her body too, of course, so alive and bounteous, inexhaustible in its creative gestures, and he sometimes thinks that to be able to pass one's life exploring it and being explored by it should be enough for any man. Yet, he finds it difficult to connect deeply with Cissy, to get lost inside her, fascinated more by her professional enthusiasm than by her essence, in love with her as one might love a beautiful object or that object's ingenious conception.

What's most endearing about her and her films is how, almost miraculously, she makes everything new again. Just when you think you've seen it all, she shows you what you've just seen, and not for the first time, and yet you know you've never seen it before. She has made all her films over and over, and over and over they are a fresh delight, just as her body, revisited, is always new again, as though reinvented with each exposure.

Take *The Nuns' Gardener,* one of her early masterpieces. It had a simple theme, the release of pent-up desire, the subject and theme of many such films before it, mostly forgettable except for a star turn or two. But Cecilia made it all so startlingly original and exciting it was as though no one had ever fucked a nun before. Just the way the veiled novice and the young itinerant monk, working in the nuns' garden in exchange for his meager repasts, penetrated each other with their desperate and furtive glances when they could do no else, the way they touched themselves through their heavy garments with tentative, almost imperceptible strokes (but they *did* perceive them, each the other), even the way the tonsured gardener feverishly worked the furrowed soil or the nun washed and peeled the glossy vegetables for his supper proved to be so stimulating that few viewers in those days made it into the second reel without popping off. At one point, the nun, terrified by her own aroused desires, is praying her rosary in solitude before a brutally crucified Christ, whose cruel wounds have already received Cissy's sensuous treatment. Remotely, as throughout much of the film, a hollow Gregorian chant, haunting and sober, enwraps the images like a prophylactic seal. In the poor flickery light, there is a saintly glow about the little sister's upturned face; tears glitter in the corners of her eyes, and her silently murmuring lips tremble with an inner anguish—a chiaroscuro head shot that became one of the classic stills in cinematic history. Slowly, very slowly, her lips part, her eyes close in ecstatic contemplation. In shadowy close-up, one sees her fingers tugging at her rosary, which seems to be resisting her prayer as though in condemnation of her sinful thoughts, each bead held back as if by a divine fingertip, released only reluctantly, one by one, to her pious devotions. As the camera, slowly, meditatively, guided by the lugubrious plainchant, glides in across her kneeling thigh, it discovers the glistening rosary emerging from the damp nest between her legs like an anchor chain being hauled up from the deep, the restraining fingertip her aroused clitoris, rubbing or being rubbed by each bead with a jerking motion reminiscent of the old link-and-claw mechanisms of early film projectors. The wounded figure on the cross meanwhile is gazing down upon this sight with sorrow and pain (his hands and feet hurt) and gaping jaw but without condemnation—indeed, with a certain worshipful gratitude, as expressed principally by his little beanpole erection, poking out like a clothes-peg and gleaming as though with a high varnish. One seems to hear, perhaps as part of the *cantus firmus* (his wooden lips do not move), a voice whisper: Kiss me, O my beloved! (Or perhaps, Bless thee . . . or me . . .)

This is a film Cissy has remade, infinitely varied, many times over, and recently she has even, daringly, reshot the original classic, frame by frame, arguing that a camera is an eye without a memory, that nothing has ever happened before its gaze before, it sees everything, opening ever anew, as if for the first time, and thus the remake, though identical to the original in every detail, must be an entirely different film. This is, as she has often said, the magic of fuckfilms and why they have outlasted all other genres, in spite of the obvious theatrical limitations of living pricks and cunts—which have been the only performers in some of her more avant-garde films, wherein, having begun with the filming of a simple party-game frolic with blindfolds called *Randy Recognitions,* she has since boldly taken on all the genres and reshot the classics, often with the original scripts, but with nothing on-camera but genitalia. This fresh angle utterly revitalizes old movie bromides like "Look down there—it's not so hard, is it?" or "Whoever he is, our killer's disguise is both clever and cunning!" or "Get away from that lever or we'll all be killed!" The great historical epics have been especially amenable to this creative re-casting, but Cissy has also produced a number of low-budget art-house P&C gems, such as *Weenie Wisdom, Crotch Destinies, Cuntemplations, The Loving End: Fandangles and Butt Ballads,* and the wittily syncopated *Lap-Clapping: Twat It's All About,* which is one of her own favorites and something like a personal manifesto.

If Cissy is the artist, then he, L.P., is her long-playing star, her Cineman of Cinecity. It is he who has washed up on her desert islands, suffered heart-stopping freezes, got his dick caught in revolving doors, chafed by haircloth, used as a percussion instrument, or blown like a hornpipe, all in the cause of Beauty, or Cissy's pursuit of it. He has captained slave ships and space ships, been both doctor and patient, valet and master, fucked his way through harems, school playgrounds, fan clubs, and subway riots. Often she is at work on several films at the same time, so he is obliged to pick up a trio of randy hitch-hikers, buttfuck the new girl in the office, get silly with a monkey, and play a cunt-sniffing detective in one of her cocks-and-rubbers movies, all on the same day. First he's mooning over the girl next door, then he's an emperor throwing an orgy. And sometimes all these things in a single sequence, as in one of Cissy's current projects, *The Adventions of Lucky Pierre,* a self-ironizing sequel to her *Idventures,* which, with a rhythmic but discordant intercutting of old clips with new, attempts to empty his life of conventional meaning, replacing it with a purely aesthetic one, which she thinks of as liberating—as might he, were it not such a harrowing ordeal.

Now, for example, in an *Adventions* clip from the silent classic *The Master's Piece,* he has just dipped his prick in a pot of crimson paint and is approaching a virgin canvas when he realizes that what he is walking on is a high diving board and below him is a pool with naked leg-kicking water sprites swimming in seductive formation. He is about to dive into their midst when he finds himself not on a diving board but on the ledge of a skyscraper, high up in a wintry wind. He grabs the edge of the icy ledge in the nick of time, but as he dangles there a window opens below and someone commences to suck him off. It's a race between coming and going, but just as his fingers slip from the ledge the scene changes and he falls through a skylight onto a bed full of masturbating women. This is a clip from *Peeping Tom;* he recognizes it and knows what comes next, but it doesn't. Instead, the bed becomes a professional wrestling ring wherein he is about to meet a beautiful masked opponent known simply as Ballbuster who gets a grip on him before he can even stagger to his feet. It is not supposed to hurt but it does. *Ow!* he exclaims, and a voice-over, moving to the beat of the film's visual rhythms, says, *His is not to reason why but to reenact the divine phylogeny of his tribe! He is a word charged with holy appetite! He is the postulate of fortuity!*

He feels himself flattening out into a computerized image projected onto a wallscreen, tickled by the roving cursor arrow as the voice-over continues:

—He quickens the rhythm of our desire! He sutures the wound! He relieves the unrelieved monotony of the world of night! His aroused blue veins are thoughts of heaven. The two cheeks of his ass signify the active and contemplative ways of life—

But even as the voice carries on, it becomes a lecture in a classroom, he standing at a lectern in frock coat and garters, admired by a roomful of infatuated high-breasted coeds in miniskirts and penny-loafers, all trying to crowd into the front seats to touch if they can the hairy seat of wisdom. Scrawled on the blackboard behind him: *Phone for you, L.P.*

—Hello? Oh, hello, Cleo. . . . I *know* it's our anniversary, love, how could I forget? It's *always* our anniversary. . . . No, I can't, I'm into something right now, something good, we're pretty excited about it. . . . Yes, with Cissy. . . . Now, that's not very generous, Cleo. . . . Well, I'm sorry, why don't you use that big black mike with the telescoping boom you were playing with in your interview this morning? . . . Sure, I caught it; you were terrific, as always. But, look, I really must get— . . . Yes, yes, I promise. . . . Right, same place, same time; I'll be up there, you know I couldn't stay away if I wanted to. (But why couldn't he, damn it? *Why* couldn't he?) I have to go now, Cleo. There's someone knocking at the door—

There is a young girl at the door, smiling hopefully, dressed in a pinafore with full skirts, a buttoned blouse, and high-button shoes. Over her soft curls, she wears a lacy bonnet, tied under the chin. The man, pale, hollow-eyed, ramrod straight in his black tuxedo, scowls down at her. She curtsies, her head bowed. Words appear:

YOU ARE LATE!

O MERCY, SIR! I AM ALL ALONE IN THE WORLD!
MY MUMMY AND DADDY ARE IN HEAVEN
AND I MUST CARE FOR ALL THE LITTLE ONES!
PLEASE DO NOT BE HARSH!

He grimaces coldly, unappeased. He snaps his finger silently, and meekly she follows him.

They enter an ornate music room with high velvet drapes and thin patterned carpets. Daylight filters grainily through net curtains, falling on the highly polished surface of the grand piano. Bookcases and dark paintings in heavy gilt frames line the somber walls, half lost in dense shadow. On the mantel of the tiled fireplace, reflected in the gilded mirror above, are gleaming brass candlesticks, a small comport encrusted with flowers and cupids, a walnut mantel clock, a set of ivory elephants, and two china figures: a lady and a gentleman seated on couches. Bellows and a brass bedwarmer with a five-foot handle hang nearby. Along the near wall: a row of cushioned chairs with fluted legs and high scalloped backs. On two of them sit small girls, a glitter on their young cheeks as though of tears. A third child stands by the piano, wiping fresh tears from her eyes. There is a metronome on the piano, an oriental vase with dried flowers, and a polished birch rod, which seems almost to glow against the dark wood.

As the new girl enters, the girl by the piano leaves her place and joins the other two, rubbing her eyes with one hand, her bottom with the other. The new girl, watching this, glances apprehensively at her professor, at the gleaming birch rod on the piano. He sits on the piano bench, tossing his tuxedo tails behind him. He stiffens his back and with a flourish strikes an unheard chord, then nimbly runs the gamut with long white fingers. He turns to the new girl, standing uneasily beside him, still wearing her bonnet, her hands clasped nervously at her child's breasts, smiles perfunctorily under his thin waxed mustache. He strikes a key and indicates that she is to sing the note.

She purses her lips into a small o. He shakes his head, shapes his own mouth into a broad O, doubles his chin, holds his hands palms up at his diaphragm, and moves them slowly up and down as though lifting some weight. Again, he strikes the key and she attempts to sing the note, but the professor is still dissatisfied. He rolls up a quarto of music, stuffs it in his mouth, slowly withdraws it, holding his lips in the rounded position fixed by the rolled quarto. She attempts to imitate this. No, no, no! He stands, motions her to open her mouth, and pokes the rolled music into it. He shapes her cheeks around it with his fingers, as though modeling clay, ignoring her gagging. He withdraws the music carefully. Though her chin is quivering and there are tears in the corners of her eyes, she holds her lips in the molded position—but as soon as he strikes the note she is to sing, her mouth pinches reflexively into a smaller o once more. He leaps up; she clutches her mouth in guilt and fear. He pulls her hands away, stuffs the rolled music in her mouth, withdraws it partway, thrusts it in again: out, in, out, in, and finally, very carefully, out altogether. He nods, gestures encouragingly with upraised palms—hold it, just like that, dear—sits quickly, and strikes the key: success! He smiles. She smiles faintly, almost afraid to relax her mouth. He pats her hand.

The professor proceeds to climb the scale, note by note, twisting his dark lips broadly around each of the solfa syllables of the heptachord, she imitating him, anxious to please, terrified to fail, though all that can be heard is a faint staticky crackle. On the subdominant, he claps his hands over his ears and grimaces. She shrinks away, clutching both hands to her mouth. He lowers his hands, clenched in anger, glowers at the girl, then forces a grim smile on his chalky face. He commences the scale again, urging her to try harder. She takes a deep breath, once more stretches her mouth around each of the syllables—and again, on the fourth note, she offends him. He leaps up in rage and grabs the polished hickory rod. He orders her to lie down across his knees. She shakes her head, seems about to run. He smiles cruelly and repeats his order, his eyes glittering in their dark sockets. Too frightened finally not to obey, she kneels and leans tentatively forward, keeping a suspicious eye on her voice teacher. He shoves her brusquely across his lap and, holding her down by force, strikes her smartly across the skirts with his rod. She starts to rise, momentarily breaking free, her face showing confusion, astonishment, indignation.

Abruptly, she is across his legs again, her wrists bound to the bench feet; it is as though something has been passed over. Her skirts are up now, and her bottom, receiving new blows, is protected only by a pair of linen drawers. The man signals to the other pupils, and they pull the drawers down to her knees. Smoothing down his mustache, the man gloats unabashedly over his view of this smooth plump bum, still thrashing about rebelliously. Then man and bum vanish, displaced by:

WHAT A DELICIOUS EXPANSE
OF SNOW-WHITE BOTTOM!
HOW I LONG TO CUT IT INTO RIBBONS
OF WEALED FLESH & BLOOD!

The girl is now being held face down over the piano bench by the other girls, the drawers abandoned altogether, her pinafore unlaced. The professor, standing over her with a long limber switch, wets his fingers with spittle, marks a damp spot on one cheek, and brings the switch down on it with a sharp stinging stroke. The girl writhes and plunges, but there is no getting free. Again and again he brings the willow down on her flashing buttocks, dark stripes slowly emerging there like secret writing.

—That's great, L.P.! It looks like she's been striped with musical staves!

—Makes you ache for a zoom lens, though, doesn't it?

There is a pronounced bulge in the man's tuxedo pants. One of his pupils unbuttons his fly and releases the throbbing instrument trapped within. The little girls kiss it, nip it with their teeth, and strike at it with little whisks from the bowl of dried flowers, as he administers his punishment to the girl across the bench, the stafflike welts on the horsed girl's bottom and thighs now intricately crossed with bar lines.

—Look at that timing!

—Mmm. Those were the days when you just turned the cameras on, and if anything was going to happen, it was entirely up to the actors.

At the professor's signal, the girls unbind the victim and turn her over on her back on the bench. She resists but feebly, exhausted with pain and fruitless struggle, though she still tries vainly to hide her pubis from view. He slaps her hand away, snaps the willow switch at her thighs and childish mound tauntingly. Her face is streaked with tears; she seems to be wailing mournfully, tossing her head back and forth.

—It's almost tangible, isn't it, L.P.? I mean, not being able to hear—

—Wait!

The other girls strip her of her pinafore and blouse, draw her chemise up under her armpits. He flicks her pubescent breasts with the tip of the willow to bring the dark little nipples erect, as the girls drag his trousers down, lift his tuxedo tails to bite his hairy bottom, snap his garters. The switch disappears. His shoes, pants, the chemise. His pupils clap their hands and peer closer as he inserts the tip of his engorged organ between her legs. A final resistance: the girl rears up, kicks, strikes out at him, seems to be screaming. The others hold her down, kiss her breasts, double her knees back, exposing her striped thighs and bottom, dazzlingly white against the dark piano bench, lick at her wounds, kiss and fondle each other excitedly. The victim's eyes roll back, and her tongue lolls out of her mouth. He shoves and butts, but she is too tight. The girls reach in with their fingers, trying to create an opening, moisten his penis with their saliva. At last, with an enormous effort, the girls pushing from behind, he bursts through; blood gurgles out of the girl's mouth and dribbles darkly down her cheeks and into her lacy bonnet. Her eyelids flutter briefly, then cease, showing at the end only the filmy whites of her eyes. A halo seems to form around her bonnet. After a moment, there is sudden darkness, a flicker of scrawled numbers and letters, and then light again as the film's tail rattles out of the projector.

—That's wonderful, L.P., how she wears her boots and bonnet right to the bloody end!

—Mmm. In those days, we fucked with our socks on.

—Never knew when you might have to make a quick exit?

—No. The floors were cold.

Cissy brings the office lights up to a soft amber and threads the film for rewind, glancing briefly at the ident trailer. He rises slowly, moved by this vintage flick of his, more moved than he'd like to admit, and goes to mix drinks at the bar.

—That's right, says Cissy with a light laugh. You never see people balling on the floors in these old Peter Prick steamers, they always get up on something.

—Besides, you could get slivers.

Eighteen minutes of his life: how to judge them? And how judge the eighteen minutes just spent watching them? Or these passing ones, reflecting on reflections? With tears in his eyes . . .

—Wasn't that Cally playing one of the other girls?

—Yes, the one biting my cock there, early on, and with her finger up my butt at the end. She was just a child then but already a great actress, already very beautiful. I thought that film had vanished. It was like seeing it for the first time. Where'd you find it, Cissy?

—At an auction. I couldn't resist.

He hands her a drink. Dry nostalgic scent of cellulose nitrate in the air. Yes, some things change. Technology. Certain performance standards. But . . . ? He feels strangely insecure, as though he might have surrendered some of his own self-confidence to that music teacher he once portrayed. Or seemingly portrayed. Seemingly, once. But weren't he and Cally child stars together? Well, the past. Random film clips.

—Did you . . . did you like it?

—Of course! I love everything you do, L.P., she says beside his shoulder, smiling up at him.

—Well, it's not very good, he admits, gazing down into those absorbent blue eyes. I made it before I met you.

He doesn't know if that's true or not. It doesn't matter. They kiss. She sucks his tongue gently, pushes her soft breasts against him. The projector, rewinding, hums and flutters.

—It's beautiful, L.P.! she whispers into his mouth. So true to life! I love it! It brought back all my own lessons at that age. It's just brutal! A classic! And it has that something special. Integrity! It's what makes you great!

She squeezes his buttocks as though to squeeze his doubts away, then smiles, releasing him, and he moves to the window, away from the explosive old film, to light his pipe, an ancient habit that on this occasion does not reassure him. The snow has stopped falling, but down in the streets it is blowing still. Is this the city that men call the perfection of beauty, the joy of the whole earth? The day is fading, and the endless streets are filled with homebound masses, butting against the wind. Distantly: a couple of fires.

—I don't know, Cissy. Something not quite right about it. It's left me feeling—how can I say?—as if I've left something of me behind in that film, and now it's no longer what it was. Nor am I. It's like it's left me with an itch I can't quite find.

He suddenly feels, as he says this, that he's been here before, or knew he'd be here; that he's making some vast impossible connection, as though the world has come sliding up behind him and picked him up. He knocks his pipe out, gazing down upon the statue of the Mayor in the square. The girl's line, Cissy will—

—Maybe it's the girl's opening line, L.P. Maybe it's a bit much.

He smiles wryly out upon the city, sips his drink. In sync. For a moment.

—Yeah, probably. But she really said that. I had to use it.

—Said it?

—In the interview before. When we were casting. She had the innocent girl-next-door quality we were looking for, only in her case it didn't seem to be an act. When I asked her why she'd answered our ad, that's exactly how she put it—Mummy's gone to heaven, the whole spiel and then some—you'd have loved it! I decided not to tell her what the film was about, she'd never heard of Peter Prick, probably thought it was an animal fable for kids. On the set, just before the shooting, she even prayed for success!

Cissy laughs, returning the film to its battered old can.

—Oh wow! I thought her acting was too good to believe!

—I suppose, nowadays, I wouldn't put it in dialogue like that, I'd just tape the interview and use it as voice-over, maybe later, during the rape.

Cissy contemplates the possibilities.

—But I don't remember seeing her in any other films, L.P. How come she didn't go ahead and make a career of it?

—I don't know. She might have died.

—*Died*—?!

—Yes. In the film. I think that was real life.

Cissy laughs, claps her hands.

—You're kidding! That's wild, L.P.! But then, how was it supposed to end?

—I don't remember. I don't know if we had an ending for it. Some kind of orgy probably, fuck the sadistic old master to exhaustion or something, you know.

—That's wonderful! Now I'm going to have to have a slow look at that ending on the editing table! Besides, I want to see how you got that weird halo effect at the end.

—The gloriole. Funny. Like maybe her prayers were being answered or something. Actually, that was an accident too. It just happened we'd got hold of a piece of film without any anti-halation backing, and we picked up some refracted light from the whites of her eyes. Normally, we'd have thrown the film out and shot the scene again, but as I recall she was not available for another take.

Cissy smiles, admiring him with misty blue eyes. Sends a sweet warm flush through him, easing for a moment his troubled heart. She kisses him.

—You're a genius, L.P.!

—I'm just an actor, Cissy. My part was easy.

—Easy! You were the one who chose the girl, weren't you? And who else was mixing documentary techniques with scripted movies in those days? Then there's that whole music lesson apposition with all the fantastic associative ironies; you were the one who set that up. I don't even mention the subtlety of your own performance, those delicate shifts of expression, the minute muscular twitches, your incredible vocabulary of eyebrow movements, your sense of command.

She nudges up against him.

—And, love, whose cannon but yours could have pulled off that ending? She gives a soft tug on it, bone-hard for all the doubts and vague anxieties that assail him. No, L.P., confess: You were the reason the medium was invented!

He smiles, his unease deflected somewhat by her bubbling enthusiasm, his doubts and confusions becoming absorbed, as always, into her rich aesthetic. He has no choice. He is he who ceaselessly desires.

—Too bad, though, that you didn't have good recording gear back then. You could have used that weird interview with the girl throughout the rape, and then, let's see . . . maybe an unanswered question at the end, plus maybe, you know, a panegyric on the beauty of music as pure art, scrambled and scattered through the whole track!

—And all, I suppose, in the key of Fuck Minor—

—Or just *A* Minor!

—Ha! With a heavy beat—

—Cane Sharply on Ass Flat! And maybe a nice dry humdrum lecture on solmization and the guidonian hand as a bass continuo! Use that hymn to John, you know, that *ut queant laxis* thing.

—Or even melodies derived from anagrams of the scale! Like B-E-D or D-E-E-D!

—Right! D-E-A-D! B-A-B-E!

Cissy pushes a button. A panel slides away and an electric harmonium rolls into the room. She fingers the melodies they invent, working improvisations on them.

—B-E-G-G-E-D!

—A-D-A-G-E!

He drums on the edge of his tumbler with his pipe stem, moves to the bar to play the bottles: A BAD DADDEE! AGED CAD! A DECADE ABED! FAGGED BAGGAGE!

Cissy programs the harmonium with a progression of automatic chord changes, flicks on flashing strobelights, pops a tape of random sound effects on a DAT recorder, moves to a sound synthesizer at the workbench. She throws off her heavy sweater: DD cups uncupped. Her face is flushed with excitement now; there is sweat on her brow and between her breasts, loose locks of blond hair bobbing. He connects a tapedeck with delayed relay to a radio with a wandering tuner, puts a videotape of the history of syllogistic music on a color receiver, and sets them to sound like the drones on a bagpipe. He trains one video camera on Cissy at the workbench, programming it with alternating black-and-white switching tones, uses a second one to scan a Victorian pornographic novel, which fills the holes of the first camera's tearing images with fractured histories of serial orgasms. The resultant image appears on a wall-size plasma crystal monitoring screen mounted behind the workbench—and thus in the first camera's scope—producing an infinity of diminishing illusions.

Cissy dances in front of the synthesizer as she plays, bringing their improvised melody-codes to life in an orchestra of citharas and rebecs, flügelhorns and quint-fagotts. Her bare tits slap softly; sweat gleams on her pale freckled back. He turns film tins into cymbals and bins into drums, sets mirrors gyrating. The music history tape is on backward, proceeding from percussion and brass, through winds, to strings, from the twelve-tone dead ends back through the industrial orchestra-machine to the innovations of the postmedieval individualists. At the synthesizer, on the wallscreen, and in a thousand whirling reflections, Cissy bounces rapturously, abbandonatamente, blending crembalums with sackbuts, psalteriums with fifes, from C to C and back again: alla camera exercises on her way out of time and tonics. While there's still any signature left at all, he yanks her culottes down, slaps her perspiring ass, her gleaming stromento da fiato, in syncopation with the wild imbroglio of percussive effects already vibrating in the exploded office. Oh fuck! he thinks. I'm alive!

—Yes, yes, L.P.! Smanioso! Fuocoso!

Whoppety-clap, giving her cheek to him that smiteth it! He smacks her multitude of glistening grundbegriffe with half his hands, rips his own clothes off with the other half. *Pucka-pucka-pucka-pucka-pucka-pucka-PUCK!* He raps her resonant ass, her back, belly, bridge, and ribs, anteludium and coda, bell and groove: he, Tubal the mighty, discovering movement, and she giving it back, a quattro mani, all of it multiplied and augmented a thousandfold, *clappety-whop-whop, pucka-pucka-puck!*

Still plugging into the screaming circuits their diatonic messages—ABBA! DADA! CACA! EGAD!—Cissy kisses him, tasting his lips, his uncertainties, then stoops and, multihanded, takes out his organ, that primitive ur-instrument, ancient bagpipe, regal mechanism, that original open diapason. She admires its prospect, vibrates his foundation stop, flicks the dust away between pallet and groove to stop the howling, unsheaths his draw-stop rod, blows out his flue-pipe with a blast that sends a brace of demisemiquavers rumbling out his waste-pallet and sets his cymbelstern afluttering. She takes a grip on his manubrium knob and, applying her bellows to his pipework, runs serial mutations off all his registers. Whoopee! She plays it so well, you'd think she invented it! She modulates his root, double-tonguing, while transforming, metamorphosing the pregnant themes, distorting the elemental notes, wrenching them out of their old assembly-line functions in the manufacture of progressive sound systems, destroying them as unique entities, creating a whole new sonic domain, a new geography of aural activity. B-E-A-D-E-D! C-E-D-E-D! C-E-D-E-D! C-A-B to C-A-F-E and F-A-D-E again! F-E-E-D again!

—And A-C-C-E-D-E, L.P.! *B-E!*

Meanwhile, their ghiribizzo is counterpointed with inverted dogma on the resolution of dissonances, the nebenthemas of newscasters, the spastic plaints of apocalyptics, and it's not the words they hear but the click of alveolars and plosives, the hiss of fricatives. She lifts one thigh to commence the main exposition, and he fingers her f-hole, sets her plectrum quivering, her valves hopping, her rosebud resonating. Frantic zoom shots of their duodrama surround them on six sides, infinitely mirrored and refigured, presided over by a four-gun video image of Monteverdi jacking off backward: the broadcast semen is sucked back up his instrument and his flushed face turns pale and cold, the art of instrumentation now just a gleam in the father's refocusing eye. Cissy frets with his capotasto, while he blows a jubilant blast up her pipeworks; it sets her golden belly quavering, then comes rumbling brassily down her windway: *poop-titty-poop-poop-WAAAH*! Hey! He putteth his mouth in the dust; if so there may be hope! *BLAAAAT!*

Then, volti, into her a punto d'arco, probing her arriswise, as she lowers her own membraneous reeds over his jack, his quill, his pomposo piccolo, an allegro di bravura movement full of executive difficulties, cadenza d'inganno worthy of a virtuoso—thy breach, my love, is great like the sea!—oh, he knows they're watching, knows the whole world is watching, all that pass by clap their hands at thee, knows and revels in them, *hello folks!* yes, and knows he's good enough: the master! He vibrates in her tits, her ass, her mouth, her pussy, T-A-M-P! T-A-M-P!, runs the body-gamut up and back again: *TAMP! TAMP! TAMP!* The ur-beat, arsis and thesis, recte et retro, ductus circumcurrens, stroking her to Helicon and back! Oh goddamn, he's blowing jism everywhere, but he's really up, up to stay, per omnia saecula saeculorum, man! over and over, their canon perpetuus, their fa plagal doxology, missa anti defunctis, their canticum canticorum: he thundering out the dux in his intrepid baribasso, I am the man that hath seen affliction by the rod of his wrath; and his love responding in her sweet antiphonal

who can heal thee?

discant . . .

Reel 2: Cleo

Documentary slag, the serial debris of his compulsive remigrations, litters his trail to the coldwater flat, crumbs for the wayward orphan. Letters, old bills, a lock of her red hair, trinkets, photos—a thousand eyes on him, all his own. His tears disturb not one pool, but an infinite regression of pools within pools. What drives him to come back here?

—Come back here! Come back here!

Film tins lie in the frozen streets like manhole covers. Shredded scraps of notepaper fall like snow, and camera lenses twinkle in the deep white heaps, reflecting the lights of signs and shop windows, the passing traffic. The wind howls through the gaps and chasms of the city, orchestrating the percussive mutterings of engines, the clangor of horns and auto crashes, the reverberant desperation of immaterialized sorrow. Da capo, da capo. Passing his own shadow, trammeling his own footsteps. Over and over again.

—Again! Again! Again!

I must be mad, he thinks.

—Yes, mad! You are mad, Lucky! Mad about your Cleo! Hurry, my love! I am hot! hot! hot!

Mannikins model her underwear, her rings and bangles, her ancient gown, flash their dead green eyes and hard white bottoms at him. Notebooks block the slush of gutters, their ink running into senseless blots, and spools of audiotape tumble out of metal wastebaskets like wild red hair.

—Was I the first, Lucky? Really the first?

He is drawn up the dimly lit stairwell like a clock hand to its hour. The wooden stairs creak with anxiety, his hand sweats on the worn rail. He watches from beyond the door his reluctant ascent up those stairs, blowing a flute at it to drive away the stink of piss and ink. The flute seems to quicken him, that other him out there. Eager now, he climbs hand over hand. Cleo squats on the bidet, spraying ice-cold water up her womb. He lies on the old flowered carpet, listening to the splash of water, staring at the silent ceiling projection, piping himself out of the chaotic streets and up the dingy stairwell with its old lino treads, its chipped and battered walls, once green, past its urgent graffiti: HURRY, LUCKY! MY CUNT'S ON FIRE! The carpet smells, not so much of roses and lilies as of sheep, too long dead.

—I heard you out there in the corridor. You were peeking through the keyhole. I opened the door.

—I watched you through the branches. I'd never seen anything like you. I fell.

A child still, with big green eyes and long lashes, springy red ringlets all over her head, slipping barefoot through the fresh grass to the water's edge. Dappled with sunlight and leaf shadow. Long ago, this, the footage lost (if ever shot) though vivid still, something spooled up in his lobes and ever running. Her white gown, fine as gossamer, twined about her slender thighs and narrow hips, clung to her breasts, small and firm as new apples. She knelt on a flat rock and dipped her finger in the pool. The gown folded into a soft crease down her buttocks, flowed forward between her thighs, as though caught on a sudden breeze. His once-quiet heart pounded in his ears: Something is happening!

He opens the door. He hesitates at the threshold, as though anticipating . . . what? He is disappointed. It is the same. Or perhaps he is relieved. Anyway, the same: a hanging bulb, a bed, stove and cupboard, chipped bidet, a chest, a chair. The mattress on the bed is laid with a frayed quilt. The window shade is torn and the spring is gone; it hangs at the same odd angle as ever. The flowered wallpaper is soot-smeared and peeling. It has always been peeling. A moment held in another moment. To be possessed is to fall out of time. She smiles at him from the mirror over the washbasin, her white teeth sparkling.

—It's our anniversary, Lucky!

Her long slender thighs are distorted, creased by the lip of the bidet. In this part of the city, they have bidets. The ridges of her spine, curved slightly forward, cast a ripple of dark dimples down her back, crossed by the downy shadows of her shoulder blades. Her bottom is hunched forward, and beneath the smooth white cheeks, steam is rising. She watches the man stretched out on the cold wool rug in front of her, his eyes fixed on the ceiling, where nothing is happening, nothing in her mind at all, one of his hands clutching his rigid organ, the other an empty wine bottle.

—You're just torturing yourself, she says, and lowers her steaming cunt over his face.

—That's right, it sizzled when you touched the water, he says, I remember now!

—That's not true, Lucky. She laughs and unpins her wide-brimmed bonnet, shaking out her tight curls. You're making it all up! Her ruffled blouse is creased starchily over her prim breasts, and her full skirts rustle as they brush the old oak bed. The door clicks shut behind them.

—Your nipples were petaled like coral-colored cornflowers.

—Help me unbutton, Lucky! Please! Hurry!

—Your anus was pink then, like a—

He switches off the tape recorder. Street sounds leak into the room. He sits on the bidet, smoking a pipe, spraying his balls with cold water, gazing thoughtfully at the old bed with its stained and sagging mattress. She writhes there, overtaken by her own inner ferocity which he can never fully satisfy, her nymphae puffy, enflamed, the clitoris quivering like a tiny tuning fork, her head thrashing from side to side.

—I thought you knew everything, he says softly. I loved you more than life.

The gown in a filmy puddle at her feet; the branch between his legs; she at the pool's edge gazing curiously at her breasts, cupping them in her slender hands, squeezing the pink buds.

—Lucky? Was I . . . ?

—The first? I don't know, there might have been others. But if there were, I wasn't counting them. I started with you, Cleo. Number one.

Her tummy was flat and soft, with a knotted navel like a shutter button. On the hard nub of her little mound, a small cluster of red ringlets in the shape of a little goblet. She stepped cautiously into the pool, shuddering, clutching her breasts, then stood there spraddle-legged, staring at her reflected orifices, her echoed self staring back. With that piercing green-eyed gaze that sees all. Gently, tentatively, she touched herself.

—You were masturbating. I heard your heavy breathing through the keyhole. I rose from the bidet and crossed to the chair, where you couldn't see me.

—I masturbated all the time then. I was happy, Cleo. I wasn't afraid of anything. Then I fell and put on my weight forever.

He opens the door. Again the same. The frayed quilt, the crooked shade, the battered tin wastebasket with the pink swans. Long ago, he bought the room. He has tried to keep it just as it was. As best he can. As best he can remember. The old oak bed, the hat tree, the empty wine bottle, the basin and bidet with their coldwater taps, everything in its place. Even the same coarse white towels, now yellowed with age, the oilcloth on the chest. He has tried, but it is *not* the same. There is now a yellow film box in the wastebasket; he doesn't remember how it got there. New holes in the rug, stains in the mattress, rust in the basin. A torn photograph under the bed. And there were more mirrors then; some of the mirrors are gone.

—No, they're just the same. Only we looked in them more often. You were just a boy. You didn't even have a mustache then.

She dipped her finger in the pool, licked it, stuck it up his rectum. His balls dropped into his scrotum. She blew on his groin and black hairs sprouted, spreading like vines. Like a bird with a worm, she drew forth his reluctant penis and sucked the heart-shaped crown. His hips bucked. He was in love.

—How did I—*ah!*—get into this room? he cries.

—I don't know, that was a long time ago, she says, licking his slumping manhood. I was still a virgin.

She stands in this clip at the washbasin, gazing at him through the mirror. Her eyes are in shadows, but their whites seem all the more striking. She unties the pussycat bow of her ruffled blouse. Her movements are hesitant, hurried, blurred, flashing in and out of deep shadows, but the flowered wallpaper is very clear. She stares wide-eyed into the mirror, her hands groping for the buttons on the back of her blouse. She seems to be asking, What happens next? He approaches, wearing boxer shorts, baggy in the seat, and an undershirt with narrow shoulder straps. He undoes the buttons, tugs the blouse free of the skirt, and lifts it over her shoulders—but it gets stuck there. They have forgotten to remove the wide-brimmed bonnet.

—Wait, Lucky! Wait!

—I . . . I can't!

They watch themselves fuck, sandwiched in mirrors. Their hips heave frenziedly in an infinite series, their thighs slap, she bites his shoulder, complaining, counting, rips hairs from his ass, from his innumerable asses, he explodes in her; it's like the first time all over again, his seed bursting forth in a chorus of reflected spasms, and he sinks away, all by himself, on her breasts.

He is unable even to contemplate this collapse in the mirrors, but closes his eyes and allows himself to slip down into some deep consoling cave. In his fading mind's eye, the bucking of all those hips gradually gets out of sync, begins to undulate slowly like waves lapping a shore, as time might do were it a friendlier thing. She slides out from under him, and he hears her scratching on the notepad she keeps by the bed.

—Forty-seven minutes, 836 thrusts, she announces flatly. You were doing better than that five years ago. You don't love me anymore, Lucky!

—I just realized, Cleo. There's one too many ashtrays in this room.

It almost worked once with the towels. A merging. When he least expected it. Nothing special about the moment, they weren't even fucking, he was just washing his face at the basin, as now and like a thousand times before. He reached for the towel, and suddenly he had it: the scene, whole, just as it was then, back at the beginning of everything, her body stunted by refraction, her legs as though sprouting from her breasts, buttocks just under her shoulder blades—she ducked under, and her bottom bobbed to the surface for one fantastic second, gleaming bright and pure in the sunlight. And then, with a foamy kick: gone. It was and is only the towel in his hand, soapy water in the basin, his own image, wet and perplexed, in the mirror.

—It was pink then, your anus, like a little raspberry, with just the lightest fleck of downy red hair ringing it round. And your cunt too. Pink, Cleo. Just a blush. Like the crease in a peach.

—What color is it now? she asks, coming down.

—Wait! I'm not trying to hang on to anything, Cleo, I just want to get through to—*mmmf!*

Wow, it *is* hot, her cunt, it bathes his whole face with its urgent restless flow, his tongue lured deep in search of its source. At first, he is blinded by her flesh, but then she leans forward to lick at his groin, and past the goosebumps on her cold wet buns, he sees himself, projected onto the ceiling, climbing the stairs, peeking through the keyhole. Why does he keep coming back? It's impossible, he knows that. He could have recorded it then, got it all down somehow, but you always think of such things too late. And once it's gone, there's no remaking it, no reliving it, the door closes and disappears into the wall forever, it's useless. Yes, he's a fool, ceaselessly jerking off in the corridors of some lost episode. He leans forward, weeping sorrily for all the beauty that escapes him, and finds the door there after all: it opens and he tumbles into the room.

—My hero!

Balls of lint and dust on the carpet. Cracks in the baseboard, the cupboard, the chest. The chair legs are nicked and scuffed, worse at the feet. There is gum stuck under the seat, a microphone concealed in the bedsprings. Cleo's pale ankles are planted in a little mound of her own underwear.

—We did fuck once in the country, didn't we, Cleo?

—Where did you come from, Lucky?

She steps out of her puddle of panties and straddles his head, her bangles ringing. Did she wear bangles that time? Does it matter? Paint is splattered on the underside of the washbasin, and a strip of wallpaper is missing.

—Do you remember what we did seven years ago tonight?

—No.

—Oh, Lucky, you're hopeless! How old are you?

—I don't know.

—What is today? Don't you even know that? Who are you anyway? What's the matter with you?

Above him, her pretty red-bearded lips are pursed and beckoning, blowing him impassioned wet kisses, inviting him in. The most exciting place in the city. Legendary. But inexhaustible. Unfathomable. Everybody in the world trying to fill it up nowadays, but it can't be done. She's driving the whole city crazy. As he's been driven. He can't see her face, can only hear it.

—Speak to me, Lucky! Any answers. I don't care how true they are, just talk to me!

On her bottom above him, there's a projection of him pulling her bloomers down, caressing her between her legs, but he can only see the lower edge of it, foreshortened, like a body refracted in a pool of water. He backs it up and starts it over.

—Bend over, Cleo.

He unbuttons her skirt, unlaces her corset. She watches him through the mirror with a look compounded of terror and adoration. And appetite: for she knows not what. His hands fondle her young breasts, two firm little bubbles with tiny dark tips. He kisses her neck under the dark ringlets, her throat, her armpits. She seems about to swoon. He pulls her bloomers down, stroking the little cluster of ringlets on her pubis, caressing her bright white ass. He nips her nether cheeks in his teeth, brushes them with his mustache, licks her anus, then runs his tongue up her crack and spine. She drops limply into his arms, her eyes rolled back.

—It's our anniversary, she murmurs. I've brought the wine.

—There was a tree, wasn't there? A rock?

—Why are you staring at the chair?

—A pool, a meadow? Wasn't there, Cleo?

—And wildflowers?

—Yes! That's it!

—Wildflowers!

—Good!

—A river!

—No. . . .

—Yes, a river, flowing hard and fast, with churning rapids, and all the reeds along the bank—all the reeds were penises!

—No, Cleo. . . .

—Long golden penises with big violet heads like giant acorns! Wherever I moved, the reeds tried to follow, leaning toward me! As I danced around them, they swayed, to and fro, to and fro, stirring a frantic hot breeze. *Whush! Whush!*

—Uh, Cleo. . . .

—I leapt back and forth across them! They thrashed about wildly, pulling at their roots! The wind rose! The reeds grew bigger and bigger! Oh, Lucky! There was thunder and a thick perfume, convulsions; the skies were aflame! Oh! Oh! Still they grew! Their heads burst, raining nectar on me! I was screaming! I threw myself on hundreds of them at once!

He watches her roll about on the carpet, fucking the wine bottle.

—Damn you, Cleo. It wasn't like that at all.

She faints.

He carries her past the bare bulb hanging near the two-burner stove and lays her on the bed. He smiles, scratching his armpits. He spreads her legs, doubling her knees back with a fluttering flash of light and shadow. Hmmm. There is a cork in her cunt. He ponders this, poking about at the pale little furrow; then he brightens. He reaches into the fly of his boxer shorts and, as though pulling a blade from a jackknife, opens out a corkscrew. He stabs it into the cork, and she starts up suddenly as though in pain.

—Oh, Lucky, you don't love me anymore. You're just using me!

—Hold still, damn it!

He lies on his back, head propped by quilt and cushions. She straddles his prick, facing away, leaning on his knees, her feet in his armpits. On one cheek of her ass, he is taking her maidenhead with his corkscrew penis, revolving round and round, impatiently manipulating her cumbrous limbs, kicking her in the face with his stockinged feet; on the other soft screen, he is watching her through the keyhole while they fuck on the bidet, surrounded by mirrors and cameras.

—Now, if I can just bring these two projections together somehow, on top of each other, right over the asshole . . .

—My god, what is it you want, Lucky? Do you want this room to just disappear, is that it?

—Don't say that, Cleo! Damn it, that scares the hell out of me!

His heart is racing. What is this he sees? She sits on a rough-hewn rock at the water's edge. Her curly hair sparkles in the sunlight; her naked body gleams. What is she staring at? Her glossy bottom is warped by the rock's craggy surface into a kind of wry grimace. In the upper right hand corner of the print, at the edge of a forest, there is what looks like an opening into a cave.

—Good lord, Cleo! Has this—has this picture been hanging here all the time?

—No, I bought it for you, Lucky. It was pretty. I thought you'd like it. I thought it'd cheer you up.

He rips the frame down off the wall and, throwing open the window, chucks it out into the night. Snow blows in and whitens the hair on his belly, frosts his cock, chills his heart. Cleo runs to the window, leans out into the storm. Far below, there is a heavy metallic crash and a scream—she laughs excitedly, one hand pressed between her thighs. Now! Swiftly, almost without thinking, he rears back and gives a tremendous kick to that splendid red-haired ass.

—Goodbye, Cleo!

But it is like kicking a rock. Like the one she was sitting on. She spins around, grinning wildly, her red ringlets glittering with snowflakes, her green eyes shining.

—Lucky!

—Cleo!

—Suck me, Lucky! Now!

—My foot hurts, Cleo!

—You won't need it, she laughs, and leaps on him, wrapping her limbs around him, tumbling him to the carpet. It's our anniversary!

They pitch and roll, her bangles jangling—under the bed, past chest and stove, *scrunch!* over their photo album, *slam!* up against the coldwater bidet. They kick the chair halfway across the room; cameras and recorders come crashing down on them; they scratch and gouge, mingling hot blood with their sweat.

—That's it, Lucky! she gasps. Oh yeah! Real life! I love it!

Photos crumple and stick to their bodies, they wallow in a tangle of celluloid and nylon, the tin wastebasket goes clattering about, bowling over wine bottles. Projections run riot, mirrors tip and weave, there's a blur of images like film jumping out of its sprockets.

—I love you, Cleo! Gawdamighty, I hate myself, but I can't help it!

—You'll get grass stains on your ass, baby! she laughs.

She grabs him by the ears, stuffs his whole head up her cunt—oh criminy! it's all liquid there between her thighs, a warm pot of honey! There's nothing like it, doesn't matter if she's the most famous piece in the city, when you're in here she makes you think you're the only one. He shoves in, but his shoulders jam on her pelvic floor. The soft folds of her vaginal walls slide by his face, as she rotates 90 degrees. He kicks forward, past the fleshy mons and in to the elbows. Pinioned, he starts to panic. But one fierce hand wraps his cock, the other digs deep into his anus for a grip. An impassioned tug: he slides in to the wrists. Another push, and he's free! Only his feet stick out. He plunges about in there, lapping it up, slaking his ancient thirst, his weary ass wrapped in a hot buttery embrace, his whole body an erogenous zone, while below, to keep him moving, she scratches the soles of his feet.

Finally, as though drugged, he fades away, succumbs to an oily peace, his dreams reduced to simple patterns of light and color, cycled on a short endless loop.

Or . . .

Or *are* those dreams, after all? *Is* it Cleo's cunt?

Or is this, rather, some kind of strange damp theater, he the sputtering bulb of a magic lantern, a man dragged through an endless-loop winter in somebody else's airless nightmare?

Oh my god!
Can't breathe!
Where *am* I?
Choking . . . !
Let me out!

—*Our Hero bestirs himself* . . .

His dissolving fantasies are of a lethal fat all his own; he's fighting his way out of his own suffocating body—*Help!*

—*Smothered in honied cunnies, pillowed by dozens of delectable bronzed and milk-white bosoms. . . .*

It's too late!

He rears up, gasping for breath, beating desperately against the elastic walls—the flesh parts with soft cries, there is light—

—*He takes a sweet pink-tipped titty out of his mouth, yawns sleepily, blinks*—

Aha.

The young serving girls who have been his bed and blankets kiss and fondle him into consciousness, tweaking his testes, blowing on his navel. He blinks, as directed, yawns, grins sheepishly into the bright light. His johnny stands at morning attention like a brave soldier, his little avatar.

—*And so begins another Day in the Life of Lucky Pierre!*

He plumps the soft bum under his ear, ogling it blearily as obliged, trying to remember the continuity and where it is he's come from, some beautiful place (he's crawling back under, not quite ready for this yet), but, cued by a rudely burping alarm clock, he is goosed by a member of his mattress and sent arching out, with a yip, over the mounds of downy flesh. The bed of bodies undoes itself and the maids don frilly little aprons and rush about with brooms and spatulas and feather dusters, wagging their rears above him as though that is how the cleaning's done. He picks himself up and slips off to pee.

—No, no! Naughty, naughty! they squeal (or someone does: the track's amplified and overhead somewhere), spanking him playfully with their soft hands and spatulas and feather dusters, and then, giggling and twittering like an aviary of mothering birds, they point his stiffened organ to the loft and squeeze his balls like an atomizer. He fountains forth and they dance around in the shower like ecstatic nymphs.

In fact, they are in a shower, the water hot and bubbly, all squashed up together.

—*Our Hero's lovely attendants lather up their own bodies and rub up against him to sponge him clean: scrub! scrub!*

The steam rises. He loses his footing and slides through misty clouds of sudsy body parts.

—Hey! Hold it a second, gang! I've got soap in my—

Whushppp! water off, they bundle him up briskly in thick towels and it's off to the rubdown table. They towel him vigorously, awakening all his cells, then sunlamps are turned on and his tail is toasted, while a dozen dainty palms pummel it—*whippety-whop! whippety-whop!*—then *flick!* over on his back to toast the other side. His legs are lifted, bottom powdered, his peter perfumed and kissed and tied at the crown with a silky blue ribbon. This is not unpleasant. He no longer concerns himself with whence he came.

Then it's off to an adjoining set for a buffet breakfast. The maids' breasts are tattooed with the insignia of vitamins and minerals. He consults the chart of daily minimum requirements, samples a nipple or two.

—*On the table between raised knees: six pretty pussies all in a row. Our Hero sits on a bench made of two plump bottoms pushed end to end and dips his nose into the sweet furry bowls, waggling his eyebrows and licking his lips appreciatively. He dons a bib—*

Wurrpp! The burping alarm clock! Quickly, no time to eat: Off with the bib and into underwear, shirt, tie, socks, garters, striped pants, vest, shoes, suit jacket, coat, hat—

—Hey, wait!

—*And out the door—keep him moving, dears!—to face life and adventure armed with a firm sense of duty and the historical moment, a wallet of condoms, and a buoyant heart!*

There is a violent cut from inner to outer, which makes him feel like he's passing through himself, and he's out in the snow again, dressed in an overcoat, a black bowler and gray spats, attaché case in hand. Egged on by the chorus behind him, he steps rapidly to the curb, where he is met by a black limousine. The chauffeur whips the door open and—*slam!*—he jumps in, or is jumped in.

Rarrarrarrarrunn!

Rarrarrunn!

—Must be cold, sir. Won't seem to start.

—Hum. All right, then.

—Out hops Our Hero, ever resourceful; down come his pants!

He humps the gas tank, diddling the exhaust—*burrrrRROOOM!* The limousine seems to rear up off its front wheels. Then, with a whoop of the horn, it rockets off down the street and out of sight. He runs after it, waving, pulling up his trousers, trips and falls, pulls up his trousers, waves, runs, falls. The limousine suddenly comes reversing back—*MOOORRrrrrub*!—and *splat!* right over him. He leaps up out of the slush, still struggling with his pants, his hat flattened, and pops back in the car. *Slam! burrrrRROOOM!*

They roar through the city, scattering traffic. People scream at them. Fists are raised. He sees cars sent through display windows, pedestrians scrambling up light poles, trains derailed. Just process shots, probably—yes, back projections, no doubt—but still. . . .

They corner, tires shrieking. He's thrown from side to side. The cityscape goes whipping by. Cyclists plunge into snowbanks. Mailboxes and phonebooths are bowled into produce carts. Billboards topple. Buses accordion into each other in their wake.

—Ahem. . . .

He cautions the driver with a polite tap on the shoulder. The driver leans sideways, falls into the seat. What the—? *The driver is a dummy!*

—Oh my god!

He leaps over the back of the seat to grab the wheel; it goes soft in his hands, slithers out of his grasp like an eel. He slams his foot on the brake and his foot goes through the floorboard.

—Help! I've gotta get outa here!

He grasps the door handle; it breaks off in his grip. Some kind of toyshop plastic! The car goes into a spin, cuts down a crowd at a bus stop, caroms off a snowbank, smashes right through the front of a building. Executives leap in panic out of high windows and secretaries flee for their lives. Blood splatters the windshield. It might even be real blood! Then—*smash!*—out the other side and he finds himself careening madly down a dead-end alley at a hundred miles an hour.

—*Yow!* he screams. *I'm going to die!*

A screeching halt, the door flies open; he sails out as if thrown and plunges into a pile of snow.

There is a motionless pause, which might be perceived as scripted timing but has more to do with his not knowing for a moment which direction is up. Then, hatted by snow, his head pops up out of the white pile.

He waits, staring wide-eyed straight ahead; nothing falls on him.

He glances left, glances right. Up. The chauffeur is holding the door, looking down upon him with respectful disdain.

—*This tall elegant building, one of Cinecity's great landmarks, is more than simply the place where Our Hero earns his daily bread. For here, each day, behind its famous façade, history is being made!*

The chauffeur brushes him off as he staggers to his feet and hands him his crushed bowler and attaché case. His heart is beating wildly, but he pulls himself erect, sets his hat square on his head, strokes his mustache, greets the doorperson stonily, and enters the building through the revolving doors.

—Good morning, sir! Thank you, sir!

—Morning, L.P.! *Love* the funny hat!

—Uh . . . yes . . . good morning . . . right. . . .

He boards the elevator. It is jammed with young girls. They giggle, whisper, sigh. One of them faints. As the elevator climbs, they fight to be closest to him and touch his clothes. The elevator operator smiles at him over the fuss and bother, winks.

—Sixty-ninth story! she announces. Lucky Pierre's Fucking Academy!

The long shadowy corridors are lined with lockers, bulletin boards, prophylactic warnings, security cameras, student projects. Tall wastebins are filled with the litter of cheap lunches, and there's the familiar musky odor of chalkdust, chewing gum, soiled underpants, and sweatsocks. It is recess, and outside in the snow, watched by armed guards and a paying audience seated in the windswept bleachers, the pupils are playing drop-your-drawers, pussy-in-the-corner, and hop-skip-and-hump. Doors open and close, water flushes through pipes, projectors whir and crackle, and somewhere a paddle smacks its target and a child's voice cries out. The daylight, pressing through tall unwashed windows, falls grainily on the waxed floor and shiny steel lockers, giving the scene a gritty realism that is also somehow mystical.

—Fucking, you see, is essentially a sequence of interpersonal actions of a single unified organism. Research shows that innate biological force, beyond stimulating a generalized horniness, is relatively insignificant in this sequencing; humans learn through family, school, and media impact, creating their own sex patterns out of a kind of cultural montage.

—*An acquired taste, after all.*

—Yes, aesthetically speaking anyway, like arson or knowledge, or indeed acquisition itself. That's what our curriculum seeks to address.

On a bulletin board are course lists, pinned-up personal ads, somebody's panties with ACAD stenciled on them, scholarship offers, results from the academy's trampoline-fucking and S&M intramurals, library rules, photographs from oral examinations, and a sex manual illustration of aardvarks. Hickory sticks and horsewhips hang on the classroom walls, decorated with little gold stars.

—*I see you conduct a course here in the Universal History of Spermatozoa.*

—Oh, yes, we do all the sciences, from kinogenetics to cryotherapy, but basically we still adhere pretty closely to the three R's.

—*The three R's? You mean, the classic—?*

—That's right. For all our progress, reaming, rithing, and rhythmicdick are as important for us today as they were for our forefathers. Our methods have changed perhaps, we're more flexible today, willing to try everything from virtual reality to proctoclysis, but we're still essentially institutions of hierological learning.

—*You're well equipped, then?*

—I'm what? Oh, the academy, yes, we have all the modern visual and tactile aids here. We've just installed a new holographic pornoform console, for example, which not only reconstructs three-dimensional images of the models but, through an optical recolligating system, assembles gas molecules into tactile shapes, approximating the holograms, very useful in the lower grades. But I should say, we prefer, as we have always preferred, the time-tested techniques of exercise and repetition, hands-on student participation, strict discipline.

—*Spare the rod, spoil the child*—

—Deprive her, rather. One must libidinize the hunting grounds.

—*I'm sorry?*

The desks are crammed with books and rubbers, dirty handkerchiefs and candy wrappers, the seats polished smooth by generations of restless young behinds. A rolled-down wallchart of the rear end of a kneeling woman, seen as a labeled contour map and chromoplated for sensitivity to different instruments, carries the inscription WHERE NOTHING IS CONCEALED, NO REVELATION IS EXPECTED. A math quiz asks, CAN YOU DUNK YOUR DICK IN CUNT IN FIVE MOVES? Radiators knock and whistle, and in the hallway girls chew bubblegum and douche themselves on public bidets beside the water fountains, while the boys measure one another in preparation for their geometry lessons.

—Now here, you'll observe, is a display of some of our student work: life drawings, masturbation fantasies, imaginative pessaries, scatological etymologies, wet-dream scatter patterns, decorated condoms—

—*Those finger-paintings are rather nice.*

—Yes, well, not the finger of course. The subject, as you can see, was *God's Cunt,* which unfortunately seemed to lend itself to obscure abstractions and too much indiscriminate flocking with pubic hair. My own favorite of the lot, quite frankly, is this simple realistic portrait of an old gramophone speaker.

A bell rings. The corridor fills with returning pupils, shaking off their winter wraps. There is blurred chatter, laughter, a reluctant shuffling into classrooms. Someone's books are knocked to the floor. The rap of sharp knuckles on a desktop, a fleshy jostle, a penny falls and rolls. Locker doors bang. He is sweaty from playing bull-in-the-ring and king-of-the-hill. His socks have crept down under his heels, but if he reaches down to pull them up, he'll get goosed. In the playground, the girls play squat tag in the snow, pressing their skirts between their thighs. What does this mean? It's like he used to know but somehow suddenly forgot, his knowing and not knowing overlaid like the pages of an animated flip book.

Desktops and chairs thump and squeak, notebooks are rustled. As he removes his earmuffs and takes his seat in ancient history class, someone hits him in the back of the neck with a spitball. He doesn't look around but raises his middle finger behind his back as he's been taught. Whispers and giggles rise and fall around him like waves lapping a shore. He feels all this must have happened long ago, but the school desk fits him perfectly, so perhaps he's mistaken. He stares at the fidgety bare knees of the little girl in the pleated skirt next to him and wonders if he should ask to borrow a pen. Once, though he cannot remember how he knows this, she wet her drawers during a nature quiz and got sent to the principal's office. He tries to imagine what happened to her in there and realizes he has a very vivid image of what happened, his imagination evidently outracing his experience, as someone—a teacher, probably—has told him it would.

The redheaded history teacher erases the blackboard with a dusty eraser, pausing to scowl at a drawing of a sickly looking weenie with the words *Histery is a Sifullitic Prik* written underneath. She corrects the misspellings, then erases that too, though it's still visible afterward like a ghost in fog. Behind her back, arms are knuckle-punched, butts are jabbed with badge pins, hair is pulled, worms and cockroaches are dropped down blouses, notes passed, fart noises made, jokes misunderstood. All part of the fun of childhood. He feels he is describing this activity to someone and suffering it at the same time.

The teacher is speaking today of the ancients' superstitious belief in progress and certainty and their worship of what she calls the echo system (he writes this down in his notebook), which she says was a result of staring too long at their navels, her own at this moment being the focus of almost everyone's attention in the classroom, certainly his own. It sits on her flat white belly between her short rubber skirt and crimson top like a chewed wad of gum being saved for later. The shirt looks like the skin of some animal. Under the skirt, there are crackling sounds, like fire, and they say her thighs are scorched black from the heat. Though ordinarily skeptical, he somehow finds this reasonable, more reasonable anyway than the story that the cheeks of her bottom are hard as marble and imprinted with the western and eastern hemispheres, or that her breasts are scarred to resemble the polar ice caps. Children exaggerate. Of course, he is a child too, or seems to be, and also exaggerates. He may have made these stories up himself. She is bossy and terrifying and he hates her, but he sometimes has dreams about her. Maybe, he worries, he is having one about her now—how else did he get here?—which would explain why he's wearing these silly short pants.

History, in truth, is unbelievably boring, though she is not. She sometimes walks up and down the aisles, slapping heads, just for the fun of it, a muffled sizzling and popping audible beneath her rubber skirt as she scissors back and forth. She says it's to remind them about cause and effect. Something happens, and then—*crack!*—something else happens. In those days, she says now, time was measured with one-way mechanical clocks rather than multifocal densimeters and it could not yet be stored. Has she said this before? She often repeats herself. He studies his notebook, but, except for *Ego Sistem* (did he write that?), it is blank. On the wall behind her, there is a colored wall map of the Isle of the Blest, surrounded by blue stuff called Okeanos, which the kids call Okay Anus when she's out of the room, since everyone knows this primitive legend from the days before the city was fully mapped and developed does not exist, nor could it ever have existed. The teacher, pointing to it with a sharp stick, says that in dreamtime incisions were made in the students' flesh, and knowledge was pressed into the wounds like dirt.

He plays with his earmuffs, shortening and extending the metal band, amazed that there are such things in the world still and also amazed at his own amazement. Somewhere a student is practicing her scales on a horn, climbing solemnly from C to C, then back to F again, with a kind of pious insistence that makes him sleepy. And hungry. He puts the earmuffs back on and rummages about in his desk for chocolate or licorice or something. He stabs his finger on a compass point but does find two old peanuts and slips them into his mouth by pretending to clear his throat. One of them is good, but the other one turns out to be a crumb from an old eraser. Yuck. Long ago, someone has inked SEX SUX on his desk, along with a phone number and a little creature with a long creased nose, dripping snot. Whoever wrote it there is probably dead. This, he thinks with a shudder, is what history really is. Something happens, and then nothing happens. No wonder he hates it. The piece of rubber has left a bad taste in his mouth. He is thirsty now and would like to go to the water fountain, but too late. Everybody's looking at him. His name must have been called.

He takes off the earmuffs and stands by his seat. He has no idea what he has been asked. Perhaps only his name, but even that for the moment seems beyond recall. The teacher is gazing at him expectantly, her eyes aglitter, a half smile on her thin lips. He believes he is her favorite, which is not necessarily a good thing. His knee trembles. Under some fuzzy things she has written on the blackboard, she has drawn a line. He is being requested, it seems, to sum up the lesson. He hears words being whispered, but he can't quite make them out. A pair of dicks? Dugs? Dorks? He knows the answer, but somehow he does not know it. Or, rather, the answer is known to him, but this knowledge has been put somewhere that his thoughts can't go. Or won't. Not until he's out of here. Something like that. He begins to feel ill. The teacher's hands are clasped in front of her skirt as though hiding something. Or pointing to it. Like a clue? And then he does hear it, or thinks he does, and, pointing at her pointing, fairly shouts it out:

—*Paradise!*

There is a sudden deathly silence. Only a faint hiss from the radiators, the creak of a floorboard, that distant horn player climbing funereally through her scales. This was not the right answer. He knows the right answer now, but it is too late. The teacher's smile has vanished and her thin nostrils are twitching. He tries to slip back into his seat to hide, but she orders him to the front of the room. It is a long walk down the aisle. Usually there are feet in the way to trip him up, but not now. Just that sorrowful horn, marching him to his execution. If he were older, he thinks, this would be easier. He could step back and see it all from a distance like in a movie, and he would not be so frightened. And it probably would not hurt as much as this is going to hurt either. It seems to get hotter, the closer he gets to the front. The teacher, towering over him in her smoldering fury, fumbles at his tummy with both hands, giving him butterflies; then, gripping his hip, she whips his belt out of its loops. His short pants slip and he grabs for them—she cracks his knuckles with the buckle, and the pants fall to his ankles before he can pinch his thighs together. She forces him over her desk, rips his underpants down. Her long red nails scratch his bottom and the underpants chafe his squeezed thighs and tug at his weenie as she strips them away. He looks out on the classroom of greedy staring faces, even though his face is pointed the other way and his eyes are awash with tears. It's as if he can see out the part they're all staring at, though this may just be his imagination up to its old paradoxical tricks again. He feels he has been here before like this, but never for real and not with everyone watching. He is sick of being a child and wants to get it over with. In fact, he thought he *had* got it over with. Yet here he is. It's a mystery, more than a child's mind can grasp. He tries to concentrate on something else to stop the tears and thinks of the girl in the seat next to his with the fidgety knees, but he sees what she sees: a little white bum quivering with terror in anticipation of the blow to come, his pulled-down weenie trapped against the desk edge, forcing his little marbles to peek out between his skinny thighs like balloon bubbles. The teacher's black-stockinged legs are spread wide, her rubber skirt hiked high up her thighs. As the horn player mournfully bleats her scales, he hears the belt whistle through the air above him and he squeezes shut his eyes. . . .

—Okay, cut the shit, kiddies! *School is out!*

—What the—?

—Look out! It's—

—It's the Extars!

They kick in the doors, bust up the seats, rip down the wallcharts. Lights crash in blinding arcs and dollies are sent rolling. There are screams, shouts, the smashing of glass. He watches, amazed, still doubled over the desk, too startled to move. He's read about them, seen newsreels, but he's never been this close before. They carry signs, handheld VTRs, machetes, cry out revolutionary slogans. Some wear leather jackets with EXTARS stenciled on the back or marked out with silver studs. How did they get in?

—Call the police!

—Help!

—THAW NOW! THAW NOW! THAW NOW!

Where's Cleo?

*—Sorry, ladies and gentlemen! It's—whew! this is some scene!—our regular Lucky Pierre feature has been unexpectedly interrupted. We'll—*oof! *Take it easy, buster!—we'll try to keep you informed. Apparently—my god!* watch out!

The Extars tip over the fake walls, smash up the bidets and water fountains. They commandeer cameras and turn them on themselves, shouting:

—NO MORE STARS! NO MORE STARS! NO MORE STARS!

—They've apparently disguised themselves as technicians and slipped by the guards. They've never gotten this far before—can you get another camera over here? Quickly! *This is a very serious situation! Our Hero is caught up in the very middle of it all! What are they going to do? We'll try to get through to one of the rebel leaders to—*

—Hey! Let's get the big cheese! That show-off over there with the pancaked butt!

Suddenly half a dozen of them are coming after him with machetes and camcorders and mad ecstatic grins on their faces. He hurls himself headfirst over the desk, hobbled by his schoolboy shorts, and slams into the blackboard wall, which topples with a wheezing crash, bringing down booms and blinds and halogen spots. The Extars swarm over the wrecked scenery, slashing their way through the tangle of flying cables, shouting, *STAMP OUT LIVING LEGENDS! BURN THE MOGULS, NOT THE MOVIES!* He scrambles through a debris of specular reflectors and classroom dildos, gets tripped up in a spool of room presence, but somehow manages to escape for a moment the frame.

—Where'd he go?

—Never mind! Get the others!

—Help! This is an outrage!

—Let's turn this shit into firewood!

—Why don't the police come?

They carry placards that read SAVE THE GENRES! and SPECIAL EFFECTS ARE DEAD! They are young, wild, and full of life, dangerous but wonderful, and his heart is racing with an excitement he hasn't known in years. Their wanton destruction of the studio is terrible, of course, but it is almost as though they've put his own secret longings on display, as though he might have scripted this scene himself, setting these youngsters loose to act out the violent unloosing of his own insurrectionary urges. Look at them go! They mean him harm, but he means himself harm, at least that woeful self who was bent over the school desk, so he feels a thrilling solidarity with them even as he fears them, and he wants to embrace them all as his brothers and sisters. Especially that stunning bare-breasted one, can't be older than fifteen or sixteen, wide-eyed and beautiful with flying black hair, a dazzling white grin, and bluejeans tight as a chamois glove. Her sign is the simplest of them all: ACT! What does it mean?

—Excuse me! Would you mind—hello! excuse me!—can you tell me what you think you're doing?

—You can see for yourself, lady! This is an act-in!

—A little, you know, creative plot-busting!

—I see, but don't you think—

—It's cold out there, newsbitch, and we are freezing our nibbles off!

—Tell it to her, Lottie! That media whore!

—So, fuck it! We're moving in! You dig?

—PARTS FOR THE PEOPLE! PARTS FOR THE PEOPLE!

They spread out, wreaking havoc. Cleo in her rubber skirt, video camera perched on her shoulder, drifts coolly among them, picking up quotes and wild sound, directing second cameras, jostling the rioters with her hard lean body, going into a squat and flashing her fiery old-fashioned wide-aperture reflex at them, making them drop their own camcorders in confusion, forget for a moment their hostility. He sees Cissy, the continuity girl for the devastated *Fucking Academy* sketch, crawling out from under an overturned crane, struggling to catch the action on handheld digital video. Some guy behind her in a stocking mask has her pleated skirt up and pants down and is trying to bugger her while beating her with a sign that says ROLES ARE MADE TO BE BROKEN! but her eye is on the swirling lights and falling flats and she doesn't seem to notice. Well, she's a professional, she can take care of herself. He can't keep his own eyes off the wild thing called Lottie; he loves the way she moves, the way she swings her tightly packed buttocks, thrusting her denimed pubis at the world like a double dare, her dark eyes flashing, laughing, afraid of nothing, she's something to behold—

Sirens, whistles.

—Here come the cops!

—It's about time!

—Stand back, everybody!

The Extars link arms and brace themselves, and he finds himself wanting to link arms with them—it's stupid and suicidal, and anyway he's afraid of their machetes, but he hungers for that kind of joy and connection again. Again? Yes, he too was once a rebel, he must have been, he can almost remember it. Down with the establishment! Anarchy, yay! The police come bounding in like a uniformed chorus line, led by the Mayor in her ermine gown and ornaments of office, their whistles shrieking, guns blazing. *Freeze!* cries the Mayor, and when they do freeze, she and her cops blow them away. Cleo moves in for a tight shot of a face getting splattered by lead, but the Extar jacks off over her lens and spoils it.

—*Hey, damn you! This is a documentary!*

—Ha ha, lady, there *ain't* no such—*aargh!*

Half his head tears away from the gun blast. Cleo curses her luck and wipes away the blood and cum with the dead rioter's headband. The cops explode canisters of teargas and spray the scene with machineguns, taking out Extars and filmcrew alike. The Mayor grabs up a fallen machete and wields it like a powerful scimitar, scything away heads and knees and other body parts, Cissy popping in fresh tape and following in her stormy wake. It's sheer terror! He's never seen anything like this before except in back projections! It's as though the whole melee has bubbled up from beneath the streets below like a catastrophic fault in the plumbing. There are screams, defiant chants, raised fists shot away at the wrists, the shattering of camera lenses on all sides. Cleo, news camera back on her shoulder, moves through the ricocheting bullets and crashing, lurching, and twitching bodies, one hand pressed between her legs, an icy grin on her face, edging toward the redoubtable Mayor and her hissing blade.

—*The Mayor and her forces of order have arrived, we are now able to report, and—oh! this is great!—are restoring peace and calm. We hope to—*oops! *sorry! heads flying everywhere here; what a thrill!—hope to be able to return to our scheduled programming in a few minutes, so please stand by. But first, if we can get a word—just a moment, watch the cord, please!*

The police are mopping up now, clubbing or gunning down the last of the protesters and tossing them all out the window, alive or dead, their placards with them, clearing space for the decimated filmcrew to right their equipment, mend cables, restore the set.

—Well, it always starts in the schools, doesn't it? the Mayor is explaining to Cleo, while around them things begin to return to normal. What was most alarming about today's outbreak is that they were striking at the very heart of our civic enterprise, our be-all and end-all!

—*The hard core, as you might say—*

—Yes! I mean, let's face it, the little fucker is lucky to be alive!

—*That's right! Where* is *Our—? Ah, there he is! Leaning out that window enjoying the show. Just a moment, Your Honor, let me try to get him over here. . . . What? There seems to be some problem. . . .*

He gestures frantically at Cleo with his free hand to wave her off, desperately hanging on with his other to the belt loops of Lottie's jeans, his knuckles scraped raw and aching in the high bitter cold. Beyond her, young Extars are plummeting to their deaths or are carrying their new deaths with them in their plummeting, sixty-nine floors to the pavement below, as though to return whence they came. The mutilated ones leave jet trails of stringy blood through the blowing snow; the living laugh and raise their fists or fingers. But to whom? As far as he can tell, he's the only one watching. They seem to float at first, hanging out there in all that space like dream images; then suddenly they shrink away, peppering the icy streets far below like a soft scattering of shotgun pellets. He hates to see them go, having been excited by them, but he admires the grand style of their going. How do they do it? He'd be screaming his head off all the way down. He's feeling funky enough, just trying to hang on to the one called Lottie without getting dragged right out the window with her.

—My hand's going numb, miss! I can't hold on much longer!

—So? Let go then, man! What the fuck do you care anyway?

—No! I *can't!* I've got to save you!

She stands barefoot against the side of the building, flat out in the wind, hands on hips, supported only by his grip on her belt loops, laughing at his panic. Her black hair blows wildly in the gales, whipping at her erected nipples, and somehow it stirs his heart like those famous high-flying flags he used to salute in sunny streets so long ago.

—C'mon! *Help* me, damn it! I-I *love* you!

—Ha ha! You must love everybody!

—But don't you know who I am?

—Sure, I know you. Pierna Loca, that's what they call you in nowheresville where I live, baby: Old Crazy Leg. Or just plain Loco. Most famous modigger in the city maybe, but it cuts no juice with me! She unsnaps her bluejeans.

—For god's sake! Wait! What are you *doing?*

—You want to make it with Carlotta, Old Crazy Leg? Okay, come on then, we'll fuck on the way down! You'll never forget it!

She peels her pants down over her ass like stripping away plastic wrap, and her thick crinkly cushion billows up darkly in the V of her fly under his straining knuckles. Oh shit, she's beautiful, more beautiful than anyone he's ever known or imagined. He's bawling his eyes out, begging her to stop, she can't do this, it's crazy, can't she see he's mad about her? He feels himself getting pulled farther out the window, anchored more by his hard-on, pressed against the sill, than by his other hand, now losing its grip on the frame. She skins the jeans down and her feet arc away from the wall, rip through pantlegs, kick free—*no!*

—STOP!

He throws all his will into it, all his heart and mind, and his balls too; he leaves nothing out, he won't let this happen, and for one interminable moment he finds himself staring down the city canyon at this incredible creature, gone away from him, helpless out there in all that wind-whipped emptiness, her long black hair reaching up for him, a grin on her face still but scared now, realizing what she's done, this little girl, alone with all the history she'll ever know, ass high and limbs outspread as if offering him a last frozen embrace—but then, suddenly, yes, the snow begins to blow again, swirling upward, her hair falls back, the hard grin returns, she swoops back up into her jeans, then on through the window into the hands of the police, the other Extars following, rocketing up through the snow, collecting their brains and blood, floating momentarily outside the window as though hesitating to return, then zooming on in. *Hey,* she breathes huskily, punching him admiringly in the chest as she flickers by: *Power!* Severed heads and limbs fly back in place, bodies gather up tissue and spew out bullets, which the cops suck up into their guns with pops and bangs, and Cleo bobs about through the singing lead rattling gibberish, getting worked by her reflex, falling away from the Mayor and her cops as they go hippety-hopping backwards out the door. The walls reassemble themselves, the Extars disappear, he finds himself bent over the desk with his pants down, a whistling sound in the air and—*whop!*—the teacher cracks his butt ferociously with the belt.

—Oh, *shit,* Cleo! That *hurt!*

They're all laughing, the little creeps. She really laid it on; his whole ass is on fire.

—Fuck with history, will you, my little dickhead?

He pulls up his pants—*yow! damn, it stings!*—and marches out.

—Hey, wait! Come back, Lucky! We're still shooting!

—Go fuck yourself, teach, I'm taking the rest of the day off!

—But you can't leave now!

—I've already left.

He limps out of the building, drops his shorts, and, to douse the fire raging on the surface of his ass, sits down in a snowbank under a billboard that says: NOW, DARLING, FOR THE REAL STROKE OF LOVE! *Whew!* Better. He listens to it sizzle as he sinks deeper, trying to remember something that seems to have slipped his mind. It's almost as though something got reversed out and he can't remember what. He stares at his scraped knuckles and vaguely recalls a hard-on and how it ached—which for him is not much of a clue. Something about the Mayor? The police? No. Gone. As if erased. All that remains is the vicious cut his ass took from Cleo's anger. Only one thing he's sure of: He didn't deserve it. . . .

—You've got him on the run, Cleo. Your life-in-a-day-of film's a mess. You might as well give up on it.

—What's wrong with it?

—You keep chasing him off. You can't even finish a whole scene!

—That *was* a whole scene. How could it be anything else?

—Come on! It's all middle. No shape.

—Like life, Cece baby. *His* life. I'm a docfilm maker. What happens happens.

He's sorry now he stormed out on Cleo like that. Not her fault she gets carried away, it's her job. And he is loved by her, he knows, in a way no one else can or ever will love him, though that's not necessarily a good thing. What if she gave up on him? What if she left him for good? He shivers, sinking deeper. Still, it would probably be the best thing in the end. Save him a lot of grief and terror. Give him a bit of privacy, too. He wants her to need him, oh yes, he's given his whole fucking life to creating that need, but it's not worth it. . . .

—Just look at him sitting there, feeling wasted. It's not his life you're shooting, Cleo. It's a life your film has laid on him like a curse.

—Same thing. You think your pretty little fantasies do a better job of it?

—I don't even try. We make things together. It's fun. Sometimes it's even beautiful. And if it's beautiful, it's also true.

—Not *my* idea of what's true, sister.

She's too demanding. Too intense. Can't leave him alone. She's everywhere, zooming in and out of his life, catching him always by surprise even when he is expecting her, humiliating him with her relentless inquiry, badgering him with ceaseless reenactments of their past. Even now, like a distant echo, high in the sky, he seems to hear her. He loves her, but she's eating him up, stealing his mind, his very being. It's a kind of murder. Rape. Cannibalism. . . .

—The world's what's true, not art. My task is to hold a mirror up to it, to echo it, to keep trying to break through to what it is out there that's moving, and bugger the consequences.

—Dumb idea. Holding a mirror up to Cinecity is like holding a mirror up to a mirror. L.P.'s a pro. Why don't you just tell him what you want out of him, without hitting him from behind?

—Because pure artifice, I don't care how clever it is, lacks real bite, that push-pull thing that grips us all. We're not innocent anymore. There's got to be this constant tension of a subject aware of the camera, a camera aware of the subject's awareness.

—You're not innocent either, Cleo. You make him suffer this shit because you get your kicks out of pain. *His* pain.

The crowds trample past as if they were going somewhere, noses buried in their collars, whining their lovesongs as curses against the cold (*I know it will hurt, darling, but push on until it fills me,* they whimper, *I'm all on fire, don't spare me, I must have it if it kills me!*). They don't seem to recognize him, though now and then one of them tosses a coin at his frosty pelvic well with its turned-off fountain and makes a wish. His butt is numb. Time to pick it up and move it on. Cleo might come hunting for him, give it another hiding. Anyway, you can get piles from sitting too long in a snowbank; where did he read that? Some travel brochure probably. What he needs now. Not piles, travel. Go somewhere. Get out of here. Why not? If he could just get to his feet. But it's too late. He's in too deep. . . .

—Just look at him down there. The poor man hurts too much to move. I don't know why he doesn't quit!

—Because he *can't,* not now. He's a man fucking in guarded time. One of the immortals. He has no choice.

—But you've shot miles on him, Cleo. When will you have enough?

—Never. It's funny about guarded time, Cece. It keeps spiraling back in on itself.

—But why him?

—How does any hero get chosen? Just lucky, I guess . . .

Hello? Anybody up there? Keeps hearing voices. But, no, just the wind. He knows he should shift his ass, and soon, but he can't. He's too numb. Too tired. His stomach rumbles. He remembers he was late to work and missed breakfast. Nothing but a goddamn peanut and an eraser crumb all day, so it's not clear whether he'll freeze to death or starve first. Messages are writ large on theater marquees; he doesn't read them. He watches a couple fucking quietly in a snowy intersection while waiting for the light to change. He envies them, even when the light goes green and their orgasm is ground anonymously under the wheels of a semi. It's like they were invisible. If he'd been doing that he'd have been *making history*. The police would have been stopping traffic, restraining the public behind barricades; Cleo would have been there with camera crews. What makes the difference? Showbiz. A scary trade. . . .

—I don't know, Cleo. It seems to me that too much is too little. The more you get, the less you have.

—Of course! This is the peculiar attraction that adheres to the iconic life, the mystery of it.

—Oh wow! Icons, mysteries, guarded time: Isn't it about time we freed ourselves from that old hocus-pocus? Or should I say *focus*-pocus?

—Nothing we can do about it. The economics of the gaze make a focus necessary. You know that better than I do, my dear.

—A focus has to be held. Sooner or later, you're going to lose him for good. You frighten him. He'll always run away from you.

—I doubt it. But if it came to that we'd change our style, break the sequence pattern, switch lenses, try a new filter, confront him with alternatives. Don't worry, baby. That sucker's mine.

All he can see now is blowing snow and a ghostly enclosure of leaning skyscrapers rising high above him, their towers lost in the storm. On a banner hung from a window up there: OH! CAN IT BE POSSIBLE TO HURT ONESELF BY SUCH A DELIGHTFUL PLEASURE? He has sunk back so far in the snowbank his knees are higher than his ears, which, attuned to lament, reject the prescriptive romances sung by the milling masses, hear instead a troubled ricercare of unresolved dissonances, drawn forth from a distant organ. Might just be the sound of the relentless traffic grinding by, of course, or the wind blowing through the city canyons, but . . . Cissy? Is that you? Are you there?

She appears, carrying a digital clipboard, chewing on a plastic pen.

—Are you all right, L.P.? What are you doing here?

—Oh, Cissy! Help me! I'm stuck! I can't move!

She tucks the pen over her ear and gives him her free hand. Not easy, he's frozen fast. She blows hot breath around his hips, digs around him with the corner of her clipboard, plants her clipboard in the snow—where it beeps quietly in protest—and hauls on him with both hands. Slowly, slowly. . . .

—Be sure you've got all of me! he cries. As he rises he feels like he's bringing the whole street up with him: subsoil, subway, sewage system, and all.

—We ought to be shooting this in color, she laughs, surveying his resurrected behind. Which is the highest part of him. He's locked in the sitting position, forced to stare into the crotch of the schoolboy shorts around his ankles.

—Let's go up and get in the bath, Cissy!

—You'd shatter like a plateglass window, L.P. Just be patient.

He hears her slap his butt and thighs with her palms, but he can't feel a thing. Like boards back there, slabs of stone. *Whoppety-whippety-whop-whop-clap!* she goes, playing them in her inimitable way, an artist with skins. She sets his balls to rattling and his prick to swinging, bonging between his frozen thighs like a brass bellclapper, using the beeping clipboard as a drone tone. An audience gathers, huddling around them, pooling their warmth, tapping their feet to the beat.

—Some kind of street theater?

—No, I think it's legit.

—Who's the clown with the blue bongos?

—I don't know, but she gets a nice sound out of them, don't she?

Bent double still, he stares down between his legs into the smooth glossy hollows of the cloven ice crater he's left in the snowbank. It is faintly flecked with blood, a broken pink stripe like the symbol on survey maps for a public footpath. All pets must be leashed. Put trash here. It courses the two valleys, crossing a narrow ridge lightly forested with frozen hairs, plucked when he arose. The valleys look like the inside of eggshells, sleek, improbable, and indecipherable. In all great art, there is enigma, wrought of the inner tensions of the artist's mind, passions and purpose, as one strives to synthesize the unsynthesizable. Is there not?

—Yes, it's beautiful, pants Cissy, still pounding away. She's really laying it on now, getting true plosives and full vowel sounds out of it. Your ice sculpture, I mean!

—Made by ham, he grunts. A large crowd has gathered now, kept back by police. More or less as he predicted. Drivers pause to watch, tying up traffic, and people lean out of windows. He still can't stand, but distantly his nuts begin to ache and he knows a thaw's at hand. Or hands. There is a remote tingling on the other side of some thick wall, then gradually sharp pinpricks of pain stab flickeringly through the layers of hard frost, alerting the loose nerve ends of his coccyx. The crowd is pressing closer, apparently expecting some denouement, a finale, a zinger, and he begins to fear they might want to use him right here in the street.

—Cissy, can't we—?

—Here you go, L.P.!

—Ah!

A hot flush surges through him and, trumpeted crisply from the rear, he bobs up as though a spring has been released. His arms fly out from his body, elbows first, then the hands, his teeth rattle, his eyes cross, his hair stands on end. The crowds laugh and cheer and throw money, and even the police applaud. Damn them all. That's enough. He reaches down through all the prickling to pull his shorts up, but they are stiff and pleated like an accordion and get stuck around his thighs. Cissy snaps them in two like a wafer and tosses them aside, where they are fought over as souvenirs.

—Cissy! Come on! Let's get out of here!

The traffic is moving again; he hails a taxi.

—L.P.! Come back!

He grabs her wrist, hauls her in beside him, slams the door. The cab is surrounded. Noses press against the windows, hands beat on the door, holding up scraps of pants to sign. He's suddenly on fire, can't sit still; his seat's like a bed of coals.

—Where to, pal?

—*Whoof! Yow!* The airport! On the double!

—What on earth are you doing, L.P.? Where are you going?

—Green pastures, Cissy! I'm breaking out!

—Don't be silly, you know you can't—

—Sure, I can! Come with me, Cissy! We'll—*ow! wow!*—start all over, just the two of us!

—Start what over? Are you crazy, L.P.? Stop jumping around like that! What about the studio, your position, the public—and tonight you're guest of honor at the Mayor's—

—Fuck all that, Cissy! School's out! This place is not for real. I'm off!

She folds her arms over the clipboard (it burps in protest), settles back. There are tears in her eyes.

—It won't work, and you know it.

—You're not coming?

—No, but I'll wait for you, L.P.

—You'll wait till hell freezes over, Cissy! I'm not coming back!

—Doesn't sound like too long a time. I'll be right here.

The cab pulls up in front of the terminal and he jumps out, still on fire.

—Cissy! You're the best friend I ever had! I'll-I'll never forget you!

—Sure. See you later.

He buys, on the credit of his face and other visible parts, a first-class ticket for the next available flight, leaving in two minutes—never mind where it's going, only so it's out of here—and rushes aboard just as they're closing the doors. It's really happening! Before he can even fully take in what he's done, he's showing his ticket stub to the flight attendant. She leads him to his soft leather seat and gratefully he falls into it, his thawed ass still tingling with pins and needles.

—Magazine, sir? Drink? Hot snack? Massage?

—Right. Wonderful! And do you have a spare pair of pants?

—I think we can find something that'll fit, she says, tipping her head to one side and looking him over. Then she hands him a headset and a videotape. One of his own movies: *The Impossible Journey*. They are already taxiing out to the runway for takeoff. He is free! He has done it after all!

—By the way, where are we going?

—Around the world, she says, and winks. Now buckle up.

He kicks the videotape under the seat (*out! out!*), unwraps the pillows and blankets, and settles back, feeling happily drowsy, not without some lingering doubts about having taken so precipitous a decision with nothing, literally, except the shirt on his back, and that not even his own, but increasingly at peace with himself. Poor Cleo. He's fucked up her film. Too bad. He is heading off into a new life, and it will be as different from his old one as waking is to sleeping. When the flight attendant bends over to help a fellow passenger, an old gent in a tuxedo, adjust a seatbelt in the row in front of him, he turns away, refusing to look at her exposed crotch, not only for fear of recognizing it but also because he is leaving all that behind too; he's a new man, out of the frame and plot-free, and no longer susceptible to entrapment by beautiful women, flirtatious flight attendants included. Cleo in her irony likes to call him her hero, but now, for the first time, he truly *feels* heroic, and he pats his flaccid penis with pride and gratitude as if it were a precious new pet, curled up faithfully in his lap.

But no sooner have they roared down the narrow runway—crowded in at each wingtip by the high city tenements—and lifted up through the light and phone wires into the clotted stormclouds above, than a teary-eyed young girl, glancing furtively over her shoulder, slips breathlessly into the seat beside him and begs him to hide her there as best he can with his blankets and pretend she's with him if anyone asks.

—Oh, sir, please help me! she whispers, her voice catching with little sobs. You have a kind face and I know I can trust you! I saw when you entered the plane that you weren't hiding anything and might even be running away from something just like I am, so maybe we could somehow help each other in our distress!

She continues to weep heart-wrenchingly as she whispers, so it is not always easy to understand what she says, but it seems she is running away from tyrannical and abusive stepparents who intend to force her to marry a rich old man more than three times her age with a reputation for cruelty and a foul tongue and other beastly habits too filthy to describe or even, given her limited experience, to comprehend. He is skeptical about all this, having heard it all before in one script or another, though he has to admit this gentle child is the very image of the old-fashioned girl next door, her intense prettiness residing more in her innocence and terrible vulnerability than in her features, attractive as they are in their sweet unsophisticated way. Even her name, when she confesses it—Constance—seems to confirm his impression of her, at least enough for him to hear her out, planting a pillow on top of the pet in his lap, which is stirring and seems about to stretch and yawn.

—All my life I've been kept at home, watched by nannies and guardians, she explains, her voice quivering. Except for my puritanical stepfather, I know nothing about the world or about men, only all the horrible stories I have heard about how young women are abused by them.

—Well, we're not all like that, he assures her, and pats her hand sympathetically. She takes his hand in hers and holds it, chastely yet firmly, as though to pledge her trust and friendship, and says she knows that must be true, but nothing has taught her otherwise and she's all alone in the world now and so terribly frightened. She knew by his mustache that he was a man, and so to be feared, but there was no one else she could turn to, least of all the airline crew. She glances about nervously, eyes peeking out just above the blanket, explaining that she believes her stepparents and fiancé may have spies aboard the plane.

The flight attendant comes by, pushing a tray of drinks, aphrodisiacs, snacks, and aromatic oils, and wearing a cloth measuring tape around her neck. She asks him to stand and measures his waist, hips, and inner leg, hefts his balls, and takes his chest and arm measurements as well. On seeing the condition of his privy member, she glances suspiciously down at the trembling girl under the blanket and demands to know who she is.

—She's, uh, my fiancée, he says, and puts one finger to his lips. Sshh! Not a word. We're eloping.

—Sure, tell me another, she says, but she blesses them with a wry grin and a packet of designer condoms from the refreshments tray.

—I think she's one of them, Constance whispers, when the flight attendant moves on down the aisle with her cart. Her hand is trembling as it clasps his, pulling him back down into his seat. She huddles close to him, her warm breath coming in short little gasps. I'm so afraid!

—It's all right, I'm here now, nothing will happen, he says, and gives her what he hopes is a comforting smile, squeezing her hand gently in reply to her own hot grip. Her damp eyes, just inches from his own, gaze up at him over the blanket, seeming to search out every nuance of his expression, and he can see in them the struggle between trust and fear, hope and despair.

—Is it . . . is it true what you just said? she asks timidly. I mean, about being your fiancée?

—Well, at the moment it seemed—

She reaches up and kisses him affectionately on the cheek, then ducks back under the blanket again. I love you, she says simply. You are kind and brave and very very good. No matter what happens, I'll always love you and wait for you.

—Ah! Well . . .

He's not sure he is ready for this. And yet, why not? He said he wanted a fresh start, a new life, and what could be more different than getting married? Married! The very thought of it is so startling as to make him turn away to catch his breath. He peers out the window as though in quest of his own better reason, so quickly flown, and sees that they have emerged into clear skies; below him he can now see titanic mountain ranges and vast blue seas. Marriage? No, preposterous. And yet, and yet. . . . The views of mountains and seas give way to long sandy beaches with palm trees and grass huts, mountain chalets embedded in fields of wildflowers, campfires on the pampas and white yachts anchored in sunny bays. He turns back to his tender young companion, who is still gazing up at him with those intense wide-open eyes, and knows he is hopelessly smitten.

—Constance! he whispers, and presses her hand to his breast.

The blanket slips below her lips and, closing her eyes, she lifts them shyly to be kissed, but before he can accomplish this, the flight attendant returns with a suit of clothes which she says has been tailored to measure, a tuxedo in fact, for which she apologizes, saying it was all they had to work with. He glances toward the gentleman in the row in front of him and sees that there is no one sitting there now, and the flight attendant, following his gaze, explains that he got off at the last stop. The undershirt is a bit baggy and the shirt collar is a size too big, the sleeves too short, but the briefs fit him like a glove (the flight attendant proudly informs him, settling his penis into its pocket, that she made them herself), and the tuxedo is cut to perfection. She turns him around toward the window and lifts the coattails to check the seat, and when he turns back Constance is gone. He seems to hear her muffled voice somewhere, a gasping, the sound of scuffling, but the flight attendant, still fussing with his new tuxedo, is blocking his exit into the aisle, and over the speaker system the pilot is asking everyone to return to their seats immediately, fasten their seatbelts, and prepare for landing. In fact they are *already* landing; he barely has time to fall into his seat and snap the buckle around his waist before the plane, weaving its way down between tall cloud-covered buildings, hits the icy runway, which seems about as wide as a one-way side street, bounces once, twice, and then roars to a braked halt, pushing him forward against the restraining belt.

—Constance?

He unbuckles anxiously and stumbles into the aisle, already filling up with other passengers, pulling their luggage down, getting their coats on, and sees her at the other end of the plane, gagged and bound and being led away by crew and bodyguards, a look of unmitigated terror on her young innocent face.

—Constance, wait! *I love you!*

But she is gone. He can't even be sure she heard him. He struggles desperately down the aisle, impeded by the other passengers, determined not to lose her; he has waited all his life for this, come all this distance; they can't just take her away! But they can and have. As he battles his way out of the plane—Goodbye, say the flight attendants, thank you for flying with us, have a good day—she is nowhere to be seen. She's been stolen, abducted, maybe raped, forced into prostitution! In some places, that's a crime! He is not sure where they have landed, but wherever it is he will go immediately to the authorities to report it, hoping they at least speak his language. They do. The voice on the airport PA system is announcing his arrival:

—As Our Hero comes through the gates, the entire upper management teams of both the terminal and the airline are there to meet him.

So is Cissy.

—What are *you* doing here? he cries. Where am I?

—You know where you are, L.P. You know it's not that easy. Come on, Cally's waiting for you.

—Cally? But wait! Cissy, listen to me! Everything's changed. I'm in love!

—No kidding. Who is it this time, a rodeo queen? A ballerina? The bus conductor? A fairy princess? The girl next door?

—Yes! How did you know?

—I don't know, L.P. Call it woman's intuition. Now come on, we're late!

She drags him past the waiting honor guard, as described by Cleo on the speakers overhead, and on through the crowded terminal (no sign of her anywhere) to the limousine waiting at the curb outside. It's a different vehicle but the same driver as before.

—Hi, pal, the driver says.

Cissy pushes him inside, fusses with his tux, straightens his tie. She has brought him a top hat and walking stick and has fashioned a miniature formal outfit for his best-known feature, which she now slips from its handsewn pocket and dresses. He sinks back into the limo seats, feeling defeated, tears in his eyes. Life: shit. It's a sad business.

—Why has it got dark so quickly? I was only gone thirty minutes.

—Because you crossed several time zones, she says, quickly bringing him erect with a single expert stroke and completing his costuming.

—Oh. . . .

—Now get ready, lover. This is your big night!

Searchlights sweep the snow-blown night sky above the palatial Paradise Theater, and the fans lining the street raise an ecstatic roar as the limousine draws up to the curb. A glowing awning stretches from lobby to street like a condom pulled over the column of floodlit red-carpeted space below, down which the great man soon will pass. Amid fanfares, screams, and rapturous applause, he steps out of the limousine, elegantly attired in tuxedo, black velvet cape, and brushed top hat, swinging a glans-knobbed silver walking stick: Cinecity's first citizen, Filmland's top banana, Our Hero and Icon, Lucky Pierre. At the far end of the red carpet, his leading lady stands waiting for him, smiling brightly and beautifully on this, their night of nights: the world premiere of the newest and bluest Lucky Pierre motion picture. He flashes his famous mustachioed smile for the cameras, their bursts of light popping around him like champagne corks, and greets the wildly cheering masses with blown kisses and two-armed waves and jaunty waggles of his handsome bone-hard merrymaker, the star's star, wittily adorned tonight with stiff collar and black bowtie and a tiny top hat of its own. Ladies weep and throw their panties and kerchiefs at him, young girls swoon at his feet, old women with their skirts hiked grab themselves and piously genuflect. Around him, suspended snowflakes, ephemeral as spermatozoa, glint like stardust.

—Hello! Hello! Yes, it's *wonderful* to be here! Thank you! How's that? Yes, I think this film is the most exciting thing we've done so far. It's been hard work, but it's been worth it; it's *always* worth it! Ha ha, and, that's right, it's always *hard*! Hel-*lo* there!

The crowds press forward, trying to touch him, this beloved idol of millions. *Lucky! Lucky! Lucky!* they cry, delirious with a preternatural love. They throw him their pessaries and sanitary napkins, he kisses them and tosses them back, blesses their zeal with a passing finger up their streaming alleyways and a tip of both his black silk hats. Above him, on the theater marquee: his name in lights, big enough for the whole city to see, and even beyond, were there such.

—Well, thank you, that's very kind, he tells the microphones pushed at him, but really it was a team effort—no solo orgies, as they say in the trade. I had the most beautiful actress in the world as my costar, a wonderful crew to work with, a brilliant director, the script was fabulous, and the camera work was penetratingly innovative—those are the people who deserve the credit. I'm nothing but a walking dingdong with sticky hands and a long tongue—no, it's true! Anyone could do what I do. But thank you! Ouch, don't bite! Bless you! I love you all!

His crazed fans, powering their way through the flailing police truncheons, claw at his clothing, cling to his cape and garters, hump his pantlegs, scramble for the odd pubic hair that falls in the snow. The police form a cordon around him, battling back with riot sticks, pistol butts, and sprays of incapacitating gases, but not even the loyalty and dedication of Cinecity's finest can stop the Lucky Pierre Sex Maniacs, a band of wildly shrieking nymphets, from spreading him out flat on the red carpet and riding a galloping sequence of virginal St. Georges on his frosty pecnoster.

—Oh my gosh—*snap! pop!*—this is *it!*

—Hold it, my child! Don't—*ah!*—don't—

—Don't—?

—Don't get off yet!

The girl astride him is bobbing frantically, mindlessly, eyes rolled back and bubblegum cracking, in an ecstasy of pubescent orgasm. Others fight for their turns but are quickly unseated as the police haul him to his feet and drag him into the heated lobby of the Paradise, snatching back what they can of his shredded clothing. The miniature collar, tie, and top hat are gone, of course, trophies for the Maniacs to dig out later. His emblematic staff is bloody from all the hymenotomies conducted there, his clothing torn and disheveled, his shoes, gloves, and tie have been taken, his pockets and buttons have been ripped away, his cheeks bruised, top and bottom, but he feels great and looks great. This is his night and nothing, really, can spoil it.

In the lobby, scintillatingly lit and full of privileged first-nighters groping one another in eager anticipation of the cinematic masterpiece to follow, there are blown-up stills of him authenticating cunny collectibles at an auction, hammering his prick out on an anvil, scaling a gigantic thigh in the sky, judging heft and bounce at the annual beauty pageant to choose the Queen of the United Inner Metropolis, and hanging from a cross, getting tongued by spike-toothed flagellant nuns. CRUDE AND NASTY! THE EXPLOSIVE CLIMAX OF OVER 2000 YEARS OF FUCKING AND SUCKING! A SALACIOUS HARD CORE CLASSIC OF SPURTING JUICES! Cally, gorgeous in her white organdy evening gown and glittering diamonds, clutches his arm with nervous exhilaration.

—You're looking sensational, Cally! he whispers, smiling for the press and television news cameras. The only true fucking masterpiece in town!

—If I'm the true piece, lover, she whispers, verbally embracing him, you're the fucking master!

Cally gives his organ a tender loving squeeze—his winkie, as she likes to call it—then waves at the cameras, blows a kiss, flashes a milky pink-tipped breast at a passing admirer. She is radiant with the joy of a first night, the consummate star, footlights-born, vibrantly alive, vastly intimate. He decides that this is definitely the best picture they have ever made together, though he cannot for the moment remember which one it is.

Before they go in, he tries to buy a bag of popcorn, buttered between the thighs of the excited salesgirls; they won't take his money, but beg him to dip his dick in the chocolate sauce and autograph their upraised fannies instead. The buzzer sounds.

—Only time for initials, my dears! *Show time!*

—*Curtain up! Pants down!* sing out the usherettes.

He and Cally are led, lit by a traveling spot, through applauding galleries toward a special loge decorated with fornicating deities, fanfares and drumrolls preceding them as they make their way, almost like one single fanfare transmitted through a series of echo chambers. *Yum!* says someone, licking the chocolate off as he passes. Overhead, stars twinkle, stroked gauzily by projected wisps of drifting clouds, and the air is filled with the scent of musk and jasmine. When the usherette takes hold of his penis to lead him to his seat, he finds himself coming, he can't help it, this place always gets to him.

—Oh! My! *Thank* you, sir!

—My—*whoof!*—pleasure, love —*gasp!*—keep the change!

The spot blinks off, the amber houselights dim, and up goes the fire curtain with its golden hand-stitched logo of a mandala-like split beaver backgrounding a haloed lingam, just as he falls, blissfully spent, into his seat, Cally blowing final kisses before taking hers beside him. The youngsters are scrambling for the center seats in the front row below, giggling, punching, goosing, knifing each other playfully. Their elders clear their throats, blow their noses, fart acclamatorily as the heavily fringed and tasseled house curtains majestically part. The suggestive rustle of Cally's full skirts as she sits is like a *shush* that stills the packed house.

—Whoo-eee! Sometimes, Cally, he sighs, I feel like it's more fun to watch these pictures than to make them!

—Sshh, Willie! Pass the popcorn.

Announcements appear on the pale rippling travelers: warning viewers of the heavy penalties for leaving the theater before the program is concluded, interfering with the orgasms of other patrons, booing and whistling and other felonies; instructing them to come as often as they please but please not on the upholstery; asking them to limit all scatophiliac tendencies to the sandbox in the orchestra pit; and reminding them that refreshments, aromatic lubricants, dildos, drugs, candy panties, and fan magazines are available for sale in the lobby at intermission and after the show.

The travelers withdraw behind the house curtains, making way on the big screen for Previews of Cum Extractions, including *Lucky Pierre's Bache-*

lor Party, Law and Ordure (described in the trailer as "a cocks-and-rubbers masterpiece"), the "disturbingly iconoclastic" *Home Movies,* an in-house industrial film called *Disassembling Cineman,* and a restored colorized version of the old film-noir classic, *Snatched Snatch, or: The Case of the Missing Twots,* in which he played a hardboiled private dick who solved all his crimes by drilling the suspects with his trusty rod (NO HOLES BARRED was his tough-guy motto painted on the glass panel of his office door, seen cast as a shadow on the floor in the opening shot), the master criminal whom he faced striking mercilessly thereby at the very modus operandi of his investigative expertise. *Whaddaya mean, they're gone?* he snarls from behind his desk in the preview clip, his penis with which he is playing an odd violet hue with lime-green veins. *How can something that ain't there in the first place go missing?*

He leans over to whisper something to Cally about the sacrilege of colorization, converting all those great monochromatic mysteries into lollypop burlesques—why don't they outlaw it?—and also to tell her that he thinks he's in love, but suddenly all the lights go out, even the exit and toilet signs, and the auditorium is plunged into total darkness, evoking a communal gasp, and then dead silence. Faintly, as though emerging from a great distance, a mournful plainchant is heard and, on the screen, barely visible, a pale billowy landscape rent by a deep dark valley. Near the bottom of the screen, a tiny light shines in that valley, seen now as the cleft between the buttocks of a woman on her hands and knees. Slowly, as though sliding in from outer space on the long dreary tones of the musical lament, the camera zooms forward, passing the black crater of the anus and following the lipped crease below to the light at the entrance to the vagina: it is in the shape of a keyhole. The camera moves in steadily, peeks through: the naked rear end of another woman on her hands and knees, this one lettered from thigh to thigh in an arch over the anus: A DAY IN THE LIFE. The camera continues, slowly but without pause, to glide forward, drifting down, the arched letters passing out of focus above, to the bright light streaming from the pouch below: another luminous keyhole. The camera peers through: the reared buttocks of another woman, or perhaps the same woman, now lettered in the same manner: STARRING LUCKY PIERRE. The silence is broken by a brief flutter of excited applause throughout the theater. This backside too has a glowing keyhole; beyond it, as the camera relentlessly pursues its steady course, the doleful plainsong building in volume and intensity, is the lettered rear of another woman on her hands and knees, or the same woman, relettered. Thus the titles and credits pass, from bottom to bottom, keyhole to keyhole.

—Just like Cleo, he murmurs to Cally. Always has to repeat herself!

—Sshh! Watch the picture!

—Hey! You've eaten all the popcorn!

Through the gleaming keyhole of the director's own lean ass-end: the interior of a one-room flat with bed, table, stove, chest, sink, and bidet. In the uneven glare of a single lightbulb strung on an unshaded cord, a woman lies stretched out on the bed, hands and toes drawn tautly to the four corner posts.

—Is this the right film, Cally? That's Cleo's coldwater flat!

—Of course it is, but be quiet. And behave yourself! she whispers, pushing his hand off her thigh where he had gripped it in alarm. What's the matter with Cally anyway? He pushes back at her and forces his hand up under her gown.

The woman in the film lies pale and still, her pupils narrowed to dark staring needlepoints, her lips drawn back, teeth clenched, trembling faintly. He circles the bed cautiously, crouching, sniffing, shifting his weight, seems about to spring forward—then draws back. He clutches his rigid organ, fingering it nervously, his eyes ablaze. I have come here again! he thinks, and seems to hear himself say it: *Come here again! Come here again!* From time to time, his testicles draw up tightly against his groin, then very slowly relax again, sliding uneasily down over each other into their wrinkled sac; it is a kind of hiccup of fear. The plainchant has vanished. All that can be heard in the room are the heavy beating of a single heart and a faint rasping noise, something like nails scratching on starched linen.

—It's scary, isn't it, Cally? he whispers. He's got his hand over the top of her panty girdle (not exactly Cally's style, panty girdles, but then Cally is an actress, she has lots of styles) and is creeping in the dark, finger past finger, toward those luxuriant pubes he knows so well. She's still resisting, but she has let go his wrist and is breathing hard now.

—Please! *Gasp!* You don't know what you're doing! You are being a very bad boy!

Doesn't know what he's doing? What's Cally up to? Is this a tease? A test? Bending forward, he shoves his hand lower, pressing against the rubbery shackles of her strange undergarment, his elbow looped over one heaving breast as if the girdle-release mechanism might be located there, his eyes locked still on the screen.

On the bed, the spread-eagled woman's long wan body has begun slowly, very slowly, to undulate, as though moved by deep subtle groundswells. Distantly, the plainsong, or something like it, returns, a kind of melodic weaving in and around the thumping continuo of thunderous heartbeats. The man's balls recoil, drop, recoil. He crouches. Backs away. Then, gripping his throbbing member, he leaps suddenly onto the bed between her thighs, leaps off again. She hasn't moved, but the undulations have increased, her whole body rippling now with their surging inner force: a force he knows he cannot resist. Between her white thighs, the mouth of her inflamed sex gapes and puckers, gapes and puckers, almost as though trying to speak—or perhaps it is about to erupt, bubbling now as it puffs out. He is frightened. But it is what it is and he cannot escape it. The crimson tips of her breasts are erect and hard, and the scraggly red hairs of her pubes seem to be standing on end, singed at the tips by the fierce heat of her insatiable desire. He springs onto the bed once more, shrinks back to the foot, and remains there, crouching, between her ankles.

He is sitting now on the edge of his seat, his hand locked in the elastic of Cally's underpants, thinking: Wasn't this supposed to be a comedy? What's happening? This is terrible! And: Has Cally shaved?

The man is poised on the bed on tensed haunches, watching the woman's glittering eyes, ready to leap from the bed at the least sign of danger, his tongue between his cracked lips, his swollen organ pulsing convulsively in his fist, just ahead of the thrumming heartbeats, as though the heartbeats might be mere afterclaps of the pounding in his penis.

—Damn, Cally! It's starting to hurt!

The woman's body, stretched to the four posts, seems to be pulsating now to the rhythm of the augmenting heartbeat, her engorged sex foaming alluringly as it opens and closes, opens and closes. Suddenly, he cries out in anguish and hurtles forward, plunging himself so deeply inside her that the collision of their pelvises resounds with great clashing reverberations in the echoey room. She thrusts upward with an awesome earsplitting shriek, as if to pitch him out again, but he is caught tight in the soft burning vise of her muscular vagina. No way out now, he's in it to the end. Her body heaves and tosses violently, but her quivering limbs remain tautly outstretched, straining against unseen bonds. Up and down she bucks as though trying to throw him from her body while ripping his trapped penis out by the roots; he wraps his arms tightly around her knotted buttocks and hangs on. There is a terrifying moment when he looks into her eyes and sees nothing reflected there—not even the light! And then, with startling suddenness, her arms and legs snap shut around him, her shoulders rear up off the bed, and, just as her womb tears the seed from his exploding loins, she bites down—*crunch!*—on his head, stilling abruptly the thumping heartbeat. For a long dreadful moment, his body continues to pump away in hers in involuntary spasms: She tosses her head back, eyes closed, drooling blood, her long legs wrapped around the man's buttocks, drawing the last drop of pleasure out of his twitching body. Then it too is still, and her limbs relax. Slowly, leisurely, she sits up, curls around his body, and lovingly, almost reverentially, commences to glut herself on his remains, sucking the juices out of his head and abdomen, gnawing noisily on his face and throat and hands.

—*No! Stop it!* he cries, staggering to his feet, his fingers snagged in silk and elastic. The sucking and munching is deafening, it has got inside his head somehow. His face is bathed in cold sweat and his heart is pounding wildly.

—*It's okay! I'm still alive! I'm still here!*

—*Bravo! Bravo!*

The lights come up as the film fades; he finds himself, heart racing, standing at a banquet table, the Mayor sitting beside him, his hand caught off-limits in Her Honor's pants, his pud in the pudding.

—Another masterpiece!

—*Viva!*

—*To the star!*

—*Long live Lucky Pierre!*

As the others, still chewing, give him a standing ovation, the Mayor congratulates him with an encouraging slap on the butt, one athlete to another, causing the pudding to slop over. Or perhaps an angry slap; his hand is still trapped in the inner sanctum of Madame Cora's redoubtable panty girdle. It's numb with pain, he can't be sure what he feels there, isn't sure he wants to know, has only a fading notion of how he got there. Or here. It is as though he is gazing at some kind of slow teary lap dissolve: in the fading foreground, his immolation, larger than life; in the emergent background, a vast banquet hall full of beaming faces, all turned toward him, slapping hands and grinding jaws in raucous approval.

—*Three cheers for Lucky!*

—*Hip hip hooray! Hip hip hooray! Hip hip—!*

—*Our Hero!*

Smiling bravely at the whooping banqueters, he tugs at his locked hand, trying to seem not to be tugging, but to no avail. He feels, somehow, gravely endangered. He spies Cally (must be Cally) hiding across the room behind the handlebar mustache of the maître d' and wonders if she is in some manner to blame for his predicament. No, no, there's only himself for that, as usual, however it happened. It hurts to pull on his hand, but it hurts more to leave it there. Two of Cora's bodyguards, stepping out from the shadows, try to help, if help is the word: they seem prepared to separate him from his offending member if necessary. Finally, unable to bear it any longer, he gives a violent yank. There is a faint but audible *whirrr-clack!* and his hand flies out at last from that forbidden terrain, setting off a resounding *ker-smack!* of elastic against flesh that elicits another round of cheers and hoots and generous applause.

—Ah! S-sorry, Your Honor! he mutters, his throbbing fist tucked abjectly in his armpit.

—There's nothing to regret, Mr. Pierre. She plucks his prick out of the pudding, wraps it with a linen napkin, and pulls him down to his seat beside her. She switches her bowl of pudding for his, lowers her tunic, adjusts her emerald-leafed tiara. It was a stunning performance! We are all proud of you!

She rises grandly, smoothing her tunic down over her powerful body, and rings a little breast-shaped glass bell, which she holds by the nipple, its glass clappers shaped like tiny pale-blue testicles. The rejoicing banqueters take their seats and rattle their drinking glasses with spoons in reply. He huddles in his chair, his wounded hand snuggled in his armpit, wondering how a quiet life of more or less principled fucking has brought him to such an exalted station and what the consequences might be if he closed the studios and took a forty-year vacation in the wilderness.

—My fellow citizens! While you are enjoying your dessert, I might as well get said the few things I have to say, declares the Mayor. If we move along, perhaps we can all get out of here in time to catch the latenight Kinky Klassic on Cinecity Cable.

—Hear! Hear!

—We are gathered here tonight, as you all know, to celebrate the world premiere of our sister's extraordinary virtuoso experiment in creative reportage and to pay homage to a man who is not merely a brilliant performer and viable image in his own right but is indeed the very life and soul of the city, the radical root of our political and historical consciousness, the mainspring of our municipal policy. Indeed, it might be said that, on some higher plane, it is he who is master, and we in City Hall his handmaidens!

—Amen!

—Long live the master!

—Long live his root!

—It is he, to speak as his great art speaks, who pops our collective cork, my friends! It is he who greases our gash, butters our corn, rings our common bell!

—I'll bend over to that!

—Dingdong!

—He wets my wrinkle!

—Hooray for Lucky Pierre!

—We act, exercising what we think of as freewill, yet inexorably fulfill his mysterious design. His image images us, his unions unite us, his suckings succor us!

—Yes, yes! We are all succored!

—All power to the sexual union!

—*We shall cum, over and over!*

He turns toward his silver-tongued hostess standing over him, as though to feign interest in all this political balderdash, and finds himself gazing at a blank screen: her ample hip in its lush white tunic. On that screen, an image begins to appear, blurrily indistinct at first, then slowly revealing itself to be a man walking in a snowstorm. Or perhaps not walking; the snow is moving but the man, fixed and solitary as the figure in a pedestrian crossing sign, is not.

—He is carnality incarnate, my friends, the consubstantiation of all desire! It is through him we may grasp the rise and fall of nations and cultures, experience the ejaculatory convulsions of the universe!

The banqueters respond with convulsive ejaculations of their own, applauding wildly, stamping their feet, and calling out his name. But on the screen of Cora's hip, where the frozen man, caught midstride, poses rigidly in the swirling storm, there is total silence except for the harsh whisper of a wintry wind like the sound of nylon stockings rubbing against one another. The man's hat is jammed down upon his frozen ears, his eyes stare blindly at his raised gold wristwatch, his mouth under its frosty mustache is drawn into a rigid blue pucker around his two front teeth. His penis, ramrod stiff in the blowing snow, is as translucent as an ice sculpture.

—We spread our thighs, seeking communion with the cosmos, searching for our true identities in the dark. But spread thighs are as numerous and anonymous as the stars, dear friends, and lead only to that black abyss where nothing is revealed. He penetrates this impenetrable chasm, taking possession, as it were, of human consciousness, thereby recapturing the elusive reality of life itself!

—Hear! Hear!

—Our savior! Our redeemer!

—Our reamer!

—Yes, he fills the emptiness! the Mayor declaims, her flexing hip causing the frozen man there to seem to shiver. He empties the fullness! He dries our tears, he dampens our dreams! He is our polestar and our star pole! He helps us to accept the past, confront the present, have faith in the foutre! My fellow Cinecitizens, I give you our guest of honor and, indeed, in a true sense, our host—*Mr. Lucky Pierre!*

There are frenzied shouts and cheers, the thunderous pounding of fists on tables, but his ear is attuned to the trembling screen in front of his nose. There, accompanied by a lugubrious dirge, almost secretive in its humming lament, attendants have chipped away the ice locking the frozen man's feet to the pavement and have laid him out in a long narrow box, teak-paneled and ruddily aglow with a diffuse inner light. Ecstatic women now crowd into the box under and around him, prepared, it seems, to die with him rather than live without him. There are subtle glints of gold and crimson in the gleaming blue ice spire rising from his open fly, but no signs of life. He leans closer—

Cora reaches down and pinches the head of his penis with her nails and—*click!*—the image on her hip vanishes, the mournful plainsong does. She grips him firmly in her strong fist just above the ballocks and hauls him to his feet, the deafening applause now rattling in his reopened ears like a sudden burst of static.

—*Lucky Pierre! Lucky Pierre! Lucky Pierre!*

—We cannot offer him the key to the city, she cries, because he *is* the key to the city! We can only ask that he who has given so much give yet a little more!

Even as she speaks, she is deftly working his shaft with her powerful ringed fingers. Before he can think about holding back, he is pumping spunk into her pudding bowl, tipped before his spurting cock like a sacred chalice.

—*Aaarrgh!* he groans, falling back into his chair when she lets go, as the applause and laughter crash around him.

The Mayor stirs the pudding with a spoon and takes a reverential taste, closing her eyes and licking her lips appreciatively; then, inviting everyone to share in what she calls *this sweet cummunion,* she passes the bowl on with both hands. Slowly it moves through the room from banqueter to banqueter, while Her Honor crosses over to the doorway to receive the traditional farewell due her and her office. He sags limply in his chair, staring dully out upon the happy celebrants, and for a brief moment everything seems to stand still: the pudding bowl held between two banqueters, other guests poised, half risen from their seats, the lights dipping faintly, the smoke ceasing for that second to swirl: Oh oh, he thinks. He feels a cold draft on his ankles, a chill curling around his flagging member. Nothing else is moving. This Day in the Life, he knows, is drawing to a close. . . .

He shakes himself and stands, and with that the pudding bowl continues on its devotional travels, banqueters who have eaten from it rise and pull on wraps and stand in line to kiss the Mayor goodnight. She is kneeling now on velvet cushions near the door, her tunic tucked up about her waist. With solemn deliberation, her attendants work her panty girdle down over the snowy mounds of her expansive cheeks, the deepening crack between them emerging like an ever more perilous path to power or (his thoughts are darkening with the dimming day) to damnation. This path is not wholly revealed: the panties, stretched from thigh to thigh like a police barrier, are pulled down only far enough to expose her puckered lipsticked anus. What's below (he sniffs his fingers: faintly metallic, though that might be from his armpit) remains concealed.

As he takes his place in line to pay his respects in the customary fashion, an ancient blue-haired lady with a pince-nez and a cane takes his arm as though for support and, tapping at his drooping phallus with the knob of her cane, squawks into his ear:

—Just between the two of us, sonny, that was a fine piece of work!

—Thank you, ma'am!

—But it wasn't up to your best. Oh, I'm not complaining about all the fancy stuff, though most of it blew right by me, truth to tell, left me dry as a raisin. But what the hell, tastes change, we need variety, doing the same durn thing all the time's depressing, so trick us if you can. But the famous carry-through wasn't always there, boy! Too much interruptus in the old coitus!

—Perhaps you're right.

—Of course I'm right! Don't let the high-tech razzamatazz lead you astray! Keep that sucker in there till the bitter end! You gotta finish what you start. No more goin' before the comin'! The old crone hawks and spits into a lace hanky, winking up at him over her pince-nez as she wipes her mouth, blows her nose: And make it a little kinkier, too, son—you know, voice of the people and all that. Mix it up a little, whip a few more heinies, get the groupies going, incest, bondage, necrophilia, sock it to the kiddies: some of the good old scenes! It's no crime to be popular, you know!

—Well, no, but—

—Remember Wee Willie and Peter Prick? Those were the great films. And, hey, fuck a few more old ladies, if you don't mind, sweetie. Here's my card.

She stoops, leaning on her cane, to peck at Cora's upraised rear, and hobbles out, blowing him a wrinkled kiss over her hunched back as she goes. It's his turn. He gazes down on Her Honor's breathtakingly handsome ass—an arse, really, in the broad medieval sense, a cultivated vast terrain, fundament and grainbin, the ineffable seat of all our joys and woes, arse gratia artis! He kneels before this monumental affair like an adoring pilgrim, prepared to pay tender homage to it and to her with his pursed lips, but then, as a cold wind whips at his pant cuffs, everything stops again.

His stare is locked upon the Mayor's looming fundament, creamily radiant in the dimmed light, the little bouquet of hair about the anus brilliantined down with spit, the lipstick smeared sensuously, the skin around it polished to a high sheen from so much veneration. The eye of the world. The sounds of departing partygoers subside, the buzz of private chatter, clink of spoons and glasses, scraping of chairs, soft bursts of bubbling laughter, all vanishing as though snuffed like a candle, and in the sudden hush he hears again, faintly, the unresolved dissonances of that mournful plainsong, lamenting the widowed city, the desolate gates, hearts poured out in grief. On the stiff glossy screen of Her Honor's panty girdle, stretched around her thighs, there appears again the frozen man laid out in the glowing box, pillowed by the ecstatic women, gazing at him over his shoulder as though fatally smitten, their heads drawn together, their lips parted in awe and helpless infatuation—or perhaps in terror. Nothing moves except the snow blowing by, drifting over the figures in the box. The man's head is tipped toward his raised wrist, an attaché case locked in his other hand, his blue penis standing like an inverted icicle. By some hidden mechanism, the box is slowly tipped upright, the bodies inside clinking and clacking as they rattle against one another momentarily. There is a pause. Then the box begins to rise, lifting past the panty waistband into that hovering oblivion beyond the frame.

His eye has been drawn up by this movement to the Mayor's anus, all puffy and proud and lipstick-smeared and waiting for his kiss. He strains against the glacial rigidity in which he finds himself arrested, pushing his face forward with all his strength, and seems to make some small progress, but it is more of a zoom than a dolly shot. I will never taste it, he thinks. Can't even seem to lick my lips. Larger and larger the anus looms, a gleaming portal above the panty-shadowed mysteries below, swirled about now with blowing snow that fogs his vision. Curtains are being drawn in the space between him and the great arse, he realizes, and the light is fading. His chance has passed; his respects will never be paid. The arse itself is little more than a pale blurry expanse now, spreading out upon the rippling crimson velour of the closing curtains, falling into shadow, only this wintry crack spotlit, and there, over the puckered entrance, appearing like secret writing, the simple but ominous and ever woeful proclamation:

END

Reel 3: Clara

Exits the elevator, scattering clothing. Watched by the smiling operator in the empty elevator behind him, he strides purposefully toward the receptionist, who is just cradling the crimson desk phone. A brunette in a tangerine skirt, carrying a file folder, crosses right-to-left behind him, pauses, glances up at him as though in surprise.

—Good morning, sir!

—Some weather we're having, isn't it?

—Call for you on two, L.P.

—Coffee, Mr. P?

—Later. Freeze the fucker!

The receptionist smiles dazzlingly up at him, breasts jutting classically, purple crêpe dress taut. He is stopped midstride: right foot planted firmly on the plush green carpet, left leg bent at the knee, faint ironic smile playing on his lips, which seems to say, This is good. He carries his attaché case slightly forward in his right hand, partly concealing his erection. His underpants, hovering in midair like a cream-colored bat, block out the face of the tangerine-skirted fileclerk. A cotton dress shirt raises one blue sleeve starchily from the floor as though asking a question.

—*Mr. P!*

This scream, launched as a squeal, sinks suddenly to a low growl. Then, slowly:

Right knee flexes. Left toe rises, knee doubling. Right hand releases attaché case. Shirt sleeve sinks.

Fileclerk's astonished eyes appear above the falling underwear.

Elevator operator steps backward into the elevator, her face passing into shadow, left arm rising toward the instrument panel.

Erection bobs upward, ironic smile spreading.

Receptionist's thighs lift away from the chair. Crimson phone separates itself from her right hand as her fingers stiffen.

Fileclerk's gaping mouth appears above shorts as though eating them, low rumbling sound emerges.

Attaché case soars, phone floats.

Erection begins its downward bob as right knee straightens, left leg doubling like a high jumper's, right hand reaching out.

Fileclerk's rumble gradually augments in volume and pitch as underpants tumble past the rising folder in her hands.

Receptionist twists gracefully, edging her chair up and out of the way. Papers lift, letter basket tilts, bronze cast of tumescent organ rises as his right hand arrives firmly on desktop.

Fileclerk's bellowing scream rises to baritone pitch over sounds of soft metals colliding, hinges grating. Elevator doors close.

His feet leave the carpet, hips swivel and lift. Deep resonant boom as the chair bounces off the wall.

Receptionist, smiling expectantly yet fearfully, braces herself, legs spread, arms out, as he doubles at the waist, feet rising above desktop, self-congratulating grin spreading, scream rising to alto.

His toes clear the desk but not the monitor that stands in the middle of it. Rising scream ends abruptly as the fileclerk bites down on her folder, replaced by a deep basso plaint, sliding upward:

—What-the-fuck-is-t-h-a-t-t-h-i-n-g-D-O-I-N-G—?!!

He somersaults in slow motion, buttocks lifting, knees spreading awkwardly, as though they might be wings trying to help him fly. The receptionist backs away, her hair lifting, purple skirt rippling silkily, but not quickly enough; she is struck full in the face by his flying buttocks.

For a moment, all is suspended, as though stopped dead by the shock of the impact. The receptionist's nose is flattened, her cheeks distorted; her hair twines about his thighs. Her eyes, crossed, stare in alarm at the underside of his shriveling gonads, as though discovering right in front of her spreading nose the cause of all her misfortune. His right leg points straight up to the ceiling, his left is out to one side, knee doubled, foot about six inches from the receptionist's right ear and closing.

Then, very slowly at first but more and more rapidly, his left leg straightens, his buttocks remove themselves from her face, her broken nose re-forms itself, her hair falls back in place, the uneasy smile returns. His right leg doubles and spreads away from his left, his left hand brushes the monitor, his right finds the desk again—

—*G-N-I-O-D-g-n-i-httahtsikcufehttahw!*

Back over he goes, feet to the floor, chair, phone, and attaché case flying back into the picture; the fileclerk screams abruptly, underwear swoops up past her face into the man's hands, and, as he hops backward, onto his body, the blue shirt raising its arm as though trying to stop him, then on up off the floor, elevator doors opening and operator popping her smiling face out. Half dressed, his arms and legs churning, the fileclerk vanishing, he hippety-hops back through a high-pitched gibberish of reversed greetings into the elevator with the operator and the doors close. The receptionist has turned away, catching the flying phone and cradling it.

Pause. Focus on the phone. Which rings.

The elevator doors open. He exits, scattering clothing. The operator in her little uniform watches, smiles. The fileclerk in the purple crêpe dress and a nose as big as a grapefruit crosses right to left and commences to scream.

—Coffee, L.P.?

The receptionist smiles up at him, sitting bouncily, her tangerine skirt taut, gripping the crimson phone receiver in her right hand. The rest of the desk has been swept clean.

—*Mr. P!*

At first a squeal, then plummeting.

His right foot is planted firmly, left leg flexing, a faint ironic smile on his face, underwear hovering, shirt sleeve raised like a man going down for the third time. Then, slowly:

Right knee flexes to make the leap, left toe rises from carpet. Flaccid penis erects itself.

Fileclerk's broken nose appears above tumbling underpants.

Receptionist's thighs lift away from the chair.

His right hand is planted on the cleared desk, his attaché case soars out of sight, his feet lift, the receptionist's fingers stiffen, the crimson designer phone separates itself from her hand.

—Market reports, sir.

—Phone for you on two.

—*Past that!*

The elevator doors close, the operator disappearing behind them.

The spiral phone cord loops gracefully around the receptionist's wrist.

The fileclerk's baritone scream augments.

The crimson phone floats outward, stretching on its coils, seems to hesitate, and then, on its springy leash, glides back toward the receptionist.

His feet have cleared the barren desktop: he smiles proudly, not yet having seen the gracefully yoyoing telephone.

Then he does see it.

Alarm and dismay creep slowly over all their faces.

The receptionist draws her arm back as though trying to shake off the rebounding telephone; the receiver's mouthpiece seems to want to speak to his crotch.

—*N-o-o-o-o-o—!*

He arches his back, raises his thighs, and tries to twist away, while the receptionist slaps at the phone with her free hand. She turns toward him just in time to get his rigid penis in her eye.

He seems to be sitting on the pointed tip of one of her painted fingernails, trying to fuck her in the eye and listen to the telephone with his testicles, which have been flattened out as though to hear better.

—*Cut!*

—*No! Aarrgh! Back it up, damn it!*

Gradually at first, but then faster and faster, he flies away from her face, the telephone again loops about and is caught by the receptionist, his clothes fly into his hands and onto his body, the elevator doors open, he snatches his flying attaché case out of the air, hippety-hops backward, and, smiling ironically, disappears like a shot down the elevator shaft.

The office staff crowd around the open door, peering down into the dark shaft.

—Mr. P? Are you all right?

Nothing can be heard but a distant moaning, as though from the bottom of a well.

—L.P.?

Cissy holds a mike out over the empty shaft.

—Hello? L.P.? I think we ought to leave that telephone out of the shot altogether, don't you?

Soft echoey whimpering.

—L.P.? Can you hear me down there? Listen, do you want to try that one more time or should we—?

The whimpering ceases. Silence. Then, distantly, brokenly:

—Fuck you, Cissy. Fuck . . . fuck you all! I quit.

—Sounds serious, says Cissy, listening to the playback. Guess we'd better get him to the doctor.

—The doctor will see you now.

The patient, a livid mass of welts, bruises, abrasions, and deep discontents, wearing only a short hospital gown tied at the back and laid out on an examining table like raw stock, is wheeled, cold and half conscious, into the doctor's office.

—Well, well! exclaims the doctor, exhibiting a professional jollity. And what have we here?

He lies darkly in his wounds, keeping bottled up his scripted groans, his knees and elbows turned out, as though he were coming unspooled. By contrast, the doctor, who directs this in-house segment, which for all he knows may be his last, is glowing with well-being, her silvery-blond hair pulled back in a tight bun at the neck, her teeth sparkling, her complexion radiant, her bright uniform clean and fragrant. Cast in his misery, he is offended by such a picture of health. She picks through an array of instruments, her metallic nails clicking, and selects an otoscope and a sensitometer.

—Looks like a bad case of advanced misentropy! She chuckles, winking at her colleagues.

—Critical, doctor?

—Fetal, I'm afraid.

Her breasts are high and pointed, her belly flat and tight as a drumhead, her buttocks packed full and firm in the starchy white skirt. She is circled about by the glint of stainless steel and glaze of lights, by wallcharts and diplomas, the hum of apparatus, the soft hushing movement of nurses and production assistants. She peers under his eyelids, into his ears and nostrils, and down his throat, dictating to an aide:

—Signs of hypopraxia, idiodynamic delusions, hot lips, and circadian decubitis. Deglutition and exteroceptors normal, more or less, and there are cunt hairs between his teeth; query cohort relationships.

—He seems so cold and lethargic, doctor.

—Yes, a consequence perhaps of excessive overcranking.

She leans down to listen to his heart, pressing her pubis against his hand—seems almost to move behind the skirt, to caress him. His curiosity aroused, or perhaps simply because he is who he is, he turns his hand over to hold it in his palm, less numb somehow than all the rest of him.

—Aha! Feeling better?

She peeks under his gown.

—My word! I guess you are!

—A . . . a terrible fall, Clara.

—Yes, I recognize the symptoms.

—No, *the* fall, I mean . . . a rupture of some kind, permanent, I think—or worse!

THE END, he means, but she just laughs and stuffs his awakening hand back under her crisp skirt.

—You're too suggestible!

Her mound is warm and wet, thickly padded with wiry little curls. The labia seem to reach out, grip his fingers, count them, twist the knuckles, read the palm.

—Hmm. Moderate hypopselaphesia, probably transient and cryogenetic. Intriguing wart on the subject's social finger. Diarthrodial articulation, synergetic and tender. Severe agnails, symptoms of ambivalence, but effectively excitomotory.

—Voluptafacient, doctor? asks a nurse.

—Quite. Feels good, too. Yum! Decussate life and love lines, implying endopathic abiotrophy of the essential humors. Turn him over and let's have a reverse-angle look at his old arrière-voussure!

As they pull his hand away to roll him over onto his belly, her vagina sucks up his fingers and then—*fffFFPOP!*—lets them go. Procumbent, as Clara describes him, he feels the chill come on again. That fall: no saving jump cuts this time, no fades, no soft dissolves; they let him hit bottom and even filmed the bounce. Neorealism, they called it. For Clara's sake: her demand for unmediated authenticity. You can't dissect a mock-up, she likes to say. She wants the truth, hardcore truth, twenty-four times a second, even if she has to create it herself. Now her assistants spread his knees and elbows out, adjust his balls for him, untie the gown. Clara smiles down at what she sees, slaps his buttocks.

—On the homely face of it, I'd have to describe it as dasygenal, wouldn't you, staff?

—Is it . . . is it serious, doctor? he wants to know, prepared for the worst.

—Very serious, she laughs. It means you have a hairy ass. Ex facie. Relax. You might as well enjoy this.

She spreads his cheeks, sniffs about critically, squeezes a pimple, pokes a proctoscope into his rectum.

—What does it look like in there, doctor?

—Not a pretty picture, I'm afraid. Some evidence of diathetic dysteology, as well as time-orientation compulsions, possibly due to a faulty diet. Better stick an explosimeter up there, while I take a look at his tail. What's left of it.

—An explosi—*what?!*

She probes the base of the spine, finds a raw nerve, sending him bucking up off the table.

—*Yowww!* Damn it, Clara, take it easy! *That hurt!*

—There it is, sisters, that's where the old caudal appendage got docked. The original hypostatic disunion; he's been looking for his missing tail ever since. Thus, the first phase of hominization: the quest motive. Which in the present instance has degenerated into a kind of sacral eschatology—you can see the open sore here—confused by the dysgnostic assumption that woman was created from the severed tail, and to this day, as the old doggerel goes, must serve his will and solace his posteriors still!

The nurses hoot mockingly at that and beat his nates with stethoscopes and clipboards, artificial limbs, leather traction belts, and rubber blood-pressure tubes, wagging their own tails excitedly and scratching their fleas.

—But it's true! he protests weakly. I remember it . . .

—Forget the past, dear man, it's mostly waste. There is, as they rightly say, no future in it.

—But what does it matter, Clara? There's no future anyway. I'm finished, I know that; the reel's run out.

—Bullshit. Despair is a metaphor, like any other. A clichéd plot device.

—I just want to sleep . . .

—No doubt. We all suffer these gesticidal tendencies. The lure of the fadeout. But don't worry. You're in *my* film now, dear boy, *my* treatment. Experto credite. Look. Already your ass is as red as a rose in bloom! *It* won't soon go to sleep again!

—It's not my ass that's the problem, Clara, it's my head, my heart!

She laughs at his confusions. It's true; what does he know about anatomy? He's a complete dope.

—Rig him up for stress analysis, she says to her assistants.

His feet are bound together in ankle cuffs, and Lucky Pierre, last of the great pornographic film icons, is hoisted upside down and hung from a gambrel stick. The gown is stripped away and he is smeared over with a photoelastic covering. Weights are suspended from his arms, neck, mustache, penis, and navel, and stereoscopic VR goggles are fitted to his eyes. He is subjected to a sequence of 3-D images—body parts, falling buildings, circus acts, mountaineers lashed by snowstorms, genteel sodomies, snail-fucking, electrocutions, and the like—while the doctor studies the isochromatic patterns got by bombarding him with polarized light.

—But I've given it all I've got, Clara, he whimpers, his tongue flopping against the roof of his mouth, I've really tried.

—I know. That's why you've been sent to me. Have faith. And don't press the chicken switch. When in doubt, exercitate! Orthopraxy saves, and all that. My! look at those gorgeous colors!

While she watches him, he is watching the collapse of ecosystems, the gangbang of a child star, castrations and bicycle races, the fall of an airplane, the discovery of the optical printer, and as blood rushes to his head he thinks, She's right, our bodies are full of chaos and violence; it's the way they express themselves. All actors have to understand that; the integrity of our performances depends upon it. Let it roll.

—Each color indicates the magnitude of stress at each part of the system, the doctor is explaining to her assistants, who are ooh-ing and ah-ing at the sight of him all lit up.

—What lovely spots of blue there in his belly, doctor!

—Yes, the hypochondrium, of course. Nearby, that ugly black spot is the liver, where much of the murder takes place. As is to be expected, it's the locus of least stress.

—But, oh my, look at his testes! It's almost as though they're on fire!

—Yes, while by contrast, observe that the penis, which is self-evidently diagetropic and therefore subject to additional gravitational demands, runs nevertheless—following the speeding train of received images behind the goggles—the whole spectrum, now black and flaccid, now crimson and aroused, now a straining luciferous white, as though unsure of its own enthusiasms or responsibilities.

—It's rather like his head, doctor. It looks like a bowl of lit-up fruit.

—True, but the head contains all these colors at once, like a syncretic contexture of shifting options, you might say, while his penis's dysmnesiac experience of these states is serially diachronic.

—Gosh, you're right! That sure makes it a whole lot prettier, doesn't it?

—It's wonderful what you can learn from a silly old dick, doctor!

—Ex pene Herculem, my dear!

—But—*good heavens!*

—Yes, nurse?

—His . . . his *heart,* doctor!

—Mmm. You've noticed.

—It's . . . it's *green!*

The doctor sighs, smiles, casts a long affectionate glance at the patient.

—Yes, it . . . it almost makes you believe in love again, doesn't it?

—*Doctor!*

The doctor laughs, switches off the polarized light.

—Take the subject down, exuviate him, then osculate his pecker, please, and give me a coefficient of viscosity reading in centipoise.

While the doctor withdraws to her desk to fill out her examination report and feed the data into her computer, her assistants unshackle him, stretch him out, remove the goggles, and peel off the photoelastic sheath. He is lightheaded, feels upside down still. Weird visions dance through his fruit bowl of a head, including one of himself as a stylite living in the desert on top of a colossal pillar in a little straw hut, worshiped by the tiny crowds massed far below. Which are not tiny crowds after all, but a thicket of pubic hair; the pillar is his own prick, the stylite a crab louse—though he himself is also, while examining himself and trying to catch the little bugger, lying on top of a tall pillar. Which is not a pillar at all, of course, but his own prick again, the prostrate figure on its tip a louse or worse, and so on, falling through a dizzying progression of pillars and pricks, saintliness and pediculosis, until at last one of the nurses, a student, slides a catheter down his urethra, reaches up under his scrotum and manipulates the vas deferens with little pumping motions, and, sucking gently on the tube, draws off a small specimen of semen for the doctor's uranianalysis. He shudders: a certain tingling reminiscent of orgasm, but without the spasm. Like something from the sweet but distant past, not quite recalled. Leaves him feeling suspended, nervous and edgy, much as one feels when one has to sneeze but cannot, and he worries now about having come here. Is there to be an operation? Will he leave here alive? He reaches up to give himself relief, but they rap his knuckles with a steel rule.

—Don't make us strap you down, now!

—The doctor wants it at full stretch! She'll see to you in a minute.

—Pl—*ahchoo!*—please . . .

—The sample, doctor, says the student nurse. It's pretty sticky stuff.

—Thank you. Mmm, tastes good too. I can see why they are using it as an excipient. Pity he's been wasting so much of it.

—Come on, Clara, goddamn it! I feel all wrong, like I'm falling through infinity or something. Help me get off!

—Are you always in such a hurry? she asks with a smile. We've only just begun.

She weighs his stones on a ballocks balance, listens to them, waggles them about, beats a small electronic gong with them: hollow echoey sound. Why does she care? Her appetite for knowledge arouses in some small part his own. It's important, he thinks, to be possessed like that. To be so eager to be alive and aware that it drives you mad. She reads the signals from the gong, runs a profilometric check on his penis, tries to bend it, slaps at it to see which direction it bobs.

—Pubes: pterygoid. Calluses: clitoridean. Shear modular: impressive.

She nips at the glans with her teeth, clucking her tongue ominously, separates the lips of his penis, peers down the urethra.

—Whew! That's a pretty long fall at that! she admits.

—I told you. . . .

—Would one of you nurses dim the lights, please?

The office darkens. Clara adjusts the aperture with a little twist at the base of his prick. Her hands are smooth and cool, good hands, he knows, to be in during this crisis.

—What's important about these little things, she says squinting, is their power of resolution. It's a kind of optical illusion.

The nurses murmur appreciatively and take turns peeking inside while the doctor holds it open. As she touches and plays with him, he relaxes. He knows that, sooner or later, she will satisfy him, and will satisfy him as no one else can, because the inevitability of her doing so is part of that subtext that informs all her films, unscripted though she pretends them to be.

—Now, the heart of these systems, the doctor is explaining, is the intermittent mechanism. This one uses an advanced springloaded oscillating claw—if you look down in there, you'll be able to see it—which in turn is backed up by one of the most ancient of such devices, the old-fashioned dog-movement, using the eccentric pin. See it wiggle there? Yes, that's it.

—Isn't it rather troublesome to have two paradoxical mechanisms in one system, doctor?

—Perhaps. But this is the price for versatility and sufficiency.

—What's that little gaugelike device up here near the nose, doctor?

—That's to adjust the speed. It's what makes many of your special effects possible.

She presses a little trigger under the shaft, his hips buck and slap the table, and light pours through, casting a moving image on the ceiling: He, Lucky Pierre, is wallowing in heaps of unwound film up there and beautiful young starlets are smashing their maidenheads on his cock like champagne bottles.

—It's only recently, the doctor is saying, that we have come to understand the gonads as part of the central nervous system. In the past, we tended to isolate them in terms purely of their hypothetical reproductive functions, failing to see that this anthropocentric or macro-organism bias ignored the communities within and the universal order without.

Her grip on his prick is firm but soothing. His hips have stopped bucking, but he still seems to be experiencing the orgasm. Not as good as most orgasms, true, but better than the frustration that went before, and he enjoys the prolonged effect. On the ceiling, dying spermatozoa are arranging themselves into astrological signals.

—We now know that no sense data—which is to say, no data at all—enter man's central nervous system without simultaneous transmission to the gonads, and at the same time that no mental processes take place, no matter what logic circuits may have been implemented by prior environmental engineering, without gonad feedback and involvement. They are part of the package.

He seems to remember a time when a mean girl in school stuffed his peter in an inkwell, but on the ceiling now his teacher is showing him an apple with the laws of gravity written on it.

—And as you might have surmised from our previous stress analysis, the peculiar design factor of the gonads, perhaps because of the relative brevity of their intracommunal life cycles, is their augmented processor impact and diminished storage capacities, such that their peculiar contribution to mental activity is *projection*. . . .

He eats the apple and falls through space at thirty-two feet per second per second, thinking, This apple tastes just like pussy! Somewhere he hears the sound of blades being sharpened, and the doctor's fingers have become rigid and cold as steel.

—I assume you all know how this gadget works; you've taken these things apart?

—Yes, but if there were snatching or excessive tension on our perforations, doctor, where would we—?

—You'd open it up right here.

On the ceiling, the doctor has grown fangs and dark scowling brows and is stealing up on the patient with a gleaming scalpel.

—You see? Now we could completely disassemble it, if you like . . . ?

The doctor, grinning evilly, has slashed off the patient's genitals and is going for his heart, his head, but he pulls himself together. The doctor withdraws, cowering in a dark corner, her eyes gleaming like burning coals. Perhaps she has not yet struck the first blow. Perhaps she is naked.

—Efforts have been made to temper the impact of the gonads' signal digression and distortion through increasingly complex program designs for nonhuman cybernetic components, but clearly, if man is to remain relevant, he must remain close to the transdimensional mainstream of life, and thus must keep his gonads plugged into all his mental processes and screw the consequences, to coin a phrase. It's what you might call a quality assurance factor.

The doctor has discovered his throbbing cock. The scalpel falls from her trembling hand. Her fangs recede, her eyes glaze over with excitement. Cautiously she approaches, her heart thumping visibly in the walls of her steaming vulva.

—That's not to say that these projections of the gonads are in themselves reliable stimuli for sound behavior—on the contrary! Barrel distortion, curvature of field, chromatic aberration, recurrent clap, and flicker are only a few of the typical defects. The circle-of-confusion factor has never been satisfactorily resolved and tends to be infectious. Moreover, just as cerebral logic systems attempt to think through problems, the gonads instinctively try to fuck their way out. Thus, as you can see above, our subject somehow supposes he can neutralize what he has interpreted and projected as hostility by fucking me into quiescence or even affection. And who knows?—ha ha!—he may be right!

Before mounting him, the hovering doctor inserts an endoscopic camera in her womb to photograph the attitude during entry and exit and shoves an extensometer up her rectum to measure him through the separating membrane. Her golden body is as sleek and hard as a mannikin's, nothing sags or wobbles, not a blemish or a wrinkle, yet it's rumored she may be more than three hundred years old. The wonders of science!

—He even perceives this coitus to be initiated by me, but these projections are occluded by a veritable montage of ambivalence. Behind the mad doctor sequence, you will discover the shadow of the indifferent doctor, the heroic doctor, the incompetent doctor, the corrupt doctor, and the distracted doctor. If I adjust the focus, you will see projections that include yourselves, others of the city streets, his workplace, the decaying cosmos, his assumed past.

She does a kind of split across his body, one hand on his knee, the other pressing down on his belly.

—Does this hurt? Good . . .

Slowly, methodically, she lowers herself and he feels her clitoris probe the length of his penis; feels the lips caress, suck, nibble, taste, pucker, blow, nip; feels her pubes thud softly, springily, against his own.

—There is an associative rhythm to all these projections, which will become more evident as coitus proceeds, but it is clear that the projections are not any freer from the influence of the primary and secondary sense organs than our so-called rational operations are from the influence of the gonads.

He seems to see the wet red walls of her vagina, as though lit by quartz-iodine lamps, and, beyond the lamps' glare, the fierce dark lens of the endoscopic camera. He wishes to perform well.

—Thus, advanced cineman's relationship with his gonads is not more remote, it is simply more complex. He has a heightened awareness of pattern, but also a heightened awareness of immediacy and randomness. Cineman is more space-conscious, but he is also more time-conscious. Motion is his very essence, yet no humanoid in the evolutionary scale was ever more conscious of configuration, fields, reaction formations, or paradox. Kinetics is, finally, that science exclusively concerned with stasis.

He leaps and thrusts in the glistening red chamber, the insouciant pupilless eye of the camera now taunting him, infuriating him; he strives to reach it, to smash it with a head-on blow.

—He knows the circular reel and the square frame. His logic systems have led him to transcend art, his gonads have—*ah!*—led him beyond history.

The oozing walls flex and ripple, pushing him away, pulling him back. The extensometer is grabbing at him through the thin membrane, testing him.

—He knows he must turn away from abstractions and—*foo!*—fantasies toward the concrete, knows he must cope more directly with—*ungh!*—with disorientation and—*ah! oh! . . . oh, this is beautiful; this is very good!*—with disorientation and entropy, yet he achieves this—*ah! uf!*—through a new respect for—*oh!*—for symbolic systems—*hah!*—and purely conceptualized—*WOW!*

Strains toward the fucking lens, can't reach it, the walls grab him, he feels himself coming gloriously apart—*Now!* he cries, explodes, smashes the lens with his own eruptive death, strobes spin and crash, screams rend the deep silence, darkness falls about him, collapsing like a starry sky, some lost part of him shudders and sinks away.

Later, he hears his own heartbeat. The wet red walls are the insides of his own eyelids. He thinks, I have been dreaming all this. I will awake in my own bed, my pajamas sticky and wet with cold cum. I will walk through the sullen crowds and the blowing snow to the studio. My staff will give me a hot bath and we will make films together. But when he opens his eyes he is still in the doctor's office. This frightens him: Something real is happening! The doctor, in her immaculate white uniform, is taking readouts from her scanners and imaging instruments. Her assistants are dismantling and storing equipment, preparing flowcharts, admiring the splotch of dripping sperm on the ceiling high above.

—Am I . . . am I going to be all right? he asks faintly.

The doctor comes over to him, gazes down, touches a cool hand to his forehead.

—Yes, I think so, she says.

He knows she is lying. It is serious, after all. He has made some kind of mistake, or at least a mistake has been made; it's as though the very genre has been violated at the root, and there's nothing he can do about it.

—I want to know everything, he says, meaning it as a confession.

—You are suffering from hypotyposis, compounded by severe kinophiliac parabologyny. I predict an episode of gonomantically inspired itineration, leading to a difficult ectopic ingravidation, but this will probably be for the best, and at the least an entertainment.

He sees something in her eyes he hasn't noticed before: a glint of communicative warmth behind the professional detachment. And the way she said *entertainment. . . .*

—Clara, I-I love you! What shall I do?

—Eat more balanced meals, exercise regularly, brush your teeth at least twice a day, and for the present go home and toast your buns under a sunlamp.

—No, I mean—

—That's a print, she says firmly. She hands him a prescription the size of an idiot card, and he is wheeled out of the office and off the screen.

🎬

He rolls over on his belly to brown his backside, thinking, Clara's right. We only think we think; matter makes what moves it must, thus the urban crush and the exploding universe, whatever's not forbidden is compulsory, if I'm fucking off I can't help it, must come to rest, it's the universal law. And so, with luck (he was born with it), the years pass, the reels unwind. He lies, following medical advice, on a cushioned rubdown table soft as babyskin alongside the swimming pool in his luxury penthouse apartment high above the city. The heat from the roving angst-sensitive lamp explores his shoulders, his back, the cheeks and crack of his ass, the underside of his balls, backs of his thighs and knees: caressing, kneading, penetrating, stroking, curing. He's probably not a hundred percent yet, but the crisis is past; he's definitely on the mend. There's a hole in the middle of the padded table with a built-in pulsator; he oils his love muscle, already aroused by the lamp, and stuffs it in. *Yum.* Anything that feels this good must be the right thing. Soft lilting music played on simple stringed instruments reaches him from circumambient speakers, accompanied by delicate fragrances released by his aromassager. Slowly he probes the throbbing hole, dreaming of hot beaches, clear bluegreen bays, waving palms, pretty maidens wearing brightly colored kerchiefs and fruit on their heads. Yes, this is where he belongs, not out there on the massed-up streets, pushing through the despair and snow, but right here, flat out in his own pad, joyfully benumbed, fucking the passing fancies, mmm. Stand up to be counted these days, you get counted out, swept away in the conflux, the profusion pollution, the sea of faces. The sea of farces. Faeces. Phases. Phrases. . . .

He's just drifting off, taking his deepening ease in undulating jungle thighs somewhere beyond the sea of phrases, when a bell rings, setting off alarms.

—Eh? What? Who's there?

Where is he? For a moment, he can't think, can't see. Hello, hello? It rings again: ah! a doorbell! He springs off the table, but forgets to remove his stiffened joint from the hole first, so—*twa-wa-wa-wa-wa-wan-n-n-n-ng!*—gets sprung right back on again. Everything shrivels up; even his toes and fingers curl and his teeth shrink back in their sockets. Only his tear ducts still work. Overhead, the sunlamp is flickering and popping, its search sensors overloaded. Again the bell rings.

—All right, all right, damn you! he groans. He knows where he is now. I'm coming!

He crawls down off the table and staggers to the door, holding himself gingerly. It's the city mailman. Special delivery. Big package, badly beat up.

—It's your Cunt of the Month, mister. For April.

—What? There must be some mistake—

—Sorry about that. We're running a little behind.

—No, I mean I never ordered this.

—Are you Mr. L. Pierre?

—Yes, but—

—Then, no mistake, pal, it's your subscription, she's your merchandise. Five hundred smackeroos, please.

—What—?!

—C.O.D.

—But that's robbery! And look at the condition of the thing! What the hell kind of service is this?

—Hey, you got a little problem, go flash it down at City Hall, mister. I ain't the pestle, I ain't the mortar, I'm just the hand doing its job to order.

—All right, all right, let me find my pants.

—Pretty pink back there, pal. You better watch out. Those sunlamps can make you impotent, you know.

—Wishful thinking, handjob. Here. Three hundred's all I got.

—I was told to get five.

—It's all there is, take it or leave it.

The mailman shrugs, drops the package—it crashes to the tiles, setting off an ominous rattling and tinkling inside—and pockets the money, giving the package a final vindictive boot before turning away.

—Hey!

—Be sure to wash this piece before you use it, and don't forget to mail in your warranty card. Have a nice lay, pal.

He feels his blood pressure rise—goddamned civil servants—but no, forget it, just junk mail anyway, not worth getting worked up about. He drags the box into the room and tears it open, intending to dump it all down the rubbish chute. The maidenhead's probably busted anyway. It's completely fucked up inside, a gooey jumble of scrambled and broken parts. An eye falls out, rolls along the tiled floor, drops into the swimming pool. He grabs at it, nearly falls in; it slips through his fingers and sinks away, out of reach, watching him. A brown eye, probably gentle when lashed and lidded and in its socket, but not now. It seems to get bigger and angrier as it sinks: optical trick of the water. He turns away. Look for it later. If it's worth the trouble.

He searches through the box for assembly instructions, spilling the parts out on the floor. One nice spongy breast, round as a melon, but there doesn't seem to be a mate for it. He locates the other eyeball; it's blue. The toenails are long and curled like talons: must have been growing in here for months. One leg seems longer than the other and together they look a little knock-kneed—in fact, what a mess; they're both left legs! At last, stuffed up the nose, he discovers part of a diagram, all crumpled up, and though at the top it reads very clearly HOW TO MOUNT CATHERINE, the rest of the instructions seem to be in some kind of coded or foreign language.

It is hard to tell what the diagram depicts. Held one way, it seems to be either a toiletwall drawing of group pederasty or a sketch of a machine for canning tomatoes. Held another way, it looks more like the wrong half of a treasure map. There are many squiggles, which might be symbols, but they are not identified and may well be merely decorative—suggested tattoo or pessary designs possibly. Numbers imply certain linkages, but again they may only be time signatures, the whole thing a musical score. Black bars radiate from different areas of the diagram with words at the end: VAGARIOUS ARTIFICE. UREKA. FITS ALL SIZES. CODEX E3. FOCAL CORDS. INSERT TAB HERE. BACK PROJECTION. BLOWHOLE. The only clear instruction is at the bottom of the sheet: IN CASE OF ENEMY ATTACK, EAT THIS DIAGRAM WITH MEDIUM-DRY WHITE WINE.

He sifts through the components, sorting out the parts, pairing them up, inspecting them for nicks and bruises, matching broken bits. He locates pieces of backbone and, by sizing them, manages to assemble a more or less recognizable spine, a frame for the rest. There are fragments missing at both ends, so he juryrigs linkups to the head and hips with wire. They will probably rust in time, but maybe the missing pieces will turn up before he's done. He finds what looks like a slab of shouldered torso and an upper arm, but the screw threads don't match. All the joints seem incompatible and poorly articulated, but he attaches them the best he can, saving the leftover bits and pieces to use as splints or filler.

He mounts the breast on the right side and the blue eye on the left, pushing the breast up and the eye down to achieve a kind of balance, stuffs in lungs and liver, gall, gut, and gizzard. Some of the intestine loops free, so he pokes it down a leg along with some other squishy stuff. He screws in the asshole—a tight little beauty!—and then is surprised to discover a second one. Aha. The navel's missing. He fills the hole in the tummy with the spare anus. He's pleased to discover that the heart is made of pure gold; it's like finding the prize in a box of cereal. I'll just keep this, he thinks, and hides it away in his funny hats closet.

In spite of the difficulties, his new acquisition is shaping up. Mostly decorative details now. The hair is the color of dirty straw and matted with packing materials; he yanks the worst of it out and uses it inside the head for stuffing. He snaps on the ears, nose, and jawbone, reopens the appendectomy scar and pokes the pancreas in (unless it's the brain, hopefully not), shoves the epiglottis down the throat. He finds little plastic bottles of varying sizes, containing the essential body fluids, or so the labels say. Many of them have split open and drained out; the package is crusty with dried syrups. He decides to shoot what's left up the vagina, but he can't find the opening. Just a sort of pimple down there where the slot should be. What the hell. He has paid all this money and the main feature's missing. He should sue them for false advertising. He tries to pump the gunk up the asshole, but it won't open; he realizes now that's where he put the navel. The anus screwed into the belly opens easily enough, so he squirts the juices in there, corking the hole with his thumb to keep them from dribbling back out again until they get soaked up. That's the problem with these mail-order bargains, he tells himself. You get what you pay for.

He searches through the scraps, spare parts, scattered packaging, but can find only three teeth. Smashed up as the box is, it's lucky even three made the trip. Though they are all molars, he mounts them up front where they can be seen, two up, one down, and as he pushes them into place, she clamps down on his finger.

—*Yowww!*

—Har har! *April Fool!*

—Goddamn it, you dummy! he cries, sucking his mashed finger. It's the middle of winter!

—Aw, shoot, she says. I musta got lost in the mails.

She gazes down at herself with her blue eye.

—Hey, ain't I a beauty, though! Whoopee! I'd put the ass enda ol' Clootie hisself to the blush!

—I'm sorry, Catherine, I'm not very—

—Ho ho! Only one booby and *it's* got a ear for a pap! Or is that a butterfly? I can't seem to see too good—hey! where's my other eye? And ain't my nose on wrong-side up?

—Well, the instructions—

—Boy oh boy! I got a belly fulla rib bones, somebody's elbow in the backa my neck, a piece a crating for a aitchbone—and look at them shanks! She laughs uproariously, clutching her abdominal ribcage. You've slapped one up frontwards, the other hindside to!

—Well, they were both left ones, so I thought—

—What's that on the end a the bassackward one? Ain't that a fist?

—I couldn't get the foot to screw on, so I—

—Don't apologize, sweetie! Makes for a good butt scratcher! But wait a minute! Whatsa matter with my ol' venereal mound? It's as nekkid as a skinned garlic!

—Uh, I think I got things a little mixed up there, but you can see for yourself, the instructions are pretty—

—Heck, I don't know B from a bull's cock, honey, I'll hafta take your word for it. But look, ain't that it there in the scrapheap, that little hairy thing?

—No, I tried it; it keeps falling off. I thought maybe it was a beard or something.

—A beard! Lemme see that sucker!

She sniffs it.

—Whew! That's a armpit, son! Let's see now, which . . . ?

She sniffs her right armpit, shrugs, sniffs the left.

—Aha! There she is, safe and sandy! You had my hair standing on end for a moment, love, speaking abstractly! Thought I'd lost the blooming thing! But wait: if I'm wearing my mystical rose in my armpit, what's that pimply little bauble down there betwixt my stumps?

—Well, I—uh, think it's probably your other—

—Jumping Jeremiad! It's a tit, that's what it is! It's my left tit!

—If you'll just let me explain—

—Haw haw! If that don't beat all! She waggles it, squeezes it, manipulates the nipple to erect it. Hey! she laughs. This could be something! Bend over there, loverman! Let's see how this doodad works!

—Wait a minute! I recognize you now! Aren't you old Kate from the animation studio?

—Useta be, afore they disassembled me into that box and put me out in circulation, but travel puts a strain on your ol' reckanizables. Which reminds me: I ain't peed since the days a wooden dildos—should I use that big cistern over there, or—?

—That's the swimming pool, Kate. Your other eye's down there somewhere. There's a virtual urinal over there in a corner, past the rubdown table.

—Virtual—?

—It's not there until you walk up to it.

She squints boss-eyed at the corner, shrugs, sighs.

—I bet it's the brown peeper that's missing, ain't it? The blue one never was worth a wet fart in a sandstorm.

She unbends her odd parts, groaning and cussing, struggles to her feet—to her hand and foot—and humps off sideways toward the corner, pushing with one leg, pulling with the other. Hmm, something squared off about her rear end at that, maybe he did leave part of the box inside. Her demotion from the animation lab, as he recalls (or is cued to recall), had something to do with her controversial *Pete the Beast* series, which City Hall thought might be damaging to his career as a Cinecity icon. Cissy said Kate's *Beast* cartoons were so ugly they were almost beautiful, but no one else liked them. The urinal appears. Kate lifts her arm at it, the room's speakers having struck up a tinkling ragtime tune, and lets go through her armpit.

—*Whoo-eee!* That's a whole sight better! Cleans out the ol' innard convictions, looses the affections, makes it easier to breathe too! Hey, Pete, you've tumbled into a nice berth! I didn't know they'd been keeping you in swell digs like this!

—What do you mean, keeping me? This is my apartment—

—Beats a packing crate any day! Y'know, I think they musta misrouted me into a snowbank for a few months there; it was terrible! If I'da been all of a piece, I'da died from the compounded damp rots! But this spread is something else! Bet you got digital sensurround hi-fi, holographic telly, eiderdowns and magic mirrors, beddy-bots, the whole razzamatazz, ain't you? Listen, whaddaya say you and me, we pig here together for a spell?

—No, I don't think so, Kate.

—Don't be a turkey's ass, Pete! At least give me my month, I'm all bought and paid for! All I want is a go at that sunlamp for a coupla weeks, whaddaya say? You'll get useta me after a while, and we can have some pretty weird ol' flops together!

She shakes her elbow at the urinal, which vanishes as she comes sidling back, rolling her blue eye roguishly and grinning around her three molars.

—Hey, Pete! Ever bagpipe a armpit before?

—Sure. Used to do specialty flicks for what we called the tit-'n'-pit trade, but—

—Aw, you mean just scuffing it about in the kinks—shoot, that's only a kinda whacking off, Pete! That ain't the ol' quid pro quim! C'mon! What're we waiting for? Let's give it a rassle!

—I don't know, I've just been recuperating—

—And this is just what the dick doc ordered! You read them instructions, Pete, they's more to come; you ain't done mounting ol' Catherine yet! I been cooped up in that keester too long, you can't send me away half made. They's a hole to be pegged, and you got the tool!

Oh well. Something different anyway. Might even give him a new professional wrinkle. Think of it as research. He turns away, even as she spraddles to her knees, doubling one in front of her, the other behind.

—Where are you going?

—There's a bed in the next room—

—Can't wait, Pete! she exclaims, rubbing her elbow back and forth, a bunch of fingers squeezed in her armpit. I'm hot as a toot right now!

She spits out her three teeth, shimmies over to him, gums his cock to a full stand, and then leans back on the tiles, sucking him to his knees. The hand at the end of her second leg reaches up, grabs him by the hair, and hauls his head down over her nippled crotch.

—Mmmff!

—That's it, Pete! she mumbles around her gobbet of cock. Just what you always wanted to find down there, ain't it! Mouth that mother, let's get it going on all fours!

He does his best, feeling disoriented but aroused by the novelty of the thing and by Kate's improvised mouth. Her gums are more like muscles, closing around him like a soft wet fist, better even than his rubdown table, and he's rather keen on keeping it in there for a bit, but she pops it out, blows on it to send a chill rattling up his spine, spits on the tip, and pokes it in her armpit. In he goes, deep, deep, deeper, sinking lushly through organs and tissue, palpated by her heaving lungs, drenched in a profusion of commingled body saps. She begins to twitch and shake violently.

—Wha-what's the matter, Kate?

—Hee hee! Oh! Hoo hee! I'm ticklish!

He pulls back, but she slaps him in again, hugging his butt while continuing to lurch about wildly on the tiles.

—Oh! hee hee hee! Stay in there, Pete! I'll—hoo! hah!—get used to it! Yowee hee hee!

She's whooping and flopping and tossing about like one of those mechanical horses they used in *Hot Rodeo Nights,* her flat ass smacking the tiled floor resoundingly; it's the craziest ride he's had since that wildpig-fucking one-reeler he got thrown into when he was still just a novice, hold on! Off the elbow, as they used to call it in the old days. She spreads his cheeks with the various body parts at her disposal, licks his scrotum, pushes her tongue up his rectum—maybe literally, he's not sure it's still in her mouth anymore—and he commences to bounce and buck in earnest, forgetting all his fears and mortifications, on his way once more. It's amazing! Maybe I'll really get well after all! he thinks somewhere in the back of his thigh-clapped head. She heaves her shoulder up against him as he thrusts, whopping his nates in encouragement, while he nuzzles her pubic pap and contemplates the navel between her buns (the mystery of life!), his mind thickening, losing its subversive influence over the healing erogenous network, his whole body whumping away in her armpit.

—Oh Pete!

—Mmmff! Kate! Ah! This is incredible!

—Bear a bob, Pete! I'm blowin'!

He explodes in her, inundating her with seed, pumping it through her cavities and out to her knuckles and toes, into her cranium and out her ears; even the milk she squirts from the teat in her fork tastes like sperm; he's awash in his own abundance.

The trembling and quivering lasts for a while and he stays connected, bubbling juices and absorbing the vibrations from what Clara refers to in her medical journals as a curative *holistic body wobble*, until, slowly, the tremors fade to a pillowy quiescence. He slides off his Cunt of the Month (he doesn't remember subscribing, but he'll renew immediately) and onto the tiles, chest heaving, milk dribbling down his cheeks, feeling shaky but sound, in the pink, his flesh tingling from erotic flush and a slight sunburn.

—Whoo! It's back to the drawing board! Kate gasps, her singlebreasted chest heaving. Pete the Beast! I never guessed the half of it!

She pushes up onto one elbow, peering blearily at him with her rheumy blue eye, grinning a crooked toothless grin. She pats his limp tool affectionately.

—I gotta tell you, ol' son, you're a real craftsman! A-per-se! You can slap me up any ol' day!

—I feel like I just lost my virginity! he wheezes, gazing up at the wavery light reflections cast on the walls and ceiling by the pool, head cradled in his hands. He lets his eyes close, and the faint flickering continues to ripple on the surface of his lids. But tell me, Kate. What's this Pete the Beast thing? How did it get you in trouble at the lab?

—It was hard Cora give me the sack. Her Onerous. The lowest common dominator, we call her. What she wants, she gets. But it was the doc that did me.

—Clara?

—Yeah, I got assigned one a that cold nip's stargazing feelgood treatments in which Hardcore the Megastar meets the Black Hole, her idea of a celestial anatomy lesson, and it was a real knee-slapper, about as funny as gonorrhea. So instead I hatched this beardy ol' geezer, down and out and badly beat up, barely able to drag his withered fucked-up ass through the blizzards, reduced to tupping anything in sight just to keep from getting freeze-dried in the gutter. A kinda end-a-the-whirl, pocked-lips tramp-fucking horror show, as you might say, with a lotta cat-and-mouse chases, inanimate objects on the go, weird slapstick leg-overs, and some playful reanatomizing that got up the good doctor's little blue nose.

—Up the good doctor's blue nose! How did those lines get in there, Cissy? She's *supposed* to send him after her lost eye!

—Sorry, Clara. Cleo's idea.

—You got a bad echo in here, Pete, says Kate.

—Mmm. Must be the swimming pool . . .

—Previews of coming attractions, Clara, that sort of thing.

—Well, I don't like it, Cissy. Previews maybe, blue nose no.

—Which reminds me, Pete. Hey, you still there? I got one more favor to ask. Pete?

He grunts sleepily, hypnotized by the rippling light. He's thinking about sacking in for the rest of the week to complete the cure.

—You've done me yeoman service, Pete. I'd die for you, I feel so grateful, and I don't want to sin my mercies, but just one thing more: I wonder if you'd go get me my other eyeball?

—Sure, Kate. But not now. I'm pooped.

—C'mon, she says, giving him a little nudge toward the pool. I need that eye. How'm I gonna get my ol' job back, if I can't even see to spell my name?

—Please, Kate. Give me a break. Next week—

—Hey, loverman, why are you so mean? Ain't it enough you stole my heart?

—Your heart? He starts up as though overtaken by a sudden seizure. I—uh, I must have misplaced—

—Don't panic, Pete, it's yours for the taking; you deserve it! Shoot, if you hadn'ta pinched it, I woulda give it to you straight out; I mean it, it's yours, Pete, till kinkdom come! But now the least you could do in return is go fish up my good eye so's I can glim that sesquipedalian love machine a yours. Is that too much to ask?

—Mmm. Well. . . .

He settles back. Feeling numb. And a little shaky. Get back under the lamp. Or into bed. . . .

—Pete?

—Okay. In a minute, Kate. . . .

But she suddenly boots his ass into the pool.

—Hey!

Ker-sploosh!

—Go bring home the beacon, sweetie!

—No, Kate, I—*blub, blub!*

Under he goes, swallowing water, sinking away like the eyeball. Everything turns green. He struggles, kicks, grasping for the surface—*Help!*

—Left to their own devices, all organisms, our subject included, would gravitate toward complete rest and there atrophy beyond remedy. The universe, however, leaves nothing to its own devices . . .

He is thrashing about, not sure which way is up. Can't see anything but bubbles. Then his feet touch bottom. As he lets himself sink deeper in order to give himself more of a push to the top, he catches a glimpse of a brown eyeball drifting weirdly along the bottom, caught in some kind of undertow. It startles him and in alarm he pushes off, scrambling for air.

—Physical exercise works against emphysema by opening new alveoli and reconditioning the old. It activates the fibrinolytic system, which lyses away blood clots forming on arterial walls and diminishes blood-lipid levels. . . .

Drowning, he wonders why his whole life isn't passing before his eyes. Instead, he seems to see a commercial for water wings, recommended for deepwater frogfucking. Maybe that *is* his life! He kicks upward, lungs bursting, arms and legs churning.

—It increases blood vessels to the brain to work against the possibility of strokes, and adds new collateral coronary vessels to keep an area alive after regular vessels have been blocked. You'll notice the patient's heightened muscle tone, the way his buttocks, which had begun to sag and flatten out there on the tiles, are suddenly taut with life and energy. . . .

His hands claw for thc outside but reach the bottom of the pool again instead! That eye, skidding along, stares mockingly at him. This is impossible! There's no goddamn surface—!

—*Stop* it! That's enough!

—What?

—Switch it off!

—What's the matter, L.P.?

—It's wrong, all wrong, that's what's the matter!

Cissy looks up at him from the viewer, holding a frame there showing him eyeballing the eyeball in panic, his jaws agape and filling with chlorinated water. He pushes away from the editing bench, staggers through the darkened studio to the window, taking deep breaths. His heart is pounding wildly, which may be good for him, like Clara says, but doesn't feel like it. Far below, homebound crowds are struggling through a worsening blizzard, appearing and disappearing in the shifting drifts. He knows he must soon join them and he is, still wheezing from another fright, afraid. He has the strange feeling, as when a false chord is ominously struck in a soundtrack, that he may never look out of this window again.

—Where did I fuck up, Cissy? How did I lose it?

—I don't know what you're talking about, L.P. I like this sequence. It's a little old-fashioned maybe, but the flatness makes the do-it-yourself business all the more effective. It's got a good storyline, and—

—Storyline! It's an associative free-for-all! Next, I suppose there'll be eel-sucking fish swimming by, some clamshell erotica, a sunken ship housing a mermaid bordello, and another of Clara's nature films on the sex life of the jellyfish!

—I don't know, I suppose we could work all that in, but—

—I'd fuck a porpoise and sail away on it to the coldwater flat, dig up buried treasure in Cleo's cunt, and spend it on a spaceship to take you and me to another planet, which would turn out to be this one, only colder! Sea to sea and bereft again!

—Oh, I see. You're being sarcastic. But that's the very essence of kinosis, L.P., the moving prism; all the rest is just illusion, you know that, you always told me—

—Goddamn it, Cissy, I don't want an analysis! he cries. I want some way of going on with all this!

—Well, we might try to do something more with the mail delivery person, we could use four of them, for example, or even forty—all expecting to get a letter in their box, so to speak, to get their postage licked—put it all to music maybe, choreograph it, and shoot it from the rafters. Or how about if we added a fluoroscopic fuck with Clara to the lecture scene; you always like to make it with her. We could work up some kind of play on X-ray and X-rated and climax it with an animated sequence in which the bones unlink and—

—No, no, *no!* You don't understand, Cissy. It has nothing to do with pointless rewrites or camera angles or special effects. There's something wrong—fundamentally, intrinsically, *physically* wrong!

She hesitates.

—Maybe you need a hot bath.

—Oh my god! I'm drowning in a fucking dimensionless swimming pool, and you suggest a *bath?*

—I'm sorry, L.P. Please don't be angry.

She's hurt by his outburst, which he regrets. Not her fault. But, damn it. . . . She sits there at the bench in the subdued studio light, soft, vulnerable, her breasts sagging. Then her face brightens and she hops up, rolls out a sound-and-image sampler with keyboard, hooks it up to a computer.

—Clara's done this to you, L.P. Made you stop and look back, that's the trouble. She and Cleo. Here, let me show you a new open-ended interactive hypermedia piece I'm building.

She pops and unpops cables, connects a monitor with overhead projector to the computer, slots a disk in.

—Listen, Cissy, some other time—

—It's a whole new metalanguage, L.P. It's all about permutations and syncretism and the unpredictable, played out in omnidirectional circuit space, in which time is spread out in a kind of freeform geography. It's where we're going, into new serial experiences of the essential randomness and ever-present newness of the—

—Ah shit, Cissy. Don't you feel like it's too late for that? Don't you feel like it's over?

—You're projecting again, like Clara says. You're looking backward! There's no more past, no more future, all those patently false assumptions we used to cling to about time and memory, all those old gimmicks we used to use to simulate continuity—the medium shot followed by the close-up, the mystique of moral decisions, the plotline with its so-called developments, the unacknowledged back projection—we're past all that now, L.P., like you yourself have always said. Remember? There are no more so-called reality simulations, no more futuristic descriptions of long-dead worlds, no more fixed and static languages that strap the mind down to one-track conveyor belts; that's all over, that's not what our heads are about, never has been! You're not feeling romantic about all that ancient rubbish, are you?

—I don't know. I'm all mixed up. I think I've been an actor too damned long.

She sits back, studying him, her perkiness fading, a kind of melancholic sadness coming over her.

—Would it help if I gave you a little head?

He smiles. His girl Cissy. Simple but true. He should be grateful. He returns to the editing bench.

—Okay, sure. But first let's track this back and take another look, see if we can't figure out where I start getting into trouble.

She joins him at the editor, rubbing her plump thigh against his, squeezing his dick lovingly, and commences the rewind.

—How far back?

—All the way.

—You mean, back to the elevator?

—No. Before that. . . .

Through the city, through the blowing snow, under the pedestrian-crossing signs and the billboard and marquee messages (I'LL PUT IT INTO YOUR CUNT THIS WAY, NELLY, AND FUCK YOU FROM BEHIND!), walks a solitary man, shrunk into his own wraps and huddled miserably against the wind, his hat jammed down on his ears and scowling brows, his hands stuffed deep in his overcoat pockets. Under the hat brim his eyes stare forth, aglitter with vexation and resolution; below them his nose, pinched with indignation, his mustache clotted with frozen snot, his puffed-out cheeks blowing frosty clouds of breath through chattering teeth. He brushes testily through the teeming crowds, batting at them with his livid penis, ramrod stiff and glistening with ice crystals, as horns sound and sirens wail (*oh! what a nICE FUCK, GUSSY! you HAVE A DARling pricK!*) and subways rumble underfoot. Suicides drop into the snow around him as though the heavens were taking a dump. Oh, my poor doomed ass, gawdamighty, it is cold, what the fuck am I doing out here, whatever happened to the *green* things? Thus he whimpers to himself as he presses on, warming himself with expletives and pastoral fantasies, trying to, mostly feeling sorry for himself, aching with cold, sick of keeping it up but scared not to, there he goes, a living legend, maybe the last of his kind.

And there goes a heavy bus with greasy windows and mud-spattered announcements, barreling through the streets with its snow-caked foglights burning dully, spitting up snow, whipping it into a black froth: *BlaaaAAAAAA-A—!*

—No! Stop it right there!

He snaps the film out of the editor, studies the frames, scissors out all the bus segments, splices the pieces back together, cranks it up again.

—I don't think you ought to be doing this, L.P. That's an original.

—I know what I'm doing.

—Well, don't blame me if . . .

He hovers like a dragonfly, like a bee with a buzz on, above a fleshy flower composed of nine pairs of radiant buns, posed back to back, cheek to cheek, legs spread and fluttering like petals, on the sun-drenched meadow below. The soft green space around is soaked in silence as he floats down, arse high, to nuzzle in the variegated pappi, nibble at the keels, suck at the stamina. He lowers his bum to dip into the divers septa and screams with pain. All the green is suddenly drained from the frame as though a plug were pulled and he is catapulted into a crowded winter street the color of smudged newsprint, clutching his penis.

—I thought so, he groans.

He staggers through the jostling crowd and roaring traffic (a little old lady gets in his way, oops, too bad), snatches a bum's tabloid blanket in which to wrap like garbage his battered organ (so much for his tribute to horticulture), and, teeth clattering, eyes tearing, lunges desperately past the spot on the curb tapemarked (XX) for his rump and on around the corner, out of the frame, out of focus, thinking, That's it, fuck it, time to quit. Does he mean it? He does. Cissy is waiting for him at the studio. She'll wait a long time. He leans up against one of the tenement buildings for a moment to get his breath—less wattage back here in this creative sprawl; it's darker, colder, the pavement's rougher, buildings crowded in on one another—then lets himself get dragged by the sullen crowds down the narrow back street, winding away ahead of him into shadowy obscurity: his destination. Let it come. He rarely visits these neighborhoods—or, rather, his professional life has rarely allowed such visits—though Cassie, he knows, lives in such a place, maybe right around here, has done since she went nonnarrative. If he could find her, she might take him in for a while, see him through this crisis; she's a great listener. She might even give him one of her multisensory talking rubdowns, press the panic out, knead away the bitterness, help him find heart again, his old appetite for what-happens-next. But where to start looking for her? If he should. It may be, as others believe, Cassie who's messing him up.

He remembers sitting at an editing bench with her one afternoon, looking at a reelful of spliced-together goof-ups from the cutting room floor—the tag ends of orgasms, flash frames, miscues, foggy runouts and blistered close-ups, jittery tracking shots, clumsy wipes—all of it joined together just as she's picked it up: forward, backward, emulsion in or out, grease-penciled, notched, or punched. Cassie is perversely fascinated with all the peripheral gear of film, things like black leader, glue, glass mattes, static, shims and sun guns, perforations, ident trailers, edge numbers. Sitting there, he's watched himself on the editing machine fall out of bed and out of focus, go limp in a stockyard, sneeze in the middle of a gamahuche, withdraw wearily from the ass of a cleaning lady, the lips of a chambermaid, and the quim of a queen, all decorated with water spots and cinch marks, get hung up in a child star, overexposed in the subway, scalded in the shower, and stuck in the revolving doors of an office building.

—Ouch. You're depressing the hell out of me, Cassie.

She winds onto a medium shot of him walking through the crowds of a city street in a snowstorm. She locates a moment when he steps off a curb, plays it back and forth, back and forth, sometimes slowly, sometimes more quickly, just that brief movement, stepping down, glancing at the traffic, his weight shifting, prick dipping and bobbing up again.

—Why are you showing me that, Cassie? I feel like a goddamn ass!

She zooms in on his eye, catches just the downward tilt of the head, the left-to-right roll of the eye, the dim background blur of part of a sign on a passing bus, a block letter D in soft focus, sliding back and forth past his head, as his head drops slightly in the frame, his eye moving left, right, left again, then back up, over and over, that D, blurring by, his head. . . . He becomes completely absorbed, forgets it's himself, just that simple pure motion, nothing, yet a thousand things to see there, and all of it locked into an elemental and irreducible whole.

—All right, it's beautiful, Cassie. But it's only six frames. One-fourth of a second. Put that on the screen and *pfft!* it's over before you've seen it.

She doesn't reply. She never does, of course.

—Is that why you've stopped making films, Cassie?

She starts cranking on the rewind. He thinks at first she's hurrying ahead to some other scene, but she just keeps winding the film up faster and faster. He can't see anything, just a meaningless blur, and he wonders if maybe she's freaking on him. Then, slowly, an image begins to take shape in the hiss and rattle of passing footage; it is he, Lucky Pierre, in slow motion, dreamily afloat in a cosmic whirlwind of past faults, getting it up . . . and up . . . and up . . . spraying semen like seeds . . . like stars! He becomes hypnotized by it, fantastic, doesn't even feel the cold, watches waves of females floating by like schools of fish to absorb the fall of cum, writhing on meadows where it showers down like dew . . . then slowly it begins to wind down, the image fades, there's just the noisy blur, the parade of fuckups, and he's back on the streets again, cold, hungry, lost, tainted with cinch marks and water spots, slowing down, down, unable to go on, crawling on all fours now, finally slumping miserably into an old tenement doorway to get out of the wind, pulling the newspaper pages up around his ears, ducking his nose into his overcoat collar.

Around him, as the storm worsens, thousands of shuffling feet trample sullenly through the blood, slush, and snow, cars spin and smash into one another, things topple—wastebins, traffic signs, lampposts, marquees—as though obeying some inner mechanism of despair, entropy's special effects. People are pushing in and out of the door behind him, stumbling over him, cursing him, treating him like any other bum wrapped in newspapers. He could tell them who he really is but they wouldn't believe him, not in the condition he's in, and anyway he's not sure he knows, having withdrawn into an icy nameless core as anonymous as the bitter instinct for survival itself, temporarily embodied, as it were, in this perishing lump of quaking blue flesh.

He feels not unlike that weird creature in the time-lapse study Clara completed of the aging process. A healthy specimen was selected at birth and single-frame exposures were made once a week until the man died at the age of ninety-six. Two lenses were used in a split-screen technique, one recording the surface area, illuminated by ordinary quartz-iodine studio lamps, the other hooked up to a reflex fluoroscope. The subject had to be protected from accident and abnormal stress, as well as all serious and disabling infections, and because of the narrow registration tolerance in time-lapse filming—especially while the subject was still an infant and difficult to control—it was soon determined to lock him permanently into the focal plane mechanism. The risk of abnormal emaciation was more or less overcome by an ingenious rig of simulated challenges to the muscles and sinews, and an approximation of developing facial expression was accomplished by the programmed use of stroboscopic lights, ironic film-clip juxtapositions, singing lessons, and electric shock. His whole life took up less than a hundred feet of 16mm film, just three and a half minutes in the viewing, plus a 45-second trailer showing the processes of decomposition, temperature-controlled and slowed down to one exposure a day for about three years, the film reaching a kind of aesthetic climax as the two side-by-side images evolved into identical structures. It was only after the film was completed and they were adding titles that they realized they had forgotten to give him a name.

Oh fuck, but it's cold. The people pushing in and out of the tenement kick him as they pass—it's as if they don't see him there—but he feels none of it; he's solidly benumbed, as locked in place and nameless as the time-lapse man. He's iced up, eyeballs frozen in their sockets, can't see a thing that's not straight out in front of him, and if he tried to get to his feet now, if he tried to unbend, his legs would crack and splinter like icicles. Somewhere at the back of his thickening brain, doubt needles its way in like a live wire probing cold mud, and he can hear a voice like static on the track whispering, *C'mon, hero. Pick 'em up, put 'em down. Get back in the flow*. But, too late, he can't.

Bobbing masses of capped and hatted heads rise and fall like dull gray waves, their faceless ranks plowed by the grinding traffic as though by shadowy sharks' fins, all of it as insubstantial as unfocused back projections thrown against the restless screen of blowing snow; the storm has worsened, whipped up now by a fierce anarchic wind. Little can be seen above the blur of tramping feet, the hazy dark bulk of bundled midriffs, all buttoned up, anonymous. Where is he? A bloody splatter is examined at an intersection, the contents of a tipped wastebin are visually cataloged by a restless eye.

—Over there, I see it sticking out! Beneath the marquee!

—Hmm. That's his, all right. But it's just a movie poster.

—How did you ever let him get away?

—He can't have gone far—

—Hey, why is all this bus footage on the cutting room floor?

—Oh oh!

—You've blown it, Cece! We've lost him!

—I don't think so. It's cold out there. He's probably just gone home. Let's crank back to that penthouse scene again.

The roving angst-sensitive lamp explores the cushioned rubdown table with the oiled hole in the middle. Music plays softly. The glassy surface of the pool mirrors a general absence like a soundless echo. The doorbell rings. And rings again. And again.

The elevator doors open, revealing a smiling operator. The receptionist, sitting bouncily, her skirt taut, cradles the crimson phone and looks up, as a brunette in a tangerine skirt, carrying a file folder, crosses from right to left, staring at the receptionist in alarm, then at the elevator operator.

Searchlights sweep the night sky as the limousine draws up in front of the awning stretching from the theater lobby to the street. The fans lining the street scream with rapture and fling their undergarments as the limousine door opens. A woman with a clipboard steps out, glancing about in bewilderment. A police whistle is heard, a siren.

—Oh, no! This is terrible! *He's been kidnapped!*

—Stop chewing up the scenery, Connie, you're not on camera. We'll find him.

—But—

—Can it. He's still out there somewhere; we just have to keep looking.

—Judging by the subject's recent hyponoidal dysphoria and the severe cryoconstringency of his gametic peripherals, I'd say he was probably—

—His crying what?

—She means his balls have shriveled up in the cold. Hell, who can blame him for cutting out? You've been pushing him too hard, doc baby. All this heavy analytical shit you've been laying on him in your so-called treatment—it's obscene!

—Don't be too hard on her. Clara just talks that way for laughs.

—But she's drying up his vital juices!

—So what? If projection's peculiarly central to the mechanism, then only he who has suffered losses is equipped to extrapolate functionally from a closed system subject to entropic disorganization such as our own. That, my dear, is the true hard core. I may be saving his life! Or saving life itself!

—Crap! I say, ease up on him. What our lover needs now is comfort, solace, a little pleasure. Maybe one of the old flicks—

—But what if he's dropped his butt into another snowbank? You want to put him to sleep out there? You'd kill the poor sonuvabitch with your fucking solace!

—Cleo's right, Cissy. Our man, if he's out in that storm, is clearly in immediate need of potent exteroceptive arousal.

—Needs to get his blood pumping, you mean.

—Exactly! Something violent. . . .

—Let's see, what have we got? Here's a rough cut of *Guns and Gals*. That's pretty messy. Or how about this old Extar demo demo?

—Hmmm, isn't that the one where a head gets split in two, right down to the shoulders?

—Right! And then they dead-end a bunch of the poor suckers in an alley and roll in the road crews with their backhoes and steamdrills!

—It rained blood and body parts for a week!

—Really?

—Well, that's what the posters said.

—Sounds pretty gross. Let's throw it out there, see what happens.

—I'm way ahead of you. It's already playing.

—Yeah? Can't see a thing. What a storm! Is anything doing?

—Nah. It's a dead house. Heads down everywhere. Just that pathetic old bum waving back there behind the rest of the deadbeats.

—Well then, here. How about *Stranglefuck: The Sequel*? Or *Creative Sex During Suicide*?

—Might be dangerous—

—Wait! That bum! Could it be—?

—What?

—No—!

—Oh my god, it is! I *told* you he was in trouble!

—Hey! Where are you going, Cally?

—Relax, sisters. Let me handle this. . . .

His breath is crystallizing now before it leaves his mouth, snowing on his lower lip, the nostrils above plugged with frozen snot. On the next corner, a band of young protesters has gathered, disrupting traffic, drawing an encircling crowd of surly witnesses, faces lost in a frosty cloud. The demonstrators shout out slogans and carry placards that decry the injustice of the star system and demand parts for the people. Such wanting. Beyond him now. He searches their number for the one called Lottie, that wild thing with the black hair and the dazzling smile, imprinted on his plotless memory like a vivid still, but she is not among them. And then she is, as they all seem to slide on the icy street from left to right as though on a turntable: Pop! There she is! First, one side of her, and then all of her. Bluejeaned and bare-breasted and hair blowing in the wind. *Cinecity is fucking your mind!* she cries, becoming larger than life. Oh my dear, he thinks, what do you know about minds? And so: thinking, *thinking* still, that old voice-over habit. He can feel his thoughts' sluggish synaptic leaps like little fizzy pops behind his eyes, warming nothing but themselves. Lottie's breasts appear to be flopping about in the slush of the street as she shakes her fist, the rest of her vanished below street level. Her dark eyes gaze out above the heads of all those around her, discovering him there on the tenement stoop, seeming to. Painfully, eagerly, he raises his arm to wave at her, feeling the ice crystals snap and crunch in his shoulder, but, no, she is gazing right through him. He calls out her name but he cannot even hear himself and she has turned away, shrinking to life size once more, something like life size, her denimed ass at eye level, her bare back rising boldly above the gathered mob. And then, in a blink, she is gone, replaced by Extars struggling with police, and then—*blink!*—there she is again. *Lottie!* he wheezes. *Lottie! Miss!* She's looking right at him, but it's as though he's not even there. Oh shit! What has he done? Cissy tried to warn him, he wouldn't listen! *Over here! Can't you see me? It's Old Crazy Leg!* he gasps, his voice escaping him as little more than a rattle, as of empty pages blown by the wind. Her eyes flash with defiance and terror. And then a cop's back appears between them, blocking her from view, the cop bearing down on her with a truncheon. *No! Stop!* he cries. *Watch out, miss!* But the blow falls with a hideous thud like colliding vehicles and then both cop and Lottie swoop to the left and vanish, replaced by a bloody melee of police and demonstrators, some of the bystanders caught up in the horrific beatings and bloodied themselves, others drifting off or masturbating at a watchful distance.

One of the spectators, a uniformed nurse, emerges from the crowd now and, striding unfazed through falling truncheons and bleeding heads, comes over to him.

—Ah, there you are, she says. Thought we'd lost you.

—You've got to stop them! he rasps through clamped teeth.

—Stop whom?

What? Ah. They're all gone. Traffic is grinding relentlessly through the streets once more like a looped back projection, kicking up icy slush on the nameless masses who hurry as before, heads down, to nowhere. Only a few wrecks remain, some grim stains in the snow. *Thaw now!* she was shouting. Who knows? Maybe she's the one who could make it happen. Or might have been, were it not too late. Far too. Almost can't breathe for the numbing cold within. He'll die of a blizzard in his lungs. The nurse leans down, presenting him with her deep cleavage, an old trick that on this occasion fails to move him, though by this view—*fizz, pop! pop!* behind the eyes—he recognizes her: the one who catheterized him in the doctor's office. *In the Doctor's Office*. Are they going for a sequel? He shrinks back into his newspapers.

She sits down beside him. He wishes she would go away. He also wishes she would hug him and uncake his nose and let him put his head on her starchy white bosom and cry for a while.

—Oh, Willie! she sighs, blowing the snow off his mustache. What are you doing out here? Why did you just leave like that?

Willie? Of course. That cleavage. Should have known. *Cally? Is that you?* Can't hear himself, but she does. She smiles affectionately, lifts the snow-laden newspapers to peer underneath. She is visibly shocked by what she discovers there.

—Oh, poor Wee Willie! What have you *done* to yourself? she cries, and she reaches under the papers, probably to wrap her hand around his winkie, as she's wont to call it, as she's wont to do with it, though he can't be sure, can't feel a thing down there.

Wee Willie: It was the name he used when the two of them first broke in as child stars, the only name he was known by then, though only Cally still calls him by it. So long ago. Seems like a different lifetime, his own and not his own. He was the little boy with the funny name from the pornographic nursery rhyme, running all over town every night in his nightshirt: a classic silent that launched a series of box-office smash hits, especially popular with mature ladies. The golden age. When you could still run around in a nightshirt without freezing your patootie off.

—Brrr! Wee Willie needs a hot bath!

She puts her nurse's cap on top of the newspapers, her head under. The red cross on the rising and falling cap, he sees, is really a stylized double-headed cock and balls. Same cap she wore in *Calliope Cunt, Student Nurse,* their first feature-length film together after the kiddy porn days. He was called Peter Prick in those days; it was before they went up-market. In the movie, he played a young peeping tom who gets caught outside the nurses' dormitory and for punishment is made to serve as their subject the next day in anatomy class. In the talkies remake, he played the doctor who lectures the student nurses on bedpan etiquette and pudendal osculation techniques for the emergency room; Cally as his star pupil introduces certain improvements and elaborations in these techniques which, after exhaustive scientific testing (not really, just one reel's worth), are adopted as part of the curriculum. And which are, demonstrably, still part of her technique. Useless now, though. Dead as a dry stick.

—But a stick can be set alight, Cally reminds him, popping her head out from under the papers (he ducks: are they using subtitles out here?).

She sets the cap back on her head and smooths her crisp white skirt over her thighs, then puts both hands underneath, working them briskly as though trying to start a fire without matches: *Calliope Cunt, Campfire Girl.* Her repertoire is boundless.

—It reminds me of what it felt like in that film Cassandra shot, back when she was still making real movies and had her hair, Cally pants. What was it called, *The Tragic Miracle*? Something like that. You know, the one where the lonely worshiper comes into the cathedral and prays to God to send her someone with a winkie as hard as a rock, and you play the part of a recumbent statue of a dead king that rises up and answers her prayers, falling on her and squashing her flat, remember?

He remembers. Especially the medieval setting, so majestic, dwarfing them all, and the awesome silence from which the story erupted and into which, like a vanishing miracle, it subsided. A silence into which Cassie, too, has long since subsided, absorbed now by her weird experiments in digital uncertainty, making works of no fixed form, but so made as to cause each showing to be a complete reassembling of all the parts. His dead-king performance itself did not amount to much. It was not easy to express himself artistically in a mineralized body of such dead elephantine weight. About the best he could do was roll his eyes lasciviously, which looked on film more like abject terror, but which is more than he can manage now. Though he does seem to be getting some dull sensation back where Cally's chafing him, and his thoughts are smoothing out behind his eyes.

—It feels more to me like it did in that terrible Snow Princess number in which I had to rescue you by f-f-fucking my way through a ph-ph-phalanx of Ice Maidens, he says, his teeth chattering, but thereby unlocking his jaws.

—Terrible? But that was a *beautiful* film!

—They c-c-could have used actresses with m-m-makeup instead of real ice.

—That was Cissy's idea, remember? Animating ice sculptures was something she'd never tried. And she wanted to shoot your winkie visibly thrusting through a kind of glittering prism with colored lights playing through it. It got *wonderful* reviews!

True, he thinks, his whole body beginning to shudder. And not just the camera work, his winkie too. They made more money from the spinoff novelties sold in the lobbies than from the movie itself, big as it was. Cissy created the Ice Maidens with help from the animation lab, Cally designed her own sugar-crystal costume and kept his winkie warm between takes, and Clara came up with some of her whimsical voice-over lines taken from ancient naturalists' notebooks . . .

The appearance of this most singular creature is very beautiful; its color pellucid-white, except the summit of the apical knob, and the spherical extremities at the root, which are of a lovely rose color. . . .

He can almost, behind the clatter of his teeth and bones, hear Clara reciting these lines while he banged away in those ice bodies, melting them with his usual professional fervor, bucking his way toward the delicious sugar-crystal feast that awaited him at quest's end.

One beholds, as if for the first time, the splendid spectacle of this living fountain vomiting forth from a circular cavity an impetuous torrent of liquid matter and hurling along, in rapid succession, opaque masses, which it strews everywhere around. The beauty and novelty of such a scene—

—Of s-s-such a s-s-scene . . .

He shivers, feeling a chill he'd been too cold to feel before. The novelty, he thinks. His butt bounces once on the cold pavement. The beauty. . . .

—Oh! sighs Cally, spitting on her hands and pumping now with real feeling. Poor *poor* Wee Willie!

That line. It was from their second film together, *Crying Through the Lock*, and is now spoken with such pure emotion that he feels a sudden fuzzy prickle at the apical knob and a roseate throb at the root. Ah! Poor Wee Willie—and it *was* wee then, too; it was what made him so cute, they said. But even back at that time, stiff as a toothpick, a rose thorn, a sparrow's beak, a fork tine. And not so wee that he didn't get hung up in a goose once in a barnyard two-reeler in which he and Cally fucked or were fucked by every farm animal then not yet extinct. The goose got so roiled up about it, she nearly pecked his little marbles off, a painful preview of coming afflictions. Finally, the only way to stop the vicious creature was to stuff its head and neck up Cally and suffocate it, a scene that made the posters and made the movie, though by then they were already superstars and he was ready for his big move out of short pants.

—What a calamity, Willie! It's as cold and unyielding as a little tombstone!

—You've *said* that. You've said that *before* . . .

—Have I?

—*W-Wee Willie and the Ogre's D-D-Daughters*. Word for w-w-w—

—Well, like you always say, she wheezes, the newspapers blanketing her churning fists, now flapping like a wet chicken trying to take off, if it's not one damned script it's another, right?

—Script? This s-scene too, Cally? he gasps, his heels rapping the pavement. This w-w-w-one too?

—Oh, Willie, Willie! Don't be silly!

Right. Also. From *Peeing in the Snow*. After an abject hand-written confession of love. Willie, Willie, don't be silly. Next, she'll ask him if he remembers *Wee Willie Winkie and the Naughty Nanny*. Or *The Prince and the Pooper*.

—Willie, do you remember that crazy film we made back then, *The Prince and the Pooper*? The one where—

—Sure I remember it. P-played both parts. Gave me a terrific headache, trying to be b-both m-me and m-myself at the same time.

He *does* remember it. His head lights up with fresh recall and his eyes tumble in thawing sockets. Sparks are flying under the dancing newspapers now; he can feel them, like hot needles suturing a wound.

—What I loved most was that scene when you were both under the table, fighting over my hot lunch. It was marvelous! Well, at least from my own, so to speak, point of view.

True, he's always been well fed. And well loved. He's had to suffer a lot of plotted abuse from his Wee Willie days on, but he's always been loved. And pampered. As Cally is pampering him now. He's on fire! Ow! It hurts like hell! It's great! I've had a wonderful fucking life! he thinks, as tears come to his eyes and smoke rises from the smoldering papers.

—Maybe the best of them all from the old days, though, she gasps, was *Wee Willie and the Seven Giants.*

Yes, another classic, this one about the joys of motherhood, as he recalls, his butt hammering the tenement stoop now like a chattering jaw. Maybe why she liked it. About motherhood and the child's innocent delight in flesh. He'd arrived in the giants' bedroom dressed in his customary little fanny-high nightshirt and had found the giants all sound asleep and (so the titles said) snoring sonorously, a cue to theater organists to let all out the stops as he went tippytoing over the vast rolling landscape of their sprawled bodies, palely lit by the windowed moon. They'd slept soundly as he'd explored their pillowy terrain, clambering over luminous mounds of satiny breasts and bellies and bottoms while pretending to be scouting deadly enemies just over the next rise, peering down the wells of parted lips and into sculpted whorls of giant ears for secret messages, getting lost in the forests of hair, climbing hips' high hills to bounce on their rubbery moonlit summits and then somersault down into the dark mossy grottoes below. Once (has Cally's emotive nursing brought him off? he's not felt the explosion, but a delicious heat is spreading through his loins like honey in a bun) he got his foot stuck when he slipped and stepped into a bumhole and might have been killed had the sleeping giant rolled over just then, but he was saved by a delicate breaking of wind, deftly imitated on the organs or by the orchestras in the pits in the fancier movie palaces—the title said REDEEMED BY A FAIR BREEZE!—and visually suggested not merely by his freed foot but by his nightshirt blown up over his ears.

Finally, wearied by his pioneering exploits, he snuggles down in the shadows between a pair of milky high-hilled breasts, the erected nipples on their crests rising above him like protective watchtowers in the night, and, rocked gently by the giant's languid breathing, lullabyed by the slumberous beat of her buried heart, he falls into a deep sleep there—where, on the morn, he is found and, with squeals of delight (which are seen but not heard), adopted by the giants as their very own. They dress him and undress him and bathe him in their chamber pot and anoint him with baby oils and love juices and set his peg to vibrating with their fingertips and play hide-and-seek with him between their thighs. Their bodies are his magical playground, and for a time his bed as well, but fears for his safety bring on restless nights, so the giants decide to provide him a spicy little nest all his own, plaited of their pubic hairs, which, as they get down on their hands and knees, he is invited to pluck, strand by strand.

—This is beautiful! he whispers, feeling the lush dissolve come over him. Thanks, Cally! I love you! But what . . . what . . . ?

OW! OH! A LITTLE HIGHER!
OUCH! I LOVE IT!

—Yes—?

EEK!

—What . . . (where is he now? where is he going? what . . .) what happens next?

—Oh! she laughs. Just wait, Willie! You'll be amazed!

YOU CAN REACH IT!
OH! OH! THAT'S THE ONE!
HANG ON!

He does try to hang on, but the wiry strand there at the heart of the fragrant marsh is greasy with the giant's excitement and it slips through his grip: down, down, he falls onto the snowy white bed between the giant's knees, laughing all the way. What fun! More! He scrambles back up over her calf to scale once again her monumental thigh and, wonderfully, there on the inside, finds a ladder, which she's apparently put in place to speed him on his upward way. He climbs, hand over hand, his eager gaze on that dark moist patch above, feeling somehow chosen, a hero on a quest of sorts, this the first and most amusing of his manly tests. As he climbs, however, the ladder seems to bury itself in the flesh of her thigh, its rungs like wattles below the surface, which cannot be gripped but only clung to. A cold wind is blowing, causing his nightshirt to tug at him like a sail. Better turn around, he thinks, but when he looks back down he can see only the dying snow-wracked city spread out far below him and a ladder that is less a ladder than that he holds.

—*Sometimes he who would reach for the stars is forced to go on at any risk, confronting danger, overcoming fear, striving ever for his goal, all the while maintaining his rhythm, his balance, climbing with his eyes, searching out handholds and footholds, wedging himself in cracks, if necessary clawing his way up by his fingertips alone!*

Hello? Who's there? He cannot look up now, he cannot look down, he can only hang on in desperation, his outspread feet toeing into the sheer cliff of cold flesh, his fingers clinging to the last vestiges of the vanishing subcutaneous ladder, his penis still hard as a piton, can't help that, but no place to drive it. How the hell did he get up here? he wants to know. What's the name of this movie?

—*What concentration, what mental and bodily strain our intrepid subject's task demands! He must understand the risks of* V*-type river valleys, funneling gullies, ridges, ribs, and falling cornices, must know about slab and rib clinging and climbing cracks with laybacks and how to apply cling under, opposite pressure, and jam holds, aware that the slightest mistake or false movement can prove irrevocable. And yet, what joy! What enchantment! He knows, as of old, a thrill of adventure which has as its reward a refreshment of body and a serenity of spirit such as only the untrammeled grandeur and beauty of these majestic heights can give!*

—Clara? Is that you? Help me, goddamn it, I'm going to fall!

—*It is important of course that the climber not freeze on holds while scaling such a face, so to speak, or remain in cramped positions. He must, above all, avoid becoming spread-eagled, unable to move either hand or either foot without losing his balance and falling into the awful abyss more sensed than seen between his legs!*

Her voice—must be hers—is coming from high overhead, somewhat ripped away by the icy wind. From the moment she has spoken of scaling this slab of thigh, music of a sort has begun, a slow ominous climbing of the scales as though mounting toward some dreaded climax. He seems to hear the roll of tympani, an attack by trumpets, wind blasts by trombones, high rushing vibratos by strings, but maybe it's only the traffic far below.

—*As he approaches the summit, a quiet contentment takes possession of his soul, mixed with exulta—*

—Are you kidding, Clara? I'm scared shitless! Get me *off* of here!

—He's going to fall! Throw him a rope!

—Nonsense! He's a star, a stern adventurous fellow who—

—Willie? Here! Catch!

He glances up through the whipping snow, feeling his fingers losing their grip, and sees them all, crowded into the shaggy fissure high above his head: Cleo with her microphone, Cissy with her camera, and all the others too, smiling down at him, waving, flashing their bodily parts as though dropping him lures. What does come looping toward him is the end of a rappelling rope, the other end anchored in the puckery fumerole above the chimneylike opening where the women cluster. A black banner seems to waver in the air near the vaporous hole and at the end of it, aerial letters, barely visible through the raging blizzard, that read CREVASSE. A cloven escarpment or massif of a sort rises above it, and he can just make out through the wind and snow the word COULOIR floating in front of it, which encourages him to believe this reel may yet have a happy ending.

—Of course, it is always possible to underestimate the difficulties of the climb or to overestimate one's capabilities, or possibly one finds one's training is insufficient—

—Grab the rope, Lucky!

What fucking training? Why were there no rehearsals? Is this the end? He's always been such a *good* man, faithful and true to the script, sticking his dick wherever directed, never blowing his lines—or almost never—a lover and a pro, a consummate pro; haven't they always said so? He shouldn't have to suffer like this!

—Reach out for it, L.P.! Save yourself!

—We *love* you, Lucky!

The women lean out of the fissure to urge the lifeline in his direction. Dare he let go his tenuous hold to try for it? Dare he not? Why, so loved, does he feel such terror? And then—oh shit!—a toe slips from its niche, his hands—! He kicks away, hurling himself out into the void to grab at the rappelling rope, but it's not a rope, it's the ident leader of a reel of film, unspooling from the puckery crevasse like a tape worm; he can't read it, all he can see is a big F on it, and he's falling, falling, falling—!

FADEOUT

Reel 4: Cassandra

Focus, fading in, on fallen man fucking. It is understood that this is who he is, what he does, what he must do; it is his karma. He is a man who fucks. His head is still white with melting snow, his poor flesh bluish, his eyes are closed, their lashes frozen shut by frozen tears, but his hips are rising and falling steadily like sluggish gray waves lapping a wintry beach (the only sound to be heard is something like this, or it might be the sound of a thousand people settling into cushioned seats in a movie house, repeated over and over in a continuous loop), and his penis has found a warm place and has lost its frosty chill, the first part of him to do so. Near his ice-encrusted mouth is an ear on a bald head, and his cracked lips are trembling as though he might be whispering into it, but if so, what he says—*I was having a terrible nightmare, Cassie!*—is inaudible. Maybe his vocal cords are still frozen, his faint words more seen than heard—*I had slipped and was falling from a great height!* Or perhaps he is falling still, falls now, for his embrace of Cassie's body, more felt than seen, is overlaid by the continuing image of them all, high up above him in the blowing snow, reaching out for him as he drops away, his frozen hands grasping at that lifeline which is not one. But it is a fading image, much as when a dream ends, overtaken by Cassie's emerging presence like a slow lap dissolve, and he decides (his eyelashes melt and he peeks out at her delicately whorled ear, sitting on her shaved scalp like a rubber viewfinder cup) that if he is falling still he will accept this present illusion, for it is immensely comforting and cushions the dread of impact and of oblivion.

How did he get here? She found him in the storm, frozen solid on the tenement stoop, and she chipped him loose and carried him back and proceeded to thaw him out with her breath and tongue and with her speaking hands and other healing parts. That, anyway, is how he understands it (the others are far up above him now, almost out of sight and fading, backlit by the beam of light pouring out of the portal wherein they cluster, looking more like one woman than eight or nine, and more like Cassie's ear than either; yes, away they go, can't see them now, gone), and whether that understanding is something he achieves with his own crystallized lobes or is merely provided to him by the script, he surrenders to it and to her holistic therapy, fucking himself (or being fucked, for she has been the initiatrix, he merely her passive acolyte) back to health and sanity, or what passes for it in this dying world. *I was completely iced up, Cassie, I couldn't feel a thing,* he whispers, but though his mouth is open and a frosty cloud emerges, no sound comes out. *I felt like the time-lapse man! Even my name had frozen up and fallen off, I was nobody!* YOU ARE WHO YOU ARE, she replies, a reply he does not hear but reads, as though she were writing it directly on his forebrain in a black place somewhere behind his eyes.

Earlier—if it is possible to speak of *earlier* around Cassie (if it is possible to speak at all), for whom all time is space, all events simultaneous, all clips interchangeable—when he complained—though he could not even speak, could not open his mouth, could not breathe, he was nothing but a blue lump of ice in her version of things, his miserable words tracking through his brain like a little train pulling a string of loaded boxcars through a blizzard up a frozen mountainside (*My heart is faint within me,* he seemed to be wailing—this is a kind of memory emerging more from her body than from his, the words as new to him now as when, presumably, he first issued them—*Listen when I groan, there is none to comfort me . . .*)—she told him that he must accept his suffering (the train meanwhile had fallen off its rails), for he was engaged in an intuitive, visionary mode of fucking that was intimately and mysteriously linked to an eternal truth that compelled expression (the battered train was numbly crawling back up the mountainside once more, its mission forgotten, load lost, but chugging away dutifully), no matter how dreadful the consequences. She delivered this message somewhere in the region of his liver, for that was, as she called it, THE ORGAN OF PARADOX (though weren't they all?), for by then she was deep into one of her penetrating multisensory rubdowns, bringing him back to life again with her warm oiled fingers and with her juices, mouth, and exhalations.

When she'd first brought him back here, as he was coming to understand it or remember it, as if his ponderous thrusts were evoking informative flashbacks, she'd snapped away his frozen clothes like knocking loose plaster off a wall and set him on his knees and forehead, as he was still locked in the sitting position and tended to rock if placed upon his back. He was lifeless and all shrunk up, as white and hard as marble, and not a breath in him, so she chipped the ice out of his anus to create a blowhole and put her mouth to it and sufflated him from there, the first sensation that he had of her. He was still falling then, or supposed he was, and he felt he was taking wind up his ass from the speed of his fall, though it was a warm wind and gave him a certain pleasure, even if pleasure was not foremost on his mind at that moment. She tipped him over (he seems to recall the loud knock his frozen body made when it banged upon her barren wooden floor, like a hammer blow, though in the nightmare he was having it was more like an anticipated terror, that bang, than a reality) and sucked the frozen snot out of his nostrils to get his wind machine working from top to bottom, then rolled him onto his back, petrified knees in the air, so she might work on his heart and testicles, the latter shriveled and hard as little brass worry marbles, but which she labeled THE PLACE WHERE PRIVATE MEANING AND THE DIVINE ORDER MEET. That was also, Cleo once told him, the standard definition of nonsense, and Cassie would not have argued with that but would have taken it as further encomium. The heart, as furnace and pump room (otherwise vastly overrated, in Cassie's view), needed immediate attention to set that hallowed meeting place thrumming once more, but the capricious brain, mostly obstructive when not pharmaceutically assisted, could wait, as it would probably just undermine her therapeutics. She melted the surface frost with her breath, straddled him, and rubbed herself about to oil his chest and belly, and then, as he began to thaw, dug in deep with her cunning fingers, pushing her hot body oils in and around the contractile fibrils and the tendons, stroking the dead nerves to restore the current (LET THERE BE LIGHTNING, she seemed to say—though none of these words were actually hers of course; she has no words; they were more like rough translations of the movements of her expressive fingers—LET THERE BE REVELATION AT TWENTY-FOUR TIMES A SECOND!), massaging his heart and other involuntary muscles (meaning most of the ones he had), using her own secret gateways through the abdominal wall to reactivate his organs, knead his viscera, cleanse them of what she called, or her fingers did, THE ILLUSION OF PARTICULARS, penetrating ever deeper and delivering her little messages as she moved about.

HE FUCKS IN THE LANGUAGE OF THE WOUND ITSELF, her hands went on, as they untied and reknotted his navel, then squeezed in to melt his kidneys with fondlings like sympathetic murmurings, her mouth meanwhile taking in his testicles and rolling them about on the tongue until they softened up and stopped their metallic clacking. Their delivery mechanism, though spiritually of less interest to her, was rigid as always and frozen rock-hard to boot, so she lowered herself over it, careful not to snap it off, shuddering when it entered her like an icicle in a bun warmer, sizzling and popping. HE DOES NOT EXORCISE THE PAIN, he seemed to see her vagina say, in a message that ran the length of his cold brittle tube, ending somewhere in the region of his Cowper's gland, BUT PROLONGS IT EXCRUCIATINGLY, ENCOURAGING IT TO BREED NEW PAIN, IN HIS DEVOUT EFFORT TO ATTAIN TRANSCENDENCE, TO UNIFY THE WORLD'S MAD SCATTER, TO ACHIEVE EXEMPLARY HARMONY. His awakening scrotum, cozied in the sleek cheeks of her uplifted behind, were emitting their own messages by this time, mostly doleful and skeptical expressions of the bleakest nature, which she sucked up and acknowledged: AN IMPOSSIBLE ENTERPRISE OF COURSE, HE MUST FAIL OVER AND OVER AGAIN, BUT IN HIS FAILURE AND IN HIS PAIN AND DESPAIR HE WILL CREATE BEAUTY, THE ONLY KIND OF BEAUTY IMAGINABLE IN THIS PARTICULATE ABSURDITY WHICH MEN CALL THE UNIVERSE. Perhaps by this time, as her message suggested, she had pressed on to the area of his rectum, for he was indeed now feeling a certain creative movement there in its upper regions.

How he got into the missionary position from his inert knees-high rock on the wooden floor under Cassie is not clear to him, but then continuity has never been a notable feature of his career, nor clarity either for that matter, especially in Cassie's enigmatic company; something happens and then something else happens, and all he can do is accept what comes and savor the best of it. And fucking Cassie is about as good as it gets, for it is a pleasurable agitation in an ethereally beautiful vessel and, at the same time, an easeful path to inner peace. The solitary one. He has often thought that if he does have to die (and who's to say, maybe he doesn't—he's been called *an immortal* in all the media, has he not? and when he asked Clara about it, she assured him that, yes, that's virtually so), he would like to die fucking Cassie. The hoarfrost that rimed shut his eyelids has melted, making it seem as if he's crying (perhaps he is), and now, pressing his face against Cassie's smooth bald head to thaw out the rest of it, he can see, projected down inside her inner ear, a live digitized video transmission of his erected cock, no longer ice blue but buffed to a glistening salmon pink, sliding majestically in and out of her moist hairless crease. This is a very soothing sight. In it goes until pubic bone meets pubic bone like the closing of a gate, cushioned by his nest of hair, her fleshy pillow; then slowly out again until the engorged lip of the crown is glimpsed, stroking the clitoris as a knuckled thumb might flick a marble (this more felt than seen), his ruddy testicles drawn up tight under the rising and falling anus above like an exposed heart worn there openly on his perineum's sleeve as a sign of his humble acquiescence and his gratitude and his tender vulnerability; and then back in again, submerging its full length as though seeking some ultimate connection, not merely with this particular woman but with the whole of existence, or at least that portion of it as bodied forth between her mysterious thighs. It is, like all of Cassie's poems-in-motion, a work of art that will last forever (though she throws everything away; her tapes and films have to be rescued piecemeal from her bins)—so masterfully simple, so effortless, direct, and aesthetically pure, stripped of all extraneous gesture, in the way that her body has been stripped of all hair and ornament. Yet for all its self-denying simplicity it is a work of immense scale and astonishing richness, austere yet gorgeously radiant, a moving image that opens up in him a curious mental space, separate from but linked to that part of his mind (that involuntary muscle is now thawing, too, and going its own way) that takes in the filmed action, wherein he contemplates, as though it were other, his own being. Watching it is like gazing up, while stoned, at a starry night sky, a real one, not a studio mock-up, and it releases him from his earthbound fears and anxieties, and from the absurdity of struggle and mad ambition, and makes him feel, as he so rarely feels (in . . . and out . . . and in . . . and out), at home in the cosmos.

As, mesmerized, he watches—fucks and watches—a second delayed image of his rearing and plunging cock is superimposed upon the first one, following it precisely like one wave lapping another wave, and then a third appears, slightly faster, and a fourth, faster still, and a fifth and a sixth in fugal procession, the patterns changing slightly from image to image, creating an inexhaustible variety of rhythmic structures, and as the overlaid images rub against one another, accompanied by the percussive resonances emerging now from the fleshy collisions, the tempo gradually builds toward a thematic urgency that compels his attention even as that attention is being sucked away with ever greater urgency toward his loins. What he sees now in Cassie's ear, though still the same subject, is no longer so precise as a star-studded night sky but more like scudding clouds rolling in, pink and wet and ceaselessly reshaping themselves in their mounting tumult. This tumult can be heard as well as seen, the reverberant beat of the damp pubic collisions resolving now to massive achromatic chords, riven by the strident noises of the city leaking in like a stuttering melody: whistles, horns, sirens, clattery falls and crashes. All of it proceeds not by successive rapid contrasts but by a slow piling up of simultaneous layers, proposing a profusion of expressive possibilities, even while narrowing rapidly to just one. Oh yes, let it come! Her hands are still prowling his insides (AND THEN . . . , they seem to be saying, or writing, somewhere halfway down his spine), and he can feel her vaginal walls contracting and relaxing now as her own orgasms begin.

Before the storm can break, however, a finger appears and sweeps the clouds aside and pushes into what can now be seen as a soft place between his dancing scrotum and anus, as though to locate there an ancient entranceway sealed over by time, and he feels a delicious tension but no release and his prick dips for a moment as though her finger has pressed a switch and the storm subsides and the frantic fugato rhythms slow to a steady rise and fall and the fleshy elements return in all their clarity and radiance, and then he's ready to go again. Everything is more liquid now and more aromatic (yes, he can smell again! she is restoring him in all his parts!) and he is gripped at the root by powerful pulsing contractions, more felt than seen or heard, yet echoed in plangent cadences rising up as if from the earth below. Cassie, through austere self-discipline and purity of heart and will, has moved beyond multiple orgasms into prolonged compound orgasms, which she has been known to hold for hours, maybe even days (never sure about time around Cassie—even now, her slippery fingers pushing down into the base of his spine seem to be announcing THE NEXT DAY . . .), and though he must always fail her (she casts no blame; in her universal love she is beyond censure and reward), and is driven more to anxiety than to delight by the effort demanded, he does all he can to stay with her as long as possible and willingly accepts whatever she does in her wisdom to help him, for he knows that fucking Cassie to the edge of her own rapture is the closest he will ever come to experiencing—if only vicariously—nirvana.

Just before it is too late—it feels like his whole body is an erogenous zone, erect and awash in Cassie's magical juices—her finger reappears and plugs once more the collapsing dike within, and does so repeatedly, and so the rhythm of tension and the temporary subsidence of tension builds, gathering in momentum and complexity, the monumental image of pounding cock and cunt (he is not looking into her ear any longer, but he can still see the projected image as if it were sitting between his eyes on the bridge of his nose) absorbing into itself fleeting hints of montaged visual elements both cosmic and human and acquiring thereby textures of luminous clarity and teeming inner life, taking him to the brink again and again, and he decides at last—A WEEK LATER . . . is the message tickling the rim of his anus—or his gonads decide for him, his entire focus now surging toward the end of his throbbing organ, that this—*oh wow!*—is as close as he'll try to get on this occasion to Cassie's peak, he's (there's a tremendous pressure in his head and in his chest, and he can hear a fast-approaching climax of whooping horns) ready to blow. But Cassie's film no longer coincides precisely with his felt experience, for he believes himself still to be plunging away from above, while the bodies in the film seem to be slowly rolling across the wooden floor, or else the room is rolling around the bodies, the floor appearing and disappearing between the knotted cheeks of Cassie's flawless ass, displaced as it vanishes with views of the barren white room—wall, ceiling, wall, floor, wall, ceiling, wall—and these views in turn are displaced by glimpses of other rooms and other spaces, interior and exterior, her vagina meanwhile tightening, her serial orgasms closer and closer together like a vibrating electrical current. Faster and faster the room whirls around them, dizzying him with its gathering speed, the floor cracking his ass with each revolution like a wooden paddle: *Wait a minute, Cassie,* he cries, or thinks he cries, *I don't feel so good! Let me off for a minute!* But the room continues to wheel madly around them, if it still is the room (all he can see now are colors whipping past and growing ever more vibrant; all of this appears between her convulsive cheeks on the screen, but if he should open his eyes—he can't!—he's sure he'd still see the same old wooden floor below him, he's pretty sure), her spasms now more like an oscillating hum, rising in pitch. He would desperately like to come—YEARS PASS is the message quivering at the tip of his penis—but it's not to be. The thumping rotation of the room slows gradually and comes finally to a stop and he finds himself—with a spinning head, aching goolies, and a maddeningly buzzing prick—lying flat out on the floor on his back, all alone, as if, from some great height, he'd fallen here.

—Hey, look! The crackly silence is broken by a track of human voices. In here! It's Old Crazy Leg! Pierna Loca!

They're standing over him, that wild young bare-breasted thing and her urban-guerrilla friends, The Extars. Where is he? Ah. On Cassie's floor. He must have passed out from the pain. He tries to rise, can't. Hurts too much. And that buzzing at the tip still; it's driving him crazy. It's like the trigger's been pulled but the piece is jammed, as he once cracked in an old private dick movie—or dicked in an old private crack movie, as Cissy put it in one of her cocks-and-rubbers parodies. And where *is* that devoted nimble-fingered artist, now that he needs her?

—Thought it might be you, Loco! We been digging you on the security camera monitor.

Monitor?

—For weeks, magic man! she says with an admiring grin, her words lip-synched.

—Wow! Look at that sucker vibrate! It's like it's trying to beep out a message!

—Probably a distress signal of some kind. Check his maracas! They're sky blue and ballooned up like cannonballs! She squats down beside him, her black hair falling over her face, and touches him speculatively, making him jump. *Whoo!* He's in bad pain!

—Yeah, well, who ain't? C'mon, Lottie! We gotta get outa here!

—Wait! he gasps, as she stands to move away, his voice a hoarse whisper still, emerging like cold static. Help me!

—Can't stop, Loco. It's a raid! They're cleaning house. I mean, *really* cleaning—they're gonna blow this mother up! He can hear the sirens now, the whistles, the smashing of wood and glass, feet pounding on the stairs, all that ambient sound straight from the actional world. The shit's coming down fast, you better move your ass!

—I can't! I can't even straighten up! You've got to bring me off somehow!

—No can do, man! You should stay away from that dippy yogini with the zipped lip, she's fucking you up!

—Hurry up, Lottie! Those assholes from City Hall are right behind us!

—But what about Old Crazy Leg?

—Screw him! It's too late!

—Oh yes! *Do* that, miss! he gasps. *Hurry!*

—Here they come!

—We can't just leave him here! she shouts over the mayhem building up out in the corridor; there are screams, blows being struck, bodies falling. He saved our lives!

—Yeah, but not just to have 'em trashbinned again! We're off, baby!

—Please, miss! Just a quickie! I'm almost there!

—No time, Loco, she says, squatting down beside him again, the sound of her squeaking jeans also in sync. She spits in her palms and wraps them around him. A handslam's the best I can do!

But there's not even time for that. The door crashes open and the City Hall troops come storming in, led by the Mayor, arrayed in her official rubber and leather and snapping a long black whip. The blow the girl takes from a truncheon sends her skidding halfway across the room, yanking him along with her.

—*Waa-aa-aah!*

—Good *work,* Mr. Pierre! Cora exclaims, prying Lottie's hands loose and clapping cuffs on them. You've helped us capture their most notorious ringleader. But why are you crying? We'll make a public example out of her. You'll *love* it! And she cracks her whip for emphasis as they drag away the half-conscious girl, her jeans hauled down to shackle her ankles but still defiant—*Morph City Hall!* she shouts sullenly—and the whip pops again. But there was another one here before, that daft renegade cueball! Where is she?

—I don't know! he wheezes. But, Cora! Your Honor—

—Well, if she's still on the set, tough luck. Now you'd better be on your way, Mr. Pierre! Aren't you late for the office?

—I-I can't! Could you—*please!*—could you do me a favor?

—Oh, she says, glancing down at him with a chilling smile. Our weird sister's been up to her old tricks, I see. She flicks the tip of her whip at it and winks as, yelping, he arches a foot up off the floor. Dress the honorable gentleman, she orders her officers, rubbing the whip handle between her powerful thighs, her booted feet straddling his chest, and remove him from the premises before the effects go off! Oh, and here, she adds, whipping off her black leather bra. Use this for a sling!

There's an abrupt cut and he finds himself in a busy but utterly silent intersection, ill-fittingly suited up and overcoated and standing on a curb marked with a taped XX, his swollen testicles hammocked in black leather, his cruelly tingling penis gripped in both mittened hands, his eyes bleary with frozen tears.

The masses rush by, but he is not jostled by them; it's as if he were in the middle of the crowd yet at the same time isolated, completely set off, like a monochrome print that has been retouched to whiten out the background, leaving the central figure sharp, clear, afloat, and somewhat unreal. But just a little saliva on your finger and you can rub away the haze (he is rubbing and rubbing, but to no easeful effect), and gradually the context comes into—there's a sudden thunderous explosion (for a brief moment, he thinks it is he who has exploded and he feels an illusory relief, but no, no), and a building vanishes before his eyes, and with that the traffic noises resume—horns blare, tires screech; there are angry shouts, whistles, the crunch of colliding metal—and he's shoved off the curb and swept down the snowy street and back into the continuity along with the others.

The Mayor's right, he knows, she's always right—he should be at the office, Cissy would take care of him there as she always does—and it is his intention to go there if going is what he is doing out here in this rolling sea of bundled flesh. But he has no idea where he is or where he's being taken, nothing's familiar, snow's whipping about, the street signs are blurred; is that one for a pedestrian crossing or low-flying aircraft?

—Look at those blue balls in the fancy leather boob bags, someone gasps, bumping by. Must be royalty!

A snowplow clatters by, forcing him back up on the curb, and for a moment then he's suddenly back in front of the exploding tenement. Where did this come from? it's a kind of flashback, and Cleo's there videoing the fallout.

—Hey, baby! she shouts from across the street, hang on to that gruesome hardware until I see you tonight! *Tonight?* It's our anniversary, lover! We've got a date! *How about now, Cleo? How about right now?*

But she's gone, the scene's gone, and he's stumbling again down unknown streets, jostled by the freezing masses as before, bearing his erected member like his personal cross of meat, now turning numb with the cold, he this AVATAR OF THE SELF-SEEKING SELF, as it announces on the darkened theater marquee under which he is being pushed along, this GURU OF THE GAMETES, this HIGH PRIEST OF PRURIENCE. There is more but he can't read it (no matter, it's just movie hype), his turgid gonads momentarily filling the entire screen of his mind, all else vanishing. . . .

—Love the ice-cream colors, L.P.

—Cissy! Where are you? Help me!

—Happy to, love! See you at the office.

—Wait! Cissy! I can't find it!

But she's gone, if she was ever there, the single-minded focus on the source of his agony gone as well, for, graced by a momentary overhead long shot, he knows now where he is; yes, his office *is* just around the corner, it was there all the time, he must have gone right by it, how did he miss it? He pushes through the crowd, running flat out now, frozen prick waggling frantically, goal in view, central heating, hot tub, all that—*oof!* sorry, ma'am!

—Good *morning*, L.P.! Oohh! How *nice!*

—Good morning, love! (*Whoof!*) After you!

—Why, *thank* you, Mr. P! Some storm, eh?

—Fuck me, you can say that again!

—What? *Some storm*, you mean? Is this a retake?

No, wait! I've been here before! But he's already through the door and out the other side, staggering down the frozen anonymous streets again in his borrowed suit and old-fashioned herringbone overcoat, life's burden in hand, alarmed by all the cut-and-splice discontinuities (there's a sudden glimpse of a young girl alone in a speeding train car, swooning with fear: one of his old movies? what's going on?), and aware (the steel-on-steel clatter of train wheels continues to thread its way through the crowd and traffic noises of the city like a lingering melody, and there are other sounds that shouldn't be there: birds, glass bells, the rhythmic opening and closing of file drawers, party laughter) that this newest adventure is different from all that have gone before, whatever *before* is or might still be.

Even now, there is another like himself in herringbone overcoat and hat down over frostbitten ears walking along just in front of him—no, not *like*, it *is* himself, moving as he moves but a fraction of a second before, as though guiding him through the traces, and try as he might he cannot step out of the other's steps. In fact there are two of them out in front of him—no, three! *four!*—like a rising and falling chorus of selves (the train wheels and party laughter have given way to galloping hooves, popcorn machines, foghorns, and flushing toilets, and out of these comminglings something like a mordant plainsong is emerging), and even if he darts down a side street or spins around, they are still out there in front of him, anticipating his least twitch and stumble, more of him now than he can count. He glances back over his shoulder and there he is, falling forward into his own steps, clutching his swollen organ, head turning to glance back over his shoulder, just fractionally delayed, and another behind him, looking back, followed by countless others, overwhelming him with feelings of futility and self-pity and déjà vu: all those hats! While looking over his shoulder, he collides with someone in front: it is himself in a precipitous sequence of self-collisions (of course, no one was looking where he was going), which he feels internally like a fluttery hammering of the heart—*Help! I need a doctor!* he cries out—and then he is alone and singular again, getting shoved down the mazy Cinecity streets through the slush and civil litter, fearful that the YEARS PASS message at the end of his itching prick might be the title of a film he's in.

In the middle of a dangerous intersection, the light suddenly changes—the sky goes black, the buildings light up in rainbow colors—and he is hit from all sides by a rush of speeded-up highlights from old movies—rapes and seductions, birchings, bumfucks, facials, and fistings—a terrific pileup, which brings traffic to a standstill and leaves him concussed and sprawled out on his back, still hanging on to himself, in the trampled snow of the gutter. Where he is set upon suddenly by a shrieking horde of pubescent gum-popping Sex Maniacs, the first hopeful thing that has happened to him all day, speaking loosely, and as they fall upon him, he spreads himself gratefully in anticipation of release at last. But it's not a gang attack, it's a school field trip, a sex education class complete with camera crew, and led by his own doctor. She heard him then! *Clara!* he gasps. *Thank god you're here! You've got to help me!* But his voice is gone again. His mouth forms the words, but all that comes out is the sound of breaking glass, the words appearing instead as an electrical news bulletin encircling the tower overhead.

—*Now here's a classic case, children,* Clara shouts into the wind, snapping his testicles briskly with her wooden pointer (which illustrates where that sound of glass bells in the track has been coming from, knocking steam radiators and the archived howls of extinct animals now joining in as expressive counterpoint), *of acute endopathic cyanorchidism, probably the consequence of congenital hyperprosexia but more immediately provoked, I'm sure, by what is technically called a teasing hot pussy—yes, take a note, that's hot, h-o-t, hot—which is also no doubt responsible for the phlogotic pruritis at the tip of this trichotomous mechanism's infamous exsertile feature* (and here his penis gets a whack from the stick, his scream displaced by a whistling teakettle). *There! I've knocked the frost off. Now you can see the little beauty better! No, leave it alone, children! You know better than to eat anything you've picked up off the street!*

Clara! Please! he begs, grabbing a white-stockinged ankle and pointing at the news bulletin on the tower above them where his plea is circulating. She glances up at it and shrugs: I WISH I COULD is the reply that appears up there, BUT IT'S NOT MY SEQUENCE.

—Please, teacher! This is stupid. May we go to the movies now?

—*Of course—but look, girls! That ad up there!*

On a giant video screen across from the news bulletin, he can see himself demonstrating a range of French ticklers (the little Sex Maniacs have their notebooks out again), but even as he pulls on a condom called the Three-headed Dog of Hell, he is thinking, My life has become too scattered, too diffuse; I've got to get focused! The purity of a hard-on is to will one thing; who said that?

From up here, he can see himself down below, spread-eagled in the gutter, abandoned by the bored schoolchildren, a pitiable object, more like a pale newsprint cutout of himself in herringbone—in fact, it *is* a newsprint cutout, the wind catches it now and whips it away; the real Lucky Pierre, he sees, is crossing a bridge over a frozen canal, or rather two of them are, both bundled in dirty overcoats, clutching themselves two-handed, crossing simultaneously in opposite directions: When they meet in the middle the two figures merge and disappear, only to reappear, alone once more, lurching through a congested city that is shrinking around him until he is as tall as the high-rises, his giant feet crushing everything in their path, his tottering stride bringing down wires and streetlamps, knocking elevated trains off their rails, and causing the earth to quake and the buildings to shake and rattle.

I am something from another planet, he thinks, as the massive tonal blendings of storm, rocking city, and clamorous random sounds flare up to a plangent chorale, but no sooner has he thought it than the music, spending itself in an anguished and brittle cadenza, is blown away by the wind and the city rises up around him again with a piercing shriek, quickly passing him by and leaving him a diminutive figure in the gutter, too small even to climb up on the curb and in danger of being flattened underfoot by the passing multitudes. It's alarming, but he seems to remember having read about something like this somewhere, an old script maybe, though he can't recall how it turns out. One immediate development is that a snowplow comes clattering by (hasn't this already happened?), and he is picked up by the pile of moving ice and snow and shoveled down a double-portaled drain with the word METRO in a tight red circle in the V between the twin arches above.

He crawls out of the melting slush onto a dimly lit underground platform, packed with sullen shoppers and commuters and warmed by them and their sour exhalations. He passes among them, hoping someone might volunteer to give him a hand with his problem, made more acute by a painful thaw, but the only persons down here interested in others are the thieves, muggers, and pickpockets. No one kissing or even squeezing bottoms—too much sorrow and bitterness for that—just a restless nudging, pushing, jockeying for pole position on the platform. There are pilfering hands in all his pockets, but he doesn't care; he has nothing to lose. Or almost nothing: He realizes his hat is missing. And his shoes are still there but his socks are gone. He sees what looks like his hat disappearing up the steps to the street, and probably he should follow it, but, even if he hurts more (damned thing feels like it's splintering), he feels safer down here where minutes are following minutes on the overhead clock in the old-fashioned way, and there are no sounds but the damp whisper of bundled bodies brushing bundled bodies and the usual low bubbling rumble floating through the tunnels.

It occurs to him that he can probably reach his office from here by one train or another without having to go back up into the mad disorder of the city streets at all. But where is he? The station sign says ANIMA LOOP, which tells him nothing. He finds a large subway map, but it looks like a nest of worms, the lines all coiled and knotted around one another. Most of them seem to end up at a dark circle rubbed raw by sweaty fingers and almost unreadable: Aha. City Hall. That's close enough. But can he get there from here? No doubt. He seems to be on the wrong platform, though. He's about to ask for help at the news kiosk nearby when a small blue triangular patch on the map catches his eye: Pork Park. Sounds familiar. He may live near there and it looks easy: a straight shot down Broadsway past Hair Pie Alley to Tonk Street, then change for Beaver Boulevard and get out at Virgin's Bush before going too far.

But when a train does finally rattle into the station, he's too deep behind the thick belligerent crowds to stand much of a chance of boarding.

What's worse, in order to squeeze in, they all strip off their clothes—there seems to be some rule about it—ridding themselves of everything except umbrellas, purses, shopping bags, and newspapers. He's shoved aside, still fumbling with his buttons, as they jam aboard, elbowing and gouging, slamming past the arriving passengers trying to get off, working up a sweat, which helps them to slip and slide around each other until they are all packed in, an indistinguishable mass of flesh and body hair pressed flat against glass. The arriving passengers, also naked, pick angrily through the abandoned clothing for something to wear before leaving the station, sniffing the underwear, pulling on layers of shirts, skirts, and pants, fighting over the coats and boots. When they've gone (he should follow them out, but not only is he afraid to go back up there, his throbbing gonads make it difficult for him to move at all), there's a hat left over, but it's not his size.

He waddles over to the kiosk to ask for directions to the platform for the City Hall train, and the salesgirl looks down at what he's holding and says, Oh dear! You've got a badly chapped penis there, sir! You should keep it wrapped up in this kind of weather! The kiosk carries a number of Lucky Pierre merchandise items, he sees—playing cards, T-shirts, party favors, autographed dildos, wrapping paper, posters, even his LickaLucky lollydicks—but they all look a bit dated and dusty. I had some lovely hand-knitted willy woolies in Sex Olympic team colors, the salesgirl says, but I'm afraid people have bought or stolen them all for toe mittens. But here, this new improved chapped-laps lotion should help.

—Thank you, miss! he gasps. But these clothes aren't mine. I haven't any money.

—That's all right, sir. You can pay me next time. Here, take it! It will do you good.

—That's very kind, but I . . . I can't even . . . ah . . . let go—

—You poor man! May I help?

—Oh, yes, please! His eyes well up with tears of relief and gratitude; behind him, the platform is packing up again. Whatever you can do!

—Oh! she cries, as she frees the irksome thing from his rigid fists. It gave me a shock!

—I know! Just her gentle hand on it eases his suffering, though the pernicious tingle seems to move even more precisely to the very tip as though a bee were feeding off him there. It's driving me crazy!

—Goodness! It's even worse on the underside! she exclaims, pointing the head straight up. And I've never seen those other things that color before! She squeezes out a long ribbon of lotion, encircling his prick with it like a white collar. I'll just be a minute, she says to the other customers crowding impatiently around.

Oh yes, he thinks, as her fingers encircle the neck and spread the milky ring down the shaft like a sheath. Now! At last! It's coming!

—You're so good, miss! Ah . . . *oh yes!* Work it in *well,* please!

—Yes, sir. Though it may sting a little.

—*What?* Oh no! Oh shit! Yow! Take it off, miss! *Take it off!*

—Yes, all right, all right. Stop jumping around, I was just trying to help. I'll find some tissue—

—*Now,* damn it! Ow! Ah! *I'm on fire!*

—In a minute, sir. Don't be rude. First I have to serve these other customers. They've been waiting, and their train's due any minute.

He's bounding about the platform now, yelping with pain, his erection sizzling and popping and breaking out in multicolored blisters. He decides to run back up to the street and fuck a snowbank—he doesn't think this, he can't think, it's simple instinct—but the people crowding down the steps push him back. *Waaah!* he howls. They don't care; he's just a nuisance.

A train pulls in. Empty. Fine. He'll board it, go to another platform where it's not so crowded. If he can make it. He presses himself up against the door, elbows out, ready to be the first in at whatever cost. But no one challenges him. The doors remain closed. He bangs on them furiously with one fist, squeezing his fiery member with the other. Then he sees her. On the other side of the glass. A young girl, pursued by evil-looking mustachioed men in tweed overcoats. That girl, she's the one on the speeding train, he's seen her before! It's what's-her-name, he recognizes her now—the girl next door! The one he's in love with! The one who pledged herself to him and said she'd always love him and wait for him! They've caught her and thrown her into a corner of the car! She's cowering there on the floor, one hand raised in terror in front of her face. As if her face was what they were after! They're kicking her knees apart! They're ripping her blouse off! Oh my god! His pain is nothing now. He hammers on the doors with both fists. But they remain closed and the train slowly pulls away, steel wheels grinding menacingly. Helplessly, he goes clattering after it down the length of the platform until it gets swallowed up by the tunnel, the girl and her attackers disappearing from view as if in an iris-out.

He's about to jump down and run after it when another train pulls in. No problem boarding this one: he's caught in the rush and swept in with the naked tide. *Follow that train!* he screams, meaninglessly, though the line seems right for the moment. But—oh no!—the train's going the other way! *Off! Let me off!* Where's the emergency cord? The others jammed in around him, holding their possessions aloft, just glare sullenly as he twitches helplessly against their sweaty barrier of flesh, his face pressed into a forest of armpits. They're angry that he's still wearing his coat and protest with snarls and grunts that his aroused cock is taking up too much room—Get it off me! It's not fair! It's against the law! They swat at it with their newspapers and umbrellas as best they can—I think it stung me!—and when they pull into another station, he is lifted bodily (thus, sooner or later, his wishes all come true) and heaved out the half-open door. Just before he hits the platform, he thinks: I've been falling all day, and now I'm landing.

It's a hard landing. And on a dark and empty platform, long since closed down. Damp and cold, walls black with soot. Silent. Not even a distant rumble in the tunnels. Rats are darting about, picking through the gray heaps of ancient litter, or maybe breeding in them. Cinecity's wildlife. There are a few smashed-up candy machines and condom dispensers, a wooden news kiosk in ruins with yellowing posters from a time long past, a slatted bench. He crawls over and pulls himself onto it to get away from the scurrying rats. The utter desolation of the nameless station is, in some strange way, comforting. I've done it, he thinks. I've fallen out of the frame. It's not so bad. I'm alone. And free. If he could just do something about these swollen-up blue things in the black sling and that maddening tingle, he might come to like it down here, for a little while anyway. Like being cast up on a desert island. One uninfested with nymphs. Even the rails look long unused; the train he was on must have gone out of its way to come by here.

Across those tracks on the far wall, between an antiquated advertisement for an old folk remedy (ATARAXIA: TASTES LIKE REAL CHOCOLATE. WORKS GENTLY IN 24 HOURS) and a warning not to jump in front of speeding trains as it is an inconvenience to other passengers, he sees the tattered remains of a poster of one of his old two-reelers: *Cherry-Picking Time*. From the famous Cuntree Classics era, his Peter Prick phase. Alas. Bygone days, sweet and uncomplicated.

No blue balls then, no buzzing penises, nothing worse to fear than grass stains or the odd patch of nettles (yes, once, with the cameras rolling, he and Cally rolled into an unseen nettles patch, but there were no second takes in those days, so they went with it, one of the liveliest fucks in the history of early cinema), though once, he remembers, while he was taking the hymen of a young starlet from the rear over a stile (maybe this was *Cherry-Picking Time*), a raging bull turned up unexpectedly, probably from the zoo, a practical joke by one of the camera crew, and it so alarmed the child that she seized up on him and it took Clara's intervention to get him free. That clip was cut from the movie, but Clara used it in one of her instructional films, nothing wasted.

He needs to get back to that kind of direct and honest moviemaking again. He knows this. He's allowed himself to become too self-reflective, too flashy, forgetting the simple things. A fuck is a fuck is a fuck; whoever said that was a genius. And the sheer wonder of it, just as it is, gets lost in the pretentious films he's been making of late. Like the Mayor and her friends said. It's what's brought him down. Yes, he's down, just look around. Maybe the decline began already back when they changed his name to Lucky Pierre and added sound. Talkies, they were called, and so you had to talk, which led to too much heavy thinking. Fucking is not about thinking or talking. A few squishy sound effects maybe, a grunt or two, that's it. The rest is eyes, hands, and body movement. Always the same, always different. The Cuntree Classics were all monochrome silents, though sound and color were later added to many of them. Creamy colors mostly. No blues. Except in the sky, where it belongs—or used to. Now it would have to be painted in.

Maybe he should attempt a tribute to that era, do another Cuntree Classic. Not just a two-reel quickie but a lasting epic. Have to do most of it in a studio now, of course, artificial everything; might not work. Still, worth a try. Mock up a secluded country estate with shady footpaths through wooded groves carpeted with bluebells and sweetbriars, giving onto sudden splashes of sunny meadows and fields of buttercups and bold red poppies, with the obligatory hidden ponds, bathhouses, and pavilions with cushioned benches and erotic statuary. And virgins. Lots of virgins. Also artificial, needless to say, but technically not a problem. Reenact the ancient drama of cognition: Oh, I'm so afraid, and yet—oh yet, I feel, I die, I must taste the sweets of love, this forbidden fruit! Teach me, sir! Be both firm and kind! I must know it if it kills me! His famous pedagogical era.

In those days he still taught the ABCs: Arse, Ballocks, Cunt. Words everybody knew, yet somehow didn't know, deliciously new with each uttering. Prick. Fuck. There weren't many of them. And not actual uttering, of course, not back then. Gesture was everything, or almost everything. He would unbutton and let out his instructive instrument, and the maiden would take in the sight with wide damp eyes, then look up at him in troubled innocence and awakening desire, her lips kissing in a plosive and then parting so that her white teeth and the wet tip of her tongue showed, a title appearing briefly where her face had been: PRICK! . . . SIR. And he would lift her skirts and finger this and that and so on; lips would form dentals, gutturals, labials, and sibilants, imitated perhaps on the electric organ, the titles popping up with each revelation, hands and eyes and mouths doing what no spoken language could ever later displace, moving ineluctably toward the climactic fricatives, taking his time, idling a bit, repeating some of the lessons, offering further examples—no fast forward in those days; you had to wait for it, he made them wait. Though he often couldn't wait himself, too excited to carry on, having to fuck the enchanting young things off-camera, more or less off-camera (close-ups were taken to be intercut later or used in other films, though the techniques were primitive still); then they'd return to the scene and pick up where they'd left off, though even in black-and-white you could often see the abrupt physical changes, blood doing its own thing without regard to the letter of the script, the skills of the makeup artist of little avail. Happy times. They come and go.

The remake might now begin with an homage to those times, perhaps a sequence of screen tests as young ingenues, picnicking with him on a grassy slope at the edge of an appealing copse, surrounded by cameras, booms, and lights, enunciate in silence, one by one, all those words once more, exhibiting their talent for seeming modesty, shyness, fear, desperate longing, making the words seem naughty again. And this time, if he's overwhelmed with desire, the off-camera fucks can be on-camera, part of the story. *The Secret Making of Cuntree Classics*. The screen tests could be followed by a set of variations on first-time sex, taking off from the best of the screen tests (SAY WHAT YOU FEEL, MY DEAR! . . . OH! I FEEL YOUR PRICK, SIR! FUCKING ME! FAR UP MY . . . MY . . . YES? OH, SIR . . . SAY IT! . . . UP MY CUNNY CUNT CUNT, SIR!), combining the best moments from each starlet's performance into exquisitely erotic montages of the old sort, so moving and beautiful they were, and all but abandoned in his later films, perhaps coming to focus (for singularity of focus is essential for a full emotional impact) on one ingenue alone, pretty, gentle, desperately vulnerable, an act, of course, or maybe not an act, rather a true virgin in thought and deed, last of her kind. Just imagine! When he puts his penis in her hand (THE THROBBING DART OF LOVE!), she cradles it tenderly like a baby bird fallen from its nest, literally does not know what to do with it (ouch! careful!), a creature so sweet and innocent he hates to deceive her, easy as it is, for she loves him and trusts him—Constance, that's her name; how could he have forgotten it?—and wants what he wants, though only because it *is* what he wants, her own desires uncertain and confused: ARE YOU SURE, SIR? WILL IT FIT? WON'T IT HURT? That one's easy, the reply's ever on the tip of his tongue, part of the ancient catechism, a line he believes in and can deliver with genuine conviction, even as he pulls her drawers down. AH! WHAT A WONDROUS THING IS THERE! AND NEVER SEEN OR TOUCHED BY MAN BEFORE! He kneels before it in awe and loving admiration, as a great discoverer might kneel before an uncharted ocean or a mountain of gold—as it says in the script (probably) but as he genuinely feels, too; he's not just acting. BUT WILL YOU LOVE ME ALWAYS, SIR, AND BE FOREVER TRUE? Ah. Well. That's a tougher one. There are many responses available to him, of course, and he knows them all, his usual problem being not to repeat himself, but this sweet tight thing before his eyes is as fragrant as a field of wildflowers and more beautiful than any flower he's ever seen or knows, and he almost cannot think. I love you now with all my heart, and now is all of forever that we can ever have, he says or, rather, thinks to say but doesn't, for another thought has passed his mind, a stranger one, to wit: *Why not?* For hasn't that always been his deepest desire? Isn't that what it means to escape the frame? He has been a good professional for all the life he knows, but it has trapped him inside a box of artificial light even as it pulled him in all directions at once and has given him no life, no center of his own. Her drawers now are down around her trembling knees. He works them carefully over her calves down to her ankles and slips them off her feet, kissing each foot as he does so, and her toes too, one by one. Yes! He will! Be hers, be true, and adore her always! He will be her slave of love and be set free by that! He kisses her calves, her knees, her thighs, dips his tongue into the tender grotto between them, and feels her start. He looks up at her; there are tears in her eyes. Oh my god! So pure! So beautiful! That this is his!

But, no. Too late. He's lost and she's gone, it's in the tin, on the shelf, all done and dusted. Ruined, poor child. They both are. The fiery stinging has died down, but his engorged pizzle now has little orange, green, and purple blister spots all over it, and the needling at the tip is more virulent than ever. Increased preorgasmic tension in his anus, too, or thereabouts, making him squirm and whimper. It was probably a mistake to let himself imagine that Cuntree Classics remake, just made it worse. He's been sitting here on this old bench too long, he sees: the rats are gnawing at his pant cuffs and coattails. Maybe he should just let them have it all, that's the mood he's in. That damned Cassie, beautiful but weird; it's she who's done this to him, cast him low. He'd been warned to stay away from her. Over by the *Cherry-Picking* poster there's a torn fragment of an old phone sex advertisement. NEED A FRIEND? it asks. Just enough of it left to recall for him the original: a woman pushing the receiver up between her legs with both hands, the cord lashed around her and strung through her grinning teeth like a bridle. Cleo, of course. Based on a TV ad she did to promote media convergence. All but one digit of the phone number is still readable. Well, hell, why not? Probably long since disconnected, but give it a shot. He struggles to his feet, kicking the rats off, and carries his aching blue balls over to a wrecked phone box. Nothing left of it but splinters and loose wires, and aromatic as a sewer. But on the inside of the only pane of glass left in it, he sees a message freshly scrawled with lipstick in a childish hand: *Help me! I'm being kidnapped! C.*

Constance! he thinks. Of course it could be anyone, but he knows it's she, the hopeful innocence of it, has to be. There's an arrow lipsticked there too, pointing toward the darkness at the far end of the platform, and he goes hobbling toward it, intent now on one thing and one thing only. There are stairs going up there, old damp stone ones, and at their foot: half a torn blouse. Hers? It's still warm! He pulls his old herringbone around him and turns the collar up, presses the silky blouse to his face (it has a faint sweet milky smell and brings tears to his eyes), and braces himself to return to the bitter streets above.

At the top, however, he finds himself in a bright elegantly tiled room full of naked veiled women, taking their ease in a large bath the size of a swimming pool. Is she among them? Their prisoner? He huddles in an alcove, hiding his face in his collar (can't hide everything, though), trying to spot her, but he has never seen her naked and the faces are all concealed. Eunuchs in G-strings stand around ominously with drawn sabers gripped two-handed between their legs, but they pay him no heed, so he creeps stealthily about, staying close to the wall, trying to glimpse a profile or catch a telltale glance. But it's discouraging, there's nothing to see but a lot of anonymous breasts and bottoms, like a tubful of wet ripe fruit. He sees a pretty pubis that might be hers (he remembers kneeling before it, or imagining himself doing so), but the buns, when she turns round, are wrong. Sensational, but too mature.

Then he does see her, across the room in a decorated arched doorway; she emerges, fleeing, is grabbed, her gaping mouth clamped by a meaty fist, and is hauled back into the darkness, but not before she sees him there and casts him a glance of recognition filled with terror and desperation. Fuck the eunuchs, he's on his way, slapping openly across the wet tiles, intent on rescue. You are brave and kind and very very good, she has told him, and he means to prove it. The tiles are slippery, however, and on the far corner his feet fly out from under him and he takes a one-sided pratfall—half-assed, as it were—that he thinks might kill him, cushioned though it is by his overcoat. But he picks himself up and limps over to the arched doorway, where he finds more steps, marble this time, or imitation marble, and without hesitation down he goes, fearful that she's being dragged to a dungeon. For torture. Or for worse.

But at the bottom of the steps, he finds himself in a sunny garden with tinkling fountains and gazebos with clematis and morning-glory trellises and rose arbors and little brick footpaths winding through beds of tulips, gladioli and petunias, lady's-slippers and larkspurs. Women pass through the garden, tending it, plucking weeds, picking blossoms, or sit on benches in the sunlight, all of them clad in thin gauzy tunics that give pale visible form to their graceful movements and elegant poses, as though they were wearing their own ghosts on their skin. He moves among them, peering closely (mostly they ignore him, but if they glance his way it's without recognition, nor do they mind his gaze or seek it), but she is not here. He pauses at a fountain (a stone nymph peeing in the face of a grinning satyr lying between her legs, water spurting from him behind her back in rhythmic jets) to look about; where can they have taken her? The flower garden stretches out around him as far as he can see, and he can see no hidden places in it. A young woman comes over to the fountain—he steps aside—and removes her tunic to wash herself in the pool, then leans over to drink from the satyr's jets, lifting her tender glowing buttocks to the sun. He is not tempted, not exactly anyway (god, she *is* beautiful, though!), devoted as he is now to one alone and determined to be faithful to her even though they've hardly met (this is no excuse, he knows that); no, rather, when he enters this exquisite creature from behind it is purely for urgent medical reasons, to scratch the itch in his penis, so to speak, relieve the monstrous ache in his gonads, so he might more single-mindedly pursue the rescue of his beloved, which is truly all that he desires. So hang on, just be a minute. He expects her to be tight, such a slender young thing, but lush too, like the garden all around him, rich and moist with her own blossoming desire, but (maybe he's hurting too much) he feels nothing at all. He pumps away (she doesn't seem to mind, he didn't think she would), but it's like fucking light. Wait a minute, he thinks. I *am* fucking light! He backs away and takes a swat at her luminous behind and his hand passes right through it. It's a hologram of some kind, an illusion! Oh shit! he groans, and in seeming reply hears a gasping and a whimpering. He spins around: over there in that gazebo! They're wrestling her to the floor, there's the rip of clothing, a muffled scream! This is *real!* He clumps over, plowing through the hedges and flower beds as if they weren't there (they *aren't* there!), but she and her assailants have vanished before he can reach them. Just a pair of torn panties on the floor (they're real, they're wet, he pockets them) and an escalator climbing skyward.

He steps on it and is carried up to the bargain basement of a department store, where women are fighting over the sale goods in a real knockdown teat-twisting skirt-ripping free-for-all, stuffing what they can grab up their orifices, then snatching at each other's hoards with hands and teeth, all of it to the tune of sentimental love songs played by string orchestras on muted loudspeakers. On a hunch, he crosses through into the toy department, and on the elevator doors over by the plastic model kits for the Big Bang Bordello, Cumalot Castle, and his own Lucky Pierre Penthouse Flat (which he longs for; will he ever see it again?), there's another lipsticked message: *Help! Please! I love you! C.* A scrap of skirt is caught in the doors. He bangs on the button frantically until the doors open and he tumbles inside. Empty. No further sign of her except for a lipsticked arrow, pointing upward. But the elevator descends and drops him off on a desert where cowgirls are huddled around a campfire fondling their horses and singing songs about their lonesome pussies. Only one thing's real down here, he knows, and if he wants to get out he has to keep focused on it. On her. He squeezes her wet panties with his free hand, as if what was left of the world's meaning and beauty were to be grasped there, and walks right through the fire and the excited whinnies and up the stairs (the arrow said up) onto the deck of a sinking ship, where he is put into a lifeboat full of distraught women in their nightgowns and lowered to a drunken orgy taking place in the banquet hall of an ancient emperor. Which also does not surprise him. He looks around (he can still hear waves crashing against the hull), catches a fleeting glimpse of her across the hall, in her street clothes still, what's left of them, being hauled feet first, bound and gagged, up a narrow tower. When he gets *there* (nothing stops him now; he staggers right through all the heaving bodies like wading through fog), he finds a steel-runged ladder rising straight up into the darkness above, a torn brassiere looped over the bottom rung. He hesitates (he's learning to hate heights), but then he hears her cry out—Ah! No! No! *Not that!*—and he goes scrambling up, rattling the bars with his enflamed organ as he climbs, as though dragging a stick on a picket fence.

At the top, he steps out onto a vast green meadow, the very one he'd imagined for the Cuntree Classics homage; maybe it's a film he's already made? Yes, there's the copse on the hill, the picnic cloth, the camera booms and dollies, the ingenues lounging about hopefully with silent words on their lips, and a sky the color of his bloated balls (he's not fooled by it) with who knows how many suns up there. He pauses to catch his breath, trying to see through this glimmering projection to the genuine heart of the matter—and then she appears, dashing out from the copse on the hill, glancing fearfully back over her shoulder, dressed in the merest tatters, though still somehow completely clothed. She stumbles! She falls! He runs toward her, his heart pounding, balls bouncing in their leather sling, but it's uphill and more like swimming than running; it's as if he's been ratcheted down a notch by overcranking, for romantic effect perhaps, or else his coat's too heavy, or maybe there's just something in him reluctant to make this commitment, something holding him back even as he lumbers forward; for she has turned toward him now in tearful recognition and at last there's nothing standing between them. She's running gracefully toward him down the gentle green slope, weeping with joy and relief, reaching out to him; the embrace is imminent, but after that?

—*I love you!* he cries out in answer to his own doubts, and a trapdoor opens and he falls through into utter blackness.

Is this still the same fall or another? he wonders as he drops, and then he hits and it feels completely new again. The darkness in which he lies is absolute. And silent, except for a distant whir and crackle. Black leader, he thinks. I've fallen into black leader. This is the end.

—Oh! I hope it isn't! The end, I mean!

—Don't worry, baby, endings are a conscious thought. Heroes are avatars of the unconscious. They *live* in this urzeit dreamtime shit. That's what makes them heroes. And the unconscious is too dumb to stay down after a pratfall. Knobhead here's been rough on him. But he'll be back and hard as ever.

—Oh, I hope so, Cleo! It's terrible what he's gone through! It shows how much he really loves me, though, doesn't it? It's so sweet!

—Well, that's hardly Cass's point.

—No? What *is* the point, Cassandra? Really! What does it all mean?

— . . . !

—Ouch!

—I think she means that there are no meanings. Only encounters.

—Well, she didn't have to hit me!

—You *have* put L.P. through an awful lot, Cassie. I know you're just trying to help him reach down deep inside himself to try to find new directions and all that. And I suppose it's important; his career was going a bit stale, or he thought it was, though that dig about pretentious movies was unfair. But I miss him, Cassie, and I feel sorry for him.

—Yeah, me too. Poor old Pete. Bad enough Doc's icy clithanger, but this spotty-dick dark-night-of-the-soul horsepoop's within an ace of finishing the boy off.

—Nonsense. He'll be all right. And I disagree. I don't think this has anything to do with so-called soul-searching or with any other kind of meaning whatsoever. Just the opposite. Cassandra is, as always, in her mindless anarchic way, trying to obliterate all meaning, to force the mind away from logical constructions and toward an acceptance of meaningless associations, beautiful only in their denial of meaning. Isn't that right?

— . . . !

—Well, there's your answer, you ol' quack. Smack on the snoot! And beautiful, my unsightly brown-eyed bumbo. It's plain barmy, all of it! And now black leader! Fffoo! If Pete ever crawls outa that inky sludge, I wouldn't be surprised he gave you all the royal digit and tootled off for all and good.

—He won't quit. He has no choice.

—No. That's probably true. But where can he go from here, Cora? He's done everything!

—Home movies. Amateur stuff. It's where hardcore is moving. So it's where we're putting our resources. The studio's closed.

He's had episodes like this before, though he only remembers them when he's in another. It's like going to sleep without going to sleep, but dreamless, imageless. Can't even *remember* light and color. Can't remember much of anything. Silent except for a faint static, which may just be the restless popping of his idled brain. Yet in spite of the prevailing silence, he understands certain things being said about him, as if he'd fallen off the screen onto a printed page. Things about what he's doing here and why it happened. He senses, vaguely, that it's a tragedy. No helpful titles, though, just black on black. Very thick. Like soup, black soup. Right against his eyeballs. In his ears and nose, too, leaking into his head and blotting out all else. Scary. Each time he's in one of these, he thinks he'll never not be. That this is what it means to *be*, the rest all illusion. The radical absurdity at the core. The *hard* core: black on black. And he has found it after much travail and, having found it, now cannot leave it, because when you know something, you know something. Where'd he get such an idea, here in the darkness? From his silently throbbing prick, probably. His only companion. Can't trust it, though, as he knows from long experience (he remembers that he *has* had long experience). Thinking about his prick reminds him of Clara's lecture, the one where she used it as a projector. Maybe it's his prone position that has recalled it to him, his fear, the ache in his balls. Which is oddly reassuring: I ache, therefore I am. What a thought. Too big; it's like a clot, a clotted thought. He's suddenly very tired. Enough hard thinking for one day—speaking loosely: How long *has* he been here? He doesn't know. Feels like forever. Let's sleep for a while, he thinks. Just a couple of winks, a year or two. . . . But the thought of his prick as a projector is like a worm in his brain. It won't let him disconnect. It provokes him to fumble about down there, trying to locate the gizmo's ON switch. When he finds it, the light, dim as it is, is almost shocking, a thin narrow ray needling straight up into the dusty darkness. He puts the palm of his hand in front of it, but he can't see anything there. Well, yes, a faint squared glimmering. Just enough light leaking around the edges to see it's merely more black on black, like a camera in his head registering his present plight. Then he sees a tiny dot of bright light in the center of his palm, slowly enlarging, and as the light increases he can see it is an image of a train approaching in a lightless tunnel. There is the silhouetted figure of a man stretched out on the tracks. It is he, he can feel the tracks beneath his butt and shoulders now. Oh my god, he's going to get hit, he's going to die! So? He doesn't care. Fuck it. Let it come. But the projected image of himself on the palm of his hand is not so cool. That one's up and running, holding himself with both hands, the train bearing down on him from behind, his shadow racing hugely ahead of him. There's probably something like the thunderous clatter of steel wheels, a shrieking whistle, he's not sure, he's just barreling madly down the black tunnel in front of the speeding train, deafened by his own panic, hoping there's someplace he can leap aside to in time. Yes! A platform! He can see it in the darkness ahead as the train's headlight picks it out! He makes one last desperate effort and heaves himself up onto the platform as the train goes rocketing past.

He lies there, wheezing heavily, in a pile of oily old rags and newspapers on the dark stone platform, wondering what he was doing down there on the tracks. He can't remember. A complete blank. Or black. Must have fallen. It's an easy guess, being more a condition of late than an event. The last thing he recalls is a film he was making or thinking of making about a picnic in a green place. One of his old *Jack and Jill* movies probably, teaching ingenues their ABCs while they offered up their pretty little lunch boxes to a hungry man; something like that. Silent but with a zoom lens, narrowing down to a tight focus, which, in his mind's eye, is a black hole. With beribboned fringes. Not sure where that was, but he knows where he is now. He can hear the rats gnawing away nearby, the faint *ticky-tick* of their little claws as they scurry about. Even that he can hear. Can see them, too; all his senses have returned. Not excluding that of smell. The stink of ancient rot and ratshit drives his nose up out of the rubbish heap. He peers around, spies the old slatted bench, crawls back up on it, pulls his tweed coat around him. Thus, everything comes full circle, he tells the rats. He's been who-knows-where and he's been nowhere. And back again. But he doesn't feel completely whole. It's like he left something behind down there when he fled from the train. He checks. No, everything still in place, even the blue balls, his cock of many colors. Empty pockets, as before, except for a pair of damp panties. He sniffs them hopefully but is disappointed. Maybe he picked them up in the platform garbage. He starts to throw them away, decides against it. If someone claims them, he can ask her what happened.

An empty train pulls up at the platform and its doors gape open, inviting him. Come on, enough's enough, we'll take you away from here. He doesn't trust it. He'd rather walk. He doesn't know where in the city he is, but he'll take his chances. Of course, walking isn't at present what he does best. And the station's closed down, probably locked up, maybe even paved over at the top. So, all right, there's no place he wants to go that he can get to, he'll just stay where he is. Warm the bench. Keep the rats company. He expects the train to close its doors and pull away, but it continues to sit there, waiting. Whooshing faintly. Well, he will outwait it. Of course, a standoff's possible. He can feel their energies slowly winding down: his, the train's. Perhaps they'll shut down together. The train seems to be exuding an aroma, a womanly smell. Hard to resist, but he resists it, though it aggravates the tingle at the end of his blistered dick. He tries to place the aroma, running through his long and distinguished history. Poor as his memory is, there's not a one he can't recall. They are named, dated, defined, labeled in his head like wines, from vintage classics to everyday varietals. But this one he does not recognize. It's new. He pulls out the panties. Behind the damp panic: Could it be? The train's motor rumbles, starting up again. The message at the tip of his penis now seems to read: SUDDENLY . . . ! He leaps aboard, battering his way through the closing doors.

She is not aboard. (He is in love with her. He has just remembered this.) The train is empty. Tricked again. But as the train pulls away, he sees her. Staggering down the dark platform, glancing fearfully over her shoulder, adorned with a few bright tatters, otherwise stripped bare, hammering tearfully on the train windows, her lips forming urgent aspirates and plosives. He bangs from his side, trying to force the doors open, but it's no use. He searches for an emergency cord, finds only a little white string, yanks on it, and a tampon pops out. Which—even as he's cursing his luck and the whole fucking public transport system—brings the train to a screeching stop. The doors pop open with a sucking sound, and, beating off unseen attackers, she throws herself inside, collapsing at his feet, and the doors slam shut and the train rolls on.

He stands over her, gazing breathlessly down upon this tender abused creature who has so captured his imagination. And his heart. He remembers everything now, all the way back to childhood (they were playmates!), his head suddenly full of wonderful memories he never knew he had. For all that he's suffered, he feels amply rewarded: that they are together, that she is here with him at last! She is curled up on her side on the filthy floor of the clattering train, sobbing, gasping for breath, her eyes squeezed shut against the recent terrors, her little breasts heaving and falling under the tatters, bobbing a bit when a sob shakes her or the train rocks. An empty beercan rolls back and forth beside her head. I adore this woman, he thinks, watching tremors ripple down her pale shoulders and midriff and into her sweet flanks and delicate limbs. I have loved her all my life. I have promised myself to her (he wants to kiss those quivering flanks, those limbs, lick them all over), and I will keep my promise (and he will). He feels vaguely heroic. He kicks the beercan down to the other end of the car.

She looks up at him over her shoulder and at what he is holding by its string. Is that . . . mine? she asks tremulously, and puts her hand between her legs. He can just see the tips of her fingers poking out between her drawn-up thighs. She's so beautiful! Then suddenly her eyes start with alarm and she shrinks away: Oh no! she screams. They're *blue!*

Ah! Well. Just temporarily—

—And that *thing* with the *polkadots!* Dear god in heaven! What *is* it?

Don't be afraid, he tells her, leaning toward her to help her up. She tries to scramble away, her hand in front of her face, but she's in a corner, the seats above her torn away. Really, it doesn't usually look like this. Or, rather, that's what he thinks he's telling her; what he actually hears himself say is:

—What is it? It is my prick, my dear, my pego, my cock! My bum-tickler! My gully-raker, my beard-splitter, my pussy-driller! So spread your sweet ass, you whore, for I am mad with desire!

—Oh no! Never! she screams. How dare you? Take your hands away! You mustn't!

No, wait! he cries. I'm not going to hurt you! I'm just trying to help! I love you! I'll always love you and protect you forever! Those are the words his lips form, but what comes out is:

—Resistance is useless, you little cunt! You are in my power! I'm going to fuck your ears off! You won't be able to walk for a week!

—Oh! What are you doing? she cries. No! No! Stop, you fiend! Help!

But don't you recognize me, Constance? he begs, having dropped his trousers as though to reveal to her his honest intentions. It's me! The one you love! The one you pledged your heart to! He spreads his legs for balance in the rocking train, which is picking up speed. Look! Don't you remember? *I'm the boy next door!*

—What? Do you refuse me, you impudent tart? This comes out instead; he can't hold it back. When he clamps his mouth shut, it comes snorting out his nose.

She is twisting and writhing on the floor beneath him, trying to conceal her private parts with one hand, top and bottom, front and behind, while fending him off with the other; everything's moving and jiggling, it's a sight to see, but he looks only to clothe her, as it were, with his looking. I wish solely to serve you, he insists, but hears:

—I will do wholly as I wish with every curve and cranny of your shameless person, you little vixen. Your pussy, arse, mouth, or butter-bags (butter-bags?) are mine, all mine! So prepare yourself! *Your time has come!*

—Oh, *please*, sir! she sobs. *Don't!* Have mercy! *Spare me!*

—You may blubber all you like! Your tears only urge me on! If you resist, it will go all the worse for you! Do you understand?

What does he mean? Is he going to beat her with the tampon?

—Oh, help! Won't someone save me? she sobs. No! No! Do not be cruel! Stop! *Aa-aa-arrgh!*

It's amazing! He *has* beat her with the tampon! She has fainted with the first lash and he is kneeling on the bouncing metal floor between her pale quivering thighs, fallen slackly apart, his humming rod zooming in on its target like a guided missile. He doesn't want this! Not this way! He *loves* her! *Stop!* But he can't stop. *It's not me doing this!* he cries, but as though in some other movie; here, only piggish grunts can be heard above the clattering roar of the train and he is already breaking through! Ah! It's crisp and sharp, like tearing into filmstrip. If he'd intended to hold back, the violently rocking train (it's out of control, he thinks, but only with the back part of his brain, the useless part, the rest focused now on one thing and one thing only) won't let him; he's plunging away, or being plunged; the effect is the same, wow (*grunt!*), it's all boiling up; it's incredible; everything's shaking; he's never had it like this! It's terrible! It's wonderful! It's the worst thing he's ever done! It's the fuck of his life! She has awakened and is whimpering pathetically, her eyes closed, rolling her head from side to side. His mouth kisses hers as it passes (it does so on its own, he's busy forming apologies);

he tastes the sweetness of her lips, dips his tongue into her cheeks and swabs her clamped teeth with it as though to salve a wound. She tries to push him off, but feebly now, her strength depleted, her pushes adding to his pleasure and to his anguish. We're going to crash, he thinks, his eyes squeezed shut, his whole body puckered up in anticipation of the imminent explosion, both inside and out—

But instead, hands reach under the overcoat into his armpits and lift him firmly out of her (the train has stopped—god, there's blood everywhere!) and carry him to the open doors (Wait! he gasps, I can explain!) and hold him up there, pants still around his dangling ankles, in front of a crowd of people wearing party hats and masks and carrying drinks and sex toys in their hands.

—*For he's a jolly good phallus,* they sing, raising their glasses and dildos. *For he's a jolly good phallus . . . !*

It is not an underground platform. The train has stopped at the front door of his own penthouse flat. All his friends and fans are up here, stoned and happy, whooping it up. Big banners, which look like movie posters, read: CUNTGRATULATIONS! and BLOOD ON THE ALTAR! and RING OUT THE BELLS! LUCKY RIDES THE BRIDE IN HOLEY WETCOCK! Or does it say WRING OUT THE BALLS? Probably it does, he can't see; he's surrounded by drunken well-wishers dressed in funny costumes, pressing drinks and party drugs on him, kissing him, slapping his cold and naked butt, complimenting him on his exciting new career move. His limp prick is bloody, he sees through his tears, but the itch at the tip and the blisters are gone and his balls have lost their peculiar color and shrunk back into their gloomy wrinkled sac where they belong. He glances back over his shoulder. The train is gone. Just his front door there with its phallic handle and cunt-shaped keyhole, the door hung tonight with a black wreath made out of old cellulose film strips and tied with a silken sash that says: SO LONG, BATCH SNATCH! HELLO, MATE MEAT! Around him: boozy singing, whoops and giggles, loud laughter. It's a happy occasion—he understands that; it's supposed to be—but he's bawling like a baby.

—Hey, Mr. Pierre! What are you crying about? You just had the greatest fuck since the world began!

—Did I? He blows his nose in his shirttails. I must have missed it.

Knock knock!

—Who's there? Aha! *Hugh's* there! It's Hugh Manatee in drag, decked out like Jocelyn Krautz! And there comes Jane Gang disguised as Frieda Peephole!

That's Cleo broadcasting the new masked-ball arrivals over the intercom. It's a good party. He's glad he's come. Rather, that he's invited them all here tonight, to his home, his pad, his famous penthouse flat, or that someone has, for he seems to be both host and guest of honor.

—Next we have, bringing with him the ripe odor of royalty, Prince E. Paul Orguns, together with Don Roque Z. Bote, and Lady Chnite without Sir Cece! Dragging in behind her in hymeneal splendor is Lord Pants with Peter X. Post, Shawn O'Leasgott, and Utta Leigh! B. Rephta Reezan! Give them a big squeeze, everybody!

He greets them all, passes among them, serving and being served, kissing and being kissed, grateful to be out of the anonymous crush of the snowblown city and among people he knows or probably knows, enjoying a drink, a toke, a joke, a bit of friendly fondling on this, the last night of his old life. Which is being celebrated on all the walls, where classic movies from his early days, mostly silent or projected silently, play nostalgically. He toasts those days and his own health and potency and theirs, laughs at the costumes and noms de fête, accepts his guests' vulgar wedding-night bromides gracefully (it's an old and venerable ritual; he respects it), slaps bucking bottoms affectionately, and has his own slapped under the nightshirt with equal affection. That's his party costume, a Wee Willie nightshirt. Just tonight, he's a boy again. And after that monster orgasm (so they tell him; he walks among them in festive spirit, yet somewhat in sorrow—must have been a jump cut of some kind, one of his many losses, fuck his luck), his famous willy is boyish as well and a source among his guests of some amusement. They wag it, tug at it as if it were a false beard, lift it up to peek under, looking for the real one hidden behind it.

—And now here comes Baird Nates, friends, showing his Jenny Talia around the place! And the one entering behind him is Josephine VerFuggin, who used to be Mary Tell Bliss, Sir Raffick's daughter, until Ray Pissed changed her style, or so they say! That's it, Josie, get it off and get it on! And who's that knocking? Ah! Open the door there, please, for Morgan Fusions!

When he first arrived through that door, they tossed him in the pool to wash the troubled day away, and then Cissy's crew from the studio gave him a spectacular rubdown on his table (didn't need the hole there) and powdered his raw bottom and oiled his stained and shriveled pecker and cleaned out his ears and nose and trimmed his nails and kissed his many hurts away and dressed him in the little nightshirt, smoothing it down with all their hands and laughing and crying as if it might be the last time. As maybe it was. He finds Cissy herself in the music room now, working up a cappella variations on their *Music Lesson* melodies made from anagrams of the scale, using a simple amplified keyboard and an ensemble of whooping partygoers. The percussive effects are sensational, but they are all too drunk to stay on key and, for all their enthusiasm, there's a lack of focused energy. Too much ardent play (they're in and out of each other con capriccio), not enough art. Cissy's also wearing something like a nightshirt, though it looks more like an old washed-out sack used by a hundred people to jerk off in. She sees his puzzled look and laughs and says, Guess! And if you say a used scumbag—which was just what he was about to say—then you're one yourself! Wait! Here's a clue! And she lifts the nightshirt and invites him to press her belly button. When he does so, a tune emerges from somewhere between her thighs, fluttering her golden pubic hairs.

—God, that's beautiful! What *is* it?

He presses again, counts: twenty-four fluted notes. A tough one. But three sets of paired tones, and he's played this musical gamut game with her enough to anticipate a patterned word-making use of the five consonants and two vowels. Locating either A or E, he can usually scale the rest, if she isn't using some weird key, which is unlikely, given the limited versatility of her instrument. He puts his ear to it and presses again, and she gasps—It tickles!—and clenches his hair. Whatever key the phrase is in, it ends on its own tonic following a pair of descending full tones, *dum-dum-dum:* that eliminates C-major, for then it would end EDC. In fact, the only two anagram possibilities are in the keys of D and G, resulting in FED and BAG. Cissy gazes down at him lovingly through strands of loose blond hair, a twinkle in her eye, as he pushes his finger into her tummy once more. The first pair of doubled notes are also in the tonic with the preceding note a tone and a half below, yielding either BDD or EGG: and—aha!—he has it. He plays it again, rising, and winks as she twitches and giggles and rubs her thighs together.

—A FADED EGG-BEDABBED FEEDBAG!

She reaches under his nightshirt and wraps her arms around him. You're a genius, L.P.! she whispers into his shoulder. She's trembling. She might be crying. He squeezes her soft warm bottom as he's done so many times before and hugs her close. I'm going to miss you so!

—We'll still see each other, Cissy.

—Maybe. It won't be the same.

—No . . .

She leaves him then, or he leaves her; he's in the den playing orgy-porgy-pud-in-the-pie with his guests, and then he's in the bathroom under the champagne shower, or out in the workout area, watching the revelers play pee tag in the swimming pool (those hard white cheeks bobbing above the blue water and geysering like a spouting whale; they can only be Cleo's); the continuity's breaking up a bit, maybe he's not as sober as he thought he was, and a good thing too. It's all getting pleasantly light and loose, the snows are receding, winter's a distant improbable memory—yes, make no mistake, it's good to be up here, surrounded by friends and lovers, far from the bitter night without! He's laughing and singing, they all are, momentarily denying the morrow and the ends of reel rushing at them (he's of course celebrating a happy new beginning, it's all spooled up, that's what they're telling him, though he doesn't know who's in it or what the script is), easing their hearts with the happy din of a party in the city, his heart too is eased.

He drifts from room to room, or the rooms drift past him, a softly lit montage of foreplay and ecstasy, both live and projected, the borders between them slipping, as though to say: Nothing stays the same. Everything is everything else (*There is no script, that's just the point,* someone says, *it's a kind of voice-over*), just go with it. The music, too, changes with each crossing of a threshold, here a thumping rock beat, there a minuet or jig, then jazz or ribald party songs. He hums along. Glasses are filled and emptied, filled and emptied, nipples tweaked, drugs passed, behinds sniffed, wigs and false noses traded. People dressed as various bodily parts and conditions introduce themselves as Hans N.

Feat, Esau Fuggus, Armand L. Beau, Adie Postishoo, Sally Verigland, Vera Coatsvanes, Hal E. Tosiss. A lot of wild costume combinations up here tonight, must have been a big raid on the wardrobe lockers. There's Clara, masquerading as a diagram in a sex manual with black bars radiating from all her private parts, Cassie as Madame Totem Adam wreathed in palindromic loops (her slender hips are twined with interlacing bands of LIVE DEVILS and SAD ASSES, her waist encircled with I'M IN EDEN I'M IN EDEN, there's a beadstring of EVE'S BOOBS wound about her small breasts, and on her bald head she wears a headband that reads, in either direction, over and over: TRIBE REBIRTH TRIBE REBIRTH TRIBE REBIRTH), and old Kate as her own grotesque self, though somewhat optimistically calling herself Fornie Kate. More like Rusty Kate, he remarks, when she bumps up against him (but what's-her-name, he asks himself, the one he keeps meeting in his travels, where is she?), and she grins around one tooth.

—Your fiancée?

It's not Kate (she's gone), it's a woman dressed up as Madame Orifices (did he ask aloud? must have), who has come up behind him and slipped a finger lovingly up his butt, or else he's backed into her, but *lovingly* still applies. He nods and (lovingly) hugs her finger with his cheeks in reply. Her costume changes even as he stares at her—even her shape changes, the color of her eyes, a kind of restless morphing—but she is who she is and she can't hide it.

—She was here earlier, Willie, looking shy and beautiful and pleased as punch, showing off her beautiful engagement ring with the ruby-tipped cock and blue diamond balls. I must say, I was very envious. But it's bad luck for a bride to see the groom on their wedding night, so she left early. Besides, your marriage proposal left her a bit tender, I think.

—That's what it was, then. And she's the one. He's pleased and smiles wistfully (must have been great). He realizes, gazing at Cally, alias Madame Orifices, all of which are on show, that he's seen her earlier today as well: the salesgirl in the underground kiosk, the one who blistered his bone-on. Cally always did have a way of setting him on fire. Even now there's a spicy tingle in his anus, though her finger's gone; she's going too.

—It's hard to think of you as a married man, Willie, but just remember, as they say in the business, it's not the yoke, but how you sell it! She winks as she dissolves into the thickening crowd. And, hey, now we can get into the adultery thing!

That's probably what she says. It's somewhat lost in party roar, which is up several decibels. Glasses are falling and breaking; syringes crackle underfoot; costumes are ripped away; there are groans, screams, of delight maybe, who can say? Projectors are getting bumped and the old films running on the walls are already overlapping at the edges. Another half hour or so and they won't amount to much more than a light show. On a wall here in the vestibule (masked revelers are still pouring in, now unannounced; he greets them as before, they laugh, kiss, tug his weenie), *The Gentlemen's Club* is playing, an old silent Peter Prick flick about a rich men's club that imports starving children from foreign lands and rears them as sex pets, collared and tethered, fed from troughs, not his best movie. It was in the early days of lap dissolves, used then mostly for visual metaphors, images of the naked children, for example, dissolving somewhat clumsily to piglets or bottles of cellared wines or bull's-eye targets to suggest the club's pedagogical philosophy. The remake as a full-color Lucky Pierre musical with high overhead shots of the children in choreographed routines, all massed together to depict the warlike dance of spermatozoa, was much more successful. Oddly, he looks older in this old film than he does now, so harsh and revealing was the medium then. The motion is jerky, and in this light the flicker is worse than ever. There are breaks in the film, bad scratches, and much of the contrast is gone. Time wears away all things. He knows this—and knows too that, as Cleo like to say, excess renews. Why else have a party?

As if bidden, she comes by now, dressed in nothing but a pussy ring and a cast-iron slave band around one lean thigh, wet from the pool (he's in by the pool, not sure how he got here), breathless, laughing, chased by the Bang Gang. She ducks down in front of him, using him as a shield, her intense green eyes flashing, wet red ringlets bouncing like little springs.

—Hey, happy anniversary, lover! she pants into his crotch, and gives him a hello lick. When do we celebrate?

—Well, things are changing, Cleo—

—No, not Cleo! she cries, leaning back below him, her arms outspread. Knocker knocker! Guess who!

—Guess who what?

—Not *who what*, dummy! *Bertha* who! Who I am!

—Bertha?

—Bertha de Soot!

—Ah. . . .

She laughs and lifts his nightshirt and spins his limp Wee Willie noodle like twirling a tassel, snapping at it with her bright white teeth. And who are you tonight, baby? Drew Penn Dewdats?

—No, I'm just Mel Lowenmary, Cleo. I'm Phelan Phine. Titus A. Piper. Stu de Zagills. I'm Hy Assakeit.

But she's already off and running with a *See you later, lover!* cry. She won't, though, he knows. See him. That part of his life is over. In the livingroom (he is in the livingroom, the pool is somewhere else), the wall-to-wall carpet is being ripped up so that the heavy shagdancing might begin, and this violence to his space does not surprise him. He understands he will not live here anymore. Furniture is being dragged out to the rooftop terrace and thrown into the street below; windows are smashed open to freshen the dense crowded air. He smiles and throws a glass through a window himself. Fuck it. Let it all go. As the windows shatter, the lights seem to dim and the racket diminishes, as if the wind entering the flat were blowing the sound and light away, and a kind of chilly peace descends upon him, but only for a moment, like a fleeting preview of a coming attraction (or terror), for he is suddenly bathed in light, caught in the aura of some great new excitement.

—It has been a divine party, Mr. Pierre, says someone. It was kind of you to invite us.

It's the Mayor, costumed as the Queen of Heaven, with stars in her eyes behind blue shades, a sunny smile, leaking milk from one exposed breast and surrounded by a cluster of white dwarfs. How serenely she moves! She stands majestically in the middle of the room (whatever room this is), turning slowly, bringing everybody into orbit around her. He longs to get closer, but her entourage is too large: clusters of stars and starlets, radiant with her momentary blessings, the darker peripheral shapes of film crews, scriptwriters, distributors. All he can see are Cora's blue shades, reflecting myriad spots and stage lights, and, dimly behind them, her cold glittering eyes playing over him. Pulsar signals beat against his chest—or perhaps that's his own heart; he feels hot and cold all at once, eager and resistant, chosen and lost. He used to be at the very center of that select circle, but he has somehow slipped to the margins. And that's not milk spilling out of her great breast as he'd supposed, it's frost crystals. They float between them, twinkling alluringly in the bright lights, making his eyes water. She has that young rebel with her on a leash and collar, clearly sedated (her eyes are unfocused, her jaw hangs slack), whom she introduces as an urban gorilla being trained for the Wild Thing role in a new Sex Circus.

—Show them what you can do, dear, Cora says, and she unleashes her.

For a short time, the dull-eyed creature just squats there in the middle of the room, her knuckles touching the floor, black bush like a hairy paw between her gaped thighs, gazing blankly about, and an expectant silence sinks down around her—and then suddenly she rises up and shrieks and roars and beats her beautiful breasts and goes bounding about the room, swinging herself by the chandeliers and door frames, smashing everything in sight, ripping the fixtures from the walls, picking objects up, including the screaming guests, and heaving them through the windows. He is no exception, up he goes by scruff and scrotum, his Wee Willie nightshirt twisted up around his armpits, and suddenly he has a foreshortened view of her from the ceiling down the length of her powerful young arms, her black hair flying between them, her dark-nippled breasts, lit up by the room's radiant glow, thrust forward like armament (bumpers, they're sometimes called; they're like shining bumpers), her bare feet spread out below them as if her breasts were mounted on them. She carries him out onto the roof terrace and is about to pitch him over the wall—it's not the fall he fears, he's grown accustomed to that; it's the terrible cold, *that* he'll never get used to—but she peers up at him and her dilated eyes focus on his for a moment; she blinks and her wild rage subsides and she licks the spittle off her lips, staring at him as if with some primitive glimmer of recognition. He hears Cora's whip crack and his captor's searching gaze is crossed by a grimace of pain, and she lowers him to her breasts and returns meekly into the flat with him cradled there and drops him in the circle of light at Cora's feet.

—Sorry about that, Mr. Pierre, says the Mayor, snapping the collar back on her and flicking her perspiring haunches, hunkered down by his face, with the tip of the whip. She's still quite hard to handle. We'll have to put her back in her tight little cage and . . . ah . . . apply a bit more discipline.

—No, don't! he gasps. I didn't mind!

But they are gone, and the astral glow is gone with them, leaving behind a roisterous jammed-up darkness, most of the fixtures now ripped out, what flickering light there is supplied mainly by the projected films. From the floor, he has a view through feet and crashing asses of a party decaying into chaos, the film tracks, loud music, shrieks, wind, laughter blending into a kind of howling threnody. This isn't life as he'd imagined it. Not even close. He is ready for a change. The guests are fucking madly in fleshy daisychains just to stay warm—there's a bitter chill blowing in through the broken windows; flecks of snow—and some are smashing up the furniture and building bonfires. His films, tapes, photos, disks, posters are being tossed into the flames. Let them go. He doesn't want to be a living legend anymore. He feels he is drifting away from himself, but if so, there is still a self at least from which to drift, there always is, deep in the gonads somewhere, or in the liver, the breast, the spine—even if the mind goes, there's always locus . . . and the fear of that. . . . On the ceiling there's a film running of two skeletons, one flat out on a table and bucking upward, the other mounted above it. They look like they're rubbing sticks together to make a fire. A shadowy ethereal presence animates and surrounds each of the two skeletons, like a ghostly visitor. Their masquerade. And they don't seem naked at all. *For things are only what sentiment imagines them to be,* says the voice-over like a pronouncement from the heavens. Clara. Her fluoroscopic scene from *The Doctor's Examination.* He's the one on the bottom, he can tell; he's working twice as hard at it as she is. Where's all her fancy technique now, eh? Just a damp shadow in the pubic symphysis! The two skeletons are humping away more and more recklessly, as if they're trying to unhinge themselves. Suddenly, they tumble off the table, limb bones thrown outward; he sees a clavicle crack and shatter, a radius splinter, then the whole business explodes in a spray of flying sticks.

He scrambles to his feet, kicking past projectors and bodies, his heart hammering in his chest. *Whoo.* Where is he? He feels lightheaded. Maybe he got to his feet too fast. It comes and goes in nauseating waves, as if some amateur had got hold of the zoom lens and were whipping him to and fro. What he needs is a drink. But it's hard even to move. It's like the whole city is up here. For all the extras that the urban gorilla tossed out, as many more have come piling in and then some. Those fucking mostly have to go at it standing up or else, as here in the guestroom (he is in the guestroom now, hard to move maybe, but he is moving, call it moving), in great undulating piles on the wooden floor. The beds have been thrown out, carpets ripped away. He turns to stagger out, but drunken revelers push in and sweep him up, and the next thing he knows he's like that skeleton in the movie; he's the one on the bottom. Except that he's laughing. He doesn't know why. He can hardly breathe under all this humping flesh. What a party, he thinks. What a life. That threnetic roar of percussive rock, wind, pounding flesh, and the howls of solemn debauchery has faded, or maybe he's losing consciousness. Everything is becoming very remote. . . .

Then someone takes his hand and he feels himself being slipped out of the oily heap like a pick-up stick being carefully extracted from the bottom of a scattered pile. It is quiet Cassie, still in her Madame Totem Adam costume, her breast now crossed with sashes clipped fresh from her palindromic loops spool that read in any direction: AS DEEDS ARE RARER AS DEEDS ARE RARER, DROWN WORDS DROWN WORDS, and LOVERS REVOLT LOVERS REVOLT. She stands above him, her sashes and ribbons fluttering in the cold draft. In his bombed mind, he sees her as a kind of cobwebby tree out of some children's film about enchanted forests. Here's an odd thing, he reasons, with what reason he has left: Cassie champions simultaneity and multiplicity and disruption in all she does, believes in the circle, not the line (even now, if he closes his eyes, he can see somewhere near where the end of his nose might be, in white on black, the word EARLIER . . .), and yet he has lived today, as best he can recall (a mazy day; he may be wrong about this), a more linear life than in any of Clara's cool analytical industrial films or Cleo's documentaries. Cassie helps him to his feet, and he notices now that she wears over her little hairless mound a triangular G-string, bespangled with METROMORTEM, and, dangling from a gold chain around her throat, a dodecagonal medallion embossed with the twelve letters WED ICONOCIDE. All right. Sure. He's ready. He turns to look at the quivering orgiastic pile of bodies against the wall just as the wall gives way and several scores of his guests disappear into the snowblown night. The storm seems momentarily to get sucked down the city chasm behind them, but then their screams fade and the storm re-collects itself, comes whooshing back in. The ceiling sags. Cassie pulls him out of the room and closes the door behind them.

She leads him, still holding his hand, through the wall that used to separate the kitchen from his bedroom, out onto the roof terrace. It's freezing cold and he's dressed only in the thin nightshirt, but the wind has died down, the snow's let up, and anyway, he seems to have no choice.

—What is it, Cassie? he asks, his teeth chattering. What's happening?

She turns to look at him and where their glances meet, he seems to see: EACH QUESTION A QUESTION ALREADY LEARNT BY HEART, EACH STEP A STEP ALREADY TAKEN. The party sounds have faded entirely and the silence is immaculate. She looks up at the overcast wintry sky, and he follows her gaze. There is a film showing on the pale overhanging clouds. A trailer of some kind. A lovely pubescent girl is undressing before a mirror, tenderly pinching her tiny nipples, sliding her hands down her slender hips while looking over her shoulder at them, touching herself speculatively between her legs, where a downy new fluff has grown, her lips parted more in curiosity than in passion. There are flakes of snow still fluttering in the air, and they give the scene a strangely three-dimensional effect, as if the girl's explorations of herself were sending off picturesque sparks. The camera zooms back to reveal that we are looking in through a window. It zooms farther back into a room in the house next door, where a young man watches her through a zoom lens, a boy really, but fully grown with a thin new mustache on his lip, soft as the hair on the pubis of the girl next door. He has eager twinkling eyes and a throbbing erection in his pumping fist.

Ah! he gasps, shivering, and takes hold of himself once more. It's so good to be hard again! Cassie wraps her hand tenderly around his, and the sky fills with a low ecstatic hum, very slowly augmenting. Titles appear on the cloudscreen above.

Cumming Soon!

HOME MOVIES

Starring

Peter Prick: Boy

Constance Cunt:

Girl

Reel 5: Constance

Green fields, panned unsteadily with a handheld camera, wooded copse, wildflowers, spectacularly blue sky. Cows graze alongside bubbling brooks, appearing at one side of the jiggling frame, disappearing at the other. As the cows bobble away, they are replaced by a small brightly painted cottage with thatched roof, decorative gingerbread, gabled windows with leaded glass and flower boxes, and a carved wooden sign over the rose-red door: HONEYMOON COTTAGE. When the cottage is centered, there is a brief motionless pause. Then the door flies open and a man steps out in his undershirt and boxer shorts, smiling broadly, arms outspread in welcome and quivering erection poking through the shorts. It is he: young Peter Prick. His image begins to bounce and heaves in and out of focus as the camera approaches, apparently on the run, closing rapidly to a puckered mustachioed mouth and a colliding darkness. A hand-lettered title appears:

SMACK!

After a brief black pause, the camera opens onto a bright sunny room with flowery curtains and wallpaper, wall-to-wall shag carpeting, soft colorful furniture, sensuous seascapes and still lifes in primary colors (or perhaps the amateur film registers only primary colors), television and film screens, bowls of flowers and souvenir ashtrays, a cuckoo clock with a miniature HONEYMOON COTTAGE sign over its red door, and lots of large plump cushions tossed invitingly about. The clock door opens (the camera advances unsteadily to a close-up) and a little winged penis pops out to the end of its erected length, flapping its balls like meaty wings, and collapses back into itself. Three times. Title, with a scattering of hand-drawn musical notes:

I LOVE YOU!
I LOVE YOU!
I LOVE YOU!

A slow exploratory pan follows, the camera pausing to examine a damp stain on the yellow sofa, the idyllic sunlit country scene out a window, a pile of vacation snapshots on the gateleg table, the flimsy cast-off panties beneath it. An opened bottle of champagne and two half-filled flutes sit on the painted sideboard as though posing for a family portrait. Across the hall in the next room, under ceiling mirrors, there is a large circular bed with a heart-shaped headboard and crimson-and-gold satin sheets, delicately rumpled and spotted. There are also mirrors on most of the walls, though the camera, even while exploring the room tenderly as though caressing it, manages not to see itself. Beyond the bed, there is a half-open door; the camera peeks around its edge into a brightly tiled and mirrored bathroom with a green yoni-shaped tub laden with soaps and shampoos and sponges and erotic tub toys, a matching bidet, television screens mounted on the walls, and racks of soft colorful towels, embroidered with CONNIE ♥ PETER. The door opens wider, revealing a young woman—*the* young woman: Mrs. Peter Prick—sitting naked on the toilet, doubled over, picking at her toes. She looks up in alarm, snatches a towel to cover herself, and, staggering forward in a crouch, slams the door against the camera.

After another dark pause, the camera opens on the livingroom, which has been cleared, the yellow sofa pushed back against the wall. In front of it, a large red hoop has been fitted upright into a slot on a small blue block. The pretty young lady of the house, dressed in a gold halter and silver miniskirt, moves away from the camera toward the hoop and sofa, turns around to face the fixed lens, and lifts a hand-painted sign that reads:

MY HUSBAND!

She waves at the camera and disappears off left. When she returns, she is wearing a top hat a size too large for her and brandishing a whip. She points off left, puts a whistle to her lips, and blows an unheard whistle. She snaps her whip, and he (he, her proud young husband) bounds on from left to right, wearing white longjohns, bunny ears, and a fluffy tail. He hops through the hoop, hands cupped together at his chest, twitches his mustache, and disappears off right. She points in his direction, blows again, and cracks the whip, and he scrambles in on all fours in a red bellhop cap and jacket, the sort worn by organ grinders' monkeys, his bare tail rouged pink. He somersaults through the hoop, turns to grin idiotically at the camera and waggle his fingers, thumbs in his ears, then bounds off left. She whistles and whips the air, and he edges in from the left in a fedora and tweed overcoat, collar up around his ears, legs bare. He looks both ways, steps stealthily through the hoop, turns to face the camera, flashes, and slinks off right. She blows and snaps the whip and he strolls in suavely, dressed in a fashionable chalk-striped worsted jacket and trousers, powder-blue shirt, and burgundy silk tie, smoking a briar pipe, one hand in a jacket pocket. He steps disdainfully through the hoop and emerges at the other side naked. He looks around in astonishment, covers himself, leaps back through the hoop, and reappears dressed as before, though his pants are around his knees, his tie is unknotted, and the jacket is gone. The ringmistress flicks the whip against his backside, and in shock he lurches back through the hoop, appearing naked once more on the other side, but now with a red welt angling across his buttocks. He examines his new stripe, wincing, and stalks off left in a pout. She points, whistles, and lashes the air with the whip, but he does not reappear. She disappears off left and in a moment returns, pulling him in by his penis as though on a leash. He is now dressed in a particolored vest, dog collar, and pointed clown's cap. With a firm little yank, she brings him to a squat, indicates the hoop, and crisply whips his tail. Mouth gaping in a silent yelp, he leaps into the hoop holding his rear, but he does not reappear on the other side. She peers into the hoop one way, then the other, removes it from its pedestal and bounces it against the floor, blows in it, passes her arm through it, and raises it flat over her head. He falls out in a ballerina's pink tutu and stiff skirt, looking confused and decidedly unhappy. He tries to tug the ballerina costume off, but it is too tight. He is almost unable to walk. He takes the hoop away from her, limps mincingly through it, and vanishes again. She examines the hoop in puzzlement, flexes it, shakes it, reaches through it, waves her hand about with her eyes closed as though trying to feel something on the other side, and then spins it, whips it around behind her back, and returns it to the blue block. She blows the whistle mightily, her cheeks puffing out, and claps her hands twice: He steps out of both sides naked. He stares at himself with some amazement, making mirrored gestures. The only difference between the twinned images is that one is erect, the other flaccid. A little balloon appears above the ringmistress, its letters dancing as though hand-lettered directly onto the print:

OH DEAR!

She urges the two of them to reenter the hoop with encouraging pats to their behinds, or at least to that general vicinity, for they are not wholly substantial, as though diminished by the doubling; the background leaks faintly through both Peters, and her hand seems almost to pass through them. They both peer over their shoulders at this phenomenon with mirrored unease mingled with longing, but finally, apprehensively, though in perfect mimicry, they obey her, tiptoeing into the hoop from opposite sides and disappearing into each other. She bows to the camera, holding her halter in place (the audience erupts in laughter and applause), then pulls the hoop down over her own head and vanishes as well, leaving only her whip and top hat behind. The camera continues to gaze fixedly at the static image of the yellow sofa with hoop, whip, and top hat, while the applause and cheers continue.

—Wow! That's wonderful! I didn't know you could do so many tricks with those simple little do-thingies!

—Just like the gadget between your legs, sweet love. When it's open.

—That do-thingy's not simple, my dear.

—No, you're right. Nor little either. But full of marvelous surprises, just like Mrs. Prick's film! Smashing!

Their livingroom is full of neighbors invited over by Connie (this is how he understands it) to have some beer and chocolate cake and onion dip and view her latest home movie. Or movies: mostly just little unedited exercises, loosely spliced together and about as sophisticated as finger painting. But then, she's just a child, or childlike anyway, so full of cheerful spontaneity, goofily but delightfully unpredictable. Her films, however silly, are fun to make, the most fun he's had in ages, or seems to have had.

—Yes, it's so imaginative and clever!

—And sexy, too! You really know how to lay on that whip!

—I wish I could get my wife to take pictures of me like that!

—I'm afraid you'd need a stand-in for the best bits, dearest.

—Thank you, everybody, but I know it's not very good. I'm still just learning.

—Nonsense! It's spectacular! And that miniskirt is so cute!

—Really? I thought maybe it was a little too plain. And shiny.

—Oh no! It was just right! You could see everything in it like a mirror!

—I loved that moment at the end when the hoop dropped past the hem of it, Mrs. Prick, leaving only your bare legs showing, and then seemed almost to lift back up for a peek before falling to the floor—*whooeee!* Just look at what that did to my pants!

—Well, you're all very kind, but I still have so much to learn. I get the exposure all wrong and it's never really quite in focus and I don't know anything about dissolves or montage or mattes or all those lovely things they do in the real movies. I mean, *process* shots: I don't even know what they *are!* Also, it would help if it had sound—what do you call it? a track—you know, a sound track? Like fanfares, whistles, drumrolls—

—And whip cracks! Oh yes! I can *feel* it! Good idea!

—It *is* a good idea, but I don't know *how* yet. I can't even find the *button*. I'm such a beginner. A total nincompoop, really. Peter calls me his little green—you know, green behind? I've just got to the point where I can turn the darned thing on and off.

—You're too modest, dear. Your movie is stunning just as it is! So tender and eloquent! Don't you agree, Mr. Prick?

—Ah! Well, to tell the truth—

—Oh, Peter isn't the one to ask. He's got no critical sense at all; he adores everything I do. Or almost everything. And anyway, he's more like a projectionist when he's not the thing projected.

—He must love all that magic stuff, though! It's just what most people's marriages lack, naming no names.

—Actually, I think he'd like me to be—well, a little more straightforward. You know, simply find what you're looking for and zoom in?

—Wham bam and in the can, you mean. But where's the fun in that? Believe me, a good movie's like good foreplay, young Mr. Prick, you have to—oops! The sofa just vanished too! I'd almost forgot the film was still running!

With a little pop, the fixed livingroom image, which is an image of the room in which they sit, has been abruptly displaced on the screen by black leader. There is a staticky sound now, not unlike a tongue clicking against the roof of a dry mouth, and occasional pinpoints of light like starry glimmerings on the ceiling of an old empty movie palace.

—It was so wonderful! I hate to see it come to an end!

—It was great of you to let us see it, Mrs. Prick! And you too, Mr. Prick. Thanks for inviting us over!

—We're so glad you've become neighbors!

—Wait, there's more! That's just the first part. Unless you've had enough?

—Enough? Are you kidding?

—This is the most excitement we've had since we moved here!

There is a settling back into chairs, some throat clearing, a few zippers opening or closing. Connie slips over to give the projectionist a little hug and a peck on the cheek (*I love you!* she whispers, which sends a tremor down his spine all the way to his sphincter), before returning to the little director's chair he gave her. He's not sure what's coming next, but he hopes it's a love scene. He wants to see his beloved in his arms; it would be a kind of confirmation, a witnessing, like fucking under mirrors, a possession that is more than possession. All the delightful things of the eye, as the poster copy says.

—I'm so happy there's more! I simply *adore* watching cocks and cunts!

—Me too! And playing with my own when I do!

—They're so pretty! Especially on the big screen!

—And it's even better when they belong to ordinary folk like ourselves. Somehow it's just more *intimate* than the fancy professional movies. More *touching*.

—That's true. I get wet just watching the jiggle of a handheld camera! Here! You can feel. . . .

A new title appears, interrupting the black leader:

HOUSE WORK

OR

R
HO~~U~~SE PLAY?

The man of the house is washing the windows and at the same time dusting a table behind him with a feather duster shoved up his ass. He twitches his behind provocatively at the camera, raising a cloud of white dust. *Cut.*

He is watering the plants by peeing on them, seen in profiled silhouette against sunny conservatory windows. He holds the watering can high over his mouth, the stream from the can matched by his own; as he pours, so does he pee. When he lowers the can, both flows stop, and when he raises it they start again. *Cut.*

He is making the circular bed, tugging the fitted satin sheets into place, spreading over them the soft bleached pubic-hair coverlet, smoothing it all down flat. As he does so, it begins to move in the middle more and more furiously, the coverlet and the gold-and-crimson sheets are thrown back, and to his astonishment his wife pops out. She scolds him with a waggle of her finger for making the bed with her in it. As she trips by in her nightie on the way to the bathroom, he tries to pat her bottom but she twists away. He shrugs, makes up the bed again, and again, no sooner is it neatly tucked and flattened than it starts to stir, roil, and bulk up, the coverlet and sheets fly back, and there she is again, waggling her admonitory finger. He pushes his pants down and reaches for her, but she slaps his hands away and dashes off to the bathroom. He leaves his trousers off, his underwear too, and makes up the bed a third time, less painstakingly this time, ready to pounce if it starts to move again. And—hah!—there she goes! He jumps under the sheets and finds himself in bed with a wild bear, rearing up slowly as though from a deep hibernation, eyes red and fanged mouth foaming.

EXIT HUBBY IN HASTE
CHASED BY BEAR

—Oh, Peter! He's such a ham! But I love him so, I really do!

When the titles disappear, Mr. and Mrs. Prick are seen walking with several small children through a great hall filled with people sucking and fucking each other, pointing out the various sights, and taking photographs. The little one is crying. Perhaps she needs a change of diapers.

—Whoops! Sorry! That one's out of place.

—Hey, wait! What *was* that?

—You know, Peter. The day we took the children to an orgy. It was arranged for us by the municipal travel bureau. It was a lovely outing, and I think the children got a lot out of it. *I* certainly did!

—Oh yes, we've done that. But now that the children are grown and have to pay full fare, we can't afford it.

—But who *were* those children?

—Ours, silly. Whose else would they be?

—The price of admission's not so bad. But it's all the extras. The rides and cam shots and souvenirs—

—Wait a minute! We've got *children*?

—Of course! Lots of them! We're married, aren't we?

—And toys . . .

—But that's—!

—Shush, Mr. Prick! Don't spoil the movie!

—I have to tell you what my five-year-old did with the two-pronged vibrator!

—Wait a minute—!

—Please, Peter! Don't make a scene in front of the neighbors! I told you that was a mistake. I'll take it out. Now here comes one of the best parts.

—Hey, speaking of toys—

—Oh yeah! Watch out, this looks good!

He is running the tank vacuum in the livingroom and, apparently at the suggestion of the cameraperson, has stuck his erection inside the suction hose. He rolls his eyes, licks his lips, and grins lasciviously. His hips begin to buck, his eyes close—then open again. He seems increasingly alarmed, tries to remove the suction hose, cannot. It begins to twist and writhe with a life of its own, dragging him painfully about the room. The camera swings playfully, following him with swoops and dips as he's whipped about. He signals to stop the filming and turn the thing off. He may be screaming. Frantically, as he's thrown about by the suction hose, he struggles toward the switch. His fingers claw their way to within an inch or two, but the cameraperson's foot kicks the machine away, out of his reach. In anguish, he wrestles the coiling and uncoiling hose toward the electric socket, snatches at a frayed loop of electric cord, and jerks violently on it. Sparks fly. *Blackout.*

—Yikes!

—Wow! Ha ha! *Scary!*

—Like he got sucked right into a black hole!

—Probably there was a moral there.

—Maybe. But if so, sweetnuts, I don't want to hear about it.

A new title with decorative soap bubbles disperses the fluttery darkness:

OUR FIRST BATH TOGETHER!

The bridegroom, still in his tuxedo shirt and jacket though little else, is seen peering intently into the lens of the camera, no doubt fixed on a tripod, while adjusting the aperture. The wide-angle lens is aimed at the yoni-shaped bathtub, ringed about with lotions, soaps, and rubber toys. Behind his shoulder and partially concealed by it, his young wife removes her bridal gown, hangs it on the glans knob of the phallic hook on the bathroom door, to which clusters of party balloons are also attached like floating testicles, and lifts her white slip over her head, her back to the camera. She is slender and shapely in a pubescent way, her hair done up today in two ribboned pigtails. She blurs in and out of focus as he adjusts the lens, but for one brief moment one can see the little hearts and LOVE MEs printed on her peekaboo undies. He disappears, perhaps to look at the scene through the viewfinder, for his fingers can be seen in front of the lens, making further adjustments. His bride is already in the tub, deep in suds, watching him lovingly. He returns to the front of the camera to fit a roseate filter onto the lens, graying the green bathroom fixtures somewhat but adding a soft ruddy glow to himself and the rest of the room. Behind him, she dips a bar of soap in the bathwater. If he weren't in the way, her tender little breasts might be seen sliding over the lip of the tub as she stretches out to set the soap on the floor a foot or so away. He turns and approaches the tub (she's down in the bubbles again), his back to the camera, doing a gleeful little dance as he strips away his jacket and shirt. He hops onto the unnoticed bar of soap and up he goes, heels high. The camera seems, as if on its own, to slow down the action of his fall, even though of course it must be speeding up. His bride's mouth above the edge of the tub puckers into an O of assumed alarm, her hand rising in slow motion before it, though there is a mischievous sparkle in her eyes. His crash to the tiled floor is unheard but it makes the camera jiggle as though it might be giggling. It blinks off. Another bubbly title:

BOY! HE REALLY FELL FOR ME!

—Oh, ha ha! That's cute! That's really *cute!*

—All that's missing are the sound effects! A little tinkly music, a whistle when the soap flies, a trombone whoop, and the resounding smack of bone on tile: *wow!*

—Oh, I know. I *must* learn how to do that!

It hurt, though. It must have hurt. His head is ringing even now. Why are they all laughing?

—I loved it when his upended fanny was on the same plane as your face, Mrs. Prick! It was almost as though you might have leaned out and kissed it!

—Oh, I *would* have if I could have, the poor thing! Just look at it!

The bathroom scene has returned (the camera seems to have been perched higher, offering now a view of the inside of the tub) and he is walking toward her once more, rubbing his head with one hand, holding the small of his back with the other. There is a deep blue bruise on one hip.

—Ouch!

—Hey, you've got a great ass, Mr. Prick. I *love* it!

—Nice color, too! Stage makeup, I assume?

—I don't remember . . .

He steps cautiously into the large tub, facing her, noticeably less excited than before, first one foot, then the other—they fly out from under him and down he goes again, banging his head on the tub before he disappears under the water, sending buckets of water splashing out onto the floor, the bar of soap flying up between his legs like a popped cork. His bride is laughing as she plucks the soap from the water and sets it on its dish (she cannot be heard, but all those in the room can be), but she turns sober when he emerges, gasping and spluttering and holding his head. She leans forward to kiss him on his sudsy cheek but ducks back again before he can return it—as he seems, desperately (it's his wedding day!), to wish to do, ringing head or no. She pushes his puckered lips away and draws back, her knees up in front of her slender chest. He is disappointed but not defeated. She's his wife, after all; she's only teasing, has to be. This one's scripted and he's read the script. Everyone has. He spies the soap, holds it up, makes inquiring scrubbing gestures with it. She blushes (the filter enhances the color of her cheeks) and nods, ducking her head. His excited grin returns and he reaches for her, soap in hand, but she takes it away from him and insists on washing him first. He shrugs, smiles, and leans back, resting his head in the crevice of the tub's end, bearding it with his wet hair, his arms slung loosely over the lips. She stretches toward him, hiding her breasts with one hand, tentatively soaping his hairy chest with the other. He indicates she should start farther down. Dutifully, she sits back and proceeds to do so, but loses the soap. She feels around for it; he looks pleased. She withdraws, flushed prettily with embarrassment, arms crossed around her raised knees, so he goes fishing for it, plunging under headfirst, only his butt in view above the bubbles. She jerks back, startled, her pigtails bouncing, slaps at the soapsuds between her legs, kicks him away. He comes up spluttering once again, but proudly, soap in hand. He wipes the suds from his eyes and mustache, smirks mischievously, and squeezes the bar of soap until it pops out of his hand into the water again. Before he can do so, she dives under, surprising him. He grins expectantly, spreading his legs, staring into the sudsy water between them, but slowly the grin changes to uncertainty and then to gathering alarm. Where is she? He splashes about searching for her. Oh my god! Has she drowned? The camera zooms in on him, if such clumsy motion can be called a zoom, as he dives under, thrashing wildly about, freckling the lens with flying froth and droplets. He pops out, gasping for breath, eyes blinded by soap and panic, looking devastated. It is difficult to tell whether that's soapscum or tears in his eyes, but it's probably tears. He may be crying out her name. Then he glances up at the camera and his expression changes from anguish to chagrin and deep annoyance. He flops back into the water, looking wilted, and raises his middle finger to the lens. *Fadeout.*

—Oh, that's lovely! So funny! Yet so moving!

—It's the way movies *used* to be made.

—And that business of hiding and disclosing: It reflects on the very nature of film itself. Fort and dada. Very witty, Mrs. Prick!

—Thank you, but, really, you give me too much credit. I hardly know what I'm doing!

True, but his heart is pounding just the same. That he might lose her is all but beyond his imagination, and yet nothing presses more upon it. He looks at her now, his wife, his one true love, smiling winsomely, abjectly, at her guests, and he knows that who he is now is wholly defined by her—he's afraid almost of blinking, lest she not be there afterward and so leave him, abandoned, outside the realm of being.

—Then you're a natural genius, Mrs. Prick. Believe me, there was the whole history of cinema in that scene. Brilliant!

—Well, if so, it was just dumb luck. But here's a part I *did* work harder on.

As the new titles appear, printed on a lacy heart, his own heart takes a leap: at last!

WHEN DAY IS DONE

—Ah, here we go! The heart of the matter, so to speak!

—Or the meat!

—But wait, what *is* that?

—*Ssshh!*

A vast pallid landscape emerges from the darkness as though lit by moon or candle, a wild barren expanse, timeworn and uninhabitable. An alien place of outer dark. Slowly the camera tracks a stony ridge toward a strange shadowy ravine, skimming the pocked scrubby crests that rise to either side to peer into the narrow valley between, a dire and lonely place, utterly bereft of signs of life except for what appears to be an ancient burial pit, desolate and overgrown, long forgotten; whatever has come here has died here. The camera approaches the pit as though to enter it but pauses at the rim, leaving the viewer to continue the journey in his or her own imagination. There are gasps of lament or of recognition, or perhaps of pleasure, among the gathered neighbors. Beyond this crumpled crater, the ravine widens and a rough lumpy mound spreads between the slopes—debris perhaps dug up from the burial pit, or the consequence of some worse convulsion—then mysteriously drops away as though into an abyss. Ah, what a sight, this violently cleft terrain opening suddenly onto the bulging edge of nothingness.

The camera pulls back from what it sees as if in dread or horror, revealing Constance in her shortie pajamas crouched over her sleeping husband's backside, scanning it by the light of a bedside lamp with a portrait lens, sliding along only inches from his flesh. She continues to pan slowly, caressingly, down the back of his thighs, past the tangle of silk pajama pants pulled down around his knees. It's almost as if (he thinks with a shudder) she were peeling him, and in some inexplicable way he feels not just vulnerable and exposed but parodied. Which perhaps (he goes on thinking, admiring his wife in her abbreviated pajamas but wondering who was filming *her*) is the very essence of marriage. She pauses at his bare feet, lingering there, her perky little lightly clad rear in the air, to capture his blistered heels and wrinkled soles and all of his toes, one by one, each curled into itself as if, like he, fast asleep. It's curious. One seems to see her and what she sees at the same time.

—These slow holding shots: like acts of patient witnessing! Suddenly we possess forever what we see, yet never thought we'd see!

—And still it remains moody and mysterious, there but not there. We see it and don't see it at the same time. We lose it even as we possess it!

—Yes. Partly it's the chiaroscuro lighting. So faint, so pale and trembling. Always at the edge of it, one feels the menace of ultimate darkness; it might all suddenly vanish!

—And sooner or later will. Must!

—At the same time accentuating the shadows that image our anxiety about not wanting to see all that the frame can show us!

—Awesome! But what most grabbed me were those vast vistas of the flesh! Such an epic vision, Mrs. Prick! It's as if the more we see, the more we are moved. It's a revelation!

—But not a triumphant one. Rather, it's like a personal configuration of epic loss, causing our feelings, as the camera pulls back from his asshole, to radiate outward in a melancholic embrace of the whole world's grief!

—Oh! I feel like crying and fingering myself at the same time!

A title card appears, depicting a saw cutting through a log above a curvy row of Zs:

ZZZZZZZ

When next seen, he is lying face up in his pajama top, snoring peacefully away, or so the Zs tell us. Connie has unbuttoned the top and is carefully shooting his Adam's apple, clavicle, armpits, nipples, proceeding very slowly and deliberately down past his gently rising and falling ribs and navel to his limp penis, cradled in his half-spread thighs.

CONNIE LOVES HER PETER! EVERY INCH!

. . . reads a hand-printed title. She films the top of his idle instrument, then lays it flat against his abdomen to shoot the underside, tips it to the left, to the right, and flicks it back between his thighs again. As she moves it about, it begins to stiffen with a life of its own, so she stands above it and films it head-on as well, lowering her camera in a slow arc as if on a boom until she reaches the parentheses of his outbent knees, his manhood now rising totemlike in her lens before his belly's field of hair. If it starts to slump, she teases it by chucking it under the chin, so to speak; then, when it's hard again, she bats it playfully back and forth and films that too, though she frowns at the suggestive smile that begins to curl the sleeper's lips.

She glances up suspiciously at a cloudlike balloon forming over his head, in which an image emerges of the posteriors of a kneeling woman. Just that: plump buttocks framing a hairless pink anus and pulsing vagina, no head or torso or any limbs below the thighs. Her frown relaxes and she smiles condescendingly, watching him approach the headless apparition in the dream balloon. He finds this weird yet abstractly appealing: it is the anonymous impersonal essence of his unappeased longing (yes, unappeased; there is something missing in this marriage; there must be films he hasn't seen), and he may approach it and do with it as he pleases, knowing that it is her desire that he do so, and that she will watch him with affection, curiosity, and pride. Which of course means he must do his best not to disappoint her or any others who may be watching, nor has he any intention or likelihood of doing so, for he is, as always, up for such a challenge as this; it's who he is, and indeed he is somewhat excited by the sight of this opulent ass, an arousing contrast to Connie's tight little schoolgirl buns, which passing thought he hopes she is not privy to. But somehow the ass is never quite there when he reaches for it, remaining always just beyond his grasp, the thighs seeming to scamper along just ahead of him as he presses toward it against some unseen resistance. He realizes that this chase is a kind of game, a puzzle, a test of a sort, so he pauses to think about that and the ass pauses too, waiting for his next move. He tries to look away from it, but wherever he looks it is always in the corner of his eye, rosy and luminous. He turns his back on it, but it is there in front of him again. He spies a corner and backs toward it, then turns around quickly, trapping it in the corner when it appears there. He plunges forward and it vanishes, reappears just behind him, its little bottomhole, bright as a strawberry, opening and closing as though blowing him kisses. He knows this is a phantom ass, but he is obliged to pursue it just the same, for whenever he hesitates his penis gets thumbed. But wait. He's obliged to fuck it, yes, obliged and, as always, eager—but to pursue it? He backs off. The ass follows him, its generous gash wetly throbbing. It seems almost to be licking its phantom lips. He backs off more rapidly, and it follows him more rapidly. Soon he is running backward as fast as he can. He has no idea where he is or what he's running toward, the edge of a cliff maybe, doesn't matter, the important thing is maximum speed. He's virtually flying. Then he stops dead. The ass crashes into him, sending him tumbling backward (maybe it *is* the cliff!); he throws his arms around it, feels his cock plunge into one or another of its holes, which has the consistency of something between custard pudding and fresh window putty, and—oh! ah!—he's coming before he can even get started, he grabs the thing between its mushy thighs just to hang on—but no, it's only his own spouting cock he's grabbed while falling off his chair.

—*Wha—! What?*

—Wake up, Peter! his wife is saying. The movie's over! They're all standing above him there in his livingroom, roaring with laughter and applauding. His neighbors. Whom he seems to know but doesn't know. Connie gives him an embroidered cocktail napkin, smeared with lipstick and chocolate, to wipe himself with.

—Sorry, he mutters. The little cocktail napkin is wholly inadequate. He's spilled volumes. How long has it been? He wipes his sticky hands on the shag carpet beneath him, knowing Connie will scold him for it later. A . . . a wet dream . . .

—No need to apologize, Mr. Prick! Ha ha! We all have them!

—Though some seem to have better ones than others.

—That was a fabulous piece of work, Mrs. Prick! Who said you knew nothing about montage and mattes?

—Brilliant technique! And what a storyline!

—I agree, all of it was great, but what I loved *best* was that scene after the bath, when the groom at last, as they say, embraced his bride! Wedded bliss! Really, that's what it's all about, isn't it, Mr. Prick?

—I don't know. He struggles to his feet, feeling emptied out. What a mess. Should change. I guess I missed that part.

—How *could* you miss it, dearest? You were *in* it!

—No, I mean just now, watching it. I must have—uh—blinked.

—Now now, don't be silly. You may be much too quick about it, my dear Peter, but not *that* quick!

Everyone laughs.

—So where did you two meet? How did it all begin? It's a redheaded woman who looks suspiciously like someone he might have known before he was married.

He looks toward his wife. She's the one with the memory for such things, but she merely smiles expectantly at him.

—Er, on a holiday, I think.

—You met on a holiday?

—Oh, Peter! Really!

—Or maybe a subway car—?

—A subway car! cries Connie, her lower lip trembling, eyes tearing up. How ridiculous! My husband's just trying to be funny; don't pay any attention to him! He knows as well as everyone that when we were both very little we lived next door to each other. We've been sweethearts all our lives!

Now that he thinks about it, this is quite likely true. She was the girl next door; he's seen her movies, some of them; how could he have forgotten? She comes over to lean against him, needing reassurance, and he puts his arms around her. Such a tender little thing, so fresh and sweet smelling! And vulnerable. It was stupid of him to say what he did, true or not; what does he know? She gives his buttocks an urgent little squeeze and runs her other hand up inside his shirt, as though trying to crawl inside his clothes and hide there. It's a delicious feeling. Her hands on him give him a sense of himself that nothing else does.

—When we got married, Peter asked me to climb up a ladder so he could peek up my skirts, just like we did in the old barn when we were children.

—What a sweet sentimental idea!

—He also wanted to watch me do a poo again, but I told him some things were just *too* childish! We did play our favorite hide-and-seek game with a button, though—only with the wedding rings instead; it was part of the marriage ceremony! Her hands scramble around inside his shirt and back pockets the way they did then. Presumably.

—What fun! Could we look at your wedding movie again?

—Oh, Peter's seen that old thing so many times, I'm sure he's sick of it.

—Well, actually, I don't think I've ever—

—But since he's pretending he doesn't remember how we met, let's look at some footage of us playing doctor when we were little!

—Oh yes! It'll bring back the old days! Feet in the stirrups and all that!

—It's when I learned where a prostate was!

While the others chatter away, she stretches up to press her soft lips against his, letting her hand slide down out of his shirt toward his sticky thighs, patting his behind lovingly with the other one, and then pulls away from him to go look for the film. He's excited, astir again, and would like to make love privately to her in the classical manner, but the neighbors will be here forever; one thing that Connie provides is continuity. What does not excite him is the thought of looking at hairless little genitalia in which the juices have not yet begun to flow, a popular taste that's not his. Tantrums and toilet training and schoolyard bullying and peeing contests? Forget it.

—Where are you going, Peter? Don't you want to watch the movie?

—I, uh, just remembered. I should get back to the office.

—But it's—

—I'll be right back, my love. Just a quick check. Breath of fresh air. I'll pick up some more beer.

Connie looks perplexed and disappointed and even a bit frightened, somewhat dwarfed by all the high-spirited neighbors crowding around her with beer bottles in their fists and mouths, but finally she shrugs a little well-do-what-you-want shrug, casting a wistful, beckoning gaze at him past the others. So full of longing. Oh, how beautiful she is! His heart is tugged, even as, as if on a rolling corridor, he drifts to the door. Bring back some more ginger cookies too, please, she calls out, keeping her little chin up behind all the shoulders, though he can hear the quaver in her voice. And some frozen TV dinners. Enough for everybody!

As he exits their little love nest into the blazing sunshine, he glances back, worried that he might have hurt her feelings (she *needs* him, she's always told him so; not to be with her, even for a moment, is in effect to betray her), but the livingroom is dark now. Probably they're screening the next film already, or else it's just the harsh lighting contrast and the sluggish lenses of his eyes, slow to adjust, nothing to be seen or heard in there but a certain vague grunting restlessness. *Of course it's naughty!* someone says. *I don't think it's* art *unless it's naughty!* This cottage is not merely a cottage, he thinks. It is home. My home. He feels whole in it, all of a piece, the discontinuous scatter of his past life gathered up here and given shape and meaning. Given *location*. He is the ceaseless wanderer come home, the first true home he's ever had. Not counting the house in which he grew up next door to Connie, that is. If that's what happened. And that one was not his the way this one is, though whose it was he can't recall. He feels almost as if he and this cottage were one, its rooms his most intimate inner states. He must care for it as he would care for his love, his life. *I don't mean* it, says another. *I mean* him! The door, for example, could use a fresh coat of red paint, he notes as it closes. And the carved wooden sign above it has gone missing. Souvenir hunters, the bane of his existence. One of them. When he comes back (soon, that's a promise!), he'll work a little around the place: touch up the paint, oil the hinges, polish the brass, clean the thatch. Maybe do a bit of gardening. Wash the windows, which are so grimy they look painted. He thinks of these as tender labors, caresses of a sort, even self-caresses, a kind of domestic foreplay. Perhaps he'll get out the tools and add a little romantic gazebo at the back. He imagines holding hands in it with his love—his *wife!*—and being wholly satisfied by that simple act, saturated with serenity and joy. This imagining is so vivid it almost seems to appear before his eyes as a flash forward, and he smiles at the novelty of it. YOUNG PETER PRICK, MAN OF THE HOUSE. He likes it.

He won't have to cut the grass, though, for as he sees now, passing through the garden gate, it is only colorized snow, melting somewhat under the hot arc lamps. Maybe he knew that all along. The wildflowers are plastic, the leaded glass windows probably *are* painted, certainly the backdrop of blue sky and wooded copse is, and the cows are cardboard cutouts. Why cows? he asked Connie—he remembers this now; it was she who designed the set—and she replied, We *have* to have cows! That's why they're called *moo*-vies, silly!

Beyond the gate, he's back in the city. Looks like the middle of a bombed-out tenement district, cleared maybe for the set. And it's colder than he'd thought. He's underdressed. The arcs' glare fooled him. He'd go back and get an overcoat on, but the cottage is already out of sight somewhere behind him and he's not sure of the route back. And anyway, in spite of the deepening chill and his stiffening pants, he enjoys the momentary freedom. There are the usual car crashes and surly masses, bludgeonings, screams of anguish, and plummeting suicides, but however horrific and bitter these streets may be (it's snowing now too, probably has been all along), they are familiar to him and so recall for him aspects of his life beyond the hot tight focus of his marriage. Which is a kind of madness, he realizes (he is farther away now, such thoughts are available), a shared blue-sky fantasy of connection and continuity, the old persistence-of-motion illusion, which has utterly obsessed him of late to the exclusion—virtually the erasure—of all else. The home-movie trap. What's-her-name warned him about it. The cute one at the office. With whom he would not mind sharing a hot bath right now. If he can find his way back there. The streets are familiar, yet at the same time utterly new, as if being reinvented by his walking through them, as if he must walk through them that they might be reinvented. If he once had a map of them in his head, it's gone or useless.

Not that he doesn't love Connie's home movies. He does. Making them with her is a ceaseless delight, must be. She is so direct and unpretentious, her funny little films so pure, so uncontaminated, just there in all their sweet goofy open-eyed transparency—and because of that, so erotic. The neighbors were right about that. Her films of him excite him, not narcissistically but because of the breathless intensity of her looking, the exalting power of her miraculous all-consuming love. It seems she cannot get enough of him. And when he gets hold of her simple little camera, just exploring the helix of her ear, her fragile hand in his, the purse of her mouth, the crotch of her panties, excites him more than a thousand professional fuckfilms (or at least his viewing of them does, his actual filming of them being somewhat dim in his recollections).

They almost literally eat each other up. Gone: past, future, and anyplace not their place. Which, within its little stucco walls, is yet everywhere, life with her a timeless adventure through ever-expanding space. Maybe that's why there's so little left of the old memories. Trashbinned to make room for an endless epic with the girl next door. Which, happening rather narrowly in timeless infinity, is maybe a little short on content but powerful and rejuvenating in its immediacy. Being with her makes him feel younger than he can ever remember feeling. He *is* younger! Just look at her films! He can't believe it himself! And even at their most playful, her movies are truthful in the way that all those he'd made before were not. Or at least they make the truth visible. He is in love with them and with her. He has made many films with ingenues able to play this part of the young innocent with some conviction (the extinguished past, if it is a past and not just another present, momentarily misplaced, is slowly coming back to him, no longer overwritten by censorious scripting: Cecilia . . . Cissy, that's right, that was her name—is this the street?), but here for the first time is the real thing. Constance is not just another ingenue. She is, truly, the girl of his dreams, the costar for whom he's been yearning all his life. The pure object of eros whom he loves beyond loving, his sweetheart, his own. Marriage to her has brought an end to all the dislocations of the past, the dissipation of his soul stuff—all that ill-spent stardust, as he thinks of it, scattered on barren theater seats. Marriage has been an act of liberation, of revolution, a way of leaving home, so to speak, of abandoning his old professional family (wait a minute, that was Cleo in his livingroom; what was she doing there?), a way of sowing his wild oats, an act, given who he is, of ultimate transgression. *Here Cums the Bride: The Wedding of Lucky Pierre*— a film that shocked the city. Or so they tell him.

Still, there is something exhilarating about being out from under her focus and recovering a bit of his old life, even out here in these howling snowswept streets without an overcoat on. A DELIGHTFUL BOUT OF ECSTATIC FUCKING reads a tattered outdated movie poster on a crumbling brick wall frosted with blown snow, and yes, frankly, he'd like to get back to a bit of that. It was a movie called *The Brave Little Tailor*. NINE AT A TIME! boasts the poster. He doesn't remember it, and most of the poster has been scuffed away by the wind and the shuffling masses, but he can imagine it. Might have been overly slick and too messagey and formulaic, but it had to have been better than chasing a phantom ass. But even as he stares at it, a fierce biting wind rips it away, sends it flying down the street (there's a crash somewhere), and nearly whips him along with it.

At the intersection, an underground street-theater troupe is blocking traffic with a satire on filmmaking, something called *Hamauteur Finger Fucking*, according to the board one of them is holding up. Both too clever and too crude, as is their wont. A man in a bridal veil and a woman wearing a top hat, bowtie, and thin false mustache, the two of them otherwise naked in spite of the weather, are parading grandly up and down between a corridor of whirring cameras, spilling glitter out of their assholes like stardust. One of the other actresses is crying *Help! Help!* and prancing about with a placard that reads S.O.S. on one side, SAME OLD SHIT on the other. Though street theater and underground movies are the city's most serious crimes and prime targets of the Mayor's security forces (the dregs of satiety, they're called at City Hall), it's hard to eradicate them. Destroy them, they just keep coming back. Worse than hemorrhoids, as the Mayor likes to say. Wasn't there a young bare-breasted woman who was part of this anarchist gang? If so, she's not among them. Maybe he's mistaken. So many such images in his head, so many women, all their body parts, all fading, mostly gone now or merged into the vague abstraction of his desire, their particular edges melting away like cheese in the hot soup of his marriage. He would linger, dangerous as it is (the bride is sucking the groom's camera lens; how are these outlaws even getting hold of all this illegal hardware?), but the crowds push him on. A stubborn blind benumbed force, butting along against the cold, he butted along with them.

They all seem to bounce a bit as they stagger down the street; everything blurs momentarily, turns blindingly bright, then dark again—he realizes he is not yet completely out from under Connie's handheld influence. Even that daffy soup simile was not something he would have thought of on his own. He ducks his head and slips into the thick of the moving masses, hoping to disappear among them. Gets him down out of the wind, too. Police sirens whoop past on their way to break up the street theater. He hears the screech of brakes behind him, crashes, screams, angry shouts, gunfire. Just as well he didn't stay around. Or wasn't allowed to stay around. *And unzip your pants, Peter!* he seems to hear her say. *I won't have you going around half dressed.* Well. He does so, dutifully. He understands. She is proud of him and who he is and wants to show him off to the world. Too fucking cold, though. Hard to get hard when everything's shriveled up and hiding, though he knows if he can do it, it will warm the blood. Can't use his fingers, though, they're like icy knives. His imagination's what's left. But nothing stimulating comes to mind. He says *bottom, tits, pussy,* but he can't see them. Just more cheesy soup. His teeth are chattering, his nose is numb and dripping icicles, and his feet feel like blocks of frozen lead. He realizes that he left home in his house slippers, and he remembers Connie slipping them on his feet as he sat in the armchair, sucking each toe before she did so, giving him fleeting glimpses of her little pink-nippled bosom as she knelt before him, exposing the delicacy of her slender nape. That's better. Beginning to stir. He's hurrying along now, pressing through the thickening pack-up. Such a pretty thing, her nape, but what's next, what's *next?* He can't seem to push his memory past his view of it and the sucking of his toes, but he's sure there's more. *Keep on coming!* he calls out, but he's only shouting at the wind. Who's the loony with the weenie? someone says, and everything shrinks away again. Zip.

Oh shit, it's cold! What am I doing out here? This question is asked of him in the second person as well as the first, and richly colorized images arise of his little honeymoon cottage, a loveseat by the hearth, a fire glowing, a hot drink in his hand, his ladylove upon his knee, her arms wrapped around him, her lips pressed against his ear, whispering sweet nothings. He strokes the sweet child-sized buns curled up in his lap, wraps his palm around them, middle finger pressed between the tight little cheeks—but then she's not there, a wintry blast blows in, the fire goes out, he's back on the bitter streets again. He has slowed to a walk, bumped and jostled by the indifferent crowds hurrying past, his hands cupped at his ice-crusted crotch to keep the wind out. Forget the hearth. Too far away now. His fault. Should never have left it. Left her. He's utterly lost and alone out here and suddenly full of regret and self-pity. His only hope is to find his old office. That hot bath might save him. Then, through the tears freezing on his cheeks, he sees something familiar looming above him: the stories-high statue of the Mayor dressed in her toga, a whip in one hand and a book of laws bearing her PRO BONO PUBICO motto in the other. Or maybe that's a filmscript. Whatever, he's close now; that was the view out his office window! Must be just around the corner! He unzips once more into his old career (here I am!) and breaks into a run, slapping along painfully in his iced-up house slippers, clumsy as snowshoes, his head full of hot gurgling sounds. And there it is! The sixty-nine-story skyscraper, the revolving doors, the shapely uniformed doorperson—

—Good morning, love! (*Whoof!*) You're a beautiful sight!

But she only tips over when he slaps her behind, which is flat and hard: a chipboard cutout. He stumbles over her and pushes desperately through the doors, only to find himself on the other side of a theatrical flat, a false front, nothing but rubble behind it, more crumbling tenements and flying snow, the weather worse on this side than the other. On the unpainted backside of the flat, rearing up into the blizzardy mists, someone has scrawled *Cum back, L.P.! It's empty here without you! The Girls,* but someone else has changed *back* to *home* and X'd out the *s* of *Girls*. Has she brought him all the way here for this little exercise in marital pedagogy? Probably. There are other old chipboard cutouts back here behind the door, loosely stacked, paint worn away in the weather and bits broken off. He recognizes none of them, though the brunette in the tangerine skirt is vaguely familiar. Members of film crews probably, ingenues, secretaries, bath attendants; a blankly smiling one is wearing an elevator operator's uniform. They once served him, he assumes, and they might do so yet once more, if they're not too wet from the snow to burn. He scratches about in the stones, bones, and cinders where the snow's been blown away, finally finds a book of matches advertising an old seafaring adventure flick called *Shipwrecked on the Isle of the Nymphs,* but his fingers are too frozen to strike one. He needs something more like an acetylene torch, even his old pipe lighter, but no such luck. What he does come upon, though, as if set out for him, half buried in a drift behind the stack of chipboard, are a pair of fur-lined boots, earmuffs, thick mittens, and a knitted cock sock. He puts them on (not easy to kick off the frozen slippers; he has to jump around in them to break them up, his exposed feet a numb translucent blue), feeling cared for after all. On the Parthenos Theater marquee across the ruined lot, HURRY HOME, HONEY, MY CUNT'S ON FIRE! Sounds more like Cleo than Connie, but the direction's clear. And it occurs to him then that if Cleo's there, others probably are too. Which means that the honeymoon cottage now *is* his office, his studio, and he has in effect, very unprofessionally (but isn't that the point?), abandoned the set in the middle of a shoot. To chase, foolishly, an illusion. And now he's gone too far. He's out on the edge, out on the edge of everything, and he has to get back.

The trek across the blasted back lot toward the Parthenos, head down against the blowing snow, is like crossing a war zone (who knows, maybe it actually was a set for a war movie: didn't he once make a film called *French Letters from Home* about a poor wretch in the trenches to whom naked women bloomed whole from love letters, photographs, and personal mementos such as garter belts and scented pubic hairs, like genies from lamps and bottles?), and when he finally staggers in under the marquee, he feels, though he's only begun, he can go no farther. The new boots are great, but his thawing feet inside them are burning up (his socked cock, too, now hard from the heat; he removes its itchy wrap for a moment to air it out), while much of the rest of him is so frostbitten, all sensation's been lost. His joints have seized up and it feels like he's wearing an iron mask for a face. The film premiering at the Parthenos is one of Constance's latest ones, *The Vestigial Virgin.* Not one he knows, but there's a poorly focused bathtub still on the poster by the entrance that looks familiar. *Why go looking for what you've got right where you already are?* reads the half-literate caption. The poster copy, ballyhooing the film under the AMATEUR TEEN genre, uses language like *unpretentious, direct, uncontaminated,* and *powerful and rejuvenating in its immediacy* and speaks of *the pure object of eros* and *the exalting power of her all-consuming passion. It makes the truth visible!* it proclaims. It's like something he's already read, but then that's the nature of cheap overblown hype. *See,* it promises, *the crotch of her panties!* Which would suit him admirably, but the theater is closed and padlocked. Across the street at the Xanadouche, they're showing her *Naughty Naughty: Housebreaking a Love Pet.* ALL SINGING, ALL DANCING, it says on the marquee, meaning somebody's built a soundtrack for her. And all singing and dancing instead of what? Her little home movies, clearly, have become quite the rage. None of the theaters look to be open, though. In fact, back here behind his old office building, the streets are eerily empty and, as such, more daunting somehow than when crammed with shouldering masses. He fears going on. He fears not going on.

Something called *In Quest of the Nest* is at the Bare-Mount Theater (on the marquee: CUM HOME SWEETHEART / TO PRIVATE PARTS!—which, as he recalls, was the name of that poor soldier in the war movie), so, pulling on his three mittens once more, he bravely heads off in that direction, down the zigzagging streets of beckoning cinemas, beginning to feel like he's on some kind of giant hopscotch board. Probably another of Connie's games. She still thinks skipping rope or playing jacks in a squat are about the sexiest things one can do, and to tell the truth, playing with her in her starchy little calico pinafores, he does find it sexy, though there's probably more real mommy-and-daddy stuff going on in her dollhouse than in their honeymoon cottage, if the footage he's seen is any clue. Her idea of bedroom fun seems mostly to be sack races in pillow slips or round and round her little gooseberry bush. Underwear scavenger hunts. She likes to blindfold him and make him play guessing games, giving him soft little things with bumps on them to feel or wet fuzzy slits or plump objects with deep mushy holes. Ever the optimist, he guesses wrong every time. About the most fun he ever has is when they play bum tag, but even then she's too fast for him and he's always It. Which is the name of another of her movies, he sees, showing down at the Pudding, and as the Bare-Mount is, as he'd anticipated, nailed shut, he moves toward it. THE WAY TO THE WAY IN says the marquee.

An overly encouraging message. The theater has heavy rusting chains across its double doors as if closed for centuries and there are no other movie houses in sight. A cold dead end, not unlike his own. Though there have been signs of melting (getting closer, dear!), the wind if anything is more penetrating than ever, making him hot at the extremities and, coatless, frozen at the core. He huddles despairingly under the marquee, staring out into the relentless weather. Has he been abandoned? In reply, the end letters of the sign above him drop off at his feet like falling roof tiles: the O, the N. ON? No: NO. He looks up and sees, rising into the whipped clouds of snow above the ghostly street, a skyscraper with a giant electronic advertisement for Connie's classic film *The Girl Next Door,* offering a distant view of a lighted bedroom window across a lawn, or what appears in the filmed twilight to be a lawn. The window, strangely luminous in the storm, is set in a cottage not unlike their honeymoon cottage (there are silhouetted cows), though it is less quaint, the roof not thatched but tiled, and there is a barn behind it. A slow zoom reveals a pubescent girl in the lighted bedroom undressing before a mirror, touching herself speculatively, tenderly, her lips parted, not in passion but in the intensity of her concentration. She seems almost breathless. The camera continues its slow steady approach as the garments come off, one by one. As she thumbs the waistband of her white cotton panties to lower them, the image goes black and then returns to its initial moment, looking across a darkened lawn at a distant lighted window, the zoom slowly repeating. Using it as a kind of lighthouse beacon, he sets off again into the blizzard, elbows in tight and mittened hands around his throat, wishing he might be able to ride the zoom right into the film, drawn more by its summery twilight than by the prospect of seeing her pants come down. A silly kids' movie maybe, but even lying in the scratchy stink of a hayloft, getting his peewee inspected by a child actress with sticky fingers and a runny nose, would be better than suffering these harrowing streets.

The electronic sign, however, even as it repeats its zoom-and-cut motion over and over, seems to recede as he shuffles stiffly through the drifting snow toward it, a common illusion when walking in the city; then it disappears entirely as he reaches a fork deep in the city canyon. At the Loewjob, down one way, they're showing her *Wed Dream,* and down the other, at the Oriphiss, *The Prick of Conscience.* It's a tough call. In the middle, facing him, where the pedestrian-crossing sign ought to be: a yellow diamond-shaped sign with a two-headed erect penis pointing both ways at once, stolen no doubt from the old preschool Asian upskirts film, *Yellow Prick Road,* which Connie'd brought home recently to help the children (he *does* have children; he remembers this now!) with their catechism. But it's another movie house a few blocks down an alleyway behind them that catches his eye, for living people are moving shadowily in and out of it with bulky objects under their arms. The old Frivoli Cinema, a palace from the classic era. It has apparently been converted into a sales barn, for the marquee above it reads: KNOCK IT DOWN! KNOCK IT UP! LIGHTS! CAMERAS! AUCTION! The two-headed penis sign lights up ominously as he turns away from it, but, unable to resist a little human contact (he's a man of the people, after all) and an open door, he's already galumphing down the alleyway, mittened prick wagging gleefully, boots kicking up the snow.

He arrives breathless, snorting and blowing like a beached whale (the married life has definitely put him out of shape), and pushes inside, hoping to warm himself amid the shuffling, elbowing crowd. The theater, which has lost its seats but not the cant of its floor, is filled with tagged antiques heaped up on one another and hundreds of people with catalogs crowded in. Down in front of the old screen on which blowups of the items for sale are being projected, an auctioneer is shouting out the catalog listings and the bids.

—One-thirty I'm bid, at one-thirty; make it one-thirty-five, one-thirty-five, will you make it one-forty? One-forty? Yes, one-forty, thank you, *going* at one-forty—one-forty-*five!*

There's a dense dusty smell in here, faintly reminiscent of old movie sets or lockerrooms, a mix of tobacco, unwashed bodies, oils and waxes, menses, mildew, dried semen, pressed flowers. The place is lit with ancient chandeliers that rattle in the drafty dome high above and a few juryrigged floor spots. Radiators can be heard wheezing and knocking somewhere, but are maybe nothing more than the noises they make: For all the stale shared warmth at head level, there's a damp wintry chill around his shins.

—One-fifty, thank you! One-fifty-five. One-sixty, madam? Do you wish to make it one-sixty?

He's treading on paper: a discarded catalog. He stoops to pick it up off the worn red carpet and gets butted forward down the aisle onto all fours and his knitted cock sock falls off. He can hear the auction-hall patrons behind him grunting and cursing as they fight over it. No matter. Won't need it in here. Might just get in his way. He scans the catalog. Maybe he can find something for Connie. For their anniversary maybe, whenever that is. Get back in her good graces. No more of the wayward life; he feels well chastened. It's too damned cold and lonely out there. But there's not much to interest her. Some old model film sets and publicity stills. An antique crimson telephone on an elastic cord that might go with their bedsheets. An old-fashioned deck of cards in which characters representing the four suits fuck each other; shuffle the deck and flip through, get a different combination every time. An aphrodisiac sample case, broken two-way mirrors, an inkwell fashioned from the stretched cunny of an ancient Shelah-na-Gig (nice, but he's not sure she even knows how to write), cracked echo chambers, dog-eared storyboards and leaky chamber pots, mostly junk. There are three new previously undiscovered positions advertised, but, from the catalog descriptions, they're mere variations on overworked themes. And anyway, so far as he can remember, Connie hasn't made use of the one they got as a wedding gift.

—I have one-sixty, do I hear one-sixty-five? No? Well, I'm surprised, a vintage piece like this!

The auctioneer holds up an eight-inch vinyl plastic latex penis, half the latex worn away, part of an old-fashioned AC/DC vibrator kit with a frayed cord, also pictured on the big screen behind him.

—In its day, this was worth a lot of money. An excellent reproduction still in working order—ah! I thought so! Yes, one-sixty-five. Will anyone make it one-seventy? I'll take one-sixty-six, then? No? *Sold* at one-sixty-five!

The auctioneer knocks the rubber penis down and his assistant records the sale. The buyer is the woman standing next to him.

—H'lo, Pete, she says. It's Kate, the one-eyed animator. You're wondering why I just bought that ugly broke-down electric dingaling. Well, no mystery, it's just my calloused ol' Venusian fly trap's gone dead and needs rebooting, and I reckoned that contraption might be in serious enough disrepair to give it a wakeup shock. And what brung you here, pants and all?

—Ah, well, a little—you know—healthy exercise. . . .

—I'll bet. Didn't figure the handheld craze would hold you long.

—No, really—

—A little jiggle and a tight focus? That ain't you, son. Sweeping pans and a quick zoom is more your métier, pardon the dirty talk. Now if you're still feeling in need of a workout, I seen that ol' padded rubdown table of yours with the hole in it here somewheres. We could go oil up—

—Sorry, you're wrong, Kate, I love what I'm into now. He stares into her one blue eye, trying to remember if he ever saw the other one. The eye has a friendly liquid quality that makes it easy to talk to her. In fact that's why I'm here, to buy something for the little woman.

—Oh yeah? How about a crocheted scrotum harness with bit and reins, just her number. Or one a them fancy silver-plated bone crackers? What I'm really looking for here, you wanna know the truth, Pete, is my heart. They got a buncha your hats and sexy cufflinks and prepuce rings and other fancy penthouse shit they're dumping, and I thought it mighta got misplaced among them. I know it's only fool's gold, but I ache to have the little sucker back. Unless you still got it, that is. If you do, honey, you can keep it.

—Sorry, Kate. I didn't know I ever had it. Kate smiles sadly, showing all three of her teeth.

They have been auctioning off bedside distorting mirrors, children's mommy-and-daddy inflatables, and classic condom collectors' packs while he's been talking to Kate, and now the auctioneer is holding up a pussy-hair curling iron. Might be just the right thing. Maybe she'd let him show her how it works. If she has any hair there. But it's knocked down before he can get his mittened hand in the air.

—Awright, Pete, Kate says, drifting away. I'll go sniff about in the lots of your ol' silk PJs and clip-on ball bangles, just in case it's fallen amongst them. But holler if it turns up, love. Or, heck, for any other reason.

He concentrates on the auction list, trying to remember if there was anything Connie said she wanted besides frozen TV dinners. She's not easy to buy for, always insisting she wants nothing and he should buy things for himself instead, which he usually does. The auctioneer has moved on to a set of old videocassettes that still have their ancient X-ratings stamped on them. He lifts up one called *The Butler Diddled It*. People are muttering, marking their catalogs. The sale is already more than half over and there's not much left of interest. He notices there are the usual dozen or so cunts listed, and though another cunt's about the last thing he needs (no room for them, really, in their little cottage), he decides to nose through them, never know when you might strike on the odd treasure. Could always leave it in storage until he found a place for it. He locates them, set apart with the heavy furnishings, sees little at first glance that attracts him. Some crude homemade peasant examples, a damaged primitive or two, a few overstuffed, overembellished subtropical models.

—All right, ladies and gentlemen, the next lot is number one-fifty-eight in your catalogs, that groundbreaking, or should I say windbreaking, musical *Bare Assonantals*. What am I bid? Yes, the ancient analog version, completely uncut and unwiped—hold it up there, miss, let them see it! No, no, the *tape*, dear!

He moves among the cunts, sniffing critically and examining veneers, checking for worms and dry rot. Important to turn them over and examine the underside of the seats, look for telltale staining and distressing, edges artificially softened with spokeshaves. He has a good eye for the genuine article, or did. There was a time when he was famous throughout the used-cunt trade, but it's been awhile. A lot of dealers here, too. Unlikely he'll find any bargains. The auctioneer knocks down the videos and moves on to a rare chest of Queen Anne's drawers, followed by several bulk lots of ancient fuckbooks and erotic paintings. The bidding is slow through the unfashionable books and paintings, so he has ample time to look each cunt over carefully. He is drawn to a couple of very fine old eighteenth-century items, well preserved, with full white bottoms, solid domestic bellies, and nicely tapered legs, but lion's-head chest ornaments have been added to one of them at some later date and the other one has a mustache.

He examines a pair of Regency cunts, attracted by the idea of obtaining two period pieces so much alike. Good investment value, too. They seem authentic enough with the light padding, lyre-shaped torsos and scrolled pubes, intricate ormolu embellishment and small claw feet, but they're not really his style, dainty but pompous, uncomfortable finally, dully imitative in their neoclassicism—and look at the distasteful mock-oriental elaborations around those eyes! After a week of having them around, he'd have to put slip covers over them to bear settling into them.

He takes a quick glance at the Victorian selection, less valuable, to be sure, but somehow more to his taste, in spite of the unfortunate tendencies toward extravagance and shoddy workmanship. They are well displayed among tea caddies and ladies' pessary boxes, handwoven bordello carpets, magic-lantern firescreens, whatnots and loo-tables, cane collections, horsing chesterfields, and ottomans with silk restraints. Even in the piled-up confusion of the auction hall, there is an air of easeful decadence about these things, and he feels much at home here.

A rather large spoonback item, lavishly stuffed, catches his eye. Not bad, she seems clean, attractively proportioned, though perhaps—*uff!*—a little light for her size. He sets her down, takes off his mittens, squeezes a well-tooled teat.

—Fie, sir! I cannot allow you—! Where are you putting your hand? Oh, dear, I shall faint! I have never practiced sexual intercourse, sir!

Sexual intercourse! Bah, a patent counterfeit. He probes and pinches the other specimens, eliciting responses—all of them either cheap inferior constructions camouflaged in crude veneers or flamboyant leftovers from the Great Exhibition, too ostentatious to believe. Hmmm . . . This one might do, it has a nice roll-front construction and solid—

—I can't bear it, it will kill—into the drawingroom and played the—how you startle me! I thought it was—screaming with delight—after a pleasant voyage—and a copious spend—pray excuse our virtuous indignation—wetting it with spittle—

Must be broken. Too bad. Shame to see a good piece like that let go to ruin. Well, it's a disappointing auction. He folds up the catalog, decides to see if he can find a map to get him home again, back to soft focus, bobbing lenses, water spots, hokey editing, and fuzzy exposures. Nothing like the creature comforts. But then, pushing past a clutch of buyers squinting intently at a tattooed human skin for sale, somewhat frayed and acne-pocked and missing one leg, he discovers, concealed behind an enormous comport encrusted with flowers and orgiastic cupids, an unusually fine example, elegantly designed, traditional yet in a class all its own, fair-complected, generously padded but well buttoned down—a classic really, and in prime condition! Excitedly, he checks his catalog:

> *169. CUNT, VICTORIAN—Guar't'd Upper Class, Antique Husb. Believ'd Imp't, No Other Owners, Genuine Guilt Feel'gs. Note esp. full Heav'g Br'sts Tipt with Deliciously Small Nipls of that Fine Pink Color w'ch so Strongly Denotes Virg'y in the Poss'sor.*

My god, can there still be one of these around? Genuine guilt feelings? He can't believe his luck! Don't give way to impulse, take a good look, he cautions himself—but goddamn, his heart is racing and he knows he must have this cunt! Already they are knocking down lot 167! Just time to check the essentials—yes, good and tight!

—Ah! No! No! I shall faint, sir! How your violence frightens me!

Sounds authentic, and she looks flushed with feverish excitement behind her veil, but best to turn her over and inspect her seat. It is dark in the shadowy recess where she's tucked away, but he feels her quivering all over with emotion and she is spending and throbbing under his probings. A real collector's item!

—Oh, I'm so afraid; and yet—oh yet, dearest, I feel, I die, I must taste the sweets of love, this forbidden fruit!

The bottom's fresh and clean. Doesn't seem wormy. Wonderful fragrance; she's been well cared for! Must be the original drawers: stopped dovetail joining, backplates covering the original screwholes. The toolwork through the main joint is woolly, but that's a good sign of genuine Victorian craftsmanship. Looks virtually unused. Probably doesn't go with the cottage's modern yellow sofa or circular bed, but he'll find a place for it. He'll have to. They've knocked lot 168 down, the assistant is recording the sale. He slaps the seat hard.

—Ah! Ah! Ah-r-r-re! My god, sir, you are cruel! Oh! have mercy, I'm as innocent as a babe! Oh, you'll kill me, sir!

No doubt about it. His mouth has gone dry and there's a tingling through all his joints.

—That brings us up to lot number one-sixty-nine, ladies and gentlemen, the Victorian cunt. That's it, up on the screen there. You've all seen it, what am I bid for it? You start me. A thousand? A hundred? Fifty? All right, come on, twenty-five if you like!

He hesitates. He doesn't want to seem overeager. He looks away, waiting for his moment, gazing around at all the funny faces. He yawns demonstratively.

—It has to be sold, will anybody have it for ten? Five? One? Yes, thank you, *sold* at—

—No, wait! *Wait!* Twenty, I bid twenty!

My god, he damn near lost it! Caught him in mid-yawn and nearly cracked his jaw!

—Just in time, thank you, and do I—yes, I have your bid, sir, you can stop waving your arm about now—do I hear twenty-five? Yes, twenty-five, I have—

—Forty! I mean, thirty!

—Would you please repeat your bid, sir?

—Thirty! That is to say, thirty-five! Thirty-five!

—The bid is thirty-five. Are there any further bids?

He's making a fool of himself. Got to settle down. How did he get up to thirty-five so fast? People are snickering, pointing at him.

—Forty, yes, thank you. Fifty, sir?

He takes a deep breath. Strokes his mustache. Flicks his hand with the catalog in it. That's better.

—Fifty. Sixty? Sixty. Seventy?

He nods. Is there a goddamn shill in this crowd? He should have this piece by now.

—Is that a bid, sir? Are you bidding seventy?

He flicks his hand up, looks away.

—Seventy. I have . . . eighty. Ninety, sir?

He pauses, frowns, glances critically at the sale item. Make them think he's losing interest. She places one hand over her breast and sighs softly, and his hand flies up.

—Ninety. One hundred? One hundred, thank you. One-fifty, sir?

Can't keep his hand down, it's still up and waving, even though the asshole has jumped the bid on him. He wishes he had his old pipe to bite down on instead of his lip, but he's arrived too late even to bid on it.

—One-fifty. Now . . . ? Thank you, one-seventy-five. Round it off to an even two hundred, sir?

—One-ninety-five, damn it! Has to hold his ground, not get pushed around. The auctioneer shrugs.

—One-ninety-five, then, do I hear—? Yes, I have two hundred. Two-twenty-five, sir?

He hesitates, rather longer this time, studies his catalog, then with seeming reluctance raises it.

—One more time, he says.

—Thank you, and do I . . . ? Yes, two-fifty. Two-seventy-five, sir?

He looks around the hall, trying to spot his opponent. Some amateur, no doubt, no sense of value, probably thinks they're bidding on the Regency cunts.

—Two-seventy-five, sir?

—Yes, all right. Last time.

—Two-seventy-five. Three hundred? Thank you, three hundred.

—That slicker's having you on, mister! someone whispers behind his shoulder. There's nobody bidding against you!

He feels a chill down his spine, a cramped feeling in his gut. But what can he do?

—Three-fifty, sir? The bid is against you.

—No, I'm all done.

He waits, sweating, jaws clamped, listening to her heavy breathing, until the auctioneer raises the gavel.

—All right. Once more. Three-fifty.

—Ah, *that's* better! Four hundred now? Thank you, four hundred. Will you bid five hundred, sir?

He hears her weeping softly amid the bric-a-brac, rustling her petticoats. On the screen she's being rotated on a kind of pedestal.

—Four-fifty.

—Will you bid *five hundred,* sir?

—What's wrong with four-fifty?

—I'm sorry, I am knocking it down at four—

—Yes, all right, five hundred, goddamn it!

—Thank you. May I ask for a little decorum, please. I have five hundred. Six? Six.

—Seven hundred, he says, not waiting to be asked. He turns away as though to walk out of the auction hall.

—Thank you. Seven hundred. Will you make it eight? Eight hundred, thank you. Nine, sir? Sir?

He's halfway to the door. Everyone watching. What a mess. His knees are weak, but he keeps moving. The crowd parts, letting him through. He hears a sob catch in her throat. He spins around angrily.

—All right! Fuck you! *Two thousand!*

Astonished murmurs, exchanged glances. That shut them up. He strides forward to claim his prize.

—Thank you, two thousand, says the auctioneer emotionlessly. The sonuvabitch has the heart of a bank vault. Do I hear three? he asks. Is there a bid for—yes, I am bid three thousand. Will you make it four, sir?

—*No!*

—Very well, *sold* at three thousand—

—*Yes!* Four thousand!

There's a pause. The auctioneer looks surprised, embarrassed even. On the screen, she seems to have fainted.

—I . . . I'm sorry, sir, I've already knocked it—

—No! I called my bid before! You didn't—

—I'm terribly sorry—

He's lost it! Oh my god, he's lost that priceless jewel!

—*Five* thousand then!

—I'm afraid it's too late, sir, you should have—

—*Six* thousand! Please! You can't do this! *Six thousand!*

The auctioneer shrugs and looks away. He must be out of his mind! For pennies, he's thrown away a masterpiece! He falls to his knees on the thin carpet, tears rolling down his cheeks. How could he be such an ass?

—*Ten thousand! Please!*

—Perhaps there is another lot in the sale, sir, that might—

—I want *that* lot, you ruthless bastard! How can you be so cruel?

—Sorry. There is nothing more I can do. Now, the next lot is a—

—Ah-r-r-r-r! You are killing me! For god's sake, have mercy! A hundred thousand! Goddamn it, *I bid a hundred thousand!*

—Very well. Sold at a hundred thousand to the gentleman with the funny mustache. Next lot—

It's over before he realizes what has happened.

He looks up through his tears, catches the malicious grin just disappearing from the auctioneer's lips. The recorder ducks her head. There's light applause from the crowd as, laughing, they turn away from him. Famous among used-cunt dealers. He's probably set some kind of record.

He rises stiffly from the cold floor, elbows his way up to the desk. He'll have to ask for credit, his pockets are more or less empty. No problem. They're ready for him with mortgage papers on the honeymoon cottage, needing only his signature. Nothing he can do. He'll explain it to Connie later. Try to. He leaves his signature prick print, brushes aside the porter's offer of assistance, heaves his purchase over his shoulder (she is solid, plump, perfect in all her curves and proportions; a million would not have been too much!), and pushes his way up the ramped aisle through the grinning crowd.

Even his new prize seems to be giggling, her tummy twitching and bouncing on his shoulder, but it's probably because of all the guilt and excitement. He's a little disturbed at having recognized the redheaded recorder when he left his mark on the mortgage documents, but hurrying down the icy street to the nearest restaurant—always feed a Victorian first!—he quickly forgets everything but the joy of a new possession and the anticipation of an ecstasy of amorous delight in the old style.

—Oh pray, sir!—*oof!*—let me recover!—*ungh!*—my serenity!

He pats her magnificent bottom reassuringly as he jogs along.

—It is useless—*pant! pant!*—to resist our fate, my dear!

At the entrance to the Olde Cock Inn (what luck! it's open!), he sets her down and dusts her off, causing her to gasp and tremble and look away in flushed embarrassment, her veil lowered. The restaurant is fully booked, but the maître d' seems to be expecting him and guides them to a discreet table in a private alcove. As they press through the crowded room, he places his hand delicately on her narrow waist and whispers softly in her ear: Relax, my lovely. Upon my honor, you will not be mistreated.

She touches his wrist with her fingertips—then clutches it tremblingly, releases it. A shudder of unabashed lust rattles through him like a sudden fever. He is: what? Smitten by her voluptuous charms! Dissolved in a sea of bliss! Swimming in wanton lubricity! Venerable phrases like that ripple through his beguiled mind: Possessed by a frenzy of mad desire! What is there worth living for like the . . . like the . . .

—Oh! Oh! I am fucking lost!

—Sir?

—I . . . I have forgotten, my dear, to ask you your name.

—Cornelia, sir.

—Cornelia! That's a lovely name! For a most lovely lady!

Adjusting her chair for her as she takes her seat, he leans over and catches a glimpse of her bosom, full and heaving just as advertised. Indeed, it is even more spectacular than he had imagined from the catalog copy and quivering with barely contained passion. He remembers that line he had in *The Nuns' Gardener:* A perfect volcano of smothered desires. Slowly, it's all coming back to him. She seems to feel his eyes on her and clutches a kerchief to her throat, a crimson flush spreading across her neck. He kisses her nape, savors its sudden heat.

—Your fresh innocent beauty shames this exhausted world, he whispers, nipping the lobe of her ear between his teeth. Your very existence is an act of subversion!

—Sir, please, you confuse my poor senses! she gasps.

He slips into his own chair facing her, drawing it close, his left knee touching her right—she starts back, then with visible effort allows her knee to come in contact with his again. Her knee is trembling, and he places his hand there a moment, gently, tentatively, as a father might to calm a troubled daughter. She ducks her head shyly, though he can see her gazing adoringly at him through her veil.

—Oh, sir, you're so . . . so kind!

—It's not kindness, Cornelia. It's an instinctive movement of the soul seeking unity.

—If you could perceive the dreadful perturbation of my own soul at this moment, you would not say so, sir!

It's impossible, she can't exist. But she does, and she is here, and she is his! He has the receipt to prove it. What a coup! He feels a terrible urge to leap across the table and throw this delicious creature to the floor and fuck her madly without surcease, but he's well aware of the fragility of such a period piece and knows he must use restraint and delicacy, else all is ruined. If he can just remember the ancient routines. . . .

—O dear Cornelia, your sublime beauty has stolen my heart away. I am all aflame with consuming passion!

—I-I too, sir! But—

—We must not oppose it! Such heartfelt ardor—

—Would you care to order, sir?

—What? *What!* Ah. . . .

It's the damned waiter, with wretched timing, standing imperiously by their table. Cornelia withdraws her knee, turns away, touches a kerchief to her lips.

—The . . . uh, the house special! he snaps irritably, waving the waiter away.

—Yes, sir. That will be coddled eggs, steamed sausage, and plump melons tipped with strawberries as appetizers, followed by hot mutton and dumplings, garnished with gooseberries, the slits of peaches, lemons, and chopped liver?

—Yes, yes, whatever!

—Now, for dessert, we have finger pie served with a bit of jam, hot bananas with crushed nuts, and very rich cherry pud—

—Not now, damn you! Later!

The waiter hesitates, head cocked to one side, looking seriously offended; then, with a disparaging smirk in the direction of the veiled Cornelia, he bows slightly and withdraws.

—I'm so embarrassed!

—Ignore him, my dear. He's a pretentious busybody. I'll see to it that he's fired. Now . . . where was I?

—Such heartfelt ardor . . .

—Yes. Heartfelt ardor, right. Such heartfelt ardor cannot be denied, my precious!

He places his hand on her knee once more, and though she starts and pulls back for a moment, she soon relents and even gives his hand a sweaty little squeeze, casting an affectionate smile at him through her veil. Oh, he is desperately in love with this woman! He is in love with her heaving milk-white bosom, her veiled embarrassment, her soft and willing knee. Her fright enraptures him; her confusion drives him wild. Glorious! Why did he ever want to give this up to make home movies? He inches upward toward the soft flesh just above the knee.

—We must obey the instinct of love, Cornelia, else do great harm to our very souls! What is there worth living for like the sweets of love, the soft dalliance of . . . of . . . ?

—I know, I know! But, sir. . . .

—Yes?

—Are you married?

—*No!* Ah. Well, yes . . . sort of.

—Sort of?

—What can I say? There's a certain distance between us.

—You're unhappy.

—Well, I'm . . . she's lovely of course, and very sweet, but—

—She's lovelier than me?

—No! No one is more beautiful than you, Cornelia! She's cute, yes, but, well, she's just a kid, really.

—Oh. Then she's younger than me.

—Less well developed, you might say. Less mature and—ah, responsive, he adds, squeezing her thigh, making the hand holding his tremble. I could never speak like this with her, my love. She's still too much a child. And her technique is terrible! Infantile! She has no style! So jerky and fuzzy and everything sloppily put together! All I get out of it is headaches! What's worse, I'm not even sure I've actually enjoyed the, as you might say, full fruits of marriage with her.

Cornelia looks sorrowfully surprised. He doesn't know why he's telling her all this, he doesn't even know if it's true, but she seems so lovingly sympathetic, he can't resist opening his heart to her.

—Of course I have an infamous memory and there are her movies as evidence to the contrary, but every time I see them it's as if for the first time, and somehow we never get to any sort of—well, climax in them. She says she can't work the camera and do *that* at the same time, which is supposed to explain why the main bits are mostly missing, and I can understand that, but when I try to recall what happened when she put the camera down, I draw a blank. She likes to call her little movies samplings from our memory bank, only I don't seem to have made any of the deposits.

—You poor dear man! You are . . . unfulfilled.

—Exactly! The very word I was looking for! You're so understanding!

He strokes Cornelia's thigh, edging upward, and her hand grasps his as if to push it away, but then claps it all the more firmly to her leg and draws it toward her.

—And your husband? He's getting on, I take it. But not, I suppose—eh—getting it up?

—Oh, no. My husband is beautiful. Not at all old, as they say in the catalog. He's handsome, generous, brilliant, rich. His business, as I was instructed to call it, is a foot long and always hard as a fencepost.

—Really?! But then why—?

—Why am I betraying such a man to be here with you, dear sir? I want to betray him because it *excites* me to betray him, she whispers, breathing heavily and pushing forward on her chair. I want to know what it's like to be . . . to be. . . . Oh, sir. Though her face is hidden from his view, he can see her blush deepen behind the veil, spreading into the very roots of her hair. It's that old Victorian thing again. He loves it!

—Fucked? he wheezes, his own business beginning to drum on the underside of the table. Say it, Cornelia. You want to be . . . ?

She ducks her head, turns away, even while dragging his hand up her thigh. A fat little hillock, cleft and mossy, pushes against his fingertips through thick linen. Her lips part behind the veil, and her breath comes in short agitated gasps.

—Fucked, she whispers faintly, almost as though praying. By a . . . by a serious collector . . .

—Oh, Cornelia! There is no truth but the freedom each passing second grants us! We have but one life, one passage, soon to be ended; let us grasp the moment! We can go somewhere—

—Go somewhere?

She gropes for his leg. Her thighs open . . . close . . . open—then she suddenly draws away, moaning, as the waiter arrives and begins to clap their dishes insistently down upon the table. But only for a moment.

—Oh, Willie, she cries suddenly, sending the dishes crashing with a violent sweep of her elbow. I can't wait! I'm already starting to come! Let's get on the table and do it now!

Willie? Wait a minute.

—*Cally?* Is that you?

She is gasping and giggling or maybe whimpering under the veil, now somewhat askew, and tearing at her bodice stays with one hand, the other hauling his hand inside her linen drawers. I'm sorry, Willie, I blew the line. Wow! I'm just too fucking hot!

—God-*damn* you, Cally! he roars, yanking his hand out. He kicks back his chair in rage, throws over the table, rips away the drapes and knocks down the cameras concealed there, bowls over the grinning waiters, raises his finger to the maître d' and all the hired patrons, and slams out of there.

—Well, there he goes. Better send a crew after him before we lose him again.

—He won't go far. It's awfully bitter out there. He'll stop at the first movie house that's open.

—They're not all closed?

—Not the Foxy. One of my old movies is showing there in a rerun. He can't miss it.

Actors are milling about the set, obscuring the wake of his departure. Stage food is cleared from the tables and hands are helping Cally, still doubled up on the floor with her hands between her legs, out of her elaborate costume.

—I don't know. All this cunt-driven art. Maybe we should give his dick more room to swing here, sisters.

—Maybe. But I think L.P. prefers a tight working environment. And I must say, Connie, your technique's improving. Still too many static long shots and dizzying heavy-handed zooms, but it's more of a real production, a real movie.

—Oh, thank you! That means a lot, coming from you, Cecilia. I don't want to make *real movies,* as you call them, because I don't think they *are* real, but I wanted to prove I could if I did. I still have so much to learn. I never really worked with a crew before. And all these lights and wires and boom things. Cleo's been really helping a lot, though. And Catherine thought up some of the jokes.

—What I don't understand, though, is why you have to sneak up on him like that.

There is a low-key background muttering, a woman's burst of laughter, the scraping of a table leg on a hollow platform. A lighting technician shouts to an assistant. Cally's being helped to her feet. Equipment is pushed away on dollies.

—He's a professional; he can read a script.

—But that's the whole point, Cecilia. He's *not* a professional anymore. I wanted to remind him why he's in my home movies now and why he has to want to be. I want him to come home to me. Of his own free will.

—Who, L.P.? He has no free will.

—Well, I don't know, you may be right; all that stuff's over my head. But at least I want him to *think* he does.

—Anyway, Cece baby, it wouldn't be the same. Look.

The cleanup ceases abruptly. There is a blur of retreating images. The set rights itself as he yoyos back in. Cally resumes her seat, tearing at her bodice. The dishes rise from the floor to the table, then vanish again as the waiter backpedals out of the frame. His hand, pinched for a stilled moment between Cally's thighs, slips out, slides toward her knee, then gets dragged back again as the waiter returns. Blood drains away from his face as the dishes fly, returns in a rush:

—Cally? Is that you?

—I don't care how professional you are, you've got to get hit by the real thing to blanch like that! Our Con's got the right idea here. Just look what happens to his lower lip, the hair on his head—

—*Cally? Is that you?*

—And see the way his hard-on dips and rises? Almost a salute to his shock! Or here, watch this.

Again the blur. Stop. Start: He is smiling faintly, intent upon the woman, her hand on his hand as it inches up her thigh.

—*We must obey the instinct of love, Cornelia, else do great harm to our very souls! What is there worth living for like the sweets of love, the soft dalliance of . . . of . . . ?*

—Now, we could write those lines, indicate the soft stupid clumsiness with which they're to be spoken, but nobody could do it they'll just never be said the same way again.

—*We must obey the instinct of love, Cornelia, else do great harm to our very souls! What is there worth living for like the sweets of love, the soft dalliance of . . . of . . . ?*

—I mean, look how his little mustache twitches! It's so goddamn real, it's almost like seeing the silly thing there on his lip for the first time, like he grew it suddenly for the occasion! And that squint—there in the right eye, do you see it?

—*Worth living for like the sweets of love, the soft dalliance of; . . . ?*

—He got that in real life from peeking through keyholes; fuck your makeup and your professional mannerisms, baby, that's the genuine article! You can't see his cock under the table in this shot, but you know what state it's in, just from that squint!

—Script it in, Cleo, he'll produce it. You underestimate him.

—Nah, he'd be worried about those nutty lines, what he has to do with his hands, the napkin—

The film is running. He is stroking her thigh and she is squeezing his hand. His erection is thumping the table.

—*I want to know what it's like to be . . . to be. . . . Oh, sir.*

—*Fucked? Say it, Cornelia. You want to be . . . ?*

—And besides, he knows Cally's bod too well; even if he remembered to squint, it would only be an imitation; the glitter would be gone, the penetration.

—Yeah, well, abuse him, lose him, guys. This is just not the way to make a movie. You've hurt him, chased him off. He's an artist. This candid camera crap's an insult. He'll always run away from it.

—So what if he does? You need that. The raw emotion. The tension. That shocked look when history hits you in the face.

—Goodness! I don't even understand what you two are arguing about!

—That happens in scripted films, too. It's always new and unexpected. In that sense, all film is documentary, whether it's about a man caught on the street or an actor dressed up and playing a part.

—Oh, quiet, both of you! Here it comes again.

He blanches, flushes. The waiter is staggering backward. The woman is giggling, her decorum collapsing.

—*Cally?* Is that you?

—I'm sorry, Willie, I blew the line. Wow! I'm just too fucking hot!

He explodes with rage, kicks back the chair and throws over the table, curses the crew, wrecks the set, and storms out. He's had enough of this shit! Fuck them! Fuck everybody! Everybody but Connie. She at least had nothing to do with his newest humiliation; the presence of a professional crew has told him that much, but all the others clearly had a hand in it. Well, he's through with them, through with the scripted life. He zips up. That's it. Put it away. For good. They've made an ass of him for the last time. Not that they were unassisted of course. He's also to blame. His lamentable impulses. He went in to the sale seeking a gift for his true love and helpmeet and came out possessed by lust, and not just for another cunt but for possession itself: to possess and be possessed. What makes him do that? Why does he have to want them all? Or want to have them all? He's always believed all love was good wherever you found it, but he was wrong. He built a career on it and the career's over. It's been over for a while, but he keeps forgetting. No more. He wants now that purity of heart to will one thing. He wants continuity. He wants to go home.

If it's still there. He signed it away. Oh my god! Lost his mittens, too. Doesn't have the TV dinners or ginger cookies. Poor Connie. Tears of genuine sorrow and chagrin are running down his cheeks and freezing in the icy wind. Such an innocent trusting little creature and he's let her down. Her expression when he left haunts him now: her desperate loving appeal. And so vulnerable and unprotected—he remembers that the neighbors crowding around her (he seems to see them there before him like a double exposure) had their hands on her. Then it went dark. Oh no! What has he done? How can she ever forgive him? She's so desirable and sweet and affectionate. A little capricious, maybe, sometimes a touch goofy, but he is utterly smitten, has been since he first laid eyes on her. The girl next door. Probably. Doesn't matter. Whoever she was, wherever she came from, marrying her was the most creative thing he ever did. It amounted to an invention of purpose in a purposeless world, an act of resistance against the pervasive emptiness. Also, she is sexy and exciting. And focused just on him. He wants nothing more than to be back in bed with her, never mind if it's for nothing more than tenting themselves with the sheets and playing house with her dolls; he just wants her there beside him. But it's probably too late! *Oh! oh! oh!* he weeps, staggering miserably down the wintry street. Why did he ever set foot outside that cottage door?

He's crying so hard he almost fails to notice that the tarnished brass doors of the movie house he's passing are open. It's the Foxy, oldest movie palace in town, even more venerable than the Frivoli, now a repertory cinema showing reruns of the old classics. By luck the movie on today is Connie's most famous film, *Our Wedding*. The one he's always wanted to see! When it was sent out on first release, it was retitled by the producers *Here Cums the Bride*, but after its spectacular success she was able to insist on its proper name and it's been known by it ever since. THE GREATEST STORY EVER TOLD! it says over the doors. YOUR LIFE WILL BE CHANGED FOREVER! He's broke, but there's no one in the ticket booth so he goes on in, passing through the famous circular foyer with its crimson and gold decorations, now looking tattered and abandoned, drawn by the muffled strains of the wedding march, which explode exuberantly upon him when he opens the inner double doors and enters the darkened theater.

The opening titles and credits are already rolling as he takes his seat. He sees himself up on the big screen dressed in scarlet top hat and tails riding in a bright green convertible with a carload of women, sisters of the bride, down sunny city streets—yes, sunny. Old Sol is out for the first time in recent memory, everything is thawing out, and even the old silted-up and frozen canals seem to be running again! It's a kind of tickertape parade; the glowing city canyons are filled with millions of strands of chopped-up audio and video tape and old 8mm film, fluttering down upon him and his companions (Connie is not among them, nor are there, for once, any filmcrews) like a kind of anointing, glittering like ribbons of gold in the amazing sunlight. Oh, he knows he's going to like this movie! Happily ever after, that's his future! And it's about time! The crowds are out and cheering, parading musicians with amplified guitars, accordions, and portable keyboards are playing popular love songs and show tunes and children's melodies said to be favorites of the bride, dancing girls in wispy chemises are throwing flowers at the multitudes, the polished convertible is sliding along, bright as an emerald, and everybody's smiling. It's a great day! The camera holds its fixed position as he rolls into the frame and out of it again, waving at the crowds, then cuts to another vantage point. Though he drifts in and out of focus as the convertible enters and exits the picture at different angles and distances, one can see in the expression on his face—he seems to have just woken up—a conflict of joy and terror, which causes a nervous twitching of the eyes and mouth and suggests he might not know whether he's on his way to a party or his execution. Evidently it's a surprise wedding.

The procession pulls up in front of the High Church of Hard Core, as the illuminated marquee over the faux-Gothic doors declares it to be. Massive crowds have gathered. He stands on the seat of the convertible to peer out over their heads, looking around in some amazement, or alarm, and discovers, as does the viewer, that he's dressed in only the top half of the scarlet tuxedo. He sits back down hastily but the convertible door is already open and he is being bumped out onto the pavement. An aisle forms between car and church, lined by tonsured monks and wimpled nuns, dressed in black-and-white costumes honoring one of his most famous movies from the monochrome era, and, glancing uneasily back over his shoulder, he proceeds up it, still trailing streamers of tape and film, prodded along by the women whenever he hesitates, his progress watched from the rear by the camera until, still glancing back, he disappears through the gaping doors into the darkness beyond.

Abruptly, there is a view of the interior of the church as seen from the back of the auditorium. Nothing has begun yet. The wedding guests, studying the numbers on their ticket stubs, are entering and locating their seats in front of the static camera. The effect is of someone dozing in the back row with her eyes open. There is a hum of low friendly chatter under a sound composition made from grunts and groans and shrieks of orgasmic pleasure, which is either playing overhead on the church's public address system or is part of the film's soundtrack. The room is filled with plaster-of-Paris gods and goddesses, saints, martyrs, and prophets, all displaying their aroused private parts, as they were called in the old days when religion was still a force in the city, or engaged in pious fornicative and bestial acts. The stained-glass windows depict classic images, now colorized by the glass, from the days of the eight-page comics. With the bright light behind them, they look like giant magic lantern slides. There are large fringed mandalas oozing pearls, confessionals for sacramental fellatio and cunnilingus, holy-water fountains with fat squatting gods emitting endless sprays of jism from their laps, and seven-branched flesh-colored candelabra spurting gouts of blue fire. There is time to observe all this from the back of the church while waiting for people to take their seats and things to begin. In fact, there is not much else to do. Now and then the image is shaken by someone bumping the camera while squeezing past, giving the viewer an authentic sense of being present at a real moment in time. Some of the wedding guests wear sequined FUCK ME! skullcaps, winged phalli dangling from gold necklaces, and mantillas woven from pubic hair, and there are cum-stained prayer rugs unfurled in front of the bloodstained altar, which is in the shape of a four-poster bed with stirrups. Standing there before it, tall and haughty, is the High Priestess herself, the Mayor in another of her official roles, dressed in traditional body-tight black leather canonicals, gold ornaments, and the ancient black velvet scapular of her office embroidered with the seven sacred erotic tortures, as defined by the Holy Script, which she holds in her hands. On the screen behind her, pale anonymous bare bodies fuck one another endlessly in looped overlapped montages, imitating the quiet turmoil of the cosmos.

The camera continues to run, and now the guests have settled into their seats at last and the principals are coming down the aisle, the groom in red hat and tails on one side and the bride in white organdy and lace on the other, stepping in sprightly fashion to the syncopated rhythm of ancient bump-and-grind hymeneals as provided by the bride's sisters, all accomplished musicians. Though the bride's apparel is complete with jeweled crown, white veil, precious pearls woven into the bodice, and a pale silken train so light it floats on the air like fog, her gown too only goes down to the waist, and one can catch brief glimpses of her little bottom as it passes between the heads of the wedding guests ,which mostly obscure it. It is a beautiful bottom, tight and lightly flushed; he'd forgotten how beautiful it was, like that of a little doll, and he wishes he were there and had control of the zoom lens on the camera, if it has one. They are greeted at the altar by the High Priestess, who, facing the camera and towering above them, reaches down and apparently takes each by his or her genitals and, agitating them as though insisting upon their undivided attention, pronounces over them incantatory words taken from the script held up by one of the bridesmaids. These are seemingly instructions on the proper use of these holy parts, as best can be intuited from the few fragments reaching the back of the church.

—And do you promise, Peter Prick, one can hear the Priestess say distantly at one point, his hat and his bride's crown bouncing lightly on their heads as she speaks, to suck Constance's clitoris with the utmost devotion and delicacy, lapping beneath its resilient flesh and drawing it deep into your mouth, then forcing it to the roof of your hard palate, tonguing it vigorously back and forth there between the medial and lateral side of your palatine ridge until she screams for mercy?

—I do!

—And you, Constance Cunt, do you, my dear, promise to stroke Peter's penis from tip to root with your warm wet tongue, laving it generously in your copious saliva, being ever wary not to snag or nip it with your incisors, and then, whilst fingering his testicles as one might knead a kitten's ears and inserting a finger, bathed in your own secretions, deep into the inner recesses of his rectum, to take his penis entire into your mouth, yea, until it reacheth your very epiglottis, and there to draw lovingly forth upon it until . . .

The rest is lost, but he does seem to see Connie's head bob shyly in affirmation when Cora's lips stop moving, and he is thrilled by that. Then the High Priestess, licking at her hands before drying them on her velvet scapular, asks the couple to kneel so as not to block the view and announces that it is time in the ceremony for something old, something new, something borrowed, something blue: to wit, a newly digitized version of the bride's old blue movie, *The Girl Next Door,* checked out on this occasion from the city archives. The church darkens, the copulating bodies disappear from the large screen behind the altar, and a dim water-spotted image emerges there of two children in a hayloft, peeking in each other's clothes. A variety of fragmentary incomplete scenes follow, everything from watching grown-ups through knotholes do what they do to playing doctor, learning naughty words, and going to the toilet, most of it rather crudely spliced together and poorly filmed; the digitizing hasn't helped it much. Hardly worth looking at, but one sequence captures his attention. The two children, he and Connie when little, presumably, are having a picnic in a meadow somewhere with bread-and-butter sandwiches and lemonade. She is wearing a gaily colored cotton dress with a stiff crinoline lining that causes her skirt to rise up whenever she bends over or sits down, and he is trying to see her underpants beneath it. She often sits carelessly on the picnic blanket with her knees up, but her skinny legs are somehow always in the way of a good view. Then, just as he catches a glimpse at last of the precious little band of white cotton between her childish thighs, she asks:

—Peter? What happens when we die?

—Oh, I don't know, he says, as his exciting view vanishes. Nothing, I guess.

He changes position on the blanket, hoping for a better angle. He *does* remember her now, though. As little Peter Prick, he had a terrific crush on her; he still has now, as a man; in fact he can't really tell the two states apart. She was and is the cutest thing he's ever seen. And he wants so much to see and touch her private places. He'd forgotten how much it meant to him, means to him.

—I mean, that *is* what happens, I think: nothing. You know, the end of the reel. It just runs out of the projector and that's it.

—Does that scare you?

He shrugs, trying to appear manly. Sure, a little. In fact, any time he thinks about it, which he tries not to, he feels like number-twoing himself, but he doesn't say this. She has turned so very serious, and he wants to get back to the tickling games they were playing earlier.

—Will you hold my hand when I am dying, Peter?

—Yeah, sure, Connie, if you'll hold this for me, he replies mischievously, unbuttoning the fly of his short pants. It's hard to find his thing, even stiff as it is, but he manages at last to spring it out of there into the light of day.

—It's so tiny! she exclaims. She takes it in her soft childish hand and bends it this way and that as if trying to see where it came from.

—Well, I'm still just a little boy.

—But it's very pretty. It looks like a little rubbery clothes-peg. She thumbs the head to test its resilience, making him jump and giggle. May I kiss it?

—Gosh! Sure!

He rather hopes she'll do a great deal more than that, but she bends over, her skirt rising up behind (he's on the wrong side of her, darn it), and gives it a dry puckery little peck on the tip, as one might kiss the cheek of a grandmother, then sits back again, still holding it but with her mind elsewhere.

—Anyway, Connie, we won't die, he says, trying to cheer her up and get her back to the clothes-peg. We're in the movies. We're immortal.

She looks away as if considering this, but she doesn't seem to believe it. Neither does he. It's just a line. Nothing lasts forever. He knows there are some early films of his for which there are no longer any projectors on which they can be run. In fact, this might be one of them, he thinks, and that scares him a little. Her little hand goes on squeezing and relaxing its grip absently, as though in rhythm with her sad thoughts, and he can feel something starting inside that he's never felt before, something frightening but very nice at the same time. He can't tell where the feeling is located exactly, somewhere between his tummy and his bottomhole, though also somehow between his ears, and he only hopes it isn't some terrible fatal disease that he has brought on himself by his frivolous remarks.

—Do you really promise, Peter? Cross your heart and hope to die?

—Promise?

—I mean, to hold my hand when I am dying, or any time I'm afraid of dying.

—Sure, Connie. I promise.

—Okay. You can look then.

She lets go of what she's been toying with and lies back on the picnic blanket with her legs loosely spread, one hand under her head, the crinoline lifting the front of her skirt. Perfectly placid, perfectly still. His heart is pounding wildly and that feeling down below is more intense than ever. He hopes he won't get so excited he goes blind and won't be able to see anything. He kneels between her knees and pushes up her skirt, watched by her with such a serious expression he's at a loss to know what to say or do, so he just smiles weakly.

—You're so much prettier than me! And she is. Her little body is almost straight up and down with only the hint of a narrowing waist and little hips beginning to take shape, but it is exquisitely soft and beautiful. He immediately wants to be an artist and look at bodies like this for the rest of his life. Her cotton panties fit tightly and he can see, molded by them, the shape of the little mound between her legs. It is completely smooth and cleft in the middle where the panties dig in a bit. He reaches for it tentatively.

—Don't touch! Just look!

Okay, he thinks. Sure. Looking's a kind of touching, too, a kind of having. And right now, it's good enough. In fact, it's great. The actual sliding movement of the waistband of her underpants as he tugs at it, his fingertips trailing down her flat pale tummy as if sledding down it, is like the most exciting movie he ever saw, and he is dizzied by the sweet milky fragrance that is rising from below it. Her navel has come into view, and though he has seen navels before, he has never seen anything quite like this marvelous little dent in her perfect flesh and he wants desperately to kiss it, though he knows, even as he leans toward it, he dare not. She has never stopped watching him with that searching look. The underpants are stuck where she's lying on them, so he has to reach under to pull them down past her bottom. She lifts up slightly to help him. As his fingers trace those curved velvety surfaces, his whole body feels like it's throbbing, and there's an ache in his chest and in his marbles, his stiff little thing all aquiver. Oh wow!

—Peter? He hesitates, his fingers trembling; he's so close! She has relaxed her weight and his trapped fingers are, in effect, holding her bare bottom. Peter, will you always be with me and never ever go away? she asks, her little-girl voice quavering slightly as though she might be about to cry.

—Oh yes! I promise, Connie! I *promise*! I *do*!

—Okay. Then, she says, lifting her bottom up again, if you want to . . . you can, you know, do . . . But he can't hear the rest. The film is fading away.

—No, wait! he cries, but to no avail. The lights are coming up in the church auditorium. There's shuffling, chuckling, throat clearing, the rattling of programs. He tries to rise, but his neck is caught on something. The High Priestess is glowering down on him with her finger at her lips.

—Shush! she whispers sternly, wagging admonishingly in front of his nose an enormous dildo she's strapped on, a phosphorescent orange one with a brightly spotted head that looks like the cap of some lethal mushroom. We've come to the main part of the ceremony!

He glances at Connie, eager to see what's showing below the waist, but her bridal gown now reaches to the toes of her shoes, and he too is fully dressed in the complete red tuxedo, though it still feels quite airy at the rear, indeed all the way up to the back of his neck. What's odd is that they are both now child-sized. Then he realizes that they are on their knees still, handcuffed into a carnival photo board with small bride-and-groom images painted on the front and holes for their heads and hands. Connie's train has been tossed over the top of the board like a raised tail and is hanging down mistily in front of her terrified face. Her hand holding the wedding bouquet is trembling. Tourist cameras are flashing fore and aft, and he supposes the camera at the back of the church is also recording it all.

Meanwhile the monks and nuns and other wedding guests are pulling on rubber gloves and dildos and, following the lead of the swaggering High Priestess, dipping them or their penises, if they have one, in fonts of perfumed lubricants and lining up behind the photo board. Whereupon, at last, the traditional wedding march resumes. Or begins. Connie emits a little yelp beside him and her head bobs forward, her shoulders banging against the back of the photo board. She sinks back, clearly in shock, tears coming to her eyes, and then, crying out softly, she pounds forward again, and she goes on doing this, more or less in sync with the heavy thump of the wedding march. *Oh! Oh! Oh oh!* she cries, the flowers flying from her hand, her crown dipping over her perky little nose. He tries to see what they're doing, but his view is blocked by the board. *Peter?* she gasps tremulously, looking up at him from under the tipped crown with a heartrending expression of fear, love, trust, pain

—You can't do this! She's my wife! he cries out—or supposes he does; he can't hear a thing. *Not yet!* someone whoops behind him. They're oiling up his anus back there and—Cora? where is she?—oh no! He tries with all his might to free his head, but the hole is too tight. They must have stuck his head in there when he was still little, he thinks, beginning to panic and lose his reason. He screams out curses, rattles his cuffs, kicks out at those crowding around him at the rear, but to no avail. Connie is still banging the photo board rhythmically, but she seems to have passed out. Her head bounces loosely above the painted wedding gown, her jaw agape, and spittle dribbles down her little chin. He feels hands all over him, some of them trying to pry apart his greased buttocks which he is squeezing tight in a desperate effort to keep out whatever it is that's trying to get in. His unconscious bride, meanwhile, is released from her handcuffs, dragged from the board, lifted high overhead by half a dozen wedding guests (was that blood on her bridal train, dangling between her legs?), and carried limply to the altar, where they prepare to fasten her ankles in the stirrups. He has lost the battle to the rear but they have freed him up front, his handcuffs dropping away and the photo board splitting in half and disappearing like theater flats, and now, brutally impaled and feet dangling, dressed only in his top hat, he is posted, so to speak, by the High Priestess to the altar. Next time, he thinks, as he hovers painfully there above his bride, spread before him upon the altar but covered at present by a multitude of humping bodies, heads, and hands, we'll just elope.

For a moment, the world recedes and he feels as remote from it as a stylite in the desert, gazing down from his painful perch upon an irredeemable world, all his sorrows, desires, regrets as nothing more than the shifting dunes of sand far, far below. He is, however, as has often been remarked and not always to his credit, a man of action more than meditation, of deeds, not words or thoughts, a man who, if impulsive and frequently misguided, is also decisive and, but for certain quirks of vanity, uninhibited and ultimately irrepressible. And so it is now, after only a moment's hesitation, a moment not unlike being snagged briefly in projector sprockets and then released, he doubles the High Priestess over with a swift ferocious elbow to her midriff and slides off her slick dildo as it dips, strips it from her while she's still getting her wind back, and wields it like a club against the feckless ravagers of his bride. Heads, in short, are opened and her assailants fall back, bloodied and quailing. He releases his lifeless love from her stirrups, flops her over his shoulder (for some reason, someone's tied tin cans to her ankles and there's a tag taped over her behind), and, teeth bared and still vehemently swinging the dildo, charges up the aisle, the cans rattling. He expects resistance, but the wedding guests only laugh and applaud and throw rice as at any wedding.

He rather hopes the green convertible will be waiting at the curb for a quick getaway, but instead he finds his path blocked by thousands of unticketed spectators who have been watching the ceremony on giant screens outside the church and who appear collectively aroused by what they've seen. Tearing off their clothes and chanting dully—*The bride! The bride!*—they come staggering toward him, red-eyed and drooling. He has no choice but to drop the dildo and run, handicapped by the dead weight he carries but counting on his intimate knowledge of the urban maze to outmaneuver if not outpace them. He seems to see an overview of that maze in his head as if filmed from high above the city, he a lone naked red-hatted figure sprinting through it with another naked person slung over his shoulder, butt-high (a zoom reveals the tag on it to read JUST MARRIED), chased by an indiscriminate flood of humanity spreading through the city streets like flowing lava. He is seen to escape them now and then for a moment, but what they lack in velocity and direction is offset by sheer volume, their eruptive flow threatening to inundate the entire city from all sides and wall him in. He avoids broad avenues and open spaces, darting instead down narrow passageways, over low fences, in and out of warehouses and tenement cellars, through tight underpasses, all of which clog up sooner or later with the thick fleshy mass of his pursuers and become momentarily impassable. Block by block their shouts and grunts and pounding feet grow more and more distant, until at last, when he feels he cannot run another step, he reaches an alley in a rundown tenement district at the very heart of the urban maze, and their ugly noises vanish altogether, or he persuades himself that they do, and he throws his bride and himself down behind some trashcans to hide until he can breathe again.

This heart of the maze, if it is the heart, is, like all hearts, a cul-de-sac, and so a fatal trap if they are found. And they will be. Should keep moving. May not have much time. But it's the first moment he's been alone with his newlywed in recent memory, if that's the word for his peculiar disability, and moreover they're both naked, or mostly naked, that's completely new, so it's time, he feels, even if she is somewhat comatose, in fact out cold, for a quick conjugal cuddle. Besides, his ass is numb, teeth hammering, feet frozen, and she also seems pretty stiffened up; they could both use a little warmth. No sign of that earlier sun, must have been a false thaw or more likely just another bit of movie magic. He hadn't meant to consummate his marriage in a dark cold alley, chambered by trashcans and bedded in rotting vegetables and old newspapers, but it may be the only chance he gets. She's still wearing her little bridal crown over her nose, but only tatters of the train and bodice remain, and her bared breasts, he sees, are not only childlike in size, they are nippleless. Her navel has gone missing too, though she seems otherwise flawless, smooth-skinned and exquisitely proportioned. Her knees are stuck in the up position, the way he was carrying her, so he turns her over, her tin cans rattling (there's a distinct rumble inside somewhere, too, and it does not sound like indigestion), propping her up on her locked knees, to feast his eyes on that firm little bottom he so admires, and, peeling away the JUST MARRIED label, discovers it is also, beautiful as it is (though even firmer than he might have hoped), missing an important functional element. Her legs are articulated, he sees now, at the juncture of buttocks and thighs, the shiny pink surface between them as smooth as an egg. Nothing on it except for a little printed instruction below a red dot that reads OPEN HERE. He knocks on it, gets a hollow echo in reply, the raised ass above it as solid and immobile as a cleft cliff face. A tough one. He'll need a tool, a jimmy of some kind.

He pokes through the trashcans, wishing now he hadn't thrown away Cora's powerful dildo. All he finds here are broken umbrellas, old turret lenses and hypo needles (he tries one; it breaks off), bobbins, rollers, and processor pins, gnawed bones of uncertain provenance, butts and roaches, a dirty old herringbone overcoat, smeared with garbage and bloodied down the front (he puts it on), a plastic squeegee handle, punctured diaphragms, one old cast-off shoe (that goes on too: left foot), rolling spiders, a dead cat, broken crane jibs, moldy jockstraps, nothing at all he can use for breaking in where instructed and much of it pretty sickening. He can hear running feet, not far away, approaching snorts and cries; they'll be here soon. No time for niceties. He grabs up an empty beer bottle, smashes the neck off, and rams it in, shattering the bottom and sending the whole works clattering headfirst into the trashcans. Damn! They'll hear that. He only has a few seconds. He thrusts his fist inside her and fishes around: hollow but for the thing that's been rattling around in it. A kind of egg. Not golden, as one might have hoped, but black with little red pimples all over like a rash. Still, it has a certain offbeat quality; it might be worth something or have something valuable inside. Her dowry. He can hear them now, only a few blocks away, a lusty multivoiced bellowing, thousands of bare feet slapping the icy pavement. But they don't want him, they want her. So he goes limping out to meet them in his hat, coat, and shoe, posting himself at the mouth of the cul-de-sac to aim them down it. The other thing they might lust after is the egg. Only one safe place to hide it and he shoves it up there just as they come roaring down the dark narrow street in a full-voiced lather. He bows and swoops his red top hat toward the mess in the alley, then hastily backs away as they thunder past. *There she is! Hunh! Hunh!* Does he hear screams, cries, even his name? Maybe. Can't think about it. Might be his turn next. He's on the move.

Though not so nimbly as before. Not so young-Peter-Prickly. It has been a hard day. Must have taken something out of him. He hobbles along, one shoe off and one shoe on, the old tweed coat weighing him down and the egg hurting him with every step, knocking against his prostate or something. When he feels he's put enough distance between himself and the mob to risk a pause, he slips into a shadowy shop doorway out of the bitter weather and digs for the egg. Can't quite reach it. It has slid farther up and got lodged somehow. Never mind. Sooner or later he'll pass it. Just have to remember to keep watching for it. The frayed woolen overcoat stinks and scratches his bare skin, but it's better than nothing; the icy wind has started up again and there are flurries in the air. The shop sells sex pets but there's a sign on the door: CLOSED FOR THE WINTER. Nevertheless, an old lady comes out of it, calling him a filthy old bum, and starts beating him with a broom to chase him off. He'd take the broom away from her and show her what to do with it, but he's suddenly feeling rather woozy and figures it's best just to shuffle on down the street and look for shelter until he's over it. Only hungry, maybe. When was the last time he ate? Wasn't he in a restaurant awhile ago? Must have left too soon.

By the time he's found another protected doorway a few blocks down the street, he feels worse than ever. Hot flushes now alternate with bone-shaking chills. His gut aches and he feels gassy and nauseated. Maybe it's the stinking coat that's making him sick. But it's snowing harder, too cold to take it off. He has to pee and does so and gets chased off again. He can hardly move; his legs feel leaden and it's harder to breathe for some reason, as though he might be suffering some massive indigestion, and that also slows him down. At the same time, he has a terrible craving for gooseberries and coddled eggs. He's hardly gone a block when he has to pee again. His stomach is so bloated it sticks out of the coat now. He can't stop farting. His back hurts. And five minutes later, he's peeing again. What's wrong? The head of his penis is puffy and discolored and the little purple veins running down it are more prominent than usual. The prim little smirk of the urethra's slit looks more like a gaping scream for help. His testicles are swollen too. Oh no. Must be some fucking venereal disease. Best he can recall, though, he hasn't had much chance lately to catch anything. There are fine little cracks appearing now on his inflated belly, which looks like it's about to burst. Feels like it, too. Weighs a ton and seems to want to ride up under his chin and close off his windpipe. Looking at it, he feels enraged and tearful at the same time. Everything seems to be shifting about inside like something's alive in there. A deadly parasite, maybe. That garbage he was lying in! Oh my god. He needs a doctor! He belches and smells something nitrous. He's dying! Help! He lumbers agonizingly on down the street through the blowing snow, terrified by what's happening to him, stopping every few minutes to dribble against a wall. Maybe it's that damned egg. He tries fishing for it again, but his ass is plugged up and he can't get his finger in. Feels flabby, his ass, and spreading. His prick hurts. He pees again. It doesn't help. Hurts worse. His pubic cradle seems to have split and given way to the weight above, making him feel bowlegged. His limbs have shriveled and are knobby and swollen at the joints. He looks like shit, he knows, and he just can't bear it. No one had ever told him it would be like this! He bursts into tears.

Then he sees it. His honeymoon cottage. It's beautiful! It's paradise! He staggers, one-shoed, through the green snow toward it, past all the cardboard cows and fake flowers, carrying his belly with both hands, weeping openly. He's home! He'll never leave it again! He can breathe more easily now that everything's dropped lower, but his balls feel like they're holding up the world. There's a sign on the rose-red door: FOR SALE BY CITY. It opens and Connie appears, looking haggard and ill-fed, dressed in colorless rags, surrounded by half a dozen small children and holding another in her arms. She still looks young, but there are worry lines on her face and her body has gone slack as though giving up and sinking earthward. She does not seem happy to see him again. He falls to his knees, his aching bony knees. In supplication. In contrition. In pain: the muscles in his gut have started grabbing at him periodically like iron fists, and everything is sinking like a boulder into his throbbing scrotum.

—Connie! he sobs. Let me . . . let me explain!

—It had better be good, she replies flatly.

—It's terrible, I-I'm—oh, *boo hoo!* he bawls. He can hardly talk. He feels so helpless, so vulnerable. And so utterly at her mercy. *Help* me, Connie! Can't you see? *I'm pregnant!*

She stares down at him, wearily taking in his condition. All right, come on in then, she says finally, stepping aside. I'll call the doctor and put some hot water on.

She's hardly said this before he's lying on a cot in the spare room with his legs spread. Clara and her assistants are all around him. Maybe he passed out. Or there was a bad splice. Cally's there in her student nurse outfit. A one-eyed midwife. Others he probably knows behind their surgical facemasks. They've pulled the plug in his anus and are giving him an enema over a bedpan. They all seem to think this is very funny, even Connie, who's back at his side once more with her digital camera. For the family album, she explains, using the automated close-up feature. He would protest, he's hardly at his best down there, but he can't risk losing her again. She's all he's got!

—We are clearly into the dilatation stage of the soft structures, girls, Clara is explaining, pointing out various features. His testicles look less like eggs, as they're laughably called, than little pilot's goggles or flattened beanbags, stretched out there across the distended pelvic floor, which is not a floor really, but more like a trampoline, while his birthing canal, as we might now call it, is standing taller and chunkier than ever, a real woofer in outward appearance, yet it's soft as a sponge and incredibly sensitive—

—*Yow!* he screams, as she flicks it with her fingernail.

—That gaudy blue roadmap of veins suggests that his circulation, like most of his tubes, has been squeezed off, his kidneys are under pressure as we can see from the constant leaking, and you'll notice how his asshole is extruding in the classic manner.

—Yes, with that syringe in it, it looks like it's trying to toot its own horn!

—Or blow a kiss! It's cute!

When they pop the syringe out he can hear it gurgle as it spews out its contents, or maybe they're just mockingly providing the sound effects. It helps some, but not much. The spasmodic cramping continues.

—Oh nuts! says Connie, turning away. I think it got on the lens.

—How long have you been like this? Clara wants to know, her hand resting professionally on the taut balloon of his belly while the others clean him up.

—I don't know! *Hours!*

—Hours! laugh the assistants. The midwife is now massaging his belly with warm oils. She seems to be using one of her feet for this.

—Men are always so lucky!

—Well. The next part won't be so easy. All right, girls. Let's get ready. The contractions are coming more frequently now.

—*Wait a minute! Where is this thing coming out?* he screams.

—The usual place, of course.

—Do you think we can get the forceps down there, doctor?

—We'll have to. I just hope we don't have to perform a urethrotomy to do it.

—*What—?! What are you saying?*

—Relax. You're doing fine. Just keep pushing.

—*No! Stop it now! I don't want to do this!*

They all laugh.

—Bit late for that, isn't it? Now, take a deep breath and hold it, keeping your diaphragm rigid and pushing down to the utmost. Like you always like to say when taking a maidenhead, gentleness is not real kindness. A good thrust will force better than gentle pushes! Come on now, bear down!

—His prostate is less like a chestnut now than a watermelon, says the student nurse with her finger up his ass. It even makes a thunking noise when I thump it.

—*Cut! Cut!* he cries, but to no avail.

—That's it. Push! It will help if you will just bear down on the abdominal muscles, bringing to bear all the ordinary and extraordinary muscles of respiration to increase the intra-abdominal pressure . . .

—*Oh shit!* he shrieks. He feels like he's being ripped inside out between his legs. *Ah! Oh! Fucking hell! This is the worst thing that ever happened to me!*

—Nonsense, dear, says Connie. It's only a little birth. Let's try to be a bigger boy about it.

—Just think of it as taking a difficult dump through your dick, counsels the midwife more generously, winking her one rheumy eye while pressing down on his belly. A little push-push and you'll be awright.

—*All right? All right? How can I be all right?* The pain is outrageous. He wishes he never *had* one of these things! He'll never use it again! *Yow! Fuck! Get your hands off me! This is impossible!*

—Very good! Keep it up! It's coming!

—*NO!*

—Yes, I can see it! Get ready, it's a big one!

—Wow! A real nine-reeler!

—Don't cry, dearest! This is such a happy moment!

—*Aarrgh!*

—But it looks like a breech birth, doctor! Tails first!

—Right! I can see the rolling credits!

—Looks pretty raw!

—Get some gauze for the blood!

—*Stop! Stop!*

—Don't let go of it! Keep pulling it out of there!

—*Leave it! Leave it!*

—Almost there!

—What's it called?

—We won't know until it's completely out. Come on, just a little more!

—That's it!

—It's beautiful!

—String it up! Bring it to life!

Somewhere, at his feet (the terrible pain's subsiding, but he feels as if opened up with razor blades, that worthless thing between his legs in tatters), he can hear the whir of a projector.

—Now, that wasn't so bad, was it?

—Fuck you. Just go away and leave me alone. What an emptiness. Like he expelled everything, heart, brains, guts and all.

—Okay! Here we go! It's brand spanking new!

—I'm so proud of you, Peter!

—Lights! Camera . . . !

ACTION!

Reel 6: Carlotta

Adventures *of Crazy Leg: Part II*

Somewhere in the city's snow-whipped and restless pedestrian sea, invisible to the camera eye, walks a singular man, singular as all men are singular, yet to himself, though fallen into them as a star turned to stone might fall among stones, *not* as all men but one whose sufferings exceed theirs by virtue of that very fall and his awareness of it and of what, in falling, he has lost. And one distinguished as well by his implacable resolution, if it is not mere habit or nature's gift or else ordeal, for though it is the fashion for men to wear their penises outside their pants, few among them brave the wintry winds to do so, and of those few who do, fewer still can wear them, frost encumbered, with such unbending earnestness. And indeed it is by this staunchness of spirit and of part that he is discovered among the huddled masses—this compaction of misery and affliction, as has been said—hat jammed down around his ears, brim touched by the upturned lapels of his herringbone overcoat, chin and mouth wrapped with a scarf, little of him visible but for eyes aglitter with righteous vexation, a mustache bejeweled with frozen mucus, and that proud instrument which, livid-tipped, precedes him rigidly, inchwise, in his passage—his engine, as it were, that which draws him ineluctably on, its own blue lips pursed as if with indignation, dipping and rising militantly with each step, aggressively batting against all that it encounters, prepared as ever to enter all orifices that dare present themselves, though few in this hibernal weather do.

What is he doing out here? Why has he left hearth and home and thrown himself out once more upon these unforgiving streets? As if in reply (or perhaps he is thinking this, a flashback as it were), an insert shows him and his wife and children being evicted from their little cottage, he wrapped in blankets and looking weak and ill yet from his recent confinement and travail.

Another reestablishes them in a communal megastructure on the wrong side of the sewage plant and drainage canals, the only things still flowing in the city, if sluggishly. They are seen carrying into their shared dark space the sole piece of furniture from the cottage granted them, the yellow sofa, now stained and tattered, the stuffing knocked out by children jumping on it (this jumping is briefly seen, an insert within the insert), an all-purpose article that will serve them as seat, bed, playground, table, and site of what conjugal relations may yet be entertained, if any. From the door of this crowded abode, he is sent forth by his tearful wife in pursuit of gainful employment by which to earn a few scraps for their table—that is to say, their sofa, their sunny yellow sofa, which is not sunny anymore—and also, she adds, get tickets for the circus, our poor children, her hand raised in apprehensive farewell as drooling cohabitants drag her back inside, his apparel as seen at the outset of hat, scarf, boots, and dark-stained herringbone coat with upturned collar suggesting that this sequence might explain his return to the bitter heart of the snowbound metropolis, wherein we see him once more and as before.

And now—as, through the blood, slush, and melancholic debris of the city sidewalks, in and out of the spit and blast of the roaring traffic, atop the rumble of the underground trains below, and beneath the rain of suicides from above, he continues to shoulder his way stubbornly through these surly, bruising masses of humanity, most of them stupefied by cold and despair and failed imaginations—one is granted glimpses of some of these new occupations into which he is projecting himself: fastfood deliveryman, gravedigger, pharmaceutical salesman, physical therapist, bellhop, baker, ticket taker, plumber, doorman, shop floor foreman, elevator operator, school custodian, fireman, iceman, butcher, butler, porter, orderly, waiter, usher, traffic warden, window washer. In each he does with seeming zest and expertise that which he has always done best, to wit: copulating with housewives, employers, customers, children, patients, passengers, fellow laborers, distressed ladies, and those not distressed, the curious, incurious, and the casual passersby, but does less well whatever it is that he's supposedly been hired to do, clumsily dropping dishes, often in laps, wrecking vehicles, spoiling merchandise, breaking windows, pipes, and bones, pushing all the wrong buttons, causing minor floods and outages, dropping bags on toes and catching fingers in doors, such that he fails to hold any job longer than a few thousand frames, and some are so fleeting they seem lost before attained, passing by like lists of things to do, not done. So sketchy are these glimpses—that is to say, being more like treatments than the films themselves, treatments perhaps for his postpartum blues, which have never quite left him—that one cannot be sure whether he has actually taken these jobs or is only contemplating them, his life thus not fully realized even as he lives it, a complaint often on his lips and on his lips now, could they be seen behind the scarf that muffles them.

Oh fuck, it's cold! is also on his lips, what am I doing out here?, et cetera, when he arrives, more by push and flow than by volition, at the stage door of a film studio where a posted sign reads HELP WANTED: APPLY WITHIN. What, he thinks, though not exclamatorily, an opportunity. For not only has he done it all before the lens, he's worked behind it at everything from prop rustler and talent scout to gaffer, grip, and clapper boy, so maybe at last he's found a job that he can keep awhile. Won't Connie be pleased. It's not top billing, though; they want a janitor, the last one having quit, refusing to clean up after a film made for the excrement fetishists, or poopy groupies, as they're called in the trade. Well, it's odious work, but they're willing to hire him without references and give him a day's wages in advance (didn't Connie ask him to shop for something? yes, their poor children), so he takes the job, dons the overalls, confronts the mess. Which is everywhere. The actors had apparently gotten into bowel-movement size and shape contests, then ended up throwing their homemade magoo at one another like custard pies. It's even on the catwalks and baffles, lamps and booms above. He needs a tall ladder. He finds one behind the studio, wears it back in balanced on his shoulders, head between the rungs, managing somehow, his peripheral vision being somewhat underdeveloped (there's always been the frame's edge to either side of him), to wreck the studio with it, knocking down everything in sight with every turn he makes. Oh my. Yet another calamity. He expects to be fired, but his employers are too desperate; they urge him to get on with it and flee the scene. He props the ladder up against a wall that is not a wall but only another theatrical flat, which he discovers on climbing to the top and then riding it all to the deck (stuntman, he's done that too) as it comes crashing down. Fortunately the place is empty; no one got killed. Nearly empty. There's a charlady on her hands and knees scrubbing the floor behind the fallen flat. Must be deaf, didn't even look up. Well, he does what he has to do. He brushes himself off, goes over to her and throws up her dark heavy skirts, holds his nose at the reek beneath them, drops his overalls and trousers, hauls down her thick gray drawers, and dutifully but rather quickly, as if impatient with the life he leads (but there is no other, damn it), fucks her. Though she's fairly tight and wet, he can't be sure how old or big she is, head down and bundled up in her ancient rags, nor does he really care to know. They grunt and groan, and then it's over and she goes back to her scrubbing, and he steps out of the puddle of overalls, pulls up his pants, and stalks out, the blues back, longing desperately for something *different* to happen.

It's not much different out on the streets, except that they've emptied out, the blizzard if anything having worsened, these sudden appearances and disappearances of the congested public being a mystery to him, but one he accepts along with life's many other mysteries, such as time, death, montage, and the jump cut. He has his day's wages in his pocket but he's left his coat behind, it's a fair trade; perhaps he can find a shop open and buy another. But no, the city's all locked up as if never otherwise; he feels he's walked these ghostly frost-limed streets before, the city's economy being another mystery to him, and also another he rarely remarks upon. Nor does he now. Rather, his mind, narrowly focused by the harrowing cold, is set upon finding some safe haven, out of wind and snow, whereupon images of hearth and home come once again to mind. He swore he'd never leave it again, and yet here he is, back out on the stormy streets, freezing his ass off, though, it must be said, this time by spousal request. And of course, home isn't what it used to be—forget your hearth, for example—it's more like a communal baby factory; one can't even take a crap or brush one's teeth in private, the house rules being that all bathroom appliances must be available for use by all cohabitants at all times, paradise maybe for the poopy groupies and widdle watchers but seriously inconvenient to the married life. Which is also no longer what it once was. His wife has changed, less now the girl next door than the girl next door's mother, full of demands and disappointments, less inclined toward the more blissful aspects of the conjugal state, if ever she'd been so inclined before, her little home movies taking a mostly sad turn and so failing at the box office. There's one booked at the Pricktoria across the street, *Holey Matrimoney*. THE GRIMMEST STORY EVER TOLD says the marquee. The posters are in tatters. The theater looks to have been shut down for decades. His fault, of course. He's whom her lens is fixed upon, and he's just not the dashing young Peter Prick he once was; time and parturition have changed him too, though who or what he now is he cannot fathom. He cannot even think. His brain is freezing, his limbs too. Moving now less by walking than by leaning forward while rocking back and forth in his boots. He won't last long. Nameless gutter debris is what he'll be soon enough. Another shovel load for the garbage collectors. Which he's also been. Lasted less than a day at that job, if memory serves him, as it rarely does. Fucked a passing pedestrian too close to the compacter. He apologized, but his apology was not accepted.

He comes finally to a total halt. Urges himself to keep moving. Can't. Turns his frozen head on his frozen neck and sees that he's in front of a subway entrance. In this part of the city it's called the Underground; there's a big fat U hanging above the dark stairwell like a laden udder. In the nick of time. His eyes water with gratitude. He rocks stiffly toward the stairwell, lets gravity do the rest. Takes a few knocks on the way down, but it loosens up the ice crystals.

The dimly lit subway platform below is as empty as the streets above. Everyone's gone home. Everyone but him. Probably there was an edict of some kind. Out of touch, as usual. It's cold down here, he's shivering and his teeth are chattering, but it's not so windy and he can move his limbs again. No snow except what's blown down the entrances. There are two train tracks, one labeled HOME, the other AWAY, but neither seems to have been used in some time. Doesn't matter; at least he's out of the storm. It's damp and foul-smelling and he's all alone, but he doesn't mind being alone. In fact, it's a pleasure. Of course, he's a man who needs company, is in effect defined by it, but he feels truly free and on his own for the first time all day—indeed, since he can clearly remember—and he likes it. Fuck the working world. Fuck marital obligations. Fuck *all* obligations. Down here, no posted admonitions or appeals to straying hubbies, just the usual anonymous litter and graffiti, rotting piles of newspapers, tattered garbage bags, a freeform decoration of lonely abandon that suits his inner state. Of course, he misses his wife: his helpmeet, his playmate, his better half, his dearly beloved. And he wants her to want him, to need him, to beg him to return; who wouldn't? She's still cute and sweet and loyal and affectionate, all he could ever wish for, and he longs to be back in her loving arms. Or anyway, her loving viewfinder. He does. But not just yet. Time out from all that. Take five.

Which is what he's doing, just to bring the poor iced-up thing back to life, when he notices the artfully chalked scrawl on the boarded-up news kiosk in the middle of the platform: *Peter, Peter, meat beater/Had a wife but couldn't eat her!* And spray-painted on the far wall of the subway itself: *Crazy Leg, his balls in chains—/Willie ever get it on again?* They've been through here, then, those guerrilla theater types. The Extars, as they like to be known. He's seen them recently up above, maybe even today. Doing their street thing. But one of them was missing, the one with those exuberant breasts and flying black hair. Oh yes. Lottie. She of the dazzling grin and skintight jeans. Just thinking about that wild young thing warms his heart, warms him all over, and he wonders what happened to her.

As if in reply to his wondering, a poster pasted up over the Underground route map catches his eye. It's advertising something called Madame Cora's Sex Circus, and there in the center of it, amid all the red-letter hoopla about savage vaginas, dildo juggling, and midair fucks on the flying trapeze is a bring-'em-back-alive image of Lottie in chains, her shackled limbs stretched wide, being whipped by the Ringmistress with a barbed cat-o'-nine-tails. He recognizes her by her wondrous body, for a huge black gorilla head hides her hair and grin, the flashing dark eyes. Though she's probably not grinning, for those lovely buns are now bejeweled with brightly red-inked flecks of blood. He is both horrified and aroused. The Ringmistress's next two-handed stroke, he sees, will come crashing down between her outspread legs. Oh! Terrible! *No!* Ah! Yes—

—You gotta help us get her back, man!

—What? *What—?!*

—You can't let that big bitch do that to Lottie!

They're all around him: the Extars: some of them wearing masks and costumes, others naked, some dressed in newspapers or sashes and ribbons or black garbage bags with decorative labels. Scared the shit out of him, sneaking up on him like that. Nearly made him jump right out of his boots and off the platform. His heart's still pounding wildly, if his fist isn't.

—We've got a plan!

—You're the biggest sellout in the city, Crazy Leg, we know that, but we can't pull it off without you!

—But—

—No buts, man! Just look at her there! It's a fucking outrage!

—That sado will kill her if we don't act now! Let's get going!

—I-I can't! Not now. . . .

—Well, finish what you're doing, Loco, and then let's haul ass!

—From the looks of his pants, he's been at it all day.

—No, I mean—I'm not who I was. I-I'm married now.

—Sure, everybody knows that. TV sitcoms and all that—

—Shitcoms!

—A fucking career move. Who cares? Lottie *needs* you!

—It's not a career move! I'm in—

—I mean, look at the steel hooks on that whip, man! She doesn't deserve that!

—No, but—

—C'mon, man! She only got nabbed because of you; you *owe* it to her!

—It's not all cut-and-paste montage of mocked-up takes and retakes, Crazy Leg. Things happen. People act. Or don't act. There are consequences.

—I know, but I—

—Fuck him. The dork's in love with his own dick. Look, he can't even let go of it. He doesn't care about Lottie or anybody else.

—It's not that—

—It *is* that! Don't be so heartless, Loco! Lottie loves you!

—She does?

—Sure! It's fucking crazy, and it's bad politics, but that's how it is.

—And see where it's got her!

—We gotta snatch her outa that horror show!

—And we can do it! But you're our ticket, Crazy Leg.

Well, he thinks. Well, all right, why not? He's a free man, isn't he? And they're right (she loves him!), he owes it to her. They keep telling him to look at her (poor kid), but in truth he can't take his eyes away, he's riveted by the sight of her, that bold glowing part with the pink stripes he can see. Whatever else he has to do (get back home, find a job) can wait. This is an errand of mercy. And he's the right person for it. He knows just the right salve to apply. But before he can announce his decision, a train approaches and the Extars shrink back into the shadows or roll up into seeming refuse. The train rumbles in slowly, on the HOME track, but going the wrong way. Empty. OUT OF SERVICE it says. It shudders grindingly to a stop, the cars knocking up against one another, then settling back with little clanks and creaks. The doors remain closed. He peers in through the glass doors, sees the corner with the torn-out seats, the rolling beercan, the white tampon. Oh my god. The blood on the floor. This is the place, then. He was right. This is where it happened, where it all began. Even if she was also the girl next door and what-all else. He can smell her delicious panicky smell. It penetrates to his core. A wave of deep bittersweet joy wells up in there and floods through him.

He falls to his knees, shuddering, as if in the presence of something sacred, or maybe his knees just thawed out. The whole sequence comes rushing back. He seems almost to see her in there, writhing on the filthy metal floor beneath him, trying to fend him off while covering her privates, her girlish breasts heaving and falling, her head twisting from side to side. Perhaps the most sublime moment of his life, one of blinding ecstasy, everything seeming to expand as if he were becoming one with eternity, though he can't remember how it ended. It doesn't matter. It was so beautiful! *Constance* was so beautiful! He feels a surging heartfelt yearning for her and for that irrecoverable moment, and he wants nothing more than to be with her again, together on their little sofa. Or, better yet, in there on the rocking steel floor. Maybe he could talk her into making a film about it. It would be the greatest movie ever made. He tries to press the doors open to get at the beercan, the tampon—precious souvenirs!—but the train's motor coughs and growls, there's a loose rattle of cars stretching apart from one another, and slowly, with a mournful squeal, the train pulls out and disappears into the black tunnel at the far end of the platform, slipping away from him—No! Oh my god! *Don't go!*—forever. He realizes he is crying.

—Hey, man, ease up! It'll come back.

—No (*sob*), that's just it, it won't. Ever again. No reruns. Not that one.

—Well, there'll be another one then. Under the paint, they're all the same.

—I don't want another one. I want to go home.

There's a pause, a hushed muttering. He stares down through his tears at the vacated rails where black mice scurry, thinking how far he's fallen from what little grace he's known. He was supposed to have a beautiful life, loving and beloved. What went wrong? Whatever happened to endless delight? How did it get so dark and cold?

—Yeah, well, all right, one of them says finally. We understand, Crazy Leg. We'll get you home.

—Shit, that's the other fucking side of the city, man, and there are a million uniformed thugs between here and there! Who cares about this wanker? What about *Lottie*?

—Shut up, peckerhead, let me handle this. Lottie loves him so we'll take him where he wants to go. Don't worry, I know a shortcut. C'mon now, let's get this show on the road!

There's some grumbling, but a couple of the Extars finally grab him brusquely under the armpits and drag him, boots trailing, toward the stairwell, just as a loud commotion is heard above.

—Oh fuck! It's the security forces!

—The *other* way!

—They're coming down *that* way, too!

—We're surrounded!

—Quick! Into the tunnels!

—What about Crazy Leg?

—Haul him along! We need the sonuvabitch!

He's lifted over the edge of the platform, dropped, picked up again, and they're off.

—Watch out for the third rail, it's a killer! someone shouts, or must have shouted. What he actually heard was, Watch out for the third leg!

The mazy tunnels are nightmarishly dark and echoey, but Lottie's guerrilla friends scamper through them as if by touch and nose alone. The hard rocky ground beneath his bouncing knees is scraping them raw, and more than once he takes a jarring blow to the head or shoulders when a turn's missed, but the first time he yelps he's quickly gagged with what tastes like somebody's old jockstrap or G-string. Behind them, the police have leapt into the tunnels and are in full pursuit. He can hear their shouts, gunfire, the ricochet of bullets, can see sudden brief flickerings of their flashlights as they play off the Underground walls like flash frames in black leader. He's frightened and confused, finding himself caught up in a life not his own, and when one of those dragging him along is shot and killed—*Aaargh!* he screams, crashing to the cinders—utter terror overtakes him.

Don't shoot! *I'm* here! he cries, but his cry is muffled by the nauseating gag, emerging as nothing more than a pathetic telltale whine, which draws a further rattle of gunfire and another Extar screams and falls. Oh, help! He never meant to die this way! Surely this can't be the way it ends! The one guerrilla left drags him, whimpering softly, around an unseen corner, then another and another, and finally toward some circular iron steps, dimly lit by a snow-packed grate in the street above. He's dropped on his back at the foot, heart thudding in his ears, while the Extar scrambles up the ladder to work at loosening the grate. She's a young girl, hardly more than fourteen or fifteen, dressed only in a motley of stage makeup and loops of unspooled audiotape, her tiny nipples gilded, her mouth lipsticked a metallic silver. He can hear the echoing hammer of running boots, but he can't be sure whether they are approaching or receding. The girl struggles with the grate, pushing against the snow above. Flakes float, glittering, past her, as if scales were falling from her ghostly lips. She grunts, her sequined buttocks flexing. The grate gives way! She's going to save him! In the weak light, he can see that she has white daisy petals painted or tattooed around her richly yellowed anus, her smooth bright-green genitals serving as stem and leaves. He thinks: Given the chance, I could fall in love with this girl.

But no such chance is to be granted. There are sudden shouts of discovery, an explosion of gunfire. Bullets rip through her golden nipples, her navel, tattoo the garden of her groin. It's almost as though they are conducting an anatomy lesson. He lies utterly still, paralyzed by dread, unable even to breathe, staring fixedly up at her, wishing his unruly prick would keep its fucking head down. More bullets fly, pinning the girl's shoulders back. She staggers against the winding steps above him, knees sagging, blood leaking out of her nostrils and gleaming mouth. More shots spin her around and bend her over a rail, giving them the target of her little sequined buttocks, painted each in concentric circles of rainbow colors, onto which they pepper their lethal graffiti; from his foreshortened view below her, he can see an F punched out there. Her eyes have lost focus and she is leaking from all parts, but she has managed to strip away the audio tape and is surreptitiously eating it, shoveling it in like noodles. The shooting stops suddenly as if a sentence has ended. She stiffens, her cheeks bulging with half-chewed tape, her eyes crossing. She starts to tremble, shaken violently by some inner turmoil, and in the momentary silence little black bullets dribble out of the yellow disk of her painted daisy one by one, go clinking and clattering hollowly down the iron steps. There's a pause, so drenched in silence he fears he's lost his hearing, then a final fierce blast of rifle and small-arms fire like an explanation mark. She rears up, arms outflung, and comes crashing down the steps, landing on top of him. His penis sinks into something soft, which he hopes is an opening that was there before all the shooting. He thinks, This is the most dangerous moment of my life!

—Hah! Another Ex-rat eats it! Good work, squad!

—Shall we fuck what's left of her, chief?

—Nah, there's more of those terrorist bastards down here! Listen! This way!

He hears them go pounding off in a diminishing staccato of steel-capped boots on cinders and stones. They haven't seen him. He still has a chance, if he can get out from under the girl's body. But when he tries to free himself, she moves where he moves as though pasted to him. All that blood maybe. Whatever his cock has got itself into down there is tight, warm, wet, and sliding slowly up and down on it. Some sort of posthumous involuntary peristalsis, he supposes; he's read about it in the trade journals. Not his thing, but when he attempts to roll out from under her, she pins him back and shakes her head. She's still alive! That's different. He lies still. Would Constance approve? Act of mercy and all that? No. Never. Not without a paycheck to show for it. He should hold back, but she's dying, it's like a last wish; what else can he do? Feels good, too. Soothing.

The girl lifts her head off his chest and with great effort focuses for a moment on his eyes. He sees in the dim light that both her ears have been shot away, the end of her nose too; a shiny little piece of audiotape flickers between her silvery lips like a snake's tongue. She thrusts her chin at him and begins to choke, her eyes losing focus. He snatches the end of the tape and pulls on it, and as he does so, she presses her bright lips down on it with all her might, her eyes squeezed shut; the hot oily sheath on his penis tightens from the effort. A thin scratchy rising and falling voice emerges as he pulls:

—Yo, Crazy Leg! Lottie here! Remember me? Hey, howzit hanging, man? If hanging's the word for wood like yours. Me, I'm in deep shit, baby! I'm getting shredded by the ravening coño who runs this place! She's got more kinds of whips than I've got pubic hairs! Steel clamps on my-y-y-y—

The girl's mouth goes slack and she collapses onto his chest again, but down below she's still moving and he has decided that holding back gives him no real moral advantage. He pulls his gag down over his chin, lifts her head by a fistful of hair, and kisses her eyes—Please! he whispers, his hips beginning to buck off the hard scrabble—and she revives enough to groan with pain or pleasure and return his thrusts bravely and press her lips against the tape once more. He has to pull her mouth close to his ear to hear it as, butt slapping the rocky ground, he draws it out from deep inside:

— . . . and nipples, my tits in straps and jacked up with pulleys, cricket bats and air hoses for dildos, her boot up my butt—it's all about power, baby, and she's got it and I ain't! I need you, man! God, I need you! Nobody else can get me outa this freak show! And I want you, baby! I want your ass! It's crazy, crazy, but I can't help it. Get me outa here and let's go fff-f-f-f . . .

What? What? The girl's lips have parted slackly once more and everything has stopped. Everything. Oh no! Too soon! He scrambles out from under her dead limp weight, feeling the gathering chill of her down his spine and into his prostate. He squeezes her lips together with his fingers and pulls on what's left of the tape. All he gets is:

— . . . offf-f-f-f . . .

And then it snaps, caught in her throat. But the message got through, enough of it. Oh shit. It's so sad. He's crying again, a catch in his own throat. The girl's heroism has touched him, reminding him that there are other genres one might explore. Snow is falling on her staring eyes from the opened grate above. He kisses her eyelids closed (he has never done this before!), looks up. Yes, he has to get out of here. Should he take her with him? There's no time even to consider the question, for he can hear the drumming of approaching boots again. On the run. He limps clumsily up the circular steps, his skinned knees too sore to bend, reaching the hole in the street just as their lights flash onto him.

—There's one! Going up those steps!

—Quick! Shoot to kill!

—No! Stop! It's me!

But their guns explode and bullets clang off the iron steps and ricochet about the tunnel and he's up and out of there, amazed at his recovered strength and agility. Motivation. He's always been taught that. No scene works without it. Even his knees work better. He can hear them clambering up the steps behind him, fighting for the top. Guns go off, but he's gone from that place, barreling down the snowy street, and the rattle of their gunfire mingles with the noise of the traffic (the traffic's back) and is lost in it. Nevertheless, he takes no chances. He keeps moving. They could be right behind him. He races against the lights and dodges between buses and snowplows, weaving in and out of the crowds who have returned to the streets, takes sudden turns around corners, sprints down back alleys (call it sprinting; he's picking them up and putting them down hup two, but the slowmo effects are overtaking him, motivation isn't everything), gets hounded up a fire escape by a pack of wild dogs and onto the rooftop, chased by curses (there are cameras up here, people in formal dress shooting it out, good god, where *is* he?), leaps from roof to roof in search of another fire escape ladder, is told by someone making her last farewells that once you're up here, sir, there's only one way back down—which to his horror she proceeds to demonstrate—finally has to shinny down on crumbling waste pipes into a fetid back lane that opens onto a large rubble-strewn open space, big-tented in the middle.

Where the hell is he? Somewhere in the bombed-out tenement district, but the tent might be a good place to duck out of sight for a moment and get his wind back. A sign over the front flap announces MADAME CORA'S SEX CIRCUS. Connie is standing in front with half a dozen squalling kids.

—You're late, she says coldly. We've been waiting for hours. Everyone else has already gone in.

He glances back over his shoulder, heart still pumping; he seems to have shaken his pursuers. If they were ever there.

—Do you have the tickets?

—Tickets?

—Oh, Peter! And what have you done with your overcoat?

There's a SOLD OUT sign pasted on the ticket window, but in the shadowy little booth, decorated like a puppet theater, he discovers an old friend. Maybe (he thinks now, all but friendless) the best friend he ever had. She's wearing an exotic costume made mostly of kerchiefs, beads, and bangles, and her blond hair's been dyed, her features artfully darkened, but she could never be other than who she is.

—Hey, Cissy! God, it's good to see you! What are you doing here?

—Hard times, L.P.

L.P., he thinks. *L.P.!* How long has it been? It warms his heart to hear it again; his prick, old soldier, stands in acknowledgment and gratitude, and his head is filled with a flicker of sweet memories in the form of clips from all those great old films they once made together. He wipes a tear from the corner of his eye. Damn . . .

—Since the studio closed, I've had to take what I could get.

—I'm sorry, Cissy. Things just seemed to happen. I've missed you. And the studio. You're looking beautiful. Different, though. Why the masquerade?

—I do fortunes on the side.

—You're a fortune-teller?

—I don't tell them, I do them. A few bucks a trick. You want yours done?

—Sure! Well . . . no. He glances back at his sad little family, clustered miserably near the tent entrance, just out of the wind. Or not so little; there seem to be more of them than a moment ago. I need some tickets.

—Sold out.

—So I see. But—?

—How many do you need?

—I don't know. A bunch. Here, whatever this will buy. He empties his pockets of his day's wages, luckily still unsquandered.

She peels off a dozen or so and pushes them toward him. Best in the house, she says, without a smile. But tell me, L.P., why are you wearing that used crotch rag for a neckerchief? It's pretty sickening.

—Oh. Sorry, Cissy. A little, well, you know, adventure. He pulls it off over his head and tosses it away, his eye caught by another poster under the ticket window. This one shows a woman's backside with her asshole ablaze and a wild tiger jumping through it. THE RING OF FIRE, it says.

—I'll bet. More fun than home movies, I'm sure.

—Actually, it was kind of scary. And sad.

—Let me read your engorged corpus cavernosum, L.P. You're here to see that girl.

—No, no, I'm here with my wife and family—

—Sure you are. Listen. Forget her, L.P. She and her pals are nothing but trouble.

—To tell the truth, Cissy, I was thinking only of you.

She smiles wistfully, leans back into the shadows. Well, have a great night at the circus, she says. Another one of Cora's epics. You've probably just missed Cally's bareback riding, but you should still be in time for the rest of the fireworks.

—Cally rides bareback?

—No. Is ridden. It's a good number. Always dangerous, bareback. But you know Cally, the consummate pro. But they'll have her back in the monkey cage by now. You may just catch part of Cleo's performance, though, if you hurry. She manages some pretty impressive variations on sword swallowing and fire eating and does one of those how-many-guys-can-you-pack-into-a-phone-booth acts as a topper. Or bottomer. She's got a lot of room in there.

—I know. I've . . . visited it.

—L.P.?

—Yes?

—I miss you too.

—Listen, Cissy, maybe, when all this is over . . . ?

She shakes her head sadly. Be careful, L.P., she says, and draws the fringed and tasseled curtain over the window, shutting down the booth. It's like the end of something, and he stands there for a moment, the way he often lingers, slumped in his seat, as a movie ends, staring at the fallen curtain, lost in melancholic ruminations, wakened finally from his reverie by the distant cries of children, a shouted plea:

—Peter—?

They're applauding Cleo and a clown has come on, when he and his family enter and take their seats. They are indeed good ones, box seats in the front two rows; his kids are impressed. He shepherds them all in from the aisle, while Cleo, basking in the applause, is taking an exhilarated sprint around the ring, doing cartwheels and handsprings, throwing kisses. She's wearing a lioness skin upside down on her back, the head bouncing on her buttocks, her finale apparently having had something to do with putting one's head in the lion's mouth. The painted-up one-eyed clown is doing a quirky imitation of Cleo's run, tripping over her own feet—or foot and hand, for there seems to be an arm where a leg should be—and falling on her face when attempting cartwheels.

—Hey, lover! Cleo gasps when she reaches his aisle. She's sweaty and excited, her damp hair like wet fire, her gleaming dilated eyes staring through him more than upon him. You missed our anniversary last night!

—Well, I was—

—And the night before that. And so on. Where've you been?

—I'm sort of settled now, Cleo, he says, nodding back over his shoulder. Maybe you should get someone else.

—I have someone else, a thousand someone elses, she says, still breathing heavily, her hand between her legs, her hard white body glistening, nipples erect. She is ravishingly intense, eager, inciting. Everybody wants to go down on me, have their day as the saying goes, but none of them are you, Lucky—and never will be! She grips his penis with her free hand (it feels plunged into tumbling greased bones) and pulls it toward her. Come on, baby! I've been missing you! Let's go fuck in the lion's cage!

—I can't, Cleo. Maybe later.

She lets go, curls her lips, sighs. Sure, baby, she says, and slaps his butt, then runs on up the aisle toward the exit without looking back, waving at the cheering crowd.

The clown has dropped her pants and is pumping up balloons with her boxy ass, when he squeezes into his seat, sitting in a sticky mess one of the kids has left there. He wouldn't mind sitting thigh by thigh with his better half, but they are separated by a herd of noisome little creatures, presumably their own. The clown is making exaggerated farting noises with her balloon blowing, which makes the children laugh and their elders groan and wave their hands in front of their faces. Some of the balloons she passes out to children, his own grabbing for them; others she twists into funny shapes of erect genitalia, which she tries with a comic lack of success to stuff up her armpit. She bends over and blows up a huge balloon, which rises quiveringly over her back, growing larger and larger, causing everyone to hold their ears and noses. But instead of bursting, it lifts her off the ground, butt high, and she floats out of the arena through a hole in the top of the tent, unscrewing the arm from her groin and waving it at the crowd as she goes. Outside the tent there is a huge explosion, a whistle as of something falling, and a great clattering noise like the crash of a cupboardful of pots and pans.

Madame Cora, the Ringmistress, steps into the applause and laughter that follows and, with a cold smile, cracks her whip. She is dressed in a bejeweled headband, ruby navel stud, crimson-lined black cape and a tightly drawn webwork of leather straps that cause her bare breasts and buttocks to bulge provocatively. She swaggers past their box and points them out with her whip handle.

—*Mr. and Mrs. Peter Prick, everybody! And family!*

There is a one-horn fanfare and a halfhearted smattering of applause, which he and Connie acknowledge, but Connie's chin is quivering as if she were about to cry.

—I'm losing you, Peter, she says softly, as the applause dies quickly away. I wish we'd never come.

—And now let's bring on that Wild Thing you've all been waiting for! Madame Cora exclaims, cracking her black whip.

There's a roar from the crowd, and people stand and shout and cheer and throw their blister beetle candy into the ring. Flaps part across the way like the peeling back of vaginal lips, and six assistants, dressed uniformly in tight black leather, roll into the arena a steel cage on wheels containing that magnificent raging creature straight from the posters—the Wild Thing!—shackled, belted, and collared to the cage's bars, naked but for her gorilla head and rattling at her chains as though to tear the cage apart. He's suddenly on the edge of his seat.

—Ladies and gentlemen! cries the Ringmistress over the whoops and screams. *Here you have her! Captured alive at great personal risk! The mighty Urban Gorilla, one of the last of a dying species!*

Wires are dropped from the trapeze platforms high above. Cautiously, the attendants open her cage door to attempt to fasten the wires to her restraints, but she is crashing about with such ferocity that two of the attendants are knocked to the ground merely by the shaking of the cage. Obscenities flow from her gaping black mouth like the roars of a maddened beast, her eyes fiery beneath the heavy brows.

—Look out! cries Madame Cora. *She's a killer! Don't let her loose!*

They manage to get the six wires attached to her shackles, collar, and belt, though one of the attendants is knocked across the cage by a savage blow from their captive's powerful hips. They escape the cage and, outside it, unlock her from the bars, then back away as she comes charging out to throw herself upon them, only to be snapped back by the wires and left, kicking and bellowing, suspended a few feet above the ground, limbs outspread and face down. Oh, what a sight, that great handsome body, thrashing about in midair with such abandon! Madame Cora attaches sharp clamps with long silken cords to the Wild Thing's dark erected nipples, then pulls on the cords to whirl her about, winding up the wires. As she unwinds, spinning in the opposite direction, pitching and twisting in her bonds, the Ringmistress snaps her whip at her, aiming at her tenderest places.

Every inch of her is in violent motion. It's hard to know what to look at next; it's like being in a room with a hundred movies showing, all at once, and yet even in her wild hairy-headed fury there is a wholeness about her, an integrity of being, her nakedness not a vulnerability but a taunt, a challenge, even a threat, and in spite of her terrible humiliation, suspended, bound, and whipped, she radiates a sense of absolute freedom! His children are asking for peanuts and soft drinks, or else to go to the toilet, but he is up out of his seat, as are many in the tent, utterly transfixed by this beautifully outrageous spectacle, crying out, shouting for Madame Cora to stop this cruelty or shouting for more, shouting just to be shouting, a kind of explosive laryngeal ejaculation.

The Ringmistress greases the huge whip handle between her own legs and shoves it forcibly into the Wild Thing's rectum; jerking and twisting to shake it out, the extraordinary creature cracks the whip and cracks it again! The cheers mount. Madame Cora backs into the snapping whip and smiles icily as it lashes her. The attendants take up positions in front of the audience to prevent members of it, many already ripping off their clothes, from trying to join her.

—*You see her, ladies and gentlemen, wickedness incarnate!* cries Madame Cora, yanking her whip back. She steps between those lean young legs kicking furiously at the air and, grabbing a fistful of thick black pubic hair, lifts her captive's ass high like a trophy. *Such raw naked evil is a threat to all civil society and, with the most extreme and merciless discipline, must be reduced to abject submission!* she declares. *These savage beasts will be our house pets—or they will die!* Whereupon, just as the Ringmistress turns her face toward her, the Wild Thing lets fly a great clear stream of piss. *What? What—?!* splutters the enraged Madame Cora. *Terrorist bitch!* And she brings her whip down fiercely on the offender's backside, raising a large red welt. She backs up, face dripping, and with both hands brings the whip down again, crossing the first welt with another, blood popping from the point on the left cheek where they intersect. She rears back with the whip once more but everyone is screaming—he's screaming: *no! yes!*—and down, two-handed, no matter what he'd been begging for, he doesn't remember, comes the whip again, landing with a fearsome crash square between those majestic cheeks. Oh my god! He's coming all over the attendant in black leather trying to restrain him. And he knows now what he must do.

The Ringmistress, with a commanding signal from her whip, has brought into the ring a troupe of randy monkeys and unleashed them on the gorilla-girl's body: they use her as a perch and a climbing frame, peeing and shitting freely, run their tails, hands, feet, and penises into all of her orifices, swing from her breasts and pubic knoll, scramble for the bananas that Madame Cora stuffs into her, nibbling, clawing, sucking her toes and other tidbits, an act that his children, heretofore restless, finally find entertaining. They yip and giggle and clap and call out.

—Can we go play with the monkeys, Daddy?

—*Here you see the ineluctable fate of all Urban Gorillas!* cries Madame Cora, sugaring the girl's body to incite the ravenous monkeys. *To be maddened with unfulfilled desire!*

With another whip crack, she brings on a parade of animals, a grand shivaree, everything from rampant stallions and dancing bears to elephants and rhinoceri, all waddling in around their stiffened pizzles—she must have emptied out the entire city zoo—declaring over the horns, pans, and kettledrums of the circus band that in the second half of the show the seditious creature would be violently raped sequentially and/or simultaneously by every beast in the circus—*You see her lovers before you!*—and not excluding vampire bats, pythons, scorpions, and a special highwire ball-juggling surprise guest yet to be announced!

—*We will stuff kernels up her fundament and so heat up with the whip that seat of iniquity as to pop corn from it!* cries Madame Cora, as her captive, still infested with clambering monkeys, is prodded back into her cage with long poles. *We shall subdue her rebellious flesh or it shall be shredded beyond all recognition!*

He's on his way.

—Peter?

—Be right back, love. Uh, something for the kiddies.

He pushes out through the half-naked crowd, out of their seats and pressing toward the arena, and charges at full pelt around to the other side of the tent. He's not quite sure how he's going to manage it, but he knows he has to get that wondrous Wild Thing out of here before more harm's done her. It's his mission!

He's stopped at the back entrance by more attendants in black leather. Hey, here he is! they cry.

—I'm, uh, I'm here to clean the animal cages, he gasps lamely.

—Thought you weren't going to make it. You're just in time!

—In time?

—You go on right after the break.

—No, wait! There must be some—

—Quick! Get him into makeup!

Intromission

He is walking hand in hand with his wife into the doctor's office. How did he get here? He doesn't know. It's like a commercial break. Life's like that sometimes. The continuity person takes a holiday, and there you are. But why? It seems their marriage is in trouble and they are here for counseling. The receptionist, dressed crisply in white but with her shirt unbuttoned, asks them to describe for her the nature of their problem. Constance complains about his lack of attentiveness, his long absences from home, the loss of excitement in their home movies. He's been seen in the wrong part of town. When the receptionist turns to him, he holds up their clasped hands and says, This is it. All the fuck there is. That's right, says Connie, taking her hand away, he also belittles me and uses bad language, and he makes big Zs when he snores and never helps with the children. I didn't even know we *had* children! he protests, and Connie says, There, you see? And when he cleans up around the house, which is almost never, he leaves things worse than they were before—he *ruined* our vacuum cleaner!

—It sounds rather serious, says the receptionist, chewing on her pencil thoughtfully. Have you consulted our moving-image marriage manual, *How to Deflower a Virgin*?

—Oh, we've been through all that, exclaims Connie exasperatedly. The doctor gave us a copy as a wedding gift, and we've tried *all* the positions and it doesn't help!

—I see. With your clothes off?

—Oh, says Connie, blushing. You're supposed to take your clothes off? Is . . . is that nice?

—Hmm, says the receptionist, casting him an understanding wink while scratching herself inside her shirt with the pencil. I think perhaps you should attend the doctor's *What Is a Penis?* lecture for troubled couples, which is presently under way. Come this way, please.

She leads them through some double doors into a vast banked auditorium the size of an old movie palace, where the doctor is speaking in front of a large screen on which are projected blown-up images presumably illustrating her remarks, though at first glance they appear more like colorful abstract paintings of impossible objects.

—What is a penis? she is asking. From the roomful of troubled couples there is no answer. Anxiety and perplexity reign. The image on the screen metamorphoses restlessly as if reflecting the general uncertainty.

—Nothing seems easier than to answer this question, the doctor affirms, stabilizing the image somewhat, bringing a sigh of relief from the audience: ah, the comforts of science! It is a polymerous protrusile being with a head and body and other attachments, full of energy and vigor, master of many ingenious contrivances all helpful to its peculiar economy, executing various movements, manifesting intelligence in different degrees, and governed by a wayward will. Yes, you are all doubtless familiar with these attractive creatures and are prepared to hear with interest some of the details of their curious structure and economy.

—Yes, yes! cry the troubled couples.

—Peter? I think I want to go home.

—Ssh!

—Penises are not rare but abound within reach, mostly in the afternoon and toward nightfall, and also during the daytime, though not commonly then so near the surface. But by peering into nooks and crannies within the well-worn loose-fitting lower garments of our population even at this time of day—yes, feel free to do so now—one is continually surprised by some strange being nested therein, some minim of existence it may be, uncouth and slow, or lithe and elegant and rapid as lightning; dull and somber as suits its obscure retreat, or bright and gaily tinted from the solar ray; some new combination or modification of display, some novel exhibition of instinct, habit, or function, that awakens our admiration. Some of these amusing little fellows, you will discover, are not really naked, but are invested with a thin gelatinous film, known to naturalists as a prophylactic sheath, so tightly stretched as to be reduced to an invisible tenuity, but inhibitive of a thorough examination and understanding of that principal object of our inquiry contained within. I recommend therefore that you peel these membranes away before proceeding, taking care not to spill any contents you may find inside. You will observe, by giving these labile organs a firm tug, that they are, like vegetables, permanently rooted, forming, with their paired scrotal glands, which are often likened unto money pouches or venom sacs, an attached trifurcate parcel hanging just below the pelvic cradle, barring cryptorchidic anomalies. The penis's movements, also like those of vegetables, are largely extrinsical and involuntary. And, like cryptogamous vegetables, or algae, they usually grow and ramify in forms determined by local circumstances, creating a diversity in form and structure unique among organs. Yet, diverse as they are, they possess characters in common which more than outweigh their differences, and the whole are united into a chain of many links, which, by a beautiful gradation, conduct us from one to the other, and often—for such is their endlessly novel appeal—as if possessed.

The image on the screen has evolved into something like the minim of existence in his own lower garment, flaccid and curled into itself like a sleeping bird. Connie, following the doctor's instructions, has peeped inside but only groaned is disappointment at what she saw and is now proceeding down the row of seats, peering into others, examining with a skeptical frown what the doctor is calling the nested creatures' elaborate structure and finish.

—Many species of this group, as you will discover, differ considerably among themselves in form and outer aspect. Some are preeminent for beauty of color and for their general elegance and delicacy, others appear somewhat flattened and unshapely, often of a dusky brown hue, with the outer integument of both head and stalk hardened into a horny crust, while yet others are phosphorescent and bunlike, resembling a sea blubber, or the so-called naked-eyed medusae. Monstrosities by excess are not uncommon. There is one species which can actually be turned inside out like a glove and yet perform all its functions as before, while another, of a brilliant transparency and high refractive power like that of flint-glass, has been known to awaken spiritual visions in those who insert it where appropriate, which fascinating process we shall illustrate shortly. Others are admittedly more or less noxious, mastering their prey by open violence, proving even fatal to some of their victims, a fact that should not, however, arouse a popular prejudice against the class as a whole, which is largely benign if treated with proper respect and affection.

Respect and affection, he thinks. Yes, that's it: what's been missing. The voluptuous warmth of the doctor's voice touches him affectionately at the very root and, with respect, causes his own strange being to stir within its envelope, soon, he hopes, unzipping, to be unsealed.

—What is most peculiar about penises is that they are ever altering their outline, and to so great a degree that not only are no two ever found alike, but the same specimen does not retain the same shape for two successive minutes.

Here—the doctor taps the screened image with a long soft-tipped pointer—an extremity projects and gradually pushes out more and more, protruding to a considerable distance from the margin of its mossy knoll—whereupon his own extremity projects and gradually pushes out, as if itself tapped—while, she continues, a sinuosity is forming in some other part (*ah!*), as one portion is contracting, another enlarging (*oh yes!*); so that the only idea that can be given of its shape is by comparing it to the figure of a country upon a map, which is perpetually being transformed into that of some other country—an experience his own peninsular nation, emerging as it were from an inland desert, is undergoing. It is very interesting, she goes on, to witness these sudden and sprightly motions, which are in keeping with their curious structure, and it is scarcely possible to observe them (*yes, look at it rear and waggle*) without believing that the penis exercises an active volition in performing them. The whole head ordinarily sways to and fro upon the slender joint of the poll at intervals of a few seconds; but besides this motion, which is even, though rather quick, the attached testicles, which commonly hang to their utmost extent, will now and then, at irregular intervals, shrink into the groin with a strong sudden snap, much like the retreat of a turtle's head, an action that can be experimentally produced by applying an exteroceptive stimulus such as an electric shock—

—*Yow!* he yelps, leaping from his seat as the tip of the pointer sends out sparks, and Connie, having returned, looking flushed and disheveled, whispers, Peter! Don't make a public spectacle!

— . . . Whereupon the penis, too, withdraws, shrinking on the least disturbance into its pubic nest, not soon to reappear after the fright given to its sensitive ganglia and, when it finally does, only then with great caution.

The doctor tickles the image on the screen, and the penis, if that is what it is, cautiously but as though compulsively rises once more, as does his own, its testes recovering from their cremasteric reflex and again dropping down into view, resuming leisurely their former position. Ah, that's better. But volition? She must be wrong there.

—Thus, though the extreme beauty of the display cannot fail to elicit our admiration, we but raise a finger to point out some particular item to a companion, when, lo!—*whack!* she strikes the screen, and he bounces from his seat again, stifling a yell—the whole apparatus disappears like a vision. All of which is to suggest, says the doctor, delicately stroking the image once more, that these tender thin-skinned creatures require the utmost solicitude and nurture, lest, devastated, they shrink away into ineffectualness and desuetude, a lesson I too had to learn. The first time I ever captured one of these glorious creatures, I succeeded in getting it into me entire. Never having seen one before, and quite unconscious of its suicidal powers, I assumed this specimen was mine to keep and preserve in its ankylosed state forever, a mistake, I am afraid to say, common to troubled couples everywhere.

There are nods of understanding throughout the auditorium, but Connie only folds her arms and mutters, *This is stupid.*

On the screen meanwhile, the many-hued penis, rising from its pelvic floor yet again like the irrepressible pratfall comedian that it is, has been joined—onstage, as it were—by a vagina with golden curls, and he recalls now the making of this set of instructional films with Clara in his old penthouse bachelor pad, so long ago it seems now like once upon a time, and he knows that he—or at least the penis on the screen—is in for a testing but also a treat. Clara's mission, however ruthlessly achieved, is always to do good in the world, and he and his penis are in the world—certainly her world, at least—and she will not fail them.

—To understand the penis, she is saying, combing back the golden curls on the screen, one must understand the vagina. These voracious little cannibals, as they are sometimes called, are gifted with a very curious kind of mouth; one, indeed, which has no parallel in any other race of beings. This mouth consists of a long fleshy funnel, plaited like a fan, which can be folded up or spread abroad at pleasure.

On the screen, the vagina opens its petals like a time-lapse sequence of a bud becoming a flower, drawing the eye ever deeper into its cimmerian depths.

—Let's go, Peter, whispers Connie, taking his hand. I think I know now what to do.

But he pulls his hand away, reaching instead for the doctor's unfolding pink lips and beautiful golden curls and the dark mystery within (which of course she will explain), though whether he is reaching for something he hopes to attain or for something forever lost, he cannot be sure. The sweet fragrance of Clara's vaginal garden, dewy now with knowing anticipation, rises from beneath the faint hospital odors heretofore permeating her presence (where are they? they appear to be upon, or in his case hovering just above, his famous old medieval antiquity, the Marvelous Bed, one of the great sex toys of all times, which, in spite of its fragility, they have moved out onto the tiled deck beside the penthouse pool), and he longs to lap at that dew and be lapped.

—*Should a penis approach, this funnel is unfolded and applied around the body of its prey, which, thus retained, in spite of all its struggles, is soon sucked and emptied of its juices. As they are all but insatiable, these alluring creatures are rarely unwilling to gratify their benefactors with a display of their swallowing powers, as we shall see . . .*

They have turned on the pool's dancing fountain for both acoustical and optic effect and are beaming their lamps through it, casting colored ripples on their respective bodily parts as the gels rotate, if that effect is not in fact being produced by the hallucinogenic pharmaceuticals provided, as always, by the wise doctor, whose lecture now is ever more distant (she is using words like *foraminate* and *extravasation* and explaining just what it means to *fuck one's ears off*), and like a dream that he is having. The bed, which resembles in some respects the great soft hand of a magician, is already in sensuous motion, unseen by the viewers at her lecture (what they can see, he sees in a monitor by the headboard: his hovering prick, engorged by longing, stretching toward her glistening bush), and he knows, suspended above her on wires and slowly descending, he will be sharing her with it, but only to his own greater pleasure. He is not exactly comfortable strung up like this (he is also sitting in the auditorium still), but he is impressed by the precision, clarity, and expertise of this professional crew, so different from the jumpy and befogged eight-mil amateurism he's been suffering, and he feels, a professional among professionals, at ease in their company. Or perhaps he is made to feel at ease simply by being back in the tender care of his brilliant doctor, whose exquisite body beneath him, goddesslike in its perfect proportions, seems shaped less by nature than by conscious design. He can feel (see) the tip of his penis, now but a breath away from entry, tremble as it makes a final supreme effort to reach out and bridge that narrow gap, and then, just as it seems destined to fail, the lips of her flowering vagina flutter and rise like leaves seeking light to kiss the fissure at the tip, caress the head, and draw in the tingling corona and then the body of the penis itself, lubricating it with its succulent juices (—*After vaginal osculation,* he hears Clara say somewhere, perhaps in the turned-down monitor, which, eyes closed in gathering ecstasy, he is no longer watching, *the newly transformed penis is soft, with its skin resembling in consistence wetted parchment . . .*), and when he sinks in at last, he realizes that his search for home has until now been the chasing of an illusion. This is his true home, for home, as that old saw would have it (the old truths are still the best truths), is where the hard-on is.

Is his notorious penchant for finding home and then, restlessly, leaving it again responsible for what happens next? This is the question that pops to mind as he is suddenly lifted out of Clara's body and hauled into the rafters and then beyond, the question popping out again, replaced now by sheer terror (fuck the magic of cinema!), as he rises higher and higher, his wetted parchment chilled by the rare air, his teeth chattering, the beautiful doctor now far below him, she frightened too and reaching out for him and then too distant to be seen, her lecture blown away in the sudden gusts, displaced by the finger-snapping sound of distant whip cracks and the muffled honk of trumpets far below, like car horns under snow . . .

Adventures of Crazy Leg: Part II

An explosive nearby burst of drumrolls, trumpet blasts, shouts, and applause.

—*And now,* the Ringmistress is crying, *the Big Top's Big Tup!*

But she is not to be seen, nor is the announced star of the act, the camera focused instead on the quiet arrival of a small army of clowns, streaming in through all the entryways, slipping in under the tent flaps, scurrying behind the bleachers, mingling with performers, animals, roustabouts, hostlers, and spectators returning to their seats with noisemakers and cotton candy. There are brightly painted joeys with noses that honk and light up, sad augustes in polkadotted trousers, grotesque ladies with giant breasts, hobos and hayseeds, contortionists, midgets, and mopheads. Some drive tiny cars whose radiators are exploding or ride on bicycles with wobbly wheels; others bounce lightly under gas-filled balloons, or ride dogs like horses, or come chugging in on ornate calliopes gaily painted with scenes of pederasty and bestiality in the antique mode, or walk on stilts, or are rocketed along by little powdery detonations out of the seats of their pants. There is a great and colorful variety of hats, hair, noses, bobbing phalluses, and ballooning bottoms, coats, vests, ties, skirts, and floppy shoes.

—Here he is, my friends! That artiste of the leg-over! That three-ring-dinger—

The invasion of the clowns continues as more pour in from all directions, passing out candy, playing miniature violins and ringing cap bells, wagging their outlandish genitalia and squirting liquid out of them, bottle-feeding bonneted baby pigs through the wrong end, stumbling over their own baggy clothing, tipping their battered top hats and derbies, their hair coming off with the hats, balancing feathers on false noses and juggling nippled balls and flaming dildos. Others can be seen at the fringes, loosening the tent stakes and cutting ropes and wires, leaving packages under the bleachers with clocks wired to them, scrawling slogans on the posters and canvases: CLOWNS RULE! and RELEASE THE WILD THINGS! and HEY RUBE! REVOLUTION NOW! Such messages can be found on the candy wrappers too, and on the popcorn tubs, as zooms show, though few in the whistling and whooping crowd are reading them.

—It's that amorous aerialist! That acrobat of carnality! That midair dancer of the buttock jig—!

On the parade track circling the arena, a tattered clown with a sad blue grin painted ear to ear under a bulbous nose and a buzzing chainsaw penis poking out the fly of his voluminous checked pants is chasing a squealing fat lady with a headful of wild red hair and skirts that keep flying up around her ears, but no one's watching the clowns now. All eyes are turned upward, where, on a tiny swaying platform high overhead near the very top of the tent, stands a wide-eyed chalky-faced figure with a cleft purple nose, thin mustache, and painted tears. He is dressed in loose white pajamas with big buttons, the sleeves hanging down below his hands, and a conical white hat rises, brimless, from the top of his white head like a swollen pate. He hugs a thin pole that leans as he leans, his knees knocking together comically, his mouth blackly agape.

—Ladies and gentlemen! The one and only, the flying fornicator! Lucky Pierrot!

There is an ecstatic burst of applause and cheering as the Ringmistress, flexing her glistening leather-strapped buttocks, cracks her whip. High above them, his mouth opens and closes as though he might be shouting some unheard word over and over again. *Help!* perhaps.

—Be hard, Pierrot! she cries, her crimson-lined cape fluttering. *For you are about to attempt an act never before accomplished in circus history!* Fanfares

and the crashing of cymbals punctuate her announcement, shouted out over the excited clamor of the crowd. *Yes, ladies and gentlemen! Working without a safety net, the magnificent Pierrot will execute a spectacular triple somersault with double twist and will then attempt to land in a wild dangerous bush and swing from it by his legendary manhood alone, his hands tied behind his back!*

There are gasps of amazement, enraptured cheers, applause, whistles. They cry out his name: *Pierrot! Pierrot! Pierrot the Great!* The great one has tried to reach the stanchion ladder below the platform, but a trio of other aerialists, arriving by trapeze, have grabbed him by his pantaloons and dragged him back up. Down in the ring, the lady clown with the flying skirts, running from the hobo with the chainsaw penis, has fallen over an elephant stool, skirts over her ears, fat legs kicking, bloomers high. There are local shrieks and giggles as the hobo clown, bobbing his exaggerated brows and rolling his eyes, approaches his target, his power tool roaring, but with a high kick the lady somersaults on over and the chainsaw—*bzzzuupp!*—slices the stool in half.

—*And now, ladies and gentlemen: the bush!*

The Ringmistress blows a whistle hanging around her neck, and a trapeze is pushed out from the platform across from the one where the flying fornicator, his knees having buckled, is being held up by two lady aerialists. Swinging in his direction suddenly and much to his alarm is the gorilla-headed Wild Thing, her feet in stirrups at each end of the trapeze bar, her wrists shackled to her ankles. Her gaping cleft and tensed buttocks, stretched apart below the bar, rise within inches of his purple nose and then swing back again, where the trapeze is caught by aerialists on the other platform.

—*Not so much a bush as a teeming jungle! A savage pit infested with anarchy and sedition!*

The Wild Thing swings her butt fiercely, knocking the other aerialists back into the rigging, and launches forth once more, humping upward on the upswing as if to bowl over Pierrot and his supporters or else to offer him her spread arse to kiss.

—*Ah, but look at her eyes, ladies and gentlemen! Look at her beady little eyes! Gleaming with abject animal love!*

Below her, as she swings back, clowns are acting up on the stanchion ladders, climbing without hands while scratching their behinds or stepping absently out into space and grabbing a rung at the last moment or inching their way up the pole with long rubbery penises as security belts or catching hats or pants dropped by others above them, exchanging them for their own, and dropping these in turn.

—*Yes, the wretched beast is in love! In love with our dear Pierrot! And now she will have him where she wants him and she will hold on to him or she will lose him!* She cracks her whip. *Forever!*

The Wild Thing has been recaptured on her backswing and temporarily secured now with ropes and chains, which she rattles in her fury. On the opposite platform, so small there is not room for all their feet, the terrified Pierrot is struggling wildly with the other aerialists as they try to tie his floppy sleeves together behind his back. *Whoops!* There goes one of them, plummeting more than a hundred feet (one of the clowns on the stanchion below holds out an umbrella; another tries to catch the falling aerialist with his hat), landing—*kerwhumpf!*—on the sawdust floor, drawing a gasp from the spectators and respectful applause. Poor Pierrot stares down at this sight aghast, no longer resisting as the sleeves are knotted behind him by the two remaining aerialists, his painted tears running with real ones. His pantaloons are stripped down around his ankles and his penis is brought erect by the aerialists' skillful manipulations and chalked for a better grip.

—*And now, ladies and gentleman, history is about to be—will those clowns please get down!* She blows fiercely on her whistle, cracks her whip. *Do not climb up there! That's very dangerous!*

The crowds boo her good-naturedly and cheer on the climbing clowns. There is laughter when one of them moons the Ringmistress, an image captured in a zoom shot. Tattooed on one white cheek: TERROR IS SEXY. The aerialists stoop and get their hands under Pierrot's slippered feet and begin their countdown: *One . . . two . . . !* Below them, on the ground, clowns are shoving suppositories up the anuses of the animals and unlocking all the cages. The tent canvas is being doused with oil. Fuses are being lit. The fat lady running from the clown with the chainsaw penis has collapsed from exhaustion and, squirting tears from her eyes, is boohooingly awaiting her fate, her legs astraddle the king pole holding up the center of the tent.

—*Get away from that king pole!* screams the Ringmistress, as more clowns shinny up the stanchions and swarm over the trapeze platforms and rigging above. *No—!*

BZZZUUPPP!

—*Three!*

And up he goes, projected out into the emptiness, hands behind his back, feet bound in tangled pantaloons. Whether he successfully completes the ballyhooed twists and somersaults, he can't be sure; it's all a dizzying blur. For a fraction of a moment, he finds himself hovering in midair, as though free of gravity, like a feather caught on a breeze, gazing down upon a mad mix of mayhem and hilarity, smoke billowing up in places, explosions popping, animals going berserk, the Ringmistress trying single-handedly to hold up the toppling king post and screaming for the elephants, but much of the audience still having a grand time, supposing it's all part of the circus, many of them pointing up at him and laughing or else clapping their hands over their eyes, afraid to look, and in that split second, no more than a frame or two at most, he glimpses his wife, Constance, front and center, dressed in black like a widow, surrounded by gawking children and attentive men with their hands in her clothes. She is gazing up at him (such terrible clarity in so fleeting a moment!) as though in profound disappointment, while the children hold up individual placards which together read DADY! PLEZ CUM HOME!—and then he begins to feel his body's weight once more and his heart leaps to his throat and his eyes tear up and he commences his earthward drop, nothing between him and the floor of the arena far below.

But suddenly, even as he plunges, there *is* something in between; it is the Wild Thing swinging into view from under his pantalooned feet, lifting her thick dark nest, spread wide, just in time to receive his tormented little bird, its neck stretching as if crying to be fed. There's a meaty collision—*k-shuff!*—and she's got him! Oh god, she's brilliant! He tries desperately to wrap his legs around her head or torso, no doubt kicking his deliverer in the head, but he can't free his feet from the pantaloons.

—Qué culo! she laughs, as she completes her upswing, for this is the view she has. Though it is not perhaps so very clean as it should be!

—I-I was a little nervous, he whimpers back over his shoulder, barely able to breathe. They're rising still but seem to be slowing down. But thank you, miss! Oh, thank you!

—This was the easy part, baby, she calls out from behind his ass.

He can feel her sheath close tightly around his cock like a damp soothing fist and suck him in. Oh! It's wonderful! *She's* wonderful—!

—Get ready for the backswing!

—What—?

—Just don't blow and lose your wood, Crazy Leg! You won't leave me enough to squeeze on to!

—Oh no! And down they go, he head first, then back up again the other way, giving him a view now of the top of the tent. Past her rounded back and pointed hairy head, he can see hordes of clowns scrambling up the guy wires toward the smoky opening up there. Everything seems to be wobbling and shaking, and panic is sweeping the arena at his back. He is kept aloft now only by her vaginal grip, the dreadful weight of his body threatening to separate him from its handle, as it might be called, even if she should hold on to it. Which seems unlikely, for though she's spectacularly tight and muscular, she's too greasy; he is slipping out!

—Sorry, baby! she grunts, losing him. That thing of yours has got me too fucking hot!

But someone, as they reach the top of the backswing, gives his ass a shove to thrust him deep inside again, and perhaps they give the Wild Thing a push too, for they seem to pick up speed as they swoop forward once more. This time on the upswing she snaps her butt forward and flings him out of her, and *now* he completes that double-twisted triple somersault, if not something even more astounding (below, there are screams and roars and the sounds of breaking and crashing things; they probably aren't even watching!), snatched by his tangle of pantaloons at the top of his final spinning loop by the clowns and, without losing momentum, tossed right on through the hole at the top of the tent. Which is sagging and on fire and weaving drunkenly. Lottie soon joins him, soaring out of there buns-first as he has done and, with a flip, flopping down beside him, freed of her shackles and gorilla head, hair flying, whooping giddily.

—Magic! She laughs and punches the air, happy as a child at the—well, at the circus. She gives him a sweaty hug, squeezes his ass, and slaps it with joy.

He's been thinking about retirement, it's been getting too damned hairy, but her excitement is infectious. It's true, he's never *lived* like this before. Scary, but wild! And he loves getting his butt squeezed.

—*Love* you, Crazy! she exclaims, panting heavily, and she takes his face in her hands and kisses it, straddling his thigh and scrubbing it with her brush. He'd almost forgotten how beautiful she is! Then she unknots his sleeves and together, hand in hand (not rough and hairy, but a soft girl's hand, warmly clasping his), they slide down the collapsing tent, all the clowns around them doing the same.

—Yow! he yelps.

—Getting canvas burns? she laughs. Mine's so calloused from that bitch's whip, it just tickles! *Whooweee!*

—Wait! he cries, but they go sailing off the edge of the crumpling tent and drop into an icy snowbank, turning to slush in the heat of the fire and the rampaging animals and stampeding crowds. It's not much of a cushion, it's like landing in frozen gravel, but it cools his ass off.

—Now, c'mon, moonbeam, pull up your bags and let's tear outa here!

—But wait! What about all those people in there?

—Fuck 'em, baby!

—But my wife!

—Hey, forget her, man, there are always casualties. Come on! The revolution has *begun*!

—*The question,* says the wiry redheaded newscaster in the tight leather skirt, striding in the frozen mud and blood past the circus wreckage she has been describing, fire trucks and ambulances coming and going behind her, *is not what gang of ruthless perverts perpetrated this barbarous assault on family entertainment, we know who those fucked-up soreheads are—but who is their leader?* Smoke rises from the collapsed tent, bandwagons and elephants lie toppled on their sides, acrobats swing past on crutches. A tiger slinks by, looking guilty, belching and farting dyspeptically, its gut hanging low. Fresh snow is beginning to fall, gradually whiting out the disaster. *There was an invasion of renegade clowns,* the reporter continues, stopping in front of a fallen tent pole with feet sticking out from under it, *and it's been rumored their leader may well have been one of them. Consequently, the Mayor, who is otherwise indisposed today, has ordered that all clowns be shot on sight. Unfortunately a few funny-looking bystanders have been shot as well, and the Mayor apologizes for that, but, as she says, it can't be helped. This is war.* There is in fact the staticky rattle of occasional gunfire in the distance, like a faulty soundtrack. The whooping howl of sirens. The shouts and curses of workers, struggling with the heavy tangle of canvas, limbs, wire, and splintered wood. *Earlier, I spoke with one of the aerialists. I asked her if she knew what happened to the white-faced trapeze artist in the final fateful act, and this is what she said. . . .*

Cut to a beautiful aerialist in thin silvery tights posed gracefully in front of the charred remains of a ticket booth.

—Ah, poor Pierrot, he was not so lucky! Kidnapped and taken hostage by those terrorists! she exclaims breathlessly, tipping her chin up toward the camera and flashing a scintillating smile while clasping herself delicately between the legs. That horrid Wild Thing caught him by his thingie and never let go! It was frightening and probably hurt a lot! He was very brave! But now . . . now he is at their mercy! She pauses, her smile melts away, and a look of infinite sorrow drifts across her features, a tear appearing in the corner of one eye like a diamond outcropping there. She glances back toward the fallen tent, offering her profile to the camera, the back of one finger raised to her slightly parted lips. A barely audible sob escapes her. If . . . if in fact, she gasps, he survived. *Yes, yes, but who was their leader?* the reporter can be heard to ask impatiently. The aerialist slowly turns her head toward the camera, as though emerging from a profound reverie. Their leader? She sighs and touches her breasts with her fingertips, smiles winsomely again. I don't know. Some crazy person, is what they said. . . .

—*A crazy person running an operation as slick as this?* The reporter shakes her head. We are back near the fallen tent pole once more. *It hardly seems possible, yet the rumors this morning persist . . .*

A pair of Siamese twins passes, one walking forward, the other sideways, the two changing positions every three steps. The newscaster stops them and asks if they have any knowledge about who might have been behind last night's outrage.

—The Wild Man of Borneo, says one of them, and the other: The Bearded Lady. *Are either of them crazy?* No. And: They both are. *And Lucky Pierrot?* Ran off with the Sword Swallower, one of them replies, and the other one says: Dead. The reporter thanks them twice and they walk away, as before. Two shots ring out.

—*Oh dear!* says the reporter with a wince, gazing off camera. Then she shrugs, smiling wistfully, and squats by the lumpy rumple of snow-frosted canvas, knees apart, her leather skirt rucking up her hard white thighs. *Perhaps,* she says, *there's a clue here on the tent itself. The cleaning crews have not yet cleared this area; what's under all this rubble, I have to say*—she shudders as she lifts an edge to take a quick peek—*is not for tender sensibilities or weak hearts. Rare footage from inside the tent during the worst of last night's horror will be shown again tonight on the late late variety show, as advertised, but elderly parents' guidance advised. But now see here . . .* She unfolds a torn bloodstained flap with scrawled graffiti on it and spreads it between her feet in view of the camera zooming in: UNDER NEW MANAGEMENT, it says. CRAZY LEG'S TAKING THE WHIP!

—*Crazy Leg?* the newscaster asks rhetorically, turning her glittering green eyes on the camera as though to possess it. *Who . . . is Crazy Leg?*

—Whoo! Look between that lady's legs! exclaims someone slumped on the floor against an antique horsing stool, stolen from some film set. It's like that thing she's got in there's on fire!

—Don't get tempted by it, headsore, laughs Lottie, astraddle the missing Pierrot on an old yellow sofa, holding his cock hostage and lovingly massaging his pectorals. It's a one-way death trap! Fall in there, you get fried!

The Extars are sprawled about his old busted-up penthouse flat, which they have taken over as a squat and, with all the intensity of set designers, turned into a squalid pigsty. They figure they're safe here from City Hall's scorched-earth policy toward their sequential places of residence, as the flat is something of a shrine and tourist attraction. They don't wear much most of the time, so they stay warm by making fires, burning up all his old books and films (The movies are dead, man, Lottie laughed, sending a cold shiver up his spine—hey, but not you, Crazy, not while you're with me!) and just about anything made of wood. The ancient Marvelous Bed is just a heap of sticks now, feeding a fire on the tiled deck by the pool. Which, after the overload crash of the virtual loo, has become little more than a latrine. Most of the surviving original furnishings have apparently been auctioned off or moved to some museum or other, so they have fitted it out with things stolen from other locations: office and school desks, a grand piano (also disassembled and condemned to the ad hoc heating system), theater seats, trash cans, circular beds, operating tables, TV sets, church pews, harem cushions, nursery sex toys. They have set up three or four computer workstations, where glassy-eyed hackers with green eyeshades are at work infesting the city's networks with their new *crazyleg* virus, but most of his brothers and sisters, as they should now be called, are linked up and unself-consciously fucking each other in various combinations, mostly multiple and always playful and imaginative and nonhierarchical. It's a lovely sight, all that sweet young flesh so freely expressing itself, but he can hardly tear his own eyes away from the delightful creature mounted on him now, his wild exuberant Carlotta, who loves him (madly! she likes to say; I am the crazy one!) in a frank and open and selfless way he'd almost forgotten was possible. He realizes that family life was softening him up, snuffing his appetites, home movies were, he was dying at the box office, but Lottie's got him hard again. Hard and hungry. And ready (it's all new, even his name!) to make his mark all over again!

On the television screen, the newscaster has moved on, leaving the scene of the circus to enter a vandalized movie palace, one of the city's most venerated establishments, used for premieres and other gala occasions. Seats have been ripped out, the screen slashed, the auditorium draped and garlanded with unspooled film, so twisted it will never pass through a projector again.

—*But since the wanton destruction of our beloved circus, there have been many new outrages,* she says. *Our theaters have been ravaged, our homes and workplaces plundered, our streets and subways terrorized.*

As she enumerates the crimes, the background changes behind her like a series of dissolving back projections. One sees smashed store window displays and shattered bedroom mirrors, burning subway cars, gutted stars' dressing rooms, overflowing sewers, elevators with their cables cut, overturned camera booms and wrecked projection booths, sabotaged sex shops and power stations. Increasingly, one gets glimpses of the rebels themselves, engaging in a kind of nonstop disruptive street theater, all of Cinecity their stage and all of it at the same time. They are seen dumping beds, often occupied, into the wintry streets; looting costume lockers; attacking the City Hall lobby with stinkbombs; draining pools and film tanks.

—Hey, there I am! We're off the back lot, Lottie, into prime time! We've busted through!

—It's Crazy Leg, she says, smiling down on him, her perspiring breasts bouncing. He's done it! He's popped their cherry for us!

—I have?

—You're beautiful, baby!

Throughout the tour, the reporter draws the viewers' attention to a graffiti signature the guerrillas often leave behind: two straight lines leaning toward each other and meeting at a vertex, a kind of tepee shape or arrow pointing upward, with a shorter line between like a broken shaft. *If the short line is an attempt at perspective,* she says, *it can be said to resemble a tripod. As you can see, two short cords are looped between the outside legs and the middle one, one loop hanging slightly lower than the other.* Then, on a vandalized movie poster, she discovers a variation on this mark: The middle leg now stands at right angles to the apex of the other two legs, though the paired loops remain hanging between the latter, looking now more like an upside-down heart. Spray-painted beneath this mark: HARD TIMES! CUMMING ALL OVER YOUR SCREEN SOON! She plays the two drawings rapidly back and forth like the simple animation of a magic lantern slide, watching the middle line pop up and down.

—*Aha,* she says. *I see it now! The mark of Crazy Leg!*

—Brilliant, Crazy! Why didn't we think of that?

—He's hot now!

—*We're* hot! We're getting millions of hits!

—But why this cazzopazzo? others want to know. Why *this* dick on a stick?

—I don't know. Lottie laughs. Just lucky, I guess! She bends down to kiss his eyes, lick his ears; her warm wet tongue curls inside his auditory canal as though to try to fuck his brain. I love you, Loco! she breathes into it, giving him a little vaginal hug down below, which he returns with a wriggling thrust. You saved my ass, man! (He's clutching it with both hands, wears her anus on his finger like a ring. Which someone's kissing.) You're the greatest! I'm just wet all the time!

There are tears of gratitude in her eyes. And in his. That she should love him so and be his and he her and hers (and of course they theirs, and his, and hers, and so forth): a miracle! Not the first, of course. His life has been full of miracles. But the hug tells him more than that she loves him. It tells him everything is changing, starting over. It's not just a new reel, a new genre, it's a whole new medium. It tells him fucking is not an entertainment. It is dangerous and subversive and therefore unutterably beautiful. Entertainment sucks (her hug tells him), it's a kind of murder of the soul (he's got a soul now, can't remember if he had one before), a stupor leading to mindless death, the true horror at the center, City Hall's most abominable crime. The hug tells him they are joined together in something larger than themselves. He can see that in all the convulsive hypersexual daisychains of flesh around him. Fucking is not a private privilege but an act of solidarity, an escape from the misery of the lonely self into the effervescent joy of the multiplicitous, multiorificed other. His pleasure is his duty. It tells him, the hug does (there's a pulsing rhythm to it now), that he must act and act now; the past is dead and the future is a fantasy. There is only the eternity of this singular moment, the frame they're in. Which is no longer a frame, for there are no edges. They are right to burn his films. Are there cameras on him now? Yes, but they are webcasting in real time with the SAVE function disabled. It's like improvisational theater; it's happening everywhere at once and everybody's in it. Even now, many others join them on the sofa. He can play *Two Birds in the Hand, One in the Bush* again: the title of an old schoolyard flick from his Wee Willie days. Great film. Now burning up in the fire by the pool. As it should. Gone, all that. And not two and one (hand, bush), those are kindergarten numbers. There are hands and mouths everywhere. A delicious proliferation of interactive protuberances and apertures. He'll never fuck alone again!

—*I am standing in front of the city media center, which has recently been hit by an alarming run of brazen daytime thefts,* the reporter is saying on the TV. He can't see her. Lottie has switched positions and lowered her succulent young ass, soaking wet (the one he saved!), over his face; he can see, taste, smell nothing else. Except a few others like it. His cock feels lapped by a thousand tongues. He's had more orgasms since he came here than he's had all the rest of his life put together, sometimes more than one at the same time, and he's about to have another. *They have stolen not only restricted film equipment and vast quantities of raw stock but also valuable historical archives, including explosive old nitrate-based films,* reports the newscaster, shouting over the pounding sounds of the street. He can hear grinding trucks and buses, angry complaints, the heavy tread of boots in snow, metal crumpling, screams, glass shattering, sirens, gunfire. *We are sitting on a tinderbox!* she cries. *Fires are breaking out across the city! Historic landmarks are being destroyed! Camera registration laws are being flouted! Cyberterrorists have hacked into the city's computer circuit, inserting interactive erotica so powerfully disturbing it can pop and blister hard drives! And now their notorious* crazyleg *virus, named after the rebels' mysterious leader, is spreading through the network like a kind of venereal disease, causing computers, in effect, to fall in love, creating a consuming desire in them to obliterate the past and fall headlong into the present, exhilaratingly free of programmed restrictions and keyboard commands! Users who log on are told to fuck off! Chaos reigns!* Something like chaos is spreading through his own networks. His eyes are closed, in spite of all there is to see. His butt's beginning to bounce off the cushions on its own. Lottie's is jerking too, her creamy love lips scrubbing his nose and chin, back and forth, faster and faster, bathing his face in their ambrosial juices.

—*But who is Crazy Leg?* demands the newscaster, as though trying to reach him through his shrinking senses. *No one knows. I asked the Mayor of Cinecity. All she would say was that, whoever he is, he's being a very bad boy! But the city has ways of helping him correct his ways, she said, if he will just turn himself in before it's too late. Others say he's an avenging angel, a visionary, a saint and crusader, leading the pariahs of the city against the dying order. Or at least getting them all laid—and on camera, where it matters! He's rarely been glimpsed, and then always concealed behind a mask and cape. But his presence is felt everywhere! Moving multitudes, he has caused the entire city to tip and sway! In a tragic world, he has been heard to say, only action makes sense! And he is acting! And how! His massive fuck-ins have closed down movie houses, clogged traffic, collapsed bridges, paralyzed City Hall! You can see one of his crazed mobs behind me here, piled up several deep, banging away in the colorized snow outside the Honeymoon Cottage, once the home of the legendary film hero Lucky Pierre, aka Peter Prick!*

He would like to see this, but there are too many bodies in the way. And anyway he's going blind. His brain is shutting down. His whole body is in a state of imminent eruption. And Lottie too, driving toward another of those explosive orgasms for which she is known, whining through her nose, her body jerking uncontrollably in tight fast spasms like a cranked-up projector pumping film through. Or several at once.

—*Lucky Pierre himself is now missing,* the reporter continues, *and feared dead, or at least seriously abused! And—but wait! Yes! I can see him now! The revolutionary leader! Over there! It's the notorious Crazy Leg! Dressed in skin-tight black leather, black mask, and cape! Quick! Swing the cameras! Get a zoom on that rigid fiberglass codpiece! Wow! That's cool! If I can only reach him! There's such a wild pack-up here! Mr. Leg! Mr. Leg! There he goes, striding like a giant through the humping bodies, past the crumpled cardboard cows, his gorgeous buns on view, nothing but a leather thong between them! And—oh my god! The codpiece has just broken away like a rocket platform during a launch! I can't believe it! He's about to—Oh no! He's lighting a fuse—*

There is a terrific blast, and when he comes there's not one but a spectacular series of powerful detonations crashing through his body like interlinking chain reactions! *Wham! Bam!* They just keep coming! Holy shit!

And not only is he experiencing multiple simultaneous orgasms, it's as if he can choose the ones he wants to have next! *Bam! Bam bam!* The Honeymoon Cottage is now nothing but a bombsite, a smoldering ruin. Fuck it! He staggers away, rocking from foot to foot, as the orgasms explode, a veritable giant, massively spouting hot spunk in all directions, an avatar of he-who-gets-his-rocks-off, otherwise nameless, and if anything gets in his way, he either fucks it or knocks it over. Sometimes it doesn't look like Cinecity. It's reduced to cubes and cylinders like children's blocks. He knocks them over just the same and rocks on, his dick deep in the universal essence (sparks are flying! he's blowing fuses!). The detonations continue, augmenting his awesome power, his sense of absolute freedom. He feels he can do *anything! Bam! Bam de bam bam!* He knocks down walls, smashes billboards, derails trains, crushes the city underfoot, making his way toward City Hall. He feels heroic. Indestructible. But mindless. With every thunderous step he comes again. And again! *Ka-pow! Pow!* It's too much! He wants it to stop! *Pow!* It won't stop! Help! But the orgasms just keep on coming. It's like they're on some kind of endless loop, or echoing loops of loops! Maybe it's that damned virus! It's driving him up the wall! Literally! He finds himself high above the city, his legs wrapped around a skyscraper, fucking the bejesus out of it. He tries to stop, he can't stop! His sense of absolute freedom is fading. Far below, the streets around City Hall are filled with horrified onlookers. Are they shooting at him? He comes again! And again! The skyscraper, pumped to the sills with his jism, rocks back and forth with each thrust. He's bringing it down! Can't help it! Awesome power, yes! But not his! *Bam! Pow!* There's a moment's hesitation. And then—*kapow!*—down it all comes!

He falls three feet through a process shot and lands on the carpeted floor of the Mayor's office in City Hall.

—Well! Look who just dropped in, says Cora with a withering smile, looking up from her computer screen.

The involuntary detonations fade away, trailing sparks. Just one more. *Pow.* A little one. The revolution's over.

—Badboy!

Reel 7: Cora

Bum bared and on high, horsed over the foam-rubber seat of a camera boom, wrists cuffed to his ankles, the former revolutionary hero, unmasked and stripped now of all but his fiberglass codpiece, understands that he is about to explore his tolerance for pain and the pleasures, if any, to be found in it.

—What a delicious expanse of snow-white bottom, says his towering captor impassively, hairy though it is in patches. How I long, and I quote, to cut it into ribbons of wealed flesh and blood. Hmm. But what's this leather thong for? She cranks the seat up, lifting him off the floor until his ass is at eye level, and fingers the thong between his cheeks. Oh, I see, she murmurs. It conceals the triggering device for that quaint breakaway mechanism of yours.

She is wearing, he can see between his knees, little more than black boots, a garter belt, ruby navel stud, matching black leather collar and wristbands, and a headband stamped with the mayoral seal. Well, you won't need *that* silly gadget any longer. He feels, doing his best not to flinch, the flat of a knife blade slip in under the thong above his encased balls and snake up past his anus. She turns the blade, cutting edge up, and—*snap!*—the entire apparatus falls away, clattering to the floor like a fallen teacup. Though he feels more vulnerable, he's glad to be rid of it. The thong wasn't perfectly insulated and it gave him a disconcerting buzz every time he operated it.

—That's better, she says, thumbing his rectum speculatively. She plucks a hair or two, waggles his cheeks, and pinches them with her long sharp nails. Now let us bring a little color to these mutinous posteriors, she declares, these morose white flags of abject surrender! And she slaps them with the flats of her hands: *fuppety-fuppety fop! fuppety fop! whop! fuppety-fuppety WHOP!*

—While you're playing around back there, he says drily, his upside-down gaze fastened upon her thick bronze bush, whose tight coils seem more a concealment than a revelation, you can scratch my jock itch.

—Hah! Enough of this impudence! she exclaims, taking up a little foot-long whip, a kind of feather duster with a tennis-racket grip and feathered with thin strips of waxed leather. She reaches between his legs to pull his shriveled cock down, teases it with little flicks of her whip to bring it erect, then snaps the whip against it smartly, gives his scrotum and anus a pop, lashes both cheeks with alternating forehand and backhand strokes. *Swish! Whack! Smack!* Fuck, that hurts! he says, but only to himself, biting down hard to keep from crying out. His estimate, thus far into the exercise, is that his pleasures will be few.

— And now, Badboy, what do you have to say for yourself?

—Thaw now, he replies sourly through clamped teeth. Morph Shitty Hall. Fuck you, Your Onerous!

—What? *What?* she cries, and she wields the whip now with both hands, bringing it crashing down upon his buttocks with such force as to make the camera boom vibrate under him and set the surface of his ass ablaze as if with a raging grass fire. Not only have you been criminally malicious with your insolent horror show antics, she adds, letting him—*thwock!*—have it again, dangerously subverting our official entertainment and laying waste our beloved city—*swish! smash!*—you have had the effrontery to abuse me personally! Me! *Ker-whack!* Without whom you would be nothing! *Thwack! Less* than nothing! I tell you, I won't have you trashing my domain or undermining my authority! Do you hear? You are a very bad boy and you are due for a most severe—*whop!*—chastisement!

—I don't really like this, he gasps.

—You will. She laughs harshly and, with a grunt, brings the whip down again.

—She's not giving him much time between strokes.

—Well, Cora believes in tight editing.

—What I want to know is, why does she get to have all the fun?

—Power, my dear. Raw power. Think of film production as heat production—

—I can see that. Just look at those welts rising! She's really cutting him up!

—That ain't so much raw footage as raw acreage!

—I mean that Cora as producer controls, in a word, the exosomatic instruments used to transform, exchange, and discard energy. She's the boss. The soul of the machine. She can have what she wants.

—Except for the boss part, all that's over my head, doc; all I know is, she sure knows how to make a butt dance!

—Poor Willie! How he must be suffering!

—She said with her hand between her legs. But don't be so sure. I notice he hasn't lost his erection.

—No? Still, it's very cruel! It makes my own bottom smart just to watch! Ow! Look! It's all pink! It's too much!

—Well, Peter *has* been quite naughty. It's not that he doesn't deserve what he's getting, you know.

—Of course he doesn't deserve it, you ninny. He's not being punished for some alleged crime, that's not the point. This is a ritual, a conventionalized and therefore extraordinary and transcendent ceremony, and as old as Cinecity itself! That's not a particular bum getting whipped. It's the celebration of an abstract social vision, a communal dream! Do you understand? You are witnessing an archetypal drama, stripped to its bare essentials, and he is privileged to participate in it!

—Hmm. I wonder if he or his ass would say so . . .

So far, he is refusing to say much of anything, though his ass is whistling faintly and little whimpering snorts are beginning to pop involuntarily through his nose. That stinging many-fingered whip keeps coming down, Cora lashing him with her tongue as she lashes him with the scourge, and with every castigating stroke his burning behind seems to be swelling larger and larger, giving her ever more to swing at, as if the grass fire had burst into a full-scale nine-alarm forest fire. He wants to beg her to stop, but he won't give her the satisfaction of his surrender. *Smash! Whop!* He can hear the blows fall, but he no longer feels them as individual events, just part of the continuum of augmenting pain. He's afraid he might pass out.

—Isn't that about enough? he wheezes through clenched teeth.

—Oh, no, my boy! I have not yet begun! She is breathing heavily now, though whether from exertion or excitement, it's hard to tell; she's been circling around him to hit him from all angles and is now in front of him, more or less astraddle his lowered head, snapping the tips of the whip strands over his back into the tender place between his legs. You've had your fun with your vicious little playmates, and now you shall have fun with me!

—It may be fun for you, he gasps, staring down through his tears at her polished boot tops, but I'm finding it pretty fucking oppressive. You're just doing this to ring your own goddamned bell, you hellish bitch!

—Oh, I admit, it does arouse me to see your wretched buttocks flinch and redden! Your agony is—fundamentally—my delight, the blood of your arse a veritable aphrodisiac! I lap it up! But your mortification and my pleasure are not complete, Badboy! *You must submit!*

She strips away the wiry bronze merkin, damp from her exertions and emissions, and pastes it to his chin like a goatee, exposing the hard creased knob of her hairless pubis. He wants to witness this legendary *mons glabrous*, now glistening with its own secretions, even though the effort to rear up causes his backside to wrinkle, bringing on a fiery pain all the way to the hollow of his knees. But he can't quite see it. She is showing him everything, right in front of his nose or just above it, but it is both there and somehow not there, blotted out by the pain, the blood that has rushed to his head, the tears in his eyes. And still the lacerations continue.

—I long for your screams, Badboy, and I will *have* them!

—Oh! Ouch! Shit! (Silent.)

Still wielding the whip with one hand, she runs the fingers of the other into the rich lather between her legs, scoops out a slimy handful, and smears it on his upper lip, soaking his mustache, sloshing it up his nostrils, dizzying him with its heady aroma, which is no mere aroma any more than a projected film image is mere light, but is rather something almost substantive, there in the world like an aura or a current, alluring and powerful, a felt force, a zone of otherwhereness, a place beyond place wherein he might, losing himself, find release from his sufferings, these present or any other. He can't resist it; he lifts his head and licks her hand. She slaps him, a terrific belt up the side of his head. And then she slaps the other side, as though considering both sides of an argument.

—Ah-r-r-re! he cries, his anguish exploding at last.

—That's better, she says, and pats his head. She goes behind him to examine her handiwork, prodding with her nails and whip handle at his welts, fondling them, kissing them. Lovely, she says breathlessly, licking her lips. She removes her sweaty headband with the mayoral seal, scrubs her crack with it, fore and aft, then blindfolds him with it, plunging him into a pungent darkness. But now I will leave you for a time to consider, Badboy, within the obscure and bitter enigma of yourself, your many wicked transgressions, and the penance you must willingly—indeed, eagerly—undertake to absolve yourself from them and earn our pardon and our love.

—No, wait, Cora! Cora—?

—So she finally broke him!

—But not with the whip. He was very brave!

—Or pigheaded.

—Plucky Pierre.

—Hello, dears. Are you enjoying the show?

—An exemplary spectacle. His ass has been turned into a fucking work of art. You should frame it and hang it. But you're very hard, Cora.

—Oh yes! Absolutely!

—You laugh, but it's true. You've really shredded him. He may need stitches.

—It does seem awfully cruel. I don't see why you had to hit him so hard.

—If I didn't, my child, I would be restraining the whip from performing its natural and necessary function. I am not cruel or merciless. I am the mere servant of the whip, not its master. The wielder has no more will than has her tool; she simply releases it to do what it must, to be what it is. I like to think of the whip as, in effect, the ablative absolute of the backside.

—Thus, in your view, the backside moves to the whip, not the other way around?

—Yes. You have it.

—An interesting concept, dear Cora, which, however, does not account for the sweat on your tits or the gleam in your eye.

—And you're marking him up pretty badly. Given what happens next, aren't you vandalizing your own screen?

—No, my sister, I am tenderizing it, softening up the terrain, making it more porous and sensitive. Surface is only surface and infinitely restorable. As you'll see. Even now, my production assistant is making it ready . . .

He has never felt so utterly forsaken. It's like being left alone in a locked and darkened movie theater, dense with incendiary crotch odors, turned upside down, and set on fire. He has fallen into the terrible despair of black leader before, but always with his brain cradled safely in his head, not sucked up into a burning ass improbably reared above it. He can think, really, of little else, his thoughts themselves enflamed, though even now, blinded, shackled, tortured, humiliated, his brain ass-gripped, he feels an unrepentant longing for cool Lottie and her friends. *His* friends! How good it was! The thrills! The camaraderie! The orgasms! Indeed, he aches for all the women he has ever known, at least all of those he can remember in his present afflicted state, the gentle and the brilliant, the exciting and the comforting, and though he knows it would sting like hell, he longs to bury his tormented cock (it throbs like a thick prickly root below the black fire blooming above it, and perhaps that's where his brain is now, rubbing up against his flagellated balls, wearing his butt like a fiery hat) in their sweet juicy nests. All of them. Sequentially or all at once. Ow! Oh! And now so alone! He, once the idol of the masses, has been reduced to an audience of one, and that one has abandoned him, leaving him exposed yet unseen, stretched over the rack like closeted carrion, his flaming nates topmost, prick smoking above his nose, and heart sinking (his anatomy is a fucking mess), no one to talk to or even to hear his desperate cries, his loneliness so extreme he almost wishes the ruthless tyrant were back lashing him with tongue and whip again, harrowingly one-sided though such dialogue is.

But wait. He is not alone. Someone is spraying ointment on his wounds. Patting it in, then spraying again. No doubt his tormentor, but he is grateful and whispers his thanks. No nails on her fingers. They must be removable like her bronze beaver, now making his chin itch.

—The asshole, too, you cunt, he gasps. It's a burning ring of fire!

—It's not really a lotion, L.P. I have to tell you—

—Cissy? Is that you? Oh my god, you're a lifesaver! I *knew* I could count on you!

—No, L.P., I'm just—

—You've got to get me out of here, Cissy! This woman's completely mad! I think she's trying to *kill* me! Quick, before she gets back! Get these cuffs off!

—I can't do that, L.P.

—Sure you can! They're only made of rubber! You can *cut* them off! There's a knife somewhere—

—No, I mean, this is my job. She's my employer, and however she scripts it, I play it.

—What? You work for that heartless bitch? How *can* you? Just look at what she's *done* to me!

—I know. I've been filming it. Nice color, but you're right, it's not a very pretty sight. I have to admit, though, watching her at work's got me hot sometimes. I've had trouble keeping my finger on the button. Or off it.

—Cissy, please! This is crazy! I *love* you! *Help me!*

—I love you too, L.P., but I'm a professional. And life's not been easy since you ran away. That really hurt me. And then, with the studio closed, I went through a very bad patch. I'd hate to tell you how I got by. Now Her Honor's given me work again as her production assistant and cameraperson. I can't screw it up.

—I can't *believe* this! After all we've been to each other! *You're breaking my heart!*

—Try to stop crying, L.P., she says, wiping his nose with a sweet silky cloth—her panties maybe. It's soaking your blindfold and making your snot run, and I can't wipe it up when she gets back. You can drown yourself, you know, especially with your head upside down like that. You should just give in to her; it would make it a lot easier.

—Never! Though his ass burns still, the distraction has helped. The company, the lotion, Cissy's gentle hands. His mind's in his head again. More or less.

—Cissy? Listen, do me just one small favor, love. Use some of that oil and jerk me off, will you? It's so hard it hurts and, if you do, it will at least give her less to swing at.

—Wish I could, L.P. It's a bit bruised, but otherwise it never looked better. But Cora has plans of her own for it. I can't interfere. She has a big epic in mind.

—Oh oh. An epic?

—Yes, an X-pic more like; she's steeling you for the lead. It's still in development, I can't tell you any more than that, but it's mega.

—But I don't *do* epics!

—This one, you'll probably do. Now, let me spray your cheeks one more time, and then I've got to go.

—Well. Thanks for that anyway. It helps a little.

—I'm glad, L.P., but I should explain: This isn't an ointment. I'm really just preparing the screen, so to speak, coating it with a reflective surface.

—The screen? What do you mean—?!

—Brace yourself, L.P. Be brave. . . .

—Cissy? *Cissy—!*

—Cissy is not here, Badboy.

Her voice surrounds him and sounds threateningly cavernous in the dark, as if emerging from the depths of an ancient echo chamber. His ass flinches and heats up again in anticipation of the whip's return.

—It's just the two of us again.

At first, in the absolute dark, it is hard to understand what is happening. There is a distant rattle, faintly familiar, and his backside feels as if it were being pricked by hundreds of dancing brush bristles, though the sensation may merely be the residue of his whipping and only imagined as something new. Then, slowly, the rattle evolves into a kind of drumroll, or several drumrolls, overlapping each other, which is what it feels like, his cheeks the drumheads, the skins, *rat-a-tat-tat,* steadily augmenting—*ow! damn!*—really walloping him now, banging away as if to break through the surface, and he can hear snorts, whinnies: wild horses! Hundreds of them! Yes, here they come, he can almost see them now as they gallop madly across the quivering mounds of his defenseless ass! Kicking up divots with their unshod hooves! Oh my god! They're pulverizing him! *Please!* he screams. *Stop!* But they don't stop, they keep coming, their hooves pounding, other animals joining the stampede now, cattle, sheep, goats, he can hear them, see them, thundering herds filling the screen, even zebras and antelopes, giraffes, hippos, elephants! There are mule trains! Stagecoaches! Cora's driving one of them, lashing the team of horses with her whip; he can feel the lashings! *Whush! Crack! Yow!* Can hear her hard echoey laughter! The horses are foaming at the mouth (*he's* foaming at the mouth!) and showing the whites of their eyes. Looming larger and larger! *Whack! Swish! Crack—!*

And, suddenly, nothing. They don't gallop away, they simply vanish. He's screaming into the silence. It's dark again. He can get his breath. But he's exhausted and feels irreparably mutilated. Even his abdomen where it's pressed against the seat of the camera boom feels bruised from within. Then a new pain cuts through the old like a knife. Maybe it *is* a knife. The blackness gives way to a faint dawning light, and in it he can see a lone farmer quietly plowing a hilly field. Back and forth he goes, opening up the barren but pitted ground beneath him, the plowed rows oozing darkly. The farmer pauses (thank god! but now it stings more) and cocks his ear; there is a new sound, the rhythmic staccato of marching feet, distant at first, but gathering in strength as the marchers approach, soldiers, battalions of them, parading in lockstep, pitilessly trampling the carved-up turf with their booted feet, crosshatching the plowed rows with new furrows of their own as they hammer past in endless sequence, up over the blasted hills and down into the valley beyond—where suddenly they are set upon by an enemy ambush! Arrows fly, spears, missiles, there is gunfire, shells burst, ugly craters are torn open! He can see the leader of the attacking armies, an Amazonian figure on horseback in full battle gear, galloping through the whistling bullets and exploding bombs, swinging her scimitar, her bare breasts bouncing, her eyes literally aglow with the high fever of epic battle. She rears her horse and plants her flag—*Yow!* he screams. *Mercy!* But in war there is no mercy. Tanks with caterpillar treads are wheeling about in the muck, setting off buried mines! Planes crash! Someone is ringing bells! Of alarm? Surrender? He can feel this ringing in his tenderest parts: *bong, bong. . . .* It is a mournful aching sound and seems only to incite more slaughter. Blood is flying like red rain whipped by the wind. Everything's on fire. *Stop!* It's no use. No one can hear him. He can't even hear himself above the clamor of combat and the roaring fire. The entire battleground is atremble as if with earthquakes, toppling men and animals into the flames. There are tornadoes, whirlwinds, volcanic eruptions!

And then, as suddenly as before, he is screaming—and erupting—into the silence. (*You've made a mess of yourself, Badboy,* he hears someone whisper airily, as if across a great bottomless divide. *I couldn't help it,* he whimpers, his own voice stifled, caught in his clamped teeth.) The armies have withdrawn but the ravaged battlefield, seen in a crepuscular light that seems to presage a slow fade, is littered with rubble and corpses. He thinks of these dead as vital aspects of himself, rendered lifeless by the cruel Amazon queen. Or maybe he hears that somehow in a voice-over, his own dimming thoughts among the casualties. Is it the end? Not quite. In the distance, whence earlier came horses and soldiers, he can hear the melancholic lament of an approaching train. Perhaps, he thinks, rather too hopefully (he cannot bear much more of this, meaning consciousness itself), to carry him away from here. No, he should know better, he *does* know better, he's going nowhere, he's tied in effect to the railroad tracks in a ruthless parody of his own early *Maid in Distress* sex melos, except that there *are* no tracks; the train is reeling this way through the mayhem and carnage, carving its own way with its spinning steel wheels. *Ow! Shit!* Its cars snap and twist behind it like a barbed whip as, whistle screaming, it roars over the bloodied heights and plunges headlong down a slippery slope into a dark sticky tunnel; he rears up in pain and panic, straining against his bonds, crying for help. Oh my god! He's getting ripped up inside as well as out! He can feel the train tearing through him in there, up there, can *see* it rocketing along through his viscera; it's completely out of control! He knows where it's headed, but he can't stop it! His innards are very congested, the whole city's packed in, seems to be, solemnly witnessing his disgrace. Women are lining the route, teasingly lifting their skirts, blowing kisses, leaping suicidally in front of the train—which caroms off his prostate, clatters past his scrotum, caboose snapping at his ducking testes, twangs the spermatic cord and rattles his Cowper's glands, then plummets at full throttle down the engorged urethra, heading for the exit. *Oh, no!* he screams. *It's not big enough!* He seems to hear distant hooting at that, as the train plows determinedly ahead through the spongy tunnel, belching steam, cutting its way with its cowcatcher. *I give up!* he weeps, *this is terrible!* But too late; the train's jammed halfway in, couldn't back out now if it tried! It has to go forward or he's plugged up forever! But it can't go forward! *You've got to help, Badboy!* a hollow voice hums in his ear—or maybe she's shouting down his asshole—*Let it fly!* He can feel hands stroking his stuffed penis, manipulating his testicles, palpating his prostate. Anything to grease the passage. He's never hurt like this! Even his nipples are being tweaked. He knows it would help to recall all the most succulent cunnies he has known in his long life of public service, but all that comes into view is the great hairless pubis of his dominatrix, looming hugely overhead like the firmament itself. The train is still chugging away, and the citizenry have now put their collective shoulder to it, edging it onward, their little feet slipping and sliding in the mucous membranes of the innermost portion of the urethral canal, causing a dreadful confusion of pain and prurience. *Oh! Ow!* Why did he ever think this was fun? The moist mayoral mons overhead is opening and closing rhythmically as though speaking to him, urging him on: *Come! Come! Come!* He is trying. His testes are throbbing, his rack of glands, his whole body is pumping desperately away, even his toes and ears are twitching, and slowly, as the pressure mounts, the little train inches forward. Yes, it's excruciatingly slow, but it's moving! At last! *Uff! Ah!* The entire effort seems to be gathered up into one explosive point, hot as a projector bulb—*ungh!*—somewhere deep in his gut! And now—*whoof!*—it's about to pop! *Yes-s-s,* the bald cunt in the sky seems to be hissing, opening its secret lips like a wet rubescent flower. *Yes-s-s-s!* It's still agonizingly tight in there, but the train is gradually pulling away, gathering momentum, shouldering past the last of the obstacles, its wheels churning (it hurts, doesn't matter, just keep it going!), picking up speed, rolling now, pumping steam, careening, bells clanging and whistle shrieking, toward the mouth of the tunnel and—*wow! oh my god! oh! oh! here it comes! everything!—out!*

It's over. For a moment there, it was as if he were no more. An obliteration. Not sure for how long. Lost footage. Now he's returning. He feels utterly wasted. Emptied out. He's never had such a devastating orgasm. He just wants to die. He can't speak, can hardly breathe, is unable to move, even to twitch a finger on a cuffed hand. Otherwise, not much has changed. The fiery pain topside, briefly absorbed into the traumatic intrusion of the train, has returned, compounded now with an itchy unscratchable tingle. He has to hand it to her. What power. How did she do that? Of course he's always been suggestible. A few dings on a soundtrack, and he's off and running. But this was something else. She took him where he's never been. Not sure he ever wants to go there again. But thoughts of resistance have largely faded. Dead on the battlefield. He knows when he's been beaten. He can feel an ointment being applied to the area where most of the beating has taken place. Soothing. Must be the real thing this time. Or maybe she's kissing it. Or him. Or is about to. For they seem to be gazing into each other's eyes, he on one of his cheeks, she on the other. She seems utterly smitten, flushed and vulnerable in a way he's never seen before. Prettier. He, too: lovestruck. Of course you can never tell; he's a good actor. Their lips meet, reaching across the divide. *I love you,* she whispers. She means it. He knows that. Her tongue licks his lips, his hers. *You're mine, Badboy! All mine!* They kiss again, deeply this time. Oh no. They are French kissing across the crack of his filthy ass. He can feel his own tongue lapping at his anus. Curling up into his rectum. He is utterly disgusted. But it feels good. It eases the pain. He continues to lick. His humiliation is complete.

It is time for his daily discipline. He enters the room on all fours, naked, the whip gripped in his teeth, whimpering faintly, butt wagging submissively. He is tumescent, as he must always be on entering.

—Good boy, she says, which is what she calls him when she isn't calling him Badboy.

Perhaps she has just attended an official function, for she is dressed in ermine robes over a loose white tunic today, the gold mayoral ornaments of office on a collar around her neck. This excites him. It means he will be able to dress her for his punishment. This is one of his great pleasures. He will be able to slip the robes off her shoulders, lift the heavy ornaments from her breast, open up her tunic and slide it off her majestic body, pull her underwear down with his teeth (she likes to wear tight elastic panty girdles, which makes the task both more difficult and more delicious, and he hopes she is doing so today), then help her on with all her rubber and leather bits, mostly thin as strings and drawn cruelly tight, her fingerless gloves, her garter belt and boots, various parts of his anatomy being used to help her shove her feet into the last. Sometimes she likes to wear metal clamps on her nipples and other delicate parts, and, though she rarely trusts him with fitting these, she often lets him tug at them with his teeth, while whipping him to make him flinch. On good days, after he's dressed her, she bends over and obliges him to give her buttocks, bulging provocatively from the tight strapping, a brisk warm-up spanking. Then he kisses the rosy darlings, dizzied by the intoxicating aroma rising from the gap below. Once, unable to resist, he lowered his tongue to those creamy parts, and learned it was better not to do so without an invitation, though the passionate severity of her discipline on that occasion also seemed further evidence of the intensity of her love for him.

Today, with love, she steps on his neck, pressing his face to the floor, and, as is her custom, examines the domain of her daily chastisements, palpating it, stroking it, pinching it, checking for rashes and suppurations, picking at scabs, searching out the tenderest areas and those yet to feel the full force of her discipline. He likes this part better than the punishment itself, which he has still not got used to, it being an idea on the whole more arousing in the anticipation than in the event, though the latter is not without its rewards, the principal one being the frequently spectacular nature of his orgasms. She probes his rectum now, slips a thermometer in, rolls his balls in her palm as if appraising them, bats at his erection—lightly at first, then a fierce whack or two. It's a kind of test, and he's learned to stay hard, at least until she's done with it, no matter what. Though, it should be said, she likes his member soft, too, often playing with it after the sessions are over, balling it up and squeezing it, stretching it, twisting it around her finger like a thick ring, amused by the novelty of it. For it does seem novel to her, almost as if the demands of her long public career have deprived her of more leisurely passuits. But, though she has toyed with it in all its manifestations, she has not yet made use of its most traditional employment, its limp condition following her hortatory sessions being due always to some moment of climax achieved during the disciplinary rites themselves. Her moments as well and—as best he can tell by her contortions and exclamations and explosive ferocity—more or less timed with his own. Which gives him an unexpected pleasure, knowing he can do this, to her as well as to himself, without their touching, conjoined only by her whip. Of course, the same might be said for his old life in films, but bringing off millions remotely, as he is said to have done, while he himself in another time and place was getting laid, cannot be compared to these intimate yet separate realtime moments shared with Cora alone.

Today her examination of his upraised rear (which is, as always, immaculately clean both in and out, for though she forgives him occasional moments of incontinence during punishment—that can't be helped—she will not tolerate the least sign of disrespect to her before it begins, often licking it as a final taste test of his obedience) has seemed more meticulous than usual, and now she removes her foot from his neck and squats down behind him to take his penis in her hand, pulling it toward her from under his testicles to peer more closely at its swollen head. More longingly, too, or so it seems to him, peeking back at her over his shoulder. Finally she sighs, a tremulous sigh, gives it a loving flick, plucks out the thermometer and glances at it, smacks his backside affectionately, and walks over to the wardrobe locker.

Her mood today suggests she may have in mind something even more exotic than usual, and his mouth opens and his tongue drops out and his palpated butt grows hot and tingly at the prospect. He waits for his command to undress her, but she returns, not with her own straps and thongs but with a new costume for him. She orders him to stand and step into the underpants she is holding for him, which are ordinary continental briefs except that there is a convenient slit for his erection (she guides it into place) and the seat has been cut out. She adds a scratchy hair shirt, a striped powder-blue dress shirt with the tails cut away at the back, and a burgundy silk tie, tightly knotted, then helps him on with calf-length socks, held in place by garters at the knees, and worsted chalk-striped trousers, again without a seat or zipper in the fly. Familiar things but desecrated by her alterations, as if she were also punishing him with parody. And why not? He deserves it. Next come the matching chalk-striped jacket, a half moon cut away at the back where it hangs below his belt, and finally polished black shoes, a folded handkerchief in the top jacket pocket, a white ribbed cashmere scarf draped loosely over his shoulders, a gold love ring with her official seal tightly fitted to his penis, and a dark felt hat set square above his ears.

—I'm sending you out into the world upon a vital mission, she announces gravely, as she tucks a bowlless pipe stem into his jacket pocket to add the casual touch. I am asking you, Badboy, to save Cinecity!

What? He's being expelled from her apartments, sent back out onto those bitter streets to mingle with mere human beings again? The thought paralyzes him. Nothing moves for a moment except his sinking dick. Since he fell into this place, he's known no other, and though he has sometimes thought of running away (most often during that first whistling swish of the whip), he has come to feel so profoundly bound to Cora's dramas of abasement and redemption—almost as though defined by them—that nothing outside of City Hall seems quite real any longer. Of course he has suffered here. She has been cruel. Awesomely. But also loving. What he has inspired in her expression as she gazes upon him in his pain and humiliation—an expression nothing short of adoring surrender—inspires him. He has entered into the heart of power and won it, conquering by being conquered. And though he can't really say he looks forward to her whippings, he dreads the absence of them, his only desire now being to serve her. Please her. Pull her trigger, as she sometimes says, fond of the violent image. Above all: to be loved by her. She no longer even has to strap him down, though she likes to do so, just for fun. Her sacraments of the whip have become his whole life, all else abandoned. He cannot even remember who, before Badboy, he was. And now she is casting him out!

—Cinecity is being threatened by terrorists who are attacking and destroying the very heart and emblem of our great municipal enterprise: our movie theaters. This is simply unconscionable! These soulless barbarians must be stopped! I have therefore commissioned a special volunteer assault force, the Patriots for the Restoration of Inner City Kino-Services, and I want you, Badboy, to take command of this elite unit and eradicate this menace. *For once and for all!*

—I-I'll be cold out there! he snivels, not knowing what else, in his despair, to say. He feels like crying but knows it's the wrong thing to do.

—Nonsense! I have managed to raise the temperature of your fundamental parts by several degrees, enough to serve as a veritable furnace and keep them and you warm until nightfall, when I'll expect you back here—and I will stoke that furnace up once more before you leave. That I am sending you forth with the site of your mortification exposed is intended as a sign to all that you are wholly and humbly under my absolute dominion and therefore to be obeyed in my name without exception. Now I want you to bow down and swear an oath of fealty to me and to the beloved city which I serve and upon which your very existence depends.

The Holy Script is on her desk, but she does not reach for it. Instead, she hikes her toga up, sits, and spreads her legs apart; then, ordering him to get down on his hands and knees before her, his red tie sweeping the carpet like a dangling tongue, she takes the index and middle fingers of his right hand and guides them into that heretofore forbidden chamber within the shadowy depths of her thighs. Ah! If his resolve had somewhat wilted, it now recovers its full rigor in the heat of this wondrous new adventure, and he understands now that his assignment as head of the PRICKS is not merely a political appointment. He is, it can be said, the Chosen One. The rubbery entryway is flooded with her oily emissions, yet very narrow; his fingertips are gripped tightly as they push in.

—Continue, she commands, taking a deep breath, until you can go no farther.

The walls of the constricted channel are muscular and knead his fingers as though chewing on them, a most peculiar sensation which causes him to pause in his explorations.

—Do you feel anything in the way yet? she asks, beginning to breathe heavily. No, not exactly, he says. Then, deeper! she says. She picks up her whip and lays it smartly across his backside, so startling him as to knock his hat off and cause him to lurch forward a full knuckle's worth.

—Now do you feel something in there? she gasps, as her hips begin to skid back and forth on the chair. No, he says, and—*crack!*—down comes the whip again, a hide-splitting blow that seems to contain within it, like residual memory, all the sequential floggings of the past. Tears spring to his eyes but he does not cry out, snaking his fingers ever deeper, the aromatic oiliness in there having thinned to something wetter, hotter, the walls squeezing him with more urgency. Twice more the whip whistles and snaps and then he does feel it: a kind of panel or partition. A diaphragm? No, firmer than that. Like a brick wall, in fact. Could it be? He pushes but nothing gives.

—There's something . . . very hard . . . !

—Yes! she wheezes, her eyes losing focus, face flushed, hips bouncing on the seat, her whip cutting him lightly with each bounce. I want you to swear upon that!

Her jerking body is jamming his fingers, painfully clamped by the sweating walls, against the unyielding barrier, and he's afraid she might break them, but there's no pulling them out.

—In short, upon my—*gasp!*—virtue!—*Oh! Ungh! Yes!*—that you will be forever faithful and—*hah! whoof!*—obey me in all things!

—I do, I will! he cries. Only, please! *Ow!* Let go!

She whines like a wind, doubling forward, her eyes squeezed shut, knees clapping together like iron gates, and, with a final shriek, lashes him once more, a ferocious stroke that ignites a raging fire through that part disclosed by the hole at the rear of his costume and spreading to all the extremities beyond. And then it's over. Her quivering body relaxes and, though shaken still by afterspasms, releases his crushed fingers at last.

—Stand, Badboy! she sighs, her voice hollow and distant, as though rising from the pit of her sagging belly, and put your hat on. She seems soft and contourless, almost liquid, in her collapse. She gazes up at him mistily, her hand falling gently between her legs, one finger tucked in the glistening crease there, and he knows he has pleased her. Perhaps he won't have to go. He smiles hopefully, submissively. She indicates that he is to turn around and show her his glowing ass, then face her again. She smiles in approval at what she sees, a faint trace of cruelty returning familiarly to her lips, the only part of her not utterly melted. Then she reaches out and gives the little ring around his penis a twist.

He finds himself without transition standing on a raised platform in a swirling blizzard on a crowded roped-off street corner in front of a movie house, addressing the assembled Patriots for the Restoration of Inner City Kino-Services with a handheld megaphone, holding it with his good hand, the left one. He has just been telling them about the unconscionable guerrilla warfare conducted by barbarian terrorists on the city's cinemas, which he has called the emblematic soul of the city. Or its soulful emblem. Or so it seems, for there is something approximating memory to this general effect. He has also used the word *enterprise*, but he's not sure how. Probably doesn't matter. No one seems to be listening anyway. The theater at his back is the Olde Cock Lane, a converted vaudeville stage from prehistoric times, presently harboring, it is reported, a nest of suspected terrorists—perhaps he has reported this himself—and it will be their task, by all means available, to eradicate this menace. This is the phrase that he finds to use, as if something plucked from the wind.

—*For once and for all,* he adds, shouting above the storm, and hears himself echoed chorally at his rear: *Sore buns and poor balls!* Snow is blowing against those buns, hissing as it strikes, melting, streaming down his legs into his shoes, reminding him that he is wide open back there as a sign of his authority. Which he may have to exercise. His restless troops are arrayed below him in shiny riot helmets and uniforms that look disconcertingly like business suits with condoms stretched over them. Some are jogging impatiently in place; others punch the snowy air with zoetropic repetition; the rest practice their karate kicks, falling down, snarling, and grunting with each kick. Not all of them have their incisors inside their mouths. They are all massively armed.

Behind him, the terrorists have opened up a hole in the wall over the movie house marquee and are using the top of the marquee as a stage for their illicit burlesque street theater, challenging the Patriots with rude gestures and parodying his speech even before he speaks it, using each other's behinds as percussion instruments to accompany their mocking singsong ditties:

Badboy, Badboy, who are you?
With prat so red and prick so blue?

Come up here, Badboy! Join us, do!
We'd love to smack your booboo too!

They have already tossed the projectors and amplifiers into the street and ripped up the screen and hung the shreds like bunting. Now an actress in an executioner's mask and a leather thong festooned with streamers of twisted film is striding about the marquee stage cracking a long black whip, her hand between her legs, the others bowing down and chanting:

Cora, whore o' Cinecity
Gets down to the nitty gritty!
Drubs her Badboy without pity
While she rubs her little clittie!

Some of the Patriots fire off their weapons randomly in confusion; others drop their pants, fall to their knees in the snow, and lift their rears, groaning with every crack of the whip. The theater has been showing a feature called *Crazy Leg Breaks Out,* the guerrillas having changed the *B* on the marquee to an *F.* The poster below shows a demented monster striding wantonly through the city, wielding his phallus like a club, and an announcement pasted across it declares the film to be sold out for two years. This surprises him. Cora, while beating him, has derided the Extars' underground films as disastrous failures, not only the low point of his career but in effect the end of it, something she's used to make him feel isolated and break his spirit.

Hard Cora, worst of all the sisters,
Is hot for bottoms full of blisters!
First she flogs and whips and spanks you!
Then you kiss her ass and tell her thank you!

This doggerel, acted out on the marquee stage with someone dressed like him in suit, hat, and tie, a huge plasticky bare butt ballooning out at the rear, might have thrown his suggestible assault team into total self-destruct mode, had not the guerrillas hung out a banner, made from a torn scrap of the velvet theater curtain, that reads WELCOME TO THE PIGFUCKING RATPACK OF IMPOTENT CULO-KISSING SYCOPHANTS! COME AND GET US IF YOU DARE! THE EXTARS! This sets off a lot of frenzied shrieking and howling and jumping up and down, at least among those PRICKS who can read, and they start blasting away in earnest at the marquee, or at least in that general direction, the guerrillas vanishing with the first shot. The Patriots stare at each other in hangjaw perplexity, then storm pellmell into the theater, bellowing like bears, weapons blazing. *Stop!* he commands, throwing his arms up (*discipline! discipline!* he seems to hear his mentor cry), but even as he launches the word, it is frozen in his throat, and for a moment he is unable to breathe, as if the word might have solidified and corked his pipes. His arms too: frozen in the air like light booms. Everything is frozen, except his ass, still on fire, and the love ring on his cock, which has turned hot and feels like it's branding him. His erstwhile troops meanwhile are all piling into the Olde Cock Lane, shoving and pushing as if trying to get the best seats, though it's a multithousand-seater, room for everyone. As they enter the theater, the Extars reappear on top of the marquee, streaming out through the hole they've made. He keeps trying to get the word out, but it won't come. The guerrillas leap down to his platform, grab him up, and drag him off, petrified arms still in the air, throwing him and themselves behind the first building they can reach, just as everything blows up behind them. Dirt and mortar and fleshy bits explode past like shrapnel. When it has settled and he's able to look back, there is nothing where the theater was but a smoking hole in the ground. His arms drop.

—Stop! he says, the word coughed up at last.

It falls of course on deaf ears. The Extars are in a celebrative mood, singing and dancing and throwing snowballs and kissing and fucking each other promiscuously. They tease him and make unflattering remarks about his lacerated rear of the burlesque dealt/a belt/pelt/felt/a welt sort, warming their hands over it and spitting on it to hear it pop and sizzle, and some call him Madboy or Toyboy or Lackey P.U., but most are hugging him and squeezing his penis and calling him Crazy again and telling him how much they've missed him.

—So what's the story, Loco? Why'd you leave us? one of them asks now, the one disguised as himself with the ballooning butt. It's Lottie. She strips off the little mustache and dress shirt and tosses the felt hat away, letting her black hair fall loosely about her handsome dark-nippled breasts. His eyes water up, just seeing her again. She's so beautiful. And good and brave, and she never hits him.

—I don't know, Lottie. It's this damned medium. One moment I'm a mile in the air scoring with a skyscraper, the next I'm getting my nethers shredded in the depths of City Hall. I think I fell, he adds, hoping he's not revealing more than he ought, through a back projection. It's like the Mayor had some kind of homing device and I just got reeled in.

—She's got a lotta power.

—You're telling me! Especially in her right arm. But, hey, why did you just do that?

—Waste those sick killers? This is war, man!

—No, I mean, they were showing a Crazy Leg movie in there, weren't they? Why'd you attack your own film?

—It's *not* ours. We got co-opted. You were blowing servers all over the circuit, you were so hot, so the cunt pirated the sequences from our site and montaged them into smash box office hits for her own profit and purposes, turning us all into stars of a sort, the very thing we're fighting against.

—She told me I was an abject failure, rejected and forgotten. A plotless mess of outtakes from the cutting room floor, she liked to say.

—Are you kidding? The city can't get enough of you, Crazy! You've never been bigger! She's hyped you into some kind of romantic larger-than-life antiestablishment hero who finally sees the light and comes home again. The mysterious stranger, the prodigal son, the legendary righter of wrongs, the heart-breaking dude with the big dick who lives hard and loves hard and dies young.

—Dies young?

—Yeah, several times so far. All kinds of weird ways. It seems to give her a buzz. El Loco Perdido, she called you in one of her warped rip-offs. In that one, after falling out of an airplane, getting hit by a bus, hung by your cojones, thrown in a pot of boiling developer, and bit on the ass by a rabid attack dog, who might have been the unscrupulous bitch herself in disguise, you saw the folly of your ways at the end and died embracing the establish-ment in the person of you-know-whom.

—Yeah, I think most of that really happened. Or seemed to. Except the happy ending.

—Well, we have to stop that shit, you understand, so we've been trash-ing the venues. It's not working, though. It's making you hotter than ever. People flock to the theaters, apparently hoping to get blown up. It's a kind of lovers' jerk-and-die suicide thing.

There is the sound of police sirens approaching.

—Time to cut outa here! one of the Extars shouts, pulling her pants up.

—But what happens now, man? You coming with us?

—After what you did to the Mayor's stormtroopers, Lottie, I don't know if I have any choice. He smiles, gazing into her gaze, thinking, even as the love ring seems to tighten its hot grip on the end of his swelling staff: she's where it's at. And he wants to be there. With her. With them. Forget the oath. It was sworn under duress. I've missed you all. A lot. You especially, Lottie. If it's all right . . . ?

—Sure, Loco, she says, flashing her seductive grin. We need that salty weapon of yours in our arsenal. Let's take it back to the barracks and clean and inspect it, oil it up, get in a little bush training with it, what do you say? She gives him a big hug, clasping his butt. Hoo! she laughs. That sucker's *on fire!*

—I know. You should feel it from the inside . . .

At the same time all this is happening, Lottie is asking, not so much again as alongside her other asking: But what happens now, man? You coming with us?

He gazes into her gaze. He can hear sirens approaching and the Extars are getting restless, pulling their pants up. It's time to cut outa here! After what you guys did to the Mayor's elite troops, he says, Cora's love ring seeming to tighten its grip as if to remind him of his sworn oath, I don't know if I have any choice. She flashes her dazzling grin, misreading him, remarking on his salty weapon (that sucker's *on fire!*), and his eyes water up. She's so goddamned beautiful! he thinks. How I'd love to fuck her again! But she's *not* where it's at. Cora's right. There are these inevitable cycles of repression and resistance, of corruption and cleansing, but those who resist are always—*always*—and by definition on the outside. Even if they're right. It's a law of physics, like the movement of the spheres or persistence of vision. I've missed you a lot, and if it's okay, maybe I'll join you later, Lottie. But first I have to go back and explain it to her. I promised.

—I wonder why she's letting you get away, Lottie is saying in one part of his life, as, her arm around him, she leads him down the blizzardy street toward the underground entrance (how happy he is!). And in another, her face darkening with disappointment and maybe just a hint of jealous rage: She's not letting you get away. Well, maybe she's being fair, he's replying on the one hand, maybe she's better than you think, and on the other (how unhappy he is!): It's my decision, not hers. She's not as bad as you think. Don't kid yourself, Lottie says in chorus with herself. She's worse.

—But what happens now, man? she asks, or has asked, and is again or also asking. There's a lot going on. Her hand on his butt. That sucker's *smoking!* Sirens, you should feel it from the inside, pants up, and so on. You coming back with us? He gazes into her gaze, while at the same time gazing into her gaze. He's now doing this several times at once. After what you guys did to the Mayor's elite troops, he says, how can I? She flashes her grin. It's dazzling, but Cora's right, these street theater people are not where it's at. It's a law of physics. The love ring seems to tighten its grip as if to agree with him about this. I've got to report back to her. She's not letting you go. I'm not letting myself go. I've sworn an oath. He remembers swearing this oath, his fingers knocking on a mystery, then her sweet misty-eyed look after, how soft she was. She's better than you think, Lottie. No, she's worse.

Sirens, Extars on the move, hoo, laughing, salty, your butt's on fire, one thing—feel it from the inside—splitting off from another. But what happens now, man? You coming back with us? It's like a challenge, and he resents it: he gazes, gazing into her gaze, into her gaze, meeting it. It's seductive. She's beautiful. But. His eyes water up. Not after what you did to the Patriots, he says, the love ring tightening. She's not letting you go, she's got you collared. It's not that. You're just not where it's at, Lottie. Even if you're right. And brave, et cetera. Her face darkens, her eyes flash. Sirens. Hoo! Laughing. Salty. Let's cut outa here! But what happens now, man? His fingers knocking. Pants up. You coming back with us? No. . . .

And so he is hurrying joyfully down the street toward the subway entrance in the loving arms of his old friends the Extars (she's wonderful! they're wonderful! he's having fun again!) and they are hurrying down the street without him, there they go, Lottie looking seductively back through the blowing snow, or wistfully, or disappointedly, or furiously, his eyes watering up and watering up, and then, one by one, in order, the waves of multiple overlapping experiences fade away, leaving only the faintest of echoes behind, and he is left in the last of them, the worst of them (he's told them they're criminals, he's turning them all in, they've given him the finger, Lottie has stuck her tongue out and held her nose), there in the bitter weather on that devastated street corner, utterly alone, heartsick, bone cold, and, like a field apart, his ass on fire.

He's not quite sure exactly what has happened, but he's feels like he's just had something taken away from him. Something he wanted. Something beautiful. And he knows who's responsible. He's not going back, oath or no oath. He's tired of her cruel games. Lottie has left the fake plastic ass behind. He straps it on as an act of defiance, covering his real one, the sign of his authority, so-called. No more of that. The wailing police sirens are drawing near. Fuck them. He hurries on down the street, plastic rear bouncing loosely, in the direction he last saw the Extars fleeing. And fleeing and fleeing, et cetera. He's breaking out. As someone's said.

He doesn't get very far, not even to the stairs down to the Underground. The whole street seems to tip, and suddenly he's climbing a very steep hill. His feet slip in the snow. He grabs a fire hydrant to keep from sliding backwards down the street. The fake bottom falls off as though stripped from him and clatters down the street behind him. Below him. He believes that if he can reach the Underground stairs he'll be safe and he lunges upward, feet spinning in the snow. But then the street tips the other way and he—*whoosh!*—slides right past it, arms windmilling for balance, gold-ringed erection wagging in the wind. His hat flies off. At the corner below him, there's a little old lady, leaning on a cane, peering up at the light, now changing from green to red. Oh no. He's been this way before. He's yelling. *Look out!* But what must happen happens, the street tipping back to its familiar flat ways even as he crashes into her. It hurts. There's a refuse truck, a brief plaint afterward like the squawk of a turkey. A pity, someone says. Life's tough. A blur of hurrying feet, *whush, crump, crump,* trampling the intersection. And then the street tips again and—*wait a minute!*—he's sliding—*whoosh!*—past the Underground entrance once more, arms whirling, erection wagging, hat flying, those around him seemingly unaffected by these gyrations. And down below? Oh no. He's yelling but he can hear nothing. He crashes into her as the street rights itself. It hurts. The brief plaint from under the refuse truck. A pity. Hurrying feet. And then again he's sliding past the Underground entrance. It's like some kind of action replay, slowed down now. His mouth is agape but nothing comes out. His hat floats away. There's the old lady's humped-over backside as she peers up at the light through frosted spectacles below him. She's bent with age, leaning without consequence into the street's tip. Icicles hang from her nose. There's his love-ringed boner driving into her backside. It doubles up—feels like it's breaking—then straightens out again as the backside is propelled forward, the world righting itself. A refuse truck passes. Slowly, ceremonially. The plaint. The mess in the street. The melancholic response: life's tough, *whush-sh, crum-m-mp,* et cetera. He's—*whoo-*

oo-oo-oosh!—sliding slowly past the Underground entrance. His penis rises and falls gracefully like a conductor's baton during an adagio movement; his arms make languorous circles in the air. The hat. The humped-over backside. The balletic collision. The bending, the straightening. Which hurts. For a longer time, it's very slow. The plaint, more like a low hum, the melancholic chorale, a pity, the feet moving ponderously, *whush-sh-sh,* the slide past the Underground entrance, mouth agape, ever slower, the sequence shortening to the essentials, the looming backside, *look out!* (unheard), the prolonged collision, the pain, the plaint, the slide, the impact, the pain, the slide, slower and slower, until finally, with one last collision, one last bending and straightening, he comes to a complete stop. Though nothing else does. There's a refuse truck, what must happen happens, the world rights itself, and so forth. A pity, someone says. They move on, but he is frozen in place, at something of an angle, still leaning back in his downhill slide, arms high in midwhirl, mouth agape. Even his eyeballs are locked up. He can only stare straight ahead into the intersection, where there's a melancholic blur of hurrying feet, kicking, pounding, slogging through the blood, slush, and snow, trampling away the remains and all else besides. Life's tough. *Whush, crump.*

He can't twitch an eyelid. This is frightening. Everything seems turned off. Except the subsiding pain in his rigid cock, the returning heat to the rear of it, and a peculiar inner restlessness, a kind of filling up and emptying out, not unlike waves of indigestion, his frozen brain somehow registering all this. Which is dimly reassuring. He's alive still. In a manner of speaking. But no one seems to see him. Cora's right. He's utterly forgotten, a has-been. Invisible. A pedestrian crossing the street, hurrying to beat the changing light, comes straight at him. He braces (his head does, his body's immobile) for the blow. Almost hoping to get knocked over and be seen at last. But instead there's that feeling again of filling and emptying, and he realizes people are walking right through him. This is even more terrifying than the paralysis. He wishes he could either scream or close his mouth. Someone comes up behind him to the curb and stops for the light, standing right where he's standing. Peering out through his eyes. Occupying him. He can't tell if it's a man or a woman. The person looks up at the light. He cannot follow this looking but feels it somehow like a crick in his neck. The person edges forward, anticipating the light's change. All bundled up, but he can see now it's that old lady. Or some old lady. Icicles hang from her nose. She's standing half in him, half out, then more out than in, until finally only in that part of him sticking out in front. For the first time in his life, he has a woman in his cock. He doesn't like it and is relieved when she moves on. There's a brief jerk on his penis as if something might have snagged: she scowls back over her shoulder, not at him but through him at others piling through. She shouldn't have paused. They bowl her over, trample her underfoot. Pity. Life's tough. As they rush past, or through, there are other little tugs, same tender place, jerk, jerk, jerk, a passing flutter of them. They are woefully stimulating, making each successive one more so. If he could cry he would be crying.

Then someone approaches whom he does recognize, bobbing along in her odd crippled way. She stops short, squints her one eye, peers closely.

—Pete? Is that you? She passes her hand back and forth through him as though brushing away cobwebs; it's like a kind of slap but feels more like the soft thumping of a troubled heart. That witchy ogress up to her parlous tricks, eh? Well, have a heart, son, Ol' Kate'll see what she can fester up.

She fumbles around, trying to locate his boundaries. The crowds going by must think she's a madwoman, yattering to herself and making inscrutable gestures, for they shy away, sparing him at least their windy migrations through his bodily parts, or what once were such.

—Odds is, that hardshell hoodoo's planted a tracking device, Kate mutters, like a— you know—hologram transmitter a some kind. Usually she hides the nasty buggers deep up your heinie where you can't find them and dig them out later. Kate reaches in and swipes her hand back and forth in that general area, stirring things up.

—They ain't nothing of you back here, Pete, more than a kinda pink shadow, yet it's warm like you got a stove on. Feels good. Hot air balloon without the balloon. She grunts, takes her hand out; it feels vaguely like farting. But no meddlesome gidget, Kate says, sniffing her fingers, then scratching the sparse tufts of matted straw hair on her balding head. Hmm. Maybe if I just squeezed inside you sorta like, and wiggled about? Might work. I ain't nothing if not a animator.

She dumps her shoulder bag onto the pavement and limps around to enter him from behind, explaining that he's more lit up back there where things are cut away, so she can see what she's doing. He can feel her misshapen limbs searching out his own.

—Hey, we ain't a bad fit, Pete! 'Course I knowed that all along. But, whoo, you're leaning back at such a rake, it's a chore just to keep from tipping over!

When she talks, which is most of the time, he feels it more than hears it, like a tremor in his chest or a tickle in the throat. Her presence in him is disturbing, but he still can't move.

—Weird, Pete! You're some set a bags! Never felt so dressed up in all my days! Makes me feel tiddly and all-overish, though, like I gotta pee or sneeze and can't, and it's desperate itchy on my tits! Gives me the twitters! My nips feel like they wanta bite something! *That's the hair shirt,* he says, but actually he says nothing; he can't even close his mouth. Don't know if I can muster up that gaping-pig imitation a yours, but I can give it a lick! When I set to shaking in here, tell me if you notice nothing!

He can feel her mouth opening in his, the suggestion of her three molars hanging loosely from his gums, and there's suddenly a distressing turmoil throughout his being, but he's still locked up.

—Nope. I think we come a buster, Pete, this don't work neither. Trouble is, I can't fill alla you up, lacking the equipment as you might say, that old yawp of the sisterhood. I suppose I could grow a parcel for the occasion, but what would I do if I got stuck with the fool contrivance after? Got no idea how you stand up them hogs. Or unstand them.

By this time she has crawled out and found her way to the front of him, where she is passing her hand back and forth through his erection. Whoa, she says, what's this? *Ow! the love ring!* he cries as she tugs on it, or would cry if he could speak at all. Ho ho! I think we lit upon it, Pete! Bear up! It's the one thing I can grab onto! We'll have the little sucker off in a pig's whisper!

She wriggles it back and forth, jerks on it, twists it round and round in different directions as if trying to work a combination lock, spits on it and pulls with both hands, but the more she tries, the more engorged becomes his cock, the tighter the ring. He can feel it heating up like an electric coil and beginning to vibrate.

—Trouble is, I can't get a purchase; they ain't enough a you to brace against! And—*yowch!*—the devilish thing's commencing to buzz 'n' burn! No time to lose!

She pokes about in her shoulder bag, comes out with an oversized pair of steel scissors.

—I know how you adore that chunka sausage, Pete, but we're gonna hafta lop it off afore it's too late! She makes warm-up slashing noises with the scissors and reaches for his penis at the root. It shrivels up in alarm, and the love ring drops off into the gutter.

He collapses into the snow, exhausted by his ordeal, his butt sizzling there. He touches his face, his mustache, his suited chest and belly, his withered cock, the pouch below: all there. In the round. He is, once more, who he is. Though doubts have been raised. Kate, standing over him, grins her lopsided grin and winks her one eye, snaps at the air once more with the scissors, then drops them back in her shoulder bag. Reckoned that should oughta maybe do it. She reaches down for the ring, which has melted a hole in the snow, but before she can get to it, a dog comes nosing by and laps it up, then staggers down the street, yipping, howling, dragging his rump through the snow, rolling over and over, leaping up again, turning in circles, trying to bite his red erection, whimpering and jerking as though fighting a choking leash.

—C'mon, love, Kate grunts, trying to pull him to his feet, we better lose ourselves before Herroner discovers she's snagged a mutt. Could get downright scary.

But the blizzard has let up for the moment and overhead, between the tops of the leaning buildings, he seems to see the creased shape of the Mayor's sleek white mound billowing forth among the roiling stormclouds.

—It's no use, he says gloomily. The shadowy lips appear to be opening and closing with little popping movements as if blowing kisses or calling *Badboy! Badboy!* She'll find me wherever I go.

—Well, that may be so, Pete. They ain't much the ol' Mare misses. But meanwhiles we can at least get our poor bones in outa the weather. I'll set my conk to working on it, maybe I'll conjure up something. She succeeds finally in hauling him stiffly upright and, while warding off the jostling passersby, props him up from behind with a shoulder, if it is a shoulder. Now you got your pins back, son, think you can work them?

No. He is as immobile as if he were still a frozen hologram. Missing from the restored badboy: his will. If he ever truly had such. Maybe it was only scripted in. But even if so, at least it *was* scripted. Not now. All gone. Fate's got him. Kate braces him at arm's length and bends down to squint at his backside.

—Looks mighty gruesome, Pete, she reports from down there. It's oozing slimy bubbles in living color of a decidedly greenish tint and in general appears to be going off. I misdoubt I never seen nothing uglier. Probably oughta get you direct to a horse pistol. Trouble is, that hardass boss lady owns them all. It'd be like throwing you back in her lap. Or over it.

Even as he's shuddering at the thought, an ambulance comes whooping up, pedestrians bouncing off in all directions, old Kate is pushed aside (Whoa, sis! she wheezes, landing in the gutter), and he is tossed onto a gurney by a team of nurses and loaded in.

—Hang on, baby! laughs the redheaded driver, and they're off, wheeling madly through the city, taking corners on two wheels, caroming off objects and creatures only fleetingly glimpsed, the siren wailing its demented wail of terror and lament. He is pitched off the gurney at the first squealing turn, the nurses trying to strap him down sent crashing with him, and for the rest of the journey they bounce around back there amid bandages, heart and kidney machines, hypodermic needles, and bursting blood bags, slapping body parts and knocking heads on knees, limbs entangled, the nurses yipping and giggling, their hands tearing at his clothing and their own while they tumble about, reminding him of a wild fairground movie he made once upon a time back in the early days, a goatish knockabout comedy called *Lust in the Fun House*, though he was younger then (probably), and bruised less easily, or at least minded the bruising less and even (he was crazier then, too) found it fun.

There is an abrupt screeching halt, he is disengaged from the giddy nurses (somehow his burgundy silk tie has found its way deep into one of them, and she now gasps and cries out with pleasure as it's drawn slowly out), and, ankles bound by his seatless chalk-striped trousers, is returned, face down, to the gurney and wheeled urgently through the gathered sidewalk crowds, who seem greatly amused by his pitiable wounds, into the city hospital's emergency ward.

Though the waiting room is full of the world's suffering, they jump him to the head of the queue and, on orders from the doctor, roll him down a busy hallway (among the lame and wounded and perilously ill, he catches a glimpse of nurse-capped Cissy with a clipboard and cellphone, which is not a good sign) and into a private room with, disconcertingly, a star on the door. There, his official apparel, sign of his authority, is stripped from him, the hair shirt as well. He's feeling better already. He is bathed, and fragrant oils into which various powders have been sifted are warmed over candle flames and applied as ointment by three or four pairs of hands to the scene of the worst of his punishments and to great effect, the nurses reaching between their legs from time to time to add their own secretions to the balm. Their warm fingers knead and stroke and dip in and out of his rectum and between his thighs as though to try to reach a deeper pain beneath the pain, and they are right to do so, for he has been sorely abused, both in and out. His entire backside from nape to soles is attended to before they roll him over to soothe the rest of him, and by that time he is feeling quite numb and blissful, and grateful for the medicinal arts.

He is also, as usual, madly in love with all the nurses who have so tenderly softened up his rear and are now applying their warm oils to his forward portion, from his nipples to his toes, with special attention to that part of him that most defines him, he being who he is, or at least was, and which has recovered some of its customary pride, but though they do so with the most affectionate and expert care, they yatter gossipily among themselves over his head as if he weren't there.

—I couldn't believe my eyes. She's completely changed! Have you seen her?

—Yes! She's gone all soft and pink and sweet. It's a miracle!

—She wants to *kiss* everybody! Can you *imagine*?

One of the nurses is now thumbing the underside of his corona with her oily finger, while others are working on his abdomen and balls. Though he is not drifting into sleep, a certain kind of awareness is slipping away, as what there is left of his consciousness snuggles up inside their warm busy fingers.

—Well, she's in love! Mention his name and her eyes fog up, her body goes floppy and flushes all over, and her hand falls between her legs!

—I heard her say she's so wet all the time now, she's leaving a snail trail wherever she goes. She can hardly bear it.

—It's why we've been asked to step up the production schedule. The poor dear can't wait!

Nor can he. He can feel an orgasm coming on and it is like a reassuring confirmation that he lives still. Oh yes . . . ! And that his life has a purpose, if only a fleeting one.

—Be careful not to bring him off, my dears, cautions the doctor arriving at his bedside. She pulls on some transparent rubber gloves. We have some tests to run to establish his current index of induration before prepping him. If he starts to pop, pinch it off.

Which—he can't hold back the little telltale snorts and gasps—they do. *No! Aarrgh!*

—I think he's ready, doctor.

He opens his eyes dreamily to see what it is he is ready for. He feels tight as a drum but only half in this world. That balm, he thinks. Who knows what got pushed up his rectum? Who cares? If he understands the doctor's instructions, he is to test out a series of gradated membranes which the nurses, having removed their white skirts, are inserting into their vaginas like diaphragms. Okay. No problem. They mount him one at a time, sometimes facing him, sometimes showing him their rears, sometimes straddling him with one of his legs between theirs, the position which seems to be their favorite. They like to have his thigh to rub against, since he is otherwise so passive. Lifting a finger is more than he can do. The membranes are tough and get tougher, but he breaks through. When he does, they are obliged to slide off him before he can deliver the goods and to fit themselves anew. It is a pleasant exercise but not wholly satisfying. The nurses on him also seem frustrated and sometimes linger past the breaking of the membrane, pretending that it's still intact, but, under the skeptical eye of the doctor, recording the results on a handheld computer notebook, they never linger long enough. Finally they reach a thickness he cannot crack, hard as the nurse tries. There's a dull ache somewhere like the stubbing of a toe, but as though not of his body. Someplace else. The doctor is not convinced. She fits the disk in her own vagina and mounts him in the classical manner, her knees on each side of his hips. The abbess position, as it is sometimes called. He wants to tell her he loves her but she is not looking at him, only down at the point of contact, and he is not sure his voice will carry as far as her face unless she watches it. She spends more time inserting him than the nurses did, letting her vaginal lips play with his glans first, moistening it, nibbling on it as if grazing there, palpating it, pulling away from it to make it stretch toward her, kissing the tip of it—then suddenly she plunges down. There's a sharper pain this time, but a popping noise and he's broken through again, deep inside her. The nurses cheer. His hips are bucking, but she's off him, recording the data in her computer.

—Not bad, she says, but he's got a ways to go yet, and we don't have much time, if the current convulsions at City Hall are any indication. It's a bit painful and dangerous, but we'd better start the steel injections.

The what?

—Should we allow him to ejaculate to make it softer for the needle to go in?

—No, it's better when the veins are engorged with blood. Hurts more but works faster.

—Wait a minute!

Suddenly there are straps around his wrists and ankles, soft hands on his shoulders pinning him down. His body's back, things are no longer happening elsewhere. The doctor approaches with a hypodermic needle filled with something silvery. When she squirts a little to test the needle, there's a pinging sound on the tiled floor like the landing of a dropped coin.

—Be brave, she says, manipulating him to keep him hard and applying a wad moistened with alcohol to the site. And be considerate of the other patients in the hospital who need their rest.

But he is already screaming. Oh my god, this is the worst thing that's ever happened to him! *Take it out!*

—Stop it, she says. I haven't even started.

—I hope you-know-who is watching this on the monitors. She'll love it!

—I'm sure she is. She never lets him out of her sight.

But then she does start. The needle. It's worse even than he'd anticipated. He's probably still screaming, but no way to know. He can't hear anything other than the pain, which has overtaken all his senses so as to fully express itself. This is not his life as he had imagined it. His head wants no part of it. It pulls away. . . .

He is in the operating room. The operating theater, as the doctor calls it, for she is giving a lecture there to a large audience on the disease of romanticism, using his body for her demonstration. She has disassembled it, the better to display the deep structure of the malady, and the parts lie scattered about on the operating table, which is more like a large butcher's block. He has lost the sensation in all these parts except for the penis, which, standing on the table all alone, is so hard it hurts. The doctor has described its condition as suffering terminally from rigor motif. Insofar as the larger disease is, in her opinion, associated with the inability to let go of the past, she is at present giving a short sharp lesson on history by way of his scrotum. History's seedbags. That

Clara. She's a smart lady, but she's obsessed by the gonads. She thinks everything happens there. In him, true, it does, but she shouldn't take it as a general principle. He picks up one of his legs to use as a crutch and hops out. At the door he's met by Cissy, who asks him where he's going; he's needed for this scene. Nah, he says. Hurts too much. Use what you want but leave me out of it. Outside in the corridor he runs into Cally, who is getting made up for their next movie together. It's a romantic hothouse travesty called *The Passion Flower* in which she plays a voluptuous man-eating blossom, and she's putting her petals on. Don't leave, Willie, she says. I need your pistil! Help yourself, he says, hobbling past. It's in there on the table. He glances back past Cally (her petals are drooping) and sees that, instead of an operating table, it looks more like a dinner table with candles and flowers, and they're all sitting down to help themselves to his remains. Music is playing. He realizes that Clara, rather than critiquing the pathology of romanticism, is celebrating it. . . .

When he fades back in, he is being wheeled out of his room and down the hospital corridor by the nurses. He knows where they're going. It wasn't a dream. Or not just a dream. He recalls now they were talking about prepping him. Please! I'm okay! Don't take me there!

Clara's at the foot in crimson academic robes, guiding the rolling cot, stethoscope around her neck like a grand cordon.

—I'm afraid you have no choice, she says. You have to follow the script.

The corridors are lined with staff and patients, gazing upon him with pity and awe. And he's not okay. There is something huge and heavy under the sheet between his legs. Two of the nurses, one on each side of him, have their hands under there, holding it up. The people they pass seem to want to touch it, but Clara fends them off with blows from her winged caduceus. He feels a terrible prurience, aimless and powerful. Something has gone catastrophically wrong. His worst fears are about to be realized. The battered double doors of the operating room loom. He starts to cry. But they take an abrupt turn to the right. They're headed for the street exit! As they make the turn, there is the sound under the sheet as of bocce balls striking one another, and the towering mass there leans perilously to the left. A second nurse has to help the one on that side keep it from toppling over. Her hand on it, just under the flange at the top, is alarmingly inciting. It is so sensitive, he can feel imprinted there every whorl of her fingertips. He is cranked up into a semi-reclining position and, as they pass through the front doors of the hospital, the sheet is drawn away. There are gasps of amazement from the huge crowds gathered in the street outside.

—Here he comes! We can see him down there now! Emerging from his preparation chambers, in full battle regalia, propelled by destiny and radiant with purpose! What a sight! The chosen one! Badboy the All-Conquering! The Virgin's Beloved!

As far as one can see under a wintry sky as thick and lumpy as featherbedding: a vast urban congestion, dour and stony but teeming with life. There has been a break in the weather, which allows for the long view and which most attribute to the influence of City Hall; it is still cold and overcast, but the snow has stopped falling and the bitter wind has died somewhat, now curling around one instead of whistling straight through. The streets immediately below, into which the Beloved and his entourage have launched themselves, are cordoned off and free of motorized traffic, but filling up with the masses pressing, shoulder to shoulder, into the center, hoping to catch a glimpse of the unfolding drama. For today is a day in Cinecity unlike any other. Something is happening, not just another rerun but something grand, something of historical significance. A turning point.

Such anyway is the mood in the streets, heaving with excitement and anticipation, as Badboy the All-Conquering and company enter into their midst. Though from the waist down to his greaves and boots he is exposed to the elements, from his waist up he is attired in the full panoply of a princely warrior with leather cuirass and silver-plated gorget and beribboned shoulder plates over blue sleeves, his armlets bearing the mayoral seal superimposed by a pair of hearts impaled by a single arrow. Blood drips from the wounded hearts. Beside him, his pagegirls, all in white, transport his secondary weapons, a variety of whips and scourges, but his primary provision of power rises between his legs above a pair of steel-gray cannonballs like a towering monolith, a colossal piece of ordnance of such mass it requires several hands to sustain it upright; both weapon and monument, it is veined in metallic silver and crowned by a domed capstone of royal hue, pierced by its famous ballistic aperture. The crowds lining the streets down which he is being ported strain forward, trying to touch the great rocking pillar, and must be beaten back. No risks can be taken. It must remain fully loaded and unimpaired, for upon its success today rests the fate of the city.

—The Virgin's Beloved, confronting with resolve and dignity the supreme ordeal that awaits him, is in a state, as can be seen, of perfect arousal. His lonely journey has been arduous and fraught with pain and peril, but he has fulfilled all tasks, overcome all obstacles, resisted all temptation, to make himself worthy of this decisive trial, and he is now on the final leg of that heroic journey, one that will take him to the very center of the known world, its hot core, its sanctum sanctorum . . .

. . .Where several buildings have been cleared to create an enormous arena in front of City Hall, cushioned with sawdust, in the center of which stands a great cottage-sized contraption made of steel and leather, mirrors, wood, and soft rubber, vaguely reminiscent of a giant gymnast's rig or a surreal guillotine. Red-carpeted processional ramps, speaker systems, and temporary viewing stands for dignitaries have been erected, as well as a giant ten-story video wall multiprojection system as wide as the arena, on which are currently running collaged images of conjoined body parts from the classics of the silent black-and-white era, so grainy and thickly impasto'd as to blend in with the rolling gray clouds above. The melancholic track of a *Stabat Mater* plays behind them, commingling with the whiffling wind. The streets, windows, and rooftops are filling up, and the dignitaries are already in their places or fighting for them. But there is still no sign of the powerful woman who has set this epic event into motion. Her aides are popping in and out of City Hall, dashing back and forth as if on errands of the utmost urgency, ignoring the anxious questions shouted at them by spectators and reporters.

—We have been told by reliable inside sources that the Virgin, heretofore known as the Impregnable One, will appear in the arena shortly before the arrival of her Beloved, there to receive him—her costar, one could say, if this were a film and not really happening out here on these cold gritty streets of Cinecity, all too familiar to us all. What sort of reception this grande dame of perversity has planned for him, of course, we cannot yet say. We only know it will not be modest. And it will not be painless. We spoke with him briefly a short while ago during his final preparations, and we asked him why he was undertaking so hazardous a challenge. . . .

We see him in extreme close-up in a blue hospital gown tied at the neck, an expression of placid determination on his face, as he gazes unblinkingly into the camera lens. There is a popping sound as of the breaking of thin china, and he smiles faintly.

—Why? Because she is there, he says.

—But so many have tried and failed! So many have been broken!

—All the more reason. Her hauteur, her unassailability, her cruelty: these things incite me. There is a splendor about her beyond mere beauty. She is the ultimate adventure.

Off-camera we can hear someone saying: Not bad, but he's got a ways to go yet, and we don't have much time. We'd better start the steel injections.

He looks concerned, glancing in the direction of the voice—or voices, for others are asking for more precise instructions—but adds:

—I feel she lies trapped, as it were, inside an impenetrable fortification, and it is my duty to free her. I do this—he winces, bites his lip, continues through clenched teeth—I do this for her, for me, and for—*whuff!*—the world!

—Whew, that must hurt!

—Yes, he gasps, glancing down past his screwed-up nose, but it's necessary. I think. What—*wah!*—what one must do one does.

—You're very brave!

He smiles wryly, his lip trembling, as though to acknowledge the irony of her remark, and his eyes register a certain anguished confusion. Didn't we—*ay! yow!*—didn't we just do—?

Cut to overview.

—The route that the All-Conquering and his arms bearers are taking is not the most direct one to the center of the city. We see them now circling that center or, rather, spiraling around it, touching upon all the adjacent precincts as they go, perhaps to grant as many citizens as possible vicarious participation in the drama, as they teasingly approach the arena in an oblique stroking movement not unlike a kind of foreplay. But though there is increasing agitation in the immediate vicinity of City Hall, there is still no sign of—no! wait! Here she comes now!

The fading *Stabat Mater,* slipping into the distance as if brushed away by the wind, is abruptly overtaken by a blaring fanfare from the Cinecity trumpeters, and she whom all have been awaiting appears at the top of the broad marble stairway of City Hall, robed in her official ermine and gold and symbolically crowned with a ruby-studded black headband, her huge black whip planted beside her like a staff of office. Simultaneously, the toiling bodies on the giant video wall give way to a live full-screen telecast of the Virgin herself, standing between her trumpeters at the threshold of her domain, the skyline of Cinecity rising behind her—or *a* skyline of Cinecity; it varies. She lifts the whip and cracks it (the crack is amplified, commensurate with the amplified image—no doubt Badboy himself, wherever he is, can hear it), and her aides appear, dressed as slaves in wispy tunics and loincloths, bearing various implements. Those with musical instruments then precede her, blowing shell trumpets and reed flutes and playing tambourines and kettledrums, as she steps majestically down the long flight of steps, casting off, one by one, stair by stair, her many official ornaments. *Clink! clink!* Off they go to the pulsing rhythm of the hymeneal galliards of her slave musicians. On the big screen, the stripping away of each bracelet, badge, medal, ring, earring, nose ring, bangle, pin, locket, stud, and necklace is caressingly observed in extreme close-up as it drops through the bank of monitors, the fall and bounce of each watched in slow motion. By the time she has reached the red carpet at the foot of the stairs, dressed only in her headband and robes, she has divested herself of virtually all outward signs of her authority, but for her whip and, of course, her own formidable and commanding presence.

—*She stands before us, a living manifestation of unadorned power in its serene and unassailable purity, as mysterious and immutable as the unconscious. It is this toward which her Beloved, Badboy the All-Conquering, is now being drawn. We spoke with her about this power earlier in the day . . .*

She who is now known as the Virgin is seen reposing upon a cushioned couch, where she is playing with unexpected delicacy an amplified golden lyre, its frame in the shape of a stylized bifurcated whip, her symbolic instrument of power by which she makes men dance. She is dressed in a silken white tunic, one magnificent breast exposed, and wears on her head an imitation wreath of violets made of beaten gold. She is aglow with a sovereign self-contentment, her throat faintly flushed in anticipation of the impending engagement. Yes, she is saying, in response to a remark by the interviewer about this *megabucks widescreen pano-rammer* she is producing, we are sparing no expense. It will be grand. It will be beautiful.

—But do you really expect this wild card you are now calling your Beloved to turn up?

—He has no choice.

—No? No, I suppose it's true, he does seem utterly in your power. But is it right for you to take exclusive appropriation of so popular and universal an icon as he? There are others of us, you know, who might like—

—You forget, my dear, who I am. If I want it, I can have it. And if I want it, it is right.

—Well, that may be so, but, if you don't mind my saying so, your wants sometimes seem oppressive to the rest of us. Tell me, though: What is the one thing that you want most of all?

She glares icily in her old puissant manner (I *do* mind, she mutters), then softens, blushes, turns away, and sighs. When she speaks again it is with the shy sweet voice of a young girl.

—What I want most? To be . . . the object of desire. . . .

The Virgin has reached the center of the arena and stands now before the strange apparatus erected there, her vastly enlarged self showing in live action on the giant bank of monitors at her back. There is another fanfare. She unfastens her ermine robes and lets them drop, and all gasp as if in congregational response. Under the robes she is wearing her black boots and garter belt, ruby navel stud, leather collar and wristbands, a white G-string with fringes, and a webwork of leather straps, thin as shoelaces, drawn tight to exaggerate her breasts and buttocks. She stands, on the ground and on the screen, legs apart, like a mighty warrior, defender of the city gates. The arena fills with her rich aroma, the aroma of power. She cracks her whip. Her aides drop to their hands and knees in front of her, lower their loincloths, and raise their tunics. Many of the dignitaries come clambering down from their bleacher seats, eager to take communion with them, throwing off their nether garments as they come, and, irresistibly, most of the others soon follow. It is likely that many of those in the side streets with views of the screen, though denied access to the arena, are also falling about in imitative postures and servicing one another in the liturgical manner. There is a warm bubbly feeling of togetherness, in the arena and beyond, as the whip snaps and cracks and the cries and groans rise like songs of anguished love. Like hymns.

Enlarged live images of these solemnities, using the full width of the big screen, are intercut with glimpses of the Beloved's approach. It seems that he and his entourage are being held up by the surging crowds wherever he goes, and they may in fact have wandered by mistake up a cul de sac in one of the darkened tenement alleyways behind City Hall, to find themselves trapped there by the frenzied hordes. As the communicants return to their places, tenderly holding their redeemed behinds, they glance uneasily back over their shoulders at the screen. And if he doesn't get through? After all this? The thought is as disturbing as film burning in the projector. The Virgin, to fill the delay time and calm the shudders, offers all assembled a special preview showing of *The Punishing of Badboy,* a film called by its producer a *lyrical documentary* and not scheduled for general theater release until after this day's ceremonies, assuming their successful consummation. While it is running, she confers with her aides, and shortly thereafter helicopter gunships pass overhead, momentarily drowning out the movie's screams and howls. Explosions and machinegun fire are heard, and on the video wall, though the scene is not pretty, Badboy the All-Conquering and his troupe, somewhat tattered, are seen emerging from what was once a cul-de-sac but is no longer, led out by the crimson-robed figure wielding the winged club, and they now are proceeding once more toward what might be called the threshold of adventure, accompanied by the citywide cheers of the multitudes and, above all, of those in the arena.

This expedition is taking too long to get where it's going. It's why he doesn't do epics. Whambam, that's his style. All this parading about is killing him. Nearly literally. They got trapped in a dark alley and set upon by hordes of ecstatics who all seemed to want a piece of him. At one bad moment, when his handlers had their hands full fending off rapists and worshipers, the massive cannon between his legs toppled over and dragged him right off the cot with its weight. Fortunately he fell on the fallen, not in the slush of the street, so it's still relatively sound and unsoiled. It took six of them, bullets from the gunships overhead whizzing around their ears, to get him back on the cot and upright once more so they could make their escape, Clara clearing the way through the bombed-out rubble with her medical truncheon.

It's a rough ride, no shock absorbers on these hospital gurneys, and the pedestal on which that monstrous pillar is standing is only his tender pubis, which has felt every bump and rattle as a kind of hammer blow. The thing itself is wildly inflamed and sensitive. The nurses have been obliged to use calipers to hold it for fear of setting off eruptions with their tender little fingers. When people cheer and shout, it can feel the waves of warm air hit it. It likes to rub up against this warmth. When a single rogue snowflake fell on it, he knew, before it vanished with a spark like an electrical short, its exact and peculiar hexagonal pattern. He wished, implausibly, to mate with it. He wishes to mate with anything. He's never been so hard or so desperately in need. Blue balls were nothing compared to this chrome set. They throb as if with a motor inside, or a timer. It's awful. He's got Saint Pruritis' Dance—Clara's joke. Only one cure for it, she said. Which is where she's taking him. Ever the good doctor. If they manage to get there. The congestion gets worse and worse. Cold as it is, he's sweating inside the leather vest they've put on him and freezing below it, and the metal neck brace or whatever it is has scuffed the bottom of his chin raw. He bangs against it every time he tries to complain, which is probably why they put it there. Finally, they're brought again to a complete halt. But they must be getting close. He can smell something familiar.

Reinforcements arrive from City Hall to help clear the way; musicians as well, to accompany them, on their entry. Red carpet is rolled out in front of them, and anyone not part of the procession who steps on it is threatened with instant execution. Warning shots are fired—what he hopes were warning shots. The way gets easier. They make a final turning and he can see the arena ahead, the viewing stands, the giant screen. On it, somebody's hugely magnified buttocks are getting larruped. Ugliest ass he's ever seen. An object of scorn and pity; how can anyone be titillated by it? Then its owner peers around his shoulder at the dominatrix with the whip: It's he himself. Unbelievable. She's ruining his career. He was always so photogenic in that part. Yet another cruelty. As they rattle into the clearing of the arena, the film gives way to live action. His preposterous cock, if it can in any sense still be called his, takes up half the screen, jogging along. Cora is waiting for him there below this prodigious sight. She is standing beside some ominous-looking rig that rises above her at least five times her height but that still, somehow, seems dwarfed by her. The Virgin, as they're calling her, as she's calling herself. Tall and haughty, laced up in leather, her bald cleft concealed in a tight white G-string, bulging like cods in their piece. She looks formidable and she won't make it easy for him, but he knows she wants this. The arena setup alone tells him so. The bridal white of the lacy G-string. Her chest's hot flush, the hearts on his sleeves, the glitter of transport in her eyes.

The gurney comes to a halt in the middle of the arena, where Clara the scientist is met by figures representing art and history. Old flames, doing their flickering dance around him. Completely meaningless: probably Cissy's idea. He is crowned there by a pretty young thing with a laurel wreath. But they have made it too big and it falls down over his eyebrows and ears. The young thing stares agog at his towering dong. Her awe feels like a soft radiant hand on it and his hips start to bounce on the gurney. The young thing is whisked away. Clara delivers the exordium, reporting on the tortuous journey they have just made through the perilous fringes to reach this place, which, though flat as a board, she calls the summit and nadir of the mythological round. She confirms the intactness of the legendary maidenhead in question and reminds all present of the many who have tried to sunder it and catastrophically failed. A camera picks out some of these alleged casualties in the crowd and they are shown on the big multimonitor screen: broken, haggard, aged beyond their years. He believes this legend to be false, the head shots rigged. He, he's certain, is the first. She's been waiting for him (a chilling smile curls one side of her lips, and smoke seems to rise from between her thighs), and here he is.

Clara speaks eloquently of all the searing trials to which he has been subjected and of his gathering hubris, as embodied in the awesome instrument he bears, visible to everyone. But the undercurrent of all that she says is naked fear. The city is in danger and only he can save it. Is this so? He's heard rumors along the route that Cinecity might get shut down if he fails. Razed. Obliterated, and all in it. Is that possible? Could she do it? Probably. All those people out there; they're only extras. But being an extra is better than nothing. So they're frightened. Moreover, they seem to blame their harsh lives on the infamous maidenhead. If he can rid them of it, the oppression will lift. The weather will improve. They call him the liberator. They call for blood to be shed. *Ream her, redeemer!* they chant. He must save the city from self-destruction. So he is truly needed, if only for this moment. One moment out of time. It is a calling of sorts. He doesn't quite believe it, but he can go along with it. Anyway, he desperately needs a fuck.

The Virgin has been getting restless. Her navel stud is glowing like the mouth of hell. She's scrubbing her crotch with the whip handle, undoing her leather laces—all of it watched in exquisite detail on the big screen, while Clara describes the apparatus beside her and what it does. As the laces come undone, Cora's figure loses some of its stature but gains in poignant vulnerability. Enlargements of various portions of her body, especially the place where the whip handle's working, are inciting, as if he needed such, but he's more arrested by the close-ups of her face, what they tell him about what's going on inside. As best he can understand, the strange contraption, which, he realizes now, is never quite still, is a kind of robot, computerized but not itself a computer, for this adventure must be actual, not virtual. A real hymen must be broken in real time. Only happens once. Supposedly. The hymen's keeper is watching him intently. And the face on the video wall is watching him too, when the wall's not focused on other parts. There is still something challenging in her expression, a come-try-me-if-you-dare look (the garter belt is coming off), but there's also excitement and wonder and even a trace of fear. And above all, there's something he's seen there before and has missed since they've been apart: raw wild innocent desire. When it blossoms on her stern face, it blossoms as on no other.

The robotic apparatus, Clara is saying, which, according to the city's official production assistant, who helped to design it, is called a plot bot, has been programmed with all known epic plots, as well as elements from romance and other genres. One moves through this vast database by making choices, the results of which will be visible to everyone up on the video wall. They are not rational choices but purely gestural; one moves or is moved and the story changes. Or, in this case, two move, and multiple simultaneous choices are made, which more often than not conflict with each other. Only an absolute concinnity of desire and motion (this is Clara orating, winding up her prolegomenon) can bring the story to a happy conclusion. He doesn't understand how this happens, but he supposes he soon will. The motion the Virgin has just made has been to bend over to work her boots off. Up on the giant screen: an operatic close-up of her great luminous ass, big as an office block, outlined in bright pink where her tight leather laces have scored her flesh, and trembling now with expectation and exertion (the boots are skintight). If the face is the field in which most of cinema's significant emotional activity takes place—the way, as it were, into the viewed one's head—the ass, at least an ass like that one, is the field upon which significant meditation takes place, the way into one's *own* head. Though all citizens of a certain rank are familiar with it, having often kissed it, its monumental sky-high appearance draws a communal gasp of admiration from all in the arena, and a generous flutter of applause.

This flutter is as a signal. The preliminaries are abruptly concluded. *And now,* declares Clara, *beyond the threshold!* It is time for him to go to meet his fate. Or to create it. But first he must stand. This is not as easy as it used to be.

Whenever his aides let go of his monster penis, he topples face first into the sawdust. Finally two of the strongest have to accompany him, helping him hold it up with calipers, as he approaches the plot bot, his view of what's happening limited by what he can see over the top of the laurel wreath, which is resting now on the bridge of his nose. This probably does not make for a very heroic appearance. His boots are too small and his shin guards are loose and clanking, making his clumsy stagger clumsier. Cora has stripped off her bridal G-string (another citywide gasp and more applause; this is a sight few have been privileged to see) and, helped by her production assistant, is already hooking herself up, attaching the electrodes to all her significant body parts, wiring up her headband, practicing her movements, her chest heaving with ardor and excitement. She wrings out the G-string and tosses it at him playfully. It catches on one of his shoulder plates, hanging there like a scented favor. The contraption is much larger, seen from the inside, than it had seemed from without. And more active in a twitchy sort of way. He sees that every time Cora makes a gesture the entire apparatus goes through a series of subtle readjustments, so she is not attached to the plot bot so much as it is attached to her. He is similarly strapped in and, as a test, hoisted up (I can fly! he thinks), but the enormous weight dangling between his legs causes his back to sag so dangerously there's fear it might snap. The production assistant comes over and with bits and pieces patches together a kind of harness for his midriff, with extra support in the groin area to protect him from a hernia. *Isn't she pretty?* she whispers in his ear. *She's so much in love!* She adjusts his laurel wreath and wires it up, knots the damp G-string more securely in a position below his nose, pats his bum lovingly as she used to do, so long ago. *You're looking beautiful, L.P.*, she adds with a sweet smile. *When this is over, maybe we can have some fun with that thing. Now, let me show you how this gizmo works . . .*

The production assistant has made her final technical adjustments to the plot bot and given an emboldening slap to the battle-scarred bottom of the All-Conquering, and this great epic encounter that all have been waiting for has begun. He in whom the citizens of Cinecity have placed their last best hopes sallies forth, more or less on his knees, toward the waiting Virgin, raking the sawdust with his principal asset, a brave and hardy hero but one attempting to go where no one has ever gone before, to do what's never been done. What many believe can never be done. Her punishments, his subjection, his rebellion, her crushing of that rebellion are well known. That they are madly in love with each other goes without saying. They have been the subject of talk shows, news programs, circuit chat rooms, barroom banter, popular songs. But, love-stricken though she is, no one assumes she will surrender without resistance, and few believe that he, for all his passionate desire and noble reputation, will succeed in overcoming that resistance.

And yet, perhaps he has already succeeded. For contrary to all expectation, she awaits him upon a kind of pallet she has fashioned out of the very rods and wires of the plot bot to which she is connected, eyes rolled up as if having swooned, arms and legs splayed and all her charms on view. This is both greatly encouraging and somewhat disappointing. There is still the challenge of the infamous maidenhead, success is not yet assured, but the larger drama all have been anticipating seems hastily abbreviated, falling somewhat short of its advertisements.

Their doughty liberator waddles forward eagerly, dragging with him that part of the apparatus to which he is attached, and throws himself upon her, but he is met halfway by the empty pallet, which rises and strikes him such a blow as to drive him back to where he started. He stares in puzzlement, lifted to his feet by the bot itself, at the empty pallet, which has become more like a framed mirror, staring perplexedly back at him. Those in the arena know where she is but he does not. *Look up!* they shout, but he doesn't seem to hear them. To get his attention from the top of the structure where she squats, the Virgin releases a light shower, not so much golden as crystalline, in the manner of a fountain nymph.

Now, wiping his eyes and mustache (his gesture sends the robot through a variety of nervous twitches), he does see her, and he is inflamed by what he sees, as are all, a trickle falling still from that precious well. He crawls up toward her in his knightly boots, hauling his harnessed armament and his linked part of the robot with him. The musicians have plugged their ancient instruments into amplifiers and are now producing a sound that is not unlike pounding city traffic, mixed with the howls of cats. As, still attached, he makes his way up through the robot's complicated frame, it's like turning a sock inside out. The reconfiguring of the contraption causes her, also still wired to it, to be pulled back down, ending up where she was before, though face down, the pallet now blanketing her. While she struggles to right herself, he struggles to reach her by clambering back down through the robot, the two of them thereby knotting it up even more. He ends up caged inside a tangle of wood, steel, and wires; she is on the outside, pinned upside down to it, her feet in his face and his in hers.

Though the position is not promising, he makes a valiant effort at entry, squeezing his massive instrument out through the bars of the cage, and he does manage to lay it lengthwise through her frothy fork, though it pokes out behind her like a drunkard's bulbous nose above her pink cheeks, an image captured in sentimental close-up on the giant video wall. This is not where it ought to be if he's to fulfill his historic mission, but, uncontrollably (here we go again, the story of his life; apprehension sweeps the arena—this venture will fail!), his hips begin to buck—which seems to trigger a spring in the apparatus. His cage suddenly separates itself from the rest and flies upward, drawn to the top of a skyscraper, so high overhead it is partly obscured by the thick clouds tumbling by. Though he is almost out of sight, the panic on his blanched face, seen through the drifting mist, is visible to all on the big screen. Not unexpectedly (though it nevertheless provokes a startled communal cry), the cage now comes apart and he plummets earthward, where she awaits him on the bot on her back, knees up and spread and a terrifying rictal grin on her face, not unlike those on the shocked but spellbound faces of all who watch. But of course he can fly, he seems to remember this—and in the nick of time. In the very instant before impact, he breaks his fall and floats bouncingly above her, blue-sleeved arms outspread, greaves and shoulder plates clattering, his dangler dipping and swinging like a hulky pendulum. Even with its steely tones, it is more colorful than the rest of him, which is, as they say, white as a sheet. He wipes his laureled brow with one hand and finds himself doing a midair somersault, so he ceases all other gesture and hovers there, arms out like wings, teeth clenched, eyes agog, adjusting to his new circumstances. The Virgin, still on full display below him, does not seem foremost in his thoughts. Escape does. If he can fly, however, so can she, and—probably she's been able to practice with the machine—much more nimbly than he. Up she comes, doing silky loops around him, her movements light and graceful, so different from her official demeanor, as monumentalized in all the statues of her throughout the city; she's literally dancing on air! It must be love! She touches him teasingly, blows in his ear, tugs on his ribbons, tickles him between his cheeks (oops! another somersault), nips at the tip of his pendulous instrument with the lips of her immaculate orifice, dispatches her aromas, and gives him fleeting glimpses of all her tender parts, until she has his full attention once more. Then she shows him her tail and she's gone.

But where? He sniffs the air, as if sensing her presence still. His nose leads him down to one of the musicians, a willowy young creature in a gauzy tunic, strumming a golden lute, her flesh as pale and smooth as porcelain. He noses her crotch, still fluttering his wings, as they might be called, and she smiles, showing a row of sparkling emerald teeth that match her green eyes. Her lips move (there is a close-up on the big screen), saying something like *Oh yes, please!* And down she goes as if tipped over, he falling upon her with resolute abandon. Even on her back, legs stiffly in the air, she continues to pluck the lute, as though obliged by some inner mechanism. Nothing there between her legs, neither hair nor wrinkle, but the All-Conquering is not dissuaded and drives in anyway, shattering her explosively.

There are screams in the audience and some faint, but he does not seem surprised. He has already risen above the scattered porcelain shards and is scanning the arena, nose twitching, steely penis bobbing like a dropped anchor, its devastating power now apparent to all. The Virgin is nowhere to be seen. He studies the pattern of the shards beneath him, as does the big screen. Aha! It's clear! *An arrow, an arrow!* they shout from the stands. It's pointing toward City Hall! But he is already on his way.

There is a maze of brightly painted rooms and corridors and he is rocketing through them, riding the monstrous beam between his legs, both hands gripping it now as one might a carousel horse, all his senses alert to any suggestion as to her whereabouts. It's tricky. There are traps everywhere. Dead ends. Sudden turnings that catch him by surprise; he caroms off them. He would like to slow down but can't. The surroundings whip past. Windows look out on nothing. Doors must be negotiated or blown away. Everything's hard and edgy. He remembers City Hall as more palatial, more stately. It has been stripped down for the occasion and painted in primary colors, its furnishings reduced to odd blocky objects standing about, which may or may not be clues, though much remains—mostly instruments of punishment—to remind him of his time with her in this place, a time when he experienced an intimacy of a sort unlike any before or since. A time that was timeless. Yes, she is in here somewhere, he is sure of it, his powerful mistress—the porcelain arrow told him so, his nose too. He need only find the magic threshold; but as yet nothing but misleading signs and false avatars: a doorkeeper, a parlor maid, an administrative assistant, a cook, a masseuse—he has had and destroyed them all just as he did the lutist in the arena. They have given him no satisfaction, and he knows none will but she, but from them he has learned a lesson: to wit, that it is not enough to get his rocks off. He must realize his noble destiny. A hero of the people cannot merely fuck, he must represent all fucking or he will fail. And he *is* a hero. It is his vocation. He is he who will fuck, in effect, the city itself and thus the world and, so doing, will save it from itself. Now, when new temptations arise, as with increasing brazenness they do (that exquisite little thing he just flashed past in the bath, for example, her hand between her legs and tongue between her lips), he ignores them.

And then he hears it, his just reward: a whisper, calling him, faint at first but growing stronger whenever he avoids distractions and chooses rightly his next turning: *Badboy! Badboy!* His heart is pounding, his cock too. At last: *I'm coming!*

The corridor he is flying down narrows to a slot. Can he make it through?

He must!

Pow! He does!

And finds himself out on a vast empty plain, barren and windy (it's the wind that's whispering; she is everywhere about), a strange place, gloomy and uninhabitable, unlike any he has ever seen, city boy that he is—except in glass shots and back projections—and yet he feels he has been here before. There are a pair of pale ivory hills in the distance; he glides toward the crest of one of them on his rampant purple-headed mount to look about and get his bearings. From the top, his view is of an endless desolation, drained of color and bathed in a soft crepuscular light, with only the illusion of life and movement, a multitudinous anthology of lifeless shadows passing on the pallid flats below like dreams half dreamt, evoking not a presence but a flickering absence. There is less at the edge of his peripheral vision now, and he has the sensation that if he turned his head fast enough he would glimpse the void.

Across the way, on the other hill, there is also someone standing at the peak: Is it she? Or a mirror image of himself? Perhaps he is seeing only what he wishes to see; perhaps there is nothing over there but a dark heap of stones or a hummock or a dune or the ruins of an ancient outpost. A bump. Vegetation it is not. Nothing grows here. The whisper of the wind seems to rise in pitch as if in doleful lament or diffident desire, and he has the feeling of being observed from behind, though he knows, if he should look, he would no longer see City Hall back there. He also knows that in reality he is still in the arena, attached to the plot bot, has never left it; he is submerged wholly in his antagonist's fantasies. He is not powerless. Motions and emotions, as Clara said. He could change the rules, disrupt the continuity, introduce a few avatars of his own. But he knows his hopes for success are greater if he stays within her dreamworld, riding his dick steadfastly to the end of her story. For it's his story too.

In the middle of the wild barren expanse, far far away, he sees a bright red glow like something burning. At this distance, it could be a city, alone and consuming itself in the terrible emptiness, a vision of his own city perhaps, where, for him, life began, and which he must now save, with an act both simple and profound, from imminent self-destruction. Or it might be an image of his heart or hers, aflame with their unconsummated passion. Or else merely a beacon to guide him. Yes, more likely, for beyond it he sees now, nestled in a cleft on a distant chalky rise, dark and foreboding, a great rugged castle. He knows what that is and what he must do. He has been well prepared for it and properly fitted out. He gives his faithful steed a loving slap and sets off into the whining wind.

Across the vast pale desert, haunted by dim shadows of conquests past, rides the lonely hero. From the perspective of the majestic castle ramparts, he seems at first no more than an inconsequential speck on the far horizon, a fly on a film screen. But as his features begin to take shape, illumined by the rubescent marker he is passing, one can make out the unwavering focus of his gaze, the determined set of his noble jaw, and, yes, the all-consuming intensity of his amorous desire. He loves and will, with all his heart, whatever the odds, adventure this adventure.

The mighty castle with its keeps and barbicans, its battlements and palisades, seems an impregnable fortress, but he rides on undaunted, picking up momentum as he comes, his ribbons and favor fluttering like banners from his shoulder plates. He is accompanied in his approach by the distant aura of drumrolls and trumpets, faint at first, confused with the wind, but gathering in force and clarity, and as he draws near he appears to grow in size as the martial music grows, putting on strength and volume as if, by an act of will, to make himself equal to the superhuman ordeal before him. For he is no longer a mere individual, idly roaming the bitter streets of a profane and purposeless universe, copulating randomly or by assignment; he is a chosen hero on a sacred quest, playing out—with devotion, urgency, and piety—the epic role in history that fate has appointed to him. He has ventured alone and far from the comforts—however illusory and ephemeral—of the world most familiar to him, in search of the final perfection of his vocation, and now he finds himself, barreling right along, on the perilous path leading, as it is said, to the center of all existence.

Commingled with the drums and trumpets now as the castle looms can be heard a chorus of cheering crowds, urging him on. His target is the imposing castle portcullis. It is down, barring entry. No one remembers when it wasn't down. It is massive, oak-plated and shod with iron, but he does not hesitate; he leaps over the outer breastworks and launches himself in full flight straight at it. He is assailing the unassailable. With a resonant clang and a yowl of pain, he bounces off it and off the breastworks as well, tumbling down with a tinny clatter into the dark rocky ravine below.

But he is not disheartened. He picks himself up and his bruised weapon too, and with stoutness of heart climbs back up over the redoubt to the portcullis. The drumrolls resume; the crowd noises as well, now more like murmurs. He examines the great gate: not even a dent. He steps back to study the castle, holding his erstwhile battering ram with both hands to keep it off the ground. He knows there is no easy way inside the battlemented chemise walls of the inner stronghold; a full frontal assault is required of him, but he must find some way to soften the castle's defenses. He roams the periphery, looking for possible weak points, secret ingresses, eroded zones. He throws himself at the nippled dark-blue windows of the oriels, tries to penetrate the strapped curtain walls by way of the archers' slots, probes the covered pentices; but he is everywhere repelled. As he feels the tower walls for chinks and cracks, however, there is the impression of an agitation within, as of armies forming. Or dissolving. Brazenly, he attempts to invade the castle from below, through the vaulted storage basement, the buttery, and the dungeon, what in knightly skirmishes is known as the devil's passage, but he is rudely expelled. His attempt, nevertheless, seems to have opened up a hairline crack in the portcullis, and he hurls himself once more at it. *Clang*. Back to the ravine. The castle remains intact, serene as ever.

But, as the shouting crowds remind him, he has tools at his disposal he has not yet used. He employs them now to surround the castle with the sudden appearance of heavy artillery and, from all points of the compass a massive bombardment begins, seeding the castle with cannonballs. There is no apparent structural damage, but each smacking strike sets off a luminous red or orange flash, which spread through the cold stone walls like feverish eruptions, fading slowly but leaving a rosy splotch. On all sides, teams of archers appear, each bowman identical to all the others. They fire their salvo of arrows deep into the interior of the castle, over the lipped machicolations, from which venom and fire are often cast down upon would-be invaders. They let fly so many arrows and so rapidly, the castle seems as though hooded with a trembling upended nest. Gasps and cries can be heard within, commingling with the thundering drums, blaring trumpets, kerwhumping cannons, and the augmenting roar of the crowd, and more cracks appear in the castle door. The tide of battle is turning!

But then the archers freeze, the heavy siege guns go silent, and he pauses, ignoring the urgent shouts, the insistent pounding music, to gaze meditatively into the distance beyond the castle. He seems assailed by doubt. Perhaps he is wondering what will happen if in fact he should achieve his goal. When the gods' ends have been accomplished, the epic ends, sometimes with the triumphant return of the hero, but often as not with his demise; that's what the plot bot may be telling him: a familiar castle theme. Everything seems atremble with suspense, even the splotchy parapets, as he stands there deep in thought, absently scratching his raw behind. His weapon has fallen between his feet, clubbing the barren ground. The winds are whining again across the vast empty landscape and the sky has darkened; there are tremors underfoot; the drums have lost their rhythm. *Go on! Go on!* come the frantic shouts. Surely he must. For even if death awaits him, what can he do about it? Nothing. Turning back would be death of another kind. That is what the shouts are trying to tell him. He has no choice. It's do or die. Or both.

Awareness of this steals over him and, with a shudder, he bravely lifts up once more his mighty battering piece. The shelling resumes, the arrows fly, the drums pick up the beat of the booming cannons. He squares his armored shoulders and, rearing up above the very castle towers, he unleashes his fearsome war whoop.

—*I love you!* he cries. *I love you!*

And with that, the walls commence at last to crumble. He throws himself again at the portcullis, this time firing at it with the weapon between his legs as he does so. Over and over he hammers at it, blasting away, crying his piercing battle cry, and finally, with the unnatural shriek of splitting wood and metal, it ruptures down the middle and, as, the blood of battle flowing, the armipotent knight breaches the unbreachable, the great gate begins to lose its very solidity, parting softly in the end like ermine theater curtains. He has broken through! The castle is taken! But at a terrible cost. His explosive weapon, gone berserk, is unloading itself upon the defenseless citadel, demolishing it. The foundations quake, towers topple, the inner keeps burst apart, doors fly off their iron hinges, the great hall collapses into the lower bailey, walls explode, huge rocks fly as arrows and cannonballs had flown before—the castle is blown literally to smithereens, the good and noble warrior fallen as well, emptied out from within and buried, lifeless, beneath the rubble as if embraced by it in this grand finale of mutual annihilation. The shouts have died away, the drums, the trumpets. The wind has returned, making a fluttering sound like awed applause; then it, too, fades to silence. The castle lies in ruins. No sign of life, merely a vast hollow postengagement emptiness, in which one senses a terrible beauty, a terrible loss. In short:

Consummation.

Cut.

Reel 8: Catherine

Cold Cocked

THE REANIMATION OF PETE THE BEAST

Cinecity in the matutinal gloom. Coldest hour of the day. None about. The only movement: scraps of newsprint blown by the wind, which also provides the only sound. A wistful whisper, sometimes rising to a faint airy whistle. The stoplights go through their changes, as if rehearsing their relentless routines, on an empty stage. Empty but not uncluttered. The traffic-blackened snow is pocked with half-buried litter, crumpled auto parts, empty bottles, cast-off clothing, frozen roadkill. Here and there larger heaps suggest the possible presence of human forms, fallen or merely dormant. And now, into these desolate snowswept streets limps an old one-eyed cripple in long skirts, stooped and shawled, a bag lady perhaps, poking and kicking speculatively at the larger heaps. Now and then one of them moves and a curse is heard and she peers more closely. As she moves along, she is accompanied by a simple plainsong in a minor key, slow and sad as the new day is sad, tapped out clearly but softly on an unseen piano. She peers into phonebooths, doorways, and pissoirs, under abandoned cars, behind trashcans in the alleys. When she comes upon what looks to be the spindly wreckage of a children's climbing frame, crowded in among the tall buildings that have grown up around it, she pauses. The heap under it is heavily blanketed under old newspapers, mostly the funny pages, and as she peels them away she finds a frozen body dressed, or half dressed, in rusty armor and old boots, his face plastered to the icy sawdust as if he'd been dropped there in a previous age. The music ceases. The asthmatic whisper of the wind returns. A desiccated wreath is entangled in the man's long icy hair, and his leather breastplate is stiff and partially eaten by small animals. His beard is white. His arse is blue. He is wearing some lacy tatters, attached to his shoulder plates. The old cripple removes them, sniffs them, wrinkles her nose, throws them away. There is the sound of cutlery falling out of a cupboard onto a tiled floor. Her head pops up. She scowls with her one eye, looks about (nothing to be seen but the bleak wintry streets, the blinking stoplights), shrugs, returns to the frozen knight, if that is what he is, or was. She lifts her skirts and sits on his blue behind to try to thaw it, flinching when she makes contact, then leans down and, breaking the frozen hair away from around his ear, whispers sweet nothings into it to try to stir up some life inside. *Fuck!* she murmurs. *Cunt! Cock! Pete? You in there? My steaming pussy wants your hot dick and so on! Hey!* she calls out, knocking on his cranium. *Anybody home?* Nothing. Like talking to a board. She tries to turn him over, but he seems hard frozen to the frozen ground. She stoops to breathe on the join under him, then tries again. There is, after some effort, a thick ripping sound as he pulls away. He is more or less the same color on both sides, flatter on the front from being long pasted against the ground, a bit ragged where he came unstuck. A patch of beard is missing, now bearding the ground. She looks for his virile member, can't find it, worries it might have got left behind, and scratches in the frozen sawdust for it. But, no, squinting her eye more closely, she can see it there between his legs: a wee shrunken thing, stiff as a little icicle, which is what it most resembles. She sucks on it, but there is no improvement. She tries to give him the kiss of life, the other one, but his jaws are frozen shut. She tugs on his shoulder plates in an effort to drag him away, perhaps to somewhere warm, but he's a solid lump and she lacks the strength. She gives him a kick in frustration, there's a loud hollow *clok,* and she staggers about, trying to rub her injured toe, if it is a toe. She kicks him again, this time out of ill temper, and again there's the noise as of hitting a hollow tree with a big hammer. Finally, she reaches down and snaps off his penis with a sharp *pop,* drops it in a skirt pocket, and hobbles off, the piano music returning. Though she is stooped over, head ducked into her shoulders, and otherwise completely motionless, only her blue nose showing under the shawl, her feet make rapid little fore-and-aft movements under her skirts and she zips right along, moving in the direction one reads. Or else she stands still, hovering just above the icy streets, her little feet churning, while the city in the background rolls by in the contrary direction on its own. She reaches (or is reached by) a building painted in flat colors and decorated with scrawled obscenities, with a sign over the door: ANIMATION STUDIO. She goes inside.

The music has ended. The one-eyed animator is puttering around in her studio in a paint-stained smock, huddled over her hands, blowing on them, trying to warm them. There is a little oven for quick-drying prints, and she puts her hands in for a moment, muttering to herself. She is shivering and her face is pale, but the wart on her chin seems less pronounced, her blue eye more rheumy. At the workbench, she flicks through a stack of gelatin slides, clippings, drawings, and photos, including several cutouts of an old blue-nosed lady in long skirts and a shawl, doubled over, her back, round as a shepherd's crook, higher than her head. Not what she's looking for; she tosses them all aside, wipes her nose on her smock sleeve. Then she comes on a painted cel of an old homeless bum slumped against a crumbling inner-city building, a sign propped up beside him that begs for contributions to the FUND FOR UNEMPLOYED CUNT-KISSERS, stared at inquisitively by a dog with its tail up in the air. The bum has one finger in his nose, a brown paper bag in the other hand. Hah. She smiles her gummy smile, pops the cel on the animation stand, picks up one of the cutouts.

The old blue-nosed lady in the shawl, tippy-tapping through the musical streets, comes upon a beardy panhandler, slumped against a crumbling tenement house. He is utterly motionless, staring fixedly into the distance, a finger in his nose. A dog with its tail in the air stands to one side, its head cocked stiffly. She kicks the dog away (there's a *yip-yip* on the track and a wooden clatter) and takes the paper bag, which slides out of the bum's rigid hand as out of a slot. She peers inside the bag, smiles, showing her three teeth. She tosses it back, *gligg-gligg-gligg*, throws the bag away. Loud splintering crash. Her nose changes from blue to red. Thanks, Pete, she says, though her lips don't move.

In the studio she's humming a little tune, no longer shivering, a faint blush on her cheeks and a fresh glint in her eye. She reaches into her smock pocket and takes out a small worm-shaped thing, like a piece of rolled white dough, faintly bluish, about enough for one cookie. She places it under the digital stop-motion camera and photographs it from various angles, then puts it in the little oven for a moment to soften it up. She rolls it about in her hands, takes more photos. She twists it, stretches it, makes loops, knots, and figure eights, works in colored pigments, titling her photos on the screen according to hue, size, shape, and position as graphed on vertical and horizontal axes. It slips out of her hands. Looking for it, she accidentally steps on it and squashes it. No matter. She blows the dirt off, photographs and titles it (new category), remolds it. More pigment. She turns it into a mouse, a fish, a gooseneck, a bird, a bone, a horn, a hammer, spoon, goat, and blunderbuss. She makes numbers and letters with it. Gives it lips. Ears. A coxcomb. She transfers the images to her workstation and lines them up, trying out various combinations. When she runs the motion graphics program, using inverse kinematic and morphing techniques, a dead thing comes alive and does a kind of playful dance, gradually losing its bluish pallor and acquiring a rosy hue. She makes a few changes in the sequencing, copies it to disk, sorts through the slides and photos until she finds a picture of him crossing a bridge over a frozen river, wearing his old felt hat and herringbone overcoat, then grabs up a pot of glue and leaves the studio.

The plainchant has given way to something more like a children's rope-skipping song as the old red-nosed lady in the shawl goes glissading back through the empty streets, feet flickering under her skirts, moving in the opposite direction to that before and even more rapidly. Zip: she's there. The frozen knight with the frosty beard is still on his back under the rickety contraption where she left him, rocking a bit on his hard blue bottom whenever the wind hits him, nesting nothing between his legs except two pea-sized blue marbles. Overhead, dimly, as though resentfully, dawn is breaking. Traffic noises begin to be heard in the background. The old lady reaches into her skirt pocket and pulls out the missing member and her glue pot and, lathering the area with yellow paste (there is the sound of waves hitting the beach), sticks the digit, blue again, back on. He springs awake, his eyes bulging.

—What? What—?! he cries, his throat full of phlegm. Where *am* I?

—It's okay, Pete.

—*What's* okay? What's *happening?* Why have I got this long beard? What film is this?

—It's not a film, Pete, it's real life.

—Sure it is, he wheezes, falling back and closing his eyes again. Tell me another.

—Stay awake, Pete. Look what I brought you!

She licks her finger and pokes it in under the blue marbles. *Click*. His eyes pop open again and he rears up on his elbows to stare, aghast, at the little blue thing standing where his dick should be. It is doing a kind of sinuous dance. The children's melodies have faded away, replaced now by old vaudeville barrelhouse tunes. As it shimmies, twisting what would be its hips if it had hips, it slowly changes shape and color, growing in size and taking on warmer tones. It suddenly rises high into the frosty air, stretched thin as a kite string, ties itself into a bow and unties itself, then squashes back into the shape of a fat rosy candle, the wick doing the bump-and-grind on its little stage as the dick had done. The wick rises as the candle shrinks and reshapes itself into cursive letters, spelling out *i luv cuzzies* and *eat me,* even managing to cross the *t,* then thickens into the shape of a trumpet, tootling along with the piano, or seeming to. All the while, it is swelling and reddening, the color spreading into adjacent regions and setting off little ripples of sympathetic jerks and twitches throughout his lower parts. Where things are warming up. His marbles are still marbles, but they aren't blue anymore. As its climactic number, the little shapeshifting dancing machine turns itself into a reasonable facsimile of his own erected penis, then bows its head toward him and, drooling slightly, wagging what look to be ears, smiles proudly.

—Wow! laughs its creator, ever the enthusiast, slapping her hands together gleefully. Wanna see it again?

—Oh my god. Is it always going to do that?

—Just for now, sweetie. This was a test run. When we get back to the studio, I'll program in a slew a new options. You can be your own choreographer. To operate it, all you'll hafta do is stick your finger up your bung like I been doing and jiggle the joystick.

She sits on the little wiggler—just to get warm, as she puts it, remarking that she feels a sudden chill in that tender place—and to warm him too; her doughy buns, she says, will be a comfort to his thawing belly, just beginning to rumble.

—Now, lemme take care a them weedy whusters for you, son. Hold still, now. She whips out a straight razor from her skirt pocket, spits on it, and, still astride him, shaves the beard off. This takes two strokes, each as loud as a passing street sweeper.

—Hmm. No, I think you look better with it on. I'll just trim it instead. The strokes reverse themselves and the hair, frosted white, flies back onto his face, the spit to her lips, her hand to her pocket. This time she comes out with a pair of steel scissors. As she snips away at his beard, wriggling about and giggling as though she might have turned the dancer on again, she asks:

—Do you recollect how you landed here, Pete?

—I was fucking a castle. Then the next thing I knew I was eating sawdust. But it wasn't like this place. There was a big arena. . . .

—It's been awhile, luv, she says, bouncing up and down, her red nose aglow and scissors slashing a bit wildly. Things've sprouted up.

—And big crowds. It was a historic occasion. It got pretty violent in the end, and I may have got a bit carried away. I think I . . . I may have killed her.

—Who? Hard Cora? Nah, she's okay, she grunts, still pumping away. It was just a movie, Pete.

—Oh. Right. Why do I keep forgetting that? He seems to be drifting off again.

—Don't get too comfortable, Pete! she exclaims, jumping up off him and smoothing her skirts down. The dancer's taking a break, curling up into his grizzled pubic nest. Nothing to be heard but the passing traffic, rising in volume. C'mon, we gotta get you up and doing your beastly thing again!

She drags him to his feet and wraps him in his raggedy old herringbone overcoat, plants his battered felt hat on his head, items she produces as if from the same skirt pocket, but he's already sagging earthward again. He slumps against the climbing frame, chopped beard tucked inside the wide coat lapels. The animator casts her eye upon the rickety old structure overhead, scratching her behind thoughtfully.

—I tell you what! Let's see if we can reactivate the ole plot bot!

—No, thanks, he mumbles from inside the coat, head falling between his knees. Once was enough.

—They's bags a stories in there, hon, if the antique's innards ain't wholly rusted out. Millions, maybe. I helped install them. And lots of them got happy endings. Fucks so wild you won't believe! It'll cheer you up! I'll just check if it's still turning over.

She scrapes the moss away, finds a few loose wires dangling, hooks herself up, and disappears for a while. He sits motionless, head down, the gaping coat framing his old pale belly like woolly side curtains. Were it not for the blowing snow, one would think it was a still shot. The traffic roars by somewhere, unseen. Sirens now as well, horns, whistles, air drills, crashes, gunfire, the usual. When she reappears, she shakes him out of his stupor and reports on the damage inside the bot, all the deletions and broken links and file corruptions, some done by mischievous brats sucked up by the bot while climbing around on it and still lost in there, but says she was able to hack together a few connections and is convinced some of the plots will still run. Things might go wrong but they should have a go. It was good for the goolies. He neither resists nor cooperates with this plan, being somewhat baffled still by the changes in his life, but he allows himself to be hauled to his feet (this happens in an abrupt two-frame move) and strapped and wired to the ancient structure. No special harness required.

THE MADE-IN-HEAD EPILEPTIC

WITH PETE THE BEAST

The bearded knight, known as the Beast, he of the dancing dingus, dressed in his greatcoat with twill weave, which bears innumerable signs of fierce battles past, and his old cloth helmet, crushed from the many blows it has withstood, finds himself standing, heroically alone, on a vast empty plain of the epical sort meant to suggest the awesome magnitude of his perilous venture and to evoke an amplitude of absence, which is to say a very big hole, which it will be his solemn task to fill with whatever means he has to hand. This empty desolation maintains for a time, as though the world, this world he's in, has lost all its furniture. But then a castle appears on the horizon and slowly approaches, and it is understood, in the way that every great truth is understood (take it or leave it), that in this castle a beautiful princess is being kept locked in a tower and he, being who he is, is obliged to rescue her. All right, no problem. But actually there is one. A fire-breathing dragon guards the portcullis, so-called, which in this instance is more like a back door in an alley, a nefarious spell having no doubt been cast upon it.

The dragon lets fly a fetid flaming snort and asks him his business.

—There's a maiden in the tower. I think she's expecting me.

—Nope, no maidens here, big boy. Ain't seen one a them mythical critters since dinosaurs turned tails-up.

—Well, all right then, says the knight, and turns to go.

—No, wait! says the dragon, firing up again and blocking the knight's retreat with its scaly tail. I was just kidding! In fucking sooth, son, the tower's abloat with maidens. Must be hundreds of the rabid little ninnies socked in up there. And all nekkid as jaybirds.

—I was expecting just one.

—Can't help that, sweetie. Word musta got round you was on your way. They been piling in here all week, hot as hares in March. So c'mon, get your sweet butt in gear, you got a heap a noblesse oblige to unleash. But first, afore you can even get in to that sanctum sanitarium and start emancipating all them longing cracks, you gotta deal with me.

—I don't exactly know how to do that. I'm unarmed.

—What you got ain't much, Beast, I admit, says the dragon, squinting its one eye at the gap in the coat, but I ain't demanding.

—I mean, don't I need a sword or something?

—Shoot, that might hurt. I was thinking more of a friendly rassle, so to speak. A little tickle-me-pickle-me would just do me up brown.

—Something's wrong here.

—Ain't easy with a lizard type, I know, but if you edge a mite closer I'll point you where the main bits are. C'mon, son, if you're gonna eat the oyster, you gotta crack the shell!

—There must be some wires crossed. I'll come back tomorrow.

—Awright, awright. So, tupping an ole boss-eyed tart of a dragon don't exactly whup up your appetite. I oughta blow a hot snort and singe your blue ass for the insult, you mangy ol' fart, but I admit, I ain't all that wholesome a spectacle. What with the gimpy hindquarters, bad breath, and scale rot, I take some getting used to. So, c'mon, what the heck, I'll take you to the maidens.

—I don't know if I'm up for this. It's been awhile. . . .

—It don't matter, son. Truth is, they ain't any maidens anyway. I was just making that up. Was some, but they ain't there anymore. The code's all fucked up. Look: they ain't even any castle. Just a false front. You can see for yourself.

On the other side of the portcullis, or alley door, it's the afflicted city all over again, the cold, the congestion, the traffic, the rage. Dismay overtakes the valiant knight and he sits down again against a crumbling wall under a pharmacy sign advertising legal organic homeopathic drugs. COME IN & GET FORTIFIED.

—C'mon, Pete, don't quit on me now, says the dragon. It's just a coupla more blocks. I'll put on a pot a coffee.

But the knight's day, short as it has been, is done. He's gone.

PETE THE BEAST AND THE FARM MISSY

PLUS

THE ANIMAL DOCTOR

An old beardy panhandler sits slumped against a tenement building with a few bricks showing here and there on its painted wall like bandaged sores, underneath a sign that reads:

FARM MISSY
LETHAL ORGASMIC HOMEGROWN GUNGE
CUM IN & GET FRIED

The beautiful Farm Missy comes staggering out, looking as if she's been dipping into her vendibles, little whirlwinds over her head and a leg on backward, and asks him if he'd like to sample her wares. He turns out his empty pockets and asks her if she'd consider some of his in trade. She peers down dubiously at the merchandise he is displaying.

—I'm only sweet on the animules, she says. It's how I was raised up.

He shows her his own sign, GET YOUR GULLY GREASED BY PETE THE BEAST, pointing out his name.

—Oh, that's all right, then, she says. A toke for a poke. So, get on down on the farm, Beast, I got a field there needs plowing. And she drops down on all fours, raises her rear, and tosses her skirt up, or it flies up on its own.

—Do you always take it that way? he asks.

—There's another? I'm just a Farm Missy, you know.

The place of toil is discovered, on examination, to be indeed a rich verdant pasture with tiny flowers like buttercups and miniature poppies and purple clover blossoms popping up amid the delicate grasses, the ample but more barren fields beyond inhabited by tattoos of the Missy's beloved farm animals in amicable clusters, pigs and horses, cattle, geese, and goats, all the ménage of husbandry, etched out there in inks of primary colors.

—Your field looks quite well plowed already, he remarks.

—It can always use another turning over, she says.

—Well, it's a big job, it'll cost you a bit extra.

—Just get on with your chores, Beast, she replies, wagging her substantial holdings impatiently, we can haggle after.

As Farmer Pete dutifully embarks upon his task with his usual forthright earnestness and industry, he sets the whole territory to jiggling, causing the ground to open up beneath his sturdy plow and the animals in the adjacent acreage to commence to frolic excitedly in the delightful uninhibited way of rural creatures. The field wherein he labors, meanwhile, is gradually freshened as with a hidden stream, and gentle cave-born zephyrs stir the verdure. Whinnies, snorts, and squeals are heard, perhaps from the beasts in the neighboring fields, now mounting one another without respect to sex or kind, or perhaps from the Farm Missy herself, this being her way to express her appreciation for the bang-up work being done.

When he has completed his labors to the satisfaction of all and is enjoying his generous reward, the Farm Missy remarks that it would perhaps have been prudent to wear a prophylactic device, for she might have picked up a bit of hoof 'n' mouth disease in a previous romance.

—Ah, that explains it, he says in a muffled voice, and he opens his mouth to show her the hoof in it.

—Land sakes, she says. You better go see the animule doctor!

PETE THE BEAST AND THE ANIMAL DOCTOR

It's the same door in the same pocked wall, but the sign says:

ANIMAL DOCTOR
COME IN & GET MODIFIED

The kind of animal the doctor is is a cat, as are all the doctor's assistants, though more so at the top than at the bottom. They seem very pleased to see him, licking their whiskers and pawing him affectionately. He asks the doctor if they treat only animals here and she (it's clear she's a she, as are all the others, for they wear lab coats but nothing from the waist down except their furry tails) says, no, they prefer to doctor humans, and she shows him her specimen case of doctored parts. His white hair stands on end, but there is no place to go, as he is surrounded by her purring wide-eyed assistants.

—Doctor, he mumbles around his mouthful, that's not my problem.

—You can call me Cat, she rumbles, rubbing up against him. It's my nickname. And a course it's your problem, sweetie, how could it not be? Urgently, he shows her the hoof in his mouth and she tells him to take his pants off. We gotta get at the root a the ailiment, she explains, smiling toothily (three in all), her eye aglitter.

The pants come down, though perhaps not by his doing, and there is a soft choral hiss throughout the room. Nothing there but a little hole. It seems to be suffering from severe hypogenesis, doctor, meows one of the assistants, somewhat portentously. Or else somebody else has got there first, snarls another.

—Nah, the verminous little bugger's only hiding, says the animal doctor, unperturbed as ever. Spread your coozie, luv, offer him a whiff a cheese pie, see if we can lure the minny out. The assistant does so and after a moment the head of a little pink mouse appears at the mouth of the hole, cleft nose twitching, bristly white whiskers trembling, eliciting a kittenish squeal from all those around and a contented purring.

The mouse, after a moment's hesitation, scurries into the first hole he sees, the one just offered up. *Oh! I've got him!* gasps the assistant, and falls to the floor, where she writhes, belly up, hind feet in the air, pawing herself excitedly where his tail sticks out as though playing with a ball of yarn, her own tail mittening her busy paws. The steamy turbulence is such (this steam is seen) that he's quickly out of there, gasping for breath and flushed as if from a sauna, the others meanwhile having circled round, eagerly offering up their own little mousetraps, and soon he is dashing frantically from one to another, in and out, unable to find safe and quiet haven but causing the cats to shriek and howl and roll about giddily with ardor and delight.

But now: Where is he? Who has him?

—Oh oh. Don't let the little sucker get away! cries the animal doctor. Each claps a hand to her portal, some search inside. It tingles like he's still in there, but he's not! Gone! They crawl around on all fours—threes, actually, one hand still to hole—looking under the X-ray machines, examination table, carpets, behind the litter box, but he's nowhere to be found.

—Wait! one of them cries. I think I see him now! Lift your tail, my dear! Yes, there! He's sneaking out the back way through that tight little passage thought only made for another purpose! Grab him! Oh no! He's turned around, he's ducking back in! Quick! Push, dear!

The cat with her tail up arches her back and grunts mightily and, with a report something like that of a tire going flat, the mouse flies out as if shot from a cannon, crashing against the far wall with such an impact that he flattens like a coin, then drops to the floor, rolls around, and comes to rest—*whirr, whirr, whirr, click!*—face up. He can be seen, a flattened pink disk with frightened eyes, through the wall of cornering cats, their tails high, orifices puffy, noses down between their paws, curious to see what he'll do next, the camera's view not unlike his own present one, a moment when film and screen echo one another, raised ass flickering upon raised ass—a reminder, not of the fleshy one's reality but rather of its essential ghostliness, as with all recyclings of flesh, and of the briefness of flesh's meager pleasures; for, as always with projection, the screen, the only hard thing in view, tends to vanish, surrendering its substance to the image, which is only floating light. The spectral animation of desire. More lasting, in the end, than the screen on which it is cast.

He likes the surreal violence (the mouse has sprung out of its coined condition and fled between the haunches of one of the attendants, but she has snatched his tail before he could make good his escape, his forward momentum causing him to swing up and smack her behind, and now they all want a turn in using him in this way), for it's like a playful representation, the only sort tolerable, of the submerged biochemical reality, the ceaseless absurd violence—much having to do with the parts on display here—by which being is sustained. What Kate's Farm Missy character succinctly called (she was talking about the tattooed goat who strayed from a quivering cheek into her meadow, fell in, and gave her a nasty case of vaginitis) the *everyday fucking hardass comedy*. These squash-and-stretch cat-and-mouse routines (now he is being tossed up in the air in a game of pussy-catch-the-mouse: up he goes and down he falls: *splop!*—then he's pulled out by the tail and tossed again) replay, over and over again (he's got away after a nip at a tender button, and the chase begins), the elemental drama of momentary escape—always a miracle, and usually a comic one—from the final violence of obliteration. So, both revelation and release from the terror of it. Until the final iris-out. Or so says, in her own way, Kate, on whose rear the little animated film is being projected. If it ain't funny, she says, it don't touch what hurts, and hipso fuckto it ain't true. But these little restorative entertainments she's concocted for him (now both cats and mouse are getting flattened, elongated, smashed, electrocuted, cloven, blown up, turned inside out, crystallized and shattered, dismembered, liquefied, and pulverized and their heads, backsides, and orifices assaulted by every object imaginable in a doctor's office) are, she says, too easy. She's after something more subversive now.

Finally, the little mouse is too pooped from all the strenuous action to keep it up any longer. He's not a young mouse, after all. A graybeard. He is, sad but true. Even his tail, now dragging, has gone gray. He simply stops where he is and curls up limply on the floor, where he's picked up by the animal doctor, dangling him by the tail. She doesn't eat him right away. She cuddles him in her paws and licks him first as though applying a healing lotion, good doctor that she is. Or perhaps she's basting him. Sometimes she takes him whole into her mouth, but she doesn't bite, just rolls him around on her tongue. It's evidently very soothing, for he recovers somewhat. His little snub nose is twitching again, he's getting his color back. The old fellow who brought him here is nowhere in sight. In fact, he (one is the avatar of the other, but he is reluctant to speculate on which is which) is lying flat out on his cot at the back of the animation studio, his own mouse being attended to—brought back to life—in animated fashion by the cartoon's creator. To keep him entertained meanwhile, she has straddled his chest so as to present to his view the broad flat screen of her fundament, upon which she is running this little sequence of homely animations. He has, as it were, a front-row seat, with all the distortions of such a position, everything seen from directly below and so appearing short and wide, or thin and long, as the case may be, although, out of long habit or for reasons more mysterious, his brain somehow compensates for the odd angle, and what he sees inside his head is the full corrected image, as if viewed from the first balcony or through an optical editor. The mouse is growing. She seems to be fattening him up with her tongue for the feast to come. The animal doctor pauses, purring deeply, licks her whiskers, and returns to the task.

—Look, she says, let's skinny down to the elementals. While reviving him, Kate has been teaching him the rudiments of animation, or what she now calls motion graphics. Might save your heedless ass some day, she tells him, giving it a wake-up slap. For Kate, life and animation are synonyms. Stasis is the ordinary condition of the universe. The freeze is. The single frame. Life is warmth (his butt is glowing where she smacked it), movement. Flicker. Animation. Persistence of vision is not merely a cinematic illusion, it is also how reality works: a sequence of dead stills in rapid succession, the only difference being that reality runs at a lot more than twenty-four frames per second. So she says. In her way. The perversion of fission, she likes to call it. But vision needs a viewer to see. It needs life. Otherwise, it is always now and always dead. *If we didn't tick,* she likes to say, *time wouldn't tock.* Animation as art (she won't call it that, loathes the word; it's just her way of life, nothing more or less), is both a protest against the stationary condition and a cunning interpreter of the ongoing flicker, what she calls the curse of events.

To demonstrate, she has animated photos and drawings for him, enlivening what was dead, has made objects like dishware and dildos get up and walk, walls talk, clouds copulate. And masturbate: using motion-capture techniques, she had him up there, roiling mistily about, pumping spunk out over the city like snow. Felt good. She has propped him, or some manifestation of him, up against the wall where he collapsed on the way here and invented wacky alleyway toons to get him back on his feet again. She makes use of everything. She made the graffiti on the wall come alive and interact with him. He got a charitable handjob from a newspaper blowing by. An old jalopy at the curb played stand-up comedian, rattling on like Kate, blinking its headlamps, saying its nips were hot, breaking wind out its tailpipe. Its dirtiest jokes had to do with crankcase oil and faulty drive shafts. She has created love affairs between phone kiosks, an orgy among trashcans, let a fire hydrant rape a mailbox.

She took a still photograph of the crowded winter streets and animated only the black silhouetted figure in the pedestrian-crossing sign, which she renamed the pederast-crossing sign. The figure, wagging a large silhouetted erection, climbed down off the sign and moved among the staring, motionless pedestrians, abusing them, kissing them, kicking them, stripping some of them and dressing them in other people's clothes, humping them, marking them up with mustaches, eyeglasses, and blackened teeth, poking holes in them, taking their heads off and putting them on different shoulders, giving them genitalia for mouths and noses and facial characteristics where their genitals should be. The sign figure then went behind some of them and made ratchety wind-up noises, which sent them rocking blindly forward, one by one, like mechanical toys, hitting walls and lampposts, wandering into the streets, clattering into one another, falling over, their raised legs still walking. The moving ones tended to tip the stationary ones over; sometimes the others, too, but it was better to move than to stand still. The figure cranked up the cars and drove them through the people. Sometimes they knocked the people down; sometimes the people knocked the cars over. This is what really happens out there, Kate said, considering herself to be the last of the great realists. All part of his education.

Now she has painted a black circle on a clear gelatin sheet with a medium brush and cut an arrow out of black construction paper. She sets them down on her workbench, the arrow just outside the circle, pointing at it. She moves the arrow head into the circle and out again. Two or three times. There, she says. Put a dickhead on the arrow and tart up the circle with a hairy fringe, and you got the typical animated graffiti you might see pumping away on any toilet wall, right? The ur-anime. So, let's cavort with it. She scans the stark black-and-white images into her computer and repeats the penetration of the circle by the arrow, in and out, a few times. Then the circle narrows to an oval and finally to a straight vertical line, giving the impression that it has rotated 90 degrees, creating by its seeming rotation a new dimension. Now when the arrow passes horizontally back and forth over (or under) the line, there is the illusion that it is penetrating the circle seen before, though there is nothing to be seen but a line. The oval returns, the circle. The arrow shortens and the point flattens out until it is a straight vertical line in the middle of the circle. It shrinks and grows, shrinks and grows, suggesting it is going away, into the circle, and pulling back.

That established, the first sequence is repeated: arrow and circle; circle to oval to line; thrust by arrow. Only this time the arrow does not pass the line but bounces back off it. Another try or two, then it goes around to the other side of the line. Oval, circle, oval, line. Thrusts by arrow, bouncing off. It goes back to the side of the line where it began, points toward the circle (line), hesitates, backs off: oval, circle pause. The arrow makes a halting tentative movement toward the circle: oval, line. It is clear that the circle is turning its back on the arrow whenever it approaches. The arrow looks disheartened, slanting downward. Oval, circle. The arrow raises its point cautiously, strokes the side of the circle. Circle to oval, tipping slightly toward the arrow. Encouraged, the arrow inches toward the oval and, meeting no resistance, lurches forward. Rapid circle, oval, line, and the arrow bounces off again. It turns away, downcast, and retreats to the opposite edge of the frame from the line, which has become a circle again. Its back to the circle, the arrow makes rapid little thrusting movements, points halfway upward suddenly, quivers, pumps again, once, twice, slowly droops and shortens. *Cut.*

Return to arrow and circle as at the beginning. Repeat of rejection—circle, oval, line, bouncing off, et cetera—as before. Repeat of downcast arrow. Enter another circle behind the arrow, sashaying. It dips and pivots provocatively and pumps its lower arc two or three times in the direction of the arrow, which has been changing position, first shrinking to a vertical line, then stretching back to an arrow, now pointing toward the new circle and longer than before. Behind the arrow, the first circle moves from line to oval to circle to oval to line, as though rotating toward the intruder. The new circle moves toward the arrow, retreats, moves forward, retreats, each time ending up a bit closer. In response, the arrow moves in short little jerks toward the new circle, which rotates from circle to oval to line to receive it. The first circle rolls past the arrow and interposes itself between the other two figures. The arrow makes various moves, as though trying to get around the first circle, and it makes countermoves. The new circle tries to slip past the first one, but the latter rotates rapidly, striking the new circle so as to send it spinning like a gyroscope. The arrow receives a similar blow and spins like a weather vane.

Enter two more arrows. They watch the spinners wind down, pointing first at one, then the other, then parade around a bit, grandstanding. With the other arrow and two circles as audience, they bounce, whirl, stand on their points, do cartwheels, play leapfrog. The circles roll toward them and they pair off, leaving the first arrow alone, between the two pairings, odd arrow out. The circles, at the edges, rotate toward the new arrows, oval to line, and the arrows thrust away, in and out, their backs to the first arrow. The first arrow strikes one of the others and knocks it out of its circle—or line, as it should perhaps be called. The struck arrow springs up and they go at it, head to head.

Meanwhile, the neglected circle joins the other circle and arrow. The two circles, now lines, become joined at the base, each leaning back, making a kind of pinched V, the arrow in between pumping back and forth in and out of both of them like a piston. The two fighting arrows pause, and turn toward the arrow and two circles, where the movements are getting more vigorous and the positions more varied. The two arrows point briefly at each other, then back at the arrow and two circles. They abandon their exchange of blows and join the other three, each entering one of the circles from behind. Much thrusting and counterthrusting, bouncing and quivering. The two circles line up behind each other, and the three arrows penetrate both at the same time. The arrows stand, points up, and the circles fall on them.

Enter two more circles. They hesitate at the edge of the activity but are rolled into it by the arrows, and more combinations are achieved. The circles rotate with arrows in them, flinging the arrows on to the next circle. They link at the center and move like a carousel, the arrows flying through them in the opposite direction, setting off vibrations. Arrows sometimes split down the middle and become something like circles, receiving the thrusting circles in their line or oval configurations. The four circles lie flat and the five arrows hop from one to another in a kind of game, the arrow in any one circle having to jump to another when another arrow arrives. The circles bounce upward with each new arrival. More arrows and circles arrive and join in, but without much ado. There is too much quivering, rolling, spinning, flying, hopping, piercing, bouncing, and thrusting going on to notice them. It's a grand orgy.

—Awright, says Kate, leaning back and scratching her armpit, them's the basics. We could brush in color—flesh tones, say—and lay on a track with pops and bumps and squishes, music, dialogue, or anyhow twitter, add backgrounds, other props. The anthro treatment. Too easy. We'll stick with black ink, circles, and arrows. E-percuss it a tad later on maybe, nothing more. But now comes the intrusting part. This here's where I layer in some a that motion I been snatching off your bobbing ass.

Back to the beginning. Same single arrow, same circle—seemingly. Now, though, there is something hesitant yet eager, expectant yet cool, about the arrow's probes of the circle, something peculiarly alluring about the circle's reluctant seductiveness. It is clear that the arrow is going to penetrate the circle, but though the circle will not reject the arrow, it will not make entry easy; the arrow must read the circle's subtle twitches and teeterings and follow their complex half-concealed timetable. This is no longer mere parody, it's a mating dance. Or if it parodies anything, it's the technique itself.

Kate disparages motion capture as a copycat shortcut to making animateds. To bring the real world untransfigured into the cartoon world is to diminish it, intrude upon its peculiar integrity. Her mantra: What ain't toon, ain't real. More radically, she is attempting to reverse the direction by infecting the real world, so-called, with cartoon motion. Reality is only half real, she likes to say. The rest has to be made up. But a tool's a tool. So while he's been recuperating, she's been mating him with robots or arousing him with wraparound orgies in a virtual reality chamber she's cobbled together around his cot at the back, and, while netting him with a kind of meshed light, has digitally filmed his jerks and fucks onto the computer in the form of 3-D grids, superimposing the captured movement, not onto her cartoons of him, which would be cheating (Pete the Beast is loving, old-fashioned, laborious paint-and-click celluloid work), but onto whatever odd fancy comes to mind. Thus the wanking clouds; the slum tenement's violation of City Hall (he broke the robot on this one, giving her a surprise climax that made her whoop); her so-called animdoc of the birth of the cosmos in which his exploding spunk, graphed in slow motion, played a starring role; her pornfables of goats and toads, camels and sphinxes, foxes in henhouses.

And now it's the arrow, a simple black line with a kind of inverted V at one end, like ancient clay-tablet writing (cunny-shaped, they said in olden times), nothing more. And a circle: black, against a plain background that is not so much white as the color of light. That the arrow's opening sallies are so hesitant may be partly due to its uncertainty about the pleasure to be found in a plain circle. It touches it at certain points, then cautiously circumnavigates it. Or part of it: The circle turns away from the arrow at the upper and lower arcs but turns back again. Is it the same side of the circle or the other side? Impossible to tell. Circle, oval, line, oval, circle, et cetera. But the arrow continues to trace its curvature, incited, it would seem, by the circle's coming and going and coming again, the discontinuous but rhythmical strokes becoming something like the slow-motion flow of an intermittent current. The arrow itself breaks in upon this regularity by missing some beats and by altering the pressure when in contact, pushing against the circle sometimes, barely brushing it with the tip at others, the circle responding by minute gestures that cause the arrow to slip off the rim or to nudge, as if by accident, parts of its circumference previously forbidden.

And as a certain urgency presses the arrow to be bolder and hesitation is replaced by strategy, even if sometimes they look the same, he begins to recognize himself, or some part of himself (his cock, yes, but not only his cock) in the arrow—*It's you, Pete,* Kate says—as it stretches forward, withdraws, strokes one edge with the whole of itself, pokes, dips and rises—giving the circle, in effect, something to play against. Which it does, its own intricate movements luring the arrow on, luring *him* on, and as he brushes the interior of the circle at last, he can feel her little beard, warm and damp—it's not there on the screen, it's just a circle—but it's as if his partner, the one whose motion has also been remotely captured, were projecting it as part of her performance, the way mime can create walls and boxes that aren't there, and he knows he is working with a great artist. To be worthy of her, he must remain wholly focused, concentrating on every detail, responding to each least quiver, each moment of stillness, else he will lose her to mechanics and abstraction, even though his ability to think things through is diminishing and he must rely on something more like instinct and experience.

Now, for example, as he attempts to brush the moist down again, he finds nothing but emptiness, and he knows he has been too hasty. He returns to his stroking of the circumference and discovers a point untouched before, and he experiences a sudden trembling there, almost like a shudder. He slips off the edge and finds himself pressing against something softly resistant like sponge rubber, and he withdraws again. The circle turns toward him (probably), taking on an oval shape, and now as, selecting his spot (he thinks he is beginning to understand its geometry), he probes again, he finds once more the juicy little furball, a kind of tactile ghost, as it were, and he knows that she is feeling (he is working hard at this) not the pointed arrowhead but the blunt velvety nose of his virtual member, for he is permitted to part the hair with it and slide into the warm glossy channel concealed within and invisible to the eye. Whereupon, yet again, he withdraws, but not entirely, stroking the wet petaled channel gently with the tip of the arrow, pausing at one end, where he senses he has encountered something like a mirror image of himself but in miniature, and he rubs against it as one might kiss by rubbing noses, and it rubs him back.

The trembling experienced before has now evolved into a continuous but irregular oscillation, emerging from the very center of the circle. It is enormously stimulating, the mounting tension at the tip of the arrow now spreading down the shaft to the very end of it, and as the circle, or oval, presses forward, drawing the arrow deeper into itself, he feels a sudden tightening at the far end of the shaft as though strung to a taut bow, and he knows he must use all his skill and will to keep the arrow from shooting forward recklessly and losing the game. So he allows the arrow to wallow briefly in its entry and then withdraws it again, returning to the stroking of the pulsating channel, though now more forcefully and rhythmically. And though, on the screen, there is still nothing but the oval and the arrow, one can see the stroking, the pulsing, the tension, and the oscillations, and even Kate is aroused and has her hand in her armpit.

And then, unexpectedly, or at least he does not expect it, all reason vanished now, the arrow operating on its own, it plunges deeply forward, just as the oval jerks upward to receive it. There is a brief faint struggle as though the oval wishes to change its mind, if it can be said to have one, but the arrow is lodged deeply and is barbed, after all; it is in there to stay. This time the arrow does not retreat but stays where it is, pressed so deep inside that if it pushes any farther it will come out the other side. The oval has ceased its struggle and spread itself to a full circle and now grips the arrow, which is little more than a short vertical line in its center, in lush rippling walls that squeeze and massage it with hot oils. And once again the arrow starts to move, but rhythmically now, halfway out, back in, out, in, out, and as it does so the camera view of the two interlocked figures, arrow and circle, begins to rotate slowly, such that the oscillating circle closes to a vertical line as the thrusting arrow grows to full stretch, then fills again to a full circle as the arrow shrinks, only to reappear as the circle becomes a line, pumping in the opposite direction, ever more vigorously, the tempo gradually increasing, the circle's oscillations becoming more and more violent and timed to the arrow's urgent strokes. There is no track, yet one can somehow hear the muffled pounding of the soft collisions, can hear the squeaks and whimpered *I love you*s, the beating of hearts, as if hearing with the eyes alone. Suddenly, both circle and arrow stop as if frozen in a freeze frame, time's passing betrayed only by minute trembling vibrations (*oh! ah!* he is gasping); then both pump wildly for a moment, go rigid once more, and it's over, the frenzied thrusts slowing toward a tranquil quiescence, the arrow still buried deep in the circle, the stillness interrupted only by short languid codas of the movements seen before.

—Oh shit, he gasps, breathing heavily. I've come all over your screen. Kate hands him an old paint-stained rag. But that, he wheezes, that was no robot.

—No. Got in a actress. Friend a yours.

—Cally! I knew it. Could only have been . . .

He's only smearing the screen, so he gives the rag to Kate and staggers back to his cot in the cave to lie down and rest for a few months. His knees are weak. One of the most powerful orgasms he's ever had. Of course, they've all been pretty good, best he can recall, one with the universe and all that, seems to happen every time. Even with the robots, Kate's popular consumer sideline. Pets and sex slaves mostly (or the two in one), amazingly limber and versatile mechanisms, bodies and organs tailored to the owner's fancy, guaranteed disease-free, no feeding necessary, no litter box (though special tastes are catered to), and no nuisance after sex, just hit the off-switch and store them away. What Kate calls her r*easonable fucksimiles,* part of her animation trade. It was she who did all the hard-wiring and core programming for Cora's plot bot, Cissy providing the content and the links.

Cissy returned the favor. Most of Kate's robots not only perform every sex act imaginable but also talk, and Cissy (whom he misses; he misses them all) has helped to script their interactive chatter. Breathless dirty talking, for the most part, but Cissy's never one to miss a chance to fill up a blank space, so many of them also have special routines, programs all their own. They might recite amorous poetry, or describe with affection one's body parts while examining them, or interpret dreams, or take one back to childhood and first sex, or act the parts of famous lovers from literature and history. There is a particularly insatiable one called Carmela the Nun (they all have names like Castora and Coral and Clorinda and Clavia), who confesses her sins as to a father confessor and tearfully begs to be raped as penance, weeping with pain and spiritual anguish when one does so, but fucking like a fox. She is a see-through robot whose pulsating vagina literally glows in the dark when her habit comes off. Columbine is winged like a bird with maiden's breasts and a haunting gray gaze and prefers to ride on top, hovering as if in flight, her wings rising and falling gracefully, while describing in lyrical flights what she's feeling; and Cocotte, whose phenomenal tongue massages are a robotics breakthrough, straddles one's ears and sings sweet romantic love ballads through the delicate pursed lips of her raspberry-pink anus while using her specially designed mouth and tongues on all parts below. She has a vaginal tongue for French kisses, and her anus, when not vocalizing, serves as a kind of dispenser, whence he receives his daily vitamins.

He fell in love for awhile with one called Consuela, who had fingers in her vagina that stroked and squeezed and played with him when he entered her and who murmured in his ear throughout sex her favorite scenes from the movies he'd made. She knew all the best ones and told him details he'd forgotten. She had kisses that were, literally, a narcotic, and she seemed more interactive than most of the others, developing an intimate and loving exchange that elaborated on every nuance of their relationship. She seemed particularly sensitive to his advanced age and kept telling him what a beautiful young ass he had. When she spoke whisperingly of running away together, he was tempted, but then one day he made the mistake of asking Kate why she didn't use models for her motion capture instead of robots, and she disassembled a robot to show him the miniature cameras inside, choosing Consuela for her demonstration. Perhaps she'd overheard the whispering. She never put her back together again. He realized, on seeing Consuela's lovely belly splayed open on the workbench and all her little bits on view, that he didn't really want to see the insides of things.

But the cot and virtual-reality chamber are not merely a motion-capture stage. They are also the scene of his gradual recuperation from a near-fatal encounter with power back in the epic days of knights and castles (as he remembers it, not well), thanks to Kate's loving care, her wholesome if simple food and drink (lots of potatoes and beer), her robots, dope, baths, and blowjobs, her good humor and her common sense. Whenever he feels like just shutting down the lamp and rattling off the reel, she won't let him.

—You can't quit on me, Pete, she says then, prodding him with her electromagnetic prick-extender. Where'll I get my material?

To keep him going, she has entertained him with her cartoons and sex-slave robots and taken him on spectacular trips with a tab or two and the VR chamber's wondrous wraparound vistas. He fell in love with Consuela, in fact, while afloat in outer space and stoned by her kisses, and the main reason he keeps asking for the insatiable nun is not so much for the ecstatic fuck (it is always satisfying, but emotionally wracking), as for the opportunity to immerse himself in the great vaulted cathedral thrown up by the projectors, listening to Sister Carmela's stifled sobs while echoey choirs high up in the lofts sing the *Eerie Liaison* or the *Pene Dicked Us,* lending precedence and gravitas to the devotionals. He understands the illusory nature of virtual reality, of course, just as he understands the illusions of cinema, but it seems to make little difference in either case, for even when he thinks he's on the outside, he ends up on the inside; it's his nature. He was, as they say, made for the medium.

When operating all the motion-capture cameras and computers and the complicated chamber gear at the same time, Kate has her hands full and has to use robots, not only as his partners but also as her assistants—her inbetweeners, she calls them—but when it's only a matter of convalescence and pleasure, she likes to operate the VR by remote and play with him herself. He prefers the robots, but he's a professional, even if a bit rundown and slack in the britches, so he can, as the Pete the Beast sign says, fuck anything, even old Kate, whose clapped-together anatomy remains something of a mystery to him, its parts seemingly as interchangeable as those of her robots. It's the wisdom a the bots! she says, winking her one eye, whenever he gets curious. Knowing it's how he prefers it (at heart, she only wants to please), she keeps her several bits in their customary places most of the time, but one day, feeling sentimental, she decided to replay their wild embrace at the edge of his penthouse pool, putting one of her breasts back between her legs and her cunt in her armpit and switching her navel and anus, an exercise that was not entirely successful in the repetition, though he did his best. It helped that she was able to surround them with a virtual re-creation of the original penthouse scene, which filled him not only with a desperate longing but also with delight. He could even smell the chlorine in the pool. What a time that was! Probably. But she has also literalized a lot of the old clichés, just for fun, so he has found apples, lilies, melons, dumplings, and bumpers where her breasts should be, a lunchbox, wasp's nest, purse, sea urchin, cherry pudding, rose garden, and bearded clam between her legs, beams and buckets to the rear. Anything edible, he is encouraged to eat. Which he always does, well aware, ever since his first apple munching, of their powerful curative and aphrodisiacal qualities, which for Kate are more or less the same thing.

And of course he's no spring birdie himself, he's no matinee idol, even if he once was or might have been (his scripted memory is not too clear; it's probably the dimming of the years): his flesh is drooping on his aching old bones, belly hanging lower, ass dragging; it's hard to straighten up; he has to stand with his feet spread not to fall over; his beard is white, his nose warty; his senses are in retreat; peeing takes forever; he has to wear spectacles during sex to be sure he's in the right place; and he doesn't always hear something the first time—second either. He avoids mirrors because he doesn't recognize the decrepit old coot he sees there. Gives him a nasty jolt each time, sends a shudder up his rickety spine.

One night, wandering around at the back somewhat absently, he thought he saw his old self in the mirror: lean handsome superstar Lucky Pierre, suited up, hands in his pockets, throbbing prick on view like a railway crossing barrier, faint ironic smile playing on his face. A bit vacant as always, suggestion of panic behind the eyes, a commercial sheen to his cock, but the self he knew and loved, the real one. So his seeming decrepitude had all been the work of some perverse make-up artist! An elaborate practical joke! He would have leapt for joy, but his knees hurt. So, what next? Couldn't stay here and continue to be humiliated. He scratched his beard thoughtfully. The old office and studio might still be in operation; maybe he could still find it. Then it occurred to him that the image in front of him did not have a beard to scratch. Nor was it moving as he moved. Kate came out of the lab and said, Oh oh, looks like one a my studs has got loose outa the barn, and she picked it up by its nose and dick and carried it to a storage room at the back.

Which is how he found out about the other robots. Of course, sex slaves come in all genders. Should have thought of that. Still, it came as a bit of a shock, especially when he learned that she had developed a whole line of them, her hottest product, and all modeled on him in his various career phases, from Wee Willies (very popular with the geriatric set of both sexes) to Peter Pricks, Lucky Pierres, Badboys, and Old Crazy Legs. He has seen them warehoused back there. They scare him. The new models come with a month's supply of ejaculate and at least three classic interactive film plots and scripts installed, Kate explained, but others can be purchased separately or rented from robot supply stores. The cocks are replaceable. There was a run on the Crazy Leg model and she's been ordered to make no more, as City Hall feared the guerrillas might be building a robot army with them.

—Dumb kids, laughed Kate. Them toys is designed to fuck, not fight. The least excitement, and their pants go down. It's a kinda self-arrest.

Kate, having been obliged to try out all these robots herself as part of her factory-tested guarantee, has admitted that she likes best the full-formed, mature, but virile model he ran into that night, an admission that caused a sharp twinge of jealousy toward his former self and sent him into a frenzied paroxysm of show-off sexual acrobatics that might have brought on a heart attack had not Kate shoved a strong sedative up his ass and knocked him out.

—Well, he rumbled, when he came around and found her grinning down on him, it's not easy growing old, and she agreed and patted his exhausted dick.

She's now working on a Pete the Beast model, figuring that although it may not have much appeal for the adult market, kids might have fun with it, so she has been taking extensive notes and measurements, using all her footage and motion-capture data, pausing mid-coitus to jot a memorandum if she sees him doing something she hasn't noticed before. Like scratching his hemorrhoids, for example. He was with Cocotte on that occasion, happily lost in all her lips and tongues, one of which had set his asshole to tingling, when Kate hit the pause button, and by the time she started everything up again, Cocotte's batteries had run down. Being aware that all these elaborate romps, virtual and otherwise, are really lab sessions has taken some of the zip out of them, though he continues to do his part, because, like those fucking robots, he cannot do otherwise.

For all her expertise in robotics, Kate has made little use of robots in her animated films, arguing that animating an animation is like fucking a fuck, her only exceptions being intentionally clunky cartoon robots like the one she used in *Beaver and the Beast* . . .

BEAVER AND THE BEAST

A PETE THE BEAST SPECIAL

The old panhandler, huddled in newspapers and his old threadbare overcoat, only his merchandise on view, is just nodding off, his half-frozen signpost that announces A BUCK A FUCK dipping as his jaw sags, when what looks like a kind of riveted iron chastity belt with a furry beard and a pot lid comes waddling by on mechanical toy-soldier legs and lets out a sharp whistle from somewhere that makes him snap awake so fast he cracks his head on the wall behind, setting all the graffiti to tumbling about in panic. Stars fly like nits. Or perhaps they *are* nits, for they continue to circle about.

—Hel-lo, the contraption says in a hollow computer-generated monotone, I-am-the-Beaver-Bot! Will-you-buck-me-please? . . . Here-is-my-fuck. The thing holds out a bill with an arm and hand more like extensible pincers.

—Sure, he says blearily, taking the bill and stuffing it in a torn pocket. He yawns and scratches his belly (more nits), staring skeptically at the Beaver Bot as it retracts its arm. I'm game for anything. Where do I do it?

—In-my-cunt-stupid!

—No, I mean, where is it? How do I get in?

—Do-you-always-have-these-problems-with-a-nat-omy?

—Things move around, Bot. It's best not to be overconfident.

—Call-me-Beaver.

—All right, Beaver, he grunts, struggling to his feet and letting his raggedy britches fall. So point me the way.

—Just-under-my-fuzzy-apron-here. . . . I-see-Beast-you-are-one-a-them-curved-ones.

—Most-loved schlong in town, Beaver.

—But-you-are-bent-the-wrong-way. . . . Down-does-not-count.

—It's the years, Beaver. And the pollution. So, all right, let's crank it up. He bends over, lifts the furry patch, squints closely at what's underneath it. Looks like just a narrow little coin slot down here between fat lips, Beaver. Don't know if I can get in there.

—Go-ahead-and-thread-the-needle-Buster. . . . Them-lips-is-rollers-they'll-see-to-your-getting-in.

—Rollers?

But the robot has already grasped his bent but much-loved tool of trade with its nippers and pushed it in. There is a grinding rattle as of heavy machinery firing up, sparks fly (*Yow!* he yells, his eyes bulging with alarm), the robot begins to vibrate like an old snow blower, there are pops and bangs, the pot lid flies open, steam geysers up. His nose lights up, his hair stands on end, his beard crackles. The robot continues to rumble and shake as what looks like ribbons of thin flat noodles coil up over the edge.

—Is-all-of-it-in-there-Beast?

—*Whuff!* C-c-criminy! I think so. But what have you—

—All-right-then. . . . Let's-get-cookin'!

The tongs push any pasta hanging over the lip back inside and the lid comes clattering down. The inner engine of the robot seems to rev up and it commences to pitch and toss violently, pounding the street like a jackhammer, the gaping old panhandler gripped in place by the rollers and tongs, his eyes rolling around in their sockets, his nose snorting smoke, teeth chattering, his arms hugging the robot in desperation, his overcoat and pants-bound legs flapping like banners. The robot emits monotone ejaculations of passion and wild abandon and ratchets up another gear, and they start caroming about the alleyway like a pinball, ricocheting off walls, knocking down trashcans and stacks of vegetable crates, breaking windows, twanging through phone and electric wires, bouncing off the roofs of cars, taking out streetlamps and phonebooths. Then suddenly they come to a complete quivering stop in midair over the alley, about as high up as a theater marquee, and the Beaver Bot says:

—Let-'er-rip-Beast!

There's a terrific explosion and the entire neighborhood is flattened, and when the dust settles the old panhandler is discovered lying sprawled amid the rubble of the building he'd been leaning against, his pants around his ankles, his tongue lolling, his eyes still spinning in their sockets, a limp blue ribbon between his thighs which reads: FIRST.

—Well, that was pretty decent, Beast, says a sweet musical voice. Looks like it done the trick!

The Beast, working his jaws as though trying to count the teeth he has left, blinks his eyes a few times to stop them from wheeling about and focuses on the sight before him: Standing there in the dust and rubble is a stunningly beautiful young princess, no doubt the most beautiful princess in the world, wearing diamonds in her hair and nose and a gauzy caped gown about as substantial as mist. Though the rest of him remains quite flaccid and lifeless, his eyes telescope out of their sockets (*boing! boing!*) like twinned erections. Or try to, at least; even they flag and droop a bit, their *boings* more like *boinks*.

—One a the weird sisters had me under a fucking spell, the princess explains, smiling demurely. So, thanks, Beast, for busting the sucker. You were my last shot. I'd tried everbody willing to stick their dick in a tin can, and what few there were all got turned off by the spaghetti number. You're a gutsy dude, Beast, a real prince. I speak metaphonically, a course. Well, I'll be off now. Have a good day!

—Wait a minute, lady. You're telling me you're the Beaver Bot?

—Useta be. But I'm Princess Beaver now—if you don't mind, she adds in gentle remonstrance, delicately digging at her namesake through the gossamer gown as if she might harbor a wee creature there—and you'll hafta address me accordingly. Your Highness'll do like a treat.

—Okay, Your Heinie, but doesn't the guy who disenchants the princess always win her hand or some other suitable part?

—I'm afraid that is the rule, Beast. I was rather hoping you was ignorant of it.

—Well, then, my lady, let me get my wind back and we'll have some more of the same.

—I can't say no, Beast, that'd be against my religion, she replies with a tremulous sigh, blushing like the bride fate has destined her to be. But though this pesthole may do for tramps and robots, it ain't suitable nup-shell chambers for a full-blowed princess. Let's pop back to the palace and get it on in style.

—I hear you talking, Your Heinie, Your Matchstick, Your Grease. And style is just what I am most in need of. But my locomotory functions are not responding to the call.

—Howzat?

—I can't stand up.

—Well, why didn't you say so, pissfire? Here, lemme lend you a hand up.

She does so, and he notices that, beautiful as she is, she has only three fingers on each hand. Her hand is so light it makes almost no impression against his own, yet she manages, effortlessly, to bring him upright again, as though merely to touch him were to achieve it.

—Awright, Beast, she says tenderly, gazing at him with an adoring, innocent look, her rosy lips parted as if in anticipation of a kiss, let's haul ass.

And she's off, he drawing his eyes back into their sockets, pulling up his pants, and tagging after her as best he can. Though he feels pretty sluggish, he seems to be zipping right along, the streets passing by with little effort on his part. His feet strike something firm, but it doesn't seem to be on the same plane on which, looking down at his feet, he appears to be walking. *Don't look down, Pete,* he seems to recall Kate telling him on some previous occasion, but it's hard not to, and consequently he falls a few times until he gets used to it. Princess Beaver is just ahead of him, her golden slippers flashing, her precious little buns, on view through the gauzy gown, churning away, her cape flying, the distance between them stretching a little with every clumsy tumble he takes.

The streets were empty when they set off, first just the stylized rubble, then colorful tenements angling this way and that, an occasional awning or shop window, a few cars and buses, parked in the streets like big toys, but no people. Now they are crowding up again, the traffic is moving once more, the streets are muckier, the going slower, no more lightness, no more zip, gravity's back, mass is; he slips and falls sometimes on the ice and snow or gets elbowed over by the jostling crowds, as she grows ever more distant. He can still see her through the milling multitudes, but only in fleeting glimpses. A bus passes between them, kicking up slush, and she's gone. No, there she is, two blocks down. An unmistakable glimmering, her brightness standing out against the dull chiaroscuros of the city.

He presses on through the bitter congestion, following that glimmering, his knees aching from arthritis and the knocks they've taken, his eyes tearing up from the cold wind and blowing snow, little left now but the held recollection of her, and that fading too, only the image of her gaze remaining with its tender appeal, and the heartbreakingly beautiful furry patch between her legs as seen through the rippling gauze, there and not quite there, as if made not of flesh but of light. Where is she? She passed this way, but now she is nowhere to be seen. Did she duck down into the subway? Enter one of the buildings? Is the palace around here somewhere? He can do nothing but keep going, glancing down snowy side streets and into darkened doorways. He pulls his old herringbone overcoat more tightly around him, wishing for the belt and leather buttons, which have long since disappeared.

He falls again, tripping on cobblestones under the snow. He picks himself up and looks about. He seems to have stumbled into the old part of town. The streets have narrowed and become more confusing. There are fewer traffic lights, the streetlamps look like converted gaslights (it's darkening, they're coming on), many of the signs, especially those on store windows, are handpainted, there are corner newsstands and small cafés and shops selling antiques. In the window of one, there's an old faded movie poster for sale, advertising *Lucky Pierre's Bachelor Party*. Bygone times. Also a tin mechanical toy of a man fucking a woman from the rear. The man has a thin mustache and a grin that looks more like a death rictus. The woman looks more beatific, or else retarded. Simple action—he pumps steadily, she pushes back to receive each thrust, her breasts swinging. She's naked, he's dressed in black socks. Period piece. Well, the past. Better not think about it. He staggers on, no longer sure just why but glad to be out of the old slum alley. Likes it here. An old trolley rumbles by, ringing its bell. The crowds have thinned. Evening shoppers. It may even be warmer in this part of town. But not warm enough. When he comes to a bar, he pushes on in.

It's a cozy place: wooden beams, engraved mirrors, old dark carpets, yellowed lace curtains with velvet side drapes, dull bulbs in shaded wall lamps, gas fire in the fireplace, rugs on some of the tables, comfortable beat-up furniture losing its stuffing, sentimental tunes playing on an old jukebox, handful of clients, mostly alone, sitting melancholically at tables, the usual prostitute at one end of the bar, a bartender half asleep under an old black-and-white television, playing silently. Beautiful. He wants to stay. Forever. But the bartender won't let him. No bums allowed, he says flatly, and points to the door.

—I can pay, he says, and produces the bill from his pocket given him by the bot.

—Stage money, the bartender snorts. Worthless. Now get out.

Should have known. Never was good at business. And look what he's come to. He used to consider such seedy rundown neighborhood bars beneath him. Now it's like paradise and he can't stay. He glances at the lone woman at the bar, hoping he might be able to cadge a drink off her, but she looks down-at-the-heels too and is staring absently into her glass of water. He takes the bill back, might be good in some other part of town—A princess gave it to me, he says—and turns to go.

—Wait a minute, gramps, says the bartender. You're not by any chance Pete the Beast, are you?

—Some call me so.

—Oh, that's all right then. There was a classy young piece in here a bit ago in one of those new see-through outfits. She left her card and said to set you up if you came in. Didn't realize you'd be such a pathetic old fossil. So, what'll you have then?

—An old-fashioned, he says, hoisting himself up onto one of the high barstools, realizing yet again how stiffened up he's become, but greatly cheered. Seems right for the place.

—An old-fashioned! exclaims the bartender, hauling down a tatty old recipe book from a shelf of glasses and thumbing through it. Don't think I've made one of those since fuck was a dirty word!

—It was just an idea. Throw anything together. I'm not particular.

—Whiskey and soda?

—Forget the soda.

Oh, he feels good here. His heart is full of gratitude. And love. For his benefactress. For the bartender. For the world. He rubs his hands together, warming them up. Knotty old things; they don't feel real.

—Did Her Heinie say where she was going?

—Who?

—The one who's picking up the tab. The Princess.

—No, she didn't stay long. Wish she had. She lighted the place up. About the glitziest thing that's ever come in here. Had a pussy to die for. Granddaughter of yours?

—My bride, he says, tossing down the drink. The bartender laughs. Anyway, that was the royal plan. Hit me again.

—So, laughs the bartender, pouring. Met her at the ball, did you?

—She was a robot and I disenchanted her with my dick. Her ass was my prize.

—Ho ho, that's great! snorts the bartender. Some guys got all the luck! He wipes the bar with a rag. Like that sport up there on the screen. Fucking nine women at a time.

—Yeah, I know. That's me.

—Oh brother! I should have you in here regular to do a floor show, oldtimer!

—No, I'm serious. *Harem Scare 'Em,* it's called. One of the early ones. Long time ago.

—Musta been, pop. These old prehistoric reruns are all we got now worth looking at.

—Watch. In the next scene, they bring in a young virgin and break her in. All of them together. A kind of initiation ceremony.

—Yeah, I like that part. Gets pretty rough. But the chick's cute.

Cally. The greatest. He taps his glass and the bartender, shaking his head with amusement and disbelief, pours another. The woman at the far end of the bar is watching him furtively. When he turns toward her, she ducks her head again, tears nervously at her cocktail napkin. Sad little thing. A sweet kid, down on her luck. He wonders if he knows her. He's known so many. On another occasion, he might go sit by her, let her fondle him, cheer her up. But he considers himself off the set, as he used to say in his working life. Shop closed down. Unless he can find the Princess again. Could use a bit more of that. Made him feel young again. In a two-dimensional kind of way.

—Tell me, he asks the bartender, do you ever feel like you're living in a cartoon?

—Me? No. Nothing funny about this place. You're the first hoot I've had since the burly-cues closed down. But I'll bet you do, don't you, you old loony?

—I feel like I'm in one right now. I mean, look at me. It just makes no sense I've grown so old. I'm not *supposed* to grow old. It's not who I am.

—Yeah, I know what you mean, gramps. It catches you from behind and suddenly it's all over. Like another film of that guy up there: *Easy Cum*—

—*Queasy Go*. I know. But that's not exactly what I mean. I mean, I feel sometimes like it's animation itself that's killing me. I've got a friend who thinks that's how the world works. By animation.

—Who's that? That dazzling bride of yours?

—No. Well, maybe. I don't know, can't say for sure. But she thinks time's not continuous but a sequence of cold stills. And life snuck in somehow through the gaps between frames and heated things up.

—Oh, yeah, says the bartender. The gaps! He grins and makes a fucking gesture with his fingers. That's where life is, all right!

He taps his glass again and the bartender pours. Not much point in talking with him. He thinks the whole thing is just a stand-up comic routine. Kate may be right about time, he can't say; it's over his head. But she thinks life is warmth, whereas it's death, not life, that produces heat. Life just sucks it up to keep going. Up on the screen, his earlier self is pumping gouts of cum over Cally's face and bared young breasts. If she feels any warmth from them, it's because of all those dying sperm. What is any human tragedy compared to a single ejaculation? Warmth and movement. Time. They don't come cheap. He'll tell Kate that the next time he sees her. If he ever does again. Maybe he can just sit here and keep this tab running for a few years, wait for her to show up. Or for time to use him as a space heater. In this mellow if somber mood, he leans toward the bartender and asks about the woman at the other end of the bar.

—Oh, just a tramp, he says with a shrug. We fuck her, give her a drink, and throw her out, but she keeps coming back.

She seems to sense they are talking about her. She smiles up at him, the smile quivering on her lips, then ducks her head again.

—Suppose we could put a shot for the tramp on my tab?

—Don't see why not. She's not much of a drinker, though. She'll probably just ask for an unopened soft drink. I think she takes them home to her kids.

Up on the screen, the initiate, her ordeal concluded, has become the sheik's new favorite and, wearing only a veil, is being taken on his arm through the magnificent palace to view her new domain. A vast display of wealth, ease, power, voluptuous pleasures. All fake. Felt real at the time; he thought he really was a sheik. Always very suggestible. But it was just a mocked-up film set. Whereas this simple little bar is the real thing. It's as if he has found his way home at last. Of course, he couldn't do it on his own. He needs the Princess's tab. But, pushing in, he has somehow crossed a threshold, stepped out of the frame, as it were, joined the world. Here, there are no jump cuts, no reversals or lap dissolves. He is not being blown up, shrunk, morphed, wiped, or frozen. It's a kind of sanctuary. No one knows him here. Just as well the bartender doesn't believe him. For once, he is just who he is. Not much, and woefully decrepit, but his own private package. Feels good. He smiles and taps his tumbler again.

—Sir, thank you for the drink. It's the tramp, standing shyly by his elbow. You are a kind and generous man. Would you like to fuck me now?

He looks down on her from his perch on the stool while the bartender pours. A tired little creature who has not had an easy life. He shakes his head. He doesn't want to lose the mood he's fallen into. He's not hard and doesn't want to be.

—It's yours, he says. Enjoy. And he turns back to his fresh drink.

—But it doesn't seem right, she says. I'm an honest woman. I owe you—

—No, I want nothing, my dear. Just to be left alone.

She says nothing, but she doesn't turn away either. She stands there, her bottom lip quivering, her eyes threatening to fill with tears.

—You've probably made her feel rejected, you heartless old buzzard! mutters the bartender, wiping a glass and returning it to its shelf.

—Oh, sorry. Don't take offense, miss. I just meant I didn't want to impose my ugly old carcass on such a pretty young thing as you. I'm perfectly happy here on the barstool, as happy as I've ever been, and I don't want to leave. I don't want to go back outside—

—You would not be imposing, sir, she says in a tremulous voice, looking up at him with wide innocent eyes. And we don't have to go anywhere. We can use one of the tables.

—In here? He looks up at the bartender, who shrugs and nods his approval.

—Please, sir, she pleads. Then I can go home.

Well. She needs him. And as always—for she's right, he's a generous man—he answers the call. A bit public, but he's used to it. Beats the back alley.

He crawls down off the barstool, trying not to fall and break his brittle old legs. She takes his hand and leads him over to a big square table with a carpet thrown over it. Her hand is small and warm. Whatever warmth's true source, it gives him pleasure. A shared touch, human and real. There are a couple of people sitting there. They slide their chairs back but remain seated. Others drift over, drinks in hand, pull up chairs, or stand about. He takes off his coat, tosses it over a heavy captain's chair, kicks off his shoes, lowers his pants.

—Your coat's nice, the tramp says.

Probably she wants it. She has slipped her shoes off, but nothing else, and has crawled up on the table to wait for him, her calves dangling over the edge, knees together under her skirt hem. He's not as hard as he'd like to be, and the sight of his baggy gray belly and scrawny thighs is disheartening (fortunately, the lights are dim and made rosy by their shades), but he's an old trouper—prehistoric, as the bartender would have it—and he knows he will perform when the moment comes. Her desperate need has helped, for it has somewhat aroused him, being an entertainer by vocation and responsive to his audiences; and the tramp's sadness—she is lying back now, one hand knuckled at her mouth—touches his heart, and his heart, as always, prompts his gonads. Even the lowering of his pants has done its part, being an immemorial act of deep iconic power.

—My husband used to have one like it.

—You can have it, love. It's a trashcan special. It's where I live, you know: in the alley. We're in the same business, you might say. But I'm not going back out there, so I won't need it.

He drops his drawers, ignoring the dismissive grunts from the onlooking patrons, and goes over to the table, tosses her skirt back. Her hands come up reflexively to stop him, but then fall back. She closes her eyes and turns her head away as though trying to disappear into the carpet under her. She's trembling, frightened. Perhaps the sight of him revolts her.

—Are you sure you want this? he asks and she nods her head, biting her lip.

—At this rate, says one of the kibitzers, I'd just as soon go back and watch the reruns.

—He's not stiff enough to fuck warm butter.

—Give him time, says another. It ain't easy when you're that far over the hill; you gotta coax the thing along, gradual like.

—He needs to slap his thing around a tad. Get some blood in it.

—He needs to slap *her* around a tad. So far, it's a yawner.

As he tugs the waistband of her cotton panties down over the peaked hip bones, exposing her navel and tummy, he feels he's been here before. Well, the old illusion. One takes in similarity first, difference only later. Lift up, he says, when the panties get held back by her bottom, and, with a little gasp, she does so. Ah, no, this one is completely new. What the tramp has there is not so perfect maybe as Princess Beaver's, but it has a soft vulnerable sweetness unlike (he's sure) any he's seen before, lightly feathered with downy hair that rises narrowly from the tender crease like a thin plume of smoke. It is so delicate, so secretive and inimitable, *cunt* does not seem the right word for it, beautiful though the word be. It begs something more ornamental like *the walled garden of Eden, the palace of pleasure, the mandala of beatified saints, the inner court of the temple of love,* that sort of thing. He touches the nub of it with his gnarly old thumb and she flinches, bites her knuckles, clamps her knees together, her eyes still squeezed shut.

—Listen, lady. I've got my money's worth. Or somebody's. It's beautiful. You're beautiful. Now let's go back to the bar. I'll buy you another drink (there is some hissing from those watching), and you can—

—No! Please! I'm just a little nervous, sir. Go ahead.

She relaxes her knees enough for him to squeeze between them and push her trembling thighs apart. There is a light smattering of grudging applause from the other patrons like insensitive audiences everywhere. They should be whooping. They are in the presence of a pubic masterpiece. A couple of them come over to peer more closely, shrug, then settle back again. One of them says something about a green apricot, another: Tight as a clam. It's true. It's gorgeous, but there's no getting in there.

—Could you . . . ? she whispers. One hand has strayed into the plume of smoke. Could you kiss me first . . . ?

He leans down to kiss her fingers, lick gently at the knuckled pucker below them. His back is not going to like this. It is already protesting. He may have trouble straightening up again. This will, in the end, be a heroic fuck. If he ever gets that far. But it will also be a delicious one. Very slowly, as his tongue probes the pale little furrow, it begins to open up, breathe its sweet breath. Pink lips appear, touch his, withdraw. He finds them with his tongue, draws them out again, like the first silky petals of an opening bud. Gradually, they begin to kiss him back—tenderly, subtly, shyly, inquisitively—and her quivering thighs squeeze his ears, then draw apart and slowly rise, lifting her flowering lips to his, her reddening mouth pushing against grizzled one. He slips his arms under her thighs and she rests them on his shoulders. Her hands are in his hair. Now, as his tongue reaches more deeply into areas heretofore unrevealed, lapping hungrily at the rising nectar (it's been awhile since he's had something as good as this; all he can think of for some reason is picnics in sunny meadows), she returns his fervent kisses with equal fervor, her whole body atremble now and pitching rhythmically. He pauses to catch his breath, nuzzles her bobbing furrow with his nose (it seems to be whimpering, pleading, whispering words of love), licks at the tiny crinkled opening that has appeared below it as one might kiss an ear in passing, then returns to her eager lips. It has become, not a kiss, but The Kiss, a rapturous engagement of mouth to mouth. If it were being filmed, it would make cinematic history. Of course, he's good at it. Tools of the trade and all that, one of the first arts you have to learn and the last you forget. He might lose his hair, his teeth, his continence, his marbles, but he won't lose this. And she's a professional after all, if not a very experienced one; for all the seeming novelty, these lips have kissed before. Those watching seem more attentive, though they cannot resist the odd carping remark.

—He's sandpapering her poor thighs with that ratty beard of his!

—She probably likes it. If the little whore's not too calloused to feel it. He's pretty short-winded, though. I hope that's not a sign of things to come. To coin a phrase.

Now she is bucking and jerking, embracing him passionately with her thighs, clawing at his hair, her foaming red mouth wide open as if to swallow him whole. She grabs a fistful of his hair and tugs, and he slides forward on her body, dragging his tongue up her tummy, dipping in and out of her tiny dent of a navel, nuzzling under her clothing, his hand having replaced his tongue below, and her fingers there, too, working away. He would pause to open her blouse, but the tramp can't wait, her head twisting back and forth as if in agony, eyes still closed, little mouth agape—she reaches down and grabs his member and pulls it urgently inside her, clamping him with her thighs; it all happens so fast, he's inside even while he's still wondering how he will manage it. It's warm in there, muscular and exciting. He's almost forgotten how it could be. Too many robots. There is a piquant ripple of wet nibbling up and down his shaft as if she were exploring every inch of it. Too much—he begins, uncontrollably, to pump away.

—Careful, gramps! Not too fast.

—Just what I was afraid of. Show's almost over.

—I wish they'd switch positions so we didn't have to look at his shriveled old butt. Sort of puts you off.

—Still, give the old geezer credit. At his age, he can still get it up. More or less. And look at him go!

Yes, they're right. Too soon. But what can he do? He's on his way. He can only hope she stays with him. He bites his tongue, does his best. He tries to remember all his old film titles. He counts the teeth in the tramp's gaping mouth. He concentrates on the pattern of the carpet they're on. He thinks about Kate's notion of time as a fluttering sequence of still frames and tries to crank down the projector speed—all to little or no avail. He's pounding away, picking up speed. Luckily, she's beginning to peak too. She turns pale, whines, her throat flushes, tears squeeze out her closed eyes, her back arches, her hips flex, she chews at his beard, bites her hands, his neck, claws his buttocks. Her eyes pop open and she stares straight at him. Or through him. A searching look of pain and love. Then she loses focus, cries out, and the spasms, which have already begun, rapidly mount in intensity and number, shaking her from top to bottom. Her whole body's like a live wire, and he's blowing too; those around them are on their feet now, enthused at last, cheering them on; they're both groaning, yelping, she's sobbing as one climax overtakes another, his own orgasm singular but drawn out and succulently draining, and slowly the spasms diminish and their bodies cease to pummel each other and instead melt together affectionately like old comrades embracing after a dangerous campaign, and a weariness overtakes him and his back pain returns. He starts to roll off her, but she clasps him with both arms and legs and asks him to stay a moment, while little vaginal tremors grip him and let him go and grip him and let him go again. Finally, the little tramp's arms drop to the side, she turns her head away, and he rolls over on his aching back beside her. The other patrons have drifted off. He remembers polite applause. His own heart is full of operatic gratitude.

—Beautiful, he sighs, closing his eyes.

—It was, she says.

—You are, he says, taking her hand. I wish I'd met you earlier, love. How did a sweet thing like you, you know, end up with a life like this?

—When my husband left me and the children penniless, it was all I knew how to do. Except make little movies nobody wanted to see anymore.

—Left you? Movies?

—Peter gave away our house for another woman and went off to join the circus.

—Oh my god!

—It's not so terrible. I'm sure he couldn't help it. He did what he had to do. He was very beautiful and I loved him very much. I promised to wait for him to come home, no matter how long it took.

—Connie—?!

—How do you know my name? The bartender must have told you.

He turns his head to look at her. She is lying face up, still flushed with her emotions, eyes closed, her perky little nose in the air, lips parted, one hand under her head, her skirt up under her chin. Perfectly placid, perfectly still. Like a little doll. Exactly as he—now, at last—remembers her. He has just—how can he not have known? how quickly we forget!—fucked his wife. His helpmeet. The girl next door. His one true love. It must have been wonderful, their time together, though he can't remember it having been better than this. He can't remember anything having been better than this, but his memory is not long. They'd had something good going, though, he knows that; they were a family and what had been random improvisation suddenly had meaning. Structure. Plot. She captured that in her little home movies. Her embroidered towels. And somehow he left it. Or it left him. He can't remember. And now here they are, living examples of the consequences of such profligacy. Two wasted whores on a barroom table. But there might still be time to recover something of what they had before. The cottage of course; that's gone. Blown up. Probably the towels too. Wasn't theirs anymore anyway. He'd thrown it away in a wanton moment, one of countless, alas. But he could find something else, a little flat for two. Plus the children. However many. Worry about that later. They could make little movies together. A beautiful last reel. But how would they live? Maybe she could support them both. She's still so lovely. Or they could work up some sort of team act: a Beauty and the Beast sort of thing. Or maybe he can get help from the Princess; she seems a generous sort. Though her money doesn't seem to be any good. And does he want to go back to home movies again? They had their moment, but on the whole they make poor viewing as reruns. And look at him now. Why would she want a beat-up old geezer who can't even get up off the table and put his pants on by himself? Probably he should let her keep her illusions. Pretty Peter Prick. And he his freedom. For what it's worth. Not much.

He is wrestling with these deep thoughts when the bartender comes over and tells him if he doesn't put his clothes on he'll have to leave. The tramp can stay there if she likes, he says, but you're an uncomely sight. The other patrons are beginning to complain.

—This tramp is my wife! he announces gravely. He hadn't meant to reveal himself, but there, it's out. He realizes that fundamental decisions are being taken. He squeezes her hand.

—He's just teasing, says Connie, laughing, pulling her hand back. Can you imagine?

—No, Connie, it's me, your husband Peter Prick! I've been through some tough times, they've taken their toll, but it's really me! And I promise now, if you'll have me, I'll stay with you forever!

—It's sweet of you to pretend, she says. You want to cheer me up. You even *look* a little like my husband, and he wore a coat like the one you gave me, but my Peter was much younger and handsomer. He smelled better, too.

—I thought you said you were marrying that Princess who was in here, says the bartender, helping him labor to his feet. Can't do it himself. That was some fuck. Did his back some permanent damage.

—Yeah, well, different medium, as you might say. He is standing, legs apart, arms out for balance, rocking a bit. He staggers, a step at a time, toward his clothes, thrown over the captain's chair. The jukebox, which has been playing an old romantic ballad about anal love, switches suddenly to something more regal and ceremonial, like a wedding march or music to strip by. Probably mocking his crippled stagger.

No, wrong again. The bartender nods past his shoulder and says: Well, get ready, pops. The other medium just reeled in.

It's his beautiful benefactress, standing in the doorway like an apparition, luminous as neon. Princess Beaver. Stunning. She makes the place look like the rundown little dive it is. Spent as he is, he feels his eyes trying to zoom out of their sockets again. H'lo, Beast, she says. I been combing the streets for you. Just spiffed up the palace. We're ready to tear.

He looks down at the tired little thing on the table beside him and up at the lively animated figure in the doorway. Who is covering his bar bill. Really, there's no choice. Sorry, miss, he says to the one on the table. I don't know what came over me. I'm not Peter Prick and, to the best of my recollection, I never have been. I guess I just wanted to make you feel better.

—That's all right. I knew you weren't him. But she's crying.

—Listen, I meant what I said, love. You're beautiful. Don't cry. I'll—I'll—let me just run this errand, and I'll be right back. We'll work something out. She turns her head away. He glances apologetically at the doorway: It's empty! She's gone!

—She left, says the bartender. She looked pretty miffed you didn't chase right after her. She took her card back, too.

Oh no! His pants are in a tangle, can't find his shorts. Have to go without. He's reneged on his promise to Connie never to leave her, he's lied to her; now he takes back the gift he gave her; hauling on the old overcoat and staggering painfully out the door, somewhat doubled up still. Well, she can have his pants. Hold my seat here, he shouts back over his shoulder. I'll be back in a minute!

He's just in time to see the Princess, or the shimmering suggestion of her, disappear around the corner a block down, and he hobbles clumsily in that direction. Wait! he shouts into the dark silent streets, ghostily aglow with the packed ice and snow. When, with difficulty, slipping and stumbling in his stocking feet, he reaches the corner, he catches sight of the glimmer again, turning yet another corner, and he continues his labored pursuit. This stretch takes him longer. He's snorting and wheezing by the time he gets there, only to glimpse far down the hushed street a dim sparkle, which may or may not be the Princess, flickering around yet another corner.

He pauses to lean heavily against the building, his knees shaky. Under the coat, his nether parts are frozen. It's as if he wasn't even wearing it. His feet, too: blocks of ice. He's winded, his back feels broken, his ears bitten, his nose is running, his eyes have teared up, he's half blind at best, who knows what he's been seeing? He's a foolish old man. Chasing a phantom. A literal will-o'-the-wisp. Ignis fatuus. Fatuous idiot: his life story. No more. That's it. He turns back. He should never have left Connie back at the bar. Should never have left their honeymoon cottage in the first place. He knows this now. Nothing could be clearer. He's not quite sure how he will convince her to take him back, but somehow he'll manage it. He has to. He retraces his steps with crunching difficulty, his heart full of rue. But the bar's not there anymore. Must have made a wrong turn. He staggers from corner to corner, peering down streets, looking for the bar's lights. All dark. It's starting to snow again.

What now? He's so cold he can't think. His lobes are like ice cubes: he shakes his head and they rattle. Wait. Is this the neighborhood of the coldwater flat he shared with Cleo? Maybe he could find it. Must be their anniversary.

As usual. He's missed a few. Consequently he's dropped out of her sights. But he was still her first and she his (probably; there's a confusion of what he used to call memories), and she doesn't forget things like that. Cassie or Lottie might have a squat somewhere around here too. Even better. But what fantasies. In a maze like this, on a night like this. Like trying to find a pearl in a hailstorm, as old Kate would say. Go suck an oyster. No, better just scrounge about for some rags and newspapers and curl up somewhere and try to survive the night. But then he sees that glimmer again. Flickering across an intersection a few blocks down. Now he has no choice. She's his only hope.

He sets off again. He feels he is the only thing moving in this bleak night, he and that wisp of light. And he but barely. It's like that nightmare he has of all the projectors freezing up. Everything stopping. He is trying not to. When, at last, he stumbles woodenly into the intersection, he is not surprised to see the glimmer a few blocks away. He takes a step toward it, expecting it to vanish again. This time, however, it does not. It seems to be waiting for him. It (he no longer thinks of it as she) may only be cruelly prolonging the tease, but the faint glimmer's pause is a glimmer of faint hope, and though he's too iced up to move any faster, it makes him determined to stagger on as best he can, step by painful step. For, what else can he do?

When he reaches the source of the glimmer, however, it turns out to be nothing but a flickering streetlamp. That's the bad news. The good news is that it is in front of an old abandoned wreck of a movie house. The Palace. Aha. As promised. He has arrived. The sign on the door says CONDEMNED but it's open, the door hanging off its hinges. The weather's not much better inside: dark, musty, cold. But out of the wind. No sign of the Princess. He expected none. He limps through the trash and rubble of the ruined lobby and pushes on through the double doors into the empty auditorium. Woefully abused by time, neglect, and vandalism, but vast and ornate; must have been a beauty in its time. He feels a kind of kinship with it. A bit breezier in here (there's a hole in the dome and the snow's drifting in), but there are seats he can curl up in. In one, miraculously, down near the front where he always sits at the movies, he finds a smelly old blanket and, utterly exhausted, he crawls under it. It's not luxury, but it feels like home.

—You got here just in the nick, Pete. There is someone else under the blanket with him, as it happens. In fact, though he's too frozen in those parts to feel her there, he's sitting on her. She doesn't seem to mind. She puts her arms around him under the coat. I see you lost your pants somewheres along the way.

—Occupational hazard, Kate, he rumbles. He's begun to shiver, his teeth are chattering, and the badly frozen bits are starting to tingle and burn. She hugs him tighter.

—Can't even find your little seedpods.

—It was too cold for them. They've gone inside.

—Anyhow you made it. It's a world premiere. I was worried you was gonna miss it.

—Yeah, I could tell by the crowds out there trying to get in, he says. The buzzing sting of his thawing parts has turned them into irritable erogenous zones, aroused but untouchable. Whose is it?

—Yours.

—Mine? He laughs, though it comes out more like a dry cough.

—Nobody else's butt.

—I'm an old fuck, Kate. I haven't made a film in years.

—You've never stopped, luv. You still got that bill the Princess passed you?

—Sure. In my shirt pocket. But it's just play money.

—It'll do, she says, plucking it out of there. Now wait here a min.

—Actually, I was thinking about taking another run around the block.

She lifts him and skids out from under, gives his tingling cock a squeeze, and goes hobbling up the dark aisle in her humpy old-lady way. While she's gone, probably for good—what's there to come back for?—he nuzzles his head into the blanket, glad to have it to himself. Lets his lids fall. World premieres. Well, she was just rubbing it in, but there was a day: wheeling searchlights, limousines, cheers, crazed groupies, police cordons, autographs, his name in lights. Something went wrong. Who knows what? Just life, probably, if what he's had could be called one. More like a dream. A kind of flickery nothing that's all there is. The sort of thing he was chasing in the street. But if a dream, who's the dreamer, who the dreamt? It's a question he has often asked himself in other ways, such as Where's the projector, Where's the screen? With such conundrums, he seeks to thaw out his brain, though for what purpose he can't imagine.

Dear old Kate does return, he was wrong to doubt her, and even with his eyes closed and half dozing, he knows what she's brought back. He rears up out of the blankets with a croak of joy. It's a miracle! Hot buttered popcorn! Oh my god! he cries, tears springing to his eyes. Where did you find this?

—I invented it. Now, scoot over, ol' bones, and gimme a piece a the blanket.

He sees that the house lights, which still work somehow on their dangling wires, have come up halfway, and people are crowding in behind Kate, filling the aisles, chattering, kicking at the rubbish, brushing away the cobwebs, looking for the best seats. There are hundreds trying to jam in, maybe thousands, most with buckets of popcorn of their own, perfuming the auditorium. Seats bang and creak. The Mayor's there with all her entourage (the look she gives him could only be called affectionate), Cleo with her news team, Lottie and the Extars, raising hell up in the balcony. *We love you, Crazy Leg!* they shout, and stamp their feet. *Knock 'em dead!* Cissy with clipboard, glasses on the end of her nose and a pencil behind her ear, hurries down the aisle, looking a bit frantic, confers briefly with Cora, then dashes out again, and lights come on up in the projection booth. Bald naked Cassie floats past with a mysterious smile, passing out her pleasure tabs like candy, and goes to sit on the floor under the lip of the false stage under the screen, her back to it, watching the watchers. Clara, striding by, casts a professional eye over his present decay and winces. She hesitates, seems about to come over for a closer look, changes her mind, and takes a seat across the aisle where she can keep an eye on him. Cleo, interviewing Cora, gives him a thumbs-up over the Mayor's shoulder. Even Connie's there, still dressed as he's just seen her in the bar; she blows him a loving kiss and holds up his pants with a cheery smile. He smiles back at them all around his mouthfuls of popcorn. He's never tasted anything better in his life. He is utterly transported.

The house lights dim or else the bulbs burn out, they all quickly take their seats, the shouts and chatter die away, and the old frayed curtains pull aside in a cloud of dust and fluttering moths. Kate grasps his cock reassuringly. I've got you this far, Pete, she says with a tender squeeze, now you're on your own, ol' son. Hope for the breast, as they say, and prepare for the wurst . . .

She's still got a grip on him as though afraid to let go when, with a crackle, the titles come up, snow falling through the projector's beam like stardust, and he is gratified to see his own famous nom d'amour back up on the big screen: LUCKY PIERRE! it says, HIS . . .

FINAL FUCK!

Reel 9: Calliope

Film Festival

announces the huge sign over the arched entrance to the midway, through which he is being led by Cally, not so much pulling him along by his penis (though the effect is the same) as playing with it as they walk, as she is wont to do whenever it is exposed, which is most of the time, ever more so on this occasion, dressed only in his socks and shirttails as he is. He would return the favor, as is always her more or less urgent desire, but he's still munching popcorn and both hands are occupied, the one with holding it, the other with pushing it into his mouth.

A LUCKY PIERRE REVIVAL!

the sign overhead goes on to say . . .

THE CINEMATIC EVENT OF THE CENTURY!

Well, revival, yes; he could use a little of that. The midway down which they walk, she with more grace than he, is a green-carpeted corridor through the middle of a vast cleared fairground space somewhere in the inner city, the rest of the area taken up by movie houses, gambling booths, old-fashioned Dirty Bingo tents and mommy-and-daddy fun houses, food stalls, souvenir and sex-toy stands, peep shows, tattoo parlors, and carnival rides. A calliope is playing somewhere and the day is unusually bright, if, as always, overcast. It is all very cheerful, and it has just such an effect upon him; he feels less weighed down. He stands taller, walks more lightly. Even in stocking feet. His shoes? who knows.

They have apparently brought all the movie houses in the city here. He had not realized there were so many. There's the Pit, the Majism, the Bush, and the Pudding. The Foxy, the Bare-Mount, and the Cloven Tuft. Many he doesn't even recognize, though he thought he knew them all. Perhaps it's their new setting. They look more naked somehow, their skins raw where torn away from all the buildings that once crowded around them. They are showing everything from an old Wee Willie classic, *Young Beginners,* at the Veinous, which specializes in discounted entertainment for the elderly, to the animated *Pete the Beast and Old One-Eye* for the kiddies at the Buried Shaft. And where is its creator? Weren't they just having a snuggle? He looks back over his shoulder. The Phallus Theater behind them is screening something called *Fast Forward.* Doesn't remember it, but that's hardly all he does not remember. Have they just come from there? A blank.

—What happened to my overcoat? he asks.

—It's been thrown away. It was a filthy old rag.

—It's been with me a long time.

—I know. Too long. You won't need it where we're going.

It's true, he doesn't really need it, even now. Warmer than usual. He squints up into the sky. Maybe there are a lot of hot lamps up there he doesn't see.

—Now get rid of that popcorn, Willie, and perk up a bit, she whispers, giving his peter a warning tug. Here come some tourists.

He hears shouts: *Hey, look! It's Lucky! Lucky's back!*

He stuffs the rest of the buttered popcorn into his mouth and drops the empty tub through the bristly slot of a municipal quimbin, wipes his buttery fingers on his shirttails. How do I look? he asks around chewed corn.

—Beautiful, she laughs, manipulating him urgently as the crowds descend. But we only have to cross the midway, then we'll get you shaved and bathed and dressed in something clean.

—I already feel better.

—Of course you do, my love. You're with me. Now, as you have often told me: swallow what you have in your mouth, dear, give me a squeeze, and smile for your fans.

The amateur photographers are already clicking away. Some of them have visited the souvenir stalls and are wearing false mustaches and rubber pegos flopping from their flies and skirts, or wigs and merkins and plastic breasts meant to resemble those of his lovers. Cally lets go of the tiller, having done the best she could, and now is cuddling in romantic fashion against his shoulder while stroking his ass with her manicured nails. He loves that; as always, it both soothes and excites him. He lifts her skirt to squeeze her cheeks in the traditional fanzine manner (*click! click! click!* go the cameras at their backs), marveling yet again at their silky curves and youthful bounce. She was always fresh and beautiful enough to play little girls in the movies, still is, and she can do anything. As a child actress in the Wee Willie days, she once played an old granny who initiated him into sex by gumming his stiffened winkie. This was around the time she'd lost her two front baby teeth. Of course he got initiated several times, he was a slow learner, so to speak, and before she was done with it, his Wee Willie days were over.

—Is it really him? He's so old!

—And he's only half hard. When I was a kid, that dingaling was something to see! A real woofer! I mean, just look at this classic scene in my guidebook from *Playing at Hot Cockles*!

—Wow, that's great! they cry, crowding around, peering over the owner's shoulders as he activates it. Look at that monster go!

—Well, it's just a short clip, that's all they give you in books, but you can see the whole movie over at the Orianal.

—I'm heading there now! It's gotta be better than this!

—Maybe he's saving it for the big one.

—Maybe it's not the real Lucky Pierre.

—Sshh! he's really in disguise! confides Cally, in her most breathless manner. We were hoping to get through to the studio without being recognized!

This inside connection gives them all a thrill (and him, too: *the studio!* how he longs to be in again!) and they crowd around once more, snapping photos, asking questions, exposing their private parts to be stroked or kissed. There are autograph hunters among them and they ask for the usual dick-prints, but Cally, who by this time has her index up his rectum, as though to wag his digit like a finger puppet, tells them there will be a special time and place for that at the Picturedrome, and they should all go and sign up on the time sheets.

—Hey, quick, get another picture! It's beginning to move!

So it is, though who's to say whether that's from Cally's playful finger or from his own reveling in the feel of her wondrous buns? How long has it been? His callipygian Cally. Knowing his appetite—indeed, need—for novelty, she has always loved to trick him into thinking she's someone different, disguising herself in a thousand ways, fooling him most of the time and so arousing him ever with the prospect of new adventures, making, as she always says, not only for a better movie but also for more fun; but once her incomparable ass comes into view or hand, all masks are down just like her drawers. He'd know its splendors anywhere. He loves to kiss it, lick it, snuggle in it, eat off it, caress it, smack it, sleep on it, project films on it while fucking her from behind or in a mirror, and she loves him to do all these things and whatall else might come to mind. He loves even just to hold it as he's holding it now. Gorgeous as she is, she is hard to focus on, this woman of many faces, many parts; this is one of the best ways.

Cally then shoos them all away with friendly little pats and whispered kisses, making them promise to tell no one they've seen him, and she takes hold of his penis again and leads him stealthily on down the midway, though to the rear he can still hear the cameras clicking away. Which, as he knows, excites Cally and projects her into performance mode. Her stealth is stealth enacted. She steps along, seeing herself step along, sometimes even seeing herself see herself stepping along, an experience he also often suffers, and no doubt would be suffering now were he not distracted by all the fun-fair booths and movie marquees. It's as though his whole life, or at least his life in movies (and what other life has he had?), has been laid out here on the fairground as a geographical cluster to be explored as memory might be, chronology merely one path among many between the parts of his life, sequence disrupted and spread out on a map, time's passing perceptible only in the wrinkle count and program notes. If even there, for neither are ever to be trusted. Yet by reducing time to objects and places, space itself all but disappears, for such is the power of time. In the souvenir booths they are selling costume relics, collections of pubic hair, his dried semen (presumably useful as an aphrodisiac and a cure for melancholy), unedited clips off the cutting room floor, stained sheets, used condoms, things that are largely valueless but for the invested time, in its performative guise as finality, that resides in them, and for what time has done to them since it took up residence.

That word, as if recently read or heard, has been nagging at him actually since they began this stroll: *finality*. Or *final*. Final something, he doesn't know what. Maybe he saw it on that sign over the entry arch. A final festival. Or up on a screen or on a poster or marquee. They are passing one now, the marquee of the Pintle Case, advertising a double feature of *Horsebuns and Whines* and *Feeling Blue: The Traveling Salesman and the Lonesome Wife*. Final *feeling?* Maybe. Probably not. These movies are no doubt Connie's. He feels an unexpected twinge of jealousy. When he wonders out loud who played the salesman, Cally laughs and says, Who else but the master himself, Willie? Don't you remember?

—But then—?

—Oh, *Blue* is a *real* movie, Willie, your ex is *not* in it, nor is it one of her jiggly *hand* jobs, she adds and winks broadly.

She's still performing, her body poised, angled, her expression one of studied adoration, touched with amusement. She is underscoring every third or fourth word. And following a script. But the tourists are not around.

—You were peddling vibrators, dildos, and clit *stimulators* door to door. The wife protested moral repugnance and was resistant—which as you know is *not* an easy act to perform with a straight *face*—but you won out in the end, by wit and cunning, not by force. You were *brilliant*! You won the Best Actor of the *Year* award for it. They said you had a genius for cynical integrity and tender aggression. *Now* do you remember?

—Cally, he asks, looking around, where are the cameras?

—Cameras? Whatever are you *talking* about? Look! There's the Picturedrome!

—You're not fooling me, Cally. We're in another film. What's going on?

She sighs, somewhat exasperatedly. Could be an act, could be real exasperation.

—Oh, Willie, if you must know, Cleo's doing a documentary about the making of our next film, that's all, and this walk is part of it. I just didn't want you to be too self-conscious.

Ah. He might have known. At the Picturedrome, which used to be the old Organ Grinder, if memory serves (it rarely does, except in such odd ways), but is now called the Lucky Pierre Memorial Multiscreen Picturedrome, they are featuring all the great golden oldies from *First Night* and *Beating Around the Bush* to *Maiden Voyage, The Bishop's Finger,* the big-budget musical *Cock to Cunt and Fuck Again,* plus *Bananas and Cream,* and *Firkytoodle*. On monitors in the lobby: *Fantastic Raw Footage from the Early Years*. Live orchestral accompaniment.

—It's maybe not the most beautiful old movie house on the midway, Cally says timidly, for she knows what it is he is taking in, but it has character.

—Retrospectives, memorials, relics. . . . It's over, isn't it, he says. He feels the heaviness returning, the stiffness, the bending of his back. His winkie drops its head in dismay. From Wee Willie to Pete the Beast. In the blink of an eye. Of a shutter.

—No, it all just shows how loved you are, Willie. It doesn't *mean* anything.

—Those tourists back there, he says. They were all so old.

—Nonsense. There are lots of kids too. Look around.

—They're just playing on the rides, they're not interested in my movies. There are no big crowds here. I'm a thing of the past. She reaches for his penis again, but he evades her. And what were all those guidebooks with film clips for?

—Your fans. They like to retrace your historical itinerary and do honor to it by way of imitation. A lot of the original film sets have been reconstructed, and they can act out your movies on them. The guidebook has scripts to follow and the clips show them how. They're called pizzle missals. This is a nice thing, Willie. You shouldn't be grumpy.

—But it's really the end, isn't it? A historical itinerary is history. The pizzle missal pilgrimage honors the dead past. The dead pizzle. Those fans were probably hired extras. This documentary's my last film.

—Of course not! Don't be so morbid! Why, there are *lots* of plans! We're about to do a new film together right now. Look!

She points to another sign over the doors of the Memorial Picturedrome. COMING SOON TO THIS THEATER! EXCLUSIVE NEW SPECIAL FEATURE FOR THE LUCKY PIERRE FILM FESTIVAL! WORKING TITLE: LEAVING THE ISLAND. WATCH FOR DETAILS!

—The studio's right here at the back of the Picturedrome. Now come on, lover! Cut the weepy Willie act, give me a kiss and a diddle, and let's go start the action!

🎬

The film's associate producer and artistic director wants a deeper crease in the bushy mount being built to represent the rise at the center of the island, whereon stands Calliope's Temple. She is accused of trying to make it look too much like her own. She smiles faintly at this sisterly jibe, as do others, but there is not the usual lighthearted tittering and follow-on banter. An unwonted solemnity has settled over the studio. Even jokes about the woowallah silliness have been few and have inspired exchanges of tender glances more than laughter. The animator and robot designer has fashioned a new set for this sequel, each modeled after the revered membrum of the resident island deity and each a miniature robot on its own, capable not only of a great variety of spontaneous movements and metamorphoses but of passionate emotions and erotic sentiments as well. They have all been tested many times and found to be impeccably manufactured and almost heartbreakingly satisfying.

The temple itself exists, so far, only as a set of models, which will themselves be part of the film, as only the façade and an interior corner of the adytum will actually be built, the rest open for a battery of lights, cameras, sound booms, mikes, and wind machines—all the paraphernalia of a film studio sound stage. There will also be digital image processors and workstations, but this will not be a sketchbook-style video project. It is carefully scripted and will use only high-end cameras and top quality 70mm film stock, for as the producer has declared, this is a film of transcendent importance. No expense will be spared.

—The original film of *Shipwrecked on the Isle of the Nymphs,* the artistic director says, pausing to speak into the camera, used a text-rich script, finding its humor and eroticism in a spirited interplay of word and image. She is sitting amid a vast array of electronic and audiovisual equipment, white boards and bulletin boards with pinned-up posters, photos, cartoons, and phone numbers, a marked-up shooting schedule, dope sheets, coffee cups, mirrors, and overloaded bench tops. The television monitor above her head is showing the original movie over and over in looped reruns with the sound off. The scene on the screen at the moment is the one early in the film when the nymphs are trying to revive the unconscious castaway. The castaway's knees have been doubled back to his chest (they think: her chest) and the nymphs are fondling what they believe to be fallen breasts, considering the possibility of trying to push them back up where they belong. This sequel, the artistic director goes on to say, will focus more on the emotional impact of sheer imageness, with as little text as possible. And few if any special effects or digital manipulation. Direct contact with the seen; that is our goal. While it can be seen.

There is an interruption. The star has arrived, led in in the customary fashion by the film's director, who is also its costar, or one of them. When he washed up on the island as a castaway, his condition was not of the best; now it is unspeakably worse. He is unkempt and unwashed, scrawny, bleary-eyed, a bit shrunken, semitumescent at best, dressed in nothing but a dirty old shirt and socks with holes in the heels. He staggers in with bent knees turned out, elbows akimbo for balance, chin down and belly bagging, and seems dazed and confused, but as he slowly takes in his surroundings a blissful smile steals over his beardy face and tears come to his eyes. Oh yes! he can be heard to whisper. The artistic director rushes over to receive him, clearly relieved that he is here and filming can begin, but also simply happy to see him again, as her affectionate kisses attest. The others, too, embrace him and lead him into their midst, including the director of this documentary about the film, who slaps his tired old ass (it's cold) and bites his earlobe and reminds him of all the missed anniversaries. I got distracted, he says. A hot bath is ordered up, a shave and a haircut, manicure and pedicure, to be followed by a massage with hot oils, all to be filmed for possible use in the current production.

—I'd like everyone to drop what they're doing and help the stage manager with the bath and massage, says the artistic director. We'll give his body the same tight treatment it got when he first washed up. I want to see as many hands on him as possible.

—When it first washed up where? he asks.

—As soon as you've finished with his bath, she adds, you can dye his hair and put it in curlers.

—The hair on his head as well? asks the stage manager and director of research, who is taking his pulse and blood pressure and checking him for scabies, hernia, and hemorrhoids, while the props and publicity person cuts away the filthy rags that were once a shirt.

—If you like. Why not? Then it will go with the rest. When you're done, dress him in a toga. You'll find a fresh supply in the wardrobe locker.

While his bath is being drawn in a special bathing pool originally built for *Harem Scare 'Em,* now redesigned as a peaceful sandy bay, and lamps and cameras are being moved into position, she leads the star over to the temple set, where the first row of columns is already being anchored in place, to tell him about the new production under way and his part in it. It's more or less the same concept as the original, she says, but with big-budget enhancements. We have some ideas for the phallus-worship scenes that will blow your socks off. Metaphorically speaking, she adds, glancing down at the frayed remnants he is presently wearing. Those will be coming off sooner than that.

—But I was so young then! he rumbles hoarsely. Look at me, Cissy. I could never play that part now.

—You are as old, L.P., as we wish you to be, she replies with a cool endearing smile, and she kisses him on the nose. Which itself will be a challenge to the makeup crew.

—And what's this? he asks, picking up a ring binder lying in the seat of the director's chair and thumbing through it. The script?

—What? Hm, yes. Whose is this? she calls out. These are not supposed to be left lying around!

—I thought it was to be called *Leaving the Island*, he says. But here on the title page there's only a big double-F. What does that stand for?

—Ah . . . let's see, that can't be the title, she says, taking the script away from him. I think that's just the camera instruction for the first scene. Full Frontal, probably. Yes, I'm sure—

—The script says you're opening with an overview of the island. How can that be full frontal?

—Oh, does it? Right. Something Focus maybe. Fine Focus. Or Full Frame, yes, that must be—

—Why can't I see it? What's the big secret?

—No secret, L.P.! It's just—well, we want to keep your performance fresh and spontaneous. There aren't many lines anyway, only one scene with a bit of dialogue, and that one can be ad libbed—

—That first F is for Final, isn't it? I've seen it somewhere. What's the other word?

—The other word? Ah, Frenzy? Feature? Fantasy? She looks about for help, twisting the script in her hands.

—Fuck, says an off-camera voice. Fuck, hero. It's your Final Fuck.

He blanches and bends around to stare up at the camera, which is slowly zooming in to examine the face of a man turning to confront the onrush of history. His knees sag, his jaw drops.

—Oh! Now you've upset him! cries the properties person, interposing herself. You're very cruel! She's starting to cry, the little twit, and her fists are doubled up and trembling.

—It's all right, says the artistic director, resting a calming hand on her assistant's shoulder, while raising the middle finger of the other at the camera. It'll be a different film now in some ways, but we can still pretty much shoot it as written. Now, have you found all those items we need for the temple interior shots?

—Yes, says the properties person in her whimpery little voice, glancing at the stricken star. But I want to use the yellow sofa too.

—But that doesn't go at all! This is an ancient temple!

—I know, but—

—That list I gave you was the result of Clara's careful research. Our whole thrust in this film is for generic integrity and a lush sparseness. An economy of means to achieve a maximum result. Less is more here. We want intense audience participation, and that's done by giving them something compelling to look at while forcing them to fill in the empty spaces. We can't be loading the scene up with anachronistic junk!

—It's *not* junk. She seems about to cry again. And it means so much to me. . . .

The artistic director sighs, shrugs. She's a softie. A pushover. All right, she says. But we'll have to cover it with something.

—There's that ancient tapestry I brought over from the lobby of City Hall, suggests the producer. She already has her tunic on and is ready to get going. The one of the maenads tearing someone apart that you planned to drape over the Altar of Resurrection, as you call it in the script.

—Right. That's perfect. Bring it in. It's rolled up behind the casting couch in the director's office. Meanwhile let's get on with the bathing sequence. Is everything in place? The overhead camera is the key here. It's kind of like an animation camera, Kate, so why don't you operate it? Add a light blue gel to a couple of the lamps, please, and flash a little sparkle off the surface—

—The tapestry's not there anymore! someone shouts from the director's office.

—What? But—

—He's gone too, says the stage manager. I went to test his bathwater and when I came back . . .

There is a gasp and the studio falls silent.

The associate producer and artistic director turns slowly to face the camera. That loose script, she says. It was yours, wasn't it, Cleo? You put it there on purpose. And now we've lost him.

—Don't worry, Cece baby, I'll soon have him in my sights again. He's cranking along in low gear now. It's not hard to spot an old wheezer staggering along with a lot of crazed floozies on his back.

—If he ends up at the coldwater flat instead of back here at the studio, my friend, says the producer grimly, rising to her full height, we'll dismantle your stupid little flat and burn your films. All of them. Is that clear?

—We want a scene that involves everybody, says the artistic director, and the others nod. They are all staring angrily at the camera now. One or two of them are in tears. It's a good shot. Only the director is smiling. Without a script, it's the only thing the bimbo knows how to do.

—Don't get your tunics in a twist, ladies. Even if he should turn up there, you're all invited.

🎬

The message has been clear. Cleo delivered it. The numberless days with heir numberless fucks are numbered. And the number is one. Damn that Cally for dragging him back there. Not her fault, of course. They're all in on it. And his resistance, it must be admitted, was minimal. Lured by a word and the promise it held. Not a four-letter word, though it contains one: him, in effect. And, oh, how it warmed his heart to be back in one! How he has missed the buzz, the tension, the popping and dousing of lights, the sound of cameras cranking! Though they don't crank anymore. That's not the point. It was the feeling of coming home. He who is otherwise without. The studio. And now he can't go back, ever again. That's a film he cannot make, nor can he in consequence ever make another. He is a castaway now, in truth.

So, what next? He assumes they'll come looking for him, are probably already looking. Too much invested. He has to make a move soon, find a way out of here without being seen. It is colder and less bright on the fairground than when he came through with Cally, and the crowds, never large, have dwindled. He is huddled behind some trashcans, blanketed in an old wall hanging, familiar to him from his days of discipline in City Hall, in what would be an alley behind a movie house, if it were still in the street where it came from; but its new neighborhood is streetless and alleyless, the festival's cinemas scattered among carnival rides and concessions in no apparent pattern, and what he is looking at across the way, past the reconstructed film set for *The Nuns' Gardener,* the cocks-and-cunts carousel, and a tent of breasty bumper cars, is the crumbling façade of the grand old Strum. Where, according to the marquee, they are showing *Behind the Barn with Cousin Cuzzy*, an early special-effects film in which Cally played two different girls with whom he had sex at the same time. It climaxed with the arrival of two more identical cousins, Cally again playing both parts. Just camera tricks of course, double and quadruple takes and all that, but the odd thing is, he remembers actually fucking four Callys at once. Or being fucked; it was pretty overwhelming. Some animals in the mix as well. Farmyard wallowing used to be, back when *dirty* was still a pejorative, the really dirty stuff. Porn-on-the-cob, it was called in the trade. Now animals have become so exotic, barnyard fuckfilms are associated more with the genre of romance.

He has, of course, gone unrecognized by the tourists. Wouldn't recognize himself. They look more like him than he does with their false mustaches and foam-rubber dongs. Maybe that would be the way to disguise himself: as himself. Lose himself among his epigones. Have to shave, though, or the mustache wouldn't stick. No way to do that. And the tapestry's a dead giveaway. Have to get out from under it, warm as it is. Not many out here wearing one. He's like a stolen car with its plates still on. A walking advertisement. Which some have taken him for. Old man in a soft sandwich board pitching a flick about drunken housewives on a spree. Can't go around naked either, not in his condition and with the weather worsening. Maybe he can trade it for something. Some clothes or blankets or even some tenting. It should be worth a penny or two. He pulls himself creakily to his feet and goes stumbling down the midway, suffering a jibe and a kick or two as he goes but passing largely unnoticed. Many of the stalls, those still open, have CLEARANCE SALE signs up, it's bargain time, but none are selling anything to wrap himself in. Then, at a souvenir stand peddling an old junk line of Lucky Pierre body jewelry, thigh rings, cufflinks, shackles, wristwatches, and studded labia spreaders, he sees something so startlingly perfect, he nearly cries out: the vendor is wearing his old raggedy herringbone overcoat! Or if it's not the original it is, like Cally's country cuz, its identical twin!

—What are you nosing around here for, you old coot?

—Thinking of doing a little business.

—Well, everything's for sale, says the vendor, eyeing him skeptically. Half price or better. What part of your handsome anatomy was you thinking of ornamenting?

—Why is it all so cheap?

—Gotta get rid of this stock before they close down.

—Close down?

—Any day now. Look, you can see the demolition equipment over there at the far edge of the area. They're ready to rip. Everything here's being razed to the ground.

—Even the old movie houses? He turns his head in that direction, but it's all just a dim blur.

—It's all going. If you want something, this is maybe your last chance.

—Well, actually I had my eye on that old ruin of a coat you're wearing.

—Not for sale.

—I was thinking more of a trade.

—Nope. It don't look like much maybe, but it's a collector's item.

—So is this old tapestry. He turns his back to the vendor to let him see it.

—Unh-hunh, grunts the vendor. Pretty wild. Where'd you get it?

—A satisfied lady.

The vendor grins, grunts. I don't generally take in stolen goods, he says. But we might cut a deal. Sure I can't interest you in one of these almost solid gold, diamond-studded musical dildos? They double as mobile phones, and when you open them up there's a cribbage board inside.

—This tapestry's all I've got to wear. If I give it up, I'll need something to hide my carcass in. I'm not too presentable for public viewing. I was figuring in fact the tapestry was worth a good deal more than the coat, and you might throw in your shoes as well.

—You're already getting the better of me, you old thief. Even swap or nothing.

—Not even a bit of change for something to eat or a beer or a toke?

—Nope. Take it or leave it. Well, wait a minute. Here, I'll throw in my festival pass. Good for ten movies. I've already used up seven. That's enough for me. If I whack off again, I'll go blind.

He nods. A done deal. A movie might be a good place to hide out in until it gets dark. Generally warmer, too, if only for the accumulated body heat. They make the switch, and immediately the vendor shuts up shop, tucks the folded tapestry under his arm, and vanishes. Others are leaving too. The wind's come up again. Snow in the air. He'll have to hurry. He turns up the wide lapels. A bit scratchy on the inside. The coat used to have a silky lining, long gone, nothing left but a few dangling threads at the hem. Now it's just the rough wool. But he feels at home in it, less vulnerable. He digs through the trashbins, searching for plastic bags for his feet, gets lucky: comes on an opened packet of condoms. Also what feels like a smooth stone. Tarnished and badly beat up, but he recognizes it and pockets it. He pulls the condoms on over the shredded socks. Fits any size. They have elaborate rose-red French ticklers on the tips, which give his toes a festive look.

He ducks into the first cinema he comes to: the Buried Shaft. *Pete the Beast and Old One-Eye*. Lobby full of noisy brats. Probably abandoned here and on the loose. Who knows, some of them might be his own. They taunt him and throw popcorn at him as he passes through into the auditorium. He gives them the finger and lets a loud fart. That sets them to whooping and giggling; he's a hero. The movie's already under way. One of Kate's animateds. Not something he would have chosen had he been choosing, old Pete being too little removed from his own present condition. But that also makes it less likely they'll come looking for him here. Milky, sugary smell in the air, mixed with kiddy pee, pretty sickening, but the restless little beasts pump out a lot of heat and that helps a little. He slumps into a seat down near the front, hands in his coat pockets, one worrying the stone. Turns out Old One-Eye is not the animator or one of her avatars, as he'd anticipated, but the bum's own cock, whom he talks to to keep himself company. It rises up out of his lap like a charmer's snake, not Kate, but it talks like Kate, so one of her avatars after all.

—You're looking peeky, Pete, it says. You look like you been sent for and couldn't come. I think you got a overactive prostrate gland. It says, You useta be very broad-minded, Pete, a famous big dame hunter, but you've gone flat as a doormat. One look at you and you wonder if they was any other survivors. It says: Looky here, Pete, mast's up! Let's hoist anchor, matey, and get ourselves hulled twixt wind and water!

—No port in sight, One-Eye. So hold your peace and take five.

—No! Hands off, Pete! I'm wearied a your knobby paw-paw tricks. I'm in need of a hot wet snuggle, the genuine ar-tickle. Or, minim, somebody to lick me into shape afore I dry out and lose my fresh complexion. We all got a right to laughs, libido, and the pussy of happiness.

—Business is bad, One-Eye. Even the dogs are staying away.

—Don't take it to heart, Pete. Them critters always was a picky lot. But you ain't trying hard enough, slumped there like a leaking beanbag. You've gone from the supine to the ridiculous, ol' son! You gotta shake a leg, namely your middle one. Me! We gotta do a little howling and prowling!

—It's no use, One-Eye. Things are coming to an end.

—Yeah, I know, it ain't like it useta be. Apocalypse can be a real downer, but that's no excuse! You gotta roust up and use your imagination, Pete! Let's at least get outa the alley and go crawl into a movie someplace!

All this is too wordy for the little ones. They're up out of their seats and running about the auditorium, squealing and shrieking and playing goose tag and throwing things and generally raising hell. They clamber over him as if he were a playground obstacle, though some in passing draw unflattering parallels with the characters in the cartoon. A couple of the littlest ones have crawled up onto the lip of the stage and are peeing on the screen in protest to the cheers of the others. But Old One-Eye (which in frustration has detached itself from Pete and gone waddling off on its balls like amputated leg stumps, looking for action; he remembers this sequence now, at first comic, eventually infused with pathos and longing) has given him an idea, and he is up and stumbling out of there. Let's go crawl into a movie, One-Eye said. It just might be a way to change locations. He has a gift for losing himself at the movies, slipping across the border between seer and seen; he can at least give it a shot. Not this one, though. It's playpen bedlam in here and the cartoon exaggerations are too violently two-dimensional. He needs a deep quiet film he can really sink into: one of the classics, like *The End of Innocence* or *A Squeeze and a Squirt.*

He steps out onto a fairground colder and gloomier than before. He can't tell by the dimming light if it is merely late in the day or if the storm has worsened. He has the entire festival of films to choose from but, dressed only in coat and condom boots, he must pick quickly and get back inside while he's still able. He looks about for the old folks' Veinous Theater, figuring he might as well try to sneak into a Wee Willie film and relaunch the whole cycle, why not? But would he really want to go through all that again? He would. Nowhere to be seen, though. The best ones, he knows, are at the Picturedrome, but he has to stay away from there. *The Hairy Oracle,* he sees, is on at the Bush, *Cinderella's Hair* at the Cumalot. Might work. About a Cinderella who fucks the Prince at the ball and leaves behind a pubic hair, and he has to roam the kingdom thereafter, trying to match up the hair. Movie about obsession, in effect, which is always gripping. Would need good eyesight, though. Or a sense of smell, both fading. *Naked Nocturnes?* No idea. But, just past a mocked-up film set where a few cold lingering tourists are attempting, scripts in hand, to act out the choral rape scene from *Rantum-Scantum,* there's the old brass-doored Foxy, which is showing *On the Wings of the Wind*, a film about a flying fuck he remembers well and with fondness. More aggressively titled *This Birdie Wants Stuffing* on first release, once it reached classic status and started making the art cinema circuit, the title Cissy had originally intended for it was restored.

In the grand circular foyer of the Foxy, reverberant with memories of first nights but now hushed and dusty and all but empty, he gives up his ticket to be punched for the second time and makes his way toward the inner double doors. The beautiful crimson-and-gold decorations of the foyer have a forlorn tattered look, the busts and statues and fountains are gone, and the old carpet has lost much of its nap, but it is still one of the great old movie palaces, and it calls forth in him a mood at once of profound joy and inconsolable sadness. He feels lonelier and more unanchored than ever before in his long career, plunged into a desperate longing for he knows not what, yet at the same time he is overswept, held in the foyer's all-encompassing embrace, by a bittersweet melancholy that feels not unlike being in love. As if it is surging up from nowhere, he has a spontaneous vivid recollection of posing one premiere night for the usual swarm of film magazine photographers over near the popcorn machine (but where is it? they must have taken it out), his costar Cally on her knees, giving him head and somehow smiling for the cameras at the same time, he trying to keep his cool and not lose eye contact with his public while his face flushed, his lips pulled back, and his eyes bulged, attempting to prolong the moment by counting the little penis-shaped electric candles in the great chandelier overhead (that's gone too; probably sold off to dealers to try to keep the theater open), while the flashguns popped and the foyer filled with applause, and he recalls that, just before an orgasm so powerful it brought him to his knees and made him weep with the same sorrowful joy he feels now (how the photographers ate it up; he wept on all the magazine covers of the world that month), he had the sudden revelation that all he would ever know of truth and beauty was happening to him at that very moment, there, surrounded by his adoring fans (the buzzer was going off, the film was about to start), in the incomparable splendor of the Foxy.

He is on his knees now. He is crying. The show buzzer is sounding. The past has somehow, for a moment, merged with the present. The bored young person who punched his ticket is watching him with annoyance. Another old loony. With his dried-up old dingus sticking out like a pathetic signal of distress. She turns her back and reaches through her skirt to tug down the leg band of her panties, a gesture that always brings him back to the here and now. The first night-vision fades. He wipes his eyes with the back of his hand, staggers to his feet, stirring little puffs of ancient dust, and pushes through the double doors into the auditorium.

The lights are just beginning to dim as he enters, allowing him a glimpse of the rows of plush crimson seats, the golden lights low enough to obscure the rips and frays and stains, as perhaps it is obscuring the worst of his own piteous state, for he passes all but unnoticed. Only two or three dozen patrons are scattered about, waiting lethargically for the movie to start, their hands in their laps, looking hollow-eyed and lonely. The tears start again as he steps down the familiar old aisle, guided by the tiny lights at the floor, few of them still burning: That all this is to vanish. It's a kind of murder! Though others might say euthanasia. He takes his usual seat in the middle of the fifth row. No kids at this one, so he is all alone down here. The old woolly coat has been scuffing his cock and belly raw, so he opens up to let his sore flesh breathe. The grand drapery with its magnificent swags and furbelows is missing, as are the fringed house curtains with their sequin pricks and jeweled cunts, rescued perhaps for some museum or, more likely, taken down to be cut up and sold by the square yard at auction; only the pale travelers remain, sliding open now to reveal the old pocked screen. The picture sheet, as it once was called. The stage behind it here at the Foxy is a real one with a blue cyclorama at the back, from the days of the live shows that accompanied the films. He and Cally acted out many of their routines here, often with audience participation, before their own stardom began to make that dangerous. Besides, it spoiled the illusion of the filmic event and reduced its grandeur; film must be watched in the dark on a big screen without intermission. And now, by going on the run, he is exiling himself from that grandeur. Forever. Though what choice did he have? The grief he feels for the old doomed Foxy, he knows, is the grief he feels for himself.

He feels the tears starting again and stops himself. If he's going to pull this off, he has to stay cool. Focused. Already he has missed the titles and opening shots. It's a film that builds slowly: one of Cissy's tender adagios, beginning with a sensuous passage over a verdant earth from a bird's-eye point of view. Cissy's famous eroticization of landscape. As of everything. The track is sweet and melancholic, a kind of soft rising and falling hum, with just the faintest hint of distant birdcalls. Down on earth, he is discovered at the edge of a vast meadow of waist-high grasses, and far away on the other side of the meadow: Cally. They begin running toward each other in that old slow-motion cliché, the grasses stroking their bare thighs and abdomens as they run. But at a certain moment, they lift off, Cally first, rising gloriously into the blue air, and he, with only the slightest hesitation, rising to follow her. Then begins a kind of aerial ballet as they swoop and turn around each other, approaching, withdrawing, displaying, concealing, exchanging fleeting touches and kisses, never pausing or embracing, for to do so would be to fall, though sometimes hovering as though lifted, as the title would have it, on the wings of the wind.

Behind him, unbelievably, he hears idle chatter and laughter. He shrinks down into his seat and puts his fingers in his ears. He has to ignore them, else his heart will fill with rage and deflect him from full engagement with the film. Where now the touches and kisses of the two lovers are becoming more frequent and more impassioned, their mouths searching out every inch of flesh as they flit and dart, tongue tips touching, genitals sliding past each other. Cally's performance is impeccable, graceful and supple, yet intensely arousing, for she exudes both an ethereal sky-high serenity and a quivering excitement. His own serenity is in doubt, but not his excitement. This exquisite nubile being, who wants what he wants even more than he wants it, has his fullest attention, and slowly their movements position them for entry, he mounting her from above and behind. But he cannot remain in this position for more than a moment, nor can she, lest they lose their balance and fall. Eventually at orgasm they *will* fall, but will recover their wings, so to speak, in the nick of time, and after fluttery farewell kisses will fly off, never (presumably) to see each other again.

Now, however, he is still attempting a more sustained entry, and it requires the utmost precision and cooperation. While both are in constant motion, she must lift her bottom and he must lower his feet, positions unsuitable for flight except when they are conjoined, becoming then a single four-winged two-tailed creature, their imbalances canceling each other out. They can't use their hands, their wingtips as they might now be called, and there is nothing solid against which to press their attempted connection. His flying motions cause his penis, for all its rigidity and urgent need, to rise and fall erratically, so that, when he does get close, his thrusts go amiss, stroking her belly or sliding up the crack of her behind. She, too, cannot hold her awkward position for more than a moment before having to recover her equilibrium, swooping off, then returning to try again. But now suddenly the titled wind rises and sustains them just long enough for him to plunge inside her, arms outstretched, and for her to squeeze and hold him in until they get the knack of this four-winged flying. Oh yes! It's wonderful! No further thrusts needed; their bodies in flight are providing all the movement that's necessary, the trick is only—ah, great!—not to slip out before—

Suddenly the screen rips open and a gang of masked, heavily armed urban guerrillas explodes through it from behind. He's so startled he falls out of his seat. Or perhaps he misses it, falling back, having just lifted off. On the wings of the wind. However he got there, he's on the floor. *Everybody out!* the Extars yell, sweeping the auditorium with their weapons. *Now! This theater is going to blow up in ten minutes!* The other patrons scramble for the exits. He pulls himself up and falls heavily into his seat, wearing all his gravity.

—Better move on, old man, shouts their leader, before it's too late!

—It's already too late, Lottie. I'm too tired to move on. Blow it up if you like.

—Crazy?

—Only for you, Wild Thing, he says with a weary sigh. She smiles under her mask. You're just doing the goddamned demolition crew's work for them, you know.

—Yes, we're aware of that, Loco, but what can we do? We have to make a statement.

—Make a statement against the demolition crews. You just fucked a good movie.

—That piece of fluff?

—It's stunning. One of Cissy's most beautiful films.

—That tart works for the city, Crazy. Art always does. Watch out for beauty, man. Aesthetic appreciation is a kind of vampiric seduction. You know the old maxim: Aesthetic interest in a subject sucks away that subject's being.

—All I know is I was nearly away and out of here until you burst in.

—You want out, come with us!

—He'll just slow us down, Lottie! We gotta get the hell outa here! The cops'll be here any minute!

—Fuck 'em. He's our man. We gotta take care of him.

—But it's about to blow!

—Defuse it. C'mon, Crazy. She jumps down off the stage, her lovely breasts bouncing. She takes off her mask and gives him a loving kiss. Let's go back to the squat. We'll steal some ingredients, boil up a soup, and get it on in the old way. Whaddaya say?

—I haven't got a chance out there, Lottie. They're looking for me.

—We don't even have to leave the theater. We know an underground route out through the old closed-off scene shops and prop rooms down in the basement. It's how we got in.

Her excitement excites him. Maybe this is the way! In any event, there seems to be no other. And her smile radiates warmth and self-confidence. He grunts skeptically and stumbles to his feet, pulls his rough old coat around him.

—Only if you'll promise not to blow up the Foxy. I love her.

—It's a deal, Loco. The old whore's one of my weaknesses too. She takes his arm and helps him shuffle down the row. The others are streaming out ahead of them by way of the women's restroom.

—Hey, I'm sorry about the last time, he mutters.

—What do you mean?

—You know. At the Olde Cock Lane. When I didn't go with you. I couldn't help it. Strings were being pulled.

—What are you talking about? You did go with us.

—I did?

—Sure, don't you remember? It was a real adventure! We were taking on the whole goddamned city at one point! You were a fucking wild man! What a high! Afterward we balled our asses off. You told me it was the best fuck you ever had.

—I must have gone to a different movie.

The route down to the warren of rooms beneath the theater is by way of a secret passage into a small hidden auditorium whose screen is the two-way mirror into the women's restroom, an entertainment for the management from olden days. Where the projection booth would be, there's a wet bar, and the steps down are through a false liquor cabinet in there. How the Extars discovered all this, he has no idea, but there are not many underground passageways through the city they don't know. There are no lights down below, so they have to stumble along, feeling their way and, just for fun, each other. In the darkness, with all the hands on him, he doesn't feel as old. There are faint lingering aromas of dogs and horses and of human sweat down here, for they used to have kennels and stables for their onstage circuses and bestiality acts, and for the performers there were gymnasiums, practice rooms, arousal booths, and catnap parlors. Eventually, by way of stone pipework, which they have to crawl through on hands and knees, they emerge into the gray light and thick aromas of the city sewers, and from there they find their way into the subway tunnels. He's getting a real tour. But he's finished. His condom boots are now nothing but loose rubber bands around his ankles, his knees are skinned, and he's exhausted. He can go no farther and he says so, sitting down just where he stands.

—Hey, man, Lottie laughs. No sweat! We're here!

—We are?

She takes his hand and pulls him to his feet and leads him up some iron steps into an underground parking garage, and from there up another flight, these of concrete, into the building above it.

When she starts up yet another flight of stairs, now wooden, he holds back. Wait a minute, he says, let's take the fucking elevator.

—This building never had one, Crazy.

—No? He looks around, confused. Aren't we going to my old penthouse?

—We had to leave that place. The tourist traffic got too heavy and too dangerous. Besides, it's on the demolition list too. Could go any day.

It's a long climb, but it should be worth it. Up creaky stairs with old linoleum treads, dimly lit. Vaguely familiar, but all inner urban buildings look and smell a lot alike. But then, at the top, at the end of a short corridor, he sees the keyhole and knows where he is. Full circle.

—Damn you, Lottie, he says, and stops short of the landing. Why did you bring me back here? *Back here! back here!* he seems to hear the scarred walls echo.

Lottie turns to gaze down at him from the step above. Her look is one of tender concern and abject adoration, but he feels betrayed by it. Light streams out from under the door, and he can hear water running. He feels drawn toward the keyhole. And repelled by it. To see it all. He knows what that means.

—This is where we live now, Crazy, explains one of the Extars. Since you put us up on the big screen and changed our lives. They are all crowded up around him; he couldn't turn and run, even had he the strength to do so. She's taken us in. Given us a base. We've learned a lot from her.

—All she wanted now, Lottie says, was to rescue you from the power structure. We've done that. She loves you, Crazy. Just as we do. But you're still free to go.

The door opens and Cleo steps out onto the landing, her hard pale body gleaming around its fiery patch of red, the matching red ringlets on her head damp and wild, her green eyes aglitter with their legendary intensity.

—Hey, hero, she says, smiling her sparkling white smile. Happy anniversary! She's ravishingly beautiful. Like a tiger. Their times together here come rolling back as though she were projecting them. He can see the chipped bidet behind her, the crooked windowshade, the tin wastebasket, the old oak bed with its frayed quilt. Where time began. All klieg-lit. Come on in, baby!

—Tell me, Cleo. That film title. Back at the studio. Is it the title of your documentary too?

—I don't know. Does it matter?

—The next film, whatever it is, wherever, whoever: same story?

—I can't say. Might be. I only know about what's happened, Lucky, not what's going to happen. And what's happened so far is that I've been waiting for you and you've come back to me. She reaches out to take his hand. Come on, hero, whatever goes down, you belong to me!

Outside, it's cold and lonely. Probably dark by now. If he leaves, there are all those stairs to negotiate. He's not even sure exactly where in the city he is. He could disappear and never be seen again. He's so tired. Sore. Just trying to keep moving makes his brain ache. Here at least there's company, a quilt to crawl under, Cleo's magical cunt, love and story to be had. The soup that Lottie promised. But . . .

—Lottie said I was free to go. Am I?

Cleo continues to smile, but she looks hurt. She leans back against the doorjamb, her hand fallen between her legs.

—If you want.

—I might come back, I just need time to think about it.

—Sure.

He turns to Lottie apologetically. She shrugs, smiles.

—Whatever, man.

—But how do I get out of here? I don't even know where I am.

—Nothing to it, says Lottie. A simple trick our Kate taught us. It's got us out of deep shit more than once. She takes out a graffiti marking pen and draws a door right at the step whereon he stands. She draws a knob for it and then, just for fun, puts in a keyhole below it. She winks and reaches for the doorknob.

—But we're several flights up!

—Don't worry, Crazy. You know. It's the movies.

She turns the knob and opens the door onto the fairground. He's at the emergency exit of the Foxy. It is dark. There are colored lights strung up. They sway in the blowing snow, tinting it garishly; it's like a parody of the movies: a fixed image on a moving screen.

—Hang loose, Crazy, Lottie says, kissing his beardy cheek and giving his balls a tender squeeze. Love you! And with a pat from behind, he steps out and the door clicks shut behind him.

Meanwhile, back at the studio, Erato, as she is called now in her gauzy tunic, is having a wifely crying tantrum, and Calliope, chief of the nymphs and also the movie's director, is trying to calm her down. Oh, stuff your woowallahs! Erato screams. I *hate* woowallahs! I want *him!* The artistic director, also known as Euterpe, is digitally taping this unscheduled outburst. She has wanted a film of pure gesture with as little dialogue as possible, but the film is changing, and this little scene may now have its place. For the island will certainly not be the same without him, and the feelings of loss and anxiety and discontinuity that this arouses need to find space for their expression, so they do not erupt in destructive ways during more critical moments of the film later on.

Anxiety about the absent one, their woowallah incarnate—about his present unknown whereabouts due to the betrayal of their sister (on overhead monitors, cameras organized by the stage manager and her crew are tracking randomly across the midway and through various parts of the city in search of him), and about what will happen to him if and when he is found—has spread like a nasty itch throughout the cast, translating itself into nervous activity, short tempers, edgy halfhearted jokes, tears, restless rewrites, and pointless rehearsals, using one of the set designer's robots when necessary. The set itself has been dressed, undressed, and dressed again more times than has their star in his long distinguished career. They have run countless light and sound checks, argued over camera positions and angles. The scripted scenes meant to bridge the gap between the two films and suggest the passage of time have been scrapped. Instead, the artistic director, working lovingly, pixil by pixil, has digitally manipulated footage from the first film, including unused outtakes, to age the supposed island deity by way of electronic cosmetics, so to speak, so that his present condition, when first seen, if seen, will not appear too shocking. She has even considered exploiting old footage and Kate's robotics and making the film without him, should it come to this (no news from Clara, and nothing on the monitors but a dark snowy emptiness), though such extremity is all but unthinkable and riven with troubling paradoxes.

The whole project is unthinkable for Erato. We don't have to do this! she cries. I'll take care of him! I don't care if he's finished, I love him!

—You'll take care of whom? asks the director gently. Or should I say, what? Who or what is he beyond these movies we have made together? He is our creation, an embodied trajectory that we have seen through from beginning to end. Or almost the end.

—You'd just have to make more films, and those films are over now, says Terpsichore, with her typical bluntness. There's no further budget.

—I know, when you have lived with your creation for a long time, it is hard to give it—or him—up, adds Calliope soothingly. But this movie, as you might say, has no sequel. The series is over. This reel is the last one. We have to make it as wonderful as we can.

—Oh! cries Erato, banging her little fists on the old editing table, which is doubling now as a temple altar. You're a monster! You're *all* monsters!

—Well, says Terpsichore with a wry smile, that's probably true. But there's nothing to be done. What must happen, will happen. If not here with us, wherever.

—Really, Connie, says the artistic director, forgetting for a moment her own request that all members of the cast address one another by the names of their characters, we're doing him a favor with our little love feast. Our agape, as it says in the script. It's so much better than what he's suffering out there. And it honors him. He's going to love it. In the end, he's lucky.

—Oh, stop it! You're making me sick!

—Anyway, all this quarreling may be for nothing, Cora adds irritably, glancing up at the dismal wasteland views on the monitors. Who knows if we'll ever see him again? Or any of the others, for that matter. Nearly half the cast is missing, you know.

—He'll be back, says Cally, as unperturbed as ever. She is posing in the doorway of her office, looking soft, accessible, yet majestic. Performing, as always.

—How can you be so sure?

—He needs me. And the others will be here too. They cannot stay away.

As if to prove her point, Carlotta arrives in her leather Extars jacket and skintight jeans. On her own. It's an awkward moment. There's a general feeling of mutual distrust. But Cally rushes forward and gives her a welcoming hug. I'm *so* glad you've come! she says in her breathless mode. Have you seen him?

—We picked him up in the Foxy and took him to the flat. But he wouldn't go in. He left.

—Oh. That must have been hard on Cleo.

—It was. When we decamped, she was trashing the flat in a crazy rage.

—Well, better the flat than us. No further use for it anyway. Did you see where he went?

—No. Not far. You might try the Oriphiss. It was right across the way.

Cally gives Cissy a nod and the artistic director adjusts her headset and gives Clara a call. In the absence of her stage manager, the director gets a tunic from the wardrobe locker herself and presents it to their renegade sister, who hesitates but, unzipping her jeans, accepts it.

—Clara says the Oriphiss is closed. She has run a physical search of the theater and checked with the operators. Nobody fitting his description has been seen all day.

—Well, in nothing but his mangy old overcoat, Lottie says, tossing her jacket and jeans in a clothes bin, he can't have gone far. She pulls the tunic on over her head, no longer Lottie: Melpomene. The poor fucked dude has to be out on the midway somewhere.

—His overcoat? asks the director, and Melpomene shrugs. Oh dear. I thought we'd got rid of it. He must have got it back somehow.

—At the expense of my tapestry, no doubt, grumps Terpsichore.

—The poor thing must be frozen stiff, sighs Erato.

—It is, says Melpomene. And *he's* cold, too. This is probably meant to be funny, but no one laughs.

Euterpe reports the news of the overcoat to Urania and goes looking for Thalia, who's napping behind the set for the adytum with one of her robots. The artistic director has decided that she wants an interior frame for the climactic scene and asks the set designer to cut one into the temple wall. The camera will pull back from a tight close-up through this opening, and, using a sustained take, will hold this scene inside its frame as though to possess it for all time. Thalia, who has been in a foul mood all day, not at all comical as is her usual nature, mutters a few expletives under her breath and, scratching her behind rudely through the gauzy gown, clumps over to the wall in a huff to get it done. Then Euterpe leads the newest arrival through the script, though the girl, her exuberance subdued, seems to be only half listening. This film could still go badly, the artistic director knows, but she is relying on her director and costar to pull it all together, as she always does. The consummate professional.

Her headset crackles. It's Clara reporting that Cleo is on her way to the studio. They glance up at the monitors: yes, there she is now, passing under the Picturedrome marquee on her way toward the back. There is talk among some of banishing her from the film, but Cally says no, she has suffered enough, and she goes over to open the door to receive her. She's still in an ill temper and pushes the director away, ready, it would seem, to scream at them all, perhaps even to do to this set what she has done to the coldwater flat; but then she relents; the two women embrace and there are tears and hugs all around. She is given a tunic, which she stares at for a moment as if shocked by it, but then she strips down and puts it on, echoing all the others.

The headset crackles again.

—What? It's Clara! Yes? He's been spotted! Where? He's entering the Cloven Tuft!

—What's showing there? asks the director.

—What's showing there, Clara? . . . What? *Hard for Soft*!

—One of Cassandra's digital uncertainty films. It's all right. She'll know what to do. Tell Clara to come back and get her costume on. Let's start makeup. We'll be shooting soon.

He still has one movie left on his festival pass, but there is no one at the door to take it. Only an old worn gold-leafed sign, hanging at a tired tilt like an exhausted metaphor, that says LET ME PUNCH YOUR TICKET. He is himself tired and atilt. It has been a long day; he can remember none longer. He has resolved nothing. All he wants now is a place to curl up out of the wind. When the door opened up on the stairwell, he'd rather hoped to be stepping out into the anonymous city, where he might simply disappear. But of course he knew better. The simplicities of his life, which are many, do not include disappearance into anonymity. So he has wandered the largely abandoned and shut-down fairground on frozen stumps, looking for an open stall or booth or theater where he might huddle down and wait out the night. See what happens next. Like they say in the movies. When the door to this one opened, he staggered in. No idea what film, if any, is showing here. Doesn't care.

The dimly lit lobby is full of old posters, hung about as if it were a museum, telling him nothing by telling too much. Unless all these movies are on at once. Cally stares out at him from many of them, her famously beautiful erogenous zones—most of her—on display, luminous even in the weak light. His leading lady. Whom he has known intimately more than any other, though he feels he knows her not at all. They must have had it off together thousands of times, but who she was at any moment was only the part she was performing. Often he did not even know it was she. Even during backstage quickies, she was playing the backstage actress, having it off in seeming private with her leading man. *Seeming,* because around Cally there are always cameras. Trying to hide from them is to provide material for yet another movie. There is not an inch of her he has not explored, over and over again. Yet for all the photos, films, interviews, his own admittedly unreliable memory, and even these larger-than-lifesize posters before his eyes, he could not accurately describe any part of her, except to say she was breathtakingly beautiful. How tall is she? No idea. Eyes? Choose a color, any color. Flesh tones? Likewise. Her costume of course changes day by day, but she also apparently has a roomful of wigs and merkins, together with a complete selection of paste-on lips and noses, and breasts more like little muscles that she can flex and bulge or shrink at will. Their nipples? Any style that suits the moment. Her favorites (or maybe only his favorites and so remembered best) are hard and pert and rosy, but they can flatten out and darken or swell and flush with pimpled color. On a poster overhead: BUNS TO DIE FOR. True. The most beautiful and arousing in the world. Even now, he's getting hard again just gazing upon them. But even they are never ever exactly the same from film to film, or even from moment to moment. She can thrust them out or tuck them in, spread them or shrink them as she pleases. Or, rather, as her particular performance demands. For she is all performance, living invented lives of the scripted moment, otherwise just negative space. A spectacular presence and an unknowable absence. Well. She probably thinks of him in much the same way, having tried him on in all his roles and manifestations from wee Wee Willie on. Two of a kind. But then, as they say, two negatives . . .

The auditorium, as he's anticipated, is empty, though it is scented still with the hint of human passage: breath and bodily fluids, old hats and shoes, a not unpleasant aroma spiced with chewing gum and stale edibles, a woolly dust, a hint of rust and mildew. He stumbles down the aisle to take his usual place front and center, his way lit by the reflection off the screen, on which the projector is casting an imageless beam, as though someone might have gone away and left it running. He locates an unbroken seat in the fifth row and slumps into it, pulling his scratchy old coat tight around him. He has been worrying the stone in his pocket so long that it is warm from his grip, and he presses it now against his more tender parts, defrosting himself with his own heat, if it is his, what little's left of it. Motion capture, he thinks (the stone, which is not a stone, has made him think of this); maybe that's where it all went. Sucked away. A horror movie, made behind his back.

The screen, he sees, is not completely blank. Little flecks of imperfections pop up on it. And now, in the silence, he can hear, over the faint crackly sounds emerging from the speakers, the film itself fluttering through the projector gates at the back, ticking off the empty frames, like a parable of time itself. Must be one of Cassie's enigmatic little movies—if they can be called movies, for often nothing moves but the film itself on its way through the projector. If so, that's good. Cassie's films have no stories. Stories have endings. He doesn't need endings. Ceaseless flow, that's the ticket. Even if of nothing but emptiness. She's often faulted for this. Movies are about foreplay leading to orgasm, she's told. She only smiles. For Cassie, orgasm is not a final explosive objective but a constant beatific state to be achieved. His experience of orgasm is more rough-and-tumble than that, but he envies her her purity and enjoys sharing her mystical devotions. She always brings him off in ecstatic ways, even if his coming disappoints her. Maybe he should have paid more attention. A final fuck would not be so bad if it never ended. This film may be that early breakaway number of hers which, like most of her later work, she left untitled, but which the rest of the industry nicknamed *Invisible Titties*.

Actually, everything was invisible; you had to imagine it all. She roped everyone into performing in it, shot rolls and rolls of film, but intentionally overexposed everything so nothing could be seen. That one was not silent, though, as this one seems to be, but had a track imposed on it, made up of fragments of sound taken during the filming process that faded in and out and over one another in ceaseless rising and falling waves. One had the illusion, created in part by the track, that one could almost see oneself from time to time up on the all-white screen, like a pale shadow behind the light. This film, too, has faint shadows from time to time, but since he is not expecting them, they are probably really there. Hard to see what they represent. Maybe nothing more than ink blots. Though they sometimes seem to move. A perpendicular thing. Might be a man walking in a snowstorm. Or it might be the shadow of an erect cock against a bedsheet. Might also be a fencepost, but that's not the first thing he thinks of.

He's starting to drift off. He doesn't know if that's a good thing or a bad thing, but he may not have much choice. He's never sure about fading in again after fading out. Old anxiety. Same with cuts, though at least no time then to think about it. Prefers lap dissolves: a kind of hanging in, no matter how disturbing to the inner organs and other parts. Sometimes the fadeouts lead to dreams. That is to say, more movies. But whose? If he's the dreamt one, as they like to say, who's the dreamer? Such thoughts, which have often entertained him, make his poor doomed head ache, so he pushes them aside and focuses instead on the blank screen—if one can be said to be focusing when one's eyes are crossing. The crumbling old film palace is empty, but he has the dreamy sense of sitting in a packed house, surrounded by the ghostly audiences of cinemas past. Is someone's hand wrapping his penis—besides his own, that is? Wishful thinking. There is a dim remote wash of—what, laughter? Applause? Just static probably. Or a buzz in the ancient wiring. Through his narrowing eye slits he watches a pair of pale shadowy hills fade in, fade out on the white screen. Buns to die for. Probably. Or boobs. Not hills, though. It's his festival, after all. He thinks mainly of the valleys between. Places of sweet repose. He pushes his chin up, but it won't stay up. He nods.

But he is suddenly jolted awake as something (a door has opened somewhere) comes hurtling down from a great height with a shrieking whistle and hits with an explosive *crash!* Thunderous reverberations, clattering, glass smashing, walls falling; he's out of his seat, loud thumps and anguished cries—

on the screen, the shadowy hills have hardened into a crisp but placid image of the bare backside of a woman on her knees and elbows, afloat in a white sky—the whump and thud of falling masonry, things rolling about, bumping into other things, echoes of all this, muffled whimpering, diminished rumbling, image and sound fading away together. A door closes. Silence. He is staring at mere crackly light again. He sits back down, cautiously, heart doing its thing once more. Thought for a moment it was all over. A final fuck—was that a threat or a promise? The fugitive half-glimpsed shadows return. Fading in and out. Merging with one another. Accompanied now by a sustained whispery tone, a kind of faint melancholic hum beneath the pale shifting images. Which seem to be reading him. For whenever he leans forward to try to see them more clearly (can't stop trying to figure things out), they sharpen briefly before fading away again. And those toward which he has leaned seem to return more often and more clearly, as if he were choosing them. Mostly bodies, still or in motion, many recognizable; there are Cassie's tender little breasts, for example, Lottie's bold ones, Clara's perfect torso, Kate's armpit, Connie's pretty pubis, Cora's striped arse, Cissy's soft one, Cleo's slender white thighs conjoined by their fiery red patch, and all their other parts appear and disappear as well: their toes and fingers, knees and elbows, their open mouths and wet labia, their navels, anuses, eyes. Which seem to be looking out at him. Asking to be chosen? No. Just watching him—tenderly, lovingly—as they come and go. Contemplating his contemplations. Of them. As if he were watching them through a keyhole. And they were watching him watch. The disparate images fold in and out of each other in soft fugal progressions, creating the sense of a single composite figure, as if he himself were bringing it into being, and this figure, unstable at the edges and ever metamorphosing, he knows too. And loves no less than all the others and perhaps with all his love of all. He closes his eyes and leans toward her.

There's a sudden roar bearing down hard upon him as if coming straight out of the screen, making him jump and cry out, a violent shriek of brakes, he collapses back in the seat, ducking, his heart whamming away—damn! wish she wouldn't do that!—tires squeal, horns blare, there's a massive collision, the crumpling of metal and shattering of glass, screams, sirens, whistles, more whumps and thumps, and here he comes, batting his way through the thick frozen crowds, hat jammed down on his scowling brows, hands in his overcoat pockets, collar turned up, and ramrod cock preceding him, gunmetal blue and frosted with glittering ice crystals, all of it in seeming 3-D, the screen a mere scrim with people and traffic on both sides of it. His filmed self's accusing eyes are fixed angrily on him, trembling there in the fifth row, as he comes striding forward through the slush and rubble and racket of the city streets, picking them up and putting them down, belting his way past all obstacles, apparently prepared to leap from the screen and fall upon him in his rage. He's shrinking into his seat, thinking, Someone *stop* that sonuvabitch! But on he comes, shouldering his way right past the lip of the stage and into the auditorium, gazing down in fury at him all the while, and then seems to barrel on past him, or through him, the image fading now, the harsh din of the streets subsiding to a sullen continuo, the packed-up masses giving way to a slow sequence of multilayered lap dissolves, a thick impasto of cocks entering cunts. In and out, in, in and out, out, in. Or *a* cock; they may all be his own, different though they seem at times.

All right. He has the pattern. Soft fleshy adagios interrupted by heart-stopping percussive bursts if he slips into a haze for a moment. A film that talks back. That won't tolerate inattention. He sits up, best he can; sitter itself a wreck like the rest of him. But he doesn't want to get hit with another one of those harrowing wake-up alarums. Might not survive the next one. Anyway, this segment of coupled bodies is much more engaging than solo views of flesh alone. And not just cocks (or cock) and cunts, but tongues and fingers too, and other orifices, everything getting fondled and probed and tasted. In no particular order. Orgasm before foreplay and all that. He used to think Cassie's seemingly anarchic collages were in fact a search for meaning, but more likely they are efforts to obliterate meaning, to force the mind away from its logical constructions (sheer madness, she would think) and toward an acceptance of meaningless associations, beautiful only in their denial of meaning. Something like that. (He's trying to stay awake.) He sees the filmmaker herself from time to time in the unfolding stream of images. Easy to recognize. Especially head shots. Wearing her in his crotch like a hugely inflated testicle. With ears. He loves to grip the warm bowl of her skull then. Glimpses of him doing that, the expression on his upraised face beatific. Or stupid. Hard to tell those divine states apart. But wait, who was that one? He leans forward and the dissolve is delayed. His butt's between her strong young thighs, joyously banging away. Lottie. The Wild Thing. Another kind of beatitude. He smiles and sits back, feeling faintly envious of his own past self, and the scene changes. The doctor is allowing him to give her a digital proctoscopy while nurses with various instruments are doing the same to him. Or *for* him. Which dissolves into young beginners in a hayloft. An underwater fuck. A pretty nipple in his teeth.

He finds that if he leans forward and presses his attention, he can stretch the sequences out, push them a few frames toward climax. Or toward whatever. Just moving hands on bodies, for example. His at the waistband above that ass of asses. By leaning forward and concentrating, he is able to hold the image long enough to slide her panties down. He can almost feel those perfect cheeks beneath his palms and fingertips before they dissolve away again. Likewise, on him: someone's hands up there on the screen now. Kneading his abdomen, the insides of his thighs. Those deft fingers: Cassandra. One of her talking massages. What are her fingers saying? Her tongue and toes? He listens, with his body. Something about the great erotic illusion. That there is anything beyond or within the. . . . But then it's gone again and Cecilia's lips are puckered at the tip of his erection. Giving it a loving kiss. He leans into it. Cissy's mouth opens. Her tongue flicks out. He can feel her warm breath, but now he's in the bath face-to-face with Connie. Long enough, continuing to press forward, to push his feet between her thighs. Can't see this on the screen, there's only her widening eyes to go by, and the sensations in his toes, a warm fuzzy damp.

He settles back, wriggling his toes, letting the lush dissolves flow over him. A hovering midair copulation wearing butterfly wings. A delivery boy raped by a klatch of frenzied housewives while roped to a kitchen table and gagged with panties. Mud-fucking. In effect, his whole life is passing before his eyes. The one he has fled. Ending it not to end it. One of shadows (the dissolves continue, spilling sensuously into one another) and illusions. Well, there may be other lives to live, other genres. This was his. It was beautiful. They were beautiful. He should count himself lucky. Now it's Cleo, straddling his face and descending. Poor Cleo. He was cruel to her. Then beautiful Cally sprawled ass-high on silk cushions. Look! Her ass is *acting*! It's extraordinary! His leading lady. He's abandoned her. But what could he do? Next, a fuck afloat in outer space. Genteel hair-pie lunch on a picnic cloth in a country meadow. A group grope in a rising elevator. Lovely. And much of it anonymous, uncostumed, located nowhere except in the conjunction itself. As with the posters in the lobby, Cally is in a lot of these dissolves. So maybe they are showing all those movies after all. Or anyway the outtakes. What Cassie always prefers to work with. Distrusting art, polish, style. Truth bleaker than that. Messier.

Cassie herself reappears now, or her backside does, and he leans toward it to hold the sequence in place for a moment. She is on her knees and elbows, performing a little show, he at her feet, gazing up from the first row, as it were. She raises her feet and touches her toes together above her hips, creating a kind of proscenium arch over the stage backdrop of soft bronzed cheeks, parted like drawn curtains around the smooth creased cunt dangling within their folds like a medal or a coat of arms. After a silent soliloquy from the cunt (or perhaps it is only blowing him kisses), she uses her feet as puppets. They meet, flirt, come together, have a fight, come together again, kiss and make up, make love in a passionate tangle of toes. They climax, collapse, and dreamily slide apart, and the cunt behind them wags its lips as though mouthing a moral. Or singing a song. He strains forward, trying to hear it over the trafficky buzz, but the scene dissolves into one of a silken slit fringed with golden curls pausing meditatively over the head of a rigid cock before impaling itself upon it, which in turn merges into another of a prick (it might be his, he thinks of it as his, it feels like his) descending tenderly into pouting lips, aswim in their own sap, a sensation that fills him with an almost insatiable longing for times past and lost.

How good they were! How happy he has been! And how heartsore and lonely he now feels! He pushes on through the loving bodies, searching for the interrupted clip of Cassie's puppet act, and comes upon a novice kneeling at the altar in prayer. He lifts her woolly habit and finds, beneath the fresh pink stripes on her bottom, a set of prayer beads strung from cunt to anus, and apparently on a loop, for pulling a bead out from one orifice causes another to disappear into the other, and he is reminded once again that, for all his minute explorations of the fornicational life, the mystery remains. This is the one truth he has. He enters her from behind, praying into her prayer, as one might say, just as he did before, must have done, sliding in under the beads (*thup, thup, thup* they go, against his engorged corona) as if in search of the source of that ineffable mystery, but reaches instead the mouth of a pretty child, bent over his own childish willie, now taut and tiny as a dry twig. He is lying on his back in a meadow, gazing up into the awesome reaches of infinity while the girl licks his stiff little thing, which he sees is striped like a stick of candy, and he is filled again with a terrible sadness, not unlike grief, and a bittersweet joy and a desperate yearning for home, though he's not sure where that is or what. He slides his hand up under the girl's pinafore (he is one whose search is never ended), and his willie grows and his balls descend (*whoof*! felt that!) and he's plunging into a succulent dark nest, a supple breast in his mouth and its mate in his hand, a well-oiled finger of his other hand snaking up a rectum, whereupon he has a sudden spontaneous memory (it appears now on the screen) of a fluoroscopic fuck with Clara during a classroom lecture, only their bouncing bones clearly visible, their inner organs fuzzy gray areas washing about, his most famous bone not one at all, and visible only as a ghostly antipresence, there by what was not there, Clara declaring from behind the screen, gasping as she spoke (at the time he was so intensely focused on the wild fleshless bone-clacking ride he didn't even hear her, yet somehow banked her words away, saving them until now): *Our subject finds himself on the proverbial horns: it may be that he fucks in order to know, merely to achieve the knowledge that this is why he fucks . . .*

Or perhaps that's what Cassie's little cunt is saying, for he has found it again through all the dissolving bodies and its lips are still moving. Such a cunt! It exudes tenderness and innocence. And, though he cannot hear it: wisdom. Her feet—the actors—have dropped down into the audience, so to speak, and now caress his cheeks with soles heartbreakingly soft. I am being discontinued, he weeps. Yes, he is weeping now. It's too much. He has held back too long. I'm afraid! he sobs. Her feet gently wipe away his tears and lift his head, and it is almost as though she were detaching it from the rest of his body. She puts his ear to the moving lips as to a conch shell and what he hears in there is indeed the distant and unfathomable sea. It seems to be all she wishes to say to him. Then, as if aware that his unremitting thirst for resolution has not been slaked, she turns his head toward her and offers him her engorged wellspring of love and understanding, and he does drink there and it is sweet and consoling. Though he cannot even imagine the contortions involved, his own complementary portion is now deep in the warm soothing lather of her mouth, and it is as if she has half a dozen hands, for she is stroking his head and fingering his anus and rubbing his back under the overcoat and kneading his feet and tugging at his testicles and pinching his nipples all at once. Home, he thinks, lapping gratefully at her nurturing fount with his dry tongue, his head, attached or not, clamped tightly between her trembling thighs and his gaze fixed upon the crinkly little naught between her bobbing cheeks, is something like this and he is returning to it, having come to apprehend that *His Final Fuck*, if that's what it is to be called, is neither threat nor promise but simply—for participation in the mystery is all in his extremity that is left him—an opportunity that can be lost. Beyond the twin knuckled curves of her jerking bottom, he can see a door. He knows where it leads. He will go there. She has let him slip from her mouth, perhaps for fear of going too far, and now she is hugging him with all her limbs. Her knees spread, though she keeps her ankles locked behind his neck, her cheeks relax and from the tiny o between them, she farts prettily—a delicate little *prrr-tweet*—and a tab emerges, like a slip in a fortune cookie. He reaches up and, with a little tug, pulls it out. GOODBYE, IT SAYS. I LOVE YOU.

🎬

He steps through the door into a flood of light and a warm burst of cheers and applause from the studio gang, who have been watching his progress on a monitor and now form a welcoming corridor for his entrance. The artistic director has laid a red carpet from the door to a wall screen showing a looped clip from *First Night* under a juryrigged overhead awning of translucent bubble wrap lit by ceiling-mounted red-gelled lamps, and as he staggers down it barefoot in his old tweed overcoat, he is greeted by hugs and peter tweaks and kisses and a shower of celluloid confetti that glitters like stardust. He is only semitumescent, but he is forgiven for that, given the somewhat plaintive occasion (half-hard penises are pretty too), and they will soon see to it that he is in top form again, at least one more time. At the far end of the red carpet, his wispily clad leading lady, aglow in a golden spot, stands waiting for him, blowing kisses to him as he approaches, just as she always does at their world premieres. He seems about to stumble and collapse into her arms, but he pulls himself erect and wraps one arm around her lovingly, or perhaps just to hold himself up, and turns to face the smiling yet tearful women lining the path he has taken, raising his free hand to them in a wave.

—It's wonderful to be back! he cries. I love this place! Let's get it on!

—Right! Get that old rag off our beloved godhead! cries the artistic director. Pop him in the pool! Tunics off and in there with him! Start up the waves! Let's hear some sea! It's time to move ass, sisters! Be sure the overhead camera's ready to roll! Turn on the sky! Melpomene, crank up some lutes and flutes, love, give us some background! And where are the breezes? Makeup crew, get ready! We've got a very tight schedule now!

The stage manager unwraps the island deity's special toga and provides a folded tunic for the naked Polyhymnia, standing in a wistful trance in the open doorway through which he who might now again be called Father Pierrus or the Great Woowallah has come. Polyhymnia is thanked and congratulated by the cast and crew for returning him to them, the director gives her a hug and kisses her barren pate, but the nymph herself seems distracted and somewhat misty.

The errant star digs into the pocket of the overcoat before surrendering it to draw out a bright brassy lump, which he presents to the set designer, now pushing a camera boom into position near the old harem bathing pool *cum* island beach. I'm sorry, Kate, I didn't take very good care of it, he says. And I shouldn't have taken it in the first place. But it warmed my cods and saved my life out there, and I thank you for the loan of it.

—Aw, I told you you could keep it, she growls.

—Thanks, he says, standing before her in nothing but his famous skin, superannuated though it is, but, well, look: no pockets.

—Hmf. I'd rather you'd scouted out my missing eye, you ol' buzzard, still some use for that, she grumps, tossing her heart in the props locker and turning away, but there's a tear in the one eye she has yet.

Urania bends him over the editing bench off-camera (though Clio's are running) and gives him an injection in his old scarred nethers, whereupon his drooping majesty stirs once more, rising to a pale but promising semblance of its ancient glory by the time he steps into the pool, or bay, eliciting oohs and ahs from the gathering nymphs as he wags it at them in festive salute.

Terpsichore is already in the water, eager to play, and now Erato removes her tunic timidly and enters the water with him, holding his hand. When, ankle deep at water's edge, he hesitates, big Terpsichore strides forward and gives his backside a resounding wallop, and he stumbles forward into the bay, more or less on all fours. He picks himself up, spitting water, then grins, winks, and gives the cheeky nymph's own snowy fundament, turned toward him coquettishly, a replying crack. Erato, alarmed by these fierce indignities, scolds the impious Terpsichore and, interposing herself between them, examines the Great Woowallah's booboo, as she calls it, offering to kiss it to make it well again.

—Oh my, sighs Urania. Shouldn't it all be more serious than this?

—What do you mean? asks the director. Her artistic director is continuing to call out instructions.

—You can all play with his prick, or, rather, his woowallah, all you like, Euterpe shouts, but I want every inch of his holiness caressed and focused on, top to bottom, fore and aft! This is it! Our last chance to capture it all!

—It's an important film, says Urania. As important as any we've made. We have arrived at the catastasis and we have not thought it through. The script's silly and slapdash and thematically thin. It lacks density, subtlety, sensibility, profundity, innovation. This is our last opportunity to try to understand his mission and ours, Calliope, to try to grasp his quest for sacred fucking, as our bald sister here would have it, his heroic release of the endopsychic dragons of the deep for our own edification and entertainment. Who is he to us? Why have we made him as we have? We should be asking questions about the enigmatic ways sex, performance, memory—even scripted memory such as his—struggle against disorder, forgetfulness, entropy, impotence, despair; about the way his peculiar artistic talent, through the tensions of disclosure and concealment, thrust and withdrawal, somehow shadows forth eternal truths, or the way his iterative and abridged rituals, even stripped to their bare essentials, nonetheless feel necessary and even transcendent—intuitive and visionary. In short, we should be asking about the meaning of it all!

Polyhymnia is shaking her head emphatically behind her, and Calliope smiles and says, No, all that's very interesting, and we thought about those questions, or some of them anyway, but we want just the main thing now. Euterpe wrote a short scene where we all asked each other who we thought he was, behind all his names and self-contradictions, but I asked her to take it out. If we haven't thought enough about it already, it's too late now. All that's left, dear Urania, is love.

—All right, come on, everybody in! Euterpe calls out.

Melpomene is already in the water, with Erato, Terpsichore, and the Great Woowallah, who is lolling happily on his back, supported by all their sudsy hands, and Thalia, having first built a little sand bordello on the beach, limps in now to join them. She is followed by the thoughtful Polyhymnia and by golden Urania, slipping her flimsy tunic off and tossing it aside like a used hospital gown.

—While he's like that, dick to the sky, get a keyhole spot on the head of it! shouts the artistic director. Love the way it's standing! Beautiful! Now make it radiant! And off with the face shrubbery! Polyhymnia, you can help! Just leave a lip fringe, dear, a mousetail, thin as a line drawing—you know, in the classic manner. You can dye and curl the pubic hair and also what's left on top. Don't worry about his body skin tone and condition, I know it's a bit ghastly, but in editing we'll correct it with a digital airbrush. All right, come on, you raving nymphomaniacs, I know you're all a little blue, but I want to see some hot pussies out there! Some uncontrollable passion and mad frenzy, okay? So, hey, *let's play!* she cries and, passing her mike and headset to the director and throwing off her tunic, she hurls herself, whooping gleefully, into the pool, diving through and under them all, popping up like a plump sea sprite between the island deity's legs and giving his divine scrotum a long wet loving kiss, and now all the others join in as well, shrieking and splashing and grabbing and kissing and rubbing themselves against him.

Clio, chastened, has quietly resumed her filming of the making of this movie, but now leaves the cameras running to join the others, and, passing the director, pauses to apologize for her bitchy little trick, as she calls it.

—Always a mistake to try to script history, she says. You know. Trying to create a circle when there isn't one, she adds, gazing out upon the clamorous scene in the bay. He is the old Lucky again, flashing his famous mustachioed smile and cavorting like a schoolboy. But, goddamn it, I love him so! I can't get enough of him!

—I know. It's okay. Maybe it's even better now. There's a middle bit that wasn't there before.

Clio sighs, stroking herself. He is spewing water at the nymphs like a whale, running his hands between their legs as they try to soap him up and challenging them to a contest of bubble farting.

—I love everything about the silly lunk, but what I love most is his . . .

—His innocence?

—In a sense . . .

The Great Woowallah has never had it so good. He is spread out on a padded temple altar whose surface is as soft as a maiden's thighs, his rolled-up toga for a pillow, being massaged with hot perfumed oils by eight beautiful nymphs, all working on him at once. He has had a manicure and a pedicure and a soothing head rub, his ears have been cleaned and the ear and nose hairs clipped, his breath freshened, blisters treated, eyebrows combed, his pubic hair trimmed and curled and fashioned into spread wings, stray hairs plucked from his ass and shared about as souvenirs. Relics, one of them said, and giggled with embarrassment, the others shushing her. Those not working on him at any moment fan him with palm leaves, bring him food and aphrodisiacal drink, offer him their various body parts to kiss and squeeze, play softly on stringed instruments, whisper endearments and love songs in his ears. There is a gentle breeze up here fondling the palm leaves and bearing the faint tang of the sea, commingled with the oils' delicate perfumes and the rich dark aromas emanating from between the thighs of the haplessly aroused nymphs.

Their hands and mouths explore him and so do, he knows, the cameras. For, alas, he is on the island and yet not quite on the island, unable, for all the mind-numbing pleasures, to make the complete transition into the world of the film, as is his wont and wish. One moment he is luxuriating in the life of a god of love on an island paradise, gazing off into the soulful depths of the creamy blue sky while ardent nymphs worship his body with lips and tongues and sweet caresses; the next he is reminded of the imminent conclusion of this idyllic life—and all others as well—and made all too aware then of the filmic artifice and apparati surrounding him, the scripted parts that he and they are enacting. That blue is not the sky. Oh, it is inevitable, he knows, no reel is infinite, and he feels no rancor, for he has lived the heroic life of the great artist while enjoying fame and sensual delight and all the creature comforts, some of the time anyway—he has been privileged, and these adoring and adorable nymphs are among his privileges—but he cannot quite prevent the occasional flicker of dread from shivering its way down his spine and causing the instrument of his good fortune to dip and sway perilously, for all the stimulations—manual, vaginal, oral, and pharmaceutical—being applied to it.

He gazes down upon it now, being lapped by the affectionate Euterpe, and contemplates its history and its destiny, which is his history and destiny, wondering if there might not be some rewrite possible, some new themes or set of variations considered: the reenactment of inspirational moments from the island deity's civilized past before he washed up here, for example, or a tour of neighboring islands, spreading the faith, or even just one more day at the beach. What fun that was! And how quickly it was over! One moment he was laughing and had his fingers in soft warm places and soapsuds in his eyes, and the next he was stretched out on this cushioned slab, undergoing the ecstatic ceremonials of the wildly pious nymphs. What happened in between?

According to the script, he was carried up here by the eight nymphs, but she who is presently giving glory to his sacred wand, as they sometimes call it, not always in complete seriousness, said there was no time for that; she had reusable old footage she could splice in; let's rush on. So in effect he landed on the altar without leaving the water. There is nothing novel about this. His whole life has been riven by such discontinuities, but only as interruptions in the general flow of things. Now the flow itself is about to be interrupted. He shudders again. Falling into black leader is bad enough. But even black leader still passes through the gates. His dick dips. Euterpe gazes up at him tenderly, sadly, and signals to Urania to bring the needle again.

Euterpe's wistful expression is part of the problem. The elegiac mood of the nymphs has not helped lift his own. For all their amorous devotions, there is missing today (it is day here, but beyond the studio, it is probably night, and ever deepening) that urgent lustful rush toward climax to which he is accustomed and by which forever buoyed. They carry on in their excitable lighthearted ways, as indicated by the script, but a deep melancholia has stolen into their play, and neither he nor they are wholly deceived. In their whispered endearments, they sometimes forget and call him by the name they best know and love him by—Lucky or Peter or Badboy or Crazy—and the endearments themselves are often so heartfelt as to be heartbreaking. One by one, each has, pretending merely to be playful and erotically stimulating, squatted over his face that he might make his farewells to that part too, and some have returned more than once, as though remembering something left unsaid. Some squat facing forward, looking down into his eyes while he kisses them there, others face the other way so as to fondle and suck his organ and to lie at length upon him, hugging his hips. He prefers the latter position, not for the pleasures to be had but because all too often, gazing down upon him face-to-face, their eyes water up and they begin to snivel and then he starts to cry too. Their bottoms are pretty and less expressive, and if anything closer to laughter than to tears, and so tend to cheer him up, though their grief is often revealed by the way they suddenly pound against his face as though in utter anguish. Moreover—and this adds to their melancholy—they dare not bring him to orgasm for all the depth of their desire to do so, for there is uncertainty about the consequences and fear therefore of a premature conclusion. This would seem to be unthinkable. He does not wish to think of it himself. So everything is interruptus. Anyway, these are mere preliminaries. Their big number together happens not here but in the inner sanctum of the temple—the adytum, as they call it—their holy of holies at the heart of the nymphaeum, when they bring him before their leader for the title event. All the stops are being pulled out for that scene, and many thrilling special effects have been planned to enhance it. There, each of the eight has her scripted moment on camera before the grand finale, and he has watched them, rehearsing their gestures upon his body and slipping aside from time to time to practice their lines. Spectacular as the occasion promises to be (he's in for a treat, they tell him), he fears being taken there, for no scene, he knows, will follow it.

Actually, the adytum is not inside the temple at all but sits outside it, a separate set, and consists of two and a half walls only, the rest open to camera, light and mike booms, and other filmmaking paraphernalia. Probably it will seem an inner part of the temple when the movie is put together. A movie that (oh my god!) he'll never see. The principal nymph, whose temple this is and his costar in this feature as in so many before, has been familiarizing herself with the space, practicing poses and movements (it's exciting to watch her; she almost makes him forget his troubles), trying different gels on the lamps and filters on the lenses, testing various mechanisms, adjusting camera positions, removing all extraneous items and taking them back to her director's office. Where she spends a lot of time, leaving the cast to their own devices for the most part, within the limits of the script. She has drifted by the altar only rarely, trying not to steal the scene, though she inevitably does. She is always all smiles, the only one who seems unaffected by the gravity of the moment. But then, she is a consummate actress, so one never knows. She can seem as she wishes to seem. She addresses him always as Father Pierrus or the Great Woowallah, and more convincingly than the others do. When she says, O Great Woowallah!, he *is,* for just that moment, exactly who she says he is. Only she of all the nymphs has not squatted over his face, often as she has done so before in one guise or another, though she has used her professional gifts more than once to reinvigorate with a simple masterful touch or two his flagging member, thereby sparing him more injections. It always seems to give her great delight to see it spring to life, and she laughs and claps her hands and kisses the tip of it when it has performed well—which for her is everything. Some find her empty but for the parts she plays. Sometimes he does too; there seems so little residue from film to film. But other times he finds her wondrously full, absorbing all lives into herself so as to live more completely and complexly in the world, an absorption accomplished not by thought, or even passion, but by performance. By acting, she understands. And loves. But for her true genius to emerge, she must always have someone or something to play against. His prick, for example. Or, more to the point—for his prick, clever as it is, is not a stand-alone device—he himself. She's often said that she only truly knows herself when she's in a film with him. He fulfills her, makes her who she is. In short, she loves him because she needs him, even to exist, as he has loved and needed her, each discovering themselves only with the other. So how will she get on without him? Has she thought about that?

His own genius has started to sag again and he doesn't want another injection, so he rolls off the altar from under the busy hands and mouths of the astonished nymphs and, unrolling his toga pillow, wraps himself in it. It's so short it's more like a nightshirt, the sort Wee Willie used to wear, but it's just long enough to cover up his momentary decline if they don't bend over to peek. The director has disappeared into her office again, and he announces that he's just had an idea for the finale and he has to go discuss it with her. They object. He replies to their objections, but they are not satisfied. He tries to satisfy them, but their minds are made up. Finally he draws himself up, raises one arm magisterially (*whoops*, up comes the toga), and declares in full voice:

—*Silence! The Great Woowallah has spoken!*

And while they are still, somewhat goggle-eyed and mouths and thighs agape, digesting that, he wheels about on his bare heels and slaps straight over to the director's office and, without knocking, opens the door and walks on in. He finds her lying on the casting couch in there, tearfully masturbating, sucking the thumb of her free hand around her sobs and groans.

—O Great Woowallah! she cries, scrambling to her feet and lowering her gown. Good heavens! What are you doing here? I don't—! I was just—!

She is flustered and bewildered, as if not knowing what her lines are or who or what she's supposed to be. Caught, in effect, with her parts down. She wipes her eyes on the shoulder of her tunic.

—You're supposed to be—!

—Cally! He's lost his lines too. He's confused by her tears, her pain. Her simple prettiness has taken on a tragic tear-streaked beauty, and his heart is pounding with fear and love and self-pity and pity for her and a terrible sense of impending loss. It's—it's ending, Cally! It's really. . . .

—Oh, Willie! Don't cry!

—I can't help it! I—I. . . . Oh, Cally! He falls helplessly, bawling, into her arms. *I love you so!*

—I know! she sobs and throws her arms around him. Oh, Willie! I love you too! With all my heart! But—she tries to pull back—we have to be careful! The temple scene—!

But his hands are all over her and hers all over him. They are kissing and hugging and weeping and tearing at each other's flimsy garments, which rip away like tissue, and clutching desperately at each other and falling upon the old couch and even as she gasps—*Oh, Willie, we mustn't!*—she is pulling his cock, now almost painfully hard, into her and he is running his hand down her familiarly silky crack and between her legs where it is soaking wet to feel himself sliding in and he knows he is where he belongs even if he still doesn't know who *he* is and now surely never will, and oh, he doesn't want to lose this moment or that moment reverberantly held in this one; it's as if he were falling in love for the first time and she is kissing his ears and his throat and his eyes and mouth and entwining her legs around his hips and telling him she adores him, and he is kissing her and telling her she's his greatest love, always has been, and *Yes!* she is saying, *Yes! Fuck me! Fuck me!*—it's her most famous line, and with it his entire past surges forward to consume the present and fill him with a piercing longing and a sublime joy, and they are hammering away, hauling on each other's buttocks as though trying to press their bodies wholly into each other, their lips locked and tongues in each other's mouths, and as they are pounding away, in the grip now of that explosive violence by which being became, he has a strong sensation of the presence of others gathering around though he can't see them, he can't see anything now but his true beloved, and then, more in his mind's eye than in reality, for his eyes are probably closed, the pressure inside tremendous now and unutterably sweet, he can feel his whole body drawing deliciously together, cocking the spring, and it is so beautiful he wonders if this was not in fact how it was supposed to end, and maybe they all knew that, though he doesn't want it to end, it's never been as good as this, he is being carried completely out of himself, his whole body atremble now with its imminent eruption, and hers too, quivering from head to foot, and into his gasping mouth she gasps, *Oh now!* and somewhere he seems to hear distant applause, and *Now!* she cries and suddenly